Praise for *Mary, Called Magdalene*

"[An] expansive, thoughtful novel."
—*San Francisco Chronicle*

"[*Mary, Called Magdalene*] evokes with great authenticity the smells, sounds and crowds of ancient Judea . . . best of all . . . is her evocation of the mysterious evil of old gods and demons."
—*The Washington Post*

"The premise of Ms. George's novel is intriguing...with rigorous research, [she] paints the landscape and rituals of Judea and makes 'educated guesses' about her mysterious subject."
—*The New York Times*

"[A] book that informs, moves, and . . . surprises."
—*Book Street*

"The setting . . . is evocatively drawn and rich in period detail. This is an exceptionally realized and eminently readable tale."
—*Booklist*

"[*Mary, Called Magdalene*] is the story of every woman who has ever been on a spiritual journey and a celebration of the heroic uniqueness of this single woman . . . The story brings to light the indomitable spirit and moving tenderness of Mary Magdalene."
—*Green Bay Gazette*

PENGUIN BOOKS

MARY, CALLED MAGDALENE

Margaret George, a tenth-generation American, is the author of the bestselling *The Autobiography of Henry the VIII*, *Mary Queen of Scotland and the Isles*, and *The Memoirs of Cleopatra*. When not conducting research for her novels in places such as Egypt, Israel, Rome, and Greece, she lives with her husband in Madison, Wisconsin. You can find out more about George, her books, and her research at www.margaretgeorge.com.

MARGARET GEORGE

Mary, Called Magdalene

Penguin Books

PENGUIN BOOKS
Published by the Penguin Group
Penguin Putnam Inc., 375 Hudson Street, New York, New York 10014, U.S.A.
Penguin Books Ltd, 80 Strand, London WC2R 0RL, England
Penguin Books Australia Ltd, 250 Camberwell Road, Camberwell, Victoria 3124, Australia
Penguin Books Canada Ltd, 10 Alcorn Avenue, Toronto, Ontario, Canada M4V 3B2
Penguin Books India (P) Ltd, 11 Community Centre,
Panchsheel Park, New Delhi – 110 017, India
Penguin Books (N.Z.) Ltd, Cnr Rosedale and Airborne Roads,
Albany, Auckland, New Zealand
Penguin Books (South Africa) (Pty) Ltd, 24 Sturdee Avenue, Rosebank,
Johannesburg 2196, South Africa

Penguin Books Ltd, Registered Offices:
Harmondsworth, Middlesex, England

First published in the United States of America by Viking Penguin,
a member of Penguin Putnam Inc. 2002
Published in Penguin Books 2003

9 10

THE LIBRARY OF CONGRESS HAS CATALOGED THE HARDCOVER EDITION AS FOLLOWS:
George, Margaret, 1943–
Mary, called Magdalene / Margaret George.
p. cm.
ISBN 0-670-03096-1 (hc.)
ISBN 0 14 20.0279 8 (pbk.)
1. Mary Magdalene, Saint—Fiction. 2. Bible, N.T.—History of biblical events—
Fiction. 3. Christian women saints—Fiction. 4. Palestine—Fiction. I. Title.
PS3557.E49 M36 2002
813'.54—dc21   2001056840

Printed in the United States of America
Set in Aldus and Kallos Book
Designed by Francesca Belanger

For Rosemary,
Favorite Sister

Acknowledgments

My thanks:

For thoughtful reading, Alison Kaufman, Paul Kaufman, and Mary Holmes. For ideas and encouragement, Charlotte Allen and David Stevens. For help in Israel, Benny and Selly Geiger, Rachel and Tziki Kam, and Mendel Nun.

For inspiration, the Isle of Iona in Scotland and the spirit that is there.

And always, Jacques de Spoelberch, wonderful agent and friend.

Pilate said to him, "What is truth?"

John 18:38

I write this history of what happened to us from that moment onward. So many will come after us, and none of them will have seen, and they must be assured of what we have seen.

The Testament of Mary of Magdala, called Magdalene

"You will know the truth, and the truth will set you free."

Jesus, in John 8:32

PART ONE

The Demons

༂ 1 ༂

She was carried to a place she had never been. It was much more vivid than a dream, it had a depth and a color to it, and exquisite detail that made it seem more real than the time with her mother in the court-yard, more real than the dreamy hours she spent sometimes looking out at the great lake of Magdala, the one so grand they called it a sea: the Sea of Galilee.

She was elevated, put on a high pillar or a platform, she could not tell which. And all around her were people, gathering at the base of it, looking up at her. She turned her head to the side and saw that other pillars had other people on them, that there was a whole row of them, stretching as far as she could see. The sky was a yellowish color, the color she had only seen once, when there was a sandstorm. The sun was blotted out, but there was still light, diffuse golden light.

Then someone came to her—were they flying, was it an angel, how did they get there?—and took her hand and said, "Will you come? Will you come with us?"

She felt the hand holding hers, and it was smooth like a piece of marble, not cold, not hot, not sweaty, but perfect. She wanted to squeeze it but dared not.

"Yes," she finally said.

And then the figure—she still did not know who it was, she dared not look at the face, only at the feet in golden sandals—lifted her up and took her away, and the journey was so dizzying that she lost her balance and began to fall, to plummet, and it was very dark beneath her.

She sat up with a jolt. The oil lamp had burned out. Outside she could hear the gentle sound of the water of the great lake, not far from her window, as it lapped the shore.

She held out her hand, felt it. It was moist. Was that why the being had let her go, had dropped it? She rubbed it hard.

No, let me cleanse my hand! she cried out, silently. Don't abandon me! I can wipe it off!

"Come back," she whispered.

But the only answer was the stillness of the room and the sound of the water.

She rushed into her mother and father's room. They were sleeping soundly; they did not need a lamp, they slept in darkness.

"Mother!" she cried, grabbing her shoulder. "Mother!" Without permission, she climbed into the bed and huddled under the warm covers next to her mother.

"What . . . what is it?" Her mother struggled to form words. "Mary?"

"I have had such a strange dream," she cried. "I was taken up . . . into some heaven, I don't know where, I only know it was not of this world, it had angels, I think, or . . . I don't know what . . ." She paused, gasping for breath. "I think I was . . . I was called. Called to join them, called to become part of their company . . ." But it had been frightening, and she had not been sure she wanted to join them.

Now her father sat up. "What's this?" he said. "A dream? A dream about being called?"

"Nathan—" Mary's mother reached out and tried to restrain him, by touching his shoulder.

"I don't know if I was being called," Mary said in a small voice. "But there was this dream, and people up on high places, and—"

"High places!" cried her father. "That is where the ancient heathen idols were. In the high places!"

"But not up on pedestals," Mary said. "This was different. The people being honored were standing upon them, and they were people, not statues. . . ."

"And you think you've been called?" her father asked. "Why?"

"They asked if I would join them. They said, 'Will you come with us?'" Even as she recited it, she could hear the sweet voices.

"You must know, daughter, that all prophecy has ceased in our land," her father finally said. "There has been no word uttered by a prophet since Malachi, and that was four hundred years ago. God does not speak to us that way any longer. He speaks only through his holy Law. And that is sufficient for us."

But Mary knew what she had seen, the transcendent glory and warmth of it. "But, Father," she said, "the message, and the invitation, were so clear." She kept her voice low and respectful. But she was still shaking.

"Dear daughter, you have been misled. It was but a dream, brought on by our preparations for Jerusalem. God would not call you. Now return to your own bed."

She clung to her mother, but her mother thrust her aside. "Do as your father says," she ordered.

Mary returned to her room, the majesty of the dream still enveloping her. It had been real. She knew it had been real.

And if it was real, then her father was wrong.

In the hours just before the sky would lighten, the household made ready for its pilgrimage to Jerusalem for the Feast of Weeks. Mary had been excited, because all the adults were so eager for the trip, and because all Jews were supposed to long for Jerusalem. But she had most looked forward to the journey itself, for the seven-year-old had never been outside Magdala, and there were sure to be adventures on the way. Her father had hinted at them when he told her, "We will be traveling to Jerusalem by the short route, through Samaria, so it will take us only three days instead of four. But it is dangerous. There have been attacks on pilgrims going to Jerusalem." He shook his head. "The Samaritans even still have idols, I have heard. Oh, not so openly any longer, not by the roadside, but . . ."

"What kind of idol? I've never seen an idol!" she asked eagerly.

"Pray that you never do!"

"But how will I know an idol if I see one?"

"You'll know," her father said. "And you must shun it!"

"But—"

"That's enough!"

Now Mary remembered this, but all her earlier curiosity about Jerusalem was eclipsed by the dream, still so vivid to her in the darkness.

Busying herself with the final preparations, Mary's mother, Zebidah, had suddenly broken off measuring grain into the travel sacks and bent down to her daughter. She did not mention the dream. Instead she said, "Now, as for this trip, you must not mingle with any of the other families coming, except for the few I tell you are acceptable. So many people do not keep the Law and only want to go to Jerusalem—and even the Temple!—as some sort of holiday. Stay with the other observant families. Do you understand me?" She looked hard at Mary. In that instant her pretty face was not pretty but forbidding.

"Yes, Mother," she said.

"We keep the Law zealously, and so it must be," her mother continued. "Let all those other . . . transgressors look to themselves. It is not our duty to save them from their negligence. And mixing with them will contaminate us."

"Like mixing milk and meat?" Mary asked. She knew this was absolutely forbidden, so much so that anything pertaining to them must be separated.

"Just so," her mother answered. "And worse, because their influence does not fade away after a day or so, like that of the milk and meat. It stays with you, corrupting and corrupting."

They were ready. The six families making the journey together waited, donkeys loaded, packs slung over their shoulders, on the road above Magdala for the larger groups from the nearby towns to join them for the trip to Jerusalem. Mary would start out riding a donkey: the youngest traveler in the family, she did not have the stamina to walk long distances. Perhaps on the return journey she would be so toughened that she would not have to ride at all. That was her hope.

The dry season had begun, and already the sun felt hot on Mary's face. It hung brazenly over the Sea of Galilee, where it had risen earlier from behind the mountains. At dawn those mountains across the lake had been the color of tender grapes; now they showed their true colors of dust and stone. They were quite bare, and looked, Mary thought, malevolent. But perhaps that was because the land of the old Ammonites had such a bad reputation as Israel's ancient enemy.

What was it the Ammonites had done that was so bad? King David had had trouble with them. But, then, he had trouble with everyone. And there was also that evil god they worshiped, although Mary could not at first remember his name. He made the Ammonites sacrifice their children to him, putting them into the flames. Mo . . . Mol . . . Molech. Yes, that was his name.

She held up her hand and squinted across the lake. She certainly could not see any temples of Molech from here.

She gave a shudder, even in the warm sun. I won't think any more about Molech, she told herself sternly. The lake, gleaming in the sun, seemed to agree. It was too beautiful for its blue waters to be stained with thoughts of a blood-dripping god; it was probably the most beautiful place in all Israel, Mary firmly believed. No matter what was claimed for Jerusalem, how could anything be lovelier that this oval body of water, bright blue, surrounded by hills cupping it protectively?

She could see fishing boats out on the waters; there were a great many of them. It was fish that her town of Magdala was famous for—here they were salted, dried, traded, and shipped all over the world. Magdala fish were a presence on tables as far away as Damascus or Alexandria. And a presence in Mary's own home, for her father, Nathan, was a leading processor of the fish hauled into his warehouse, and her oldest brother, Samuel—although he had taken to calling himself the Greek name Silvanus for trading purposes—was the business manager, dealing with both local people and foreigners to arrange sales. Thus the big mosaic of a fishing boat that decorated their entrance hall indicated the source of their wealth. Every day as they stepped across it they could be reminded and give thanks for their good fortune and God's multitude of fish in their sea.

An east wind struck the waters of the lake and made the surface of the water tremble; she could see the ripples of water that did indeed look like harp strings. The old, poetic name for the lake was Lake Kinneret, Lake Harp, because of its shape and also because of the pattern of the wind on the water. Mary could almost hear the fine sound of plucked strings, singing to her across the water.

"Here they come!" Mary's father was gesturing to her to urge her donkey back toward the others. Down the dusty road she could see a very large caravan approaching, with even a camel or two besides donkeys and the mass of walkers.

"They must have celebrated the Sabbath too long yesterday," said Mary's mother, tartly. She was frowning; the late start was a nuisance. What was the point of delaying the departure until after the Sabbath if they were to lose a half-day anyway? No one ever started a journey the day before the Sabbath, or even the day before that, if it was a long journey. The rabbinical law forbidding walking more than about a Roman mile on the Sabbath meant that would waste a day—as far as travel was concerned.

"The Sabbath is such an excuse to waste time," said Mary's brother Silvanus loudly. "This insistence on strict observance of the Sabbath is crippling us in the foreign trade; the Greeks and Phoenicians don't take one day off out of every seven!"

"Yes, we know about your pagan sympathies, *Samuel*," said Mary's other older brother, Eli. "I suppose next you'll be running naked in the gymnasium with all your Greek friends."

Silvanus—alias Samuel—just glared at him. "I haven't time," he said coldly. "I am too busy helping Father run the business. It's you, with all your spare time studying scripture and consulting with rabbis, who have the leisure to go to the gymnasium or any other place of amusement you want to."

Eli flared, as Silvanus knew he would. The younger man had a hot temper, despite all his efforts in studying the ways and whys of Yahweh. With his fine, straight-nosed profile and noble bearing, he could pass for Greek, thought Silvanus. Whereas he—he almost laughed—looked more like the little scholars who were always bent over the Torah in the *beth ha-Midrash*, the House of Learning. Yahweh must have a mighty sense of humor.

"The study of Torah is the most important thing a man can do," Eli said stiffly. "It supersedes all other activity in moral worth."

"Yes, and in your case it precludes all other activity."

Eli snorted and turned away, pulling his donkey with him, so that its hindside was facing Silvanus, who merely laughed.

Mary was used to hearing this exchange, in various forms, between her twenty-one-year-old and eighteen-year-old brothers. It was never resolved and it never even progressed. Mary's family was deeply observant, adhering to all the rituals and religious strictures; only Silvanus seemed restless in what her father referred to as "the perfect Law of the Lord."

Mary wished she could study that Law at the little school attached to their synagogue, the *beth ha-sefer*, and see for herself. Or that she could steal the knowledge that Silvanus, who did not seem to want it, had acquired from his Torah schooling. But girls could not attend the school, since they could have no official place in religion. Her father had sternly repeated the rabbinical dictum, "It would be better to see the Torah burnt than to hear its words upon the lips of women."

"You should learn Greek so you can read the *Iliad*," Silvanus had once suggested to Mary, with a laugh. Naturally Eli had countered with a shocked blast. But Silvanus had replied, "If someone is shut out of her own literature and knowledge by stupid rulings, is she not then forced to turn to another?"

Silvanus had a point; the Greeks welcomed others into their culture, whereas the Jews guarded theirs like a secret. Each action was the result of thinking theirs was superior: the Greeks thought that one taste of Greek culture would instantly win anyone over, whereas the Jews felt theirs was so precious it could be desecrated by offering it to any and all passersby. Naturally this made Mary all the more curious about both of them. She would learn to read, she promised herself, and then she could tap into the magic and mystery of the holy writings herself.

The two traveling parties met and merged on the fork of the road up from Magdala—there were now about twenty-five families to make the journey. Many were related, distantly or otherwise, so large numbers of third, fourth, fifth, and sixth cousins would meet and play en route. Mary's family was traveling only alongside other very observant families. As they regrouped to form the procession, Eli could not resist one aside to Silvanus. "I don't know why you are making this journey at all," he said, "since you have no sympathy with our way of thought. Why go to Jerusalem?"

Instead of a sharp retort, Silvanus said thoughtfully, "For the history, Eli, for the history. I love the stones of Jerusalem, each of which tells a story—and tells it clearer and finer than the words in the scrolls."

Eli ignored his brother's solemnity. "It's a story you wouldn't even *know* if it wasn't written in the very scriptures you scorn! It isn't stones who talk and tell us their tales, it's scribes who record it for posterity."

"I'm sorry that you credit only yourself with the finer feelings," Silvanus finally said. He halted and fell back into another group; he would not be traveling close to his brother on this journey.

Mary did not know which one to keep near, so she went over to her parents. They were walking resolutely, their faces set for Jerusalem. The sun beat down, its brightness causing them to squint and shield their eyes.

Clouds of dust were blowing. The startling green of the Galilean spring grass had begun to fade, replaced by a dun mat; the jewel-colored wildflowers that had dotted the hillsides had wilted and disappeared. From now until next spring, the landscape would become progressively browner, the glorious burst of nature's love merely a memory. Galilee was the lushest part of the country, the nearest thing to a Persian garden paradise in the land of Israel.

The branches of the fruit trees were laden with new apples and pomegranates; the bright-green early figs were peeking from under their leaves. People were gathering them; new figs never remained on the trees long.

The unwieldy group lumbered up over the crest of the hills surrounding the lake, where Mary could glimpse it one last time before it disappeared from sight.

Farewell, Lake Harp! she sang to herself. There was no pang of goodbye, only anticipation of what lay ahead. They were on their way, the road was calling them, and soon all the hills Mary had seen from her earliest-remembered days would vanish, to be replaced by things she had never seen. How wonderful it would be, like getting an extraordinary present, opening a box filled with glittering new objects.

They soon joined the wider road, the Via Maris—one of the main thoroughfares across the land since ancient times. It was busy, too—crowded with Jewish merchants; lean, hawkeyed Nabateans on their camels; Babylonian businessmen swathed in silk and sporting gold earrings that looked painfully heavy to Mary. Greeks were there aplenty, mingling with the pilgrims heading south. But there was one sort of traveler to whom everyone else gave a wide berth: Romans.

The soldiers she could recognize by their uniforms, those odd skirts with leather strips that bared their big hairy legs; the ordinary Roman was harder to spot. But the adults had no problem identifying them.

"A Roman!" her father hissed, gesturing for her to fall back behind him in line as a nondescript man approached. Even though the road was crowded, Mary noticed that no one jostled him. As they passed, he seemed to turn his head and look at her with a sort of curiosity. She looked back mildly.

"How did you know he was a Roman?" Mary asked eagerly.

"It's the hair," he explained. "And being so clean-shaven. I admit, the cloak and sandals could belong to a Greek or any other foreigner."

"It's the look in their eyes," her mother suddenly said. "It's the look of someone who owns everything he sees."

They came out onto a flat plain, wide and beckoning. Scattered trees made pools of shadows that looked cool; the sun was now standing almost directly overhead. There were isolated mountains on either side of the road: to the right, Mount Tabor, and to the left, Mount Moreh.

As they approached the flanks of Mount Moreh, Silvanus appeared by her side and pointed vaguely at it. "Look out for the witch!" he teased her. "The witch of Endor!"

When Mary looked puzzled, he confided, "The witch that King Saul consulted to bring up Samuel's spirit. This is where she had her quarters. They say it's still haunted. Why, if you were to leave us and go there and sit under a tree and wait . . . who knows what spirit might be summoned?"

"Is that true?" asked Mary. "Now, tell me, don't tease." It seemed an awesome thing to be able to call up spirits, especially of people who had died.

His smile faded. "I don't know if it's really true," he admitted. "It's written in the holy books, but"—he shrugged—"so is the claim that Samson killed a thousand men with the jawbone of an ass."

"How would I know a spirit?" Mary persisted, not to be put off by the jawbone.

"They say you know them by the fear they instill in you," Silvanus said. "Seriously, if you ever see one, I'd advise you to run in the opposite direction. The one thing everyone knows is that they're dangerous. They want to mislead, destroy. I suppose that's why Moses forbade any contact with them." Again he was skeptical: "If he really did."

"Why do you keep saying that? Don't you believe it's true?"

"Oh . . ." He hesitated. "Yes, I believe it's true. And if not strictly true that Moses said it, it's still a good idea. Most of the things Moses said are a good idea."

Mary laughed. "Sometimes you do sound like a Greek."

"If being Greek means thinking about things carefully, then I'd be proud to be labeled such." He laughed, too.

Down past more mountains, larger in fame than in actual size: Mount Gilboa on the left, where Saul took his last stand and perished at the hands of the Philistines; and far to the right, visible across the plain, Megiddo, rearing itself up like a tower, where the battle at the end of time would be fought.

Not far beyond Mount Gilboa, they crossed the boundary into Samaria. Samaria! Mary gripped the reins of the donkey and clung hard to its flanks. Danger! Danger! Was it dangerous? She looked around alertly, but the landscape was the same as that they had just left—the same rocky hills, dusty plains, and lone trees. She had been told that there were bandits and rebels who used the caves near Magdala for hideouts, but she had never seen any near her home. Now she hoped to see *something,* for they were venturing into enemy territory.

They did not have long to wait. They had not gone more than a short way before a group of jeering youths were lining the road, throwing stones, and yelling in deep guttural voices, insult after insult: "Dogs . . . Filth of Galilee . . . Perverters of the holy books of Moses . . ." Some of them spat. Mary's mother and father looked straight ahead, pretending not to see or hear them, which just provoked them further.

"Deaf, are you? Take this!" And they blew jarring blasts from a ram's horn, and gave shrill, unhuman-sounding whistles that must have come from someplace deeper than their throats. The hatred quivered in the air. Still the Galileans did not look at them or answer the insults: Mary was trembling on her donkey as she came within almost an arm's length of one knot of taunters. Then, mercifully, they passed beyond them—first beyond sight of them, then, finally, beyond earshot of them.

"That was terrible!" Mary cried when she could safely make a sound. "Why do they hate us so much?"

"It's an ancient feud," her father said. "Nor is it likely to change in our lifetimes."

"But why? Where did it come from?" Mary persisted.

"It's a long story," her father said wearily.

"I'll tell it," said Silvanus, striding fast alongside the donkey. "Now, you know about King David, right? And King Solomon?"

"Yes indeed," she said proudly. "One was the greatest warrior king we ever had, and the other the wisest!"

"He wasn't wise enough to have a very wise son," Silvanus said. "His son made his subjects so angry that ten of the twelve tribes of Israel broke away from the kingdom and set up their own in the north. They chose an overseer for their king, Jeroboam."

Jeroboam. She had heard of him, and whatever it was, it wasn't good.

"Since the people in the north couldn't go to the Temple in Jerusalem any longer, Jeroboam set up new altars for them, with golden calves for them to worship. God didn't care for that, so he punished them by sending the Assyrians to destroy their country and carry them off into captivity. And that was the end of ten of the tribes of Israel. They just vanished into Assyria and never came back. Goodbye, Reuben; goodbye, Simeon; goodbye, Dan and Asher . . ."

"But Samaria isn't empty now," said Mary. "Who are these nasty people yelling at us?"

"The Assyrians brought in pagans to settle here!" Eli cried, overhearing the conversation. "They mingled with the few Jews left behind and produced this dreadful mix of the true faith of Moses and of paganism. An abomination!" His face contorted with disgust. "And don't tell me they had no choice!"

Mary drew back. She had not been about to tell him any such thing.

"Everyone has a choice!" he continued. "Some members of those ten tribes were loyal to Jerusalem. And so they weren't punished and taken off to Assyria. That's what our family did. We were—we are!— of the tribe of Naphtali. But we were faithful!" His voice had risen dreadfully loud and he seemed furious. "And we must guard that faith!"

"Yes, Eli," she said, meekly. She wondered how she would do that.

"Way over there"—he pointed southward—"on their special hill of Gerizim, they carry out their heretical rites!"

He still hadn't answered her question, so she asked it again. "But why do they hate *us*?"

Silvanus inclined his head toward his brother. "Because we hate *them*, and make it so obvious."

All was calm for the remainder of the day. As they passed by fields and small villages, people lined the road and stared, but did not call out or attempt to hinder them.

The sun swung over Mary's left shoulder and began its downward descent. The tiny pools of shadows under the wayside trees, modest little skirts at midday, now stretched far out, like princes' trains, beyond the trunks.

Up ahead, the caravan slowed to begin searching for a place to camp for the night. They needed enough daylight to secure a safe place, and there was likely to be trouble with the water.

Wells were always a problem: locating one in the first place that could water a company as large as this one, and then the possibility of hostility from the owners of the well. People were killed over well disputes. The Samaritans were not likely to welcome the travelers to their wells, hand them buckets, and say, "Drink all you like, and water your animals as well."

The leaders of the group had selected a wide, flat area back from the road with several wells. It was an ideal spot—provided they were left in peace to enjoy it. For the moment there were few people about, and the Galileans were able to set up their tents unhindered, water their pack animals, and draw water for their own uses. Once everyone was settled, sentries were stationed around the boundaries.

The campfire crackled and spat, the way Mary liked it. It meant the fire had a personality, and was trying to speak to them. At least that is how she had always imagined it. The huge goat's-hair tent was big enough for all of them, and that was also as she liked it. It was good to be able to sit around the fire, to know that everyone was in the same circle.

Now, as she looked at them—at her handsome brother, Eli, and her less handsome but fascinating brother, Silvanus, she had a sudden fear that this time next year one of them would be *married*, and maybe even have a baby, and would be no longer in the family tent but in a tent of his own. She didn't like that. She wanted everything to stay just the way it was, with them all gathered together, forever and ever, protecting one another. This little family, this little circle, so strong, and so consoling, must remain forever. And in the cooling twilight of the Samaritan spring, it felt as if that could be true.

Deep night. Mary had been asleep for what seemed a long time, the thick blanket under her, her warm cloak over her. Outside the tent flap the embers of a small guardian fire were pulsing slowly, gently, like the breathing of a dragon. Then, suddenly, she was wide awake, a peculiar sort of wakefulness, like a very sharp dream. She raised her head slowly and looked around; everything was very fuzzy in the dim light, but she could hear the breathing of the others nearby. Though her heart was pounding, she could not remember having had a bad dream. Why was she so excited?

Go back to sleep, she told herself. Go back to sleep. Look, outside it's still completely dark. You can see all the stars yet.

But she was quiveringly awake. She wiggled and tried to find a completely comfortable spot, turning on the blanket and moving the wadded material that served as her pillow. As she struggled to realign the blanket, her hands felt an obstruction just beside her pillow. It had sharp edges. Curiously, she felt around it, and it did not feel like a rock, but something smaller and finer, although not an arrowhead or a sickle or anything metal. She dug a bit with her fingers, and could feel ridges in it. More eager now, she took the hardened edge of her sandal strap and used that as a trowel to excavate the object. When, finally, she had it free, she could see it was something carved. It was also pale, and too lightweight to be stone. She held it up and turned it this way and that, but could not make it out. She would have to wait until dawn.

Then, suddenly, almost miraculously, she fell fast asleep.

Daylight flooded the eastern sky, and Mary blinked awake. Her family was up and stirring, folding the blankets and tent. She felt groggy, as though she had not slept. And as she pushed the covering cloak back, she felt the thing she was clutching in her hand. Puzzled for a moment, she held it out and squinted at it.

It still retained a slight covering of earth, like a veil that hides a beautiful woman's nakedness; but shining through the dullness was a face, a face of exquisite beauty.

An idol!

Just as her father had said, she knew it even though she had never seen one.

"And you must shun it," he had said.

But instead she could not take her eyes away. The thing drew her, compelled her to look. The dreamy eyes, half lidded; the full, sensual lips with a curve of a smile; the thick hair pulled back, revealing a slender neck as fine as an ivory scepter . . .

Ivory. Yes, that was what this . . . idol . . . was made of. It was yellowed, and even had some brown spots, but it was ivory, creamy and almost translucent. That was why it was both light and delicate, and even its hard edges were not sharp.

Who are you? Mary asked it, staring at the eyes. How long have you been buried here?

Her father was stepping over the saddlebags near her, and she quickly hid her hand under the blanket.

"Time to go," he said briskly, leaning down. Mary reopened her eyes, pretending that she had just awakened.

Trudging along beside the donkey—her mother was riding him this time—Mary kept fingering the new possession, which she had thrust into the long wound bolt of cloth serving as her belt. She knew she ought to have shown it to her father on the spot, but she did not want to. She wanted to keep it, and she knew he would make her throw it away, probably with a curse.

She felt very protective of it.

This time, at noon, when the sun was at its hottest, they had to make a detour around a well guarded by Samaritans. Again there were the threats and gibes, which the pilgrims attempted to ignore. It was good that they had been able to use the wells in the place where they had stopped. Only one more night in Samaria; only one more set of wells to find.

"And to think our ancestors dug these wells, and now we are not even allowed to drink from them!" muttered Eli. "Dotted all across the land are wells that should rightfully belong to us!"

"Peace, Eli," said Nathan. "Someday, perhaps, it will all return to its rightful owner. Or the Samaritans will return to the true religion."

Eli looked disgusted. "I know of no scripture that prophesies that."

"Oh, I'm sure it's in there somewhere," said Silvanus, who had been sticking close to his family that morning. "Everything seems to be. There is a wealth of promises, from the Messiah to the well situation. The problem lies in interpreting them. It seems that Yahweh did not wish to make his messages too easy for his faithful to understand."

Eli was poised for a retort, but suddenly there was a commotion up ahead, and the caravan halted. Nathan detached himself and hurried on. But the word of what it was spread faster along the group than Nathan could walk.

Idols! A whole cache of idols!

Soon the caravan had turned into a milling mass as everyone rushed up front to see the idols. High excitement reigned—for who among them had actually *seen* an ancient idol? There were the modern Roman ones about, of course, although even they were confined to the pagan towns like Sepphoris in Galilee, which few people in the caravan had ventured into.

But ancient ones! The legendary ones that the prophets had thundered against, that had brought first the northern kingdom of Israel and then her sister kingdom Judah to ruin and exile. Even their names were tinged with a titillating sort of fear: Baal. Ashtart. Molech. Dagon. Melkart. Baal-zebul.

A rabbi from Bethsaida was standing by an outcropping of stone along the path, with a small crevice where two of his assistants were pawing and bringing out wrapped bundles. A line of them was already on the ground, laid out like dead warriors.

"The seal was plainly visible!" the rabbi cried, pointing at the stone that had covered the little entrance of the hole.

Why did he feel he had the right to open it? Mary wondered.

"I knew it was evil!" he pronounced, answering her unspoken question. "These must have been hidden long ago, in hopes that their owners would return and restore them to their—their high places, or wherever they were served and worshiped. But they probably perished in Assyria, which was only right. Unwrap them!" he suddenly ordered his assistants. "Unwrap them, so we can smash and destroy them! Abomination! Idols! All abominations must be destroyed!"

The yellowed old bandagelike cloths had deteriorated so badly that it was difficult to unroll them, so the rabbi and the others cut them off with knives. Little clay figures emerged, crude things with bulging eyes and sticklike arms and legs.

Mary clutched her own treasure tight inside her belt. Hers was not ugly like these, but beautiful.

When the rabbi started smashing the figures, swinging down on them with a club, Mary wondered if she should throw hers onto the pile, too. But the thought of that lovely face being destroyed was too painful. So she stood and watched as pieces of the helpless idols flew all around her like rain. One tiny, detached arm landed on her sleeve, and she picked it up and looked at it. Just a little chickenlike limb. It even seemed to have claws.

Without thinking about it, she stuck this in her belt as well.

"Who do you suppose they were?" asked Silvanus offhandedly. "Maybe they were Canaanite gods. They could be almost anything." A shower of idol pieces fell on them. "Well, whatever they were, they aren't any longer. Pouf, they have vanished."

But could a god vanish? Could a god be destroyed? Mary wondered.

"'Woe to him who says to wood, "Awake!," to dumb stone, "Arise!"'" cried the rabbi, pounding the idols for one last masterstroke. "'Can such a thing give oracles? See, it is overlaid with gold and silver, but there is no life breath in it.'" He paused and rested his club, nodding with satisfaction. Then he gestured toward Jerusalem, and his voice surged with joy as he quoted the next verses of the prophet Habakkuk. "'But the Lord is in his holy Temple; silence before him, all the earth!'" He raised his staff. "Tomorrow, my friends! Tomorrow we see that holy Temple! Blessed be God, the one and eternal I AM."

He spat on what was left of the idols.

⟡ 11 ⟡

One more sunset, one more camp before Jerusalem. As they settled in to pass the night, Mary could feel the excitement of the adults now that they were drawing near to the city.

This time the soil around Mary's pallet was firm and smooth, indicating there was nothing just below it. She was a bit disappointed, as if she had been expecting every stop in this alien landscape to yield something exotic and forbidden. She had carefully untied her belt, where her carving was, and kept it rolled near her head. She did not dare risk taking it out when so many people were about. And the little severed god-limb stayed in its pocket, too. But she was aware of them all the time, as if they were calling her, drawing her.

Fighting off sleep, she wondered what they would find at the Temple. Around the cookfire, Eli had said, "I suppose our entire caravan will be searched just because we're Galileans."

"Yes, and there will probably be extra guards at the Temple," said Nathan. "Lots of them."

Apparently there had been trouble recently, caused by some rebel from Galilee.

"Judas the Galilean and his band of bandits!" said Silvanus. "What did he hope to accomplish by his rebellion? We are under the control of the Romans, and if they decide to tax us, there is nothing we can do about it. He and his pathetic resistance just made it harder for all of us who are left."

"Still . . ." Eli took his time chewing before he finished his thought. "Sometimes the feeling of hopelessness and helplessness can overwhelm a man and then any action, even a futile one, can feel necessary."

"It will be quiet in Jerusalem this festival," said Silvanus. "Oh, yes. The Romans will make sure of that." He paused. "It makes you glad that we have our nice young king Herod Antipas watching over us in dear old Galilee, doesn't it?"

Eli snorted.

"Well, he *is* a Jew," said Silvanus, but in a tone that Mary knew meant the opposite.

"A poor sort of imitation one, like his father!" Eli had risen to the bait. "The son of a Samaritan woman by an Indumaean father! A descendant of Esau! To think we are forced to pretend that—"

"Silence," warned Nathan. "Don't speak so loudly outside our own household walls." He laughed, to make a joke out of it. "Now, how can you say his father wasn't a good Jew? Didn't he build us a fine Temple?"

"It wasn't necessary," snapped Eli. "The original one was good enough."

"Perhaps for God," agreed Nathan. "But people want their gods to be housed as finely as their kings. God wants both more, and less, than we usually wish to give him."

A deep silence fell as the offhanded comment struck each of them with its truth.

"Mary, tell us what the Feast of Weeks is," Eli commanded, breaking the quiet. "After all, it's what we are going to Jerusalem to celebrate."

Being singled out made her feel defensive. Anyone else could have answered the question better than she. "It's—it's one of the three big celebrations our people observe," she said.

"But what *is* it?" persisted Eli, bearing down on her like an examiner.

Indeed, what exactly was it? There was something about the grain being ripe, and being so many days after Passover. . . . "It's fifty days after Passover," Mary said, trying to remember. "It has something to do with the grain getting ripe."

"What kind of grain?"

"Eli, stop it!" said Silvanus. "Even you would not have known that when you were seven."

"It's . . . barley, or wheat, I think," Mary guessed.

"Wheat! And we are presenting the first of the harvest to God," said Eli. "That's what it is all about. The offerings will be set before him up in the Temple."

"What does he do with them?" Mary imagined that a great devouring fire would shoot out and God would consume them.

"After the ritual, they are returned to the worshipers."

Oh. How disappointing. So they were journeying all this way just to present some grain, which would then be returned to them untouched? "I see," she finally said. "But we don't grow grain," she pointed out. "Perhaps we should have brought fish? The fish we cure?"

"It's symbolic," said Eli shortly.

"The Temple," said Silvanus. "Perhaps it's better if we talk about that. It's simpler."

And so, as the sun vanished and withdrew its warm rays from their shoulders, they discussed the Temple. How important it was to the Jewish people. How this was the third one to be built, the other two having been destroyed. In fact, it was so important that it was the first thing the exiles rebuilt upon returning from Babylon, five hundred years ago.

"We are the Temple, and the Temple is us," said Nathan. "We cannot exist as a people without it."

What a frightening thought: that a building must stand in order for the Jews to exist. Mary shivered. What would happen if it were destroyed? But surely that would never happen. God would not allow it to.

"Our ancestor Huram was a worker in Solomon's Temple," Nathan said. He fumbled for something around his neck and drew out a tiny brass pomegranate on a cord. "This is what he made," he said, pulling it off and handing it to Silvanus, who studied it with a thoughtful face before passing it on to Eli.

"Oh, he made many other things, large things—bronze pillars and capitals, cast in huge clay molds—but this is what he made for his wife. A thousand years ago. And we have guarded it and passed it down among ourselves ever since. We even took it with us to Babylon, and brought it back."

When it reached Mary, she held it reverently. It seemed immensely holy, if only because of its great age.

My great-great-great—many times great—grandfather made this, and with his *own hands,* she thought. His hands, now dust, made this.

She held it up, rotated it slowly on its thong. The dying light played on its surfaces, on the rounded body of the fruit, and on the four forked protrusions at the apex, representing the stem. He had captured the shape of the pomegranate while casting it in its perfect form, symmetrical and ideal.

Not daring to breathe in its presence, she handed it back to her father. He draped it around his neck and tucked it in his bosom again.

"So you see, our pilgrimage is no light thing," he finally said, patting the place under his robes were the talisman resided. "We go in the name of Huram and the last thousand years."

Early dawn, and the tents nearby were being taken down, the pack animals loaded, and mothers were calling their children. When Mary awoke, she had the strange feeling of having actually already been to the Temple, and also of remembering rows of goddess statues . . . in a grove of tall trees, whose dark-green tops were waving gently in a breeze. The Temple was calling to her, but so was the rustle of the wind in the cypress grove.

They were up and on their way quickly. The entire caravan was moving energetically, as if they had just started out rather than having been on the road three days. The spell of Jerusalem was drawing them.

By late afternoon, they had reached the top of one of the ridges overlooking the holy city, and the entire caravan halted to look. Spread out below them lay Jerusalem, its stones tawny and golden in the evening sun. Within its walls, the city rose and fell with the changing level of the land. Here and there were white flecks, which were marble palaces set among the limestone buildings; and rising on its flat plateau in gold-and-white splendor was the Temple with its grounds.

A hushed silence fell over them all. Mary stared, too young to feel the rush of religious awe that her elders did, seeing only the pure white of the Temple, the golden light that seemed different from any she had ever seen, coming down from the sky with long hands to touch the city.

Other groups were gathered on the ridge. A number of decorated carts, containing the symbolic offerings of first-fruits from towns that could send no pilgrims that year, were also clustered together there. The carts had been loaded as tradition dictated: barley at the bottom, then wheat and dates, then pomegranates, then figs and olives, and, crowning the top, grapes. Soon they would rumble into Jerusalem and be presented to the priests.

"Song! Song!" cried someone. "Let us sing with joy that we are allowed to come to God and his holy Temple!"

And at once a thousand voices began to sing the Psalms they knew so well, the ones celebrating the ascent to Jerusalem.

"Our feet are standing in your gates, O Jerusalem.
That is where the tribes go up, the tribes of the Lord,
according to the statute given to Israel.
Pray for the peace of Jerusalem:
May those who love you be secure.
May there be peace within your walls, and security
within your citadels."

Eagerly, waving palm branches, they descended the last hillside to converge on Jerusalem. The walls, and the gate they would enter, loomed ahead.

The tumult seemed to multiply as the groups approached the city, and their ranks swelled as they were crushed together. It was a happy and joyful mass, propelled by a combination of awe and fervor. Ahead, more carts were jouncing down the incline, and other songs of pilgrimage rose in the air, to the clashing of cymbals and ringing of tambourines. The great northern gate stood open; around it beggars and lepers clustered, wailing and crying for alms; but they were almost crushed by the oncoming crowds.

Mary saw a few mounted Roman soldiers watching from the sidelines, alert for any trouble. Their crested helmets looked fierce against the bright-blue sky.

The travelers slowed almost to a tortoise crawl when they came to the gate; Mary's mother held her close as the crushing pressure built around them; an immense squeeze came, and then they were through the gate and in Jerusalem itself. But there was no time to stop and admire; the mass coming up behind pushed them forward.

"Ahh," people were murmuring all around her, in rapt admiration.

That night, they camped outside the city walls with thousands of other pilgrims, stretching almost around the city to make an outer set of walls. It was this way at all the great festivals; sometimes half a million pilgrims converged on the city, which could not possibly house them all. And so a second Jerusalem sprang up around it.

Excited laughter, song, and voices came from the other tents and campfires, as people visited one another, hunting for relatives or friends from other villages. And the foreign Jews, who had traveled great distances to worship at the Temple, emerged from their strange-looking tents: domed ones, silken pavilions, fringed-door ones. Some of them had lived away from their ancestral lands for ten generations, yet they considered the Temple their spiritual home.

Mary closed her eyes, trying to sleep. But it was hard with this great party going on all around her.

Instead of Jerusalem, she dreamed again of the mysterious grove of trees and the statues within it, the white of the statues on their marble bases visible in the dream-moonlight, floating like foam on an ocean wave. The whispering of the trees, the glory of the moonlit marble, the promise of lost secrets swirled around her sleep.

While it was still dark, they arose and began to make ready to enter the city again, this time for the observance of the feast. Mary was so curious to see the Temple, she was almost trembling.

The crowds were even thicker today, the actual feast day. Rivers of people were jamming the streets, pressing so hard against the walls of the houses that it almost seemed the stones could be pushed back. And such curious-looking pilgrims: some from Phrygia sweating under heavy goat's-hair cloaks; others, from Persia, with gold-brocaded silk; Phoenicians with tunics and striped pants; Babylonians in dour black robes. Although they were all eagerly pressing toward the Temple, they seemed less pious than ravenous, as if there were something up there they were ready to devour.

At the same time, the noises of the city mingled and fought. The cries of the water-sellers—sure to do a brisk business now—the singing pilgrims, the shouting of tradesmen who hoped to sell trinkets or headcoverings, and above all the bleating of flocks of sacrificial animals being driven toward the Temple, all created an almost painful din. From somewhere far away came the blast of the silver Temple trumpets proclaiming the celebration.

"Stay with us!" Mary's father warned her. Her mother grasped her hand and pulled her close. Almost braided together, they shuffled along the streets, past the enormous Roman fortress called the Antonia that brooded—and acted as watchdog—over the Temple and its grounds. Rows of Roman soldiers stood on the steps, in full military gear, spears at the ready, watching them impassively.

Festival time meant a full alert for the army, to head off any disturbances or misguided attempts on the part of some self-styled Messiah to cause an uprising. The key central areas of Judaea, Samaria, and Idumaea were under direct Roman rule. And that included Jerusalem, the biggest prize of all. The Roman procurator, who normally resided in the seaside city of Caesarea, grudgingly came to Jerusalem at the time of the big pilgrimage festivals.

So it was that the Temple was guarded by a fortress of Roman soldiers, with pagans looking down upon the holy site.

Mary's family was caught in the stream of pilgrims, moving more rapidly now, sweeping up to the Temple itself. Rising high into the sky, the holiest site in Judaism called to all her faithful. A huge wall of white marble surrounded the actual buildings and the platform; in the morning sunlight it was dazzlingly white. One corner parapet, where the trumpeters stood, was supposedly the highest point in all Jerusalem.

"This way!" Eli jerked the donkey's bridle and they swung toward the great stairway that would carry them up to the level of the Temple.

And then into the holy Temple precincts, the shining place.

The flat site was enormous, and would have seemed even more enormous had it not been crammed with pilgrims. Herod the Great had enlarged it to double its natural size by building a huge extension wall, as if that would double the glory of the place—and his own name. But he did not change the dimensions of the Temple itself, housing the

Holy of Holies, which had been decreed by Solomon, so it seemed small set down on Herod's vast platform.

Herod had not stinted on the decorations—the building was a jewel of architectural excess. Golden spikes protruded from the roof, reflecting the sunlight. The sumptuous building was raised above the level of the plateau so that the faithful must mount by a series of steps to reach it. The huge outer Court of the Gentiles admitted anyone. Then came an area only for Jews. The next barrier held back the Jewish women, so that only male Israelites could pass through into the next area. Finally, only priests were allowed to ascend to the altar and the sacrificial places. As for the sanctuary proper, all priests were barred except ones chosen by lot to be on duty that week; and the Holy of Holies could only be entered once a year by the high priest. Should any repairs be required on it, workmen would be lowered in a cage that prevented them from seeing anything in the Holy of Holies itself. The Holy of Holies: where the spirit of God dwelt in emptiness and solitude, an enclosed chamber at the very heart of the Temple, where no light could penetrate, windowless, and hung with a thick curtain.

But all Mary could see was the vastness of the place, and the sea of people swarming all around her. Huge flocks of sacrificial animals—cattle, goats, sheep—bleated and bellowed in one corner, while the coos and chirps from the cages of cheaper bird sacrifices sent a note of sweetness above the other noises. Merchants yelled from the covered porticoes that ran around the edge of the platform, gesturing and trying to entice customers.

"Money-changer! Money-changer!" one cried. "No unauthorized coins allowed in the Temple! Change here! Change here!"

"Cursed be he who brings in banned currency! My rates are better!" another claimed.

"Shut them up!" muttered Eli, clapping his hands over his ears. "Is there no way to shut them up? They desecrate the place!"

As they came to the gate, Mary saw that there were signs in both Greek and Latin posted at regular intervals all along it. If only she could read! As it was, she had to tug at Silvanus's coat and ask him what it said.

"'Anyone who is taken shall be killed, and he alone shall be answerable for his death,'" he quoted. "It's absolutely forbidden for any non-Jew to pass through this gate."

Had people really been killed for trying? Death seemed an extreme punishment for curiosity.

"We would like to think that God is more . . . enlightened than some of his followers," said Silvanus, as if he had read her thoughts. "I imagine he would welcome a pagan curious to discover another way of worship, but his priests don't see it that way." Silvanus took her hand to keep her close in the milling crowd. "Here, let's go in."

They passed unhindered through a huge bronze door opening into the walled courtyard, which, like the one outside, had porticoes all around it, and other structures built into the corners. But Mary was not looking at that—she saw only the Temple, elevated by a series of steps beyond the courtyard.

Great and mighty it reared up, the grandest building she had ever seen or imagined. Its white marble, hit by the morning sun, sparkled like snow, and its imposing lintel, with the gold frieze above its massive doors, seemed like a portal to another world. It projected power and cried out that the Lord Almighty, King of Kings, was far more formidable than any earthly king, any king of Babylon or Persia or Assyria. And, indeed, that was what it looked like—a huge palace for an Eastern king.

When she beheld it, all that came to mind were the stories and songs about God smashing his enemies. Here, before her, were quivering minions presenting booty to this terrible king—that was how the sacrificial animals, the offerings, and the clouds of incense struck her. They spoke of fear.

If you stepped into the wrong enclosure, you could be killed. If you used the wrong coins, you could be punished. And for anyone who transgressed into the sanctuary itself, there was punishment beyond death itself.

She wanted to feel love, possessive pride, and worshipful awe for her deity, but instead there was only this fear.

A large group of Levitical priests, clad in immaculate garments, stood on the flight of steps dividing the Court of the Women from the Court of the Israelites. To the accompaniment of flutes, they were chanting exquisitely beautiful hymns, and underlying their own deep voices were the sweet, high voices of their children, who were also allowed to sing.

Priests stood by to receive the offerings and lead the sacrificial animals away to the ramps and altars. The new-grain loaves were presented on flat paddles, to be "waved" before the Lord in a special ceremony. Behind the priests' heads, Mary could see smoke rising from the altar, where the consuming fire burned the offerings. The pungent smell of the incense mingled with—but did not mask—the stench of burning flesh and fat.

As their Galilean group's offerings (seven male lambs, two rams, a bull, a basket of fruit, and two loaves of bread made of flour from new grain) were being carried away, Mary suddenly felt that she should quietly add the ivory idol-face to them. Let her rid herself of it—now. Was it sacrilege to have brought it here? It seemed to be almost burning her through the layers of cloth in which she had hidden it. But, of course, that was her imagination.

Once I surrender it, I will never have it again, she thought. It will be gone forever. And perhaps it would be an insult to God to mix it in with his offerings. I will keep it snug in my pocket now. And when I get home, I will look at it once more to remember it, and then I will throw it out, before my father sees it and punishes me.

Winding their way out through the main gate, called "the Beautiful," Mary and her family passed through the Court of the Gentiles again. It was all so grand, so dizzying, so unlike anything in ordinary life.

"If I could go inside the Temple, would I see the Ark of the Covenant, and the stone tablets with the Ten Commandments?" Mary asked Silvanus. "And what about the jar of preserved manna, and Aaron's rod?" Just thinking of these ancient things gave her a tingle.

"You'd see nothing!" Silvanus now sounded bitter. It was a tone Mary had seldom heard from him. "It's all gone. Destroyed when the rest of Solomon's Temple was destroyed by the Babylonians. Although, of course, there's a legend that the Ark is buried somewhere on the grounds. Of course. We always want to believe that we haven't really lost something, not really, not forever." He looked sad in the midst of all the rejoicing pilgrims around him. "But we have."

"So what is in there?"

"Nothing. It is empty."

Empty? All this housing, all this grandeur, all these rules and regulations—to honor nothing? "That can't be!" Mary burst out. "It would make no sense."

"That's what the Roman general Pompey thought when he conquered Jerusalem fifty years ago. So he had to peek inside himself. And when he saw nothing, he was baffled by the Jews. Our God is mysterious. Even we don't understand him, and by serving him, we have become a people no one else can understand." He paused.

Mary was not to be put off. "But why do we even have a temple, then, if the precious things inside it that honored God are gone? Did God ask us to build it?"

"No. But we imagined he did, because all the other nations had temples, and we wanted to be like them."

"Really?" It seemed extremely important to Mary to know about this.

The noise of all the people around them made it hard for her to hear his answer. "God gave no instructions to Solomon or David about a temple. And Solomon himself, praying at the dedication, admitted as much when he said, 'But will God really dwell on earth? The heavens, even the highest heavens, cannot contain you. How much less this Temple I have built!' Now, will that satisfy you?" He looked at her affectionately. "If you weren't a girl, I would think you were bound to become a scholar—one of the scribes. They study these things all day long."

It was true she wanted to know all about God and his requirements, but she had no wish to spend all her time poring—and arguing—over documents, like the scribes and scholars they knew at Magdala, men simultaneously comical and frighteningly powerful in the community. Even Eli did not aspire to join their ranks.

"It isn't that . . ." she started to explain. What was there to worship in an empty temple? was what she really wanted to ask Silvanus. But he might not have understood.

⚘ 111 ⚘

The journey home seemed to go faster. The vast company set out from the ridge overlooking Jerusalem as soon as it had gathered itself and its leaders had counted families to make sure everyone was there. Then, with a signal, the first carts rumbled forward, headed northward, northward to Galilee. Others went west to Joppa, and others east to Jericho, but Mary's family's company was directed like an arrow back toward the Sea of Galilee.

There seemed to be more confusion now, more mixing. Mary's family and the other five observant families from Magdala drew themselves up tightly like a little knot, but Mary watched for a chance to escape. Suddenly she was curious to see their neighbors around the lakeshore, and this would be her only chance. She already knew the names of the towns: Capernaum and Bethsaida, and ones inland, like Nazareth. She wanted to meet the people from those places. There were no young children in her Magdala group besides her third cousins Sarah and Rachel, and they were as eager to explore as she.

"Let's slip away!" she whispered to them. "Let's sneak into one of the other groups!"

"Yes, let's!"

For a moment, it surprised her that Sarah, two years older, and Rachel, even older than that, would obey her, but she was too pleased to give it further thought. They were with her, and that was all that counted.

They ducked around the groaning wheels of the carts and the wheezing donkeys. It did not take them long to find the Capernaum group. It was the largest, and made up of elderly people and grownups, trudging along and sighing. There were few children in this group, so Mary and her friends did not linger among them. Capernaum was the largest town on the Sea of Galilee, situated right on its northernmost shore, but if its pilgrims were any indication, it was a staid and dull place.

The group from Bethsaida seemed to be composed mainly of the religious—had not the idol-smashing rabbi come from there?—and that also held little interest for the children.

Dancing through those groups, the band of little explorers was approaching a contingent that looked completely unfamiliar—with all the excitement that promised—when Mary became aware of a girl about her own age trailing behind them. She whirled around to face her and stood staring at a girl with a mass of red hair, ineffectively tied up in ribbons.

"Who are you?" she demanded. It should have fallen to the older members of the group, her cousins Rachel and Sarah, to demand this identification, but since they stood silent, it was up to Mary.

"Keziah," she said stoutly. "It means 'cassia'—'flower of cinnamon.'"

Mary stared at her. She was exotic-looking, with her dark-red curly hair and her golden-brown eyes. "Cassia" certainly fitted her.

"Where are you from?" asked Mary.

"From Magdala," she replied.

Magdala! "And your father?"

"Benjamin," she said.

But Benjamin and his family had never been mentioned by Mary's family. And they did not travel in the company of the six families. That meant they were not observant, were inappropriate company for her. There was so much in Magdala that she did not know, that she suddenly wanted badly to know. "And where do you live?"

"We live in the northern part of town, on the slope by the road. . . ."

In the new section. The section where the recently rich, the friends of Rome, gathered. And yet . . . if they had made this pilgrimage, they could not be entirely friends of Rome.

"Keziah," she said solemnly—as solemnly as a seven-year-old could—"I welcome you."

"Oh, thank you!" The girl tossed her glorious hair, and Mary felt a jolt of envy. If I had hair like that, Mother would make over me. She would. As it is, she can dismiss me as plain. Her own hair is thicker and more shining than mine. But if I had Keziah's hair—

"What are you staring at?" Keziah asked. Then she laughed and held out her hand. "Come, let's explore!"

They made their way over to another group that seemed self-contained, and when they heard it came from Nazareth, they laughed.

"Oh," said Sarah. "No one pays any attention to the Nazareans. They simply don't count."

"Why? In what way?" asked Mary. She kept her new friend, Keziah, close by her side, as if she had found a treasure by the roadside and would not yield it.

"Nazareth's a little village with poor people," said Sarah. "It's a wonder they could get together a group to travel to Jerusalem."

"But there are a lot of camels with them," said Mary. She thought people who owned camels must be more interesting than those with donkeys, since camels had more personality than donkeys.

"True," Keziah admitted. "All right, then, let us try to enter the group. We can judge for ourselves what they are like."

They cautiously approached the group, sidling up and falling in with one family as its members trudged along. They attempted to strike up a conversation, asking about Nazareth. They were given straightforward, dull answers.

"We don't have many foreigners in Nazareth," they said. Nazareth was quiet. Very good for raising a family, they stated.

"Perhaps because there is nothing else to do, children cannot get into trouble," a wizened woman said. "Like that family over there."

She pointed toward a large group walking together, with two young children on the family donkey. "Those people. Joseph and his kin."

Mary looked over to see who they were talking about. A young and pleasant-looking man was stepping along smartly, followed by his wife, presumably, and several other people, with the donkey and the youngsters bringing up the rear.

"Carpenter," said a youth. "He doesn't go every year, but often enough." Pause. "The rest of the time, he's overseeing his shop and his clan. He had a brother in Capernaum whose sons went wild. Joined those insurrections. I suppose Joseph wants to avoid any such trouble."

Just behind Joseph and his wife was a tall young man—or almost a man, but still a boy—with thick dark hair that shone reddish in the noonday sun, and a resolute jaw. Beside him was walking another boy, and then a gaggle of others.

Just then the young man turned to look at Mary and her friends. He had dark eyes set deep.

"Who is that?" asked Keziah.

"That's the oldest son, Jesus," said their informant. "Joseph's favorite."

"Why? Is he such a skilled carpenter?"

The lad shrugged. "I don't know. I suppose so, or Joseph wouldn't be proud of him. But all grownups like him."

"What about people of his own age?"

"Well—we like him, but he's so . . . *serious*. Oh, he likes to play and is friendly enough. But"—he laughed—"he likes to read so much, and he tries to keep it secret. Imagine letting your friends know that you really enjoy all that study that the rest of us find so tedious. They say he can even read Greek already. Taught himself."

"That's impossible," a tall girl said. "No one can teach himself Greek."

"Well, then, he had help, but he studied it himself. Secretly."

"I'm sure it wasn't secret from his real friends," said the girl disdainfully.

"Like you?"

"I'm not—"

Mary and her friends decided to see this intriguing family for themselves. It was not difficult to fall in beside them and join them. The patriarch, Joseph, was trudging along, thumping his staff energetically at each step. Mary noticed that it had a lovely carving of a date palm and its fruit on its top: an artist's touch.

At the same time, she had a very worried thought: I hope he doesn't lose it. Perhaps he should not have brought it on a journey like this one.

"What a pretty staff." Keziah used that as an opening.

Joseph looked over at them and smiled. "Do you like it? I carved the long part, but Jesus here did the date palm."

"It's lovely," said Keziah. Mary herself felt suddenly tongue-tied.

"I enjoyed carving it," the youth said. He had a very pleasant and somehow distinctive voice. "I warned my father not to take it on this trip. If he loses it, I can't promise to carve another. At least, it would be never be the same. I can't always replicate things."

My exact thoughts, about the staff and losing it, thought Mary. How odd. But, then, the other—what did he mean? Why couldn't he just carve another?

"Nothing ever turns out the same way twice," he explained, again as if he had known her thoughts. "No matter how much you wish it to." Then he smiled, a dazzling and reassuring smile. It changed his entire face, taking his deep-set eyes from dark private pools to openness.

"Where are you from?" he asked, when she did not immediately respond to his comment about the staff.

"Magdala," said one of the cousins.

"Magdala," echoed Mary.

"What is your name?" he asked.

"Mary," she said, quietly.

"My mother's name," Jesus said. "You should meet her. She is always happy to meet other Marys." He gestured farther back, toward a woman walking surrounded by her children.

Obediently, Mary, Keziah, and her cousins dropped back and waited to meet the other Mary. She was walking briskly, busy with exchanges with those around her.

She was quieter than her husband and eldest son, but warmly welcoming. She, too, asked questions, but gently and not obtrusively. She wanted to know where they were from, and who their families were. She knew of Nathan—"Indeed, who has not heard of him and his far-reaching business?"—and even admitted to "envy him his sons, who are such a help to him in the business." She had fine, even features that made her face seem classic, like a coin portrait or a statue, and her manner was calm and reassuring. She said she, or someone in her family, usually came to Magdala once a year to buy the preserved fish, which had no equal elsewhere.

"We have no fishermen in our family," she said. "So we must rely on others." She paused. "At least, so far. Perhaps one of you may grow up to be a fisherman?" She looked back at three boys trailing not far behind: a dark, brooding boy of about twelve, followed by a short, stocky boy two or so years younger, with lighter hair, and finally the youngest one. "James," she said, indicating the dark one, "and Jude. And the youngest, that's little Joseph, but in the family we call him Joses. Two Josephs are confusing."

Joses smiled and waved at them, and James curtly nodded his head in acknowledgment.

"James shows little interest in outdoor things," the adult Mary said, seemingly without judgment. "He prefers to be indoors, reading."

"Like my brother Eli," said Mary happily. Perhaps every family had one.

"Oh, is he here?" asked Mary the elder.

"Yes, over there, with the Magdala group."

"What is your name?" asked the elder Mary.

"Mary."

"Why, that is my name!" She seemed very pleased. "It is an honor to meet you." She sounded as if she meant it.

"Thank you," said Mary. No one had ever said that to her.

"We are the daughters of Miriam, then," said the other Mary, "even though our name is the Greek form of it." She turned and looked around for the rest of her children, gesturing for them to come to her. "Here is Ruth," she said, introducing a girl taller, and older, than Mary.

Ruth dipped her head.

"And Leah." Suddenly a large-boned girl about Mary's age appeared.

"Hello," said Leah. "You aren't from Nazareth."

A question? A challenge?

"No," Mary admitted. "I—and my friend and cousins here—are from Magdala."

When Leah looked puzzled, Mary continued. "It's on the Sea of Galilee. The Sea of Kinnoreth."

"Oh. Yes! It's like a mirror in the morning and afternoon! How lucky you are to live beside it!" Leah laughed.

"You should come and visit me and see it."

"Perhaps I shall." She made a gesture with her arm. "I think you have met everyone now except the baby," said Leah. "There he is." She pointed toward a dun-colored donkey with a toddler on his back, held firmly in the saddle by another cousin, walking alongside. "That's Simon."

As they walked along, talking, neither Mary nor Keziah nor her cousins noticed the sun sinking across the afternoon sky. This Nazareth family was so much fun to travel with. They—or at least Mary, Jesus, and Leah—seemed to listen intently to everything she said and find it somehow important. James was listening, too, Mary could tell, but he said little. Their questions to her were, mysteriously, ones that she wanted to answer, rather than the boring ones that everyone else asked, that made you give answers as lifeless as the questions themselves.

Suddenly the entire party began slowing its pace.

"Sabbath is drawing on," said Mary the elder firmly.

Sabbath! Mary and the other visitors looked at one another in surprise. They had forgotten all about it! And now the caravan would have to halt here, right in the middle of Samaria, to observe it! They had best return to their group.

"Stay here with us," said the elder Mary.

"Yes, spend the Sabbath night with us. We have plenty of room." It was Jesus speaking.

Mary looked at him to see if he really meant it or was just being polite.

"Please." He was smiling, a smile that was entirely welcoming.

Would not her family be angry? Or worried?

"People visit all the time," said Mary the elder. "It is a fine way to honor the Sabbath. But Jesus can go and let your family know where you are, so they will not worry."

"And our families, too?" asked her cousins and Keziah anxiously.

"Yes, of course."

"Thank you," said Mary. She bit her lip not to betray how excited she was at the prospect of spending the Sabbath with these strangers, who were both mysterious and oddly comforting.

They began searching for a place to stop for the night. With the short time left before the Sabbath began, they could not afford to be too particular. So they hastily selected an area with level ground and some clumps of trees, providing protection and a place to tether animals. All around them the other Nazareth families were settling, and soon a small town of tents had sprung up.

"Quickly, now," Mary the elder told her sons. "The fire! Get it going!" Jude and James started piling up sticks in a clearing in front of the tent, and hastened to light them. "Girls, help me get the food ready for the pot!" She pulled open a bundle of cooking pots and ladles, and then pointed to another sack. "The beans. And do we have time to bake bread?" She cast an appraising eye toward the sun.

Meanwhile, Joseph was tending to the donkeys, removing their packs and saddle blankets and leading them to a small stream to drink. Inside the large tent, the younger Mary, her cousins, and Keziah were set to work getting the blankets out for sleeping pads.

"The lights!" The elder Mary nodded to Ruth. "Please get the Sabbath lights ready." Ruth began hunting for them in one of the pack bundles, finally pulling out two lanterns. She then expertly filled them with olive oil, as far to the brim as possible, and set them down carefully.

The little clay stove was set up over the burning sticks and the beans set on to boil; the hastily made bread dough was wrapped and put beside it to rise. There was a feeling of tremendous anticipation, both in the rushing and in what was being rushed toward. More food was readied—for there had to be enough to last all the next day, until sundown—and as soon as it was cooked, it was snatched off the fire to be replaced by something else.

The sun sank lower in the sky, until it was hanging just above the horizon, casting long purplish shadows into the camp from the surrounding trees and camels. The smoke from many campfires rose, sending billowing clouds toward the sky, which was also purple-tinged, so that the whole setting seemed wrapped in a violet mist.

"We're almost finished," said the elder Mary, relief and elation mingling in her voice. "Here." She shoved some loaves of bread into the oven, after snatching out two freshly baked ones. She set them aside to cool, and they gave off a crusty smell in the evening air.

Ruth and Leah had transferred the cooked beans into the earthenware bowls and set them alongside the blanket where they would sit to eat. The two Sabbath lanterns were likewise waiting beside the blanket. The boys brought over a wineskin, and their sisters set out cups; goat cheese, dried fish, almonds, and figs were laid out on a cloth.

The sun had touched the horizon.

Now whatever remained to be done must be hurried through or forgotten. Were the tent ropes secure? There could be no knot-tying on the Sabbath. Was the fire smothered in the stove? There could be no cooking or heating on the Sabbath. Did anyone need to write in a ledger? Hurry—there could be no writing on the Sabbath, except by using impermanent ink, like fruit juice, or writing upon the sand—or using the left hand, if that was not the normal hand one used for writing.

Ruth quickly braided her hair—there could be no braiding on the Sabbath. Leah reluctantly pulled out the ribbons in her hair—forbidden ornaments. The men pulled off their nailed travel sandals—nailed sandals were also forbidden.

Jesus arrived back at the group and sat down quickly, pulling off his sandals.

"Did you find our families?" Mary asked. "Did you speak to them?" Did you get permission for us to stay? she wondered. She was ready for the certainty that she would have to go back, and quickly, while the sun was still above the horizon.

"Yes," said Jesus. "Yes, I found them all." He leaned forward, still trying to catch his breath. "Keziah, yours seemed pleased that you had been invited to spend the Sabbath as a guest." He looked around at Rachel and Sarah. "Yours were not as happy with it, but they gave permission. Yours . . ." He looked at Mary. "I had quite a time convincing them."

What had happened? she felt her heart hammering as she waited to hear.

"Your father—Nathan?" He nodded toward her.

"Yes," she answered.

"He said it was irregular, that we did not know one another, and that he was strict about not mixing with less observant families."

Yes. Of course. Mary had known it would be so.

"He needed some proof that we were respectable."

"And how—how could he know that?" Mary asked.

"He put me to a test." Jesus laughed, as if he found it amusing rather than insulting. "He wanted to test my knowledge of scripture, as if that would reveal my shortcomings."

At that, his mother let out a laugh. "Wrong test!" she said, shaking her head. "The rabbis in Jerusalem know better." She turned to her guests. "Last year, Jesus stayed behind in Jerusalem to probe the scribes and rabbis at the Temple about fine points of scripture. So I can appreciate how your parents feel, Mary, to have a child suddenly go off on his own. But no one wins a scripture contest with Jesus."

Jesus made a face. "It wasn't a contest," he said. "He merely asked me a few texts. . . ." He shrugged.

Everyone gathered around the blanket, although the smallest rays of sun were still spilling across it. Ruth bent down and lit the Sabbath candles, her freshly braided hair wound around her head. Quietly they all watched the fading of the sun.

Mary remembered doing this every week at home, but this was the first time she had ever experienced it at any other place than with her own family. Always at home there was the same exultant expectation, a sort of holding-of-the-breath for the coming of the Sabbath. And when it came . . . yes, the time did seem different, somehow. Almost magical. She could say to herself, This is Sabbath bread, this is Sabbath water, this is Sabbath light.

From somewhere in the camp came the sound of a trumpet, blowing two notes, repeated three times. It signaled the onset of the Sabbath, the twilight between the appearance of the first and the third stars in the dusky sky. Traditionally, the first couplet was to warn workers to cease their tasks; the second to tell merchants to close their businesses; and the third set to say that the moment for lighting the Sabbath light had come. The Sabbath had begun to shine, as the saying put it.

Mary, the mother, now moved forward to consecrate the already lit lights. Holding her hands over the lanterns, she said quietly, "Blessed art thou, O Lord our God, King of the Universe, who hast sanctified us by thy commandments, and commanded us to kindle the Sabbath lamp." Her warm, low voice made the words seem especially rich.

Everyone sank down on the blanket and waited for a moment. The sky was swiftly darkening, and with every moment the sturdy Sabbath lanterns were providing more and more light; other lanterns set before the tents were also burning. Except for the occasional sound of an animal lowing or bleating, a hush seemed to hang in the air.

"We welcome our guests," said Joseph, nodding toward Mary, her cousins, and Keziah. "Although we do not live far apart, we have many neighbors in nearby towns that we never get to meet. We are grateful that they came to us."

"Yes," said Jesus. "Thank you for coming to us." He smiled.

"Now we must eat and welcome the beautiful Sabbath." Joseph broke one of the loaves of bread and passed it around. .

Sitting cross-legged on the blanket, they each took pieces of bread. Following that were the beans, the thin-sliced onions, the figs, almonds, and goat cheese, and then cured fish from Magdala.

Jesus looked at it in surprise and said, "We must have known that we would have guests from Magdala." He took a piece and then passed it on.

Mary tingled with pride. Perhaps these fish had even come from her father's warehouse! She selected one herself, placing it carefully on the piece of bread.

"Magdala fish travel far and wide," said Joseph, jauntily hoisting a piece of bread with the fish. "You have made our name in Rome and even beyond." He popped a piece in his mouth.

"Yes, we Galileans are respected abroad but hardly in Jerusalem," said Jesus. He, too, put a piece of fish and bread in his mouth and smiled at the savory taste.

"What do you mean?" asked James, scowling.

"You know what I mean," said Jesus. "What is Galilee called? 'The circle of unbelievers.' That's because we have been in and out of true Israel's boundaries so often as different parts of Israel were conquered. . . ." He took a thoughtful sip of wine. "It's an interesting question—who and what are the true sons of Israel?" He laughed and inclined his head toward the women. "And the daughters, of course."

"Who is a Jew?" asked James suddenly, his lean face stern. "Perhaps only . . . heaven . . . can answer." He paused. "There are half-Jews, those whose ancestry is suspect; there are pretend Jews, like Herod Antipas; there are Gentiles who are attracted to our teachings—as who wouldn't be, in contrast to the disgusting pagan religions surrounding them—but who won't go all the way and be circumcised. Do all these quasi-Jews help us or hinder us?"

"It depends on whether God is pleased that people want to be associated with him, at least at a distance, or whether he is insulted by that."

"I don't know," admitted James.

"Nor do I," said Joseph, firmly putting a stop to the topic. "Beyond this, we are just profaning the Sabbath with idle chatter. And we are held accountable for all idle chatter. We shall have to give an account of it before God."

"What is 'idle chatter'?" asked Keziah. Mary was shocked that she would speak out like that to Joseph. "Anything not holy? But I can think of so many things that don't seem very holy to talk about." She paused. "Such as . . . deciding which clothes to wear."

"But there are laws governing all that," said James. "Moses laid down some laws, and then since then the rabbis—"

"I mean, wearing flattering clothes or moth-eaten ones, bright-colored ones or dull ones, expensive ones or cheap ones!" She looked around triumphantly. "You see, there are no laws about that."

"Well, in that case, you have to apply a general principle," said Joseph. "Will it be pleasing to . . . the Holy Name? Will it give glory to him? You see, it isn't so simple as just a rule. Does a good outward appearance reflect well on him? Or is it only impressive to men, who cannot see what's in the heart?"

"It's so complicated," Keziah complained. "How can anyone know the mind of God?"

Just then, Ruth bit into a dried date and winced. "My tooth," she said, more in surprise than in pain.

"The pellitory root," said her mother. "It is in the leather bag in the . . ." Her voice grew small. "In the large saddle-bundle." There was no need to say anything more. The bundle was tied with strong knots, and it was forbidden to untie knots until after sundown tomorrow. And anyway, even had it been handy, it was a rule that on the Sabbath no medicine might be used.

"But," she remembered, "vinegar . . . vinegar can be used for food-seasoning, and if it happens to help the tooth as well, that is permitted." Luckily, the small vial of vinegar was already out. Quickly it was passed around, and everyone added it to his food. Ruth took a large dose.

In the quiet after having just eaten, and while waiting for the vinegar to alleviate Ruth's pain, the family started reciting scripture. It had to be recited from memory, because reading was forbidden.

But at the end of the recitations, Ruth did not look any more comfortable.

"Perhaps we should ask the rabbi," said Joseph. "It may be that he can permit us to untie the knots, or to use medicine this once."

Someone scampered off to find the rabbi, and after what seemed a long while, he loomed up in the darkness around the tent.

"Let me see the child," he said. He made straight for Ruth, asked her to open her mouth, and peered into it. Then he clamped it shut.

"I do not see anything amiss," he pronounced.

"Nonetheless, it hurts," said Ruth.

"Can we not untie the bundle that contains the powder?" asked Joseph.

"Can you untie the knot with one hand?" answered the rabbi.

"No, it is a true knot, meant to withstand road travel."

The rabbi shook his head. "Then you know the ruling," he said. He turned to Ruth. "Try to be brave, child. The night is already well under way. It will not be so long until sunset tomorrow." He looked at all of them. "I am sorry," he said, turning to leave. "And in any case, even if the medicine were out in plain sight, it cannot be used on the Sabbath." He looked sad and apologetic. "You know that, Joseph."

After the rabbi left, Joseph came and sat by his daughter, held her hand as she winced with pain. He looked deep into her eyes, and finally he stood up.

He made his way over to the bundle and slowly, deliberately, untied the knot. "I'll make a sin-offering to cover this," he said. "But I cannot just stand here and wait for tomorrow."

He took out the medicine and handed it to Ruth.

Shortly thereafter, they all went to bed, stealing away quietly to the makeshift pallets that awaited them. Mary, her cousins, and Keziah were all in one corner of the tent, and it was not long before she was fighting off sleep. She had carefully unwound her belt and put it aside with her cloak. Patting it protectively, she settled down, keeping it safely near her head.

She smiled as she drifted off to sleep. It was great fun to have a secret. And it had also been a wonderful day, meeting these people and coming to know them. It was fun, she had to admit, to get away from your own family, to be someone else for a while. Or perhaps not someone else at all, but your actual, real, true self.

She slept very soundly, and did not awaken when everyone stirred at dawn. They were up and outside before she rubbed her eyes and sat up, hastily dressed herself, and joined the others.

The sky was already clear and blue; the dawn streaks had long since vanished.

They shared a small meal of bread and cheese, sitting together in a circle as the sky grew bright overhead and the sweet early-morning smells promised as fine a day as earth could offer.

"It is no wonder, if the first Sabbath was as beautiful as this, that God rested and called his work 'very good,'" said Jesus. He was slowly chewing a piece of bread and looking overhead in deep contentment.

Everyone nodded in turn. A calmness seemed to be in the very air. "Yes," Jesus's mother answered quietly, in her melodious voice. She passed a basket of figs to her left, her gesture almost as graceful as a dancer's.

Why, she is beautiful, thought Mary, only I had not noticed it until just now. She is much more beautiful than my own mother. Instantly she felt disloyal, and even guilty, for such a suggestion.

The rest of the day—and it could seem both long and short at the same time—was spent in the pleasures of idleness or in special devotions. Sitting and talking was permitted; singing, taking short leisurely walks; feeding the animals their necessary food; eating the already-prepared meal; taking time to be quiet and daydream. And then there were the prayers, private and in groups, among them the ancient, most basic prayer of all, the Shema: "Shema!"—Hear!—"O Israel, the Lord our God, the Lord is One."

Mary noticed Jesus sitting by himself under a small tree, and he seemed to be dozing. But as she watched more closely, she could see that he was not sleeping but concentrating deeply on something, something within himself. Though she started to retreat, it was too late. He had seen her; she had disturbed him. He was gesturing for her to come closer.

"I am sorry," she said.

"For what?" He seemed genuinely puzzled as to what she meant, rather than annoyed.

"For intruding on you," she said.

He smiled. "I am sitting here out in the open. It's impossible to intrude on someone in a public place."

"But you were by yourself," she persisted. "You must have wanted to be left alone."

"No, not really," he said. "Perhaps I was just waiting for something interesting to happen."

"Like what?"

"Anything. Anything that happens is interesting, if you can just look at it carefully. Like this lizard"—he inclined his head slowly, lest he frighten it—"that is trying to decide whether to come out of the crevice or not."

"Well, what's so interesting about a lizard?" She had never found them particularly interesting, although it was true she had never taken the time really to look at one. But they moved so fast!

"Don't you find lizards fascinating?" he asked, serious. Or was he? "They have such strange, bumpy skin. And the way their limbs move—so different from other animals with four legs. They move them one at a time, not two together. When God created them, he must have been

40

trying to prove that there are many different ways of traveling, and many ways to be fast."

"What about snakes?" she asked. "I don't understand how they can move at all, let alone fast, because they have no legs."

"Yes, snakes are a better example. God very cleverly taught them how to move around and have a happy life in spite of what they were missing."

"We aren't allowed to eat them, either," she said. "Was God trying to protect them, or us?"

"Now we are truly keeping the Sabbath," Jesus said, unexpectedly. "That is a pleasure, as it is meant to be."

He said such odd things. But she liked him anyway. Some people who said odd things were frightening, because you felt they were dangerous or dim-witted and unpredictable. But this boy seemed the opposite: eminently sensible and trustworthy. It seemed all right to admit, "I don't know what you mean."

He gave a sigh of pleasure. "Because we are thinking about God, considering the work of his hands, meditating—if you will—on it."

"Meditating on a lizard?" She could not help giggling.

"No less a creation of God than an eagle or a lion," he said. "And perhaps showing his genius better."

"Should we spend a year meditating on a different creature each day?" she asked. It seemed like an intriguing idea.

"Indeed," he said. "Remember the Psalm, where it says:

'Praise the Lord from the earth, ye dragons, and all ye
    deeps:
Fire, hail, snow, ice, stormy winds, which fulfill his word:
Mountains and all hills, fruitful trees and all cedars:
Beasts and all cattle: serpents and feathered fowls.'"

She didn't remember that Psalm, but now she would never forget it.

"Say praises to God!" she sternly commanded the lizard, who bolted from his crevice and disappeared. Jesus laughed.

Soon—too soon, it seemed—the sun was touching the horizon, spelling the end of the Sabbath. They stood and watched it go, listening as the trumpet signaled the close of the consecrated pause.

In spite of the elder Mary's assurance that visiting others was a fine way to observe the Sabbath, and Jesus's seeking out Mary's family to tell them where she was, when she returned to them they were angry with her.

"What were you thinking, wandering off like that?" her mother snapped. "Finding yourself stranded as the Sabbath started, so that you had to spend it with a family of strangers!" She glared at Mary. "That boy who came hunting for us—I didn't like him," she said.

"Jesus?" Mary asked.

"I could tell he wasn't raised right. He wasn't even deferential. Not the sort of people you should be associating with."

"Then why—did you let me stay?" Mary asked, in a small voice.

"What I'd like to know is, why did you *want* to stay? That's the question!"

Mary wanted to tell her mother that this family was wonderful, and how much she had enjoyed talking to them, and the adventure of the aching tooth. But she knew Joseph's thoughtfully considered breaking of the Sabbath would not have pleased her parents. So she just lowered her eyes and said, "They seemed very kind."

Her father came over. "Nazareth has a bad reputation," he said. "And that Jesus. I asked him some questions about scripture, and he—"

"He knew more than you did," said Silvanus, right behind him. "When you asked him about that passage in Hosea"—he laughed—"you know, that favorite one you like to quote, about the land mourning—"

"Yes, yes!" barked Nathan.

"He asked me to give you this," said Mary, holding out the staff that Jesus and Joseph had carved. They had insisted that she take it, as if they wanted to soothe Nathan. She had protested—it was much too fine, and they had put so much work into it—but they were adamant.

"What?" Her father snatched it away and examined it. The corners of his mouth twitched. He kept turning it and looking at the workmanship. "Bah!" he said. "Vanity!" He threw the staff down, and Mary winced.

Silvanus bent down and picked it up. "It is a sin to disdain a gift like this," he said.

"Oh, really?" said his father. "And where does it say that in scripture?"

He turned and walked away.

Silvanus stood, running his hands over the staff. "When you see Jesus again, you will have to ask him," he said. "I am sure there is something in the holy texts about not profaning a gift. And he will surely know it."

"I won't be seeing Jesus again," she said. There could be no way of that. But as for her new friend, Keziah, right in Magdala—she was determined to visit her home. Her father would forbid it. Doubtless he would disapprove of Keziah, too. But what her father did not know, he could not forbid.

Magdala was waiting to welcome them back. Returning pilgrims were always a focus of intense interest for the first few days after their return, brief celebrities of their circle: Tell us—the streets of Jerusalem, what were they like? The foreign Jews—were there many of them? The Temple—how splendid, really? Was it the high point of one's life to have stood in its courts? The fleeting attention, the momentary adulation, was sometimes more heady than the trip itself. Then, inevitably, it faded. And the next group of pilgrims—in this case, the ones going to Jerusalem for the High Holy Day of Atonement—took their place in the center of the ring of attention.

It was several weeks—measured by six Sabbaths—before Mary and Keziah were reunited. They had managed to exchange messages and arrange a time for Mary to come to Keziah's house and share a meal with them. It was to be during an afternoon when she was supposed to be watching a weaving demonstration in a neighboring house by a master rug-weaver from Tyre. She did watch the weaving for a few minutes, thinking, It is very beautiful, but I could never do such a thing. Then she scampered away, leaving the shaded workshop beside the lake, hurrying through the crowded marketplace, following the street that led north, toward the hilly section of town with the newer houses.

The streets became steep enough that she paused to catch her breath. All around her, the houses were growing larger and more impressive, presenting closed blank walls to the street, which in itself served notice that whatever lay within must need guarding.

Keziah's lay at the very end of the street, perched so that the steps leading up to it were at an angle. The front door was of ornamented bronze. Before Mary could even knock on it, it was flung open by Keziah, grinning triumphantly.

"You got here!" she said, pulling Mary in and hugging her.

"Yes, but—it was difficult." She tried not to think of the punishment awaiting her if her parents found out she had left the weaving demonstration. But she was here now, where she wanted to be. She stepped inside and became immediately aware of a large, dark atrium surrounding her. The coolness was astounding on this hot summer day.

They stood looking at one another, a little awkward. The friendship that they had forged so quickly and so fiercely a while ago seemed now, perhaps, something they had imagined.

"Well," said Keziah. "I am glad you are here. Come, see my home." She took Mary's hand and guided her beyond the atrium and into an adjoining series of rooms. There were a great many of them, as many as all the rooms in Mary's house put together and then doubled and tripled.

"You have your own room?" Mary asked.

"Oh, yes, and a second story, too, with rooms above us." Her voice was light and friendly, playful, as if this was the way everyone lived.

Mary tried not to stare. But the cavernous rooms were like something in a dream. And in spite of having only three walls, with the fourth open to a sunlit courtyard, the rooms were dark. Then, as her eyes became accustomed to it, she saw that the walls were painted a deep blood-red, and in one room the walls were even black. That was why they seemed so dark.

But Keziah kept pulling her forward, and they left the formal part of the house and entered the family quarters. Then Mary was ushered into a room with yellow walls and a lower ceiling—a room containing little chairs and a table set with miniature cups and pitchers. The floor was cool and laid with polished stone, and in one corner was an elegant narrow bed with finely carved legs, painted black but gilded on its ornamental rungs. Glistening silk covered it.

"Oh!" Mary finally said, turning to look at everything in wonder. "And this is where you live? And sleep?"

"Yes," said Keziah. "Ever since I can remember." Then they both laughed, knowing that seven or eight years is not a very long time to remember, so it was not much of a feat.

Mary could not imagine living in such surroundings. I would spend all my time just looking at it, she thought. She examined the little cups and other plates on the table—tiny sauce dishes and jugs and patterned bowls.

"Do you eat from these?" she asked, wondering.

Keziah laughed. "Oh, no, they are just for playing. I've much too big an appetite to be satisfied with those portions!"

Did she have dolls? But those were forbidden—surely there were no dolls here.

"They are for me and my imaginary friends," said Keziah. "And, now that you are here, a real friend. We can pretend to have feasts! Feasts of invisible food that never leaves a stain or needs washing up after!"

"I never had a place to set my make-believe banquets," said Mary. What fun this would be!

Suddenly the shyness between them melted. They were indeed very similar, and were meant to be friends.

"Come, now, I think it is time for our real meal, and I want you to meet my mother and father. And—oh, yes—my little brother. Omri."

Omri. Mary had never heard of anyone named Omri. Vaguely she remembered the name—some king who was bad. But, then, she had never met anyone named Keziah, either. Obviously these people did not care to call their children by common names—like Mary. Or Jesus. Or Samuel.

In another section of the house, also bordering on the courtyard, Keziah brought Mary into a fair room, its walls a deep green with life-like trees and flowers painted on its upper panels. There was a low marble table in the center, with cushions set against stone backrests. The heat of midday did not reach inside the room, but the light did.

"Mother, Father, this is my friend Mary," said Keziah proudly, presenting Mary to them as if she were a prized toy. "You remember, I told you about meeting her on the pilgrimage to Jerusalem."

"Oh, yes." A tall woman, dressed in crimson silk, bent down to meet Mary, looking at her very solemnly, as if she were being introduced to someone very important—another adult, not a child. "I am so pleased that you and Keziah have made friends," she murmured.

"Welcome," said Keziah's father, Benjamin. He was not so markedly different in age and size from Mary's own father, but there were several gold rings on his fingers, and his robe was brighter-colored than the plain ones Nathan favored.

A round-faced little boy who looked a bit younger than Keziah dragged his feet up to the table, then leaned on it. "Hello," he finally said.

"This is Omri," said the woman. "Omri, can't you smile? You say 'hello' but you aren't very welcoming."

"Oh, all right!" Omri sighed. He jerked his mouth into a parody of a smile. "Welcome," he said, exaggerating the word.

"Omri, you're a pest!" said Keziah.

"I know," he said proudly. Then he plopped down on the cushion and grinned.

Mary slowly sank down, holding herself very still. It was all so different from her home. She hoped she would not make an embarrassing mistake in front of these people. But she never ate like this, on a marble table, nor was she ever served by servants. Or were they slaves?

She stole a look at the women bringing out the dishes. They did not look like slaves: they were not foreigners, and when they did speak, they had no accent. They must be local people, hired for household duties. That made her feel a little more comfortable.

There many small dishes containing food that was unfamiliar to her. There was a bowl of some sort of white cheese with red streaks in its curds, and another of some dark-green and salty leaves, and a fruit she did not recognize. Were they . . . unclean? Was she allowed to eat them?

But, then, these people did go to Jerusalem, so they must keep the Law, she told herself.

"Keziah tells us your father is Nathan, Nathan of the large fish-plant by the lake," the man said to Mary. "I have had dealings with him, and I must say, his honesty and his high standards are rare in the fish-processing business. So many of the others are slippery characters—like the fish they handle, I fear."

"Thank you, sir," Mary said. The thought of her father just then was troubling. What if he was looking for her? What if the weaving had ended early?

"My father is a goldsmith!" said Keziah proudly. "He has a big workshop, and has lots of artists working for him. Look, look at his rings! They are from our own shop!"

So that was why he wore so many. Now it did not seem vain. He was simply showing people his own craftsmanship outside the confines of his shop. She did not want to find anything to criticize in this family, and hoped that, if she did not, neither could her parents.

"Have you ever come to our workshop?" asked Keziah's father. "It is just on the other side of the central marketplace."

Mary did not think so, but she could not be sure. Her parents did not buy gold jewelry, so they would not have had a reason to go there.

"We'll go there together this afternoon," said Keziah. "Father, you are returning there, aren't you?"

"Yes, I'll be going later," he said. "I could show you the workroom, where the smiths hammer out the sheets of pure gold, and where the filigree is made."

This afternoon—no, she could not go then. She would surely be discovered if she was gone so long.

"I—I cannot, this afternoon," Mary mumbled. How she hated to say it! How she wanted to see the workshop!

"Ah. Then another time," he said, shrugging. "Was that the first time your family had gone to Jerusalem?"

"Yes," she said.

"And what did they think? Was it as they had expected?" Keziah's mother asked.

"I don't know," she admitted. "I am not sure what they expected."

"And what did you expect?" Now Keziah's mother was leaning toward her, seeming truly interested in what she had to say.

"I expected something not of this world," she finally said. "I thought the stones would be dazzling like glass, I thought the streets would be gold, or sapphires, and I thought I would faint when I saw the Temple. But the streets were paved only with stones, and the Temple was not magic, even if it was enormous."

Keziah's father said, "You were expecting the city the prophet Ezekiel saw in his vision. But that was a promise of what may come. That is what visions are—promises from God."

Visions! Were they the same as vivid dreams? "Do people still have visions?" Mary asked.

"Perhaps," he answered. "We cannot know what goes on in every house."

"Our friends the Romans were certainly in view in Jerusalem," said Keziah's mother. "I don't think Romans were in Ezekiel's vision."

"Our friends?" Mary was shocked to hear the Romans called friends.

"She means it as a joke!" said Omri. "It's the opposite of what she really means." He folded his arms authoritatively.

"Thank you, Omri. I don't think you should apply for a diplomatic post." But Keziah's father was smiling, not scolding. "And, actually, there are some Romans who are our friends. Several patronize our shop, buying the most lovely necklaces and earrings for their wives. A man who decks his wife out in gold jewelry can't be all bad!"

Mary, used to her family's harangues about vanity, not to mention their diatribes against the Romans, laughed. Yes, it would be thrilling to be taken to a goldsmith's and told to choose something.

A cool breeze blew in from the open courtyard. Mary could see a glint of the lake from their high vantage point. The hillside house was well positioned to catch the winds of summer. But what about winter, when the gales blew?

A tinkle from a circle of hanging glass played sweet, high music as the breeze passed through it. It sounded like a harp plucked by the wind.

"In the winter we retreat indoors," said Keziah's mother. "Into the rooms painted black or red, which is all the fashion now abroad. It makes you feel very warm and cozy. But now who can think of winter?" The wind chimes sang again, a high-pitched, tinkling sigh.

Ugly winter, whipping up storms on the lake, endangering fishing boats, with its gales and fog and cold that crept into every corner of every house—no, no thinking of that now. Not now, in high summer, when the land lay open and golden and warm, and the lake was friendly and safe and covered with boats of all sizes.

"'Mary' is such a pretty name," said Keziah's father. "What are your brothers and sisters named?"

"Mary" is a very common name, she thought. How kind of him to compliment it. "I have two brothers. One is named Eli and the other is Samuel." More ordinary names. "My mother's name is Zebidah," she added. That one was unusual; it was the name of the mother of an ancient king of Judah.

"I've never known a Zebidah," said Keziah's mother.

"Well, I've never known either a Keziah or an Omri!" Mary said.

"'Keziah' was the name of one of Job's daughters," said her mother. "After God restored his fortunes, that is. It means 'cassia,' a spice. When we saw her red hair, we both thought of it."

"And Omri?" What had Mary heard about Omri? It wasn't good.

"Omri was ruler of the northern kingdom of Israel," said his father. "He was the father of Ahab."

She knew it! He was evil! It was all Mary could do not to bring her hand to her mouth in shock.

"Oh, I know he's dismissed as bad because anything and anyone in the northern kingdom is now seen as bad, but let's examine the evidence," said Keziah's father.

Mary was not sure how you could examine the evidence, but she was eager to hear.

"He founded the great city of Samaria. It was to be a rival to Jerusalem. He regained lost territory east of the Jordan and conquered

Moab. He made peace with Judah and ended the constant warfare between the brother states. He's a man to be proud of, to emulate!"

"We wanted our son to be strong and full of courage and vigor," said Keziah's mother. "And so we named him Omri. Those who know the achievements of Omri understand. As for the others, they are ignorant, bigoted fools!"

Like my family, thought Mary. They don't think much of the northern kingdom.

"Sarah!" said her husband. "That's a little extreme. They are ignorant, but let's not call them fools."

"If you read our history, you can see for yourself how blind they are."

She read books? She could read?

Keziah's mother turned to Mary. "Are you learning to read?" she asked. "Keziah has just started lessons."

"No, I—" *I want to learn, I want it more than anything!*

"Would you like to join Keziah? Lessons are more pleasant if there are more of you than of the teacher."

"Yes, please come! You'll like my tutor, he's lots of fun!"

Could she? Could she possibly escape from her family and come here and learn to read? She felt dizzy with excitement just thinking about it.

"It's twice a week," said Keziah. "In the midafternoon. When most people are resting."

"I—I can ask," Mary said in a soft voice. But she knew the answer. So there was no point in asking.

"Shall I ask for you?" said Keziah's mother. "I could extend the invitation—"

"No!" said Mary quickly. Then she would have to explain to her family how she knew them and all the rest of the story. And the answer would still be no. "I'll—I'll ask," she said.

"And how shall we get word to one another?" said Keziah. "Shall we leave notes in the tree by the lake? But—oh—you can't write."

At that moment, Mary made up her mind absolutely to learn to read and write, no matter what she had to do.

"I'll leave a red handkerchief if I can come, a black one if I can't," she said.

"And where have you been?" Mary's mother loomed over her as she stepped into their atrium—a tiny one, it now seemed.

On the way home, Mary had concocted her story: after the weaving demonstration, she had gone to look for colored wools in the marketplace, to see if any were available like the ones the weaver had shown them. She had not meant to be gone so long.

She told it, boldly. Her mother eyed her. "I came at the end. I did not see you," she said.

"I left just before the end, so I could go to the market ahead of the crowd," said Mary.

Zebidah nodded approvingly. "Yes, that is what one must do," she said. "If a large number of people crowd in on a merchant, he knows he has sales. He can drive up the price. Then, of course, you cannot buy from him. Because he has increased his price."

"But what if the price—even the increased one—is fair?" asked Mary. She was so relieved that she had apparently gotten away with her secret excursion that she was happy to discuss merchants and their prices.

"Even so, you must not reward such behavior," said her mother.

"But what is wrong with it?" asked Mary. "If the merchant sees that many people want to buy from him, what is wrong with setting a higher price? Just as, if a seller sees that no one wants his wares, he lowers his prices. I have seen you buy at such lower prices. If one is wrong, why is the other not wrong?"

"You don't understand," said her mother.

But Mary knew she understood all too well. "Mother," she said, "the weaver is going to give lessons twice a week to beginners. . . ."

The summer passed pleasantly, with long hot days and cool nights. Mary's ruse about the weaver's lessons worked well, and twice a week she hurried up to Keziah's house on the heights, going directly from the weaving lessons to the reading ones. Keziah's parents would not hear of her paying for them, they were so delighted that their daughter had a learning companion. And how eagerly she learned; how thirsty she was to master reading, so that a whole world could open to her.

It was just on the eve of Rosh Hashanah, of the new year of thirty-seven hundred and sixty-eight, when Mary was lying awake with excitement, that she heard a faint "Mary!," as if someone across the room was whispering her name.

Although the voice was sweet, it startled her. She sat up and peered into the darkness. Had she been dreaming? There was no one there.

It must have been a dream. I suppose I was asleep and did not know it, she thought.

But she was wide awake now. And certainly awake to hear the voice again. "Mary."

Now she held her breath. There was no sound of anything else in the room: no intake of breath, no rustling.

"Mary." Now the sound seemed to be coming from quite nearby.

"Yes?" she asked in a tiny voice.

But there was no answer. And she did not dare to get up.

In the morning light, she looked around the room but saw nothing. Was it perhaps just a dream? She thought about it most of the morning, and suddenly wondered if this was what had happened to the prophet Samuel as a young boy. When he was living with the priest Eli, he too had heard a voice in the night calling his name, and thought it was Eli. But it turned out to be God, and Samuel was told to answer, "Speak, for your servant is listening."

If I hear the voice again, Mary promised herself, that's what I'll say, too. She could not help feeling a tingle of exhilaration that she might have been *chosen* for something.

That night it was the dead time of deep darkness before anything came to Mary's ears, and she was sound asleep, having been tired out by her half-sleep the night before.

"Mary, Mary," it said. It was a soft woman's voice.

Fighting through layers of sleep, Mary gave the answer she had been practicing: "Speak, for your servant is listening."

A hush. Then, faintly, "Mary, you have neglected me. You have not attended to me as I deserve."

Mary sat up, her heart pounding. The Lord—the Lord was speaking to her! How could she possibly answer? But did not the Lord know everything, all her weaknesses and lacks? "I"—she struggled for words—"how have I neglected you?" It was near the Day of Atonement; was God going to call a great omission to her conscience?

"You have hidden me away and do not look upon me. It is not as I should be treated."

What could he mean? God could not be seen, or hidden. "I do not understand."

"Of course you do not, for you are a foolish girl. You were clever enough to recognize something valuable, and clever enough to protect it, but beyond that, you are ignorant."

The voice was teasing and light at the same time. It did not sound like God, at least as he was reported to have spoken to Moses.

"Then teach me, Lord," Mary said, humbly.

"Very well," the voice said. "Tomorrow, you must gaze upon me once again, and I will tell you what to do. Now sleep, foolish one." The voice dismissed her, and faded away.

Sleep? How could she sleep? Mary sank back down in the bed, unhappy. God had chastised her—and for what? She should have been honored that God had spoken to her, but he had been so disapproving.

"You were clever enough to recognize something valuable, and clever enough to protect it. . . . Tomorrow, you must gaze upon me once again. . . ."

Protect . . . gaze upon me . . .

Even before the room grew completely light, Mary was jolted by the realization: it was the ivory idol who had spoken.

Yes, it was she. That explained the woman's voice, and the complaints about being hidden away. For Mary had indeed hidden her in a box underneath a winter cloak—the box *was* across the room, whence had come the voice—and forgotten about her.

Gingerly, Mary rose from bed and pulled out the box, thrusting her hand under the folds of the woolen cloak and feeling for the wrapped bundle. Yes, here it was. She grasped it and brought it out into the gray dawn light. Carefully she unwrapped it, and beheld the face of the enigmatic smiling goddess.

How could I ever have forgotten you? was her first uncensored thought.

"There, now." The voice seemed to be right inside her head. The exquisite face was growing more visible every moment, as the true daylight came. There were the lines carved in the ivory, depicting her hair flowing down over her shoulders, the dreamy half-closed eyes, even the pattern on the dress, and the symbolic jewelry, all suggesting her power, but gently, like an ancient vision, from a time when goddesses were mighty in the land, and controlled wind, and rain, and crops, birth and death. "I am reborn, into the sunlight."

The lovely face gazed up at Mary's.

"Put me where I can feel the daylight. I have been buried so long in the dark. In the ground. Wrapped away far from light."

Mary obediently laid the thin ivory image—for it was very narrow, just a carving on a slice of tusk—on the foot of her bed, where a small band of sunlight was falling.

"Ah." Mary could swear she heard a long, soft sigh from it. She looked closely at it, seeing how the daylight revealed the delicacy of the carving.

As the sun grew stronger, the ivory seemed to glow, absorbing the very light. But then Mary heard her mother just outside the door, and she hurriedly thrust the image back under the cloak, and shoved the box into the corner.

"Forgive me," she said.

"Well, Mary!" said her mother, standing in the doorway. "Up so early? A good start for this new year!"

Soon it was night again. Mary was lying in her little bed, watching the flickering of the oil lamp that rested in a niche in the wall. As the flame rose and fell, it threw jumping shadows on the whitewashed wall above it. Before, it had always been a comfort to her; now it seemed less reassuring.

I won't leave my bed, she told herself sternly. I won't go over there. It's just a piece of ivory, carved by human hands. It has no power.

"My name is Ashara, my child." She heard the soft voice.

"Ashara," it kept whispering. And Mary knew that this was the idol's name, and that she wished to be addressed as such.

Ashara. It was a beautiful name, as beautiful as the carving itself.

"Ashara," Mary repeated dutifully.

Trembling with fear, secretly (for surely Ashara could not read her thoughts), she promised herself, Tomorrow I must take it outside and throw it away, into the ravine. No, I'll go to the village ovens and throw it in there. No, I mustn't do that—it might contaminate the bread. I'll go to the . . . I'll go to the . . . She fell asleep trying to think of a purifying, and final, fire.

But the next day they were very busy, and there was no opportunity for her to extract the carving from its hiding place and take it out of the house. Her mind was quiet; she did not sense the idol speaking to her, and her fear subsided.

The great Day of Atonement—a day of fast commanded by Moses— was quickly approaching. On this day, in Jerusalem, the priests would make all the prescribed offerings and perform all the rituals necessary to attain forgiveness for the people of Israel for their sins, both known and unknown. After all the rites to expunge collective guilt, a goat would be sent out into the wilderness, symbolically carrying the last residue of sins on its head. There it would presumably perish, expiating the sins of the nation.

But for an individual, the day was personal and somber. After a service of praise for the Lord at twilight, the faithful were to keep to their houses, wear sackcloth and sprinkle ashes on their heads, and fast and pray all day, recalling all their sins and confessing them, trusting in God's mercy to be forgiven.

It turned out to be a glorious day, making the task of atonement more difficult. To tease the worshipers and lure their thoughts, the sun beckoned them outdoors, reminded them of ripening fruit and vineyard festivals: all the pretty gifts of life that divert people from a close examination of the dark side of themselves.

But the household of Nathan stayed resolutely indoors, all the family members keeping a silent, fasting vigil in their private rooms.

The obligatory rough cloth tunic Mary wore—the traditional sackcloth to show remorse—scratched so much she thought she had fleas. She could not imagine how the holy men of the desert lived in this sackcloth; nor could she imagine why and how that made them holy or closer to God.

Trying to be reverent, she dutifully ticked off all the Ten Commandments, her head bowed.

"You shall have no other gods before me. You shall not make for yourself an idol. You shall not bow down to them or worship them."

Ashara! But I didn't make her, Mary thought, and I don't bow down to her or worship her. Besides, I will not keep her. I promise!

"You shall not take the name of the Lord your God in vain."

No, I don't do that. I don't use the name of Yahweh, except in prayer.

"Remember the Sabbath day and keep it holy."

We always do. We always follow all the rules.

She remembered her applauding Joseph's decision to violate one of the rules, though. Does that make me guilty? she wondered.

"Honor your father and your mother."

The lessons! The secret reading lessons! She felt smitten with guilt. But at the same time, she felt there was nothing wrong with the lessons themselves, only that she was forced to lie about them.

"You shall not murder."

She sighed, feeling safe there.

"You shall not commit adultery."

"You shall not steal."

Another sigh of relief.

"You shall not give false witness against your neighbor."

She was a girl, and women were not even allowed to be legal witnesses, so she was prevented from committing this sin.

"You shall not covet your neighbor's house."

She coveted Keziah's, but not because of its furnishings, only because of the spirit of the people who lived within it.

"You shall not covet your neighbor's wife, or his manservant or maidservant, his ox or donkey, or anything that belongs to your neighbor."

She had certainly failed here. There were many things she coveted, wished she could have for her own. She couldn't help it, when she looked at them and they were so desirable. . . .

That is no excuse! The stern voice of Yahweh seemed to be sounding in her ear.

But there must be more than this, she thought. These ten things are so *big*. What about smaller things, everyday things? Murder is not an everyday thing.

To me, real sin seems like . . . like choosing to do something you know is wrong, she thought. Is it wrong for me to take the reading lessons, even though I think it's right that I learn to read, if my mother and father do not wish me to?

And what about bad thoughts?

The worst things I do are the mean things I think. For every bad thing I actually do, I think a hundred bad thoughts.

Her stomach growled. She was very hungry. Her head ached. That's to remind us that we are dependent on God for food, she told herself, and to remember all the times we forgot to thank him for it. But the ache inside was making it hard for her to concentrate.

She sat obediently on the hard floor of her room, lightheaded from hunger, trying to fathom the divine commandments, pondering her childish sins.

The Day of Atonement had seemed interminable. At the quiet meal they had to break the fast, Nathan said, in a very subdued voice, "It is only through the mercy of God that we are spared to live and repent."

But, truly, would they be any better this time next year? Mary wondered. Or would they spend all year struggling to attain mastery over the same sins, only to continue in their grip?

Perhaps people just don't try hard enough, she thought. I am going to try my best. She repeated it quietly, moving her lips: I will try my best. It was a vow. She knew God heard it, and would hold her to it. I must rid myself of the idol, too. I must rid myself of everything that displeases God.

She was more than glad to go to bed, even though she had barely ventured outside this little room all day. Lying down in the dark was a way of drawing a curtain across a day that had been dark in any case—dark with unpleasant recognitions and a cloudy conscience.

I will do better, she promised herself, and God, once again. She thought about the chosen goat that was now wandering alone in the desert wastes, carrying the nation's burden of sin with it. It would be days before it succumbed to death, if it succumbed at all. It might miraculously find water and food. The mystery was that no one would ever know.

ဢ **V** ဢ

"The Roman emperor is dead." Nathan strode into the house and put down his basket. "That's what all the commotion is about."

All night they had heard distant sounds from the hills, rumblings and the vague noises that indicated that something, somewhere, had gone wrong. Perhaps it was the sound of Roman troops moving from their camps on the seacoast, or coming down from the north, gathering in case of trouble.

"King Herod Antipas has ordered us all to maintain a public mourning," he continued. "Oh, we don't have to sacrifice, not to the Roman gods, just to our own on behalf of the departed emperor." Nathan looked relieved. He was in his mid-forties now; the long hours and demanding work at the salting warehouses were telling on him. His two sons, married now, relieved him of a great deal of the burden; but there was still much work for him to do.

"It won't be long until the emperor is declared a god himself, like

56

the first one, Julius Caesar," said Mary's mother. "I wonder if they'll wait a decent interval?"

Nathan snorted. "Ah, Zebidah, what's a decent interval?" He sat down and helped himself to a fresh apple he saw in a basket. "How long does it take to turn into a god?" He bit noisily into the crisp fruit. "Is it just—pouf!—in an instant? Or is it long and slow, like bread rising?"

Both of them began to laugh helplessly. They pictured the old Emperor Augustus's body inflating majestically, his features swelling, and finally his whole body floating up from his deathbed.

Finally, after she caught her breath and calmed her laughter, Zebidah said, "He's been emperor for as long as anyone remembers. How old is—was—he?"

Nathan had to think. "He's well over seventy," he finally said. "That's a long life by any standards, but an especially long one in Rome." He paused. "For all those years, and all those intrigues, and all those marriages, poor Augustus has no son to succeed him. To be lord of the world, but the last of your family . . ." Nathan shook his head.

"Who *will* succeed him?" Zebidah grew sober.

"His stepson, Tiberius. The thing is, he never liked Tiberius. But in the end that was all he had left. Everyone else, young and old, who might have been a better emperor, had died: his best friend Agrippa, his grandsons, his nephews. . . ." He shrugged. "Very sad. It is, actually."

"What is Tiberius like?"

They both turned to see Mary standing in the doorway. How long had she been there?

"They say he's gloomy," said her father. "And suspicious of plots everywhere. He's been waiting too long for his turn to become emperor."

"Why, how old is he?" Mary had lost none of her inquisitiveness as she had grown into adolescence. Nor any of her quickness.

"Oh, in his middle fifties," Nathan said. "He's turned into a sour old maid, if a man can be called an old maid."

As soon as he said the words, he regretted them. Mary was already at the age when she should have been betrothed, but that was proving surprisingly difficult. She did not seem to want to be married, nor had the family received many offers for her, which in itself was puzzling. She was pretty and clever, and an alliance with the family offered a good prospect for a young man.

Mary clamped her mouth shut and glared at her father. Finally, she snapped, "And just how can a Roman man be an old maid?"

"All your father meant was that he was . . . fussy, and touchy, and prissy—"

"Like me?" she replied. "I heard that he had obscene gatherings where he and his friends amused themselves, so how could he be prissy?"

"Well, if it's possible to be both prissy and perverted, Tiberius is both," her father pronounced. "What a reign we are in for," he predicted. "Perhaps he'll just keep busy in Rome and ignore us."

"And where did you hear about his carryings-on?" her mother asked. And *what*, precisely, had she heard? What Zebidah herself had heard was truly revolting, unnatural.

"Oh, it's common knowledge," said Mary, loftily. She and Keziah had talked about him, and especially his orgies, endlessly; they used him as a standard of depravity to measure local men against: *Well, at least he doesn't have scrolls with obscene pictures, like Tiberius. . . . At least he does what he does in private, unlike Tiberius. . . . He doesn't issue special tokens to attend his orgies, like Tiberius. . . .* She could not help giggling as she remembered the particulars.

Her father sighed; Mary's interest in such things would make her just that much harder to marry off. Men would see her as a bad bargain, even if she was attractive and quite graceful. They would rather have plain and sweet, Nathan thought. He looked at his daughter as a merchant would, trying to evaluate her marketable qualities. Pretty hair. Pleasing features, especially the mouth and smile. A tad too tall, but slender. A pleasing voice. Could speak Greek as well as Aramaic. Good knowledge of the scriptures.

It was fortunate that most of her advantages were visible and her flaws were not immediately obvious. Flaws: A restless, questioning mind. A tendency toward disobedience. Interest in taboo subjects— like Tiberius's lust. Bouts of melancholy, which she did not trouble to hide. A certain love of luxury and precious objects. A temper that was a little too quick, and a certain stubbornness as well. And a secretive nature.

"I suppose we shouldn't be laughing," Mary finally said. "Not with old Augustus lying in state somewhere. But isn't it sad that they—the Romans, I mean—really believe he will turn into a god?"

And quick shifts of attention, her father added to his list of Mary's undesirable traits.

"I wonder if they really do believe it," Zebidah said, "or whether it's just a political convention. It seems, somehow, even odder than people believing that idols have power, when they know very well they are made of stone and wood."

And ivory, thought Mary, with a jolt. It had been a long time since she had thought about her childhood secret.

"Yes, the idol-worshipers say that it isn't the stone itself they worship, that the stone represents another power, an invisible force," said Nathan. "But to claim a man turns into a god . . ." He shook his head in amazement.

"And to think, they leave Augustus just lying about for days and days after he dies!" said Mary. "And then they burn him up." She shuddered. "I would say it's barbaric, but, then, that's what they are, the Romans. Barbarians."

"Pagans," said her father. "They are pagans, not barbarians. There is a difference."

"I suppose I would say that all barbarians are pagans, but not the other way around," said Zebidah.

"They are all to be pitied," said Nathan, with absolute conviction. "Pagans, barbarians, heathens, the whole lot, no matter what you call them."

The body of Augustus Caesar, who had died away from Rome, was transported slowly, traveling by night and resting by day, toward the capital. It took two weeks for the old emperor to reach the heart of Rome, where he had schemed and sacrificed and given his all for almost a half-century. "I found Rome brick and left her marble," he was claimed to have said, and it was true that his funeral cortège passed through the streets of a magnificent city. No rites were spared, no touches overlooked, to make his last earthly journey somehow worthy of all his others. When at last his funeral pyre was lit, an ex-praetor named Numerius Atticus saw the spirit of Augustus ascending to the skies; later he swore it before the Senate.

On September 17, almost a month after Augustus's death, the Senate formally declared him a god. Temples were to be dedicated to him, a cult of priests would be assigned to him, and festivals would be celebrated. It was now official to swear an oath by "the godhead of Augustus."

Such oaths were immediately accepted in all the outposts of the empire, including the land of Israel, at Roman administrative centers like Caesarea. But in Jerusalem and Magdala, Augustus's godhood happened to fall during the holy days beginning the new year of thirty-seven hundred and seventy-five. And those praying for their sins and examining their consciences on the Day of Atonement would have put proclaiming a man to be a god at the very head of their list of abominations, should they ever be weak enough to utter the newfangled oath, even for an important business transaction.

For Mary, the yearly ritual of atonement had assumed a certain dreary predictability. Every year, she would enumerate her sins and genuinely repent of them, vow to God to do them no more; the next year, she would find herself in her room repenting of the same ones. Sometimes they were lessened, so they were not so glaring, and she could see some improvement, yet they remained, as stubborn as rocks that donkeys trod over and wore down but did not destroy.

Now, this year, in addition to the old familiars, Mary had acquired several new ones. During the past winter, she had passed from childhood into a state delicately called "according to the manner of women." That meant a whole new set of expectations and rules, some of them going all the way back to Moses, about ritual uncleanliness, and more modern ones, about how she behaved. It meant she was now marriageable, and although her father had not insisted that they begin the search for a husband, she knew it would not be too long before he did.

She both did and did not want to be married, which she found very confusing. Because it was a disgrace not to be married, of course she did not want that disgrace. She wanted what everyone wanted: to have a normal life, to be blessed in the ways that all agreed were gifts from God. That meant health, prosperity, respect, a family, and a home. But . . . she wanted more freedom, not less, and the responsibilities of running a household meant that, in practical terms, she would be a slave. She would have to be busy every moment taking care of those under her roof. She saw how hard her own mother worked, and how hard her sisters-in-law—in other ways so different from each other— worked. Yet the only other alternative was to be a burden, the shame of the unmarried daughter. The scriptures were full of admonitions about widows and orphans and how pitiful they were and how one should take care of them, but the unmarried daughter equaled them in status, or lack of it. The only difference was that presumably a father or brother could provide for the unmarried girls.

But life seemed too sweet to pass in bondage. Mary saw how old the Magdala housewives looked compared with the Greek women who sometimes came with their merchant husbands to the salting warehouses. Foreign women could own property, she had heard, and even travel about on their own; some of them headed their households and ran businesses. They addressed men in a familiar manner and did not lower their eyes—Mary had seen them, and seen them behaving this way with the men in her family. Even Eli seemed to enjoy it, as if it pleased him in some forbidden way. They had exciting names like Phoebe and Phaedra and wore sheer gowns and uncovered hair. Names somewhat like . . . Ashara.

The name came into her head like a thunderbolt. Ashara.

Ashara, who remained where Mary had hidden her those long years ago; Ashara, who had survived Mary's resolve to remove her from the household and destroy her; Ashara, who was suddenly, powerfully, present.

As soon as this day is over, Mary said to herself, I will do what I vowed to do so long ago. I will rid myself of her. God commands me to do so. He forbids idols.

All the rest of the day, while the sun swung around the sky and the light faded from Mary's east-facing window, she sat quietly and dutifully reflected on her shortcomings. She should be more obedient, and more cheerful while obeying. She should not hinder her father's attempts to find her a husband. She should stop daydreaming and apply herself to useful tasks. She should not be so vain about her hair, or wish to put henna in it to redden it. She should stop reading Greek poetry. It was pagan, and inflammatory. It depicted a world forbidden to her, and made her covet. Coveting was a sin.

You will never be married if you do not change these bad habits, she told herself. And you must marry; it is your duty to your father. God wishes you to obey. What was it Samuel had thundered in God's name? "To obey is better than sacrifice, and to hearken than the fat of rams."

Now a thought popped into her head. God has addressed Abraham, Moses, Samuel, Gideon, Solomon, Job, the prophets—but the only time he ever seemed to address a woman was to announce that she was to have a baby!

She was, suddenly, quite distressed, even as she struggled to refute that thought. Was it true? Well, there was . . . Eve. And what did he say to her? "I will intensify the pangs of your childbearing; in pain shall you bring forth children." Hagar. "You are now pregnant and shall bear a son; you shall name him Ishmael." He never even spoke directly to Sarah, or to Hannah, although he gave them the desired children, who were to fulfill some promise or serve God. Sons, of course. Always sons.

There must be a woman he spoke to, she thought. Some woman, somewhere, with a message that had nothing to do with childbearing. But she could not think of any, even though she sat there until well past sunset.

And another thought crept into her head. Ashara is a goddess. A goddess who speaks to *women*.

Mary's life was already like a wife's, in many ways. By the age of thirteen, a Jewish boy had fulfilled all his studies of the Law—unless he was going on to become a scholar and a scribe—and taken his place in the congregation of men at prayers. He also would have begun training to follow a trade, either his father's or another. Had he a twin sister, at thirteen she would have been relegated to shouldering domestic chores at home and waiting to be married. Mary's routine did not differ from her mother's at this point. It was both very hard work and very boring, because it presented no challenge, other than the challenge of getting it all done by nightfall. Mary was very efficient and managed to complete her tasks early most days, so that she could have a bit of time to herself to do as she would.

She liked to walk south, beyond the ending of the fine stone promenade that lined the lakeshore in the center of town, out past the walls that extended into the water to make a show of guarding the town, and along the shore by herself.

She often sat on a favorite smooth and rounded rock, near the water, and watched the light fading. At twilight and sunrise, the lake seemed to glow from within, as if the sun made its secret home there. There was always a hush as breezes dropped and leaves and rushes stopped rustling, when the day itself sighed as God did in the beginning of creation and whispered, "It is good, it is very good." Then dusk would follow, quickly, like a pulled curtain, changing the light from a rosy glow to mauve.

Away from all the clanging and clamor of the town, Mary would pull out her reading and devour Greek poetry or the stories of their ancient heroes, like Heracles. There was no popular literature in Israel; everything written concerned religion. The stories and songs of the people were all spoken, not written; for tales of adventure, tracts of philosophy, history, one had to go to Greek, Latin, Egyptian. There was a lively trade in them in the markets since the people had a hunger for them, no matter what the sages in Jerusalem might think. Dog-eared copies of the *Iliad* and *Odyssey*, of Sappho and Cicero, the epic of Gilgamesh, Catullus, and Horace were sold and resold from under the tables of fish and linen before the city gates.

Currently Mary was reading the poet Alcaeus, struggling in her Greek, not to mention the poor light. It was her own brother Silvanus who had served as her accomplice and her secret Greek-teacher. For days she had been slowly making her way through the poem about a shipwreck. Today she was to complete the last sentence, with a great sense of victory. Her feeble resolve to give up Greek poetry had withered.

. . . and our boat is swallowed by the waves.

Finishing, she folded the sheet of papyrus and looked out at the lake. As a poem should, it caused her to see the storm rather than the flat, peaceful water actually before her. The memory of storms she had witnessed on the notoriously dangerous lake rose up in power, like high waves.

She stood up. Darkness would come soon, and she must be inside the town walls. But there was one thing left to do, the thing she had promised so long ago.

From out of a pouch she withdrew a cloth-wrapped object. It had been tucked in there sight unseen. The idol. Ashara. Now she would fling it into the lake and let it sink there, to beguile the fish and rocks and weeds.

She held it in her palm, hesitating. I will never see it again, she thought. I hardly even remember what it looked like, it has been so many years.

Do not look, she told herself sternly. Did it not speak to you once? Did it not insinuate itself into your mind just yesterday?

She pulled her arm back, steadying herself to throw it as far out into the lake as her strength would let her.

I am not that weak, she scoffed at herself. To be afraid to look at a heathen idol? I am ashamed of my fear. The only way to conquer fear is to face it. If I do not look at it now, I give it a power over myself forever after.

Slowly she lowered her arm. She opened her palm and let the little bundle rest there. With her other hand she gingerly unrolled the wrapping. In the purplish light she could see the ivory face again, its lips seeming to smile at her.

She bent closer to see it better in the failing light. It was so beautiful that it actually caused her to draw in her breath. It was more beautiful than the white marble statues of athletes she had seen being transported across the lake to the pagan city of Hippos; more beautiful than the sensuous silver coin-portraits of Tyre that changed hands in the foreign market-stalls.

It would be wrong to destroy it, she thought. I could sell this to that Greek merchant who comes through regularly on his way to Caesarea. It must be worth a great deal. Then I could—for one instant she thought—hide the money and keep it to save me from an unwanted marriage. Quickly she replaced it with the pious thought: I could donate it to my father's business, or give it to the poor.

In any case, it was wasteful to throw it into the sea.

Sighing at her victory over her hastiness, Mary replaced the carving in her bag.

໖ VI ໖

"He seems a worthy young man," Nathan said at dinner, a tinge of apology in his voice. He spread some fig paste on his bread and waited.

"I thought so, too." Zebidah nodded.

"The family has withstood the addition of Dinah, so we can withstand anything," said Silvanus, referring to Eli's wife. Dinah, even more rigid in her adherence to the Law than Eli, had caused both great merriment in the family, and great pain. She had rendered the celebration of the Passover, or any meal, a trial of propriety and ritual cleanliness. As a result, they seldom ate with Eli and Dinah.

Now all three turned their eyes on Mary, whose opinion was the most important of all. After all, she would have to live with him.

"I . . ." The words were hard in coming. Her thoughts seemed muddied, captive. What had she thought of Joel, the young man who had worked for several seasons at the family business and was now ready to marry into it? He seemed personable enough. He was from a respectable family in nearby Nain, was twenty-two years old, rather attractive, and seemed to get on well with everyone. Mary had hardly spoken twenty words to him. If he had been interested in her, why had he not singled her out for conversation? She had visited the warehouse often enough.

All eyes were upon her. "I—I suppose I do not mind."

That was not what she had wished to say! What was happening to her?

Her mind swam, and she was speaking words that did not reflect her own feelings. And not just today. It had been going on for several months now.

It was—it must be—the problem she had sleeping. Last winter, her gift for sound sleep had deserted her, to be replaced by horrible, vivid dreams or else no sleep at all. And the room—the room had become very cold, when all the rest of the house was still comfortable. In vain her father had searched for chinks in the wall to account for the drafts, but he could find nothing. In the end, she had just piled more covers on herself.

The lack of sleep must be taking its toll on me, Mary thought. I cannot seem to think. Or to respond. But this is marriage! The thing I both did and did not want; the thing that will ruin my entire life, should I make a wrong choice. I have been dreading this day for years. It has been postponed too long for the family—not long enough for me.

Nathan leaned forward. "A very limp answer to a very important question," he said. "'I do not mind' may be suitable for deciding whether to take a short walk or not, but it is hardly a good response to a marriage proposal."

"I—what exactly is he proposing?" Mary asked. Perhaps if she heard the details she could decide.

"That he join us in the family business, and that he move to Magdala. You would not have to live with his family."

That was good. Mary did not want to live with a mother-in-law and have to take care of a family she did not even know, though it was common practice.

"That he bring a suitable amount as your *mohar*, your marriage gift, and that the marriage take place next year. You would be seventeen, and he twenty-three. Time enough for both of you. What is it the rabbis say? Even the most liberal sets twenty-four as the limit a man can reach before getting married."

"Perhaps he is only worried about meeting expectations," said Mary. "Perhaps his father is forcing him."

There, that was a little more like her. She shook her head to clear it.

"What matter?" said her mother. "The point is, he is a good man from a good family, and you seemed to get on well together. And he has prospects."

"I don't know if I even like him. I am not sure I would recognize him if I saw him in the market."

Silvanus looked up as if he were a scribe who had been pondering all this. "I think we chose our donkey more carefully than this!" he blurted out.

His father frowned. "That's foolish. Of course we had to ask more questions about the donkey. It could not speak for itself! But a man is different."

"Is he?" asked Mary. "What has this man spoken for himself? Or is it only what he does *not* say, or what others do not say about him?"

"Then speak to him yourself!" Nathan ordered. "Yes! The next time he is in the warehouse, come down and talk to him! But in the meantime, what do I tell him?"

"Tell him—that I would know as much about him as the family donkey."

"No, I shall not! I should order you just to proceed," her father said. "Enough of this foolishness. Decide today. Forget speaking to him. If you speak to him, you may scare him away!"

There. Now he had said it. They were desperate to marry her off, and had been deliriously happy when the man of Nain had asked for her, Mary thought. She had become an embarrassment—unmarried at sixteen. This might be her last chance.

"I—I need to think about it at least until tomorrow," she said. "Please give me that courtesy. After all, we did wait longer when buying the—"

"Enough about the donkey!" spluttered Nathan.

At last it was time to retire. Mary took to her narrow bed in the cold room—oddly cold, even though winter had not arrived. She pulled the extra covers up over her head and closed her eyes. She was longing to escape the daytime world.

But now, perversely, sleep slithered away again. She was acutely aware of every shadow in her room, every minute sound, and the square of moonlight that shone in one corner, like the eye of a relentless, searching god.

What is happening to me? she asked in a tiny, subdued voice. I cannot seem to think anymore, I do not even seem myself anymore.

She could almost see her breath in the room. Slowly she blew out—yes! there it was, a tiny cloud visible against the moonlight. This was impossible. It was warmer outside. It could not be this cold inside a house.

And the oppression in her mind—as if something were weighing her down, actually *pressing* on her.

The man . . . Joel . . . try to think about Joel, she ordered herself. He wants to marry you, to take you into his home. Picture his face.

She tried to think of him, to conjure the face, but she could not. It seemed to have vanished from her memory.

Suddenly, across the room, she heard a noise. Sitting up alert, she strained to see what it was. Darkness loomed all around her, making a frame that she could not penetrate. Then, slowly, something edged out into the room—a small chest. It was actually moving, making a grinding noise as it inched across the stone floor.

She watched, filled with fear, as it moved out into the square of moonlight. Or had the moonlight moved to it?

She wanted to pray, but only nonsense words, words she had no knowledge of, tumbled from her lips.

What was in the chest? she wondered. But she was too terrified to leave her bed and go see. Instead, she watched as it sat there, expectantly.

Though she was forced to hold herself completely rigid in the bed, she finally fell asleep, strangely enough. The dreams she had were odd and detailed, involving black caves that stretched deep into the hill behind the town and whose farthest reaches could not be found. They were like the night itself.

But when dawn came and she could hear the morning noises of footsteps on the path outside and fishermen rowing their boats out to begin their work, she stepped out of the dream-cave and back into her room. In an instant she looked to the floor to see where the chest was. She knew that had also just been a dream—the moving chest.

It sat . . . not exactly where it usually did, but not out in the middle of the floor, either. Perhaps her mother had moved it earlier and she had not noticed, or noticed just out of the corner of her eye and then had a dream about it.

Or had the chest moved back again after she fell asleep?

Silently she got up. The room was still very cold. She reached for a shawl to put around her shoulders, and rubbed her forearms for warmth. She found to her bewilderment that they were covered with scratches, raised scratches that made patterns, and were painful to touch.

She almost cried out, but stifled it. She held out her hands and stared at the markings on her arms. It looked like scratches made with thorns or brambles. She tried to remember exactly what she had done the day before. Was it possible she had gone near thistles? Or had she started sleepwalking? There had once been a child in the town who walked in his sleep; he would wander out into the night and have no recollection of it the next morning. His parents had to tie him to his bed to prevent his leaving. It was terrifying to think she might have wandered abroad, into danger, all unaware.

She bent over the chest and ran her hands over its lid—a smooth surface made by the local carpenter, with a few studs for decoration. She tipped it back. No wheels or anything that would make it move easily. Quite the opposite; the sturdy little pegs on the bottom would anchor it to the ground and make it hard to dislodge.

But—and here she caught her breath—the pegs *would* make a scraping noise if they were dragged across the floor! And, sure enough, faint lines were emanating from behind the chest's resting place, proving it had moved.

But it could have been moved by anyone, she thought.

Mary opened the lid slowly, as if she expected a snake to jump out. But there was nothing there except folded linen tunics and some heavier wool scarves and, underneath those, some of the Greek writings she had hidden, as if they were something dangerous. She stuck her hand down and rummaged around, feeling bolder now. No snakes, no scorpions, nothing dangerous. She felt a lump, grabbed it, and pulled it out.

It was something wrapped in several layers of cloth, something terribly familiar. She unwound them, slowly, apprehensively. The layers fell away, revealing the smiling face of Ashara.

Mary felt a jolt of recognition. The brazen beauty of the idol, which had stayed her hand in destroying it, now seemed to be mocking her.

"*You lack the courage to grapple with me,*" it seemed to confide. "*Those male prophets, those Jeremiahs, those Hoseas, they would have made short work of me. But you, a woman, understand more. Understand that we are sisters and must help one another. You helped me, now I will help you. I will give you whatever it is in my power to give.*"

And what is that? Mary asked it, in her mind.

"What is it women want? It is always the same. They want beauty, power over men because of it, and assurance of safety. It is very simple."

But I want more than that, Mary thought. I want to reflect the glory of God in my person, to be whatever he has created me to be.

But capturing men by beauty was so much more expected of a woman. That was the temptation. It was so much smaller, and yet, in many ways, so much more prized.

"You cannot add to my beauty, or subtract from it," Mary said out loud. "I already look as I do, and nothing can change that." *Refute me, say something different!* she challenged it.

"But I can affect how others see you," Ashara whispered in her mind. *"Will they see you as the Magdalene, mysterious and lovely, or as plain Mary of the fish-salting family in Magdala?"*

Regardless of what I might wish myself, the truth is that my station in life is already set, Mary answered her. People see me as they always have.

"I can alter everything from this moment on," Ashara promised. *"I can make you as lovely as a goddess. At least in others' eyes."*

So you cannot change my features, cannot alter my eyes or my nose? Mary asked. A man has sought me out and chosen me, with what his eyes have already seen. It is too late.

Ashara sighed. *"It is never too late,"* she whispered. *"Mortals cannot understand that."*

For God it is never too late. Yahweh says a thousand years in his eyes are as a single day. But for me it is not so, Mary answered her, one mind speaking directly to another.

"You are a woman," Ashara murmured. *"I am a goddess of women, and I have chosen you. I will fulfill your dreams, your dreams of being desirable to your husband."*

How could she know? How could she know this secret and deep longing of mine? Mary thought.

Women. Men. Marriage. Love and desire. Children. Every woman wants to be Bathsheba, wants to be Rachel, wants to be the beloved Bride. *As do I.*

All my dreams . . . all my wishes to walk in beauty . . . grant them! she commanded it, roughly, sarcastically.

She clamped her fingers around the idol, as if to choke it, to remind it that it lay within her power to obliterate it. It felt so slight in her palm. "Make me beautiful, make my husband want me above all things!" she ordered it again. Then she thrust it into the depths of the chest, slammed the lid, and dragged the chest back against the wall.

I am not beautiful, she thought, straightening up. I know I am not. Yet how I wish to be, if only for a day! How I wish someone—perhaps with changed vision?—might see me so!

When she emerged from her room, her mother and father were already up, eating their morning meal of bread and cheese. They looked up expectantly; they had been impatiently waiting for her.

She quickly sat down at the small table and began tearing off a piece of bread for herself.

"Well?" her father asked. She saw her mother glare at him as if to say, Nathan, not so soon!

"I will consent to become Joel's wife," she said. It seemed the right thing to do; and she was exhausted by all the struggle and self-examination concerning it. She must marry, and Joel seemed as good as any and better than most. Her prospects would decline steeply in another year or two, and she might be forced to marry some elderly widower. And also . . . perhaps this house was haunted by some malevolent spirit that seemed to have targeted her, and she would be better off elsewhere. She was being driven away by whatever *it* was. It might have nothing to do with the old ivory idol in the chest, but be some other force. How to be sure?

Mary had seen the possessed—they should be called the "dispossessed," because they had lost everything in life—wandering about through the market, with everyone staring at them and giving them a wide berth. No one could explain why a demon singled out one person and not another; some of the best families had an afflicted person. Now it seemed that Mary's own household had been invaded. It was her duty to leave the premises and either draw the spirit after her, protecting her family, or escape its grip.

"Mary—how—how wonderful!" her mother said. Apparently she had been expecting a long-drawn-out battle about it. By yielding easily, Mary had given them an unexpected gift. "I am so happy for you."

"Yes," said Nathan. "For we thought Joel a very commendable man. We will be pleased to welcome him as a son."

"Mary." Her mother stood up and put her arms around her. "I am so—pleased."

Relieved, you mean, thought Mary. Relieved that you will not have the disgrace of an unmarried daughter. You have fulfilled your duty.

"Yes, Mother," she said, turning the embrace into a real one, holding her mother close.

Now I will leave them, she thought. Not today, but soon. And in some way the leavetaking has already begun.

She felt bereft, as if she were being cast out.

"Therefore shall a man leave his father and mother and shall cleave to his wife," scripture said. Again, it only concerned the man and what he did, Mary thought. No mention of the woman he was clinging to, and what she felt.

"Shall I go and talk to him today?" Mary asked. "Or do you want to speak to him first?"

"You should talk to him yourself," said her father. "It would be best if you spoke privately to one another. After all, we are modern people." He was smiling, clearly pleased.

Mary made herself ready to go to the warehouse. She dressed slowly, selecting a gown she knew was flattering—a white one with a banded neckline. She combed her hair and fastened it back with clips.

I suppose after I am married I will have to wear it up and braided, she thought. And cover it. What a pity. But the thought was fleeting. Everyone knew that married women had to hide their hair. It was part of the price one paid for being a respectable wife. No other man was allowed to gaze on it.

Of course, that meant that no one else outside the household ever saw it, either, not even children or women friends or men past the age of lust. A bit less beauty was abroad in the world.

She selected supple sandals of lambskin and a mantle of lightest wool. After all, this is supposed to be one of the happiest days of my life, she thought. I should wear special clothes for it, clothes that, every time I wear them again, I will think, This is the mantle I wore upon the day when . . . And perhaps I'll tell my daughter that, and show her the mantle.

She sighed. I feel old already, imagining what I will tell my daughter, she thought.

She set out for the warehouse, knowing that midday was a good time to visit. Everyone would be there, and although all eyes would be on her as she entered, the noise and clamor inside would be a good shield for whatever she and Joel said to one another.

．　　．　　．

The family business was located near the pier where the fishermen unloaded their catch in Magdala, beyond the wide promenade and the market where the fish were bought and sold.

The lake teemed with fish, and provided the people who lived in the sixteen towns around its shores with a fine diet. But fish were highly perishable and could not travel far without being preserved in some way, and for the fish of Galilee to feed anyone besides local people, they must first be treated. Mary's family had built up a business that specialized in the three known ways of treating fish: drying, smoking, and salting.

These methods were used primarily on sardines, the fish that was the mainstay of tables throughout the region. Sardines were small and easily treated; larger fish, not suitable for preservation, had to be consumed quickly. But the sardines lent themselves to preservation, and in that state, they traveled as far away as Rome, where Galilean sardines were a delicacy even on the royal table, so it was said. Once, an order had come to Nathan from Augustus's household, and he had carefully saved the letter as a memento.

They employed some fifteen men in the heavy work of moving the barrels, spreading the salt, and bottling the fish. In the hotter months, the smell inside the warehouse was oppressive; a man had to have a strong stomach to work there. Today it was relatively fresh, and the wind blowing through the open doors swept the fish odors out over the lake, where they belonged.

Mary had walked slowly through the streets, to delay the meeting as long as possible. She passed many people she knew and made a point of stopping to talk to each one, all the while thinking, At least I will not have to move away and lose all these people I have known all my life, like so many women. Yes, that is something to be thankful for.

And Joel was not a shepherd or a merchant or an accountant in the royal household, all of which would entail an abrupt change in the way Mary lived. Sheepherding was smelly and grueling and meant living out in the field. With all due respect to King David, it was not a very appealing way of life. Being a merchant meant always gambling on getting a return on already-bought goods, and it also meant a great deal of traveling. As for being associated with the royal household, King Herod Antipas, although more humane than his cruel and erratic father, Herod, was too closely bound to Rome for Jews who served him to feel comfortable. It was said that he was a Jew in one place and a pagan in another, depending on whom he was trying to please. Still, he was all that stood between the Galileans and direct Roman rule.

She could delay no longer. Mary stood before the large stone building housing the family business—and squared her shoulders. Workmen known to her since childhood were going in and out the main door, rolling barrels and pushing carts, but today she did not even see them. She had to go in there; she had to speak to him.

She stepped inside. It was dim, and it took a moment for her eyes to adjust. She could see moving shapes that gradually resolved themselves into men. Silvanus was standing near the mound of pure salt that had been unloaded into a bin at a far side. He was holding a tablet and going over figures with another man. Others were milling around.

And then Mary saw Joel, standing near the row of clay amphoras waiting to be filled with ripened garum, the fish sauce from her family's famous recipe. It came in two varieties: one for the pagans, and another strictly kosher. Many places made garum, but the Magdala variety enjoyed an exalted reputation, and its success had made Mary's family renowned.

There he is, Mary thought. For the rest of my life, I will be looking for him at the warehouse, on the street, in our home. He is . . . attractive. Tall and well built. And he seems—

Before she could ruminate any further, Joel saw her. His face lit up and he hurried over.

"Thank you for coming," he said as he approached.

She only nodded, because, quite suddenly, she found herself unable to speak. She just stared at him as he came closer, unable even to evaluate him as she usually could people and things. He stopped in front her, now awkward himself.

"I know this is difficult," he said. "Although we have met several times in passing—"

"We were not paying attention," Mary finished for him.

"I was," he said.

"Oh."

"Let us go outside," he said. He gestured toward the busy comings and goings in the warehouse, as well as the veiled staring from those who suspected. For a moment Mary hesitated, wanting the protection of all the other people present. Then she followed him.

They left the dark building and set out beyond the promenade and landing site to walk northward along the lakeshore, away from prying eyes. The path was broad and well traveled, for it followed the curve of the oval lake, sweeping along near the water's edge.

"You do not come from lake people or fishing people," Mary finally said, asking in the guise of a statement.

"No," he said, speaking as he looked straight ahead. "My family has lived in the Galilee for as long as anyone remembers—some even believe that we have remained here on this land through all the wars. The Assyrians claim they depopulated the entire land. But of course they did not; otherwise there would have been as many Israelites as Assyrians in their own country. I do not think they wished to repeat the experience of Pharaoh and be overwhelmed by us!"

He had a pleasing voice, Mary thought, and his words were thoughtful. His face was kind and pleasant to look upon. Perhaps . . . perhaps . . . I can actually come to love this person. Perhaps he is like me.

"There is a legend about that in my family, too," said Mary. "That we are—or were, because they supposedly are lost—of the tribe of Naphtali in this region. Just around the bend is the ruin of their ancient city. It is a nice story, at any rate."

"'Naphtali is a hind let loose,'" said Joel. "Isn't that what Jacob said about him in his deathbed blessing?"

Mary laughed. "Yes, and no one knows what it means!"

"Jacob also said he gives goodly words." Joel slowed his walk. "I await your words, Mary. I hope they may be goodly for us both. Just speak your heart."

He was so direct! Could they not walk farther, talk more, first? But how natural could such talk be? She reached up to adjust her headscarf in the brisk wind, in order to create some time.

"I—I told my father that I would—I would accept your offer to join our household."

"That is not exactly what I offered," he said. "Can you not speak the words?"

No, she couldn't. They stuck in her throat. The words "marry," "wife," "wedding" were suddenly beyond her. She shook her head.

"Then, if you cannot say them, you cannot embark on them." He sounded disappointed but resigned.

"You haven't said the words, either." He had avoided them as much as she.

He gave her a surprised look. "To your father I—"

"But to me all you have said is 'I await your words.' My words on what?"

He smiled. "You are right. But you cannot win this point, because I have no fear of saying: I wish you to become my wife. I wish to become your husband and for us to make a new family. There."

A bunch of rowdy children burst around the bend, chasing and yelling.

"Why?" was all Mary could ask.

"Because, ever since I came of age, I knew I didn't want to be a flax farmer like my father. I wanted to find my own trade and have my own home and family. When I saw you, I knew you were the person I wished to share my life with."

"But why?" He had hardly spoken to her; how could he know that?

"'And Jacob loved Rachel'—why did he? He had barely met her. All he had done was water her sheep."

"That was a long time ago, and is just a story." He would have to do better than that.

"'And Jacob served seven years for Rachel; and they seemed to him but a few days, for the love he had to her.' It is a true story, Mary. It happens all the time. It has happened to me." He paused, embarrassed, trying to regain his dignity. "I have already been at the warehouse for almost three years! Almost half Jacob's serving time."

Now she became acutely embarrassed as well. "I hope that is not why you were employed there."

"No, I was drawn to the trade. I like the idea of feeding people, providing a needed service, but also having the opportunity to travel and meet new customers. The world is a wide place, Mary. Too wide for me to be content never to venture beyond Galilee, beautiful as it is."

He had a desire to see the world, to venture beyond the narrow confines of their fish-processing business. He had already left Nain, had chosen another trade than his father's. That was how she felt—pulled by something far away. They were alike: restless, seeking spirits.

"I see." Now she would have to give her answer at last. "I am honored that you would have thought of me like Rachel. And, like Rachel, I will consent to marriage. But I cannot trust such means of making decisions as you have described."

"Ah, Mary. Then I hope . . . someday . . . that, when you do come to understand it, you will feel as I do. But it is enough now that you have said yes. I am a lucky man."

She did not think him lucky, but misled. And if he knew one of the reasons why she stood ready to leave her parents' home, he would not be pleased. But she was relieved. Everything would be all right. The headaches, the sleeplessness, the confusions—as she stood here in the clear light, outdoors, they seemed to fall away. She would be delivered from them. Joel would take her away from the house where they lurked.

Now, rather than less awkward, the solemn words they had just spoken made them feel even more ill-at-ease with one another. But they walked on, resolutely, trying to seem lighthearted. The bright sun was masked and unmasked by passing clouds, making the lake beneath it a mosaic of different colors. A light wind rustled the plumed reeds and nettles growing along the path.

"A cult stone!" Joel suddenly said, pointing to a rounded black object almost hidden in the wayside brush. It had a hole through the top and looked like a stone anchor, only much bigger. "Look! I have never seen one still in place like this." He approached it cautiously, as if he expected it to move.

"What do you mean? Isn't it an old anchor?"

Mary had seen similar ones elsewhere, but could not remember where. She had not paid much attention to them.

"No." Joel bent down and parted the weeds that had grown so high around it. "It looks like one, but see how big it is? No, it's a relic from the Canaanites. One of their gods. Or an offering to a god. Possibly to the sea god they imagined lived here in the lake."

"The land is full of idols," Mary heard herself saying. "Under the ground—beside the path—"

"It's good that there are still some here and there," said Joel. "Just to remind us they are waiting to take over again. We can't take anything for granted."

Mary felt a cold internal shiver that did not manifest itself visibly.

"No," she agreed. "We can take nothing for granted."

The wind whipped across the path suddenly, flapping Mary's mantle back behind her. She instinctively crossed her arms, and as she did so Joel saw the scratches on them. Too late, she tried to cover them up.

"What's that?" he asked, staring at them.

"Nothing—I was gathering some firewood down by the beach, and—"

"What did you do, fight with it?" Joel smiled. "Never gather wood with unprotected arms." But he was content to let the matter drop.

In fact, he seemed quite happy, and the mood changed from guardedness to pleasantry as they continued walking along the lakeshore path. Many fishing boats were heading in toward the landing near the warm springs just ahead, called Seven Springs. It was a popular place for fishermen from the nearby towns of Capernaum and Bethsaida, because the warm water attracted certain fish in the winter; as a result, often the small harbor facilities were overwhelmed by many boats all trying to tie up at once to sort their catches. The waterfront was bustling, the atmosphere jolly.

"Fishermen are an interesting lot," said Joel. "They have so many contradictory traits—a reputation for piety, though they deal in the earthiest matters. Working all night, sorting fish, mending nets: it's the exact opposite of the lives of the religious scribes."

"Perhaps that's why their religiosity is suspect," Mary said, "at least by those in Jerusalem. After all, how can a fisherman keep himself ritually clean? He has to handle unclean fish every day in sorting the catch in his net."

"Yet who would you rather have with you in a crisis, a fisherman or a Jerusalem scribe?" Joel laughed. "Zebedee there"—he waved at the burly red-faced man, who waved back, although he most likely could not recognize Joel from this distance—"has single-handedly brought in catches in really bad weather. He owns several boats; he has a real business. His sons work with him, and they have hired men as well."

They approached the landing, which was very busy with fishing traffic.

"Watch it, there!" A loud voice rang out. "Stay away from the basket!"

They had been skirting a large, bulging basket; between its seams slimy water oozed, and the entire basket seemed to be quivering.

"Sorry, Simon." Joel stepped back from it.

"I worked three hours to sort them all out," said Simon, a giant of a man, standing near the basket with massive crossed forearms. He looked quite fierce. Then he laughed.

"Far be it from me to undo any of your work," said Joel. He hesitated for a moment. Mary could sense him thinking. "Simon, you know the sons of Nathan—Samuel and Eli. This is their sister, Mary."

Simon looked at her carefully. He had very large eyes, and they seemed to be boring into her face. "Yes, I know. I've seen you in the warehouse." He nodded emphatically.

"Mary has consented to be my wife," Joel said. He looked at her proudly.

Simon's face lit up, and a smile spread across his features. "Ah, you are blessed indeed! Congratulations!" He winked conspiratorially. "Does this mean I report to you in the future?"

Joel seemed embarrassed. "No, of course not. Nathan is still very much in control. He is not old!"

"That's what my father says about himself," said Simon. "But Andrew and I can sense he's ready to turn over the hard work to us." He indicated another young man, standing by himself on the dock. He had dark curly hair but otherwise looked nothing like his exuberant brother. He was slimmer and smaller. "And since I've married," continued Simon, "I can feel myself becoming more respectable by the moment."

"Married?" said Joel. "I did not know. So—congratulations are in order for you, too."

Simon grinned. "Yes, it has taken some getting used to. I now have a mother-in-law, which is quite different from a mother, let me tell you." He cocked his head. "Someone once told me, 'If you wish to know what a girl will be like in twenty years, look at her mother.' Well . . . it isn't true. Or God help me if it is!" He laughed.

The loud Zebedee was now approaching in his boat, followed by a second with two young men—one broad-faced and sandy-haired, the other slighter and with lighter hair.

"You there!" yelled Zebedee at no one in particular. "Throw us a rope!" A startled lad on the wharf scurried to comply. Behind Zebedee, the other boat was pulling up.

Before they could disembark and start a conversation, Joel looked up at the sky. "It is well past noon," he said. "Time to be heading back." He waved to the fishermen and turned toward Magdala.

Mary was ready to return. She wanted to be alone to think about what had happened. She had agreed to marry this man. They had discussed it, agreed on it. It all seemed odd, unreal. She had to get away and think.

Yet already it felt comfortable to be walking beside him, to hear his opinions about the fishermen and his wishes to travel and also to help people. They were agreeable to her and reassured her. It must be right, she told herself. It has to be. We will grow together over the years, for we seem to be similar already in what we want.

Mary hurried along the street toward Keziah's house, bursting to tell her about Joel. In all the years she had known her, Mary had managed to keep their friendship secret, although Silvanus knew—and approved. The girls, having long since outgrown the miniature dishes, had transferred their attention to real ones, as they planned their future households and speculated on their mates—an endless game, as long as no real bridegroom was in sight. Keziah had conjured a rich Jerusalemite who would live in the upper section of the city and entertain many foreign guests, and sometimes be posted abroad for a diplomatic or business mission. They would also have a seaside house.

Mary had countered with her imaginary soldier—from a mighty Jewish army—who was also a scholar. He would be brave, poetic, and indulgent. Indulgent because he would be away at various soldiering duties and not able to keep a close watch on his household. Not that she would be unfaithful, but it would be delightful to buy whatever she wished without his noticing.

At the age of sixteen, Keziah had received many offers of marriage, and all had been refused. Her father had higher sights than the fishermen and apprentices who had come forward.

Mary's knock was quickly answered, and Keziah greeted her with a whoop. That was her charm; she always gave the impression that she had been waiting all day just to see someone, and that there was no other sight so pleasing.

"What's happened?" she asked. "Your face is all afire."

"*It* has happened." Mary stepped inside.

"*It?*"

"Keziah—I am betrothed."

Keziah's lovely face registered shock. "Who?"

"His name is Joel," said Mary. "He works for my father."

"Oh, no!" Keziah clapped her hand over her mouth. "We always said—"

"That we would not settle for such a thing," said Mary. "I know. And our imaginary men were wonderful. Your rich diplomat from Jerusalem, my soldier . . ." Her voice faded. "But we always knew it was not real. We always knew it could not be."

"Yes, of course." Keziah nodded, slowly. "It was always make-believe." She smiled and put her arm around Mary's shoulder and guided her into the house. "And now—you must tell me about this real man."

Now Mary wished she had not come. Their fantasies would have lived a little longer if she had not. But what was another day? For, had she not come today to tell Keziah, she would have come tomorrow. One does not keep one's betrothal secret from one's friends.

The hallway of Keziah's house was now as familiar to her as her own. They came into her dear old room, furnished now to elegant adult tastes. Keziah sank down on a bench, but not before gesturing toward the filled pitcher on an inlaid tray. "Tamarind juice?" she asked politely. Mary shook her head.

Keziah leaned forward, her eyes glistening. "Tell me, tell me!"

"There is this young man, Joel, from Nain—"

She painted Joel in as bright colors as she could, realizing all the while that they were pale beside the Soldier's. When she was finished, Keziah said gently, "It sounds as if you have made a good choice. We must put away the Soldier and the Diplomat. We will make our lives with a fish merchant and . . . My father has recently received an offer from a man named Reuben ben-Asher who fashions fine swords. Oh, no ordinary swords," she hastened to explain. "These are the most elegant blades, thin as a veil and sharp as a razor."

"But you have not decided?" Mary asked.

"My father has not decided," Keziah said. "I will not meet Reuben until after he has said yes or no."

In that moment, Mary was grateful to her family. Strict and traditional as they might be, at least they had not made the decision for her. In spite of her seeming freedom, Keziah was in a worse position than she.

"Should your father decide yes, I hope you find this man pleasing" was all she could say. The idea of being presented with a stranger and told you must live with him until death claimed one or the other of you was momentous.

Keziah shrugged, trying to make light of it. "We are women," she said. "In the end, we have so few choices."

Keziah insisted that Mary must stay and tell her mother and father. She gladly did so; she was fond of them, and also strangely curious to know what they would say.

Sarah, Keziah's mother, seemed delighted. "It sounds like a good match," she said. "He joins your family, you do not have to go to his. Is he personable?"

"Yes, I . . . I think so," Mary said. That walk along the lake seemed so little to base a lifetime on, yet she felt that she had discerned a likeness of spirit within him.

"Is he—religious?" Sarah asked. "I know it is important to your family."

"I—I don't know," she said, realizing that she and Joel had never discussed it.

When she had first met Keziah and her parents, she had known they were different from her family, but she had not realized the two families came from different religious traditions: Pharisee and Sadducee. The Pharisees were rigorous in their interpretation of the Law and held themselves aloof from all compromises; the Sadducees thought accommodation on unimportant things was the order of the day, but kept the sacred things apart. As a result, Pharisees did not consort with Romans or Gentiles, fearing contamination, whereas the Sadducees believed in knowing the enemy at close range. Each accused the other of betraying or harming the interests of Judaism.

"Surely it's important?" asked Sarah.

"He did not seem to be intolerant," said Mary. That was her first impression.

"But he may expect all his pots broken if they touch something unclean," said Benjamin, Keziah's father. "And he may make you wear those severe clothes."

Mary winced. "But he does not wear them himself."

"What does he think about the Messiah?" Benjamin asked her, solemnly.

"We didn't—the Messiah did not come up," she finally said.

"Well, that's a good sign," said Benjamin. "If he had been one of those looking for the Messiah, he could not have stopped himself from talking about it. They all do. You cannot be with them but an instant, talking about the seasons or the emperor, and suddenly they will get a faraway look in their eye and say, 'When the Messiah comes . . .' Stay away from such people!"

It is too late, Mary thought. How can I stay away now? Is Joel waiting for the Messiah? He seems too sensible. Only fiery people are concerned with the Messiah.

"I think Mary should be thankful one of those fishermen did not come calling," said Keziah. "You know, the ones who deliver to the warehouse." She tossed her head, shaking out her shining hair, uncovered in the privacy of her home. "They smell. You've said so yourself!" She pointed at Mary.

"Yes, we ran into them as we were walking along the path," Mary said. "It's those sons of Jonah, Simon and Andrew."

"Oh, him," said Benjamin. "Yes, I know Jonah." He turned a stern eye on his daughter. "You wouldn't be so haughty if you knew that Zebedee has approached me about you."

"Who is Zebedee?" Keziah sounded alarmed.

"A big-name fisherman from Capernaum. He has a house in Jerusalem and connections with the royal household."

"He has several sons?" asked Keziah.

"Yes, two," said Benjamin. "The oldest one, James, is fiercely ambitious. At least that's what Zebedee says—that his son is eager for him to step down. And there's a younger one, John. John is like most second sons—overshadowed by the elder one."

"Did you . . . encourage them?"

"Not really. I met James and found him overbearing. And John was too dreamy for my taste. He'll never make a good living—not even if he inherits his father's business. There's something about John that is soft; people will take advantage of him. No, you needn't worry—you won't have to join the family of Zebedee."

"We are remiss!" said Sarah, rising. "We have not wished Mary well, or given her our blessing. She is soon to become a wife!"

They all stood, and Benjamin extended his hand over Mary's head. "Dear friend of my daughter, like a daughter to me, may the blessings of marriage establish your home in happiness."

Mary had never seen him so solemn. Keziah squeezed her hand as he spoke the words, and her skin tingled.

After the next Sabbath, Keziah took Mary to the merchants who had shops up near her father's and introduced her to the owners. When she said, "My friend Mary, who is soon to marry Joel of Nain," the happiness in her voice was unmistakable. To be a bride was to have one of life's mysteries resolved.

This was a rarefied area where only the wealthy traded. A single necklace could cost the entire seasonal wages of a fisherman; a finely turned bowl a widow's income. It was frequented by the other Sadducee families in town, who did not mind rubbing shoulders with the Romans and Greeks.

My family would never allow me to shop here, Mary thought. But she smiled politely and nodded to the merchants.

Since her first visit to Keziah's family, long ago, Mary had realized her own family might have been as well off, but they hid their wealth. Only certain things were worthy; other things were vanity. They were generous with the poor, making large contributions to the synagogue charity-box, but would never buy the wares in the upper part of the city. A bowl that cost a workman's winter wages? Never!

As a result, although Mary liked looking at the things with Keziah, a part of her censored such indulgence. She was torn between her common sense, her family's standards, and her own desires. The bowl was so beautiful, so delicate and fine, that as the light passed through it you could see the outline of your hand on the other side. Such an achievement deserved honor. But the price! Mary could never allow herself to pay it.

"Look!" said Keziah, holding up a goblet. "Can't you see yourself filling this? Saying, 'And here is our finest wine'?" The goblet was made of gold.

"No," said Mary. "A golden goblet is not something I can ever have." She took it in her hand, examined it carefully, noting its smoothly hammered surface, and reluctantly put it down. Without ever asking him, she knew Joel would never purchase such a thing. The world of golden goblets was beyond her.

"Well, I hope he will let you choose something lovely—something to remember your wedding day by," said Keziah.

"I imagine I will never forget my wedding day, even if I had no special gift," said Mary. "I think anything I touched that day—I would remember. The day itself will make it sacred."

As the day grew closer, preparations for the marriage consumed more and more of the family's time. Mary's mother, usually so diligent in all her tasks, now neglected them in favor of plans for her only daughter's wedding. She even went about her daily chores singing—the only time Mary could ever remember her doing so.

One evening, she announced that the following day was to be entirely devoted to preparation by the women in the family.

"Your cousins, your aunts, and Joel's sister—they are all coming!" she said, proudly. "Yes, his sister, Deborah, is coming all the way from Nain!"

Mary had heard Joel speak fondly of Deborah, his fourteen-year-old sister, but she had never met her. Joel's mother, Judith, had come to Magdala shortly after the betrothal, as had his father, Ezekiel. Mary had been surprised to see how little Joel resembled either one: they were both short and round, whereas Joel was tall and thin. She wondered what Deborah would look like.

In the midday heat, the women began arriving at Zebidah's home, their heads covered against the dust and sun. Soon they were sipping their cups of minted yogurt, milling and murmuring around Mary. She felt like one of the lambs in the market, acutely aware of their inspection.

Deborah, who arrived after the others with her mother, turned out to look a great deal like Joel, and Mary found that oddly comforting.

When they had all finished greeting one another, as well as confiding the latest gossip, Mary's mother held up her hands for silence. In an exaggerated manner she looked around and said, "Are we sure there are no men here?"

"Have you checked the back rooms?" one of Mary's cousins asked. "They tend to hide in there!" Giggling, they scampered off to see, then returned, shaking their heads. "We are alone!"

"Good!" said Mary's mother. "Now we can speak freely!"

Before she could continue, there was a knock at the door. Everyone froze, then burst out laughing.

"You would think we were fearful of a Roman soldier bursting in," Mary's aunt Anna said.

Zebidah pulled open the door to find the bent form of the widow Esther from across the street. Esther's sharp black eyes took in the group, and she said, "I beg your pardon, I was just going to ask if you had any barley flour, but I see—"

"No, no, please come in!" Zebidah almost pulled her into the room. "We have need of your knowledge."

"My knowledge?"

"Of what the years mean to a man and a woman," Zebidah said. "As you know, my daughter, Mary, is to be married soon. All the women close to us in the family have come to help her and tell her what we know. But we have no elders here. My mother and Nathan's mother have died long since, as have our aunts. So, please, we need you!"

Old Esther looked around cautiously. "I do not know what wisdom I have. I have lived a long time, that is all. I have lived longer alone than ever I was married; I have been widowed for over forty years."

The women in the room tried not to look at her in pity, but everyone knew what it was to be widowed, especially if there were no children.

"Come, sit," said Zebidah.

But Esther ignored her and came over to Mary. "I have known you since you were born," she said. "And I wish you great happiness." She patted Mary's arm. Mary tried not to wince; the welts and scratches were very bad today, and she prayed no one would want her to try on her wedding robe and make her bare her arms. Only a little while longer and she would be gone from this besieged house, this house where something malevolent hovered, tormenting her. Only a little while longer . . . Joel might not be the most dashing husband for her, but he could be her salvation from the torment that lay within the walls of her own home.

"Thank you," Mary said, pulling her arm closer to her side.

"But I must tell you," Esther continued, "that much of that happiness lies within your own power. The man has little to do with it."

Joel's mother looked indignant. "What do you mean?" she demanded. "Of course my son will have everything to do with it!"

"If your son is a good man, then he will," said Esther. "But should Mary have been chosen by someone else not so good, even then she could have hollowed out her own happiness." She paused. "And should something happen and—may Yahweh forbid it!—she enter into my state, then her only happiness is in her own hands."

"I think, old woman, you forget that this is a glad occasion," said Judith. "If you were not already known to Zebidah, I would suspect you had the Evil Eye. Now take back, I pray you, what you said about my son!"

"I meant nothing evil, but pretending evil does not exist around us gives it power," said Esther stubbornly. "By whatever means I can, I wish a long and healthy life to your son, and to his wife."

Zebidah pressed a cup in Esther's hand and steered her away from the others, forcing her off into a corner.

"What shall you wear?" asked Anna, Mary's aunt on her father's side.

"I have selected a robe that is mainly red, because it is a joyful color," said Mary, dreading a request to try it on.

"And your head covering?"

"I—I think—"

"We have brought it for you!" said Judith and Deborah together, whisking out a light wool scarf, so thin that the light shone through it. "We wanted you to have something from our family."

Mary took it and marveled at the lovely weaving. It was so fine that it seemed as if a cloud had been captured and dyed.

"And your coins! What about your coins?"

Zebidah snorted. "Oh, we have something better than that, much better than those jangling necklaces and headbands that women wear covered in gold coins. I know, it's only ceremonial now, it doesn't really show wealth. If we were to do that, Mary would have to wear preserved fish as a bridal crown. No, here's what we have." Carefully she presented a cedarwood box to Mary. Mary opened it to find the brass pomegranate there, attached to a chain.

"All the brides in your father's family have worn it, all the way back to—well, no one knows!" her mother said.

Mary held it out, letting the delicate little pomegranate made by her ancestor Huram turn on its chain. Everyone crowded up to see it, and she let them all take it from her hand and pass it among themselves.

"Mother," she said, hugging her, quite overcome. She had not expected this, indeed had not even known of the custom. Her mother never spoke of her own wedding day, except to brag about the bride price Nathan had brought.

"And you will pass it to your daughter someday," Zebidah said, her voice trembling. She was close to tears, unusual for her.

"I promise," said Mary, picturing that daughter, and herself someday performing the same rite, surrounded by the women in her family, looking into her daughter's eyes. Oh, let it be so! she prayed, silently.

"Oh, this is much too serious!" said Anna. "You forget that it is a long way from the bridal finery to childbed, and further still until you bedeck your daughter for her wedding. We must ensure that Mary is prepared for what she must do to arrive at where we are!" Her eyes glistened as if she were remembering forbidden things she relished hinting at.

"I know all these things," said Mary, stoutly. Indeed, who could not know of them? Married women whispered about them, unmarried girls speculated about them, and there were always the flocks of sheep and cattle in the nearby fields to demonstrate, in glaring sunlight, how lambs and calves were created. As for the nighttime, which men and women preferred, the Song of Songs hymned its joy in detail.

"It is our duty to initiate you," said Anna, with a loud assent from Mary's other aunt, Eve. With a shy smile, Eve pulled a tiny bottle from her sleeve and waved it tantalizingly back and forth. "For your wedding night!" she said, handing it to Mary.

Mary was forced to reach out and take it. The opaque clay did not betray what was within.

"Put two drops in your wine on the wedding night, and you will conceive that very night!" said Eve.

"Shame on you, haven't you anything for the man?" asked Anna. "I think you have neglected him. Here!" She waved a vial. "I *guarantee* this! Personal experience!" She pressed up against Mary—her own father's sister, who had always seemed so proper to Mary as she was growing up. "One drop is all it takes! He'll be like a male camel!"

"Anna!" Joel's mother cried.

"Does not the prophet Jeremiah talk about the male camel pursuing the wild she-camel in heat?" she countered. "It is in scripture!"

The wedding night. Mary had tried not to imagine it, knowing that nothing was ever as one pictured. Generations of women, from the original Eve down to her own mother, had experienced it. She took solace in that, sometimes adding, Let me not be a disappointment to my husband.

"Thank you," Mary said, faintly, taking it from Anna.

"Where is the consummation handkerchief?" demanded old Esther.

"Here," said Zebidah, waving it before them all: a large white square woven of fine linen. It was to be placed under the bride on the wedding night, and retained to prove the bride's virginity, should any challenge arise.

"You do not still do that!" said one of Mary's young cousins. "It's so old-fashioned. No one now—"

"It is in the Law of Moses," said Zebidah. "Not the handkerchief, but the legal importance of virginity."

"And what if a bride is not a virgin?" asked the cousin, hesitantly.

"The Law says she shall be stoned," said Zebidah, and Esther nodded.

"But when has that happened?" asked Naomi, Silvanus's wife. She had remained uncharacteristically silent until then. "No one does that today."

"It depends on how observant you are," said Zebidah. "To some of us, it is still important."

Mary hated all this talk. Again, she felt like a lamb in the market.

Was she to stand on a stool and proclaim, "I am a virgin"? Why did she have to prove herself to these women? Suppose she were not one? She hated to think of what would happen. She would be cast out, rejected by all these loving relatives now crowding around her with gifts and good wishes.

"Here!" Her mother pressed the cloth into her hands. "Keep it until that night!"

"Have you chosen the day?" asked Esther. "No, of course you cannot yet, you need to know when your time of uncleanness is past. We must wait."

"Another few weeks," said Zebidah. "Then it will become clear. After the last fortnight of uncleanness, then we can plan the ceremony."

Uncleanness! Such an ugly word. Mary hated hearing it, but she had been taught since her earliest days that women's natural cycles rendered them unclean for at least half their days. They could not touch certain things, they could not lie on a bed, they could not come to their husbands, lest they contaminate them.

"The feast will be grand," said Zebidah. "We must think of that!"

They planned to have a roasted kid and the largest fish the lake would yield, flavored with herbs and decorated with wreaths and flowers. Since it would be midsummer, early figs and grapes and melons also would be in season.

"And there will be flutes and drums and singers?" Deborah asked.

"Oh, indeed, the best in the city," Zebidah assured her.

"But there is one ancient dance we must perform here, now, with only women," said Esther, coming over to Mary. Esther was so decrepit, her suggestion that they dance was startling.

"Clap for me," Esther ordered. "Clap loudly. And raise your voices."

She took Mary's hand and slowly turned her around. Then she moved more quickly, and their gowns began to rise at the hem and fly outward.

"Look only at me!" she ordered Mary.

Mary looked into the old woman's eyes, lost in their wrinkles and folds. In them, almost hidden, were two bright spheres, dark and shining. She could almost imagine them young, and then, as they spun around, that young girl in the old woman emerged. Time retreated, and they went backward, backward to Bathsheba, to Ruth, further still to Zipporah and Asenath, and then even further back to Rachel and Leah and Rebekah and Sarah, and they turned and turned until they were one, and one with their ancestors. Then, abruptly, Esther let Mary's hands go so she fell back against the women surrounding her, the women of this year and this life and this time.

"Join me!" Esther ordered them, and the married women gathered around in a circle and began clapping and crying out in ancient voices they did not know they possessed, blessing Mary and welcoming her into their midst.

⚭ V111 ⚭

As the time for the wedding drew near, Mary felt more and more at ease with Joel. She even hesitantly let him know that she could read, and he seemed unbothered by this—although she had not revealed that she knew Greek as well. He even seemed pleased about it, finding the good in it: that they could study and read together, write letters when separated, and each compile and check records.

I am to spend the rest of my life—may it be a long and happy one, please, God!—with someone I trust and enjoy, she repeated to herself several times a day. But she neither felt excitement when thinking about him nor longed for the day when they could be alone in the bridal chamber together.

At the same time, she wanted Joel to love her that way—to feel passion for her. She worried about all the odd things that had happened to her—the mysterious attacks, increasing all the time, that had targeted her; the mental confusion, the insomnia, plus the painful marks and scratches that would suddenly appear on her arms and legs and, lately, her sides and stomach. She could never reveal this to Joel. He would be repelled by it, and probably not wish to go through with the marriage. She looked to him as her hope of salvation from whatever *it* was.

There were nights when she lay in bed, feeling an oppression in the very air of the chamber, a heaviness that had nothing to do with heat. She almost felt that she could address it, and that if she did it would answer back. As Ashara had not so long ago.

Ashara. The ivory idol. She with the smiling face and beguiling, musical voice. The image made her think of all the things she wanted to be—beautiful, mysterious, a bride. All the things it had promised her she could be, a side of herself that wanted to rise up, like a serpent to a charmer's flute.

She sighed. But I know it is just a trinket, a little artwork, she told herself. Why don't I show it to Joel? she suddenly asked herself. She wanted to; his reaction to it would be very important to her. She would do it this very day.

In the morning, the scratches and marks on her arms now looked like welts. Outside, it was a dreary, overcast day, with patches of fog hanging like a pall over the lake and its shore. So she quickly pulled on a long-sleeved garment to hide her shameful marks. She longed for the day when the wounds would stop, as suddenly and mysteriously as they had started.

She knew she would find Joel already at work, busy in the salting house. And indeed he was there, staring down into a pickling barrel where only the silver backs of the fish were visible above the briny surface. He was frowning, but his expression changed to one of welcome when he saw her.

"What is the problem?" she asked. She could tell there was one.

"I think this salt has gone bad," he said. "It is oily, but its pickling strength is gone." He shook his head.

"Is it that dealer from Jericho again?" Mary asked. There was a certain dealer who was suspected of getting his supplies from the vicinity of Sodom; it was known that the salt from that area had a lot of impurities.

"The same," said Joel. "We'll be sure to tell everyone. This is the second time. He has just lost his Magdala business." He stopped. "But you did not come here to inspect the salt tanks." It was a question, not openly asked.

"No. I came because"—because I wanted to test you about the carving, she wanted to say—"I have heard that new shipment of rugs from Arabia is being shown in the marketplace, and I thought we might select one."

They still needed a floor covering for their house-to-be, and Mary was hoping they might get a real rug rather than just a straw mat. In years to come Joel might find such an excursion a chore, but now he did not. He was eager to bring closer the day when they would be husband and wife and living in the snug little house he had had built.

"Of course!" he said, and the pleasure in his voice was obvious.

Walking through the crowded streets, with the mist still clinging to the buildings and obscuring the lake, Mary tried to keep her mind on the task at hand. But thinking was so hard of late; her mind felt like the swirling mists on the lake. I want to tell Joel about the ivory, she kept repeating to herself. I do; I must. She wanted to bring it out into the light at last, be done with it.

But no good opportunity presented itself, and Joel was greeting people as they passed and asking her questions about the rug. What color did she want? Where had the shipment of rugs come from? How much did she think was a fair price?

"Joel, what do you think of idols?" she blurted out finally.

"Idols?" He looked puzzled.

"I mean, works of art depicting ancient gods," she said.

"Statues and such? We aren't permitted to have them, even if they aren't of gods. We aren't permitted *any* graven images. It's good that, so far at least, the Romans haven't forced them on us. The god Augustus doesn't peer down on us from every street corner."

"I'm not asking you about politics," she said quietly. "I'm asking about a person owning one. Keeping it as a . . . memento."

When he still looked puzzled, she tried to proceed. She had to explain it. She had to say: Joel, when I was a little girl I found this carving of a goddess in Samaria. I picked it up and took it home, but no one has ever known. I kept it hidden. Over the years, I wanted to throw it away, but I never could. She talks to me; I have heard her voice many times. I don't know if it is right to bring her into your house. She told me her name was Ashara.

She tried to say it, but her throat would not obey. She honestly could not form the words. All that escaped from her lips was a croaking semblance of "Ashara."

"What?" he said.

"Asha—Asha—"

"Are you all right?" He sounded alarmed.

"If you mention my name you will die," the voice said to her as surely as if it were right beside her.

"I—I—" The tight hand constricting her throat eased, and she was able to catch her breath. "I—got something caught in my throat." She coughed and took in deep breaths.

By the time she had recovered, Joel had lost his train of thought and did not remember the question about someone owning an idol.

They went to see the merchant, with his wares spread out all around his stall, and selected a finely woven rug of goat's hair with bright patterns of red and blue.

"From the land of the queen of Sheba," he assured them. "The very best!"

In the summer evening, Mary and all the wedding guests stood waiting for the late-setting sun to sink below the horizon. All was prepared: she waited now for Joel to come for her once full darkness had fallen, and take her to his home as his wife. Waiting with her were her mother, father, brothers, and sisters-in-law, and all the other relatives who had traveled to Magdala. Close friends of the family were also able to squeeze into the room where the wedding ceremony would take place, and they had begun assembling themselves some time ago. They wore their finest robes, best sandals, and most glistening jewelry, for a wedding was the highest festivity most of them were ever likely to attend.

Mary's gown and robe were red, carefully chosen to make her stand out. They were of the best linen her family could afford, and would serve as her grandest attire for years to come. Running through the material was a smaller, almost indiscernible pattern of deep-blue threads, which gave to the entire garment a richness that a pure-red color alone could not. Her thick, deep-brown hair was gathered away from her face and fastened with clips, and around her neck rested the brass pomegranate that her mother had given her.

Everything was going forward perfectly. And she was ready. She was ready if she did not think too deeply about it, but stood still and let it proceed.

"You are as beautiful a bride as anyone has ever been." Silvanus's voice near her ear broke into her thoughts. She turned to see that her older brother was standing right beside her, and he took her hand and squeezed it. "My dear little sister, your hand is cold. Are you afraid?"

No, not afraid, she wanted to say. Just numb. Instead she smiled and rubbed her hand to see for herself how cold it was. "No," she said.

"Well, you should be!" said Silvanus. "Only your birth day and death day are more momentous."

He himself had been married now for several years, to the good-natured woman named Naomi; Mary had liked her from the very beginning.

"If you keep talking like that, you *will* frighten me," said Mary.

"Then I will run out the kitchen door and disappear. Never be found again."

"And what would you do for all those years?" he asked. "Everyone would be looking for you. It would get very dull, hiding all the time."

"Perhaps I'd join those bandits that live in the caves near here. Their lives could hardly be dull." She smiled and almost laughed. Silvanus was making her forget the thing that was about to happen, and she relaxed.

"Living in a moldering, damp cave would be dull by definition," he said.

"I—" But she broke off when she heard, suddenly, the sound of singing and musical instruments coming from outside. Joel! It was Joel and his companions, coming in a procession with musicians and lamp-bearers through the streets toward her house. Now her own brides-maids, carrying torches, went out into the street to meet them.

The music and voices grew louder, and in the darkness now the guests could see the yellow glow of the lamps being carried before the groomsmen and the bridegroom as they strode along.

The musicians came up to the threshold and halted, and the lamp-bearers did likewise, taking their places at the entrance. Then Joel entered the room, broad-shouldered, laughing and high-spirited. He was wearing a very grand cloak—one that Mary had never seen before—and around his head was a garland of glorious summer leaves, which made him look both ancient and noble.

He stopped and looked deeply at Mary, then moved quickly over to her to take her hands in his.

"Welcome, Joel, son of Ezekiel," said Nathan. "Today you become my son as well."

"And mine," said Zebidah, covering his hands with hers.

"Are you ready to speak the words?" Nathan asked.

"Indeed, my son, are you ready?" asked Ezekiel.

"With all my heart," said Joel, heartily. His voice sounded very loud in Mary's ear. But she realized he was speaking to the entire room, not just to her and their parents.

"You may say them, then."

Joel turned to Mary, and his face grew solemn. Now he *was* speaking just to her, and to her alone.

"Let all these people be witnesses that today I, Joel bar-Ezekiel, consecrate Mary of Magdala, bat-Nathan, to me as my wife." He took her hand. "This is in accordance with the law of Moses and of Israel."

They placed a pomegranate on the ground before him, and Joel stamped on it heartily, sending its seeds squirting against ankles and feet and onto the hems of fine gowns—a propitious omen for fertility.

He tentatively reached out and took her hands in his—her cold hands. His around them were warm, protective.

Mary longed to say something in return, but it was not customary. Instead, she just looked directly into his eyes to show him how deeply she trusted herself to him.

All around her, her family and his were smiling, and began to clap their hands and cheer. And suddenly the solemn silence turned to a noisy celebration, and all the neighbors and friends were crowding around, offering their best wishes and congratulations, and Mary could see, behind their happiness, a wisp of sadness in her mother's eyes, in her brothers', and in her father's. An ineffable feeling of loss shadowed their joy around its edges.

"May the God of Israel, of Abraham, Isaac, and Jacob, bless this union," said Nathan, his voice rising above the noise. "May you be as Sarah, Rebekah, Leah, and Rachel, a true daughter of the Law, and a blessing to your husband." Then he raised his arms, as though embarrassed by his own seriousness. "Now, son, lead us on to your house for the feast!" He nodded to Joel.

The wedding banquet would be waiting at Joel's home—now Mary's as well—spread out and prepared for many guests. Joel would lead them all back through the streets, preceded by the lamp-bearers, the bridesmaids, and the musicians. He motioned for them to begin, to form a line at the door and file out. Mary took her place beside him, and they led the group out over the threshold of her childhood home and through the side street onto the main one. The night was warm; people lined the streets and looked out of their windows at the excitement passing by; young girls joined in the procession, laughing and skipping. Under the summer sky, the parade of celebrants passed in a bright line through the streets, illuminated by the golden lamps. Their light and pretty clothes made them glow in the night.

As Mary walked beside her new husband, she felt that she was part of an exquisite picture, that all around her was beauty and happiness, almost as visible as incense, and that, as she walked, clouds of it would roll away on both sides of her. She was not a participant, but an onlooker, observing, distant, appreciative. She wanted the walk to last forever; she did not want to arrive at her new home. But it was only a short distance, and soon they were approaching the doorway, brightly lit by torches outside, and glowing with lamps inside.

In the largest room, a long table was laid with an overabundance of food: cheeses spiced with cumin, cinnamon, and radish; olives from Judaea; brass trays heaped high with dried and fresh dates and figs; pottery bowls filled with almonds; platters of sweet grapes, piles of pomegranates, roasted lamb and kid, and honey cakes flavored with sweet wine. The choicest fish were displayed on platters, with jars of the famous fish sauce from the family business beside them. And, of course, a large supply of fine red wine, the very best Joel could afford.

As the people came pouring in, Joel took his place beside the table to welcome them. He poured out the first cup of wine for himself and drank it symbolically, then invited guests to help themselves to the feast.

"This is my wedding day, and I welcome you all!" he said in a loud voice, gesturing to the table and the flagons.

People surged forward.

"You must have some wine, too," Joel said softly to her. He poured out a cup and handed it to her, their hands touching on the wide rim. The gesture felt sacred, more binding even than the promise Joel had made before all those witnesses.

"Drink," he said, and she tipped the cup up and tasted the heavy tang of the wine; swallowing it, she bound herself to him who had handed her the cup.

Only as she lowered it did she see that everyone had been watching, and then they cheered in joy as she handed it back to Joel. She wished they would look elsewhere; she was relieved that after this there was nothing further that she must do before the guests.

In spite of the open windows, the room grew heated; guests crowded around the table to taste the generous fare and sample the dark-red wine, and flutes and lyres provided joyful music that was soon drowned out by the talking. As Mary looked around, she realized that there were a great many people present whom she did not recognize. As if he was reading her thoughts, Joel said, "I have asked some people I know through my work travels to join us." He nodded toward a knot of people grouped near the end of the table, helping themselves to the kid.

"Some of the fishermen and their families from Capernaum," he said. "We do a great deal of business with them during the sardine season. Zebedee and his sons—do you remember them?"

She had seen them several months ago on the walk with Joel, and remembered them vaguely, and Keziah's father had talked about them. Mainly she remembered Zebedee and his impatience. He looked somewhat sweeter-tempered tonight, she thought. And then she saw someone whom she thought she knew, but no . . . she must have been mistaken. Still, there was something familiar about the woman.

"That woman with the blue gown and the thick hair . . ." Mary murmured to Joel. "She must be a friend of yours, for I cannot give her a name."

"Oh, yes," said Joel. "She's the wife of one of the best young fishermen from Capernaum, Avner by name."

"And her name?"

"I'm not sure," admitted Joel. "Come, let's ask her!"

Before Mary could stop him, he had turned toward the woman and said, "I am afraid I do not know your name, although I know your husband well."

"Leah," she said. "From Nazareth."

Still she looked familiar. Nazareth. Mary had seldom met anyone from there. Except once, long ago . . .

It was hard to see the face of a child in this grown woman's face, but Mary looked hard. Wherever she had met her, she had not seen her since. But that was not surprising if she was from Nazareth, for Mary and her family never went there.

"On the way home from Jerusalem!" Leah suddenly said. "Yes, yes, I remember! You and your friend joined us, and spent the night with us when we were camped out. We were little then, only six or seven."

Now it all came back. The trip home from the Feast of Weeks. The adventure of leaving her own family and spending time with this other one. The episode with the toothache and the Sabbath.

"Oh, yes, of course! Tell me, your brothers and sisters, your parents—are they here, too?" Mary looked around at the large crowd, so many of whom she did not know.

"No. My father died last year; my mother still lives in Nazareth but does not travel much. My oldest brother, Jesus, has taken our father's place in the carpentry business, with our next brother, James, to help him. But James is not much help, he seems to want to be a scribe or something; he spends all his time studying the scriptures and debating things in the synagogue—mainly about ritual and cleanliness. It's not much fun back there anymore." She laughed.

"Are they married?" Mary asked. Today was a day when she could think of little else. "

"Not Jesus."

"Isn't he—" Mary wanted to say "awfully old to still be unmarried?"

"He ought to be married," said Leah firmly. "But he's been too busy with the business. And taking care of Mother. He'd better hurry, though. Do you have any eligible sisters?"

"Unfortunately, no," said Mary, and they laughed.

"Ah, if he waits much longer, he will be hopeless. Already he shows signs he would be difficult to live with—for a wife, I mean."

"In what way?" Mary remembered him only as the boy who had said unexpected things about lizards. Maybe he now kept them in his house?

"He keeps to himself after working hours. Mother says he seems to seek solitude too often."

"Too often?" asked Mary.

Around them the musicians wove themselves in a line, thumping their drums and shrilling their pipes and trying to attract attention.

"Often enough that people notice," said Leah. "They talk about it. You know how a small town is, and Nazareth is a small town."

Suddenly Mary felt sorry for Jesus—having to toil away all day in his father's place in the carpenter's shop, and then being the focus of gossip for his behavior afterward. Why shouldn't he want some privacy and solitude? She herself did often enough. But in teeming small towns and under a family roof it was seldom granted. Only the desert granted solitude. Perhaps that was why the holy men retreated to it.

"But you," Leah went on, "you are to live here in Magdala? I know Joel goes all around the fishing towns on the lake, making business arrangements, and even goes to Ptolemais occasionally. Will you go with him? How exciting that would be! I've always wanted to see Ptolemais."

"Perhaps I shall be able to go." All of it felt very strange; in truth, she could not picture her new life very well.

"Riddles! Riddles!" Ezekiel was holding up his hands and calling for attention. It was a time-honored tradition at weddings; the groom was to ask his guests riddles, and provide a prize if they answered correctly. It went all the way back to Samson and his wedding feast, where he put the riddle of the lion and the honey to his guests and was mortified when his bride disclosed the secret to her relatives.

"Ah, yes." Joel broke off his conversation with a guest and walked slowly into the center of the room. "A riddle." He tried to look thoughtful, but Mary knew that he had been composing the riddle for weeks.

"It is this: I am made of water and locusts. I am dangerous to approach, for I destroy; yet many approach regardless. Now tell me what this is, and I will reward you with a new cloak and a year of honey."

Everyone looked puzzled. Made of water and locusts. A cake? There were special locust-cakes made from the dried insects. Someone suggested that.

"But they are not dangerous, my friend," said Joel. "Sorry, you do not win."

"A drought?" a woman asked. "A drought might bring forth locusts, and it involves a lack of water." It was known that these riddles could use such subterfuges in language. "And it is dangerous."

"But no one approaches it. It approaches us instead," said Joel.

"What about a plague of locusts? They might go around a large body of water, so in that way the water directs them. And we approach them, to try to control them. We pull things out of their paths, burn a swath before them to rob them of food."

Joel looked surprised, for this answered most of the criteria but was not what he had in mind. "No," he finally said. "The plague is not 'made' of water, and so it does not fit. But, for your inventiveness, I think you should have at least a large jar of honey."

Several other people ventured guesses, but at length they ran out of ideas. Finally, Joel said, "What I had in mind was one of those holy men who go out into the wilderness and call for people to purify themselves with ritual washing. It is said these people eat locusts and wear rough clothing. And they are dangerous, because they put all sorts of revolutionary ideas in people's heads. Sometimes they are put down by the Romans, other times they just perish out in the desert. But as soon as one vanishes, another appears to take his place."

"But these men aren't made of water," objected one guest. "That was misleading."

"Yes, I suppose so," admitted Joel. "Still, water is part and parcel of their message. They usually preach beside a running stream and use water as a symbol of purification."

"Who's the latest desert prophet?" someone asked. "I thought it had been fairly quiet lately."

"It's just a matter of time," answered someone else. "They pop up like desert flowers after the winter rains. All promising us a new world, if we would just repent."

"And rid ourselves of the Romans!" another burst out. "Well, that will take more than a wild-eyed prophet in the desert and his band of ragtag followers."

"I suppose it's time for another Messiah," one man said, lounging on a cushion. He was quite heavy, and seemed to sink into his surroundings. "Or have we given up on that? It's rather childish, isn't it? Some Deliverer, or Messiah, or whatever he's called, who will wield the sword and show the Romans what's what." He belched, shielding his mouth with his hand, and smiled as if to emphasize how ludicrous it all was.

"Enough, friends," said Joel, fearing that the topic of the Deliverer and his war of the true believers against Rome was about to erupt. "We want no prophets at this wedding feast, except in the guise of a riddle."

To Mary's relief, people dropped the subject and seemed willing to go back to joking, singing, and feasting. Tonight no one wanted to linger on an unpleasant topic. Her mother made her way over to Mary and embraced her, whispering, "Let us know when you are ready."

Ready. Ready for the good wishes, ready for the dancing, ready to be carried on the shoulders of the guests, and ready to be escorted into the bridal chamber, where a canopy had been set up over the bed.

"I think—soon," Mary said. Yes, it had to proceed, there was no holding it back. The good wishes of the people in her life, the boisterous singing, the final time-honored raucous lifting of her and Joel on strong shoulders and carrying them about the room and then into the bridal chamber—these things must happen.

At last she and Joel were standing beside the canopied bed, with all the guests staring in from the adjoining room.

"I now claim my bride," Joel said, simply, looking first at her and then out at all the company. He moved to close the door that separated the two rooms, and in the scraping of the wood against the floor Mary heard an ending to her former life as distinct as a handclap.

The door shut. Now they were alone—or out of sight, rather.

Joel reached up to touch her hair, bound partly back but still the long, loose hair of a maiden. "I will honor you with my life," he said.

She shut her eyes, not knowing what to say or do. What seemed most natural was just to answer, "And I you, with mine."

Since she trusted him so much, it was not difficult to go under the canopy and to become his wife. She did not use the potions the women had given her, and when she tentatively held out the bridal cloth to spread it upon the bed, Joel took it away.

"We have no need of such a thing," he said. "You are mine and I am yours, and there is no other, and we need not prove that to anyone."

He enfolded her in his arms and kissed her so deeply that even the poetry of the Song of Songs deserted her.

"You are so beautiful," he murmured.

ೞ IX ೞ

The kitchen glowed warm in the autumn light. It was the close of day, and Mary was setting out the pots and dishes for the evening meal. She had felt as warm and golden as this room all day long.

The two years since she had left her father's home and made one for herself and Joel had passed quickly, and today she was mistress of a house she could be proud of, and a way of life that they had fashioned to fit themselves, like a special garment.

She looked out the window; it was a little too early for Joel to be coming home. She had labored over a dish of lamb stew with figs all afternoon, and had already set out the little bowls of condiments to accompany it. There would be good wine and fresh bread—almost like a Sabbath dinner.

Hurry, Joel, she thought. The meal awaits. The evening awaits.

Everything was perfection: the house was clean-swept, the bread fresh-baked, the air freshened with sweet rushes in baskets. Everything was holding its breath.

But when Joel finally arrived, long past the hour of dinner—which had dried out a bit—he was not in the proper mood. He was muttering and shaking his head as he stepped into the room, and barely greeted his wife.

"Sorry," he said offhandedly, "but there was a problem with one of the shipments. The garum that we were supposed to export never got picked up. Try telling that to the merchant in Tyre who was expecting it before the hot season." He looked harried. "I had to dispatch an emergency message to him. I think it will get there in three days."

He sank down at the table, still distracted. He seemed not to have noticed that Mary had not yet said a word. Finally, he said, "I hope you aren't upset."

Upset? No, she was not upset. Just disappointed. Her enthusiasm had dried out as much as the stew.

"No," she assured him, dishing up the food. He wolfed it down without even looking at it.

It could have been anything, thought Mary. I might as well have served him a plate of stale fish and two-day-old bread.

Suddenly it seemed that all this—the carefully laid table, the oil lamps freshly filled and burning, the sweet-scented rushes—was a waste of time.

"Mary, what is it?" asked Joel. He was looking at her, and he saw her glistening eyes.

"Nothing," she said. "Nothing."

"You're angry about the dinner. . . ." But he did not sound sympathetic, only exasperated. "I told you I couldn't help it." Joel stood up. "You care too much about this! Put your mind to more important things than how promptly I arrive to eat a dinner!" He paused. "Not that it is not kind of you to prepare—"

"What sort of important things?" she asked. "Without children, what important things can there be for me?"

"Children are a gift of God," said Joel quickly—too quickly. "He alone sees fit to bestow them. But there is a useful life without them—"

"Then perhaps I should be pursuing it," said Mary. "Perhaps I should be helping with the books at your work, or making arrangements for exports and shipping, or keeping the correspondence."

But none of that sounded any more important than what she was already doing—just less lonely.

"Yes, perhaps," said Joel. "The correspondence has gotten in a mess."

"Or perhaps I ought to apply myself and study Torah," she suddenly said. Perhaps then she could understand what God required of her, in this life without children.

"What?" he said. "Study Torah? Alas, they don't allow women, and that's a shame, for you would be well suited to it." They had spent satisfying winter evenings reading Isaiah and Jeremiah, and he knew what a quick and eager mind she had for studies.

"Perhaps there's a way," she said stubbornly.

"Not unless you disguise yourself," he said. "And I am afraid that would be difficult, for you are very womanly." He put his arms around her. "I wish there were something I could do." If only God would grant them children!

"There isn't." She knew that; knew that it was not Joel's responsibility, or in his power, to make her life better.

She thought back to her feelings late in the afternoon, before Joel had arrived home, about her contentment. In spite of her material well-being, in spite of the love of her husband, in spite of her respected place in the village, at the center there was nothing to take hold of. A barren young wife was the poorest of creatures, isolated from common life.

That night, as Joel lay sleeping beside her, exhausted from his day's work, she stared up at the ceiling. Tomorrow I will go to the market and buy some good things for dinner, prepare them, and wait for Joel to come home, she thought. A lonely road that stretched on endlessly.

ౚౚౚ

Six more years passed, sometimes slowly and sometimes fast, and nothing changed, except that she was aware that gradually she had become an object of pity to everyone except her old friend Keziah. But Keziah had three children now, and it was increasingly painful for Mary to be around them—and her. As she went about her normal activities, she could almost feel the solicitous looks and unasked questions from her friends and acquaintances. In her own family, they were more blunt: Silvanus and Naomi were the first to ask openly about it, and then to offer their love and support. Eli and Dinah—ah, that was another matter. From the way they looked at her and blathered pious platitudes, it was clear they thought that she was somehow at fault, or that God was punishing her and Joel. Eli often hinted that she should examine herself and search for any hidden sins.

"'Who can understand his errors? Cleanse thou me from secret faults,'" Eli would intone, quoting the Psalmist.

"'Thou hast set our iniquities before thee, our secret sins in the light of thy countenance,'" Dinah would add unctuously. Then she would encircle her three colorless, boring sons—with the comically old-fashioned names of Jamlech, Idbash, and Ebed—and, holding her infant daughter, Hannah, would look mournfully at Mary, as if to say, You see what you are depriving yourself of by refusing to live a godly life?

One afternoon, as the Sabbath was coming on and Mary was making the dinner in her home, she felt unusually downcast. Suddenly she had had something—a glimpse—it was almost a vision—of both herself and Joel living long ago, in tents with a large company of kinsmen. And in this picture she was still childless, but Joel had taken other wives, and even some concubines, and they were all sitting down to a Sabbath meal in the tent, surrounded by the host of children, ranging in age from infants to adolescents. Joel was reclining on pillows and looking self-satisfied, and she, Mary, was the subject of taunting looks and haughtiness from the other women, even the lowest-ranking concubine, the one that had to perform the meanest tasks to care for the donkeys and goats.

And because she had spent time studying the scriptures, she recognized it as a vision of her own ancestor. She and her family were supposed to be descended from the tribe of Naphtali, and Naphtali was the son of Bilhah, Rachel's handmaid.

One day, Rachel had accosted Jacob in frustration and cried, "Give me children, or I die!" When Jacob had protested that it was God's decision to withhold children, she had insisted on the substitute of her fertile maidservant, Bilhah, for herself.

I could never do that, thought Mary. I could not bear it if Joel—

Yet it is Bilhah who is your ancestor, not Rachel. You come from the line of Naphtali, whom Rachel named in honor of her struggle.

The long-ago pain of those people—the husband, his two rival wives, the maidservants—broke upon her, and she found herself crying for them.

It was so much worse than what I have to endure, she thought. So much worse.

She wanted to reach out to touch them, tell them that, thousands of years later, their own private struggle had benefited their nation, but they were unreachable, far away in the past. And she was trapped in her own kitchen, preparing dinner for people who, just then, seemed much less real.

Her parents arrived just before sunset, and Joel had already bathed and helped arrange the ceremonial items on the table—the Sabbath lamps, the special bread. Everything was gleaming, freshly scrubbed, and polished. The Sabbath would be welcomed as usual. Mary often savored those first few moments, when all was in readiness and awaiting the sunset, the actual arrival of the holy pause, but tonight she was still distracted by her ghostly visitors, and had to shake her head to clear it.

"Ah! How lovely, as always." Her mother gave a happy sigh. "Mary, you know how to create such peaceful order. It is the very spirit of the Sabbath in your home."

Mary thanked her mother for the compliment, but she could not help wishing for some of the disorderliness of a household with young children.

She lit the Sabbath lamps, saying the age-old prayer, "Blessed art thou, O Lord our God, King of the Universe, who hast sanctified us by thy commandments, and commanded us to kindle the Sabbath lamp." She held her hands out over them, feeling their warmth.

They took their places, and the golden Sabbath bread, the challah, was passed. Then came the other dishes, still warm from the preparation: herb soup, sweet-and-sour beets on a bed of beet greens, roasted barley, and a fine, plump boiled barbel fish.

"This was the largest one presented to the warehouse yesterday, and I grabbed him," Joel admitted. "I never gave anyone else a chance at him."

"I assume it was one of Zebedee's," said Nathan.

"Yes. It always is," said Joel. "He seems to know all the best fishing sites, and he keeps them secret. Well, as long as he trades almost exclusively with us . . ."

"I think Jonah may be reconsidering his partnership with him," said Nathan. "He's tired of Zebedee's possessiveness about fishing areas. After all, he's supposed to share the information with his partners."

"How do their sons get along?" asked Joel. "I can't imagine Simon just quietly stepping aside—not in the long run."

"Thus far the sons seem to get along better than the fathers," said Nathan. "Simon is good-natured but impulsive, and Zebedee's sons, John and James, are very aggressive about their rights but usually back down if Simon stands up to them. That is, if Zebedee isn't nearby. Then they sink in their teeth like mastiffs."

Zebidah stirred her cloudy green soup thoughtfully. Little bits of chervil and mint floated to the surface. "Then I would predict that this partnership is doomed, since Zebedee will always be nearby. When it ends, who will you choose to trade with? For they will make you take sides."

Joel gestured toward Nathan to answer.

Nathan waited a moment before replying. "I suppose Zebedee. It does not pay to cross him. He controls too much. And he has important commissions in Jerusalem to supply the high priest Caiaphas's household with fish. No, it would not do to cross Zebedee." He shook his head, chewing slowly on a piece of challah. "But I hope it does not come to that."

Mary tried to listen attentively; she knew it was important to their livelihood. But in the back of her mind she kept seeing Rachel and Bilhah. "How will the new town nearby affect us?" she asked, as much to direct her own thoughts to the present and future as to get an answer.

"It's difficult to know," said Joel. "When Antipas announced it, I thought it would be a catastrophe for us—another town just south of Magdala, putting us in the shade. But perhaps not. It may even be good for us. Those newcomers will all have appetites, and need to be fed."

"The man has no sense, and no shame," said Nathan. "He selects an unholy site to build it on—over a cemetery!—and then he names it Tiberias."

"He had to," said Zebidah. "He's trying to flatter the emperor. He'll do anything to try to please him."

"Then he ought to be careful with his women," said Joel ominously.

"Why?" Nathan laughed. "Is Tiberius likely to care? How many divorces has he had? Perhaps you don't really commend yourself to the Roman emperor unless you *are* divorced, or engaged in an incestuous union of some sort." He began dividing up the fish fillet he had on his plate, noting the flavor and firmness of the flesh.

"But Antipas's subjects care," said Mary. "I've heard people talking about it, about his liaison with his brother's wife. If he marries her, it's against Jewish law."

"But will anyone dare speak up?" Nathan asked. "Everyone is afraid of Antipas."

"And we don't want to attract the notice of Rome," said Joel. "Not now."

Recently Tiberius had expelled the Jews from Rome, on account of a supposed religious scandal involving a highborn Roman matron. He had even consigned four thousand young Jewish men to serve in the Roman army in Sardinia, despite their laws against fighting on the Sabbath or eating unclean food. The rest had been sent packing over the rest of the empire. Some had found their way back to Galilee, loudly proclaiming their mistreatment. Antipas had looked the other way.

"No," agreed Nathan. "The emperor is not kindly disposed to Jews right now."

"I heard from Zebedee himself that they may be getting a new procurator in Jerusalem," said Nathan. "Tiberius may replace Valerius Gratus with someone else—the Lord protect us as he decides who."

"I heard a rumor—but it cannot possibly be true—that Tiberius himself was going to leave Rome," said Joel.

"No, the emperor can't leave Rome," agreed Nathan.

"Still, he's old," said Joel. "Maybe he just wants to retire."

"There is only one way of retirement for an emperor," said Nathan. "Death."

ಌ X ಌ

Tiberius did not die immediately, although, from reports even the common people heard in Galilee, he was becoming increasingly erratic and irascible. Likewise Herod Antipas, closer to home, who was still involved with his brother's wife.

"How can such madness seize people?" Mary wondered aloud to Joel. "He is endangering his throne."

"They say love is a form of madness," Joel said.

It is a madness I have never felt, Mary thought. Would I want to? She looked around at her snug home and could not imagine jeopardizing it.

Mary kept a very tidy house—more so since she had poured so much of her frustrated energy into housekeeping—and thus, when it was her turn to provide the Passover celebration for her family, she had less to do to transform her home into a ceremonially clean setting than other women might have. She had to clean, of course, more thoroughly than usual, scrubbing surfaces diligently. The special Passover dishes had to be taken from their storage place and washed, and the lamb ordered in advance—a large one for the seventeen people who would be coming—and all the leavened bread searched out and either destroyed or sold temporarily to a Gentile. Mary always destroyed it; there was not that much of it, and somehow the ruse of legally transferring it was not very satisfying.

Mary cleaned ferociously, as if a crumb of leaven might have found its way into the most minute crack in the floor, into the fiber of a rug, behind a jar. In the furious scrubbing, it was easy to feel that she was somehow purifying her heart and life. She decided to open all the trunks and containers and purge them, too.

A wooden box yielded some woolen mantles that she had forgotten about. Perhaps she should give them to a needy family.

The next box contained some items from childhood: her lessons, some flowers she had grown in her first small garden—quite brittle and faded now—and her baby clothes. Looking at them, she felt despondent. These I should give away, so they cannot mock me any longer, she thought.

And then there was something else, something wrapped and lying inside a pouch. She withdrew it and slowly unwound its wrapping, until the face of the ivory idol smiled back at her.

A cold chill ran through her.

Ashara. Here you are again. That name, that name which sprang so readily to her lips, brought memories of both childish desires of beauty and, running alongside these, currents of fear. But that was long ago, before she was married. Her dreams of being supremely desirable had not been granted, but the puzzling afflictions had vanished, too. It had all been her imagination. There were no more oppressive dreams, no more confusion, no coldness in the room, no scratches and welts to cover up. Truly, as she had hoped, she had left all that behind, and she saw it now as just a strange illness of girlhood.

The beautiful Ashara. Mary addressed her silently: And to think I once was so in awe of you I believed that you could speak to me. Speak, Ashara! she commanded it. Speak if you can!

The carving was silent, even in her own mind. It merely lay there in her hand, looking up at her.

She put it down and went about her cleaning. She left it out to show to Joel, as she had meant to—she remembered this now—before they were married. Well, she would tonight. The sun was sinking and light fading. Time to stop. She got up to light a lamp, and saw the carving lying there, waiting for Joel.

And then, strangely drawn to it, she picked it up and looked carefully at its perfect ivory features, the inviting, half-closed eyes, the curve of the lips, the wavy hair. Here is the very personification of womanhood, she thought. She is what a woman should be, in every way. What I asked her to make me, as a bride. Now I have more important needs.

"Give me a child!" she commanded it. "Give me a child, if you have any power!"

She put it down smugly. That would destroy its hold over her once and for all. She did not even know why she had said it. But this would end her long fascination and enthrallment to it. She had challenged it only to discredit it.

Several days later—days of intense preparation in the households of all Israel—the sun was sinking toward the sunset that would mark the beginning of the eight-day festival of Passover. Mary and Joel's home gleamed. Several tables had been put together to create one long one, and all was in readiness. Her parents arrived.

"We must wait a little longer for everyone to arrive before we can search for the leaven," said her father. "Let them hurry!"

It was a ritual much loved by children—they were to search all over the house lest some small piece of leaven had escaped Mary's notice. The forbidden substance would be discovered and destroyed, and woe to any household that failed to provide the "overlooked" leaven. Mary had left some out in plain sight on the kitchen table, and had scattered other pieces about to provide a challenge.

"My dearest, how beautiful your home is tonight!" Dinah swept in, carrying her much-praised unleavened honey cakes. Behind her trooped her three sons, dressed in their best linen tunics. She carried Hannah in her arms, but even Hannah wore a special ribbon on her gown. Eli followed, also carrying a special dish to be put on the table— the bitter herbs.

Just after them, Silvanus and Naomi and their two sons and little daughter arrived, also carrying a contribution: the *charoseth*, made of apples and nuts and wine and meant to represent the mortar the children of Israel had had to use in making Pharaoh's bricks.

"Now, my children," said Nathan, "your aunt has probably forgotten about some leaven in her household. God would never forgive us. So—let us search thoroughly and make sure there is no leaven anywhere! Blessed art thou, O Lord our God, King of the Universe, who hast sanctified us with thy commandments, and enjoined us to remove the leaven." He clapped his hands, and the children rushed everywhere. Little Idbash immediately found the pieces left out in plain view, but the others fanned out over the house and searched as diligently as Roman soldiers looking for an enemy.

While they busied themselves, the adults waited and talked. Soon the children came flying back in, triumphantly carrying little pieces of leavened bread.

"We found some! We found some!" they cried.

"And this, too." Jamlech held out the ivory carving to his father.

Mary's heart almost stopped. She had left it out—but for Joel, not for this company!

Eli studied it carefully. Mary could see the alarm in his eyes, although he tried to mask it. "I can't imagine how such a thing came to be in this household," he finally said. "It is . . . it is . . ." He could not bring himself to say "a heathen idol." Instead he said, ". . . some old carving from people who lived here before. The Canaanites, perhaps."

"Let me see it." Dinah snatched it out of his hand. She scrutinized it carefully. "Whatever it is, all representation of the human form is forbidden to us. It's a graven image. Joel—such a thing in your house, and on the Passover! It's worse than leaven."

Joel looked at it. "I've never seen it before."

"It—it was something I had out to show you," said Mary. "I found it lying on the ground." She did not indicate how many years ago that was. "I wanted you to see it."

"Why?" asked Eli.

"It might be valuable. Or . . . I thought it might be interesting, if it showed us who lived here before us." Mary suddenly felt very defensive about the carving. If it was to be destroyed, it would be by her, and not because a child had barged into her room and found it by accident.

"We are not to care about those who came before us," snorted Eli. "God told us to destroy them utterly—or they would prove a thorn in our sides and bring us down to destruction."

"That was a long time ago," said Silvanus. "Others live here now with us in this land, and we must live in peace with them."

Joel held up his hands and repeated the ritual words, "Whatever leaven remains in my possession which I cannot see, behold, it is null, and accounted as the dust of the earth."

"Let's destroy the leaven and the pagan carving!" cried Jamlech. "Here's the fire!" And he flung the leaven he clutched in his hands into a brazier. The fire blazed up, hungrily.

"Here!" Next he tossed the carving toward it. But it tumbled to one side of the fire. No one seemed to notice, and the leaping flames masked it.

"Now let us begin the feast!" Joel indicated the little tables and the cushions where they were to recline in accordance with rabbinical custom for the opening ritual. He also girded himself in his traveling cloak and held his staff as commanded by scripture: "This is how you are to eat it: with your cloak tucked into your belt, your sandals on your feet and your staff in your hand. Eat it in haste: it is the Lord's Passover."

Nathan, as the head of the entire household, pronounced the blessing over the first cup of wine. Then they passed a basin of water and a towel among themselves. Custom dictated that they perform this ritual while lounging.

Once the preliminary ritual was over, the company retired to the tables already set up. Joel took the plate of bitter herbs—watercress, horseradish root, chervil—and passed it around, followed by the *charoseth*. As soon as everyone had taken a portion, the plates were removed and the second cup of wine was poured. Then the youngest son present, who was four-year-old Ebed, asked his father the four questions about Passover.

"Father, why is this night different from all other nights? On all other nights we eat either leavened or unleavened bread, but on this night we eat only unleavened bread."

Eli answered solemnly, explaining that the Israelites left Egypt so swiftly that their bread did not have time to rise.

"Father, on all other nights we eat any kind of herbs, but on this night we eat only bitter herbs?"

Again Eli explained that it was to signify the bitterness of slavery and bondage in Egypt.

"Father, on all other nights we eat meat roasted, stewed, or boiled, but on this night only roasted?"

Because those were the Lord's instructions to Moses, Eli said.

"Father, on all other nights we dip the herbs only once, but on this night twice?"

By the time Eli had finished answering the questions, he had given a short history of the people of Israel and their deliverance from Egypt and the giving of the Law at Mount Sinai.

The dishes were replaced on the table, and the second glass of wine drunk, and hands washed once again. Two unleavened cakes were broken and dipped in the *charoseth*.

Before dipping his piece, Nathan said solemnly, "This is the bread of affliction that our fathers ate in the land of Egypt."

Next the lamb was brought out, the central part of the feast. It was a particularly fine and meaty one, and everyone complimented it and exclaimed over it.

The third and fourth cups of wine were presented and drunk in accordance with the ritual observance. The traditional hymns were sung, the old words—"When Israel came out of Egypt, the house of Jacob from a people with a foreign tongue, Judah became God's sanctuary, Israel his dominion"—bringing joy and memories to everyone present. Then a portion of wine was poured into a particularly fine cup, awaiting Elijah.

Mary looked at it sitting there. How surprised we would all be if Elijah suddenly appeared, picked it up, and drank it, she thought. And yet I myself saw Rachel and Bilhah in this very kitchen. Why not Elijah?

"To Elijah," Nathan suddenly said, stealing her thoughts. "Would that he would come again!"

"Would we recognize him?" asked Joel. "Surely he would not look the same, or thunder against Ahab and Jezebel."

"Oh, we would recognize him," Eli assured him. "We would welcome him gladly."

"How long has he been dead?" asked Jamlech bluntly.

"He *lived* more than eight hundred years ago," said Dinah. "But he didn't die. No, he was taken up to heaven in a fiery chariot."

Jamlech looked skeptical. "Someone saw him go?"

"Oh, yes," said Naomi. "Many people. That's why we wait for his return. Only one other person was taken directly to God without death, and that was Enoch."

"So why don't we wait for him, too?" asked Idbash.

"We don't know much about him," Naomi admitted. "We know much more about Elijah, and we tend to want people to return if we know about them, not if they are just names. Like a friend. Or as we wait for the Messiah. We don't know the Messiah, but we know *about* him, so we know what to look for."

"Hmmm." Jamlech was carefully considering this.

While their attention was on Naomi at the other end of the table, Nathan quickly drank the cup and put it back.

"Look! He's been here, while your heads were turned the other way!" he exclaimed.

Jamlech was confounded and frustrated. At eight, he didn't quite believe it, but he wasn't sure.

"Next year, Jamlech, you'll have to watch closer," said his grandfather.

The guests gone, Mary and Joel sat in the messy room and felt the great contentment that descends after a successful gathering.

"Is there anything more satisfying than the house after a celebration has ended?" asked Joel, coming over to her and holding her against him.

"No," she admitted. She was proud of how it had gone; she liked being hostess at Passover.

"Have I told you what a wonderful wife you are?" said Joel. "And not just because of your Passover dinner."

"Yes." Joel always told her how he treasured her, unlike many husbands.

What a pity your wife is an incomplete one! she whispered cruelly to herself. You are wasting your love and devotion. She hated her childlessness as much for Joel as for herself; it dishonored him. But the words must never be spoken.

Later, their arms around one another, they went to their bed.

ꙮ X 1 ꙮ

Spring in Galilee: the most glorious in all Israel. The deserts of the Negev and Judaea might bloom in their fashion, fleetingly and sparsely, and the coast and plains had their own special flowers, but only Galilee had a spectacular spring. Wildflowers, orchards, gardens all blazed forth with every color, framed by the brilliant green of new grass growing in meadows and on hillsides. After the first white flowering of the almond trees, the others competed, opening in profusion and haste: red anemones and poppies, purple grape hyacinths and irises, yellow crowfoot and marigold, and pure-white lilies in hidden places. From Magdala the entire rim of the lake seemed to glow bright with the jewel-like flowers, and people stole away from their town tasks to wander in the fields and hills whenever they could.

Mary was among them; she walked alone through the blooming hills and then sat on the pretty slopes. As she looked down at the blue surface of the lake, it was hard for her to muster up the usual despair about her condition. Perhaps I've just begun to accept it, she thought.

Overhead the hawks were flying, and farther away black vultures were riding the warm air, slowly turning, turning in a great circle. Mary suddenly felt overcome by a strange sleepiness, as if someone had given her a magic draft. Her eyes closed, and the sky with its hawks and vultures vanished.

When she awoke, weak and trembly, it was almost dark. She pulled herself up on a shaky elbow. What had happened? Around her the wind was rising, and she could see the first star of evening in the sky above the lake.

Groggily she stood up. She would have to hurry back before it got fully dark and she could not see the path. She stumbled along, and was almost back home again before her head cleared.

The strange sleepiness descended on her many more times—some of them not so convenient—in the next few weeks. Soon other odd symptoms appeared, such as an unsettled stomach, weak legs, tingling in her arms. It baffled the physician whom Joel usually consulted; it took an old midwife to pronounce the obvious.

"You are with child," she said, amused at the stupidity of others in overlooking the most obvious explanation. "It does not take a learned doctor to know that."

Those words, so long awaited, now sounded false to Mary. It could not be. She was barren. That had become an absolute fact in her mind.

"Aren't you pleased?" The old woman looked into her face.

"Of course," Mary answered, as if by rote.

"I would guess this commenced around the time of Passover," the woman pronounced. "That means you may expect the child around the time of Chanukah. More or less. It is hard to predict exactly."

"Passover," Mary repeated stupidly.

"Yes, Passover." The woman looked at Mary. Was she dim-witted? "You can name him something appropriate meaning 'deliverance' or 'liberty.' Or just plain 'Moses.'"

"Yes. Thank you." Mary stood up, gathered her basket, fumbled for something to pay with.

She reeled out into the street. With child. Her prayers had been answered!

Oh, dear Lord, forgive my unbelief! Forgive my despair! Forgive my doubts! she cried from within. She started running to get home and tell Joel.

"Oh, Joel!" She threw herself into his arms. "You cannot—it's wonderful, it's impossible, but it's happened!"

He pulled back and looked at her quizzically.

"I am with child! We are to have a child, at last, at long last!"

A tentative smile spread over his face, as if he was afraid of believing the words. "Truly?" he finally said, in the soft, sweet voice he used only in the dark of the night with her.

"Truly. The midwife has confirmed it. Oh, Joel . . ." She embraced him, burying her face to stop the tears. It was to come to them, at last. "Next winter, when the storms come, so will our child. Our child . . ."

In bed that night, they lay together, hardly able to sleep. A child! Conceived at Passover, born at Chanukah. Could anything be more auspicious?

Finally, Mary could tell by his breathing that Joel slept. But still she lay awake, and she did not care. What did sleep matter? Her prayers had been answered. God was good.

As she lay there and thoughts drifted through her mind like leaves slowly turning, she luxuriated in them. They sank through her consciousness and came to rest gently. *Barrenness . . . God's sovereignty . . . All that opens the womb is mine, says the Lord. . . . There you saw how the Lord your God carried you, as a father carries his son, all the way you went.*

God, you did carry me, and I never saw it. Forgive me, said Mary. But her heart was so buoyant that even her repentance was pleasant.

"You utter fool!" A harsh, nasty voice sounded in her mind. It was high-pitched, and completely unlike the one she imagined God to use. "God, or Yahweh, or whatever you wish to call him, had nothing to do with it. He had denied you. It is I, Ashara, the powerful goddess, who heard you and answered. You begged me for a child, did you not? I answered. Now you are mine."

The ugly voice startled Mary so much she almost sat up in the bed. It sounded as if it were right there in the room.

Instead she lay rigid and tried to frame an answer. The silence of the night seemed very thick. There were no crickets, no sound of waves on the shore, no crackle of fire. It was the deadest time of the daily cycle.

That's a lie, Mary finally answered her. You have nothing to do with it. You are . . . you do not even exist.

She was answered by a sharp laugh. "Stretch out your hands and lay them on your belly and tell me I do not exist. You asked me for this child, and I have granted your wish. Do you deny that I have done it? Very well. I can remove it as easily as I granted it."

Mary clutched at her stomach protectively. This was insane. The little carving had nothing to do with it. The voice was just in her imagination. It was . . . diabolic. Yes, just a manifestation of the Evil One. She would defy it, prove its impotence, its nonexistence.

But the words died in her throat, her mind. She had indeed asked Ashara for a child, if only to test her. Did she really dare to ask that her wish be reversed? Did she want to risk that?

No, she heard herself murmuring.

"I thought not," the voice said smugly. "That is intelligent of you."

But you are . . . you were . . . Mary remembered that Jamlech had thrown the carving onto the brazier.

Again, harsh ugly laughter. "Do you really think that destroyed me? I took his hand and made him miss. And even had I been consumed, you had already made the bargain. That would stand, regardless."

What had happened to the carving? Mary thought frantically. Joel had cleaned the brazier; had he found it? What had he done with it?

"Get up!" the voice ordered her. Dumbly, she obeyed.

"Go out into the kitchen, where we can converse. Where you can answer me out loud."

She traced her way into the kitchen. It was dark and chilly; the fire had died out. She stood shivering, feeling very afraid and small.

"Now, then." Ashara's voice finally spoke, breaking the silence in the night. But was it aloud or still only in her mind? "I have given you what you desired, what your Yahweh withheld from you. Why did he withhold it? No one knows. He punishes those who serve and love him—strange god! No wonder people have always turned to other, more kindly gods." Now Mary actually heard the mocking laughter out loud. "And then he gets angry, and uses that as an excuse for punishment! Excessive punishment—destruction and exile. He is hardly fair. Admit it."

But Mary kept her lips shut. She did not know how to answer. And she was afraid to, as if answering would make the voice more real and give it more power.

"Think of all the other gods the Israelites have worshiped: Baal, Ishtar, Molech, Dagon, Melkart . . . and me. If Yahweh had really been a true god to you, why would you have felt the lack and needed to turn to other gods? It is his fault, not yours."

Mary knew this was temptation and blasphemy, but . . . could a god blaspheme against another god? Then she was stricken with even more guilt: she had admitted that Ashara was a god.

"Are you ready to obey me? Are you ready to submit?" The voice was relentless.

The child. She could not give it up. Mary nodded, miserably. She could not speak. It was so dark in the kitchen; could Yahweh see her little nod?

"I accept your allegiance," the voice said. "Actually, I have had it since your childhood, since the day you found me and could not let me go." The brisk laughter came again. "It took an eight-year-old child to have the courage to fling me away! But that was because I had not spoken to him."

No, it was because Jamlech did not have eyes to see the beauty of that idol, thought Mary. Oh, blessed innocence, to have blind eyes that way. And yet . . . blind eyes to that beauty meant blind eyes to all beauty. The different kinds could not be divorced.

I should have obeyed my conscience and thrown it away at the Temple, thought Mary. I should have.

Yet . . . the child. Can I throw away the sin and still retain its benefits?

I cannot take that chance, she thought. I cannot. Time enough later to abjure the idol Ashara, renounce her utterly, repent. She hastily smothered the thought to avoid Ashara's wrath.

"Speak aloud!" the voice commanded her. "I want to hear you say it. I want your god to hear you say it!"

"I . . . I thank you," Mary said.

"Thank me for what? Say it!"

"I thank you for . . . granting me this child." She whispered it, but still the words hung on the air.

Silence all around her. Silence from the insistent voice in her head, silence from God—if he had heard.

The bargain was kept, the bargain sealed. Ashara did not speak again, and the summer unfolded, and Mary now wondered if she had imagined all of it: the voice, the commandments, the certainty that Ashara was involved and that God had been betrayed somehow. Her child grew peacefully within her, and she did everything she could to assure its health: she rested every day in the hot hours, ate good soups and grains, and did not let herself become agitated. She tried to think only good and uplifting thoughts, quickly repelling any that even hinted at anything dark.

Joel must have thrown the ashes of the idol out, she reassured herself. It is gone from the house and from our lives, and that is an end to it, she sternly repeated to herself. It had to be true.

ᔕ X 11 ᔕ

It was a little puzzling, Mary's friends and family agreed. Most young women expecting their first child—especially when they had waited so long—were exuberant and excited, but Mary was so calm and detached that it was eerie. They assumed that it was a superstitious fear of something going wrong—understandable enough, but a little extreme.

Only once during the long months did she slip. One evening, as the autumn rains had begun to fall and she and Joel were listening to the steady drumming on the roof, she suddenly asked, "Do you remember Passover, and the things Jamlech found? The leaven and the carving?"

Joel looked up from the warehouse document he was reading. "Yes, I do. What a hunt that was! You really gave him something to get excited about. An idol! What will Silvanus and Naomi do to top that next year, when we are in their house?" He was laughing.

"What happened to the carving?" she asked.

"We threw it on the fire—don't you remember?" Mary seemed so preoccupied and dreamy of late. He assumed that was part of her condition.

"Did it burn up?"

"Of course it burned up. How could it not?"

"Did you check the ashes?"

"I just emptied them out later. No, I didn't paw through them."

"Where did you throw them?"

"Into the trash ravine with all the other trash. What is this all about?"

"I just wanted to make sure it was destroyed."

"I am positive it was. After all, if it had been lying there, I would have seen it—wouldn't I?"

"Wouldn't you?"

"Mary, stop fretting. It's gone, it's burned up, its ashes are out of the house. There's nothing left of it. And even if there is, it's just a little piece of ivory that some craftsman, sitting and drinking beer, and mopping his face, carved long ago and put in a stack of other little carvings he was selling at his stand. There's nothing magic about it, nor anything harmful, either." He paused. "Why is it bothering you so much?"

"I suppose because I knew it was wrong to have such a thing. I still feel guilty about it. Maybe it contaminated the house!"

"It certainly has a hold over your imagination," said Joel. "But we should be laughing about it. Remember how Isaiah mocked idols? When he talked about a man who cuts down a tree, uses half of it for firewood, and makes a god out of the other half?"

"Yes," said Mary.

"Just so," said Joel. "It could not save itself when it was thrown on the fire."

The autumn months slid past, gloomy and overcast and unusually rainy. It was the in-between season for fishing; the summer catches were over, but the intense winter fishing for sardines had not yet started. Several violent storms had already swept across the lake, piling up waves on the western side.

After great soul-and-scripture searching, Mary and Joel had decided on names. "Moses" had been their teasing name for a boy for so long that after a while it seemed obvious that that *was* his name; but for a girl, it was harder. Finally, they settled on "Elisheba," because they liked the melodic sound of it and liked its meaning: God-her-oath.

Chanukah, the commemoration of the great victory of the Jewish freedom-fighters almost two hundred years earlier, fell in the darkest time of the year, so the nightly kindling of the menorah lamps in households gave a warm glow in the rooms—from the one lamp on the first night to all eight blazing on the last. It was a favorite holiday for children. Chanukah was about miracles and the victory of Judaism. It celebrated the defeat of the Greek ruler Epiphanes by the five sons of Mattathias Maccabaeus, and the reconsecration of the Temple in Jerusalem, where the one night's store of holy oil supplied by the Maccabees kept the lamps burning for eight nights.

This time next year, Mary thought, I will have a child to watch the lamps being kindled, and someone to recite the story to.

On the first night of Chanukah, they were gathered in the warm home of Silvanus and Naomi. Outside, the chill rain was falling; but inside, the glow of lamps made a circle of light and cheer. Silvanus's children, especially Barnabas, the oldest, eagerly gathered around the waiting ceremonial lamps, squirming with anticipation.

"Blessed art thou, O Lord our God, King of the Universe, who hast—" began Silvanus, reciting the blessing. A loud, rapid knock on the door interrupted him. Everyone looked around. No one was missing.

"Hmm." Silvanus excused himself and went to the door, while the company waited impatiently.

"What—" Silvanus gave a cry, and suddenly a strange little man, dripping wet, burst through the door and into their midst.

"Hide me! Hide me!" he cried, grabbing Silvanus's robe. "They're hunting me!" He caught his breath and stared intently at Silvanus.

Joel jumped up and pulled the scrawny man off, freeing his brother-in-law.

"I'm Simon!" the man said. "Simon of Arbel! You remember me! That time you came to Gergesa, on the other side of the lake! You asked about the pigs. The pigs over there, kept by the pagans. Pigs! Remember?"

Silvanus looked confused. "I cannot say that I do, friend."

"There are no Roman agents here, are there?" The man—swarthy, bandy-legged—stepped closer into the room without further invitation and looked over the company.

"I cannot recall ever meeting you, let alone inviting you to my home on the night of a family gathering," Silvanus said coldly, backing away.

"Ah, but it should be more than just a family gathering!" The man acted as though he had a perfect right to be there, as though Silvanus was forgetting his manners in not asking him to remove his cloak and wash his feet. "This—this is the celebration of liberty! This is no holiday for children, but for men and women who are willing to give their lives for liberty!"

"I repeat for the third time: I do not know you, and you are intruding in my private home. Leave, or I shall have to have you forcibly removed." Silvanus clearly considered the man dangerous. "And show me that you carry no weapons."

The man swirled around, letting his cloak fly out behind him, ostentatiously holding out his hands. "I have nothing," he said. "Nothing that would give the Romans an excuse to arrest me."

"You must go." Silvanus was looking at Joel, signaling that they might well have to evict this stranger by force.

"Hide me!" the man said. But it was less a request than an order.

"The Romans—they may be following me. I lead a group of warriors—we meet secretly in the fields near Gergesa, where the possessed people live—we oppose Rome in everything. We are training for the day—"

"Not another word!" Silvanus ordered him. "I do not wish to hear anything of this. I will not be a party to it. Nor will I provide shelter for you. If you are hunted, take refuge in the caves outside town, in the cliffs there."

The man looked outraged. "But in Gergesa you said—you gave the prearranged code word—'pigs'!"

"I go to Gergesa on business," Silvanus said. "I never go to that haunt of possessed people on the outskirts of town—why would I? They live among the rocks, some of them restrained with fetters, all of them outcasts, and many of them dangerous. I never met you there."

"You asked someone about the pigs! I heard you!" The man sounded betrayed.

"Then you were in Gergesa itself, not the demon place. And unless you yourself tend pigs, whatever I said about them should not concern you."

"*I* tend pigs?" The man was blazing with the insult. "I would not even touch them, let alone tend them. It would contaminate me! How could I defend the true Israel if I went so far as to—"

"Enough. Leave my house. I do not know you, I did not invite you, and I do not wish to join any rebellion against Rome." Silvanus indicated the door.

The man was almost trembling with anger; Mary was afraid he was going to attack either Silvanus or Joel. But he closed his eyes and let his trembling subside before speaking. "May God forgive you," he finally said. "When the hour comes, and the war begins—and the anointed one, the Messiah, looks around and counts the ranks of those on his side—God forgive those who are missing."

"I will have to count on his mercy," said Silvanus. Again he indicated the door.

The man turned and left, as suddenly as he had come.

They all sat in stunned silence.

"Silvanus," Naomi finally said in a very small voice. "Are you sure that you never spoke to him?"

"Positive," said Silvanus.

"Is it true about the pigs?" asked Mary. "Were you inquiring about them?"

"I may have asked a polite question or two about them. The herds on the plateau overlooking the lake are quite large. I've heard them grunting and snorting, and even from some distance away you can smell them. It's hard to imagine that such an unappetizing creature could produce tempting meat," Silvanus said. "Obviously this is a trap. We must be careful. Someone may be watching us. We must avoid anything that would make the Romans suspicious."

"But what about when the Messiah comes?" asked Joel—joking. "I suppose we won't be in his good books, turning away his lieutenants like that."

"All this Messiah business!" said Silvanus. "Can't these people understand that the days of brave freedom-fighters against the tyrant are over? Rome is much stronger than Epiphanes ever was. She crucifies freedom-fighters and zealots. Now I am going to say a very unpatriotic thing, and God can punish me, but here it is: if Mattathias or Simon or Judah or any of those glorious Galilean warriors were alive today, they wouldn't last a month against Rome." He paused. "Tonight we honor their memory. But it is only a memory. It cannot be re-enacted today."

"But the Messiah . . ." Barnabas spoke plaintively. "Isn't he supposed to be different? Fight with God's power?"

"There are so many things he is supposed to do that I could spend all night listing them, and even then it wouldn't help, because some of them are contradictory. He fights—he judges—he destroys demons—he is descended from David's family, of the tribe of Judah—he comes by supernatural power, yet he's of David's line—it goes on and on."

"I'm afraid that we have created him out of our own intense longings—as a people," said Joel. "The idea is dangerous because it creates 'freedom-fighters' like Simon. That makes the Messiah much more of a problem for us—his own people—than for the Romans."

"Now, Mary," said Naomi, trying to recapture the light spirit of the gathering before Simon's intrusion, "have you and Joel considered naming the baby after one of the Maccabees, since it is the right season?"

◊◊◊◊

On the eighth day of Chanukah, only a few moments after the last lamp had burned itself out, Mary felt what was unmistakably a twinge of labor pain. The midwife had told her she would know when it came, and she was right. It was unlike anything else.

She turned to Joel and took his hand. "The time has come," she said. "At last." She bit her lip as another twinge came. The pain was very slight. Surely she could stand this. Yet everyone knew the pains could be terrible.

He put his arm around her. "Shall I send for the midwife, and the women of the family?" he asked.

Mary sank down on a stool. "Not yet. Not yet." She wanted to sit there with Joel, be quiet, and wait for the pains to change, deepen. This little time was theirs, theirs alone—and the baby's.

It was daylight before Joel sent for the midwife, and Mary's mother, and his own. Once they arrived, it was no longer Joel's house, but a house of birth, of women.

As it turned out, Mary had a very easy time of it, especially for a first baby. Before noon, a perfect little girl was born to her and Joel. And although they were supposed to be disappointed that their firstborn was not a boy, they were too happy to care. Even though there would be no elaborate circumcision ceremony on the eighth day, there would be a religious blessing read over the baby when she was solemnly named on the fourteenth day. The entire family would gather and welcome her as its newest member.

So, once again, Mary's home shone as she opened it for the proudest moment of her life—the naming of her long-awaited daughter. However, it was marred by the fact that Mary would have to stand up the entire time, and not allow anyone to touch her, since ritual law proclaimed that any bed or chair she sat on until the sixty-sixth day after the birth was unclean, and so was anyone who touched her. That meant that she could not hold her own child for the ceremony.

"The curse of Eve," Joel had said lightly. To him it was only amusing, whereas to Mary it was a painful reminder that in every way women were considered so much lower than men. Of course, within their own walls they ignored the law—as if a mother would not hold her own baby for sixty-six days! But the rabbi might refuse to give the blessing if they were so rebellious in front of him. So now they must pretend.

Little Elisheba lay in a tightly woven reed basket, lined with soft wool blankets and decorated with ribbons, a cap on her head and a long blue dress enveloping her tiny form. Mary kept bending over her and looking at her.

Her eyes were wide open and looking about brightly. What was she able to see? No one knew at what age a baby began to recognize something she had seen before. But, gazing at her daughter, Mary believed that Elisheba was seeing her, and somehow knew that she loved her. The very intensity of that love had taken Mary by surprise; she had never known anything like it. She was utterly unprepared for the torrent of feelings that seemed to swirl around her every time she looked at the baby. It was like a part of herself, but, no, not really; it was finer and better than herself, and would go on to finer and better things; yet in doing so it would take Mary along as its companion for as long as she lived, the entire rest of her life. They were completely separate, yet completely joined.

I will never be alone again, Mary thought in wonder.

Now she heard the sounds of the arrival of the rabbi. Time to go out and meet everyone; reluctantly she left Elisheba's basket.

"Welcome! Welcome!" Joel was saying. He was so excited he almost forgot to take the rabbi's cloak and offer the customary courtesy foot-washing.

Mary welcomed the rabbi, taking care not to come too close to him or to touch him. On this day, she was not in the mood to challenge the rules that dictated the behavior of a woman after childbirth.

Yes, we are one person, Elisheba and I, but she should have the higher things, not suffer any of the bad that this other half, Mary, must . . . How shocking it was to be a mother. Truly, it changed everything, giving rise to strange, startling new thoughts.

"Bring the child," said the rabbi, and Mary's mother took Elisheba and carried her up to him. Naturally Mary could not even stand close. Everyone else crowded around freely.

The rabbi cuddled the baby in his arms. "Praise be to God, King of the Universe, for giving Mary and Joel this child," he said. "We welcome you into the family of Abraham."

He gently held the baby up so that everyone could see her. She peered out, her bright little eyes looking preoccupied. What impressions was she getting of all this, of the strange arms holding her, of the other eyes staring back at her? Mary wondered.

"Solomon in his proverb says, 'Children are a reward from the Lord.' And indeed this is true. All children, not just sons. Although the book of Sirach has some observations to make about daughters. 'A daughter is a treasure that keeps her father wakeful, and worry over her drives away rest.'" He went on in a lighthearted, joking voice about all the problems associated with a daughter: how as a maiden she might get seduced, as a married woman she might prove barren or unfaithful, all a disgrace to her father. So, he concluded, "'Keep a close watch on your daughter; see that there is no lattice in her room; better a man's harshness than a woman's indulgence, and a frightened daughter than any disgrace.'" Everyone dutifully laughed; most people knew these lines by heart.

It isn't funny! Mary's newfound championing of her daughter was outraged at these lines, lines she had accepted for herself and heard all her life. So a daughter is just an object to be watched carefully, lest a man become dishonored through her! And what of the sadness of the situations he has so dismissively described? Every one of them is painful to the girl, but does anyone care about that?

"The prophet Isaiah says, 'Before I was born the Lord called me; from my birth he has made mention of my name,'" the rabbi quoted. "And what name have you chosen for this daughter of Israel?"

Joel spoke up. "Elisheba," he said.

"A godly name." The rabbi nodded.

"It means 'God is her oath,'" said Mary from the back.

For an instant annoyance flashed across the rabbi's face, but he quickly controlled it. "Yes, daughter, I am aware of the meaning of the name. Thank you."

"I—" Suddenly Mary felt a sharp, stabbing pain in her chest that robbed her of breath. The rest of the words died in her throat, and the rabbi continued.

He recited prayers and blessings before handing the baby back to Joel. Joel held her up and said, "I rejoice to have such a godly daughter! Now let us celebrate!" He gestured toward the table, laid out with food and drink, and people swarmed toward it. Some of the more religious ones came up to see the baby first, and they even touched the child's forehead and recited their own blessings over her.

Joel was looking around for Mary, expecting her to join him. But the pain in her chest was still searing, and she was having trouble breathing. She clung to a chair, gripping its wooden back as hard as she could. She could not imagine what this was.

Seeing the look on her face, Joel quickly handed the baby back to the rabbi and hurried over to her. "What is it?"

She could only shake her head, unable to reply. Truly this pain was strange and frightening. But it would pass. It must pass.

"Are you ill?" Joel kept whispering. So far all the guests were busy looking at the baby and eating; no one paid the mother any attention. But that would change any moment.

"I—I—" Slowly she felt breath returning, as if a grip were relaxing inside her. "I just—" She shook her head. "I don't know what it was. I am all right." Even as she said it, she felt a stabbing pain in her stomach. But she held on to the chair back and smiled.

"Come, everyone wants to congratulate us," Joel was urging her. She forced herself to walk over to the table, all the while feeling that a knife had lodged itself in her stomach.

Then, above the din of happy voices from the guests, she heard a very clear one right by her ear: "I told you this child was mine. I gave it to you as a gift between us. And now you flout me and defy me by giving it a name stating that it is Yahweh's. That was very foolish of you. Now you will pay the price. From now on you must be doubly mine, taking your daughter's place."

∝ X111 ∝

She did not have long to wait. The very next morning, before she had even allowed herself to think about the eerie voice—and convince herself that it had been just her own excitement at the ceremony—strange things began to happen. She had begun cleaning up: rolling out the empty wine amphora, washing the plates, and sweeping the floor. This morning, she was humming as she put away the dried platters, thinking that the figs on this one had been popular, whereas the cheese on that one had not. Except that, after she had put them away, she saw that some were still out. Wondering how she could have missed them, she put them up with the others. Later, they were out on the table again.

When she saw them the second time, she was jolted. I know I put them up, she thought. I know I did. Quickly she put them up again, fast enough to make them disappear and cease troubling her.

I must be preoccupied, she told herself. Then she went to Elisheba's basket and was startled to find it filled with toys. The little girl was almost smothered under them.

This time there was no uncertainty. I did not put those there, Mary thought. Where did they come from? Guests had brought gifts, but they had not left them in the crib. And early in the morning, when Mary had come to feed her, they had not been there.

She sank down on a stool and put her head in her hands. How is this possible? she thought. Her heart was pounding, and she broke out in a sweat. In a panic, she jumped up and started pulling all the toys out, throwing them on the floor, to reverse it and make it as though she had not seen it. Elisheba started gurgling. Mary picked her up and held her.

"You didn't want all those in there, did you?" she asked Elisheba, as if her daughter could answer. If only she could! Then she could say how they had gotten there. As it was, the baby could only lie quietly against Mary's bosom. Her warmth helped to calm Mary's racing heart.

During the rest of the day, Mary was hit with the same stabbing pains in her body she had had the night before. She was also tormented by trying to understand how the dishes and the toys had ended up in those locations.

Did I myself put them there and not remember?

That thought was almost more frightening than the alternative: that some sinister force had moved them. Losing her mind was the worst thing she could imagine.

These things kept happening—the misplaced objects seeming to have a will of their own, the frightening discoveries that were no less frightening for recurring, the sense of being pursued by something. Now she recognized that this was what had happened to her long ago, when she still lived with her parents. She could see it was all Ashara's doing. Ashara was keeping her word, her diabolical word. And there was no way to call her off. Even destroying the idol had done no good. Adding to the strain was the importance of hiding this from Joel, and trying to make sure there were no lapses in her care of Elisheba. She prayed to God, belatedly: Please, help me find a means to overthrow Ashara before her power over us grows stronger and I can no longer do anything to fight it.

Joel was perceptive, and she knew it was only a matter of time before he would notice that something was amiss. She had to playact and pretend from the moment he stepped in the door until he fell asleep at night, and the strain of that was enormous.

Playact . . . pretend . . . just kind words for "lie," thought Mary. I have become a liar, a foul liar who is unable to speak the truth. Yet there was no other way to keep going.

Secretly, when she was able, she studied the scriptures to see if there was any formula in them for combating the power of an alien god. But she found nothing; it was assumed that once the idol was destroyed its power was gone—did not God tell his people to smash and break the idols into pieces?—but she knew now that was not the case. And there was nothing in the scriptures about someone in the grip of the power against his or her will. Everything on the subject assumed that those who served the foreign gods were its voluntary servants, and must also be destroyed.

Ashara had managed already to ruin what should have been the happiest time in Mary's life, her days with her new daughter. So, just as Ashara had proclaimed, the child belonged to her, as surely as if Mary had offered Elisheba of her own free will.

A few months later, a possessed man caused a sensation in Magdala. He had arrived by boat; no one knew from where. Clambering up onto the wide promenade that ran along the waterfront, he began capering and making obscene gestures and yelling. Soon a crowd gathered to watch—from a distance.

Mary had not wished to go and gape at him, but she felt drawn to see him. This man . . . this man might be herself in a few months, or years. She needed to see the full extent of what might await her. Yet she had to disguise her interest as detached curiosity to her friends and neighbors.

They stood at a safe distance from him, as proper women should. They could see him walking on all fours, like a beast, and growling like one. He had matted dark hair that stood out from his head like a lion's mane; did he think, in his madness or possession, that he was a lion? He was pacing like one.

Suddenly he reared up and began to paw at the air, truly like a lion. And, just as suddenly, he straightened up and stood like a man, and began to speak. At first the words made aching, touching sense—to Mary.

"My friends!" he cried. "Have pity on me! Where am I? How did I get here? The wicked spirit has brought me here, I know not why!"

"Who are you?" asked one of the town elders, who often presided over court cases. It was to him, the city authority, that maintaining order must fall.

"Benjamin of—" But his voice was choked off, in a way that Mary knew all too well, and what followed was a torrent of unintelligible language. His face contorted, and he dropped to the ground as if fighting—futilely—whatever was within him.

Two young men rushed toward him and tried to help him stand up, but although they were strong and muscled, he threw them off like children and flung them back against the guard wall of the promenade, where they sprawled, dazed.

"Stand back!" said the elder. "Stand back! He's dangerous!" He motioned to some other men in the crowd. "We must bind him! Get some ropes."

The men dashed off, while the elder tried talking to Benjamin.

"My son, keep calm. The demon within you is not you. Do not let it prevail. Help is coming."

Benjamin just crouched and snarled at him. Staring out of his eyes was the malevolent force.

So that is what you really look like, Mary thought. You do not look like the beautiful ivory carving at all, but you hid behind it to beguile me. A cold column of fear spread all the way through her, gripping her as certainly as Ashara herself already did.

"A holy man!" cried the elder. "We must have a holy man! They alone are able to cast out demons."

"Perhaps old Zadok would come," someone suggested.

"What about his disciple, Amos?" someone ventured. "Or Gideon?"

"Yes, let's get all three!" someone called.

A youth was dispatched to get the old rabbi and his students. Benjamin continued to lie on the pavement and writhe, all the while screaming in the foreign tongue. Suddenly his voice changed—it became deeper and rougher, another voice entirely.

"He's speaking Akkadian!" a merchant in the crowd said. "Yes, that's what it is! I've heard it in Babylon!"

"Satan! It's Satan who speaks through him, in another tongue. Satan manifests himself this way," said the elder. "And the deepness, the roughness—yes, it's the Evil One himself!"

Fascinated and horrified, Mary stood rooted where she stood. Oh, God, King of the Universe, is this what will happen to me? she cried, silently. Oh, save me! Deliver me! Break that bondage with Ashara!

The first set of men returned with ropes, and cautiously approached Benjamin. They encircled him and tried to distract him so that they could drop the ropes over him. But this proved difficult. Time and time again, the man showed himself wily and alert, and dodged the ropes. Finally, by simply approaching him boldly and closing in on him, they managed to get the ropes around his shoulders. They tightened them quickly and trussed him up.

The anger of the demon was quickly apparent. Benjamin rose up and, arching his back and flexing his arms, broke the ropes like ribbons. Then, in perfect Aramaic, he roared, "Do not attempt to assert your puny power over me! You cannot even touch me!"

Everyone fell back, stunned. Only the elder stood his ground.

"I command you in the name of Yahweh, King of the Universe, to come out of this man and cease tormenting him!" he said, in a quavering voice.

The only response of the demon in Benjamin's body was to rush for the elder, grab him, and throw him to the ground. He bared his teeth—which looked almost like wolf fangs, although they could not have been—and sank them into the elder's neck. A group of men fell on Benjamin and rescued the elder, dragging him to safety. The men watching in the fishing boats suddenly raised their oars, dipped them into the water, and back-paddled farther out.

Just then old Zadok arrived, along with his two students.

Benjamin turned swiftly and stared at them. "So it's the old fools of the synagogue who have come!" he taunted. "As if they could have any power over ME!"

"Silence, demon!" said Zadok, with surprising volume. "You must not address us. We shall address YOU." He draped his prayer shawl about his shoulders and signaled for his young assistants to do the same. They fastened the tefillin—small boxes containing holy texts—on their foreheads and arms, and huddled together in prayer. Then Zadok, flanked by his helpers, turned to confront the demon.

"Demon, Evil One, we command you, in the name of Yahweh, to release this, your servant Benjamin, a son of Abraham and of the people of Israel, who has been caught in your snares." He stood like a column of righteousness before the stooped man.

But the demon merely laughed, showing bared teeth.

"I repeat: depart from this man, Satan. You must release him, in the holy and sacred name of Yahweh. I command it."

"And who are you?" snarled the demon. "I do not recognize your authority. I will not obey."

"I speak to you in the name of the Holy One."

"I defy the Holy One. I always have. You have no other weapons against me."

"Come out of him, demon of Satan!" yelled Zadok. "Depart, and flee!" It was inspiring to see the poor old man standing up to this force. His voice had even lost some of its power, as if it had been drained away, but still he railed against the demon.

Gideon grabbed Zadok's arm, and took Amos's as well. Together they stood, holding each other up. "We are the Lord's servants," cried Gideon. "And together we have strength against you, Evil One! We command you, in the name of Yahweh, to quit this man!"

The combined force of the three holy men seemed to have some effect against the demon inhabiting Benjamin. Benjamin shrank down, as if against some assault.

Encouraged, Gideon spoke again. "Yes, release him from your grip!"

"In the name of Yahweh, depart from this man!" said Zadok.

"The forces of darkness can never prevail against the God of light," Amos said tentatively.

Benjamin snarled, but cringed.

"Out! Out! I command you, evil spirit, depart!" cried Zadok.

And suddenly Benjamin flung himself on the ground, writhing and screaming, and great waves of movement passed through him, and then he screamed even more horribly and went limp.

"Run, run!" cried someone in the crowd, causing a stampede. Only Zadok and his students remained, stalwartly standing. Mary pulled her companions farther back.

Zadok, utterly exhausted by his struggle, was helped to a bench to sit down. People were praising him, but he deflected the praise.

"I did nothing," he said. "I only spoke in the name of Yahweh."

"The demon!" someone cried. Then they asked the question that was uppermost in Mary's mind. "Why did it get hold of him? What did he do?"

Zadok, mustering up all his energy, said, "It may not have been what he wanted, but what he did in ignorance. The demon sought an opening, an opportunity. Benjamin provided it, somehow. Demons are able to infest through the victim's activity, not his attitude."

Yes. Mary knew he spoke the truth. It was her activity, long ago, in picking up the ivory, that had brought this about, not her attitude.

And yet . . . it may not have been a single act, but a whole series of them. Picking it up . . . keeping it . . . making continual resolves to get rid of it, but always backing out . . . It may have been these cumulative acts, rather than just one. Did this mean that someday she would suffer the same fate as Benjamin? she wondered.

Just as she was wrestling with this thought, she saw Joel on the other side of the crowd. He, too, had been drawn to the excitement, leaving his workplace. His face was white and shocked. She flew to his side, threw her arms around him.

"Was that not dreadful?" His voice was shaking. "I hope never to witness such a thing again in my lifetime."

The limp Benjamin was being carried away on a stretcher, to a house of mercy where he would be treated to food and more prayers.

∞ XIV ∞

After the exorcism of the possessed man, Mary returned to her own home even more apprehensive. It seemed now to be enemy territory; although, in all truth, she had to admit that there was no place she could flee from Ashara. Had Ashara not sought her out in many places? Had she not been found in Samaria and doubtless originated elsewhere to begin with?

"The earth is the Lord's, and the fullness thereof," went one Psalm. But now it seemed only a vast canopy sheltering Ashara. The words of another Psalm—"Where can I hide from your spirit? From your presence, where can I flee? If I ascend to the heavens, you are there; if I lie down in Sheol, you are there too"—seemed more fitted to Ashara than to Yahweh. The Law of Moses set up sanctuaries, but only for men whose blood was being sought for unintentional crimes, a horned altar the pursued could grasp and cling to. For her, no such sanctuary existed.

Still, during days without incident—and there were a few such days—Mary drew closer to God in the only way she knew, through reading scripture and praying. She felt that she could approach only when she was free of the attacks from Ashara, that God would not look at her or hear her otherwise.

On the good days, Mary was able to turn all her love and attention to little Elisheba, who was now starting to sit up and already had a dazzling smile. But she never took a moment of that time for granted, knowing it could be snatched away at any instant.

In the evening of one of the good days, Joel came home and announced that he and several of the men from the company must make a trip into Tiberias to choose new transport amphoras. Would Mary and the other wives like to come? It would take a full day in any case, and if they went in a group, they might make a pleasant excursion out of a necessary trip.

"Besides, I know you have been curious about Tiberias," he said, chewing his bread. Today having been a good day, Mary had been able to prepare a full dinner, including her special bread with thyme in it.

Tiberias! Though it was only a short distance from Magdala, few from the town visited it. Its reputation as a stage for pagan activities kept most observant Jews away. But there was no arguing the fact that, in the few short years since Herod Antipas had ordered it built, Tiberias had become a major trading center. If one wanted a full selection of amphoras, Tiberias was the place to look.

"Yes, indeed I have," she said. Actually, she had been fascinated by it, and by the proximity of Herod Antipas there. He was enjoying his new city, built just as he liked it, modern and free from religious interference.

"Good. Your patience will finally be rewarded."

The trip was planned for the day after the Sabbath, the first day of the week. The Sabbath had been excruciatingly long, for Ashara decided to make that a day of torment for Mary, when there was little outside activity to divert her. As the hours crept by, the horrible accusations against herself seemed to bubble malevolently in Mary's mind. As she tried to pray, a buzzing would sound in her head, distracting her. Memories became a strewn field of shame, as she relived each stupid or bad thing she had ever done; plans for the future were overturned with taunts about how she would fail, and deservedly so, for she was both inept and hopelessly sinful and in need of punishment. Sometimes, there even seemed to be a second voice, quite different from Ashara's, that whispered foul and blasphemous words in her mind and described violent and perverted acts in great detail. It was all she could do not to scream, but that would disturb Joel, sitting and reading contentedly, watching Elisheba crawl slowly around his feet. He must not know; he must never know!

Could a second spirit have crept in? Mary had heard of people being afflicted with many, each with a distinct personality, although it was rare. When one had made an entrance, he sometimes beckoned to his fellows. It might be happening to her.

·   ·   ·

The Sabbath over, their party set out for Tiberias early the next morning, when the air was still cool and refreshing. It was not a very long journey—only about three Roman miles—and made a pleasant walk. They chose to walk along the lakeside path, where the water lapped up against the rocks and the reeds rustled, making faint music. The delicate colors of dawn were still spread out on the lake, and filled the eastern part of the sky—pale lavender shading into rose, with an edging of gold where the sun would soon appear.

Joel and his two fellow workers, Ezra and Jacob, were in high spirits. In the past few weeks, the house special-recipe fish sauce had received so many inquiries from abroad that their scribes were hard put to keep up with the correspondence. One came from as far afield as Gaul, near the very farthest reaches of the Roman frontier. It was clear that the fame of the pungent sauce was spreading in ways that took even Nathan—who had always prided himself on his good recipe—by surprise. And there had been an order from Herod Antipas. He—or, rather, his household steward, Chuza—had requested a large supply for the ruler's upcoming marriage celebration.

"His Highness will require eleven full firkins of the noted garum from his subject Nathan of Magdala's inventory, to be delivered ten days before the celebration of His Highness's nuptials with Herodias. In the name of the most potent and beneficent Herod Antipas, *magister officiorum* Chuza," the request had read.

This, of course, meant ordering special containers. The regular, unadorned amphoras would not do. Filling the foreign orders would require a different, and sturdier, amphora, one that could withstand long sea journeys.

"I hope the profit on our overseas sales will help offset the . . . hmmm . . . donation we must make to Antipas," said Ezra. For of course the garum must be furnished as a "gift" to the ruler.

"Antipas," said Miriam, Ezra's wife, "is used to having everyone bow to his wishes. What if you billed him for the garum? Perhaps he would not even notice."

"He would notice," said Jacob. "That man notices everything. We must stay on his good side!"

They were walking past the area where Mary used to go to be alone and read her poetry. Now, for the first time, Mary saw a Canaanite cult stone that had overlooked her all these years. She stiffened as she passed it—a tall, dark stone that seemed to have ownership of her.

You, too? she thought. I was surrounded on all sides, and never realized it. Are you part of the sickness of mind that has seized me?

She wanted to reject it in some way, but the group swept past, still talking about Antipas.

One of the wives tried to engage Mary in conversation, but she listened with only half her mind.

"Unlike that preacher," someone was saying.

What had she missed?

"What preacher?" Joel asked, fortuitously.

"That man who calls himself the Baptist," said Ezra. "The one who has gathered a large following down at the Jordan."

"Down at the Jordan?" Miriam asked. "Where?"

"At the ford where the road between Jerusalem and Amman passes. All the travelers go that way; it's the only route between the two cities."

"What is he doing there?" Miriam persisted.

"He's one of those old-style prophets who preach repentance and say the world as we know it will come to a sudden end, and that the Messiah will come soon." Ezra paused. "But Antipas doesn't care about that. What he cares about is that this man—he's called John the Baptist because he immerses people in the Jordan—has denounced his coming marriage. Because Herodias was his brother's wife. It's against the Jewish law, and John has said so. Bluntly. I wonder how long he'll be free to keep on baptizing?" Ezra laughed. "As for us—we'll send Antipas his fish sauce, no questions asked."

"Are we such cowards?" Mary heard herself asking.

Joel stopped on the path and looked at her, puzzled. "All we are doing is supplying fish sauce," he finally said. "He didn't ask our opinion about his marriage."

"But we are helping him celebrate it," Mary said.

"And if we did not send him the fish sauce," said Joel, "he would celebrate it just the same. And find some reason to punish us afterward. We have no choice."

Joel was right, of course. They had no power to influence Antipas, only to turn him against their family business and destroy it—influence to bring about their own downfall, but not to deter any immoral action elsewhere.

"John the Baptist," Mary asked, "is he not afraid? Where did he come from?"

Abigail, Jacob's wife, shrugged. "What difference does it make? He's doomed."

Surprisingly, Jacob reacted sharply. "Don't speak that way! The man's a prophet, and God knows we need one. A true prophet, not one that just says what Antipas—and the rest of us—want to hear. John was originally from Jerusalem," he told Mary, "but why he went out into the desert, and how he got his message, I don't know."

"We ought to go out and see him!" the empty-headed Abigail said. "Yes, make an excursion of it!"

Jacob looked embarrassed for her. "It's a long way from here," he finally said. "And those who go for the wrong reasons might get singled out. He points at those who come just to observe and calls them a 'brood of vipers.' I don't think you want that sort of attention, my dear."

She laughed mindlessly. "No, I'd rather go to the bazaar in Tiberias!"

Jacob shook his head. "There isn't any bazaar in Tiberias, it's a Greek-style city."

"Oh, with one of those agora things?" asked Abigail.

Tiberias was a modern city, laid out with all the latest planning fashion. The streets were all straight, and there was indeed an agora in the center of the city, as well as a large stadium on its outskirts, and sturdy walls on three sides that extended out into the lake on the fourth, farther out than a mounted rider could safely make his way around. They were not quite complete, but already they were formidable. Joel's party entered through the great northern gate, where a big group of workmen were preparing the gateway for the monumental door that would soon be affixed. It was a busy, boisterous place.

"Now, I was told that the amphora merchant we wanted was down this main street, past the palace, then at the fountain of Aphrodite turn left . . ." Joel was consulting his homemade map. All around them surged the merchants, tradesmen, palace functionaries, and travelers; the street bulged with them. Mary was struck by how clean everything was; its newness saw to that. The raw odor of the fresh-cut building stones, the glistening pavements, the open sky over the street—not yet shadowed by balconies and arches and canopies—made it seem so pristine in looks that it promised equal orderliness and tranquillity in all human dealings.

As they were making their way toward the center of town, they passed a shrine to some foreign god, complete with a statue. The others ignored it, but Mary stared, because around the shrine and its fountain a throng of people had gathered, chanting and moving as if in a chorus. They were leaning over the little fountain that spurted at the god's feet, bathing their faces in the sacred water, then turning with a brimming handful of it to wash the face of someone behind them. Some were moaning, and others just stared ahead blankly, and some even wore restraints. These poor people did not join in the swaying and the chanting, but others helped them, linking arms and holding them up. Sometimes a painful wail rose from the group, its anguish sounding odd against the cheerful clamor of the city.

I know those people, Mary thought. I belong with them, not with these people I am with. I am as miserable as they, as afflicted. . . .

She halted a moment and touched the sleeve of a heavily veiled woman, who was lingering on the fringes of the group. Whether she was just an onlooker or a participant was not readily apparent.

"What is this shrine?" Mary asked, softly.

The woman turned. It was highly unusual for one stranger to speak to another on the street. But she finally muttered, "Don't you know it's Aesculapius?"

Aesculapius. Yes, Mary knew his name, but she had never seen him depicted. Now she stared at the statue—so openly displayed here, so much a part of the daily life of the city—of a handsome man, partly disrobed. His perfectly proportioned body, slender and yet properly muscled, bespoke the whole Greek and Roman ideal of vigor and health. He seemed gentle. She could not look at his face without feeling reassured, as if he held the secret of life and it consisted merely of maintaining the physical. There would be no place for unclean spirits in such a pristine vessel.

"Mary, come!" Joel took her arm and pulled her away. "Stop staring at that half-naked man!" He attempted to make a joke of it.

"Isn't it shameful, with all these idols and naked statues everywhere you turn?" asked Miriam. "It's disgusting."

"Hmmm . . ." Abigail rolled her eyes. "Still, all the children must be very knowledgeable from an early age. The wives, too."

Jacob shook his head. "All it does is give people false knowledge. For, under their robes, most men do not look like that statue. So there will be many disappointed women and children when they find out!"

Joel laughed heartily. He could afford to, since he did not look so different from the statue.

"The women will be disappointed in their husbands, and the little boys disappointed in what they grow up to be," persisted Jacob. "That's just another example of why life under the pagans is so . . . so bad for you!"

Again Joel laughed. "You make it sound like handling poisonous snakes," he said.

All around them the street was thronged with people, and when Joel stopped to consult his map, their party made an island in the midst of the fast-flowing stream. Women with bundles bumped up against Mary, men leading donkeys cursed at them for blocking the way, and a group of youths shoved at them. This was no place to stop.

Pressed against the nearest wall, two men were pulling their head-dresses down farther to shade their eyes, and they started when they saw Joel and his group. One of them made a gesture to his companion, and together they left their post and slunk—there was no other word for it—toward Joel. One of them grabbed Joel's sleeve and whispered something in his ear. Joel drew back, puzzled. He started to push the man away, then stopped.

"You . . . the intruder! Simon! The zealot! At Silvanus's!" cried Joel. "The pigs—"

"Sssh!" The man hissed and made a threatening move. Mary saw his hand go under his cloak as if he was clutching something. And then she saw it—a short curved sword, called a *sica*; it could be concealed and then flash out like a serpent striking and kill quickly.

"Stay your hand, friend," Joel said softly. He even reached out and touched the weapon, forcing it down.

"Death to collaborators!" Simon threatened. "The Jews who support the Romans are worse than the Romans themselves!"

"I am no collaborator," said Joel. "I am a merchant, here on business."

The others in the group froze, rooted to the spot. All around them the crowd streamed, oblivious. That was the genius of the *sica* and the men who wielded it, called *sicarii*—they could strike in public and remain invisible. They slashed, killed, tucked the weapon away, and melted into a crowd.

"All who are not on our side are against us," said the man pressed to Joel's side. "When your brother turned me out of his house, he declared for all of you."

"He declared that he did not wish his house to be invaded," said Joel firmly. He seemed to have no fear of the man. "In that, he was but a normal householder."

Simon the Zealot loosed his grip on Joel's shoulder, and Mary saw his hand leave the dagger. "The time will come when you must choose sides," he said. "Woe to you who side with the Romans. All of you."

Abruptly he turned away, like a dog who has scented something. He and his companion rushed down the street, shoving people out of the way. In a moment there was a sudden cry, and confusion, farther ahead.

Joel sought to catch his breath. He did not want to discuss it in front of the others and have to explain. All he said was "I do not know the man, although he had the delusion I do."

They continued on their way, still going in the direction Simon and his companion had taken. When they reached a spot near their turn, they saw that the crowd had knotted, ringing something—something lying on the ground. As they drew nearer, they could see a heap of crumpled robes, with someone hidden within the folds.

Roman soldiers—appearing seemingly out of nowhere—shouldered their way through and, bending down, inspected the bundle on the street. They lifted it up and pulled away the head cloth, sadly askew now.

They said something in Latin which Mary could not understand, except for "Antipas." She guessed that this was one of Herod Antipas's staff, since the members of that household were despised by rigorous Jews as being too eager to compromise with the Romans.

One soldier dragged the man away while the other scanned the crowd for signs of the murderer. He saw nothing, so he helped his comrade pull the body off the street.

Joel had lost the color in his face. Mary came close beside him. "Was it them? Those men?" And to think one of them had actually come into Silvanus's house! They had sought to involve her family in their ranks.

Joel nodded. "I am sure of it," he finally said. "They have begun their terror here." He shuddered. Then he motioned to the others.

"Come, come!" He quickly led them away, toward the middle of the city.

Even though they did not know their way, as they passed the wide, pillared agora with its rows of stalls and neat shops, they recognized the opulent building nearby with extensive gardens and grounds—in the very heart of the city—as the palace of Herod Antipas. It was newly constructed of gleaming white limestone, and the roof glinted with gold.

They all stopped to stare, the blazing presence diverting them for the moment from the murder they had just seen.

"Do you see the gold?" Abigail cried. "On the roof itself! I had heard rumors that he had decorated the roof with gold, but—"

"And they also say," said Jacob, "that he has animals carved as decorations. Animals! Graven images!"

Ezra shrugged. "I don't suppose he has a golden calf," he said. "It is probably something more like birds or horses."

"I wonder if his new bride will bring her daughter, Salome?" said Miriam. "They say she is very beautiful."

"I would imagine she is ashamed of her mother," said Joel suddenly. "Most girls are, when their mothers act immorally."

"But then they grow up to copy them," said Abigail. "If a mother is immoral, you can count on the daughter to follow suit."

"So this is where our fish sauce is going," said Ezra. He was more interested in the business contract than the morals of those who had set it up. "And this Chuza—is his word to be trusted?"

"From all reports, yes," said Joel. "If he sent an order, it is legitimate."

"I heard his wife was possessed," said Abigail suddenly. "That she hears voices and loses control of herself."

Jacob looked indignant, but Mary could not decide if it was because he was ignorant of the fact or doubted Abigail's information. "Nonsense!" he retorted.

Mary glanced at Abigail, wondering if the remark had been pointed at her.

They continued past the crowded agora and on toward the amphora shop, or where it was supposed to be. The streets were narrower now, so that if two laden donkeys approached one would have to stand back to let the other by. It also seemed darker, more secret. Some of the foreign merchants preferred to have their stalls here, as if the sunny, open spaces of the agora were threatening and uncomfortable to them.

There was a fortune-teller at one stall, calling out softly to people as they passed: "I can tell you what awaits! I know the stars, the future! Do not face it blindly!"

Another stall was veiled and had an annex affixed, a long wooden shelter with one lamp flickering within. "My master can drive out demons," a young girl at the stall said, indicating the little house. "Are you suffering? One incantation from my master, one dose of the magic root, and you need be tortured no more!"

Jacob snorted. "And so near to the palace, too. Convenient for Chuza. He should bring his wife here."

Mary could not help herself. "Jacob," she said, "it is no joking matter. I am sure the wife of Chuza is suffering. But she should not go to a charlatan."

Jacob stared at her, surprised. "What do you know of such things?" he said. But he was only annoyed that his witty remark had been taken seriously.

"And look!" Abigail pointed to the next stall. It was very elaborate, with gold-and-blue pillars, an astrological chart painted as a background, and incense smoking from censers placed all around. "What do you suppose . . ." Her voice faded away as she suddenly wondered if it was a house of prostitution.

A man loomed up from behind the counter, like an apparition. He was wearing the elaborate high-peaked headdress of a Babylonian, and his richly embroidered robe, which fell straight from his shoulders, was made of silk dyed a deep blue, achingly beautiful, like the late-twilight sky intensified, the time when the first few stars appear.

He gestured to the tray of little amulets before him. They were of graduated sizes, and made of bronze, silver, or gold, but all had loops on the top to permit them to be worn on a chain.

"Childbirth. Protection." His Aramaic was very limited. Clearly he had just memorized a few pertinent words.

Since none of the women was expecting a child, they started to pass him by.

"Power," the man said, indicating another tray. "Power."

Mary slowed and glanced down at his wares. Spread out on a tray, on a soft black cloth, were little statues of a terrifying god. He had a hideous visage, with a snout and mouth like a lion, drawn up in a snarl, and eyes that bulged out from beneath grimacing eyebrows. His feet were not human but ended in three talons, although he stood upright and had ribs, shoulders, and arms like a man. But behind him were four wings, and one arm was raised and the other down by his side; the hands were wide and the fingers fat and flexed.

"Lamashtu," the merchant was saying. "Against Lamashtu."

"Mary!" Joel cried. "Get away from him!" He grabbed her arm and jerked her forward.

But behind the merchant she had seen a large clay representation of the god; he was much more frightening as he got larger. His ugly face seemed to glow with the faint light from the lamps lit around his base. She expected to see saliva dripping from his long, pointed teeth.

And his arms—the arms. She had seen the arms before, somewhere, the way they were positioned. And the sneering, malevolent face. Yes. The little arm that she once possessed, which had flown through the air when the rabbi smashed the idols in Samaria—it was the same palm, the same flexed elbow. She felt as if an enemy had closed in around her, encircling her.

Where was the arm? She could not remember; Ashara had always taken precedence and occupied her attention. Was the arm still somewhere in her possession? In her house? Or had it been lost long ago, in the mists of childhood?

The merchant took Mary's staring for interest. "Pazuzu," he said, indicating the idol with respect. "Pazuzu." He searched his mind for the right words and finally said, "Son of Hambi, king . . . evil wind-demons."

And at that moment, as she was staring into the bulging eyes, Mary thought she actually felt something stirring inside her, shifting, making room. There was an upheaval, and then . . . Pazuzu. She could feel the god inside her, turning, fitting himself, comforming her spirit to accommodate his presence. He was large, and demanded a great deal of room. She gasped, feeling choked and crowded.

From somewhere deep within her mind, she felt Ashara welcoming the comrade, and the other presence, the one as yet unnamed, spewing out its obscenities and filth. Three inside now. Three, and all twisting and turning to make a place for themselves.

"I said come on!" Joel said, tugging at her arm. "We will never get there if we stop at every stall."

Mary stumbled forward, feeling as if she could barely command her feet. She lurched a bit, bumping up against Abigail, who gave her a puzzled look. Mary turned back to glance once more at the Pazuzu statue.

"You seem to be quite taken with that god," said Miriam. "Why? He was so hideous. I would definitely prefer Aescupalius, if I had to choose a foreign god."

All around them, the merchants from the other stalls were motioning, promising fine things. There were brightly colored piles of unknown spices, rugs draped over dark, cavelike back rooms, dried pods and seeds from Arabia, honey from North Africa, polished copper pots. Then, looming up ahead, another stall with amulets, this time of a rigid goddess, her gown covered with rounded breasts. When they tried to pass by it, the merchant reached out, waving his hand.

"Why you stop at the Pazuzu? Bad god. Wind god—brings scorching winds and sickness. Shoots arrows of disease. Stay away!" He waved a small version of his own goddess. "Artemis! Mother! Children! No disease! Better!"

Joel's patience gave out. "We do not worship other gods!" he barked.

"Why?" The man seemed bewildered.

Finally, they emerged from the congested, dim lane and onto a wider street. "I am relieved," said Joel. "Any amphora dealer who had a shop there . . ." He shook his head.

Mary still felt assaulted and swelling with alien presence; it was all she could do to stand upright and keep walking. When she was with child it had felt similar, but then it was a happy presence, and one she did not need to hide.

"Ah!" Joel stopped in front of a spacious doorway. A number of pottery amphoras stood flanking the entrance—large ones that came nearly up to his waist; shorter, fatter ones that came only up to his knees; and some tiny ones as well. Their color varied, too, from deep earth-brown to almost red.

A rotund merchant, looking like one of his rounded amphoras, was waiting just inside the entrance to greet them. His name was Rufus, and his reputation assured that he never lacked for business.

"I am Joel, of the house of Nathan's enterprise in Magdala," Joel said. "These are my associates Jacob and Ezra." The two other men bowed. "I sent you a message regarding our needs. It seems that Antipas will require a large quantity of our garum for his upcoming wedding feast."

Rufus tried not to look impressed, but he raised his eyebrows. "Ah, yes. And what quantity are we considering?"

"Seven days' feast—I have no way of knowing how many guests, but I guess five hundred—perhaps twelve firkins? That is one more than Chuza specified."

Rufus stroked his smooth-shaven chin. "And you don't want them to run out! Do you prefer smaller containers or larger ones?"

"I assume larger ones would be more practical, since the garum will all be consumed within a seven-day period?"

"But less decorative," said Rufus. "And this is, after all, a very important occasion."

"But there is the problem of transportation," said Joel, "first your sending the amphoras to us, and then our transporting them back here to the palace—which size would be best for that?"

"Large ones," Rufus had to admit. "They are sturdier, and require less packing." He invited them inside. "Come, let me show you our selection."

They followed him into the cool, ordered interior. Mary's eyes could just make out the rows and rows of sample amphoras, some on shelves and others lined up on the floor.

Rufus indicated a group set aside in a corner. "These are very old," he said. "But the design of amphoras changes very little over the years. These are from the island of Sicily and must be four hundred years old. Aside from the fact that the clay feels fragile, how would you know?" He tapped on one and it gave out a hollow echo. "Now, then." He turned briskly to the models on the shelves. "For garum, I recommend this type."

It was a middle-sized container, in shape somewhere between the elongated ones for wine and the short, fat ones for olive oil. Like all the rest, it had two handles and a spike at the bottom to secure it during shipping and allow it to be spun around on its axis, as well as to provide a bottom handle.

It looked very plain to Mary's eyes, not fit for a king's marriage. But she was having trouble focusing her eyes, and could not trust her own impressions.

"We can offer several styles of decoration," Rufus said, "to make it more appropriate for the occasion." As he said the word "occasion," he looked carefully at them, as if trying to determine where their sympathies lay—and how safe it was to speak in front of them. "For example, we can label the contents, and the name of your business, with red lettering, right near the neck, and we can provide stoppers with a special design."

"That seems a good idea," said Joel. "For, if we do not advertise where it came from and just send it in a plain container, then no one will know where to obtain more."

"And you want the royal household to order more." Was it a question, a test, or a challenge?

"Yes," said Joel. "We would like to become more widely known."

"And the household of Antipas is connected with the wider world." Rufus seemed to be making a statement.

"Everyone knows that," said Joel.

"And with the Romans and others."

"The Romans must eat like anyone else, and so why should not an ordinary person of Galilee have some good from that need?" Joel said stoutly.

"Of course." Rufus nodded vigorously. "Of course. Here, let me write up your order. That will be eighteen amphoras, total." He went to a table where his ledgers lay and pulled out a piece of papyrus. As he bent over it, drawing up the preliminaries, he said, "Well, you may soon get your wish. Did you know that the Roman emperor is recalling Valerius Gratus and replacing him with a new procurator, Pontius Pilate? He's due to arrive just in time for the wedding festivities. Make an impression on him with your garum and who knows what sort of a standing order you may get? The Romans are crazy for garum."

"A new procurator!" Jacob looked distressed. "Why?"

"Gratus has already been here ten years," said Rufus. "Perhaps he's tired of ruling us. We can be . . ." He let his voice trail off. "Anyway, this Pilate is on his way to govern us."

"What have you heard about him?" Everyone asked the question more or less simultaneously. The news would be much fresher, and more detailed, in Tiberias than elsewhere.

"He comes from an eminent Roman family and is somewhere in his thirties. He's held some minor diplomatic posts before being appointed to this one—no great prize in Roman eyes, so I have to assume he isn't of the first rank in ability."

The listeners sighed in disappointment, yet what had they expected?

"I think his first name comes from the Latin *pilatus*, meaning a pikeman, one armed with a javelin. So he must have come from a military family. He's married to a granddaughter of the Emperor Augustus—but an illegitimate one. So perhaps Pilate owes his appointment to her influence in royal circles. He's bringing her with him—unusual, since permission to do that isn't normally granted, and the women normally don't want to come!"

"So he will be here soon," said Joel, "eating my garum."

"You hope so, don't you?" Rufus asked.

Mary tried to listen to all the details about this new procurator, but the words just swirled around in her head. A new ruler . . . a different Roman over Jerusalem . . . pray to the Lord that he would be merciful and just.

"His name will become renowned."

Everyone turned to look at Mary.

"What did you say?" asked Joel.

"Nothing. I—I—nothing." Mary could hardly respond.

"Yes, you did speak," said Rufus. "Why did you say that?"

"And in a strange voice," said Abigail. "It was as if you were imitating someone."

"I didn't . . . I don't know," said Mary. Cold fear was running through her. Why had she spoken—*had* she spoken? She knew nothing of this Pilate.

"Have you heard anything of Pilate?" asked Rufus.

"No. Not until you spoke his name," said Mary.

"Become renowned—how?" Rufus was persistent.

"My wife knows nothing of these matters." Joel put his arm around her. "I cannot imagine why she said it."

"It is because I know things," a voice in her head spoke. "And I can reveal them, and let you speak them."

"No, don't!" Mary begged.

Joel thought she was rejecting his arm, and jerked it away. But he was looking at her intently.

"It is all a mistake," Joel assured Rufus. "We are completely uninformed about all these political matters."

After the order had been written up and they left the amphora shop, everyone was very quiet. Mary sensed that, although they pretended it was because of the upsetting news about the new procurator, it was really about her strange statement and behavior. They walked along, looking at the streets and buildings, but it was not as before. Something had fundamentally changed with that utterance that had come from her mouth. They knew it was not her.

∾ XV ∾

Joel went directly to the warehouse to enter the day's transaction into the ledgers, saying little to Mary as he escorted her home. He stayed a long time. Mary, exerting all her strength of will to disguise the enemies inside her, greeted her mother in a conscientiously normal manner, thanking her effusively for taking care of Elisheba.

"Was Tiberias as wicked as everyone says?" her mother asked pointedly.

"There were shrines to foreign gods everywhere," Mary said. "And many vendors selling pagan wares. " She shivered in remembering. She then gave what she hoped was a lighthearted laugh.

Zebidah handed Mary the child. "She's been good today, just waiting up for you to return. Now she can sleep."

Mary cuddled her. The warm little body was reassuring. Her daughter asked no questions, did not look at her and wonder what was happening. Elisheba put out a plump little hand and touched Mary's face. Mary carried her gently to her bed and put her in.

Her mother was still standing quietly where she had left her, waiting.

"Thank you again," Mary said.

"Mary, is something wrong?" her mother said.

No! Not after I tried so hard to hide it! Mary thought. "No, why?" she asked sharply.

"I don't know—it's that tone you have. And you look troubled. A mother always knows. You will know exactly what I mean in a few years' time." She nodded toward Elisheba's bed.

"I am perfectly fine," said Mary. "Just a little tired. It was a very long day. We had to leave before dawn." But as she struggled to get the words out, she prayed that her mother would leave soon. She did not know how long she could keep up her pretense. Or, rather, how long *they* would let her keep it up.

"It's in your eyes," her mother said, coming over to her. She looked deep into Mary's eyes, then brushed her face gently in a gesture of concern. "They look dark."

"I tell you, I am just tired." Mary turned away. "I am not going to wait for Joel. I think I will go to bed now." How much more pointed could the invitation to leave be?

"I should go."

Thanks be to Yahweh! thought Mary. At that moment, she felt comforted that Yahweh was still there, still presiding over her life in some remote way.

She accompanied her mother to the door, and sank down on a stool in relief when she was gone.

The largest oil lamp was burning bright in its high wall niche, along with its smaller fellows on tables and lower niches, and the room took on a warm glow.

My home, thought Mary. My sanctuary. But now it is about to be destroyed.

Inside her head she could hear the voices of the unclean presences. They seemed to be holding a conversation with one another, and they all agreed on one thing: the vessel they inhabited was of no value. To destroy it would be a sport.

Why have you chosen me? Mary asked in her mind. But there was no answer. And so she said it softly aloud, "Why have you chosen me? I am only an ordinary person. I live in a small city far from the centers of power. I am married to an ordinary man who pursues an ordinary trade. Even if we disappeared tomorrow, only our families and friends would take note. Mary of Magdala? To ruin an insignificant person is purposeless."

Before she could say the last word, "purposeless," the din in her head was back, beating on her.

"It is not what you are now, but what you might become," the newest voice muttered. It was snarly and dark.

"I am an ordinary woman," said Mary, softly, but still aloud. They seemed to hear her better that way, although she could hear them well enough in her head. "Women are not even allowed to be legal witnesses in a trial. Women cannot inherit property. I am not learned; I did not study in an academy, as some pagan women do. I am no one."

"No one, no one," said the soft, teasing voice—Mary recognized it—of Ashara. "Women have their own power. It is embedded not in law but in sway over men. Think you that Herodias, Antipas's future wife, has no power? She has it through him. And why do you say you are an ordinary woman? You know full well that you are different— that you have felt a desire to serve God from an early age. And no ordinary woman educates herself secretly as you have."

"Disease brings power," another voice said: a cruel one. It must be Pazuzu's. "When I shoot my arrows of disease and destruction, the world cringes and pays homage."

"Curses to all mankind! May all the organs of childbearing fail, may the ears of grain wither, may famine grasp the puny stalks in its fists!" That was the unnamed blasphemous one. "Yahweh threatened to smite with the mildew and the blasting. I go further: I smite that upon which Yahweh smiles."

Mary buried her head in her hands. Oh, stop! she begged the voices. Leave me. I have nothing to do with mildew and blasting and disease and destruction. I am but a wife and a mother. Leave me! I can be of no use to you.

She put her head down and sobbed.

"Mary." Joel closed the door.

She jerked her head up to see him standing there.

"Joel," she said. Her heart rose just in seeing him.

He came over to her—but tentatively, she noticed. "Mary, what is wrong?"

"Nothing." She must hide it. It was her great burden, hers alone to wrestle with.

"You are crying." He laid down his sack and came over to her. "Elisheba . . . ?"

"She is sleeping soundly," Mary assured him. She took his hands in hers. They felt so sturdy, so comforting. The other presences faded.

"Mary, I repeat: what is wrong?" He took her face in his hands. "I know you so well. And what happened today—that strange voice—I am troubled by it."

I could say it was nothing, Mary told herself. I could say I had just felt dizzy. That I was not myself.

"Yes, say that!" Pazuzu—odd how distinctively recognizable that voice already was!—commanded.

Immediately she disobeyed. "It was . . . oh, Joel, I fear I am . . . beset. Possessed. Like that Benjamin we witnessed recently, with the demon."

He clearly had expected an "I am tired" disclaimer. He blinked in surprise. "In what way?"

She swallowed and tried to gather her thoughts. It did no good to be so confused that the ideas would tumble out and contradict each other.

"I . . . I . . . Do you remember that ivory carving?" she began. On the one hand, she was determined to present everything in an orderly fashion, and on the other, she wanted to rush ahead before the enemy could silence her.

"What?" He looked puzzled.

"That carving that Jamlech found," she said. "It was an idol I found years ago, when my family went to Jerusalem through the territory of Samaria. I dug it up. I kept it when I knew I should not. This is not the first time it exerted its influence. It started many years ago. It haunted my house. It gave me commands. It caused those welts on my arms."

How much more should she say? Should she even hint that she had married him to escape it? No, she decided.

"You're joking," he said. He looked both relieved and incredulous. He reached out to reassure her.

"Jamlech threw it on the fire," she said miserably. "But it was too late. She had already possessed me by then."

"But it's gone. It's destroyed. Its influence—if it even had one—will fade away."

"It gave us our child." Mary spoke boldly. "It will never be gone. I owe it a debt for eternity."

Joel looked as if someone had hit him. "What—what did you say?"

"I said that Ashara—that's her name—gave us Elisheba. And she claims her rights over me now." Mary threw herself into Joel's arms and began sobbing as she relived the terror. Now it was truly real.

Slowly, too slowly, he slid his arms up around her. "But God is more powerful," he said. "God would not permit this. Let us throw ourselves on God's mercy."

"And that is not all," Mary said. Why not tell it all? "There has recently come a second presence, one that is all darkness and despair. And today, Pazuzu—remember his huge statue as we passed on our way to the shop?—reared himself up and took me."

"What do you mean—took you?"

"I mean that I could feel him join the others inside me."

"Inside you—how?"

How actually to explain it? "I . . . I feel them all inside my head, inside my mind. They direct me. They taunt me. They will punish me for telling you about them. But Pazuzu—I think I may have a fragment of a statue of him. On the same trip to Samaria, they discovered a cache of old idols and destroyed them. One of the arms flew up in the air and I caught it. It was an ugly paw, like an animal's."

A long silence. "Oh, Mary" was all he said. "We must find the arm and its paw and destroy it. And we must take you to be treated." He paused and then said, "God is more powerful than they. But we must beg God for his help."

He tightened his arms around her. Surely—if human love and determination and awareness were worth anything—she could be delivered from this affliction. And God, the all-merciful, the all-powerful, would bend down to help her. She had confessed: she had told Joel. Now God could touch her and say, "My child, you are safe." Oh, how she longed for it.

It would be all right. It had to be all right. Once they told God. Once they sought out his servant and sage.

Joel's first thought was to confide in old Zadok. But Mary shrank from the idea; it was frightening to confide in someone who knew her family. What if he thought ill of them? What if he told people?

But when Joel then suggested a rabbi who had no knowledge of them, in the large synagogue in Capernaum, who had a reputation for holiness and surely had practice in casting out demons, Mary rejected that, too. To venture over there, look for the rabbi, approach him as a stranger, and then blurt out her problem—how horrible. How degrading.

But what could be more degrading than what the demons were putting her through, every day? Just because no one but a few could see it—yet—did not mean that at any moment it might not break out and become obvious to the entire town. Hesitantly she gave Joel permission to approach Zadok about the problem; Joel went as soon as the workday was over. He was gone what seemed a very short time.

"Zadok is coming over to pray with us," Joel announced, relief in his voice. "He will only gather up his prayer shawl, texts, and tefillin and come immediately."

"What did he—what did he say?" Mary asked.

"He did not seem that shocked," Joel said. "Of course, he may have just been sensitive about hiding his feelings."

A useful trait in a rabbi, Mary thought. But, try as she would to overcome it, she was horribly frightened and ashamed as she waited for him. Joel made sure Elisheba was safely asleep in a room as far from them as possible, with the door closed so she would hear nothing frightening.

Stay quiet, stay quiet! she commanded the demons. But she had no power over them and she knew it. And just as Joel was greeting Zadok at the door, they rose up inside her and manifested themselves.

"Mary," said Zadok, coming into the room and holding out his hands toward her. A look of deep concern, not judgment or repulsion, was on his face.

But Mary could not respond; her mouth was frozen. And when she tried to reach out toward Joel and Zadok, she could not move her arms. Then a torrent of syllables, nonhuman and guttural, poured from her lips. There was no mistaking the shock that now registered on both men's faces.

Still the sounds went on and on, and Mary could only listen helplessly as they spewed out of her, coming from the presences within her.

Zadok immediately started praying, reciting holy words in a loud voice to drown out the other sounds, as he had done on the waterfront, saying them very fast to get in as many as possible. Joel, having no defense at all, just stared, white-faced, in horror.

"Pray with me!" commanded Zadok suddenly, grabbing Joel's hand. "Say the Tephilla!" But Joel could do no more than mumble, ineffectively. Mary could barely hear him.

"—most high God, master of heaven and earth, our shield and the shield of our fathers—"

By now she had dropped to her knees and lowered her head, submitting herself to the Hebrew prayers, making it so that they could enter into her and subdue the voices and the presences. She clamped her lips shut to cut off the sounds, although the muscles twitched and fought her will. Then, quite suddenly, she felt the sounds dying out within her, like a pot of water that has ceased to boil. She felt the roiling within for an instant, bubbles still bursting, but soon the surface grew calm. She collapsed, falling forward on her knees, and was pulled up by the men. Joel carried her to a mat and let her lie quietly; he brought a wet cloth and tenderly wiped her face.

"Is—is it gone?" he asked Zadok.

"I don't—I don't know," he answered. "These forces can be strong and tricky; they are called the spirits of the air. Mary," he asked her gently, "are you all right?"

"Yes," she said, more to reassure him than out of any certainty. "I think . . . they have gone. Oh, Rabbi, I don't even know what they were saying!"

"Nor do any of us," said Zadok, stoutly. "It is better that way."

Mary slept soundly, feeling as emptied and flaccid as an old goatskin waterbag. She felt that Joel probably did not sleep well; that he kept a vigil all night in case something—whatever form it might take—came in the hours of darkness. When she awoke, dawn was just gently painting the sky visible from her little window to the east. She could hear the soft lapping of the water on the shore close to the house, and it seemed to be whispering sounds of consolation to her.

When Joel opened his eyes, she said, "I think . . . what Zadok did was effective. I feel . . . free of them. I do not think they are there any longer. But help me to search for that broken pottery paw of . . . I will not invoke his name. You know to whom I refer."

Joel looked distressed, but Mary reached out and took his hand.

"Please! Postpone going down to the warehouse and help me look! I dare not confront it—him—alone. Then we will destroy it together."

Quickly he got dressed, and they began a systematic search of Mary's belongings, the things she had brought with her from her parents' home and stored. They had to think hard about what might have happened to it since Mary last saw it hidden away near Ashara. "I put them both at the bottom of a trunk. . . . It was quite tiny, even smaller than Ashara. . . ." So easy to misplace—so difficult to find!

Together they removed the layers of cloth, blankets, tunics stored in the chest, shaking everything out carefully. But all these things had been recently cleaned and put away, with sweet-smelling herbs. Somehow Mary knew that the paw would not be among anything sweet-smelling, but would stink foully.

Yes . . . a strange odor. Where had she smelled it? A sour sort of smell that made her think of mildew, but when she inspected, there had been none. Then it had changed to a rotten stench, which made her think a mouse had died somewhere nearby. Then the smell had vanished. But it was . . . it had come from . . . the top of the storage shelf over the inner doorway. She fetched a stool and stood on it, peering up there. There were several small sacks, containing gum for patching holes in wood, leather strings of differing lengths, files. And there, among the plugs of wood and the glue pots, lay a dark-red curved piece of pottery. It almost looked like a broken jar-handle, but it was not. It ended in an ugly, square-toed paw, with claws. Pazuzu's.

She did not ask how it had found its way there. It was enough that she could reach out now and grasp it, hold it in her hand.

She climbed down from the stool and stared at it. What a small and silly-looking thing it was. It was hard to believe it had any power at all.

"Abomination! Idols! All abominations must be destroyed!" Mary could hear the angry rabbi's voice in Samaria rising once again, and the smashing sound of the clubs and staffs against the idols, the rain of polluted material all around her.

Perhaps it was the shower of idol dust that coated me, Mary thought, as well as the things I picked up. Suddenly she felt that she had been contaminated for almost her entire life, ever since that journey. And now there remained a remnant of that pollution, here in her hand.

"Joel!" she cried. "I've found it! Come quickly!"

He hurried over and stared at it. "So this is the enemy. Let's destroy it immediately. This time with awareness. Let it be as deliberate as possible."

"Should we call Zadok?" Mary asked. It seemed prudent to have as much help against the unclean spirits as possible, but Joel shook his head.

"No, it's more important to do it immediately. Our own prayers will suffice. And let us take it outside the house, smash it near the village trash-fires, and then throw it in with the offal and garbage."

"Or should we grind it up and throw it into the water?" After all, Moses had ground up the golden calves, thrown the dust into water, and made the Israelites drink it.

"No, we don't want to poison the lake," said Joel. "It would be an act of pollution, to cast such filth into it."

They left the house quickly and walked along a lakeshore path they knew would be deserted at this hour. As they walked along, Mary was able for the first time in a long while to see the beauty of the lake with unclouded eyes. Everything seemed of a brighter hue, as if somehow the intensity of light had changed. The sun was sparkling off the wavelets, thousands of them, and she could hear—again, for the first time in what seemed years—the birds as they called to one another in the newness of the day. It was the very sound of freshness, of new beginnings. The whiteness of the water birds wading near the shore seemed the purest color she had ever seen. It, too, spoke of freshness and absolute cleanliness.

Soon they rounded a bend and could see and smell the smoke from the trash pit, the exact opposite of the unspotted beauty of the lake. Here all foul things were gathered and burned.

They found a large flat rock to lay the arm down on, and it seemed to glow warmly against the black basalt. The paw looked clenched. Joel quickly called on God for deliverance: "Thus saith the Lord the King of Israel: I am the first, and I am the last, and beside me there is no God. He will guard the feet of his servants, but the wicked will be silenced in darkness. The adversaries of the Lord shall be broken to pieces," Joel said. "Molten images are but wind and confusion."

Mary repeated the words after him, then added, "I utterly condemn the day I ever touched you. I renounce your existence, and I hate all things connected to you." Then she nodded to Joel. "Now! Destroy it!"

Joel spread out a piece of cloth on the rock and then placed the paw on top of it. He raised a rock and smashed it down, shattering the brittle clay and reducing it to shards and powder. Next he ground the last little pieces into dust, and folded everything inside the cloth, even the contaminated hammering stone. Then they walked quickly to the burning pit.

A few people were there, flinging their own trash in, and the stink of burning fish-entrails was unmistakable. Joel raised the cloth over his head and muttered, "Their worm shall not die, neither shall their fire be quenched; and they shall be an abhorring to all flesh."

Mary said "Amen!" and the bundle sailed through the air and disappeared into the flames. A little sucking noise, a little flare, and it was gone.

Inside Mary there was a slight quivering, a feeling of something jellylike shifting, but other than that, nothing. Nothing but relief.

✣ XVI ✣

The cold winter wind swept down from the heights across the lake and howled into Magdala, driving waves as high as a man across the promenade and even out into the streets of the town. No one could remember such fierce storms, and they made the fishing much more dangerous at the very time when the sardines were traditionally caught.

Mary and Joel's house, being near the shoreline, suffered from flying spray and a general dampness, but with the horrible presences gone, the looming sense of oppression had fled, so Mary hardly cared if some water seeped into the house.

For the first few weeks, she scarcely dared to breathe, as if any action, no matter how small, might inadvertently beckon them back. But gradually she began to relax. She was confidently taking full care of Elisheba, and the little girl was delighting her mother with her first steps. Already she knew a few words, and they seemed the most miraculous sounds Mary had ever heard a human being say. She was now a year old.

It had been a year ago that Simon the Zealot had broken into Silvanus's home with his wild accusations; and although since then there had been some sneak insurrectionist attacks—like the murder they had witnessed in Tiberias—no one had rebelled openly. The new Roman procurator, Pontius Pilate, had arrived and already made an official visit to Jerusalem, where he was greeted with sullen faces.

There had been a great outcry about Herod Antipas's upcoming wedding to his forbidden ex–sister-in-law, but the king was proceeding with it just the same. There were reports that hordes of people were flocking to John the Baptist in the desert, where he fulminated loudly against the marriage, calling down God's wrath on Antipas.

On a particularly dark and dismal day, Mary set out for the warehouse where the large sardine catches of yesterday would be started on the process to turn them into the famous Nathan-garum, destined for Antipas's table as well as Gaul's. It was a furious operation; at the height of the sardine season, in midwinter, so many fish came in that men worked all day and all night for a time, and even then some of the fish spoiled before they could be preserved.

There were few people out, and those that were, were hunched under head coverings and hurrying for shelter. But in the warehouse, torches were blazing, and teams of workers were emptying barrels of salt into troughs, carrying fuel to the smoking-towers on the grounds, sorting fish and rolling and chopping herbs. Long rows of clay troughs were laid out at the far end of the warehouse, and Mary saw Joel standing near one and directing the actions of the workers. She came over to him.

"Is this the beginning of the garum?" she asked.

Joel turned around to see her, pleased as always when she came. "Indeed it is. In thirty days, all this will be poured into the fine amphoras we ordered, and it will go off across the sea."

There was a layer of herbs—bay, coriander leaves, sage—on the bottom of the trough, and then a layer of shiny sardines, covered with a layer of salt as thick as a man's finger up to the first joint, then another layer of herbs, and so on, until the rim of the container was reached. In summer it would then sit for seven days in the hot sun, but in winter it must ripen in the warehouse twice that long—hence the pungent aroma of the troughs already started. After fourteen days, someone would stir the mixture with a wooden stick for twenty days, until it turned liquid. Then this liquid would be poured into the proper amphoras and sent on its way. There was pagan garum, made with unclean fish, and proper Jewish *garum castimoniale*, made with only the fish the Law of Moses would allow, which naturally was more expensive.

In one corner of the warehouse were crates of the salted fish, everyday fare for common people, and also crates of the smoked fish, a higher-priced delicacy.

Mary looked around, marveling to herself that such a lowly thing—fish—could be the basis of an industry that made not only her own family but the whole town of Magdala so prosperous. All my security comes from this, she thought. But a sudden cold thought came to her. What if it failed? She had very seldom really thought about poor people, and how they survived.

"Mary!" Nathan came hurrying over. Was it her imagination, or was he more solicitous of her now? Did he know?

"Can I help?" she asked. "I came down because I knew you were so busy."

"Well, the accounts . . ." her father admitted.

"Let me look at them. You know I am good with figures."

Sitting up in the room in a corner of the warehouse, Mary was able to add up the accounts quickly and enter them into the record books. She had an orderly mind, one that liked organizing things. She also took the opportunity to look over the various accounts and try to see where their clients were located. Some of the places took her by surprise, like Carthage and Corsica and Sinope, a faraway spot on the Black Sea. She was very proud of her father's business and how he had built it, and proud to be allowed to work in it herself on occasion. Had her father had no sons, she might well have ended up running the business herself, but she did not begrudge that to Silvanus and Eli.

It was after she had finished her task and was leaning her head on her hand that the dreadful feeling returned, a familiar, nauseating presence. The buzz in her head, the crowdedness there, the horrible feeling of invasion . . . and then she saw her hand moving, taking the reed pen, starting to write obscene and horrible words on the clean ledgers. No! She wrestled with her own hand, actually hit it to make it stop, then quickly copied the damaged text and destroyed the original.

She got up, although she was trembling, and removed herself from the ledgers. *They* must not have an opportunity to destroy anything else, nor would they torment her in secret again. This time she would not hide her affliction from Joel.

Why now? Why have they come? Is there something in this warehouse? Is it an herb from some cursed place, sacred to some evil god, or unclean animals? She looked carefully around the little room. It seemed very bare. There was just a table and a chest to hold the ledger books, the pens, and the inks. A stool to sit on. She heard a slight croaking noise and traced it to a tiny frog, who was crouched in a corner and calling with high-pitched peeps. Clearly he had found his way into this quarter and was terrified at being cut off from the water. His throat swelled as he made his pitiable little noises.

Frogs . . . one of the plagues of Egypt. But evil? How can this creature be evil? He is small, and lost, and helpless, she thought. It cannot be.

She reached down to touch him, scooped him up in her palm, and lifted him up where she could look at him. His eyes bulged out, and he gave a series of peeps, then jumped off her hand.

Then his peeping seemed to come from within her own head, and she felt his terror and his panic to escape.

They were all there now, welcoming whatever new presence this was—whether truly a frog or something diabolical in its image. They were all talking at once. Ashara and Pazuzu were speaking to the newcomer, whom they addressed as Heket, goddess of Egypt.

"Heket, my dear divinity . . . friend of Osiris and presider over the births of kings and queens," the rumbling voice of Pazuzu was saying.

"My sister," the soft, caressing voice of Ashara whispered. "You who give life to the bodies of the rulers, and those whom Khnum fashions on his potter's wheel. You beautiful goddess of the water . . ."

Even as the words were running through her mind, Mary felt a tugging to go to the water and immerse herself, to plunge beneath waves. Like a sleepwalker, she arose and left the warehouse, then walked the few paces down to the waterfront. The waves, dull and gray, were dashing up against the stone wharf, spraying upward and soaking her, and each wave soaked her feet in a cold embrace. How dreadful, how chill the water was. And yet she was supposed to throw herself in, give herself to the sea. Heket was urging her to do so.

"Mary, what are you doing?" Joel's strong hand grasped her arm.

When she turned to look at him, she could see that he understood exactly what had happened. The darkness was back in her eyes, then.

"You know," she mumbled. "It is—*them*."

"The same?" he asked. She could not tell whether he was frightened or just resigned.

"And another besides," she said. "Four now." But his presence had thwarted the command from Heket that she throw herself into the sea.

"I know what we must do," said Joel. "Do not be afraid. I made preparations, in case this happened. You must go immediately to the rabbi in Capernaum, Rabbi Hanina ben-Yair. He is the holiest man close by, with the greatest understanding and training against these powers. You must do whatever he tells you. I will go with you, consign you to his keeping."

She felt relief. Joel had thought of this; Joel had prepared for this horrible possibility. And surely this rabbi knew things Zadok did not. Zadok had not been trained in such matters.

"But Elisheba—"

"The best thing you can do for her is to go immediately to Capernaum. I will make arrangements; she will be well cared for."

Together they hurried from the warehouse, ignoring the stares of the workers. The streets were still almost deserted; the nasty weather had driven everyone without a pressing task indoors. Joel kept his arm firmly around Mary, and she felt her fear and despair subsiding.

Once in the house, Mary quickly gathered up the things she thought she might need. Some clothes. Her writing materials. A little money. She went in to see Elisheba; her daughter was playing with some clay blocks and barely looked up at her. Mary stroked her soft hair but said no goodbye. She did not want to frighten her.

Soon she and Joel were on the path to Capernaum, hurrying past their own warehouse. They passed the smoking refuse-pit where they had gone with such hopes earlier. Long before they reached Seven Springs, their mantles were soaked through, but they kept up a quick pace.

As they reached the favored winter fishing spot, they thought they might see fishermen they knew, and so they were prepared when Jonah's son Simon looked up from his boat.

"Joel! Mary!" he called, waving. His loud voice would scare away any fish, but he looked as though he planned to be out there all day.

"Hello, Simon," said Joel. "How go the catches?" He stood and chatted as if this were any ordinary day, not a day when they were being driven before the wrath of the demons.

"Good. Very good. There're always schools here in winter. You can practically catch them with your bare hands." His brother, Andrew, sitting in the boat with him, waved.

Mary remembered that Simon and his family were from Capernaum. It would not be long until they heard her shameful story. But now she did not care. She only wanted to be cured. She was beyond shame, beyond wanting anything except deliverance.

"Hello, Joel!" another voice called, this one from the shore. Mary saw that James and John, the sons of Zebedee, were sorting a pile of fish.

"Great fishing in this cove today!" they said. "Expect a big shipment from us soon."

Joel nodded and made responses, but they did not stop walking.

Now silence descended as they left the fishermen behind and hurried toward Capernaum. Capernaum was the largest town at the head of the lake, with an elaborate system of wharves and breakwaters. It also was the boundary between the jurisdiction of Herod Antipas and his half-brother, Herod Philip, and so a customs station operated here.

But, most important to them, Capernaum had a very large synagogue overlooking the lake, and an authoritative rabbi to preside over it.

The dullness of the day coupled with its natural shortness this time of year meant that by the time Mary and Joel reached the synagogue it seemed to be twilight already.

The imposing building was not very far from the waterfront. By the time they reached it, the great doors had been closed for the night. All prayer services were held in daylight, and it was now hastening on toward evening. A knock on the doors yielded nothing, but an inquiry directed them to the house of Hanina, the rabbi. The house was quite near the synagogue.

Now, as they knocked, Mary felt great urgency. What if the rabbi chose not to admit them?

The knocks sounded hollow. There was no light within. Was the house empty?

"Empty, empty, empty, there's no help!" the voices within her mocked.

Be silent, she commanded them.

Finally, the door creaked open and a servant peered out at them.

"Is this the home of Rabbi Hanina ben-Yair?" asked Joel.

"Yes." The door did not open any farther, nor did the maidservant seem inclined to offer any hospitality.

"I am Joel bar-Ezekiel of Magdala," said Joel. "I have heard much of the learning and piety of Rabbi Hanina. I seek him for a personal reason."

Still the servant stared at him, and did not usher them in.

"In the name of Yahweh, we need to see your master!" Joel said at last.

Only then did the servant girl reluctantly open the door.

The inside of the house seemed pleasant enough. The first room was warmly lit, and there seemed to be a large room beyond that.

Soon Rabbi Hanina appeared, trailing his robes behind him and seeming irritated by their intrusion. But Mary was so frantic she did not care what the rabbi felt or thought, as long as he would help her. That was his mission, was it not? To help the afflicted of Israel.

"Yes?" The rabbi stared at Joel and Mary, a frown on his face. He gave no word of welcome.

"I apologize for coming to you so late and unannounced," said Joel. "But this is a matter of great urgency. We have come all the way from Magdala, for your reputation for learning and piety is known everywhere in Galilee."

Still the rabbi did not smile. "But who *are* you?" he finally asked.

"I am Joel bar-Ezekiel, and this is my wife, Mary. I am part of the family of Nathan of Magdala, who has a large fish-processing business. Normally we see our own rabbi, Zadok, and his assistants, but this—as I said, it is of great urgency, and Zadok cannot help."

The rabbi looked puzzled. "What is so urgent?" He glanced at the faces of both Joel and Mary.

"I am—I have been possessed!" Mary said, wanting to know right away if the rabbi could help. "I have wrestled with these unclean spirits for years by myself, but a few months ago I confessed to my husband, and together we asked our Rabbi Zadok to help me. To cast them out. He tried. He prayed and ordered the unclean spirits to depart. They obeyed, at the time. But now they are back. And so . . . we come to you."

The rabbi did not look surprised or worried. "It can be difficult" was all he said. "I will need to question you to try to understand exactly what has happened. But it is not hopeless."

In her relief at knowing he would not turn them away, Mary did not hear that he only said "it is not hopeless" rather than "yes, I know I can cast them out."

So, in his private room, lined with scrolls and holy writings, Mary recounted everything to the long-faced rabbi with dark hair and beard. If he was shocked or repulsed by her story, he did not show it. He did not comment on her "sin" in picking up the idol, and he took a great many notes. Mary felt safe and comforted; this man was learned and wise and would know what to do. He would deliver her.

But after listening intently, Rabbi Hanina put down his pen and shook his head. "This is a very bad case," he said. "Very bad." He paused. "Not that it is impossible, but . . . Of course, Yahweh and his power can prevail over any forces of darkness, for they are no match for him. But . . ."

"I will do anything!" said Mary. "Only tell me what to do!"

He sighed. "First we must remove all trace of sin in your life," He said. "Now, I realize that you may not even know of any sins, but they are there. No one can keep the Law perfectly. Remember when Job was smitten, Bildad the Shuhite said, 'Does God pervert justice? Does the Almighty pervert what is right? When your children sinned against him, he gave them over to the penalty of their sin.' So first you must purify yourself. Only then can we proceed to confront the presences. The human vessel must be immaculate. So . . . I would suggest that you take a Nazirite vow immediately. There is a little attached room by the synagogue where you can live until the term of the vow is over. I would recommend that it be for thirty days. And then, when you are completely purified, I will try to cast out the demons."

"Very well," said Mary. She had never known anyone who had taken a Nazirite vow, but many people still did.

"It is very ancient," Rabbi Hanina said. "The conditions of it are laid down in the book of Numbers." He took down one of the scrolls—he seemingly knew exactly what was in each one without even needing to see the labels—unrolled it, and unerringly found the passage. "Here is what God told Moses: 'Speak to the Israelites and say to them, "If a man or woman wants to make a special vow, a vow of separation to the Lord as a Nazirite, he must abstain from wine and other fermented drink and must not drink vinegar made from wine or from other fermented drink. He must not drink grape juice or eat grapes or raisins. As long as he is a Nazirite, he must not eat anything that comes from the grapevine, not even the seeds and skin."'"

The rabbi peered at Mary to see how she responded to this. In truth, she felt disappointed. Not eating raisins—how could that help against the possession?

" 'During the entire period of his vow of separation no razor must be used on his head. He must be holy until the period of his separation to the Lord is over; he must let the hair of his head grow long. Throughout the period of his separation to the Lord he must not go near a dead body. Even if his own father or mother or brother or sister dies, he must not make himself ceremonially unclean on account of them.'"

I don't use a razor on my head anyway, Mary thought. My hair is already long. How can this help? Despair began to rise somewhere deep inside her. And it was a black despair, because after Rabbi Hanina what other sources of help were there?

He droned on about recleansing yourself if you had inadvertently defiled yourself with a dead body, and about bringing pigeons as sin offerings, and then the unblemished male lamb to be offered at the end of the period, and so on. Mary jolted upright when he read, " 'Then at the entrance to the Tent of Meeting, the Nazirite must shave off the hair that he dedicated. He is to take the hair and put it in the fire that is under the sacrifice of the fellowship offering.'"

Shave off her hair! She would be bald! She would be disgraced. But . . . if that was the price, so be it.

"My daughter, are you willing to do this?" Rabbi Hanina asked. "If so, as soon as all the offerings have been made and accepted, I will proceed with the casting out of the demons."

Her hair . . . to live in a bare little room attached to the synagogue for thirty days . . . "Yes, I am willing."

"I will have you spend the night here in our spare room, and then, early in the morning, I will take you to the shelter at the synagogue, and we will initiate the vow. While you are there, you are to follow every aspect of the Law, deviating from nothing. For thirty days, you must be perfect."

"Yes. I understand."

Rabbi Hanina nodded. "I will have the room readied, and you may speak to your husband in private." He got up and left them alone.

Joel turned, and for the first time since the rabbi had started his speech, Mary looked in his eyes. What she saw there was fear.

"Oh, Joel, it will be all right. I know it will." It seemed very important to reassure him—even if she herself was not so sure. "And it isn't for very long—a month is not very long. But I will miss you and Elisheba, and I did not even tell her goodbye. And . . . what will you tell everyone?"

"The truth," he said. "The truth."

"That I have taken a Nazirite vow, or that I am possessed?"

"Only about the vow. It is no disgrace to take a Nazirite vow; many people do it. But the possession—I see no purpose in disclosing it."

"I suppose it will seem a bit out of character for me to go off to Capernaum to take a Nazirite vow."

"Yes, but we can say it had to do with your childbearing. It would be logical that you would want to assure a second childbirth, and that you would make a vow about it."

Everyone knew about her childlessness and the miracle of Elisheba's birth. Yes, it would seem natural. No one would ask questions. That seemed very important.

"Pray for my success, Joel!" She grasped his hands. "Pray for my deliverance!"

He held her to him, clasping her so tightly she could feel his heartbeat. "With all my soul," he said. He took her face in his hands and looked into her eyes. "We will defeat them, Mary. Do not fear."

He took his leave shortly thereafter, going out again in the storm to return home. From that moment on, she was on her own.

The rabbi and his wife were very kind to her. Evidently the rabbi's wife was used to having people seek him out for spiritual crises, and she dutifully made up the bed and set out the jug of water for drinking and washing as if she had done it many times. "Sleep well" was all she said, but her smile was genuine.

Lying on the little bed, Mary wondered if she would sleep at all. *They* were still inside, and she could feel them. But they were curiously subdued, as if they were stunned by her decisive and prompt action to combat them.

∽ XV11 ∽

Just before dawn, while the sky was still gray—although it had lost the inkiness of night—Mary and the rabbi left his house and walked together to the synagogue. A swirling mist was still curling about the streets, and the synagogue, fashioned of black basalt, was hard to see. They were almost there before Mary made out its walls and the court surrounding it.

"Here is the little shelter where those making vows stay," the rabbi said, leading her to a structure alongside the main building. It was a harsh little hut, plain and bare, with none of the decorations and carvings that adorned the synagogue walls. But, then, those who sought it out were on serious missions. Inside, there were just a reed mat, a little table, an oil lamp, and a water jug.

"Food will be brought to you three times a day," Rabbi Hanina said. "But it will be fasting fare—barley bread, water, and, on Sabbaths, a little piece of cheese and dried fruit. And the holy books of Moses will be brought, so that you may read them. Do you read?"

"Yes," she said, wondering if that was a good or a bad answer in his eyes.

"Good." He nodded. "That way you can steep yourself in the Law. And on Sabbaths, you are welcome to listen to the services. But on no account must you come into the congregation. No, you must separate yourself for the entire thirty days. And if this does not work, then . . . you must go to the desert, alone."

So that was what awaited her if this failed. But it would not fail, it must not fail.

She looked around the bare little hut. She hated the unclean spirits that had brought her to this. To subsist on barely enough food to keep herself alive, to spend all her days trying to fulfill the smallest item in the Law of Moses—! But there was no choice. She had to rid herself of them.

The first day was the longest one she had ever lived. There was nothing to do in the little hut but torment herself with recalling her sins. By nightfall, her stomach was rumbling, crying out for food. The Law of Moses seemed a thicket of things that had little to do with her. Leviticus outlined all the things someone must do if he detected mildew in his house. It ordered the procedure to cure a skin disease, stating that the priest must take two live, clean birds, cedarwood, scarlet yarn, and hyssop for the afflicted person, and dip the yarn, the wood, and the hyssop into the blood of the bird . . . and so on. She saw no connection with her own situation, save that for the first time she was learning how concerned God was with minutiae.

The evening of the first day, she lay down on her pallet and only wished to fall asleep, so that the day would end. "And the evening and the morning were the first day." Just to make her torture more complete, the voices and presences were silent, so that it seemed as if she had been mistaken in coming here.

The mat was hard. It was made of reeds, tightly woven together. The thin blanket they had given her was not sufficient to keep the chill away. She was shivering as she lay there, wondering how she would ever sleep. Her head was spinning. She was so hungry she could have eaten the hangings in the synagogue.

O Lord God, King of the Universe, she prayed, I am your servant. I do wish to serve you. If only I had set myself on the path to truly knowing you earlier.

Her stomach contracted with hunger. She felt as if she was going to vomit, although there would not be anything to vomit. Why was this the way to God? To show humility? To show dependence? The things of the earth—eating, drinking, sleeping—did God despise them? Or did he only require that his servants not be bound to them?

She ran her hands through her thick hair. All this would be shaved off, all this would be sacrificed.

But she could not keep the thought at bay: was this truly what God required?

The thirty days passed as slowly as an aged tortoise creeping toward a resting place. She read the five books of Moses, she fasted on the bread and water, and she prayed for hours. Sometimes she heard the synagogue services on the Sabbath, when the people of Capernaum and even a number of Romans and Gentiles, called "God-fearers," came to participate. These foreigners were drawn to the moral message of Judaism but did not wish to undergo full conversion, since it meant being circumcised and keeping all the dietary laws. They were relegated to the aisles, but still they came. They wanted the essence of Judaism, the message of Judaism, without the irksome regulations. Should they be turned away? It was difficult to know. Could not Judaism be refined to do away with outmoded laws and rituals, like the one for mildew, so that it could reach more people with the richness of its moral teachings?

At last, the day came. Her purification was complete, the ritual performed perfectly. She was allowed out of her little shelter and led into the synagogue itself—the first time she had seen it. Inside, it was rich with carvings—one of the Ark of the Covenant—and polished brass vessels and a sandalwood screen before the sacred scrolls. All was order, all was calm, and the measured and knowable Law, as handed down to Moses on Mount Sinai, held sway here.

Awaiting her before the sanctuary that held the scrolls was Rabbi Hanina. He was wearing richly embroidered robes, draped with his prayer shawl. Mary saw that he had fastened on his tefillin and held a scroll.

Accompanying him was a younger man who carried a tray with several objects on it. He stood rigidly beside the rabbi and said nothing.

"Daughter of Israel, you have completed your time of consecration," said Rabbi Hanina. "For thirty days you have set yourself apart, according to the Law of Moses, and now you stand ready for the blessings you have earned." He nodded to the man, who set his tray down and took up a razor.

"Now, in accordance with the Law, you will sacrifice your hair, and it will be offered to God."

She bowed her head and waited.

The man took a handful of hair in his hand and sliced through it with his razor. Mary saw it fall onto the floor, shining and healthy. For the first time she was seeing her own hair as others had seen it. Soon there was a pile around her feet.

Then the razor touched her scalp, and she felt the chill of its blade against her skin and then the strange coldness of being bald.

"Now gather it up and offer it," the rabbi said, and Mary bent down and took it in her own hands and then handed it to the rabbi. He turned and took it to one side of the sanctuary, where a brazier was burning. But he did not put it in.

"The intent is enough," he said. "I will complete the rest of the ceremony when there is no one else here, for the stench of burning hair is most abominable. Now." He moved closer to her. "Are you ready?"

"With all my heart," she said.

He motioned to his assistant. "The oil," he said.

A small bottle of oil was handed to the rabbi, and he removed the stopper. "This is holy oil, similar to that used in the Temple. It comes from a sacred grove of olives that has grown for centuries near Jerusalem. Legend says that Solomon himself laid out the orchard.

"The incense." Now a pottery stand was brought from the tray and placed on the floor nearby.

"Frankincense, which is also used in the Temple and for other rites," he said. He touched a glowing stick to it to make it catch fire. "Seasoned with salt, to purify it." He added a pinch. "We are forbidden to make incense of the same formula as that in the Temple, nor are we to add the same ingredients to the oil as that used to anoint priests. But this is also sacred."

Small puffs of smoke were rising from the censer; in Mary's condition of extreme hunger, it made her lightheaded.

Rabbi Hanina solemnly traced the oil on her forehead and the crown of her head.

"Daughter, do you have a head covering?" he asked, in a kindly voice. He was concerned that she not be shamed in public later for her baldness.

Mary nodded. It was one of the things she had hastily grabbed on that last night at home.

The rabbi began reciting prayers, long ones in Hebrew. He rocked back and forth on his heels, and beads of sweat appeared on his forehead. He seemed to be wrestling with the dark powers himself.

But Mary felt nothing. She did not think the spirits were affected by the prayers. Perhaps they do not understand Hebrew, she thought. But how could spirits not understand all languages? That was a human limitation, not one of the spirits.

"Please," she finally said, "could you speak in Aramaic, the common language?"

He looked startled.

"That is the language they use in speaking to me," she explained. Perhaps they preferred it.

"Very well." He paused and had to think, translating the ritual words in his head. "'Depart from this daughter of Israel, whom you have cruelly tortured with your presence. Depart back into the abyss from which you came, and trouble your servant Mary of Magdala no more. I say that your power cannot stand against the command of God, in whose name I order you to depart forevermore.'"

She should be feeling something, as she had before, however short-lived. Some relief or deliverance. But nothing happened. The spirits had been uncharacteristically quiet the entire time of her retreat, and they remained so now. Was there someplace they hid, someplace inside where words and rituals could not reach them? It was a chilling thought.

"Depart!" the rabbi called in a loud, climactic voice. "Depart!" He raised his hands high, as if to call upon all the strength of God.

Mary bowed her head and waited for some sign, some change, but nothing came.

The rabbi seemed pleased. He had completed his ritual, had encountered no opposition, and assumed it was successful. A smile on his face, he extended his hand in blessing.

"My daughter, you are free," he said. "Give thanks!"

Late afternoon. Mary stood on the main wharf in Capernaum, clutching her little satchel of belongings and holding fast to the head covering she had put on. A shaved head was so dreadful-looking it would cause people to shun her.

A fierce storm was battering the waterfront. In the winter month that Mary had spent sequestered, the weather had not improved. She could see the waves being driven before the wind, smashing up against the entire western shore, where Magdala and Tiberias lay. Capernaum, being at the northernmost end of the lake, suffered less from the storms, but it was still very dangerous there. A number of fishing boats were sheltering behind the breakwaters, and a crowd of people had gathered on the wharf.

I will return home this afternoon, she thought. I will just walk the way. With the small amount of money she had, she bought a half-loaf of bread and devoured it, then spent more money and bought some figs from a vendor. How good fresh food was!

She had been apart from the world for so long, or so it felt, that she wandered about like a dazed person. She went down to the crowd on the wharf, as much to reaccustom herself to people as for any other reason. It quickly became apparent, however, that this was no ordinary crowd, but one wildly concerned about something.

"They're missing! They're missing!" one woman cried, calling out to a fishing boat just putting in, its interior almost filled with water. "Have you seen Joseph? Have you seen my son?"

The fishermen looked up at her. They were battered and soaked. "No," they said. "After we got across the lake, and were heading for the Gergesa fishing grounds, a terrible swell caught us. We were lucky to escape. The storm is mounting."

"Gergesa!" she wailed. "That's where he was going! Oh, did you not see him? Did you not see any other boats?"

"Only Nathan of Magdala's hired one," they said. "And it is larger and able to withstand higher seas."

"It was there! He was going there!"

Mary looked across the water toward the area of Gergesa. It was on the eastern side of the lake, in the place where high cliffs came down near the water. Near all the Gentile areas of Greek cities. Where the pigs were raised. The pig-man and his signal . . . Uncleanness, and revolution . . .

And suddenly the landscape of the eastern shoreline was replaced, and she saw a small boat swamped by waves, overtaken on its way to Gergesa. She saw—as if she had flown there and been only an arm's length away—the faces of the men in the boat, terrified as they pulled on the oars. And then she saw, unfolding before her, the boat over-turned, the men flailing, clinging to the boat, and finally sinking under the waves.

"Your son has perished." A deep, guttural voice pronounced the words. "Your son is lost."

Mary heard the words but they startled her. Everyone had turned toward her. Everyone was staring at her.

And then she felt her own mouth opening, felt it moving, her tongue moving, and words issuing forth. "Your son lies at the bottom of the lake. He will return no more. Nor shall his companions."

The mother screamed, and people rushed toward Mary.

"The storm will last three days." The voice continued speaking. "It will blow for three days. Two other boats will be lost. The boat of Joshua—who has yet to venture out—and the boat of Phineas, who will go to seek the first lost boat."

The crowd rushed on her, stampeding her, and she cowered under their blows and screams.

"A witch! A witch!"

"She has caused this storm! She has an Evil Eye!"

"Kill her! Kill her!"

They knocked her down and began fighting over her, pawing at her.

A strong arm hauled her up, and Mary found herself staring into a face she knew from somewhere.

"I know this woman! She is no witch!" The tall man positioned himself between her and the angry townspeople.

"Simon?" Was it Simon, the fisherman? The one she and Joel had seen as they were rushing here? She remembered the torture of the polite conversation with him. Yes, he lived in Capernaum.

"To the synagogue," Simon said, pulling her with him. "To the synagogue."

Once there, he escorted her inside, his height and authority keeping the people at bay. Within the synagogue, she huddled miserably, waiting for the rabbi. Her veil had slipped off her head, and Simon was staring at her baldness.

"Yes, I have been here for a month, performing a Nazirite vow," she mumbled. Clearly it had not been effective; it was Pazuzu who had spoken the words out of her mouth. Pazuzu, the wind-god demon who raised storms.

"I . . . I . . ." How could she possibly explain to Simon? She did not want to. What was the point? But perhaps he could carry a message to Joel. "I have been beset by evil spirits," she said. Her own voice had returned. "I came here in hopes that I could exorcise them. But they are still here. It was they who spoke out about the fisherman; it was they who took fiendish pleasure in it. They delight in death and destruction. Now I must go far away, where I cannot harm anyone. Pray you, take a message to my husband. Tell him this treatment has failed, and next I must do something more extreme. I await the rabbi's instructions."

"I will wait with you for the rabbi." As he spoke, his brother, Andrew, came in, having followed them.

"The crowd is ready to kill," Andrew said. "They think that you somehow caused the storm. And they are terrified about the deaths, and the predictions of more deaths."

"I am ready to die to rid myself of these evil presences that have turned my life into a hell," said Mary. And she meant it. "But I should not be killed for something I did not do. I have nothing to do with any deaths; these evil spirits, my enemies, wish my own death as much as any others. If I cannot free myself of them, then I will gladly die."

Death was what the demons wanted—to take human life, any life, and destroy it. To wreck health and happiness and kill, kill, kill. The mounds of bodies killed in war, the citizen killed by the sharp thrust of a *sica*, the estrangement between brothers, between father and son, the cruel death of helpless animals, horses, sheep, lizards, birds, snakes: this was what they commissioned, this was what they rejoiced in.

The rabbi came hurrying in. He looked around, confused. "What is it?"

Simon spoke. "There was a near-riot at the waterfront. This woman cried out on the dock and revealed things about a missing boat that only an evil power would have known. And she predicted two more accidents to come in the next few days."

A look of intense sorrow crossed the rabbi's face. He was stunned that his ministrations had failed.

"She spoke in another voice," said Simon. "The voice of . . . some evil spirit."

The rabbi slumped down and covered his face with his hands. He wept.

Mary wanted to comfort *him*, to apologize for having involved him in this, which was clearly so much deeper and more dangerous than anyone had realized. "Good Rabbi, we knew from the beginning that our efforts might not prevail," she said. "God blesses you for doing your best. Now, sir, you said that there was another place . . . a place in the desert where I might go?"

He looked up at her, surprised that she was so resolute, not crushed by the failure of the exorcism. "I ask your forgiveness," he said. "I did everything it was in my power to do."

"There is nothing to forgive," she assured him. "We fight these powers, and all we can do is our best. God requires nothing more."

Simon and Andrew were standing by, their faces unreadable. Yet Mary knew that they were listening to every word.

"There is a place in the desert . . . near Bethabara," said Rabbi Hanina. "It is where holy men go to be cleansed. But the journey there—can you make it alone? It is a long distance, and a woman traveling alone . . ."

"I will go with her," said Simon suddenly. "I will accompany her. I feel—I cannot explain it—called to do so."

"It is at least three days' hard walk from here," said the rabbi.

"No matter," said Simon. "But first let me go to Magdala to tell her family of what is to happen. Wait for me, here at the synagogue. No, better yet, at my home. It is nearby. My wife and mother-in-law will welcome you."

It broke her heart that she could not go herself, could not explain everything to Joel, hold him and Elisheba close once more. But the affliction—she could not trust herself around them, could not endanger Elisheba. She had to go to the desert, and now, and with near-strangers.

The rabbi lowered his head, crushed by his failure. He was highly esteemed in the community, and he could not understand why he had failed against these powers. "But at least I can show you the way to the desert," he told Mary. "There you will confront everything. All the spirits, all the demons, and you will wrestle with God himself—like Jacob. And beware, for there are bad spirits lurking in the desert, too. They seem to frequent desolate places, the Noonday Demons, the Locusts of the Abyss, Azazel, Deber, and Rabisu, the Croucher of Horrible Aspect. But purification is also there. More purification than I was able to offer you." He looked as though he would weep again, and Mary reached out to him. Then she remembered that it was forbidden for a woman to touch a rabbi—or any other man, for that matter, among the strictly observant.

"You offered me much," she finally said. "I am thankful for all you gave me. When I am ready to make the journey to the desert, we will come to you and you may give us guidance."

Simon and Andrew motioned to her. "Come, let us go to our house. There is no time to waste."

Outside, the storm was blowing gusts of water; the sky was a nasty dull gray, like ashes from a doused fire. The crowd, cloaked in equally dull colors of brown, black, and ink, was still seething at the edge of the pier, and small fishing craft were still fighting their way to shore.

"Pull your veil down lower," said Simon, as he and Andrew flanked her. "Keep your eyes down, and follow." Quickly they left the grounds of the synagogue and made their way out onto the street, opening directly in front of the synagogue. It was an area of houses of the prosperous; Mary could see that most of them were large enough to include a courtyard and several rooms.

The men made a quick turn ahead of her, and she did likewise, and then she was stepping into a courtyard, and a door thudded shut behind her. Simon and Andrew sought one of the rooms leading off the open area, and again she followed.

"Simon. I was so worried!" A young woman came rushing over and took his hands. She barely glanced at anyone else.

"I have a guest," said Simon firmly, to warn her that there was a stranger present. "Mary of Magdala—of the family we do business with—has just completed a Nazirite vow," Simon explained. "She is here because . . . she will be going out in the desert to perform a further vow, and we will escort her." He paused. "Mary, this is my wife, Mara." Mary nodded to her. "And you needn't have worried, dear one," Simon said. "We know better than to venture out on the water in such weather."

Mara motioned to them to come into another room. "Please. We will be eating soon."

"I must go to Magdala and see Mary's family," said Simon. "So let me eat quickly; I must go now."

Mary could hardly endure the wait while Simon, a man she barely knew, went to her home in Magdala and spoke to Joel about her. The impersonal conversation all around her—anything was better than to let the demons speak. Oh, dear Lord God, my shield and protector, please do not let them speak! Mary felt her fingers digging into the finely tooled leather hassock on which she sat. Do not let them speak!

Andrew was talking about the fishing, and something else, she knew not what. The evening passed in a blur, and soon—mercifully soon—she was led to yet another guest bed, this time in a small chamber with a table and a lampstand.

Dawn. Mary could see its dull light seeping in through the little window in the snug room. She was cold and stiff. The wind had howled all night, and wound itself into her dreams. The presences. They were still with her, and she had to go on a journey to try to rid herself of them, and someone was helping. Who? She struggled to remember. The fishermen, the fishermen from Capernaum. Yes.

Flinging off the covering, she dressed herself quickly. When she ran her hand over her bald head, she cringed. She made her way out to the kitchen, where the family was already gathered. Simon was there, drinking a broth. He had returned from Magdala in the early hours of the night.

"I saw Joel," he said. "I explained everything to him. He understood."

"What . . . what did he say?"

"He was greatly saddened, of course, that the Nazirite vow had not been successful. But he said you must undertake this journey. He said never to doubt his loyalty and love, and that he and Elisheba would be waiting. He also sent this." Simon thrust out a bag as if embarrassed by it.

Mary opened its top and peered in. It was filled with coins.

"For the journey," explained Simon. "You will need shelter, food, who knows what . . . he realizes that it is dangerous."

And yet he was willing to let her go. Her desperate situation was clear to all.

"Thank you," she finally said.

"Shall we begin?" said Simon. "Let us consult with Rabbi Hanina and be on our way."

"The journey is long, and you must gird yourselves for it," said Rabbi Hanina. He seemed to have recovered from the shock of the failure of the rite, and now was all business. He was sending them on to a higher authority; his responsibility was over. He drew a rough map on a piece of papyrus. "You must follow the river Jordan southward. At least at this time of year the heat will not be a problem. You must seek out the brook of Cherith, just east of the Jordan, once you pass the ford that connects Jerusalem and Amman. There are many caves there, and holy people who seek solitude." He paused. "Then, my daughter, you must throw yourself on the mercy of the Almighty. He is powerful there, much closer than here in the city."

"Cherith?" said Simon. "Isn't that where—?"

"Yes, it is where Elijah was fed by the raven," Rabbi Hanina said.

"But today—isn't that where that prophet is holding forth? What's his name—that one who calls for repentance—"

"John the Baptist," said Hanina shortly. "But you needn't see him at all. Nor should you. He attracts crowds, and that is the last thing you need. No crowds. Just solitude." He thrust a little bag at Mary, filled with writing materials. "You must write what happens to you there; it will intensify your dedication."

They left Capernaum well before noon, and took the road around the east side of the lake. Mary did not feel she could bear to pass by Magdala, to see the warehouse, perhaps even her own house. And then to pass Tiberias, where foreign gods lurked. No, better to take the east side, with the pigs and Gentiles.

Soon they were crossing the Jordan, at the place where it gushed and flowed between the reeds.

"The Jordan is cold here," said Andrew. "The waters come down from the north. You can feel the snow in them." He paused. "Go ahead," he said to Mary. "Go down to the banks. Put your hand in."

She hesitated, then carefully made her way down the muddy bank. The water was a swirl of brown, foaming and rushing. Holding on to a branch, she stretched herself out and put her hand in. It was shockingly cold.

They continued around the rim of the lake, passing by Bethsaida, which looked very inviting and prosperous. Mary wondered if they were going to spend the night there. But before she could ask, Andrew said, "We'll make our own camp farther down along the lakeshore."

This did not seem very appealing to Mary. She would rather have been inside in such cold, rainy weather. She realized she had never spent a night outdoors in bad weather.

"We may need an inn as we pass outside Galilee," Andrew explained. "But we should save our money for the area where the bandits roam and we can't sleep safely out in the open."

By sunset, they had reached the town of Gergesa—a large, bustling one, with a busy waterfront and a tiled building to receive fish, as well as an impressive freshwater tank for holding live fish. So this was where the best fishing ground was. Mary was curious about it.

But it was also where the boat had been lost in the storm, and as they approached in the twilight, they could see that something else had happened. There were cries and laments, and it was clear that another boat had been lost.

She heard the murmurings in the crowd. It was the boat of Joshua, as the presences had predicted. And perhaps also that of Phineas, who had gone to look for Joseph. Mary could not bear to see or hear about these losses, which she was now connected to, if only as a seer. I cannot bear this burden, she thought.

It was nearly dark by the time they left Gergesa, its harbor and town, behind. The wind, whipping down from the heights above, was so loud they could not talk as they plodded along. The seashore was a roar of crashing waves. Suddenly a loud scream made itself heard even over the wind and waves. It was cutting, high-pitched, and wavering.

They stopped and looked, but could see nothing. They were passing an area strewn with boulders, some of them larger than a man. In the growing dimness these seemed to merge with their own shadows, and the driving rain blurred Mary's vision. Then a dark figure rushed out from the cover of a rock, yelling and brandishing a club, assaulting them.

He dived for Simon, grabbing his feet, and Simon let out a yelp of fear and ran away, not even looking behind him to see where his companions were. Andrew fell on the man and pinned him to the rocky ground, but the man kept beating his club rhythmically, as if summoning up spirits. A strange series of sounds came from him. Finally, they stopped, and the club lay still on the ground.

Andrew slowly released him, and they saw to their astonishment that he was utterly naked. The rain was beating down on him, his hair was matted and his beard dripping, but he seemed oblivious to it.

A demoniac! How could they have forgotten that the possessed were banished just outside Gergesa? How could they have let themselves venture there so late in the day?

Mary looked at the man's wrists, where broken chains dangled from metal cuffs.

"Peace, friend," said Simon, panting, as he motioned to the others to slip past the man and join him farther down the beach. Fear tingled in his voice. "Peace. Peace upon you."

With a growl, the man sprang up again, lunging at Mary and Andrew, but they eluded him and ran as fast as they were able along the stony shore, following Simon. The man sank back down in despair, as if he had never had any hope of catching them or making them listen to him. He bowed his head in the rain. He howled like a dog.

"That area . . ." said Andrew, his voice shaking, once they were safely beyond him. "I had forgotten that the afflicted gather there and threaten travelers."

"Yes, we usually come here by boat. Land travel is a different thing altogether." Simon looked around. He caught his breath, trying to regain his composure, smother his fear. "We must be well clear of this area before we attempt to stop for the night."

"These . . . afflicted . . ." began Mary.

"They have all been taken over by demons, and cannot live safely among normal people. There is no place for them but the rocks by the shore." Simon was still breathing hard and looking all around him.

The demons did this. This was their aim, then: to reduce everyone to such a state, helpless to the elements, cast out, abandoned.

"How do these poor souls eat?" Mary asked.

"Their relatives and townsfolk bring food, and leave it in a safe place. They dare not linger." He paused. "Some starve, in any case."

Such could be my fate, thought Mary. This time next year, I may be here with them, hiding in the rocks, no longer able to speak.

They made camp under a small willow tree, a long—and safe—distance from the area of the madmen. A single lantern provided light, and with some gathered brush they were able to make a small fire that flickered and smoldered but gave some comfort. They ate what they had brought from Capernaum, and then, folding their mantles under them, attempted to sleep.

The ground was hard and rocky, and Mary could feel every bump and pebble. The water nearby was noisily slapping on the shore, and the rain added to the din. But there was no howl from the madmen, and the willow tree, draped with a blanket to make a tent, seemed a refuge in this frightening and confusing world.

Early light showed the lake to be a quiet sheet of water. The rain had ceased, the wind had died, and the sun was struggling to emerge from the layers of clouds overhead.

They set out immediately; by midday, they had reached the place where the Jordan flowed from the lake to begin its tortuous windings down through the wilderness, leading finally to the Dead Sea. Although the area immediately surrounding the river was green, everything else was a desolate sandy brown. From now on, they would traverse a barren landscape broken up by canyons and ruled by bandits and wild beasts at night. They clutched their staffs—their only weapons— and tucked their robes close around them, hiding their money and keeping a close watch for any sudden movement. A few other forlorn travelers were visible in the distance, but other than that they seemed completely alone, save for the ravens who watched them with impassive eyes.

It was almost dusk when they saw the outlines of a caravansary ahead of them, and they stepped up their pace to reach it before nightfall. They were near the place where trade caravans crossed the Jordan in their east-west route. Travelers took shelter in these havens, though they did not offer much except walls to keep bandits and wild animals out, a place to unpack the animals and to lie down. It would be terribly crowded, and they only hoped there would be room for three more.

The owner was about to shut the gates for the night when they slipped into the courtyard with all the camels, donkeys, and mules. People were building little cookfires; they claimed their places inside the bare building or under its eaves to sleep. All sorts of people were taking refuge there, from foreign traders speaking Nabatean or Ethiopian or Greek, to a few Roman soldiers, to young men who looked suspiciously like *sicarii*. Some seemed to be pilgrims, too. They were apparently seeking the holy site where Elijah had been taken up to heaven.

Mary was curious about the others settling down for the night around her, but she was too tired to observe them. She ate very little, and then lay down to sleep, hearing the howling of jackals and other animals just outside the walls, thankful that she was safely out of their reach.

Another dawn—the third since she had begun her exile. She could hear the grunts and snorts of the camels in the outer courtyard as they awaited their food, the babble of people making ready to set out. Only then did she notice that there were no other women present. What strange new life had she been led to? To go places where there were no women, to face being left alone, abandoned in the desert?

Abandoned by my religion, which could not help me . . . abandoned to the hope of a normal life . . . and soon to be abandoned by these men, who are accompanying me on what we all fear is my last journey . . .

She shut her eyes and stood swaying, trying to get control before the sobs started. My husband! My daughter! She lamented, weeping. I had to leave you . . . for this?

An irritable camel swung around, and its tail smacked her, as if to shame her further.

And these men—Simon and Andrew. What do I know of them? I remember when Keziah used to laugh about them, say they smelled. Why are they on this journey with me? They have said very little.

Of course, I have said even less, she reminded herself.

Now they were motioning to her. It was time to set out on the road skirting the thorny thickets that had grown up alongside the meandering river. There were more people now, heading toward the ford across the riverbank that would allow them to cross and go either westward to Jerusalem or eastward to Amman.

Again it was late in the afternoon, with the light fading, before they reached their destination, a dry canyon with ravines and caves and overhanging crevices. There was some smoke coming from a few openings in the canyon wall, rising wispy and thin against the red rocks.

"Holy men," said Simon. "People withdrawing from the world."

"Let us help you find a proper place," said Andrew.

"Are you sure . . . this is where the rabbi meant I should go?" Mary asked. It seemed so forbidding and isolated. And how was she to eat? There was nothing here but some dried-up shrubs and bare, twisted trees.

"Yes, he meant this exact spot. It is here that Elijah hid and the ravens fed him."

"Are the ravens supposed to feed me?" How foolish she had been, to venture out without any preparations. The money Joel had given her would be useless here. The ravens, the lizards, and the buzzards would not take it in exchange for food. Obviously the evil spirits had sent her out, unprotected like this. The better to attack her.

."We will leave you all our food, and our water," said Simon. He yanked his bag off his shoulder and handed it to her. "Andrew!" He ordered his brother to follow suit.

"That is kind, but . . . how will you survive?" said Mary. It seemed foolhardy to her, though she was so fearful that she would accept it.

"We will—we can obtain something farther down, where the ford is. Many people cross there. It will be simple." Simon sounded so certain. By now Mary knew that meant nothing.

"Look, here's a good place!" Andrew pointed to a little cave far up the side of the canyon but easy to reach by a sloping path up the rocks.

Inside, it proved to be dry and an adequate place to live.

"How fortunate that we found it, and right away," said Simon.

Not only was he impulsive, thought Mary, but he was optimistic as well. He seemed to see no obstacles to the plan.

"Now we'll get you settled," said Andrew, unloading his pack and handing her a blanket, a waterskin, a bag of dried figs and pressed fig cakes, and salted fish. He gave her some tinder and sticks necessary for making a fire. He even gathered two armloads of brushwood for her.

"We hate—we hate to leave you like this," said Simon. "But we know it is necessary for your cure. As long as there are other people here, you cannot confront what you need to confront. But we will be down at the ford. We will wait there for many days. You can seek us if you need us."

"But . . . your fishing!" How could they stay away from Capernaum for an indefinite period?

Andrew shrugged. "Father can manage well enough. He can hire others to replace us."

Was this true? Or were they only trying to be kind?

"Stay here," Andrew said. "Pray. Do whatever you must. But when you are ready to return, come and find us at the ford, and we will bring you back to Galilee."

But that meant they must wait . . . how long?

"I cannot know how long I must stay here," said Mary. "Please, after a few days you must return to your father."

"Do not worry about us," Simon assured her. "We are curious about the ford, and the pilgrims who frequent it. So several—or even many—days there will not be a burden for us."

"Take these things." Mary thrust the little bag with her belongings into Simon's hands. "I don't want them. I don't need them." It did not matter what the rabbi had told her, she was not going to write anything down. Her battle with the demons would not allow for that. Nor would she need money. Or anything beyond strength of will.

She made her little home in the cave. She built a small fire to keep wild animals at bay, and made a place to sleep with the blanket, and a stone for a pillow. But it was frightening: the fire only served to illuminate the craggy holes in the roof of the cave, where anything could be hiding, and the solitude and night cold just encased her in a shroud of despair. She was now alone and trapped with the spirits. Why had the rabbi thought that this would help?

If God was in this place, she could not feel him. She could feel nothing but abandonment and fear. She had come to the end of her life. The little girl who had picked up the idol out of curiosity was now a demon-ridden woman who had been cast out of her home, tormented and driven to this place of no hope at all.

I will die here, she thought, far away from my home, and my daughter will never even remember me. All she will know is that her mother was unable to care for her and later died. Joel will remarry, and that new woman will comfort him and be a mother to Elisheba, and I will be forgotten. My mother and father will mourn me, but they have other children and grandchildren and will remember me as we remember other lost relatives. At first often, then less and less.

Oh, despair! You yourself are a demon, she thought. Yet, if I speak the truth, can we call despair a sin? What is true can never be a sin. It is Beelzebub who is the father of lies, and thus, if I understand the desperation of my state and feel it in my heart, it is not a sin but only the sad truth. It is Beelzebub who would torment me with false hopes. Here hope is the sin, not despair. It is hope that is a lie.

But I was sent here to pray, to purify myself, she thought. I was told to do this by someone who knows the affliction. And so I shall obey. I shall.

All that night, between fitful awakenings, she prayed. The fire had died down, and only its embers were smoking. She was cold and hungry, and it was hard to distinguish the dreams from the fatigue and lightheadedness caused by fasting. She did not dare address the spirits themselves, but prayed all the Psalms she could remember, and at that time wished she knew them all by heart instead of just lines here and there.

"I lie down and sleep; I wake again because the Lord sustains me. I will not fear the tens of thousands drawn up against me on every side."

Yes, there were probably hosts of demons, whole armies of them, drawn up on all sides. But this prayer assumed that they were only outside, not inside.

"He is my protector, and my refuge: my God, in him I will trust. He will overshadow me with his shoulders: and under his wings I shall trust. His truth shall compass me with a shield: I shall not be afraid of the terror of the night. Of the arrow that flies in the day, of the business that walks about in the dark, of invasion, or of the Noonday Devil."

That meant that God was watching and protecting at all hours, and in all dangers. But, again, those were only outside dangers—what about the terror that made its home inside?

When dawn came, she was stiff, cold, and weak. It took all her strength to crawl out from under the blanket and drink some water from the waterbag. Was she supposed to be fasting? Was she allowed to drink? Or was she just supposed to lie here, pray, wrestle with the demons, and die?

Holy men and women fasted. The prophets fasted. Queen Esther fasted before approaching the king, and Jonah had told the sinners of Nineveh to fast. God was supposed to look with favor on it. But surely there was a proper way to do it. Why had not the rabbi explained this? Simply going without food was not the same thing as fasting. Beggars went without food, and they did not call themselves the holier for it. They were anxious to end it, and anyone who fed them was doing a good deed.

She tore off a piece of the dry bread and ate it ravenously. She could taste each little grain in it, or so it seemed. She was ashamed to be so hungry, but she could not even remember her last normal meal. She stretched out her arm and was not surprised to see how scrawny it looked. With her bald head and thin form, she would not be recognizable as the Mary who was the pride of her husband and accounted a handsome woman in Magdala. No, this poor creature looked as if she belonged with the vultures and scorpions in the wastelands. Even a vulture could not look on her with desire.

She ate another morsel of bread and broke off part of the fig cake. It was thick and rich and seemed to stick in her throat. She washed it down with the water.

And now that I am sustained a little, she told God, of my own free will I will renounce food until you send me a sign—until you deliver me or purge me. I will wait on you, and will not stir forth to do anything until you reach down your hand and rescue me.

But the words from the Torah, "You shall not put the Lord your God to the test, as you tested him in Massah," suddenly rang out in her mind.

I do not seek to test you, she told him, but only humbly beg for a sign.

She sat quietly, wrapping her mantle around her, and sought to find quiet within. I have come to the end of all remedies, she told herself. Here, alone and with nothing, I cry out for help, and if there is none, then at least I know what awaits. There was peace in that, of a sort.

The dawn had long since passed; now the sun was climbing overhead, and the shadows inside the cave were deeper. Still she sat, trying to hold herself motionless, trying to keep her mind in readiness for combat. So she was not at all prepared when a little whisper came to her, saying, "It is all no use at all, you know. No use. It is foolishness and a chasing after wind, as scripture says. All that you do is foolish and fated to disappear; it amounts to nothing."

The thought—for it seemed to her like a thought, and an eminently reasonable one—came in through the portals of her mind that were guarded against more obvious and unruly intruders.

"This place is useless," it murmured. "It is hateful. Everyone has deserted you and led you to undertake these exercises for no purpose at all. In the meantime, your child languishes and misses you, and your husband looks elsewhere and judges that you were not a good wife. There is no good in anyone anywhere; if someone seems to suggest some course of action, it is to please his own vanity only. Leave this pursuit. It is hopeless."

She looked up at the sun. It seemed not to have moved at all. This day was interminable; it stretched out for a lifetime, with no ending.

"But you can end yourself," it whispered to her. "Here you are, poised over the rocky ground below. End it; end the striving and foolish life that you are wrestling with. This is how it will end in any case: in solitary death and no answers at all, only pain and wasted effort."

She looked down at the rock-strewn floor of the canyon, with its occasional twisted trees and scrub poking up. If she flung herself off in a wide arc, she would fall right down, no smashing on the way, no hitting, no bouncing, just a clean fall and a broken neck and the vultures rustling their wings.

The sun was now directly overhead, and there were no shadows at all. No shadows. Noon. The Noonday Demon—was this what they meant? "Thou shalt not be afraid of the Noonday Devil," the scripture said. This feeling of utter despair, of defeat, of knowing that all attempts were worse than pitiful, did not even exist—could this be the Noonday Demon? But it was so different from the other ones, so subtle and ill-defined. It did not seem alien at all, but part of her very own mind.

The Noonday Demon: striking at the very heart of life and action, draining it away, telling her to end her life. It sounded so reasonable when it suggested that she throw herself off the cliff.

And now she could almost see it, could visualize the demon of the hours of highest activity: it was a worm that entered into the heart of effort, a chancre that rotted existence from within, that sapped the very spirit of life at its source.

The Noonday Demon had entered into her. Now she was captive to five demons: all so different, all so unique in their torments. So coming here to the desert served only to attract more.

Demon, I give you a name, she said. Despair. For you are the very demon of utter despair, and you have entered into my soul.

The sun now moved—extremely slowly, almost held back by this demon—down through the sky, drawing the day nearer to a close.

In the growing gloom, the canyon and crevices below turned violet and then purple, and it seemed to her that there must be many spirits down there.

I know I have an affinity for seeing spirits, she thought, for did I not see Bilhah's ghost in my own home, in my own mind? But the dark spirits, the ones that are lingering in Sheol, the shades that know nothing and are only shadows—do these shadows down below echo them, somehow?

She was very hungry. All her vows and prayers did not manage to quell appetites. "But I promised," she said out loud. "I promised, and I will keep my promise."

It was dark. She would sleep: sleep to keep hunger, and fear, at bay. She moved slowly into the cave, spread out her covering, and lay down. It was dark, a deep-black darkness that seemed infinite. Yet it seemed entirely right that she be there in this utter darkness; her life in Magdala, living in the sunlight, marrying, celebrating Passover, all seemed a dream. This is what she was meant for, this was where she belonged: ravaged, shorn, hungry, lying on a cold blanket in a cave in the middle of the wilderness, with unseen presences and unnamed menaces surrounding her.

Were there bats in the cave? She could hear the rustling of their wings. Or the rustling of *some* wings. Did she sleep? Or wake?

The next morning, she opened her eyes to see a huge carrion bird perched at the edge of the crumbling ledge outside the cave. He had a curved beak and a wrinkled, naked head, and feathers that glistened and shone with a malevolent iridescence, even though there was no sun. The feathers seemed to pulsate and expand as she looked at them.

She pulled herself up on one elbow and squinted to see the bird. He cocked his head and looked back at her.

She was terribly thirsty. She tried to stand up and felt dizzy, so she just crawled on all fours to the waterbag and took a long, deep drink. The bird did not move or seem threatened by this in the least. He just kept looking at her.

She wiped her cracked lips with the back of her hand. The eye of the bird seemed to fasten on her, and she became aware for the first time how strong he must be. His eye glinted, and he seemed to flex his talons, and they were ugly, huge, splayed things. He bristled up a bit and puffed his feathers, and they seemed almost to glow.

He opened his beak, and an odd sound came out—not a croak but a cry of desire. It sounded so obscene coming from this creature that she recoiled. He hopped two hops closer to her, and now she could hear the heaviness of his body as his feet moved.

She picked up a rock to throw at him; he was eyeing her resting place and fluffing his feathers once again, as if he would move. He must not come closer; no, she would not have that. She could see he was larger than could be safe for her; he was almost the size of a lamb, although that seemed impossible. But his shadow marked the size, and he was enormous.

She threw the rock, and it struck the bird but seemed to glance off his back. It barely disturbed the feathers. And now the creature was angry, and he turned his fierce head and vicious beak in her direction and hopped over to her, spreading his dreadful wings. She had no weapon, but she took up a gnarled stick from the pile Andrew had gathered for her and held it up like a club.

With an angry squawk, the bird lifted up and flew at her, his talons outstretched. She flung herself down so he would miss, but his aim was unerring. She smashed at his talons with the makeshift club, but it barely deflected him. And now his claws were digging into her shoulder and his beak was trying to tear at her flesh, and she could smell the foul smell of all the carrion that had passed through his mouth and now wafted from him like an open grave. It was the stink of rotten goat-meat, the stench of a dead rat decomposing, the fumes from raw sewage mixed with fish guts that people dumped to be burned. The bird himself seemed to be composed of putrid flesh, for when she grabbed his scrawny neck, her hand sank into a slimy mess. Under the feathers was complete corruption and decomposition.

The bird was not real. No known creature was made up of dead flesh.

That frantic realization came as she fought to keep the bird's beak from her eyes, where he was trying to stab and peck. Her hand squeezed on the neck, but it was nothing but tendons and slime, and her fingers passed through it and closed on each other.

But none of the others was touchable like this one, she cried to herself. They were all spirits that came and whispered and swirled around me like smoke, but nothing—

The bird's putrid odor was enveloping her, making her feel faint and nauseated. She felt her fingers slipping away from his neck, felt her feet kicking at his hard, feathered underbelly, but her feet sank into it, into that mass of rotting jelly. She could not pull them out. She would be absorbed into him.

"I am all things foul and doomed," the beak was saying. "I am Rabisu, the Croucher of Horrible Aspect."

The form of Rabisu—no one knew what he looked like, or even really what he did. But had not the rabbi mentioned him? Warned her against him?

The beak plunged and seemed to sink itself into her breast. She saw the hideous slickness of it, the wattles shining like spilled guts, the bald head plunging downward.

The pain was searing, the beak as sharp as a spear. The baleful, gleaming eye rotated and looked calmly at her, as if it would fix her with its glare. It seemed to have no pupil at all, but was black, black, black.

And then . . . as it slid into her, smoothly, like a diver going into water, the pain ceased, and she heard nothing, and she fainted on her blanket.

· · ·

Noon. The sun was directly overhead again, and she opened her eyes. At first she did not know where she was or what had happened, but then it all rushed back. She gasped and was surprised that her chest was not split open. Gingerly she put out her hand and touched herself, expecting to find a huge wound. There was nothing. Not even a trace.

But the vulture! She looked quickly to see if there were marks of his feet, and, sure enough, there were several, both on the ledge and then in a fateful sequence coming over to where she lay. Big, wide footprints, each unmistakably with three large talons.

She gulped to breathe and to calm her racing heart. The bird—another demon. But where was he? Where had he gone?

As soon as she framed the words to herself, she knew. He had joined the others. Had she not seen him actually entering into her?

"Yes, that's right," his voice—wavering as if he was decomposing and melting—now spoke for the first time from within her. "I am here. I came because the others called me, and said you made a fine home for them. We like company, and we often call our fellows when we find a good host."

Who are you? she could ask it. She was not afraid any longer; she was past fear; what difference did it make if she spoke to it?

"You named me correctly," it said. "You called my name once in your mind. Do you not remember? Try."

She had called no name, except . . . the Croucher.

"Yes, that is it. But you named my proper name," it reminded her sternly. "Names are very important. Names confer power. Names differentiate. Name my real name. Come, come. You know it."

"Rabisu," she whispered.

"Yes," the voice said caressingly, like a lover, and as she heard it, she almost smelled the stench of decay, as if the voice was decay itself.

"You who led Cain into destruction," she said.

"Yes! So you have met me in the Torah," the voice said. "Very good. You know I am ancient, and you know what I have done and the curses I have brought on mankind. Among demons I am most venerable and honored."

She could hear the rustling of pride in his acknowledgment.

"The Torah says little about you," she said. "It barely mentions you. All it says is, 'Then the Lord said to Cain, "Why are you so angry and cast down? If you do well, you are accepted; if not, sin is a demon crouching at the door. It shall be eager for you, and you will be mastered by it." ' "

"And I did," it said. "I mastered him and he killed his brother, and you know what sorrow that led to."

"Are you here to kill me, too?" To meet the end at last seemed welcome. She had indeed come to the end of her resources, to the end of her hope. This last hope, to fast and purify herself in the desert, had led only to more demons. She was too weak to fight them off, and now there were so many more of them than there were of her, and, as Rabisu said, they all called to each other and invited more of their own kind. No, there was only one escape from this.

I suppose Simon and Andrew will come and find me, and then they can tell Joel and . . . this torture and siege will be ended at last, she thought.

"Perhaps," Rabisu murmured. "Killing is what we all do best, and we like it."

Then do so! she challenged it. She was ready. But nothing happened.

She sat and waited, hunched over, leaning against the rock. There were so many presences within her that she felt like a rotting animal swarming with maggots, as if Mary of Magdala was just a shell to contain Ashara, the blasphemous voice, Pazuzu, Heket, the Noonday Demon, and Rabisu. They all seethed within; they swelled her out as would a child in the womb, except that, unlike a child, they were everywhere, invading her very being.

Did they talk to each other? Quarrel? Discuss her? She had no idea what they did; they did not speak to her except to torment her, and she could not overhear their conversations with one another.

I am as destroyed as a moth-eaten cloak, a cloak that falls apart if it is held up, Mary admitted to herself. I am only a container for evil. And so I must die, here, far from where I can cause any harm. The rabbi was right to send me here.

Each of the presences came and teased her as the hours passed, whispering her name, reminding her that they were there. She had learned that each had a distinctive voice, and so she did not need to ask each one to identify itself.

"Rabisu, you need trouble yourself with me no longer," she whispered. "I am nothing; I have ceased to exist. Crouching before my door is fruitless. I have no door; the only door I have is the door of death, and that I will enter, but not emerge from."

The sun swung overhead, and the shadows changed in the landscape all around, while Mary sat like a statue.

. . .

There was another night. Another time to sleep—or, rather, to lie down. All the hours were blending. She tried to pray, but no words came to her, and she was too weak. She lay on the pallet and closed her eyes.

Just before dawn, at the hour that changed from night itself to earliest morning, the stars were still bright overhead, and a waxing moon was sliding down the sky, making half-shadows on the rocks. Mary saw this from where she lay, weak and listless. Then she saw a movement at the edge of the little ledge, a sort of shimmering and jostling. A thousand tiny bodies were coming up over the lip of the cliff.

She sat upright and stared at them. She could feel her arm shaking; it was almost too weak to lean on. She dragged herself over closer so she could see better. The moonlight shone on the surging little army that was pouring over the rim.

Locusts. Their hard, shiny armor, their waving little antennae above their head, their massive jaws . . . Mary had seen locusts before, and she knew them. But these! Their eyes were huge, reflecting the moonlight in hundreds of little prisms, and their hind legs seemed to be gigantic. They could hop enormous distances, and one of them did just that, landing far inside the cave. Some others followed suit. But the main army of them just kept pouring over the edge, coming forward.

Locusts. There could be no locusts here. There was no food for them. This was the desert. But when she heard the click and grind of their armor as they marched, she realized that, like all the creatures who had visited her in the desert, they were not real. They were another manifestation of the demonic.

She tried to back away from them, but she had no strength. And where could she go? They would follow her even to the end of the cave. So: stand here and meet them. There could be no deliverance.

And she no longer cared. Was this the work of the Noonday Demon, who taught her that everything was useless? Or was it just that she no longer could flee, or had anyplace to flee to? She had come to the end of herself, and the last place of refuge. There was no refuge. There was only this feebly moonlit cliff and whatever was coming toward her.

The shiny army of locusts swarmed across the rock, and she put out her hand and touched one: it was hard and cold. So she pulled herself as far back as her strength would allow her, and braced herself. And, yes, now they reached the hem of her garment, now they were crawling over her knees. They started eating her robe, chomping it with their quick jaws. They devoured her blanket. They stripped her of her tunic, and now she was naked, and there was no blanket or covering anywhere. It was bitterly cold, and the cold bodies of the locusts could do nothing to keep the cold at bay. She shook and shivered and screamed.

But now she could see that they did not all look like locusts. Some had human faces, and their hair was like human hair, but they had lions' teeth. They even had breastplates. And the sound of their wings! The sound of their wings was like the thundering of chariots. And their tails had scorpions' stings in them, held aloft to strike.

Then a figure appeared on the ledge. It did look like a locust, but it was the size of a man. Like some of the other locusts, it had a human face and wore a breastplate. And the tail, curled around, circled a stinger that was as large as a sword.

The locusts stopped moving when he appeared, as though they were waiting for directions. And he gave them, in a thundering voice.

"I am Abaddon, your king! And I command you to destroy this woman!"

The locusts swarmed over her. She was enveloped in the surprisingly heavy blanket of them, which felt like metal. But she would not be taken this way! She crawled over to Abaddon and grabbed at his stinger. She wrenched it around and poised it to aim at her breast.

"You destroy me," she whispered. "Not your minions."

She could feel the tail quivering, feel the stinger readying itself.

"How dare you ask anything of me?" Abaddon snarled.

"I dare because I will fight to the very last of my strength," said Mary.

"Strength? You have no strength. It is all gone. Now surrender to my army."

"No, that I shall never do." Her earlier resignation had vanished under the onslaught from Abaddon; a last bit of strength now came to her from somewhere beyond herself.

"You must. There is no other place where you may turn."

"Yes, there is. I will have a clean death, and it will not be brought about by you or your legions."

She released her grip on Abaddon and dragged herself over to the edge of the ledge.

Down below were the rocks. They would welcome her, and it would still be a victory over the forces sent to vanquish her.

"I rule the Abyss," said Abaddon. "There is no escape from my power."

"This is not the mystical Abyss but an ordinary cliff," said Mary. "And you do not rule it."

She hung over the edge, looking at the long fall below. It would be final. She did not want to die, but she wanted to kill the evil that was within her.

With all her strength, she pulled herself to her feet. Though she was so weak she could hardly stand up, she stood swaying over the long empty space beneath her and said a broken prayer.

God, be merciful to my soul, and remember that I chose to die rather than harbor these unclean spirits any longer.

Then, summoning up the last of her strength, she flung herself off the cliff.

∞ X X ∞

She fell. She could feel the wind rushing past; it was far enough to the bottom that there was time to see the stones on the cliffs fleetingly and feel as if she were flying.

But then the ground loomed up around her. It was no matter; it was all over. Suddenly she hit first a large tree that was growing out the side of the cliff, then a rock, and finally the floor of the canyon. She lay very still.

It was with supreme hope that she opened her eyes. She expected to see something unfamiliar, and to know that she was dead, that it was over. To see Sheol—a dark place of shades, departed spirits who wandered. To see Hades—flames and more shades. But no. Before her eyes were crumbling desert rocks and some struggling plants. A curious lizard was looking at her, cocking its head back and forth.

I am still here, she thought. And then she knew true despair. I do not have the strength to climb up again and try another leap.

Wretchedly she sat up, felt her arms and legs, and touched her head—bald, sore, but not bleeding. Though she was badly bruised, nothing seemed to have been broken.

A miracle? No, why would God want to preserve this demon-ridden body? It was the demons who had done it. It was her final defiance of Abaddon that had challenged him to best her. Or had God decided that he wanted her to live?

She was naked. There was nothing to cover herself with. The Locusts of the Abyss had seen to that. But she had to leave this place. She would go where Simon and Andrew had said they were going. She must tell them what had happened. And there she could finally end herself. If this holy man, the Baptist, was preaching there, then he would keep the spirits at bay long enough to enable her to do what she must.

She pulled herself up on a rock, her arms shaking. She would follow the sun, would go toward the spot that they had told her about.

She picked a path through the floor of the canyon, but each boulder she had to pass seemed like a far frontier, and she barely had the strength to edge forward.

When the sun went down she stopped. She huddled by a rock for warmth, and since it reflected some of her own feeble body heat, she survived until morning. In the darkest hour, she could hear the scuffling sound of an animal's paws nearby, knew she would be defenseless in case of an attack. But the noises faded away, and she was spared.

The next morning, she again pulled herself along from rock to rock, sometimes crawling on the rough ground and sometimes using the rocks to steady her and allow her to stand upright. The sun beat down and blistered her badly bruised and naked body.

In a fog of passing time, she approached a stream and knew that this was probably near the place that Simon and Andrew had spoken of. She sank down and drank from it. The water, warm from flowing through the desert, was like a nourishing broth. She drank and drank, then plunged her hands in and washed her filthy arms.

As she waited for a bit of strength to come back to her, she wondered which way she should follow the stream. It seemed more promising to go toward the distant cliffs. And so she stumbled along, following the rocky bed of the little stream as it flowed toward the Jordan, which she could see glinting in the distance.

Rounding a bend, she suddenly saw the place: where the stream widened out and merged with the Jordan, a large crowd of people had gathered. Some sat on the rocks, some stood at a distance, but most were close by the banks of the Jordan.

A man was standing in the running water, crying out with a hoarse voice. "I am the voice of one crying out in the wilderness, make straight the way of the Lord!" He had waded out until the water was lapping around his knees, and was surrounded by listeners, also knee-deep.

"You seek the baptism of repentance!" he shouted, but not just to them, to everyone. "Repentance! That word means that you change your ways and walk in the exact opposite direction!" He swung around, fastening his gaze on a new group. "You! Soldiers!" He pointed at uniformed Romans standing stiffly on a nearby rock. "This is what I say to you: No more accusing people falsely! No more extorting money! I say, you must be content with your pay!"

A group of men started to wade out toward the shouting man. They were well dressed, in contrast to the rough tunic of animal skins the preacher wore.

"Teacher," they called, "what shall we do?"

"Tax collectors!" the man cried. "As for you, do not collect any more than you are entitled to."

"Yes, yes!" they said, making their way to him. They knelt down in the running water and bowed their heads. He put his arms around them, one at a time, and lowered them beneath the water.

"Be baptized with the water of repentance," the man said each time he performed the rite, and one by one the people were baptized. For each he had an admonition, spoken privately.

Then another man waded forward. Mary could see that he was sturdy and had pleasing features, but that did not account for the responses of the baptizer, who seemed to recognize him and was taken aback. They looked long at one another and spoke words she could not hear, and then the man was baptized and waded back out of the water. Both he and the baptizer paused for a moment; then the man continued wading back ashore and disappeared.

Mary suddenly became acutely aware that she was naked. People were staring at her, and she was deeply ashamed, although she had thought she was past all shame. Fearfully she approached a woman who was waiting on the rocks and asked if, in the name of charity, she might have a covering. The woman gladly gave it, and Mary wrapped it around herself.

This place must be—it had to be—the site of John the Baptist. Mary looked around to see if she could find Simon or Andrew, but she saw no familiar faces. The crowd was quite large; she had been told that the Baptist drew people from great distances. What could the Baptist offer *her*? Repentance? That was a stage she had long ago passed. Simple repentance had availed her nothing. The Baptist was for people who lived ordinary lives, not for her. A tax collector who had cheated—yes, the Baptist could help him. A soldier who abused his authority—yes, that could be addressed by the Baptist. But she was far beyond that.

"You broods of vipers!" he was yelling at a group of Pharisees gathered across the river. "How can you expect to escape the coming fire? I tell you, the ax is already laid to the root of the tree, and every tree that does not bring forth good fruit will be cut down and thrown into the fire!"

She looked around at the crowd. Nowhere did she see Andrew or Simon.

She sat down on a rock, pulling the covering up over her head. She must keep looking for them, must give them the message for Joel before she went out into the wasteland again, alone, where it would—where it must—all end.

Suddenly, late in the afternoon, she saw them. They were with that man who had earlier been baptized and spoken at length with John, and several others were in a little knot around him. She hated to approach them in front of others, but she had no choice. Slowly and painfully she hobbled over to them and tugged on Simon's tunic. He whirled around. He stared.

"Oh! Most holy name! Mary!"

She could see that, in one glance, in one instant, he understood that it had been a failure. That all remedies had proved useless. And now there were no others to try.

"I was continually attacked, I had to flee." She reached out weakly for his hand. "Simon, I know what I must do. But I wished to see you, so that you might tell Joel what has happened, so that he will always know."

There. She had said it. Now she could go, make her final end. There was nothing further Simon could do for her.

Simon looked at her with deep sympathy. Slowly, he spoke to her. "Mary, we have found someone who—who will want to hear your story."

No! No. She had no strength to tell it again, and there was no purpose in it. She pulled away, sick with longing to escape.

But Simon held her by the shoulders and forced her into the circle surrounding the man she had seen earlier.

"Master," Simon said. "Can you help this woman?"

All Mary saw was a pair of sandals on feet that were strong and well formed. She dared not raise her eyes. She did not want to look at anyone, or have anyone look at her.

"What torments you?" the man was asking.

But she could not explain. It was too difficult, too involved, she had told it too many times already, and now she knew there was no help for her from anyone.

"Can you not speak?" His voice was not unkind, but it was practical.

"I am too tired," she responded. Still she did not look up.

"I can see that you are exhausted," he said. "So I will only ask you: do you want to be made well?" But his voice was now hesitant, as if he asked the question reluctantly and was not sure he wanted an answer.

"Yes," she whispered. "Yes." If only those years could roll away, and it could be that she had never picked up Ashara!

The man came forward and pushed the covering from her head. She could feel the shock of the other onlookers that her hair was gone, but in this man she detected no surprise or notice of it. He placed his hands on her head. She felt his fingers gripping her skull, surrounding it, from the crown all the way over her ears.

She expected him to begin a long string of prayers, to invoke God's help and mercy, to recite scripture. Instead, he shouted out, in a searing voice, "Come out of her, you evil spirit!"

She felt a wrenching inside.

"What is your name?" the man commanded it.

"Ashara," a surprisingly meek voice answered.

"Leave her, depart, and return no more!"

She could actually feel the spirit leaving, fleeing from her.

"Pazuzu!" he called. "Depart from this woman!"

How did he know its name? Stunned, Mary looked up at him. All she saw was a jaw that was set. She could not see his face.

Pazuzu fled; she could feel his ugly presence slipping away.

"And you—the unclean blasphemer! Depart from this daughter of Israel that you torment! And never come again!"

With a tumbling mess of curses, that spirit came out of her.

"Heket!" The name rang out like a roll call; this man knew them all. "Depart!"

And once again Mary could feel the presence actually leaving, and could almost see a slim green shadow disappearing through a crevice of the rocks.

"The demon that haunts the noon hour," the man called out. "Come out of her!"

This was the hardest one so far; it seemed embedded in her mind, it seemed to have infiltrated her very thoughts, and when it lifted out, she felt as if she were floating.

"There are—there were—seven," Mary said,

"I know," he said. "Rabisu!" His voice was like a staff thumped on the ground.

Through her own lips Mary heard the spirit answer. "Yes?"

"Depart!"

Mary expected an argument from the fierce Rabisu, but he fled, slipping out.

"And now there is only Abaddon," said the man. "In some ways the most dangerous of all, for he is an angel, an emissary of Satan. His very name means 'destroyer.' He will lead the forces in the last great battle." He paused, and drew himself up. "Abaddon! Apollyon! I say to you, come out of her!"

The hideous form of the locust-man appeared for an instant where all could see, then vanished.

The man's hands were still on her head, and she was aware of his fingers. The spirits had rushed out between them. They were gone. They were truly gone. She felt as she had long ago, in her childhood, before they had come.

She clasped the man's hands on her head, covering them with her own. "It has been so many years," she started to say, then began sobbing.

The man bent down, took his hands from her head, and brought her to her feet by holding her elbows. "God can restore the lost years," he said. "Does not the prophet Joel say, 'And I will restore to you the years the locusts have eaten'?"

She laughed, a little unsteadily. "I don't like hearing the word 'locust.'"

"No, you must not. The Locusts of the Abyss—they are worse than any earthly locusts. What is your name?"

"Mary," she said. "Of Magdala."

She wanted to ask him questions, to ask his name, to find out how he could command these spirits so easily, but she dared not. And perhaps it was not done so easily: he seemed drained.

"I was not ready for this," he said to Simon. "Not so soon. But it is not for me to choose the hour."

He had a voice that one would never forget, and Mary had the feeling that she had heard it long ago.

What did he mean? Was he a holy man who had just taken vows?

"Mary," said Simon, his voice shaking with excitement, "this is Jesus. We just met him here, when we came to hear John, and it seems—we think—that he has—that he is" —the normally talkative Simon was floundering—"someone we may follow."

Follow? What did that mean? Listen to his lessons? Try to observe his teachings? Had Simon heard of this Jesus beforehand?

"I mean—we may leave our fishing and become his students, his followers. If he allows us to."

Leave their fishing? Leave their business? What would their families say? And what did they mean, allow them to? Did not the students choose their own teacher?

"Yes, we want to learn from him," said Andrew. "And there are others from Galilee who have come, and we will band together, and—"

"Our area?"

"I mean from the Galilee," said Simon. "Philip is here—he's from Bethsaida. He came to hear John the Baptist, too, but found this man instead. And his friend Nathanael, from Cana. That's four of us already!"

"All from Galilee?" Mary asked.

"Yes, and Jesus comes from Nazareth."

"Can anything good come out of Nazareth?" A thin, wavering voice rang out. Mary looked and saw that it belonged to a slight young man. "That's what I said. I said, 'Study the scriptures and you will see that no prophet comes from Nazareth.' But there is no doubting that this man is a true prophet. He knew what I was doing and who I was before he met me. He knew about your demons."

"Nathanael only doubted until he met Jesus," said Philip. "I took him and introduced him."

"I was not ready to begin," said Jesus. "But God has given me these followers. You do not choose me, but I chose you. Mary—I invite you to join us. God surely sent you to us here. A gift from God. I wish you to come with us."

Come with them—where? To do what? She was lightheaded from hunger, from all that had happened, from the sudden space inside her freed from the spirits.

"Mary, I invite you. Join with us." For the first time, she looked directly in the man's face. His eyes held hers. There was a whole new life there, and her former life seemed mysteriously nonexistent, like a dream that had faded.

"A woman?" was all she could ask, her feeble resistance to his invitation.

"A woman. A man. God created both. And he wishes both in his Kingdom." Jesus looked at her again. He was not pleading, he was not commanding, he was simply inviting her to look at him and decide. "It is time people become aware that there is no difference, in God's eyes, between them."

She wanted to go with them. She longed to go with them. It was insane. And yet—had she not already been declared insane, given up for dead?

"Yes," she said. "Yes, I shall come with you." For a short time, she thought. Only for a short time. That is all I can allow myself.

"Then I thank you," he said. "I thank you for letting others witness your private battle between good and evil within you. I wish that everyone gathered here"—he spread out his arms—"could have seen it. But they will see others. There will be many others, because the domain of Satan is large, and our fight against him constant.

"Come," he said to Mary. "Come with me." With a glance he stopped the others from crowding around; they fell back as if invisible hands were pushing them. "Bring her something to eat," he told them. "The demons did not allow her to eat, and she is starving."

Simon held out a tattered basket filled with bread, dried dates, and nuts. Jesus took it and then turned toward the cliffs on the far side of the Jordan, far from the noise of John the Baptist and his followers, guiding Mary. In her weakened state, she could not walk very fast and felt like an old woman as she tottered along, leaning on Jesus for support.

"Here," he said, making for a steep cliff face that threw deep shadows at its base. They settled themselves on the cool sand there, and Jesus handed her the basket. She just stared at it, helplessly. She felt weak, drained, even more than when she was crawling through the desert searching for Simon and Andrew. Now there was a lightness inside her, something empty that had once been filled. It made her dizzy.

Jesus tore off a piece of the bread for her, and put it in her hand. Slowly she brought it up to her mouth, began chewing. It was dry and tasted like leather.

"Here." Jesus held out a wineskin. "Drink."

Gratefully she held its opening up to her mouth and took huge deep gulps of the vinegary liquid. It surged through her with a jolt. Some of it ran out the corners of her mouth and fell, staining the stranger's cloak.

Choking, she wiped her mouth and looked at the spots on the cloak. It was the first time she had stained something by carelessness since she was a child.

"The demons have robbed me even of my manners," she said. A tiny attempt at a laugh escaped her, ending in a smile. Shakily, she took a date from the basket and bit into it.

"The demons have gone," said Jesus firmly. "Now it is hunger that has robbed you of your manners, and there is no shame in that."

He sat silently while she ate, even though she ate slowly.

It took all her effort just to chew the food and swallow it, and she could not watch the man who sat next to her, could not look at him or think about him. Only when she was finished, when she had eaten all her shrunken stomach would allow, did she lean back against the rock of the cliff and glance at him.

Jesus. They said his name was Jesus. It was a common name, one of the many popular versions of "Joshua." And where was he from? Someone had said Nazareth. She had hardly been listening. Nazareth. Jesus. There was something vaguely familiar about the way he was sitting, and the background of the rocks.

"You asked me to join you," she finally said, breaking the silence. "I do not—I do not understand. I am a married woman, with a baby daughter. My husband is waiting for me in our home in Magdala. How can I join you? And what would you have me do?" She paused. "I owe you everything. You have restored me to life, to normal life. But now you want me to leave it?"

"No," he said. "I am come that you, and everyone else, shall have a more abundant life."

"Is that your mission?" she asked. "When you approached John, it seemed that he already knew you. Are you a holy man?"

He burst out laughing. He threw his head back, and his head covering fell off, revealing his thick, dark hair. "No," he finally said. "No, I am not a holy man. I do not think God is to be found by withdrawing from the world, or in studying every syllable of scripture to tease out its meaning. When God speaks, he is usually clear." He turned and looked directly at her, a thing no man besides her husband ever did. "People do not like those clear directions, so they search for other, obscure ones that they can follow more easily."

If he was not a holy man, who was he? A prophet? Yet he had submitted, he had allowed himself to be baptized by another prophet. Perhaps he was just a magician with special powers.

"Who . . . who are you?" she finally asked.

"You will have to answer that for yourself," he said. "And you cannot know that until you have joined me, or at least followed me for a time." He looked at her again. "Now you need to tell me who *you* are."

Who was she? No one had ever asked her so baldly. She was Nathan's daughter, descendant of Huram of the tribe of Naphtali, who had fashioned the ancient Temple bronzeworks, Joel of Nain's wife, Elisheba's mother. She started to say all these things, but the words died away.

"Mary of Magdala," he commanded, "who are *you*? Put away your father, your ancestor, your husband, your daughter. Tell me what remains."

What did remain? Her reading, her languages, her friend Keziah, her secret daydreaming. Her feeling, however faint and wavering, of being called or chosen by God long ago. In trembling words, she tried to explain this to the first person who had ever asked her about it.

"I—I was forbidden to learn to read, but I found a way to take lessons. Later, my brother taught me Greek, and without permission I began to study the scriptures. I found a friend . . . a friend who was not bound by the rules of the group they call Pharisees, which my family belongs to. This friend . . . opened her home to me and welcomed me."

"A true act of love and charity," said Jesus. "Above all the tithing and obligations of the Pharisee."

"And I always felt that God had called me, or at least beckoned to me. And yet that faded away as I struggled with the demons. The demons all came about because of my disobedience!" Now her conversation turned into a confession. "My father warned me that if we traveled through Samaria there might be idols. He told me not even to look at any. But when I found one buried in the ground I—I picked it up!"

Jesus gave a dismissive laugh.

"But I kept it! I harbored it! Over the years I made many promises to destroy it, but I never did. It fell to my little nephew to do it, and by then it was too late."

"And that is how they entered in?" Jesus seemed vitally interested, but not condemning.

"I think so. I had it in my house for so long. It started attacking when I was still a child. But I did not recognize it, did not have the strength to destroy it." She decided to be bold and admit all the truth. This man had delivered her, after all. Why hold anything back? "I even married an innocent man to escape it." She caught her breath and went on. "I thought my father's home was contaminated, and I needed to flee. I did not see that the contamination was within me."

"It was not within you, but it was following you as flies follow a pail of pure fresh milk," said Jesus. "You must never think of yourself as contaminated. Never!"

"How could I help it? The demons made me dirty. And all those rules about cleanliness and uncleanliness, which consider a woman twice as dirty as a man in the course of nature, also told me I was contaminated." What was she saying? Talking about such disgusting things to a stranger, a *male* stranger. She reached out and touched his sleeve. That, too, was forbidden, among the strict religious, at least. She might as well commit more forbidden acts, right here and now. She found it did not feel wicked but natural.

"Those rules cause only anger and sorrow," he finally said.

"But Moses gave them to us!" That was the hard part. How could one ignore that?

"He did not mean for them to be interpreted so narrowly," said Jesus. "Of that I am certain. The human drives to lie, to envy, to be violent are within us, and do contaminate us—not the things ordained of nature in their season."

How could he be certain? "But you have just said that you are not a holy man—I mean, not someone who has spent time studying these things—so how can you know this?"

"My Father in heaven has revealed it to me," he said, his voice firm.

He was one of those strange wanderers, then, thought Mary. The ones who believe they have had a revelation. He has no authority to pronounce on religious matters after all. As comforting as his words are, they carry no authority. But the demons—he drove them out when no one else could. They listened to him when they ignored the holy man.

"You are troubled," said Jesus. "Do not be. Someday you will understand. For now, I only ask you to follow me."

"But I have already explained . . ."

"Perhaps you can follow me without leaving home," he said.

How could that be? She wanted to argue, but the suggestion pleased her so much she did not want to question it further.

The shadows had begun lengthening when they rose to return to the Jordan. Jesus had asked her many questions; only when they made ready to leave did she realize he had told her little about himself. She still knew only that he had come from Nazareth. She also knew that she was reluctant to give him back to the others so soon.

No one had ever talked to her that way, wishing to know what she thought, how she felt, how she had come to be as she was. He was not interested—indeed, he forbade her even to explain about—Nathan, his business and its situation, Joel, or even her daughter. He wanted to know only about Mary, the woman of Magdala, twenty-seven years old. What had she done with the twenty-seven years? What did she intend to do with the remaining ones granted her by God? Whenever she had mentioned her "duty," he had touched her lips with his fingers. Another forbidden thing, but it made his gesture all the stronger.

"What will *you* do?" he had insisted.

After the demons . . . after the demons . . . my life is my own, she thought. It was a miracle.

She was still feeling lightheaded, in spite of the food, but she recognized it now as freedom, as deliverance. The demons were gone!

They made their way back to the Jordan, but by now the crowds had scattered and the Baptist was no longer preaching. Mary wondered where he had gone. Did he have a cave he retreated to at the end of each day?

"John is no longer here," she said to Jesus.

"He has withdrawn to his shelter, with his disciples," said Jesus. "He will spend the evening teaching them, far into the night, until everyone falls asleep." They were passing several tents with people already gathering and making their fires.

"Even in Magdala, we heard of John," she said.

"What did you hear?" asked Jesus.

"Some people thought he was the Messiah, others that he was just another wild prophet," she said. "I know many people are thinking about the Messiah. Could it be that John is the one they are awaiting?"

"No," said Jesus. "Did you not hear him say plainly that he was not the Messiah?"

"I was not there," said Mary. In the brief time she had seen him, he had not spoken of that. "All I heard him say was that people should repent and abandon their former ways." She paused. "That is why I knew he could not help me. I had already abandoned everything, and repented."

Jesus stopped walking. "John starts people at the beginning, but there is much more beyond that. The spirit of truth will reveal it to you." The dark was falling swiftly.

But how could one know the spirit of truth? Was it not easy to be deceived? They resumed walking; a bit of strength was returning to Mary, and she moved faster.

How could she trust this Jesus? All the proof she had that he knew things, that he spoke the truth, was his power over the demons: no small matter. She wanted to ask him how he could speak to his father in heaven—by that she presumed he meant God—and how he could discern the answers. But she did not, because it seemed ungrateful to do so. The demons were gone. She kept rejoicing in that, reveling in it, marveling in it, and that meant more to her than knowing the means by which they had been cast out.

It was almost full dark before they reached the Jordan and forded its shallows. Simon and the others were waiting. Mary could no longer see their faces in the dark, so she could not read their mood.

"Come, let us make ready for the night." Jesus motioned them to leave the riverbanks and follow him into the growing shadows.

He had a lean-to nestled in the shelter of the rocks. A cliff face served as one wall, with draped blankets creating the other three. He motioned for them to enter, and the four men and Mary pushed past the makeshift entrance flap and came into the place that Jesus called home.

It was close and dark. Jesus followed them and set a lighted lamp on a rock, and the feeble light showed only that the room was as rough as the cave Mary had come from. The floor was uneven dirt, and there was nothing inside but a few moth-eaten folded things that could be either carpets or blankets.

"Welcome," said Jesus, sitting down and inviting them to do likewise. "Philip, when you asked about me, I said to come and see. I brought you here. What did you see?"

Philip, a thin man whose biggest feature was his bushy hair, started. "I—I—I found an answer to every question I asked," he said.

"And for me, that is no mean feat. I can say, truthfully, that this is the only time it has ever happened."

"And why is that?" asked Jesus.

"Because I ask so many questions," said Philip, with a nervous laugh. "And people get tired of answering them."

"Can you tell the others the questions you asked?"

"Of course," he said. "I asked you where you had come from, and why you were here, and I asked you questions about Moses and the Law."

"And the answers?" asked Jesus. "Forgive me, but I don't wish to repeat them. Besides, the only important thing is what others heard, not what I said."

"I cannot repeat your exact words," said Philip. "But you said things that made me feel you . . . you had . . ." He shook his head. "Perhaps it was only my own feelings, my own desire that such a person as you would come to Israel now, when we most need you."

"Such a person?" asked Jesus. "What do you mean?" He was persistent, pursuing Philip.

"I mean . . . there has been much talk of the end times, of the Messiah."

"Ah. The Messiah." Jesus looked around at all of them. "And are you all searching for the Messiah?"

Simon was the first to answer. "I never really thought about him," he admitted.

Jesus smiled at that answer. Mary thought he was even suppressing a laugh.

Andrew cleared his throat. "It's not that we never *thought* about him," he said. "Everyone was brought up with the idea that someone would rescue us. Our father taught it to us along with the casting of our fishing nets."

"Rescue you?" asked Jesus. "Rescue you from what?"

Andrew looked down as if ashamed. "From the Romans, I suppose," he finally said.

Jesus looked at the other three, who had not yet spoken.

Nathanael, dark and nervous, stood up. "It's more than that," he said. "We want a national savior, someone not just for this time but for the future. The Messiah will usher in a golden age, an age when—oh, what is the common saying?—'God will wipe away all tears.' We want it all to stop—the evil, the sins, the pain. When the Messiah comes, that will happen." It seemed an immense effort for him to speak all those words, to string them together like a necklace, and by the end he was stammering. He sat back down.

Jesus said softly, "Behold an Israelite indeed, in whom there is no guile!"

What did he mean by that? Nathanael looked at Jesus, puzzled.

Finally, Simon cleared his throat and spoke. "Look, everything's wrong," he said. "God's chosen people are crushed under the boot of Rome. There is no meaning to it. When we were captive in Babylon, the prophets Isaiah and Jeremiah foretold it and interpreted what it meant. But what's happening today, it makes no sense, unless we just admit that we are not chosen by God, that we are just another people, a small people in a big world, and this is what happens to little people in a big world."

"Is that truly what you believe?" asked Jesus.

"What else can I believe?" Simon cried. "The evidence is all around me!" He shook his head. "Oh, the dreamers and the hotheads think otherwise, but any sensible man can see how the land lies. We are finished as a country, as a power in any way whatsoever. All we can hope is that people will tramp through our land without destroying us."

"Mary?"

It was the first time she had ever been asked her opinion among a roomful of men. Not expecting it, she had not even thought of an answer.

"I—I cannot say," she finally murmured.

"Oh, I think you can," said Jesus. "Please, tell us what you think. What do you think of the idea of a Messiah, and are you searching for him?"

"I—I think I have found him," she blurted out.

Jesus looked dismayed, almost horrified. "Why?" he said, his voice soft.

With the strength she did not know she possessed, Mary stood up. Her legs were still shaky, but she commanded them to stop trembling and they obeyed. She held her head up, her bald head. The modest head covering had been lost back in the battle with the locusts, and she no longer cared. No, more than that: she was proud of her sheared head, symbol of her fight with the demons.

"To me, the Messiah is he who can rout the forces of darkness," she said. "And if anyone knows those forces, it is I. I fought them for years, was their lover for years—yes, I loved my demons, until they turned on me!—and they were stronger than any other force I could summon against them. Until now. Isn't the Messiah given powers to defeat them? What else can I know?"

"Ah, Mary," said Jesus, and his voice was tinged with sadness. "You are like the person who follows someone only because he can give bread, or water, or money. I pray you may come to have another reason to follow."

What other reason could there be? Mary thought, taking her place again on the floor. He had power over the demons—was that not enough?

Simon stood up. His big, muscular body seemed to fill the room. "I don't know—I don't know about the Messiah. Isn't that for the scribes and those little hunched men in Jerusalem? The ones who spend all their time arguing about the tense of some passage in a verse of scripture? Look, I can barely read, and what I read is fishing reports and records. But I'm not stupid. It's the scribes and scholars who are stupid. I can't respect them. They say nothing that an ordinary person can understand, and furthermore—they don't stand up to the Romans!"

"In what way would you have them stand up to the Romans, Simon?" asked Jesus.

"They should condemn them!" Simon said. "Like the Baptist does! Instead, they just bury their noses in ancient texts and mumble about the Messiah." He coughed. "For that reason, because he belongs to *those* people, I don't care about the Messiah. If he came, I would just turn my back!"

Jesus burst out laughing. "You would, would you? And how would you know him if you saw him?"

"He comes in the clouds," said Simon. "It says so, in the book of Daniel."

"So, unless someone comes in the clouds, you cannot imagine he would be the Messiah?" asked Jesus.

"No," said Simon. "It is best to stick with scripture."

"Ah, Simon—will you never budge?" said Jesus, affectionately. "Are you that immovable? I see you are misnamed. Simon means 'hearing,' but I think you should be named 'Peter' for the rock that you are."

"Peter! Yes, that's right, for he has a hard head, too," said his brother, Andrew.

Jesus seemed disturbed by the answers he had been given about the Messiah. But had he not asked for them? They were only being honest, thought Mary. And why did he scold her about her reason for following? What other, stronger reason could she have? He had driven out her demons when no one else could, and delivered her from their bondage. Of course she wanted to follow, in case they came back, but after that . . .

Most people will follow him for the benefits he can give them. Is that so terribly wrong? She felt defensive. The truth is, people want the Messiah to give them something, they don't really want to give *him* anything, she thought. Why should a Messiah need *us* to help him?

When it was time for them to rest, she sank down on the smooth ground in the shelter. She lay directly on the hard earth, but it did not bother her. She slept for the first time since the demons were gone, and it was a different sleep, a sleep she had sought for long years.

PART TWO

Disciple

✦ XXI ✦

The next day, even larger crowds gathered to hear John. Jesus and his group also stood and listened, and Mary saw Jesus nodding, particularly when John mentioned the coming Kingdom. But when he talked about the winnowing fork separating out the chaff to be burned in unquenchable fire, the ferocious cataclysm and judgment awaiting the world, Jesus seemed to grow uncomfortable.

"I tell you, the one to come will come in anger and with his sword in hand! He is far more powerful than I. I baptize you with water, but he shall baptize you with fire! With the Holy Spirit!" John cried. "Do not think you will escape the coming fire! Repent!"

He had waded out into the fast-flowing Jordan and stood defiantly braced, craning his neck around to see everyone gathered on the banks. No one would escape his attention.

"Make straight the highway of the Lord!" he called out.

Just then a contingent of Jewish soldiers appeared on the rim of the riverbank. "Are you John, the one called Baptist?" their commander shouted.

For a moment John just stared. He was used to being the only one yelling. Then he said, "Indeed I am! And I tell you, that you too must repent and—"

"It's not for you to tell *us* anything, you fool, but for us to tell you!" the commander shot back. "And here is what we are telling you: unless you cease attacking Herod Antipas, you will be under arrest."

John cocked his head. He had wild, matted hair and a beard that looked almost as rough as the skins he wore. "And have you come from him?"

"We were sent by the king, sent to warn you."

"Then it seems our duties are reversed: it is my job to warn Antipas, not the other way around. As a prophet, I have messages from

God, messages that I am charged to deliver, whether he would hear them or no." John glared at them.

"He's heard them once, he's heard them twice, now cease. The king is not deaf."

"It seems he is, for he is proceeding with his incestuous marriage anyway."

"Cease! It's you who are deaf. This is your last warning." The soldiers stared down at John from their vantage point.

"Come and be baptized!" John called. "It is not too late to repent!"

With a snort of disgust, the commander turned, and his men seemed to vanish behind the grasses on the riverbank.

"He is a brave man," Mary heard Jesus say to Simon—now "Peter."

Simon Peter nodded. "Braver than I am."

"Now, perhaps. How brave someone is changes. It is not a fixed thing, like a man's height or eye color."

"I tell you!" John shouted. "Produce fruit in keeping with repentance! For every tree that does not produce good fruit will be cut down and thrown into the fire!"

"What shall we do, then?" the crowd cried. "Tell us! Tell us!"

John spread out his arms. "The man with two tunics should share with him who has none, and the man with food should do the same."

Taking his words literally, everyone began looking around, and it was not long before a woman was almost forcing Mary to take her extra tunic and mantle. She was moved to tears by the woman's kindness.

She looked at Jesus, wondering what he thought of John's command, and was startled to see that Jesus had a strange preoccupied look on his face. He was staring in the direction of John, but did not seem to be really seeing him.

"My friends," Jesus said quietly. "I must go now into the desert. Alone."

His band of new followers looked shocked.

"But—when will you return?" Philip, who had earlier been so happy and assured, seemed taken aback.

"I do not know. It may be only a few days, it may be longer." He gathered them around him. "You may all wait for me here. If you cannot wait, then return home. I will find you later."

"How?" said Simon Peter. "How will you find us?"

"I will find you," Jesus said. "Did I not find you to begin with?"

"Yes, but—"

"Those who can wait, please wait. Stay here, pray, listen to John, come to know one another. Whatever food and drink is in the tent, is yours. If I am victorious, I will return for you."

The sun was already halfway down the western sky. The shadows under the rocks were growing longer, and a chill wind had whipped up, blowing across the water and making John's converts shiver and shake when he immersed them in the cool river.

"Victorious?" Andrew mouthed the word as if he had never heard it before.

Jesus repeated, "Victorious. It must be settled at the outset."

Even more startling than his words was the fact that he fastened his cloak around his shoulders, adjusted his sandals, inspected his staff, and made ready to leave.

"Now? This instant?" Nathanael seemed aghast. "Wait until morning."

Jesus shook his head. "Now is the time I must go," he said firmly.

And, to their astonishment, he waded across the ford, took the eastern path which led into the fiercest desert wasteland, and walked resolutely along it, never looking back.

At sunset, John's crowd melted away. The ones with shelters retired to them, and soon little cookfires were glowing dots of red scattered all over the area. The others left earlier, retreating to the nearest villages, or perhaps all the way back to their homes elsewhere. John seemed to have a large group of permanent disciples, who followed him everywhere, as well as a number of people who came out to hear him only once.

The newly formed group of Jesus followers huddled around their cookfire and shared their food. Since Mary had none, she had nothing to contribute and was completely dependent on the others. They did not have much: only a few salted fish, some dried-out bread, and packs of dates.

"What shall we do?" Simon Peter finally said. "Shall we wait here, as Jesus told us to?"

In the darkness, their eyes looked stunned. Everything had happened so quickly, and now Jesus had vanished.

"We just came here to hear John," Andrew told Philip and Nathanael. "We came down from Galilee with Mary, who was . . . who was seeking solitude in the desert, and we thought we would listen to the preaching and then return. We never thought—there was no plan for this—"

"Nor was there for us," said Philip. "We grew restless and wished to come and see the Baptist as well. It was dull where we were; I was sick of the fishing—and of my wife, too, at least then."

When no one argued with him or rebuked him, he went on. "As anyone who's married can tell you, sometimes it grows irksome. Are you married?"

"I am," said Simon Peter. "And, yes, I know what you mean, although of course my wife is a fine—"

"Of course! Of course!" Philip laughed loudly.

"Well, she *is*," said Andrew.

"I am married," said Mary, in a quiet voice. "And I did not come to escape my husband, or my child. I am longing to return to them, now that I am restored."

"That's what I meant," said Andrew. "We didn't come to escape our lives, only to see John. We never meant to become John's disciples or anyone else's. Our life is in Capernaum."

"And suddenly we are supposed to follow this . . . man . . . about. This man from—from Nazareth, isn't it? Are we supposed to go there with him?"

"Can anything good come out of Nazareth?" said Nathanael, suddenly. "You know that old saying." He himself seemed very fond of it, Mary thought, for he kept repeating it as if to announce it.

"Of course, we've all heard it. No prophet ever foretold of anyone important coming from that place," said Peter. "But this man . . . It's hard to imagine that he's really from Nazareth. It seems as if he's from someplace else."

Nazareth . . . What was that family that Mary had met so long ago? And then hadn't she reacquainted herself with a member of it more recently, at her marriage? Wasn't there . . . wasn't there a boy named Jesus she had met at the campground returning from Jerusalem? She searched her memory. There had been a group of children, and a Jesus had been the eldest. He had talked about lizards. Yes, lizards, and God's providence. He had had a sort of presence, even then. Could it possibly be the same person?

"Yes, I agree, he does seem from some other place," Philip was saying. "But we haven't answered the question: are we going to wait for him? And even if we do, what will we do when he returns?"

"I think—I want to wait a little while, at least," said Peter. "I won't be satisfied never to see him again. He has some peculiar kind of power. I cannot explain it. I was in his presence, and I didn't want to leave. We can stay for another day, surely."

"Father will be furious," said Andrew. "We weren't brave enough to tell him we were leaving, we just left. We left Mara and her mother to tell him."

"We didn't have time to wait," said Peter. "We had to leave, that very instant. Otherwise . . ." He stopped out of deference to Mary.

"Otherwise I would have been stoned," said Mary. "Only by the kindness of Andrew and Simon—Peter—was I hidden until I could be safely gotten away."

"But how did you get the demons?" asked Philip, eagerly curious.

"I took an old idol into my house," she said. "That was the beginning."

"In the Law, it says, 'Neither shall you bring an abomination into your house, lest you become a cursed thing like it.' Is that what happened?" asked Nathanael.

"How did you know such scripture?" Mary was astounded that he should be familiar with that obscure passage.

"I want to study it full-time, and leave my fishing."

"I can guess that *you're* not married," said Peter. "Your wife would hardly be thrilled by that announcement."

"I want to stay, just to see Jesus again, to understand more about him, to thank him for what he did for me. To try, somehow, to pay him back, by helping him. He asked us to join him. . . ." Mary shook her head. "But I am longing to return home."

"You can't join him anyway," said Nathanael. "You're a woman. You can't be a disciple. There is no such thing as a woman disciple. Did you see any with John? And even if there were, you're married. You can't leave your family. Then you'd surely be stoned, as a prostitute. Jesus couldn't have meant it when he invited you. He just meant it in some symbolic sense."

"It sounded to me as if he meant it literally," said Peter.

"Well, he couldn't have." Philip agreed with Nathanael.

"If I don't wait, how will I ever know?" It was the most important thing she would ever find out. This man had invited her to be a disciple—she, a woman, who was not allowed to study Torah. She felt deeply honored, even if he had meant it only symbolically. No one else would even allow her the symbols.

"We only wait one day at a time," said Peter. "We only have to de-cide at each sunrise what to do. Perhaps that is why he left us—to teach us how to do that."

Later, they went out and met with the people camped out around them. Some came from as far north as the area where the Jordan arose, around the slopes of Mount Hermon, and others from as far south as the desert near Beersheba. But talking with them revealed that they were absolutely committed to John, and to the idea that he was the Messiah.

"We've searched the scriptures, and all the signs point to him," said one strong-armed woman who was stirring her cookpot energeti-cally. Mary could see shreds of stringy meat rising to the top of the stew.

"Like what?" Nathanael asked, eager to test her knowledge. She stopped stirring. "Well, it's so obvious," she said. "He's clearly been chosen by God, as the Messiah must be; he is helping to redeem the people, as Isaiah tells us he will; he is judging his foes; but all through the power of God, of course."

"Exactly as the prophet Isaiah says." Her husband, a huge-bellied man, was drawn to the conversation and waddled up. "The verses say, 'For he will come like a pent-up flood that the breath of the Lord drives along. The Redeemer will come to Zion, to those in Jacob who repent of their sins.'" He stopped and took a deep breath, for he had used it all up.

"But what about where he was born?" Simon Peter seemed per-plexed. "Aren't there prophecies about the birth itself?" He was unable to quote them, however.

"Oh, there are many." Another man had appeared beside them in the darkness, wrapping his cloak around himself and peering out from under a deep hood. "If someone could fulfill all of them, he would have to be born simultaneously to several mothers in several locations."

"Shut up!" said the fat man, affronted. "No one asked you. No one was talking to you."

The newcomer shrugged. "I merely ask people to think. To do more than just quote verses, willy-nilly. A trained crow can do as much. And understand as much as you, I daresay."

"Go away," insisted the woman stirring the pot. "I don't know why you came here at all, except to spread your poisons."

The unwelcome man merely said, "I can see how warm and welcoming you penitents are. It is so good that you have knelt before John and promised to change your ways. I see how effective it is. May his Messiahship endure forever!" He turned to Simon Peter and the others, as if he were with them. "I thought a sign of the Messiah was that he had great heaven-sent power. John does not seem to."

"Go away, Judas." The woman pointedly turned her back and walked away, leaving the man with Mary and her group.

"Of course, that is just one sign of the Messiah. Did you know," he asked brightly, "that there are over four hundred 'signs' of the Messiah in scripture? Four hundred and fifty-six, to be exact. My, my, what if someone had only four hundred and fifty of them? Would we be obligated to believe regardless, after a certain quota of them had been met?"

"How do you know there are four hundred and fifty-six of them?" asked Andrew. "Did you—"

"No, of course I didn't count them all! That's what the scribes do. They spend their time on things like that. I just learned it from them, that's all."

He had a very rich, smooth speaking voice. It did not seem to be Galilean; the accent was from some other region.

"Where are you from—Judas?" asked Simon Peter.

"From Emmaus, near Jerusalem," he said.

"I knew it! I knew it!" Andrew seemed pleased with himself. "I knew your accent was from Judaea!"

"And I knew yours weren't," said Judas. "You must be from Galilee."

They nodded. "I'm Simon, son of Jonah of Bethsaida," said Simon Peter. "This is my brother, Andrew, and Philip, Nathanael, and Mary, all from towns near me on the lake."

"My father's name is Simon, too," said Judas. "Simon Iscariot. He himself is one of those scribes. So I hear much from him. In fact, it's he who sent me here, more or less to spy. Father was curious about John, but didn't want to come himself. I'm not sure whether he just didn't want to make the journey, or was afraid someone would see him."

"Or that he'd be converted and join the ranks?" asked Philip.

"Not much danger of that," said Judas. "John isn't for everyone."

"We've met someone who . . . may be." Simon Peter sounded cautious. "I mean—we don't really know yet. But—"

"Who?" said Judas sharply. He might almost be a genuine spy, sent to gather suspicious names for authorities in Jerusalem.

"He's named Jesus," said Andrew. "From Nazareth."

Judas looked blank. "I never heard of him."

"He came here to hear John, but he's not like John. Not a bit." When the others remained silent, Andrew finally admitted, "Well, perhaps a bit. I think he's a prophet of some sort."

"So—what does he say?"

"We can't paraphrase him," said Philip, stepping in.

"Well, surely you can summarize his message." Judas sounded annoyed, as if they were rustics who were very slow.

"No, I can't," Philip stubbornly insisted. "You just have to hear him for yourself."

"All right, then, tomorrow. Where is he preaching?"

"He isn't. He's gone off into the desert by himself."

"For how long?"

"I have no idea," Simon Peter said. "But when he returns—"

"I can't just stay here forever, waiting," said Judas. "And I can't bear listening to John much longer. I've got all the information Father needs. No, I have to return home." He laughed. "Another prophet missed! A pity." He yawned. "I'm going to bed."

"Come and join us in our tent," said Andrew. "There's room. And perhaps Jesus will return tomorrow, before you leave."

"It's Jesus's tent," said Mary, speaking up. "Not our tent."

"Don't you think he would welcome this—seeker?" said Philip.

Inside Jesus's tent, the company settled itself. Now, slowly, Mary began to notice things. She observed that the tent had no personal stamp at all, nothing to connect it to Jesus. There were no possessions that would indicate their owner was one sort of person or another. The blankets were of the most common kind and of the most usual color, and the lamps likewise. Yet everything necessary for the guests was there. If they wished to lay their heads down and sleep, there were provisions for that. If they wished to cover themselves, blankets were at hand. There was enough light to see by.

They were subdued this evening. All of them felt different, more ordinary, since Jesus had left, and the feeling was growing. They sat on folded blankets that served as mats and attempted to talk to one another, but they were all aching for sleep.

Judas settled himself down and looked around, eager to have a conversation. He alone seemed to have a store of energy, and was keen to direct it somewhere.

"So," he began, "I see you have found your idol."

"Wrong word," warned Peter. "None of us here is looking for an idol."

"Oh, a Messiah, then," Judas corrected himself. As he sat cross-legged on the mat, his dark eyes flicked from face to face. He took an elegant, long-boned hand and brushed his hair off his forehead.

"No, not that, either," said Andrew. He was also dark and thick-haired, but he was sturdier than Judas. "We just . . . found this man who . . . surprised us. That's all I can say."

"Surprised you?" Judas arched his eyebrows. "My, my. In what way? Now, let me see. There are only a few ways someone can surprise you. He can be less than you expected, more than you expected, or so strange he is far beyond your experience. In that case, he is either priceless or worthless." He paused. "So—which is it to be? Is this Jesus priceless, or worthless?"

"What difference does it make to you?" Philip snapped. "You clearly are here to belittle. You came to belittle John, and if you ever met Jesus, you would try to belittle him as well. People like you—they see everything as mean and . . . amusing."

"But you don't even know me," said Judas, sounding hurt. "How can you be so dismissive of me? I certainly want to hear this Jesus, since he has impressed you so much."

"What we think of him is of little matter," said Nathanael. "What is more important is what he thinks of *us*."

"Oh, now, in the last accounting, it is only what you yourself think that is of value," Judas protested. "After all, no one can know another's thoughts." He suddenly looked over at Mary. "And you, a woman! Surely it is unusual for a woman to be here alone. Does this Jesus gather women about him?"

She felt singled out, shamed, as if the demons were still within her. But shamed for Jesus, as if he had somehow transgressed: Does this Jesus gather women about him?

"I am the first," she said. "How many others may come to know him, I cannot say." She paused, then suddenly asked, "And what do you *do*, Judas? You have only mentioned your father, the scribe. But clearly you are not a scribe yourself. You must not work for a busy master, or you could not have taken the time off to come here on your father's errand." Why should they all answer *his* questions but ask him none?

"I serve various masters, but at different times. I am an accountant. I keep financial books and tabulate records for businesses. It is seasonal, like many other things." He looked cocky, as if he was pleased to have rebutted her attack. Then his face softened. "And when I am not busy serving these masters, I like to try my hand at assembling mosaics."

Mosaics! Making representations of living creatures! Mary could almost hear the collective internal gasps.

"I do not believe it dishonors God," said Judas quietly. "I think all his creation is glorious, and to celebrate it gives honor to him." He paused. "Besides, the Romans pay well. I adorn their houses, and they allow me to praise God in my own way, with my own hands. The Law—fulfilling it has hardly anything to do with your own personality, now, has it?"

"That is not the point of it," said Peter, stiffly.

"Oh, but I think it is," said Judas. "I think God wants us to reflect him in a personal way. After all, why would he have created the desire in us to paint or make mosaics if it was evil? God does not create a desire unless he means it to be fulfilled, one way or another."

They all laughed, uneasily. "We must ask Jesus about that when he returns," Nathanael said. Somehow there was a feeling, shared but unspoken among them all, that only Jesus could answer this Judas. They hoped he would linger until Jesus returned and could address his challenges.

The camaraderie burned low, like the fire outside the tent. One by one they admitted that they were exhausted, and sought sleep. The high excitement of the night before had melted away.

Mary let her head drop onto the folded mantle that would serve as her pillow. Smoke from the dying fire outside made its way into the tent, as if it wanted to sleep, too. She breathed it in. She had always liked the smell of wood smoke, perhaps because it was so familiar from her father's business, with the rows of drying fish suspended over the fires.

Father . . . Eli . . . Silvanus . . . and Joel. Her mother, and her cousins, and old Esther next door. They were all in Magdala, waiting to hear what had happened to her. If only there were some way to talk to them now, to tell them this extraordinary story. She felt an actual pain in her breast as she thought of their uncertainty, their concern. She did not wish to be the source of any more unhappiness for them. And Elisheba! Too young really to miss her, and that was the worst of all.

I must see them again, she thought. I do not know what to do. If Jesus were here, then we could all leave together, all make our way in a group. But now . . . we cannot all wait and wait.

Where is he now? Out in the desert somewhere, perhaps confronting the very demons that inhabited me. They will seek him out. They will be very angry at being expelled.

She could feel the cold from the desert night seeping inside the tent. How much colder was it in the open wasteland? It was hard to survive there. Even she had had a cave to retreat to for safety.

Besides the cold, a thin line of blue moonlight was coming into the tent. The moon was almost full. She pulled herself up and edged toward the entrance of the tent, then looked out through the flap. Everything was bathed in a clear, merciless light that showed every furrow in the sand and every cleft in every rock.

Jesus was somewhere out there, in the cold, lonely reaches of the desert, the moonlight falling on him and the rocks around him. The moonlight, although beautiful, painted everything in the colors of desolation. That desolation was confronting Jesus now.

ᙿᙿ X X 1 1 ᙿᙿ

For my dearest friend Keziah bat-Benjamin, wife of Reuben in Magdala

From her friend Mary, also of Magdala, a dishonest now an honest friend—

I am writing my thoughts to you instead of to God! The rabbi gave me these writing materials so that I could write to God and write about him, but I couldn't and I didn't. I wronged God, but I also wronged you. And now I wish to ask your forgiveness, although I can already hear you saying, "But there is nothing to forgive!" Oh, you are wrong. There is so much!

Are not true friends close in spirit? True friends choose one another for that reason. Others in our lives are given to us by blood or by convenience, but choosing a friend is always something we do only to give ourselves pleasure. And yet I kept a secret from you all those years, which means that I was less than a true friend to you.

You know I am prone to secrets—just look at the reading lessons I hid from my family, and how I would break the ritual rules when I was out of their house. Because you knew those secrets, you thought you knew me. But there was a big one I kept even from you, and it is what drove me away from

Magdala and brought me here—to the desert, with a group of men waiting for another man to come back to us.

I can tell you now: I had a forbidden idol that I kept and . . . did I worship it? Now, now that I can see more clearly, I would have to say yes. When I looked at her ivory smile, a hot rush of excitement would go through me. Was it only because it was forbidden, or was it the awe of a worshiper?

This led later to my becoming possessed. Yes, possessed by demons. You did not see me in those days. We did not see each other often by the time I had become a madwoman, a madwoman who fought the demons in private. So you did not know. I tried to keep it from everyone, but finally Joel knew, and then . . . I shall tell you everything when I see you again. Perhaps I will just hand you this bundle of paper and let you read it all at once, for I can't see any way to get it into your hands before then.

The torment of the demons! Keziah, the despair of it was so crushing I wanted to die. I tried to die. The blackness in my mind, the deep darkness that enveloped me, was Satan himself. Why do they call him "the prince of this world"? He isn't of this world at all, but from a pit, an abyss.

And then someone delivered me. Someone was stronger than all the demons, stronger than Satan, and he drove them out. And now the lightness—as bright as it was dark inside before. The world seems flooded with sunlight, with colors, with sounds of beauty. And so I think this man, my deliverer, is the prince of this world, because he has restored that world to me, only now it is better than before. And I feel like a child again, clean and fresh and new, but wiser—oh, wiser than any child could ever be! I am the old Mary, the one you thought you knew. I am a new Mary, one even I don't know yet.

Keziah—I am going to follow this man. I am a disciple! A disciple—can you imagine that? Of course I am coming back home, I am hurrying there just as soon as this man returns, but after that I'll somehow become a disciple. He said I might be able to follow him without leaving home. Does that make sense? None of this does!

His name is Jesus. He comes from Nazareth. I know, already people have quoted, "Can anything good . . . ?" You know the saying. I think he may be the boy we met on the journey so long ago—do you remember? We spent the night with his family. He was about thirteen then. He must be over thirty now. I thought he was unusual then, but that is nothing compared with now. And yet, if I try to tell you about him, he will sound very odd. You must meet him! It's impossible to describe him, but if you meet him, you'll understand. I think he is going to start his preaching back in Galilee, and then you can come and hear him.

And the men, the other disciples he has gathered—you won't believe this, but two of them are Simon and Andrew bar-Jonah. The fishermen, you know, the ones who delivered so many catches to Father. We used to laugh about being forced to marry one of them, and we said they smelled bad, smelled fishy. Well, Simon is married, but Andrew still isn't. They don't really smell—actually Andrew would make someone a good husband, I think now.

And then there are two other ones: Philip, another fisherman, from Bethsaida; and Nathanael, an ex-fisherman.

Philip is full of energy and talks all the time; he also refuses to say anything is bad or annoying or can't be done. Do you know what, Keziah? Cheerful people can be depressing! Sometimes when he's whistling around, it puts me in a bad mood.

Nathanael is handsome in a broody sort of way, but he's as sarcastic as Philip is happy. Apparently he used to fish, but he rebelled against that and announced to his family that he would devote himself only to study, study of the scriptures. But not the way the scribes do. He seems to have a great thirst for knowledge and wants to learn everything in the whole world. It's lucky for him he isn't married. I'm sure his wife would feel cheated if she had agreed to marry a fisherman and then ended up with a poor scholar when it was too late to change.

A strange man appeared a few days ago; he said he had come to spy on John the Baptist for his father. I think that was a lie; I think he really came to see him for himself. This man, whose name is Judas something, makes mosaics! Yes, can you imagine, a Jewish man making mosaics? I told you he was strange. But no stranger, I suppose, than a Jewish girl harboring an idol.

And John the Baptist. He's here, too; in fact, that's why all these people are gathered here. Being near a genuine prophet is frightening. But, Keziah, he's not afraid of anything. How wonderful it would be to be like that. Soldiers came and threatened him, but he took no notice. No, that's wrong. He did more than take no notice—he threatened them back with the wrath of God.

He truly is emaciated, and his hair is wild and has briars in it, and he wears rough skins. I don't know if he really subsists on locusts and honey, but you can tell by looking at him he does not eat much.

It is obvious from my descriptions of the people I've met here that they are very different from the ones I knew in Magdala. Even the ones I knew in Magdala, like Simon and Andrew, are different here. Oh, and Jesus gave Simon a new name, he called him Peter because he says he's a rock. Surely he meant it to be funny, because Simon Peter is so changeable and impulsive. I *can never tell when Jesus is serious or not. But I do not know him very well yet. When he comes back, then . . .*

More later from your Mary—do you realize, without you I never could have written a single one of these words?

God is good, and for the first time I feel him.

∽ XXⅠⅠⅠ ∽

"I can't wait any longer," said Judas, twirling his meat at the end of a stick over the cookfire. He was busy preparing himself a meal. Evidently he had planned to eat by himself and be away at first light. But when the others emerged from the tent, he offered them food, albeit a bit reluctantly. "After all, you don't know when this rabbi, or whatever he is, is returning. At any rate, I came to see John the baptizer. I've seen him, and I've seen all there is to see. His sermons are all the same. No point in staying any longer." He pulled the stick back and examined the meat carefully, then pulled it off the smoking stick and ate it.

"No, we can't say when he is coming back," admitted Peter. "And we, too, must decide what to do. We cannot wait indefinitely, either." Peter shook his big head, and all his curls trembled. "But I am sorry you cannot meet him, Judas Iscariot. Very sorry indeed."

Judas shrugged. "Some other time, perhaps."

"It is doubtful he will ever come to Jerusalem," said Andrew, joining them. "And that is your home territory."

"Yes, from what I heard, he seems a local man from the Galilee region. I don't get there much. My accounting keeps me in the Jerusalem area, and the mosaics take me to Roman areas, like Caesarea. Still, you never know." He shouldered his pack and made ready to set out. "I wish you and your rabbi all the best," he said, sincerely. "Be careful. These are dangerous times for everyone. I think we will not be seeing or hearing John much longer."

"Because of Herod Antipas?" Peter asked.

"It's obvious. Antipas will silence him. His speaking days are numbered. So listen carefully this morning, or afternoon, or whenever you seek him out. Not that he will say anything different from what I have heard." He saluted them. "It was good to meet you."

·   ·   ·

Judas had called attention to a troubling matter. They had to admit that Jesus had chosen them, then disappeared, with no promise of when he would return. That evening, Peter referred to their quandary: "I do not want to be hasty, but we have no idea when Jesus will return. My brother and I came here on another matter, and that is settled. We must return. Jesus said he would find us . . ." His voice trailed off. "I must take him at his word. I must hope and believe he will come back to us and indeed find us. But in the meantime, since we have no direction, I am afraid Andrew and I must return to our homes, and business. Mary—will you come with us? Or shall we deliver a message for you?"

Oh, could they not wait one more day? She was longing to see Joel and Elisheba and her family, but she did not want to leave without seeing Jesus. Otherwise, she would cease to believe that all of it had really happened. And now that she was restored to herself, she needed to see this man, to see him under normal circumstances rather than in extreme, painful need.

"No," she said. "No, it is better if I tell them myself, *show* them the miracle that has happened." She turned to Philip and Nathanael. "Nathanael, you are from Cana. Philip, you are from Bethsaida. That is not far from Magdala. If you wait, I will return with you."

Nathanael's face registered his dilemma. "I do plan to stay—but how long I know not. But, yes, when I return, you surely can come with me."

John was still preaching, and the ford of the Jordan was still filled with penitents, and the days seemed interminable. Mary went out every day to hear John, but—curse him!—Judas was right, John said nothing new. He used the same words over and over, the same exhortations; only his audience changed, and to them his message was novel.

As the days passed, Mary realized she should leave. Now she felt that Jesus was never coming back. Something had happened to him. They could wait forever, but they would never see him again.

With deep sorrow at the realization, reluctantly, she went to Philip and asked him how much longer he planned to stay, and to her relief he was having the same thoughts she was. They must leave soon.

They went into the tent and looked around, wistfully, at the place that had been their home and shelter for so many days. But surely Jesus could not expect them to stay much longer. They began to gather their belongings, meager as these were. Mary kept her writing materials, returned to her by Peter, safely ready to take.

Their last night was melancholy. Mary and Philip and Nathanael sat around the fire, speaking very little. The fire itself seemed subdued; its flames were stunted, and it crackled, whining in protest.

She would return home and, God willing, never forget any of this. It was the most extraordinary thing that had ever happened to her. God was here, in this place, and he had touched her.

"It's back to fishing," said Philip, sadly. "Not a bad life." His voice contradicted his words. "Or perhaps I'll give up the fishing and pursue my studies. Like Nathanael."

"But how will you live?" blurted out Mary. When she saw Philip's troubled face, she hastily said, "I meant—scholars need someone to support them, and if your wife is not sympathetic . . ."

"I don't know," he admitted. "But after this, I feel I cannot go back to the fishing. I must make my life with what I love, and trust somehow I can survive."

"I love my family as deeply as myself," said Mary, "yet I know they will not understand. And I am frightened that I will forget all this, and it will seem a fanciful dream."

"No one's family understands."

The voice had come from just beyond the limits of the light thrown by the campfire. It was familiar, but strained.

They all jumped up and looked in the direction of the voice. But there was only darkness, and the snapping of the fire.

"Who's there?" called Mary. Now her own voice sounded odd.

"I am." A figure appeared at the very edge of the circle of light thrown by the fire. "I am."

He came forward, moving slowly, exhaustedly. Only when he stumbled out into the firelight did they recognize him.

"Master!" Philip leapt to his side, putting his arms around him, supporting him.

Jesus. It was Jesus.

"Oh, master!" Mary also came forward, eager to wipe his face or ease his weariness. He seemed weak and burned away: his flesh had retreated into folds of sunburnt skin, and his back was bowed. Out of his gaunt face, his eyes stared from deep-set sockets, and they seemed shocked by whatever they had seen.

Nathanael brought out a blanket and draped it over his shoulders. His intensity, and his faraway look, left them at a loss how to help him. Had he been hurt? Was he just weak from wandering and the cold by night and the heat by day? Or was it something more than that?

Jesus sank down before the dying fire. "You are still here" was all he said.

"Yes, we are still here," they reassured him.

"It has been many days." He spoke those words after a seemingly long time. "I do not know how many. But you are still here." He looked around at them. "Philip. Nathanael. Mary."

"Yes, master." Philip spoke. "Now you must rest." He attempted to lead Jesus into the tent.

But Jesus did not rise. He seemed not to have the strength to do so. "A moment. Give me a moment."

"Yes. Whatever you wish," Nathanael said.

"Do you know how long it has been?" Jesus finally asked.

"No," said Philip. "We do not."

"Forty days and forty nights," Jesus said. "A long time in the desert. But I have met the Evil One, and we wrestled. It is over."

Who won? Mary wondered. Jesus seemed beaten.

"I prevailed," he said. His voice was but a whisper. "Satan has retreated."

And left you in such a state? Mary wondered. Then is he powerful indeed.

"Yes, Satan is powerful," said Jesus, seeming to read her thoughts. "But not all-powerful. Remember that, keep it in your hearts. Satan's power is limited."

Mary looked at Jesus's ravaged face. When she remembered how easily he had routed her demons, she could not imagine the power that had wrought this change in him. Her demons, as strong as they were, were as nothing beside the Evil One himself.

"Oh, master!" Love and gratitude welled up inside her, and she threw herself at his feet. There were no shoes, no sandals upon them.

"It was necessary." He reached down and took her hands, removing her from his feet. "Nothing else could go forward until this was finished." He paused. "Now it can truly begin."

They led him into the tent. He sank down on a blanket. In a moment he was asleep, his feet tucked up under him, his head resting easily on a blanket-pillow.

The next morning, Jesus was awake before any of them. They found him outside, sitting by the fire, which he had restarted. He was staring at it so intently that they hated to disturb him, but it was impossible to emerge from the tent without his seeing them.

He seemed willing to be disturbed, however, even glad to see them.

"Greetings, friends," he said. "What do we have to eat?"

Of course. He must be famished. They hastily began pawing through their stores, as if this were an emergency of the highest order, until he laughed. "Do not worry yourselves so. I cannot eat much now, for I have been so long without food. A few dates, a bit of dried fish is all I can manage."

Philip handed him a sack of dates, and he opened it slowly, not like a man ravished by hunger. "Hmmm." He held one up and inspected it. Then he ate it.

"Where are the others?" he finally asked.

"Peter and Andrew had to return home," said Nathanael. "They trusted that, as you said, you could find them."

"Hmm." Jesus was seemingly directing all his attention to the date he was eating. "But you stayed, and waited," he finally said. There was a slight smile on his face, as if to say, I am glad of it.

"There was another man here, too, wanting to meet you, but he had to leave," said Philip. Philip had a hearty, open manner that would make people seek him out for requests, Mary thought. A doorkeeper. "His name was Judas."

Jesus nodded. "A common name. How shall I know him again?"

"He is the son of a Simon Iscariot. He lives near Jerusalem. He makes mosaics!"

Jesus lifted his eyebrows slightly. "Mosaics?"

"He also does accounts. He is dark, thin, rather elegant. An interesting fellow."

"But he had to return." Jesus stated it simply. "As we must."

What happened in the desert? they all wanted to ask, but no one wanted to intrude. Finally, Philip dared.

"Sir—if I may ask," he said, "where did you go, what did you confront in the desert?" His usually hearty voice was quiet.

Jesus looked directly at him, as if measuring how much he could understand. "I needed to go out, to make myself a target for Satan. I put myself in his hands. If I could not surmount whatever tests he put me to, then I had no business beginning my ministry. Better to be discredited at the outset than to stumble later. Let me tell you a story. What prince starts to build a tower if he does not first reckon the cost of it? It will be a disgrace if he cannot complete it; people will laugh at him. What king starts a battle without comparing his own troops with the enemy's? If the enemy is too great, better not to start the battle at all, but sue for peace instead. Just so, if I am to do battle against Satan, I needed to know I will not fail."

"But . . . in what way did you test yourself?" Nathanael asked, his eyes riveted to Jesus. His lean, sensitive face seemed almost to quiver.

"Satan will always come to you," said Jesus. "All you have to do is wait." He paused. "So I went far out into the desert, and I waited. And he came to me, pressing at my weakest points. That is what he always does. That is how he will attack you as well.

"Satan knows all your fears and weaknesses. Beware of him." Jesus looked around at them all. "And most important: Satan may retire from the field of combat, but he always returns. He will return to me, as he will to you. But we must recognize him. He is the accuser, the tester. He brings up past sins that have been forgiven. It is not God who torments you with the memory of past sins, it is Satan."

"But why?" Nathanael asked.

"If Satan cannot get you to commit any new sins, he will attempt to disable you with old ones. He is God's continual adversary, and if you are in God's army, he will undo you any way he can."

He stood up, and for the first time Mary saw how his presence gave him stature. He was not taller than Philip or Nathanael, but he seemed to be. The mantle was hanging off his starved frame, but it draped as if he were a prince.

"We have a mission against Satan. Each of you must go into your own desert and be tested. Mary, you have already wrestled with your own demons, and passed the test."

"No," she said. "No, I have not! They had defeated me. I was ready to die to rid myself of them. I tried to die. They won!"

"No, they did not," said Jesus. "You have just said it: you were willing to die rather than submit. You were put to the supreme test and you remained faithful to God."

It had not felt like a supreme test; it had felt like torture. Mary wondered how Jesus could pronounce this decision so authoritatively, but she dared not contradict him.

"What do you require of us?" Philip asked the question they all had in their minds. "What shall we do?"

Mary expected Jesus to give a vague answer. Instead he said, "We will return to Galilee. I will begin my ministry. You will stay with me, and I will call others. It will be a call that will challenge Satan. That is why we have to begin as hardened veterans of the fight."

"But what—if I may ask, master—will be the message of this ministry?" Nathanael looked deeply troubled.

"That the Kingdom of God is already here, and that the time the prophets longed for has come."

"Already here?" Philip frowned. "Forgive me, but how can you say that? I don't see it anywhere. Is it not supposed to arrive with celestial thunderings and be unmistakable?"

"Those predictions were wrong," said Jesus flatly. "The prophets and writers misunderstood. The truth is, the Kingdom is a mysterious thing that grows almost unseen. It is already here. But somehow it has also fallen to me to inaugurate it. Because I see it, and understand it, and am its agent."

Mary shook her head. "Are you saying that you are the Messiah? Is that not what he does?"

"I am not saying that. I am prepared for others to say that, but that is not what I say."

"Then, sir"—Philip looked lost—"what is it that you say?"

"Follow me. That is what I say." Jesus smiled at him. "It will all become clear as we walk along. It is in walking a path that we come to understanding. God says, I desire obedience, not sacrifice. Obedience means walking as he directs our steps, one step at a time. Only then will we see where we are going." He held out his arms to them. "Are we going together?" The invitation to that wider portal was made so simply. It would have been so easy to decline.

That is what Mary thought later. This momentous journey: how small it had seemed at its start. Just a few steps. Just "follow me." Just the illusion that they could leave at any time. And yet, for those he had called, how impossible that turned out to be.

∞ XXIV ∞

The journey back to Galilee was nothing like Mary's journey away from it. She remembered the terrible, driven quest, lashed by the storms and the demons within her, stumbling along with Peter—Simon then—and Andrew, completely dependent on their support, shorn of everything else.

Even, she thought, of my hair. She reached up to touch her head. She could feel her hair already growing back, although it would be a long time until she could let others see it.

Jesus seemed preoccupied as he led them along. He answered their questions and occasionally commented on something in the landscape, but otherwise kept his thoughts to himself. At one time they stopped and made camp, and it was then that Mary asked him if it had indeed been he on that journey through Samaria, if she had stayed with him and his family.

She expected him to be unsure, but immediately he set himself to the task of remembering. What might have seemed unimportant to someone else he gave great weight to.

"Yes," he finally said. "I remember. You and your friend and your cousins joined us. That was when we were all returning from a pilgrimage to Jerusalem."

"Your sister Ruth had a toothache," Mary said. "And it was the Sabbath—"

"Yes," Jesus said. "That is right. How good of you to remember."

"Your family," Mary said. "Are they well?"

"My father, Joseph, died several years ago. But my mother, yes, she is well, as are my brothers and sisters. It was difficult to leave the carpentry shop to my next-eldest brother, James. But I had waited so many years to do so. He resents it, for he wishes to spend all his time in study, and had counted on me, as the eldest son, to step into our father's place and provide him with the freedom of a second son to do as he pleases. But as I said, when God makes a request, you are not free to ignore it. And when he makes that request, often it lays a burden on other people as well as yourself." He paused. "That is what makes it so painful."

"Tell us more about your family," Mary asked. "The first words you spoke when you returned to us were, 'No one's family understands.' What did you mean?"

"I know my family will not be pleased with my new path," he said.

How had he surmised what her real question was? The question, how can I be a disciple yet still be in my old life?

"All my life I have felt called to . . . something," Jesus said, choosing his words carefully. "From my earliest days, I thought about God and what he wanted from me, and how I could reach him to find out. We were given the Law, of course, the commandments—"

"But your father, Joseph—he broke the Sabbath!" Mary interrupted him "He untied the bundle to get the medicine, even though the tying and untying of knots is forbidden. And the medicine itself was forbidden." She had never forgotten his shocking act.

Jesus smiled and shook his head, as if recalling a precious memory. "Yes, he did. Brave man. And he was right to do so. God never meant the Sabbath to seize us in iron shackles, as the rigid keepers of the Law have made it to do." He paused. "To refuse to help someone in bodily need on the Sabbath is wrong. It is wrong. There is no question."

"But as to your calling . . ." Nathanael tried to steer the subject back to the one they all were burning to know about.

"It grew, slowly," he said. "That is why I am so sure of it. A decision is not actually made once, but over and over again. It refused to go away, all through the long years of my growing up, my father's death, my mother's widowhood, my providing a living for my entire family. But your callings may come suddenly," he said, as if to warn them. "Each person is different. God seeks each in a different way. Still, since it will be so difficult, it is good to be sure. In our hearts."

Mary noticed that he said "we," as if she and Philip and Nathanael were his companions on the same path, just further back, having had a later start. And, yes, she had felt called to something from an early age, but it had been shadowy, unspoken; and then the idol had taken away its rightful place.

"Do you plan to return to your home?" Mary asked.

"Yes, I will," Jesus said. "But not in the way they are expecting me."

"We must return to ours," said all three others simultaneously.

"Of course you must," said Jesus. "But it would be better for you if you did not."

"And why is that?" asked Philip. "Surely you do not mean us to be cruel and abandon our families."

Jesus looked pained. "No, never cruel. But when you are newly set out on a path, it is easy to be turned aside. Those you love can prove your undoing. That is why I said no one's family understands. Unless they join our family."

"Unlikely," Philip admitted. "But my wife! What shall I tell her?"

"You see what I mean," said Jesus. "It is difficult. We cannot pretend otherwise. Humans are sometimes harder to serve than God. God understands all. Humans do not." He threw a few pebbles into the fire, seeming to concentrate very hard on where they landed.

"In four days we will be back in Galilee. We will come first to Bethsaida, and there, Philip, you will leave us and go to your home. Next we will come to Magdala, and you, Mary, will leave us and go to your home. Then Cana, and you, Nathanael, will leave and go to your home. I will retreat into the hills and pray. Then, on the fourth day, I will return to Nazareth, my home. I will read the lesson in the synagogue on the Sabbath. And then it will all begin. Afterward I will go to Capernaum. If you are still with me, I will seek you there, at the synagogue the following Sabbath." He looked around at them, his eyes lingering on each of their faces. "If you are not there, I understand. I will not look for you, but will rejoice if I see you."

Hearing him say he would not look for them hurt, Mary realized. How could he take them up so readily and then let them go so easily?

Again, he seemed to read her thoughts. "God loves each of us fiercely, but he lets us choose how closely we draw near to him," Jesus said. "We can do no less. We must be perfect, as our heavenly father is perfect."

"But we are human, and can never be perfect," protested Philip.

"Perhaps God sees perfection in a different way. Perhaps you are already perfect, or will be," said Jesus. "Perfection in God's eyes lies in being obedient to him."

It would be a comfort to believe so, Mary thought.

"Here we must part," Jesus said firmly to Philip, as they approached Bethsaida. He gave him no choice. "May God strengthen you in whatever you confront."

Philip was clearly distressed to have to leave them, but he squared his shoulders and, after a trembling goodbye, made his way into the town.

They continued around the northern rim of the lake, coming to Capernaum just as the fish market was in full bustle, and crowds of fishermen and buyers milled on the docks. Did Jesus look around, even for a moment, searching for Peter and Andrew? Mary watched him carefully. Would it not be human to do so? Surely he would let his eyes sweep over the docks, pretend he was just surveying the area. But as Mary watched him, suddenly he turned and looked at her, catching her. She felt as if she had been caught in a crime. What crime? Only that of testing Jesus to see if he was an ordinary man.

Peter and Andrew were nowhere to be seen. The group continued their walk through the thronging docks, through the loud voices of the fishmongers, the merchants trying to attract their attention, the hagglers yelling in protest at the prices. The smell of fish pervaded the air, and the flopping creatures in their tubs seemed to be fanning the air to spread their scent.

"Sir!" An aggressive merchant accosted Jesus. He waved an armful of sheer scarves before his eyes. "The finest! Silk! From Cyprus!"

Jesus attempted to brush them aside, but the merchant was not to be put off.

"Sir! This is a once-in-a-lifetime purchase! These came via Arabia! On a special ship, which cannot make the journey again. Cheaper than those coming by camel across the desert. Half-price! And see the fine color. Yellow the color of dawn! Rose the color of the sky over this very lake, after the sun has sunk. Sir, you know that color. It is unique to *us*. How could they have understood it in faraway Arabia? But they did. See, look!" He spread the sheer material out over his arm.

Jesus looked carefully at it. He fingered the material, appreciating it. "It is indeed beautiful," he admitted. "But today I cannot buy it."

The merchant looked crushed. "But tomorrow I may not have it!"

They passed the customs house, a large building where all the agents of tax collection had their headquarters. Capernaum was right at the boundary between the lands of Herod Antipas and those of his half-brother, Herod Philip. Herod Philip, with his Greek name and pagan territories, seemed a completely different creature from their own ruler. But whenever there was a territorial line, it allowed the swarms of tax collectors, who were more of a nuisance than swarms of flies and gnats, to set up shop. The Romans were there to oversee the general property and head taxes, and their local representatives, the publicans, set themselves up on little stools in booths to collect import and export taxes.

"If I had bought that veil from Arabia," said Jesus, "I would now have to stand in line to pay an import tax on it." He indicated the long line out in front of one of the booths. "Thus one material thing, beautiful as it may be, robs of us precious time, a free gift from God. Is it an even exchange? No, of course not."

From the looks of the people standing in line, they disagreed. They were clutching bundles of goods, and even peeking into them, as if they could not wait to see the contents again. A little man was walking up and down and instructing them how to fill out their papers.

"Alphaeus," said Nathanael. He grimaced. "A nasty man. I had to deal with him once. He's greedy, grasping, and calculating. And he's brought his two sons, Levi and James, into the business. Like father, like son, I suppose. One of them has a big mansion already."

"Some people enjoy that," said Jesus. "For some, that is as far as their vision reaches. But I think that God has something bigger in mind for them. And that they should come to know it, and hear it."

"And you are the person to announce it?" asked Nathanael.

"Yes," said Jesus. "It is as you say."

Nathanael looked taken aback. "Consorting with tax collectors?"

"In the Kingdom of heaven, you will see, many things shall be." Jesus laughed. "Perhaps even tax collectors entering before the righteous."

"Alphaeus and his sons?" Nathanael shrugged. "That will be a very odd day."

Capernaum dwindled behind. Gradually the area of the docks receded, and they came into the open stretch until the next town, which would be Seven Springs. And after that—Magdala.

Mary was becoming more and more distraught. She would have to part from Jesus and Nathanael, and make her own way into Magdala. Joel would be waiting, and her dearest Elisheba, and her parents, brothers, and cousins. They had had no word about her since she had set out for the desert, unless Peter and Andrew had come and told them. How they would rejoice at her restoration! How they would extend their arms to take her back! An inexplicable fear filled her—for the Mary who had left them was not the same Mary who was coming back.

They made their way around the upper rim of the lake, and soon—too soon!—came to Seven Springs, where the warm waters gushed out and ran into the lake. Here they should part; Jesus and Nathanael would head west, and Mary should continue to Magdala.

Jesus seemed to understand her hesitation. "Mary, your home now calls you. Go and tell the wonderful things that God has done for you. Then, if you are still of a mind to do so, come to Capernaum and look for us all there."

He made it sound so simple. But it was not simple. Or perhaps it was. It was either very simple, or so difficult and complicated it was impossible.

They stood on the lakeshore path, the very one where she had walked with Joel all those years ago when she had first considered marrying him. The wind was whipping up the water and creating little dancing waves. The lake sparkled. Her old life beckoned. I am well, she would say, flinging herself in their arms. I am here to resume what I left so long ago. I love you all. You are my life.

But now there was Jesus, and the fact that he had freed her, and invited her to hear more of what would unfold as he uncovered his own calling. It was the most exciting thing that she had ever anticipated; she did not want to turn her back on it.

"I—I cannot," she heard herself saying. "I cannot return just at this moment. I am not strong enough."

Jesus looked surprised, and because of that she herself was surprised.

"What I mean is, I am now strong enough to return, but I will not be strong enough to leave again, even for a short while, even to help you in your mission. And I am afraid that, once I am there, I will forget you! Forget all that happened to me in the desert, with you."

She expected him to frown and give her a parting exhortation. Instead he said quietly, "Wise are you that you know this. It was revealed to you by my Father in heaven." He paused. "Very well. You will stay with us and return after we have made our visits. I will help and strengthen you in whatever you wish to do."

Immense relief flooded through her. She did not have to test her strength alone! "Yes, master," she said. "I thank you."

They still had to pass through Magdala, taking the road through the town proper before setting out for the towns of the west, Cana and Nazareth. Mary pulled her cloak up around her face as they passed by the streets she knew so well, past the very corner where her house was. Her heart was torn, for she knew that within those walls were people who cared desperately where she was and prayed for her safety, but probably—she had to be honest—had accepted that she was lost.

They have gone on without me, she told herself. They would have to. I was so sick, so hopeless. And now so long without word—yes, they will have accepted life without me.

She shook her head and clutched her mantle closer. It felt strange and dishonest to pass by her own house as if she were not connected to it in some way. The shutters were closed. Why? Were they mourning her?

Suddenly a figure stepped from the house into the street. It was her mother! She was carrying Elisheba in her arms and hurrying toward them.

Mary's heart almost stopped. She wanted to call to them but could not open her mouth; at the same time, she was frozen with an odd shame, as if she were committing a crime by looking at them secretly.

Her mother was preoccupied, and fussing with her sleeve; she did not even notice the three people passing across the street. How familiar that expression on her mother's face was to Mary. Mary stole a look at Elisheba. She looked so grown up—more like a little girl than a baby. But she was over two years old now.

With a jolt of pain, Mary bent her head down and hurried past the corner. She could not look any longer. But she bumped into Jesus, who had stopped and was waiting for her. She saw both pain and understanding in his eyes. He did not need to say anything.

They resumed walking, and soon they were beyond the town, striking out for the west. There was a steep circle of hills ringing the lake, and behind that others rose. As soon as they left the land that bordered the water, the landscape changed; the hills became terraced and stony.

On a sheltered slope beneath an olive orchard, they lit their night-time fire and rested.

"Tomorrow we go home," said Jesus. "You to your home, Nathanael, and I to mine."

Mary looked at Jesus. Was he handsome? Mary knew that others would ask her this question—What is this man, that you follow him?—and the unspoken one—Are you in love with him, that you want to sit at his feet and have him as your teacher?

So she looked carefully at him. He was, in a common way, appealing. His features were regular. His forehead was broad, his hair thick and healthy, his nose straight, and his lips were full and well shaped. But handsome? No; on the contrary, he was forgettable, ordinary. You could pass him in the marketplace and never notice him. It was his bearing that would strike you: he stood straight and carried himself in an upright way. Upright. A peculiar, and particular, word that denoted righteousness in the old texts. "Lord, who shall abide in thy tabernacle? Who shall dwell in thy holy hill? He that walketh uprightly." And "Mark the perfect man, and behold the upright; for the end of that man is peace." It was more than his shoulders, it was a whole stance, immediately recognizable.

No, I am not in love with him, not in any normal sense, she thought. I just want to be in his presence.

"We must sleep," Jesus finally said. "What we face will require great strength. And much prayer."

They spread out their blankets and coverings on the hard ground. Mary could smell the olive groves all around her. In the slight breeze, the olive trees' thin silver leaves rattled and shivered, sending a cool, dry scent to her nostrils.

Jesus covered himself with his cloak and turned away from them, looking up toward the hills behind which his Nazareth waited.

The stars, clear and white, made a bright bowl over their heads.

❧ X X V ❧

Dawn seemed to come early. The stars paled and then disappeared as the sun came over the rim of hills across the lake. Mary could see the red-orange of the new-risen sun painting the field furrows that came right up to the walls of the olive orchard.

The two men were already stirring and awake, eager to begin the remainder of their journey.

The road climbed steadily. Nazareth was in hilly country, set near the brow of a cliff, and Cana was on its slopes. As they approached it, they began to see vineyards on the steep hillside; workers were busy pruning the bare woody branches.

Suddenly they rounded a bend and found themselves in Cana. They stopped and rested. Finally, Jesus said, "Nathanael, you are home."

"Yes, I must go to my house. Would you—"

"No, we must continue our journey," said Jesus, "if we are to reach Nazareth before dark."

But they did walk through the street with him, until Nathanael turned off a lane to the right and made his way on alone. Jesus embraced him, and Mary clasped his arm. He needed their support. He was going back to his old life, and what had once been as familiar as his right hand would now, abruptly, seem alien.

It was hard to turn away and leave him there. But Jesus said little as they got back onto the path to Nazareth. Was he wondering if

Nathanael would ever rejoin them? Or was he already preparing himself for what awaited him in his own home?

The path grew steeper, and Mary began to have to strain to keep up with Jesus, but she did not want to fall one pace behind.

Now they approached the area where people began recognizing him. The vine-dresser stood up tall among his vines—"Jesus! Where have you been! I need new stakes, and right away!" The laborers swaying down the slope with water buckets swinging from their yokes nodded at him and then passed on. Waiting up over the next turn of the path, on the higher parts of the hill, was home. Nazareth: with his mother, brothers, sisters, neighbors, with the workshop—the workshop that he did not want to re-enter. But the people of Nazareth could not know that.

Nazareth was a very small village—smaller, perhaps, than Cana. There were only fifty or so small houses scattered about a main street—or, more accurately, a pathway—through its center. It was not on the top ridge of the mountain but lay just beneath it. It was not mean or squalid—it did not deserve the saying "Can anything good come out of Nazareth?"—but neither was it noteworthy in any way. There were probably one or two thousand villages like it scattered over all Israel.

As they reached level ground and saw it stretching before them— the little well near the entrance, the rough path serving as its main thoroughfare—Mary realized for the first time how wealthy and sophisticated Magdala was. Small one-story houses lined the street; a few larger ones were tucked away on side streets. That must be where the rich people—such as they were—lived. Any truly prosperous or worldly person would not be living in Nazareth, but would have decamped for another, more exciting place.

"Jesus! Go straight home! They have waited too long!" One man knowingly wagged his finger as he spotted them.

Was it Mary's imagination, or did Jesus square his shoulders as if bracing himself? Surely not. Surely he would not need such a strengthening, not with such a clear vision of his mission.

Abruptly he turned onto a side street, an even smaller path. Then he made his way, purposefully, toward a certain house that stood at the far end of it.

It was a square, blocky, whitewashed building. Mary could see the small railing that made its roof safe for people to sleep or dry things on, could see the small windows that let very little light or air in. So this was where he had lived: such an ordinary house, and smaller than those of her own family. But it still was a respectable dwelling; evidently no one in Jesus's family was terribly poor or disreputable.

He entered the doorway and motioned Mary to follow. She stepped into a room that seemed very dark, and it took her eyes a moment to adjust. Just as the exterior had indicated, it was simple and had no fine furnishings, only the essentials: mats, small table-stands, stools.

The room was empty. Jesus passed into another one, then out into the inner courtyard, where Mary could hear voices. Then shrieks.

She poked her head around the door and saw Jesus being enveloped by several arms at once.

"Jesus—"

"You were gone so long—"

"I had to leave some orders unfinished—"

"What happened? What is he like?" a firm male voice demanded.

Jesus broke away from them, laughing. "One at a time! Please!" His eyes went to Mary. "I have brought a guest."

Then five pairs of eyes turned suddenly on her.

"She is Mary, of Magdala," he said. "Mother, I believe you may remember meeting her long ago, when we took the pilgrimage to Jerusalem."

An older woman, whom Mary had seen before, nodded. She had even features and eyes that were kind. "Welcome," she said. Mary recognized the voice; its sweetness had not changed. It was the only voice Mary had ever heard with that quality. If his mother wondered why and where Jesus had found Mary again, she kept the question to herself. No one else seemed to pay their visitor much attention; they were all too focused on the return of Jesus.

"Tell us about John!" The same male voice spoke again, impatient with all these preliminaries.

Mary looked at him. He had such a glowering manner that, although he was technically handsome, he was not pleasant to behold.

"That's why you said you had to go. To see John. And left me to mind the shop. All this time!" The man was clearly annoyed.

"You will be minding it from now on, James." Jesus spoke firmly.

James's face registered surprise—angry and unpleasant surprise. "What?" he cried.

"I said, from now on the shop is yours. I will not be returning to it."

"What?" James repeated, his tone combative. "You cannot just—"

"I am no longer a carpenter," said Jesus. "I have worked as a carpenter for ten years, but now I am going to do something else."

"What else?" James jumped up. "What else? I can't manage it all myself—we have too many orders—I was only waiting for you—"

"Hire someone."

"You think it's that easy? It isn't! It would have to be someone of your skills and reliability. People won't settle for less. I can't just—" A note of desperation rose in his voice.

"Look for him," said Jesus. "Somewhere he is out there waiting to be hired."

"Very funny. Very funny. And how do I find him? I suppose God will send him a note!"

Jesus's mother was the only one to ask, "What is it you intend to do instead, son?" None of his three siblings present seemed to care. All they minded was the threat to their own situation. If Jesus left, how would that affect them? Probably for the worse.

Jesus smiled at her. It was clear she and he understood one another. "I will announce it at the synagogue this coming Sabbath. Until then, it is better that I not explain it. But I can tell you this: it means leaving my old life behind."

"And us, too?" his mother asked. Her face clouded.

"Only a way of life, not people," Jesus said. "People are not fixed, like streams or mountains. They can move when they wish. You may accompany me wherever I go. I would welcome that."

"Well, I can't leave!" bellowed James. "You've seen to that! You've chained me to the carpentry shop!"

"I know you preferred that I be the one chained," said Jesus. "But you are not chained, either."

"I can't leave," he repeated. "The family has to be supported."

"God supports the family."

"Have you gone insane?" said James. "God provides handouts, all right, if you want to live like an animal. Frankly, I think Mother and our family deserve a higher standard of living than the meager one God provides!"

"Yes." One of the other brothers, a younger one, spoke up. "What is it they say? God provides for your needs, not your wants. If you need a beast of burden, he may not send you a donkey, but he'll keep your back strong."

Everyone laughed, even Jesus. Finally, Jesus said, "Well, Joses, your back looks straight enough."

Joses: Joseph's namesake. He was round and looked well fed. Mary guessed him to be in his mid-twenties.

"You still haven't told us what John was like." A thin young man spoke up.

Jesus looked at him with fondness. Which brother could this be? Perhaps it was the infant in arms on that trip so long ago.

"Ah, Simon, you know how to ask the true questions. If you wish to see a prophet like Elijah, then go out to see John. To see him is to behold someone ancient."

"What do you mean? Is he Elijah come back to life?" asked James.

A woman who had kept silent all this time, and been almost invisible in a corner, came over and touched his arm. "You know that is a superstition."

That must be James's wife. Only his wife would dare to correct him in public.

"Miriam speaks correctly," said Jesus. "No one is born in the flesh more than once. But John has the power of Elijah when he speaks. Clearly the spirit of God is on him."

"Herod Antipas is after him," said Joses. "They say his days are numbered."

"I saw his soldiers warn John," said Jesus.

"But where have you been all this time?" demanded James. "Surely you haven't been listening to his preaching for these fifty days!"

"So you know it is fifty days?"

"Of course!" said James. "Haven't I had to run the shop all this time? Believe me, fifty days of doing it all on my own was more like a hundred. Of course I know how many days."

"After I heard John speak, and felt called to baptism, I went out into the desert—"

"Oh, you went out into the desert! And never counted the days, I suppose." James obviously felt betrayed. He never asked about why Jesus had felt called to the desert, or to baptism, Mary noticed. He just focused on the carpentry shop, as if that were all that existed.

"John's message," Simon prompted. "What was it he said that was so compelling?"

Jesus paused before answering. "He believes that the days many have waited for have arrived. That time as we know it is coming to an end."

"And the Messiah—is he to usher this time in?" his mother asked.

"John did not focus on the Messiah but on reforming individual lives and preparing for the judgment and fire that are coming," Jesus said.

"Well, he must have *mentioned* him!" Joses insisted.

"He said very little about him, other than that we are all waiting for him. And that he will be a fearsome man, baptizing with fire," Jesus said. "He certainly never claimed to be the Messiah himself."

"Some of his followers think he is," said James. "That's one reason Antipas wants to get rid of him."

"John is ready for him," said Jesus. "He does not intend to flinch. Or to stop preaching."

"Son, all this is very disturbing to us," his mother finally said. "You return, weakened from your journey, clearly exhausted. You announce that you are leaving your father's trade, the trade you have trained for since childhood, the trade that supports us. Of course you have brothers who can help, but none of them have your knowledge of the customers and the business. I cannot stand in your way, if this is truly what you desire, but it frightens me." She took a deep breath. "And all this while, I thought you would return refreshed and ready to take up the yoke again, and now you have set aside the yoke. Nonetheless, wherever you go, you will need this. And when you wear it, think of us." She went into an adjoining room and returned holding a seamless mantle that was so perfect in its workmanship that Mary and Jesus just stared at it. It was light wool, of a creamy color, woven so beautifully that not one single flaw showed in it, not even as it was turned this way and that, so that the light caught it from many angles.

"Mother," said Jesus, rising to take it from her. He clasped it in his hands and examined it, turning it over and over. "This is magnificent."

"Don't say you won't take it! Don't say you want to be rough-clad, like John the Baptist! I labored too long over it, and every single stitch of it was done with love."

"I am proud to wear it. *Because* it was made with your love."

Jesus pulled it over his head and let its light folds fall around him. It fitted perfectly. He laughed and said so.

"And don't I know you, every cubit and bit, my son?" the elder Mary said. She was smiling, happy that her handiwork had pleased him.

They then went on to speak of other things they thought would concern him, such as news about Pilate and what he had done to anger the Jews of Jerusalem, but Jesus seemed uninterested. Instead, he pressed them for news of what their everyday lives had been like. How was the spring planting? Was anyone going to Jerusalem this year on pilgrimage? Were there many orders for the workshop? Yokes for plowing oxen were always in demand at this time of year.

Only at supper did the family's interest turn to Mary, and she would rather it had not. She would have been content to be invisible and just listen to them, but suddenly they were curious about her.

You live in Magdala? You are Nathan's daughter? Aren't you married? Where is your husband? Does he know you are here? Are you returning tomorrow?

Mary tried to answer the questions but found that she could not do so honestly. She did not want to recount the story of the demons, and how she had been driven into the desert or discuss Joel or Elisheba; it seemed wrong to talk about them now, when Joel himself did not know what had become of her. But she did not want to lie—at least not in front of Jesus.

"Mary was on a pilgrimage to a holy site because of an illness in the family," Jesus cut in. "Her prayers for her family were granted, and she will be returning to them after the Sabbath. She wishes to rest and collect herself first, so that by the time she arrives the cure will be complete." That certainly described it, Mary had to admit, without revealing any details.

"How wonderful that your prayers were granted," said Jesus's mother. "I know you must be relieved."

Beyond anything you could imagine, Mary thought.

"We all have prayers that are so deep and painful that to have them answered seems like a miracle," Jesus's mother continued. She took Mary's hands and held them. Mary saw how the years had not dimmed the mother's attractive face, even if there were lines around her eyes now.

All Mary could do was nod silently. This woman seemed to understand her very well, and to have her own store of secret things. Otherwise, how could she have known?

The simple supper was soon over, and just as quickly cleaned up, and twilight was already falling. They climbed the wooden outside stairs up to the roof, where there were mats and benches, and sat for a few moments watching the sky darken and the first stars come out.

"Thanks be to God for another day," said James, suddenly. "And may he sustain us through the night." He bowed his head and seemed lost in private devotions, and his wife did likewise.

So James was Jesus's family's version of Eli, thought Mary. Every family must have one. I wonder who the Silvanus is? She stole a few looks around but did not see any candidates for a life of worldliness.

At the thought of Eli and Silvanus, a great stab of homesickness tore through her. How can I ever leave them, leave my family, even for a while, to follow Jesus? she thought. Perhaps . . . perhaps . . .

She stole a sideways glance at Jesus. When he was in the desert, it had seemed so compelling to follow him. But now, here, sitting on a rooftop with his family, he did not seem so mesmerizing or commanding. Perhaps she had been hasty.

After darkness had come, Jesus's mother showed Mary to the room Leah and Ruth had shared before they had left home to marry. A narrow bed with woven strips under the mattress was waiting for her, and everything was in order and restful. It gave her a peaceful feeling to come in here, as if this was a household—and a world—where everything had always been well ordered.

৯৩ X X V I ৯৩

The synagogue was packed. It was near Passover, and people's piety was at a high pitch, particularly those who longed to go to Jerusalem this year but could not. They would make up for it with extra devotions and prayers, and attend services with greater faithfulness. The entire family had set out together from Jesus's house, but now Mary and Jesus's mother were apart from the men and sitting with the other women of Nazareth off to one side, while the men took seats down in front.

There was the usual order of prayer and readings. The first portion of the service had a fixed reading of the Torah, read first in Hebrew and then translated into Aramaic, to be followed by seasonal prayers and supplications. Then a reading from one of the prophets would follow, the "last lesson." Any man could perform this duty, and present verses—at the most three—that he had selected and meditated upon, and then comment on them. When they came to that portion of the service, Jesus stood up and went to the lectern.

He moved slowly and deliberately, not in a hurry to take his place but not holding back, either. He found the verses in the scroll, which was unrolled at the proper place. It was forbidden to quote from memory, but although Jesus seemed to be reading the text, clearly it was already in his head.

"Thus the prophet Isaiah said . . ." he began. He looked out at the gathered worshipers, who were all staring at him with happy, expectant faces. "'The spirit of the Lord is upon me, because the Lord hath anointed me: he hath sent me to preach good tidings to the meek; he hath sent me to bind up the brokenhearted, to proclaim liberty to the captives, and the opening of the prison to them that are bound.'"

Everyone sat listening comfortably. This was many people's favorite verse.

"'To proclaim the acceptable year of the Lord, and the day of vengeance for our God: to comfort all that mourn.'" He carefully rolled up the scroll. Now would follow a little homily. Everyone waited for it.

"Today this scripture is fulfilled in your hearing." He looked around the room as he made this announcement.

There was a heavy, stunned silence. For a long moment or two, there was no response at all. These verses referred to the Messiah, to the age of deliverance.

"How is it fulfilled?" someone finally asked. "I see none of these things taking place." The voice from the darkened back of the room was prickly.

"Today it begins." Jesus gripped the side of the lectern and stared back at him. "This is its first hour."

Then a swell of voices burst from the room. "Aren't you Joseph's son? Don't you run the carpentry shop here? How would you know these things?"

Jesus looked back at them all. "Because I myself will fulfill them."

Now the silence that followed was alive with hostility.

Finally, an old man stood up and said in a wavering voice, "Son, what do you mean, you will fulfill this scripture?" His tone was of profound sadness, as if he had just witnessed a disgusting and uncalled-for sacrilege, but one that could be reversed by swift repentance.

"Day by day, by following my Father's will and guidance, this Kingdom will be revealed to me, and then I will reveal it to you. What I have said will come about. And those privileged to join in this Kingdom—"

"Your father was Joseph!" someone yelled. "Is he to guide you from the grave? This is nonsense!"

"I mean the will of my heavenly Father. God." Jesus seemed to be drained of color, as if saying all this was taxing him to the utmost. But he persisted. "We all have the power to become the sons of God," he finished.

A loud cacophony of voices drowned him out.

The two Marys shrank back. Jesus's mother took Mary's hand and pulled her out the door, past the rows of benches and the dark faces of the audience, but not before they could hear, "Blasphemy! Blasphemy!" resounding within the room. Then pandemonium erupted. While the two women watched, from a distance, groups of angry, gesticulating men poured from the building.

Both women were stunned, speechless. Another knot of men exploded from the building, and then Jesus appeared in their midst, expelled as if riding on a wave of people. He was trying to speak, but they were drowning out his voice. The crowd actually carried him along, as if he were a stick caught in a flood.

"Hear me! Hear me!" he was saying—in vain.

"You grew up here! How dare you make such outrageous claims?" someone yelled.

"We know who you are, all right!"

Jesus suddenly seemed to halt and make them halt with him. "The truth is, a prophet is not without honor except in his native place and among his own kin and in his own house!" he cried.

That seemed to capture their attention. They stopped moving and stood still, surrounding him. "Remember the story of Elijah and the widow of Sidon? There were many needy widows in Israel at that terrible time of drought, but who was Elijah sent to? A woman living elsewhere, in a pagan land."

A sullen and ugly silence now enveloped him, ringing him like the crowd. "And what about Naaman the Syrian? Oh, there were many lepers in Israel at that time, but who did Elisha cure? A foreigner, and the servant of an enemy of Israel. What does that tell you?"

The answer was a growl. "It tells us that you yourself must favor foreigners and enemies over your own people!" one voice cried. "And that you equate yourself with our greatest prophets! You! Who have never done anything but work in a carpentry shop! How dare you?"

"The prophet Amos was a dresser of sycamore figs," said Jesus. "And King David, a tender of sheep."

"Enough! Do you say you are like David?"

"Kill him!"

"Stone him!"

He had no chance to answer or defend himself. The big crowd

rushed on him and, surrounding him, bore him away toward the precipice of the hill.

"Throw him down!" they were chanting.

"Stun him, and then stone him! He's a traitor, a blasphemer!"

Nazareth was high enough that to be cast down from one of the cliffs meant certain death. The two Marys saw the surging crowd, like an ocean wave, heading in that direction, but they had no chance to reach Jesus.

"Oh, most high God above!" Jesus's mother's face was ashen. Clearly she had had no premonition of this; it was as sudden a shock as if a lightning bolt had descended and struck her son.

But Mary was less surprised. Perhaps she had come to know Jesus, or this new Jesus, better than his family.

But was he to die now? Mary abandoned his mother without thinking, beyond a rote, "Return home and I will join you. It will be all right." She embraced her and gently turned her in the direction of home, then hurried off after the crowd.

All she could see were their backs, serving as a wall between her and Jesus. Somewhere, in the forefront of this crowd, he was being pushed and shoved and carried along. She could not even hear him any longer; all she heard was the shouts and curses of the crowd: dreadful words that rang in her ear with their vengefulness, as though Jesus had personally wronged them.

She could feel the ground sloping upward a bit, then leveling off. In the distance, she could see the hills and even a slight glint of water; it must be the lake glittering far away. But directly down below were the rocks and steep gullies of the mountainside.

"Kill him! Kill him!" they were shouting. There was a great cry, and then—nothing. The crowd stood knotted for what seemed forever, and then gradually dispersed.

Mary shrank back and watched the dark-robed men striding past the large boulder where she hid. What was on their faces? She expected to see bloodlust—satisfied bloodlust. Instead she saw only blank expressions, and bafflement.

Emerging from the safety of the boulder, she began to fight her way through the crowd to get to the lip of the cliff. She did not want to look down there, but, no matter what had happened, she must try to help. Her heart beating so fast it made her dizzy, she made her way slowly toward the overhang. She forced herself to look down.

There was nothing below. Nothing that she could see. Perhaps he had fallen out of sight, behind one of the boulders, masked by the shadows. Where was the path? She could see none.

She tried to pick her way down the steep cliff and around the boulders, but it was impossible without a path. She must return with sturdier sandals, and perhaps with ropes, to help in the descent. But if they hurried—if the family could come, and right away—

Only then did she realize that none of Jesus's family was there. Where was James? Where was Joses? And Simon? Had they all fled? Was she the only one to remain?

She stood, stunned. The great bulwark, the family, had failed. It had not rallied or even attempted to save its brother—the same brother who was expected to dedicate the rest of his life to supporting them in the carpentry shop, regardless of what else he felt he had been called to do. This, then, was their true feeling. Suppose he had dedicated his life to them, only to realize the truth later? Perhaps he had already known it.

She turned to find his house again, to seek out Mary, his mother. But her mind was reeling. Jesus had been attacked and . . . and . . . She could not say the word, even in her own mind: "killed." No, he must be there among the rocks. She would find him and help him.

Suddenly she did not want to return to the house. That would just be a waste of time, with Jesus injured and needing immediate help. Anyone could contribute a rope, or sandals, and much quicker and without delaying explanations.

She almost assaulted a youth who was crossing the ground in front of her. He had thick shoes. That was all that mattered.

"Your shoes! Can I borrow them?" she cried, clutching at his arm.

"What?" He looked first at her, then down at his shoes.

"Please! A man has been injured! Down on the rocks! I need sturdy shoes to climb down there and help him. Just lend them to me!"

"What man?" He looked puzzled. Was he the only one in Nazareth not to know about the synagogue and the riot? But of course. He was young, and probably stayed away from religious services whenever he could.

"Jesus. The son of Mary." Oh, what did explanations matter? "Please, the shoes!"

"But why would they want to harm Jesus?" The young man shook his head. "I thought everyone liked him."

"They did, before he went away to see John the Baptist, and—oh, may I tell you all this later? He needs help now!"

The youth bent down and began to untie his shoes. "Well, of course—but now, if I am barefoot, I cannot come and help you. And I would certainly like to help Jesus. He has always helped me." He handed Mary the two heavy shoes.

In other times she would have asked how, and learned more about Jesus before she had known him, but now nothing mattered but finding him.

"Thank you, thank you!" she said, fastening them hastily and hurrying back to the site of the cliff.

Now she could descend, and she picked her way carefully on the steep and treacherous ravine where they had thrown Jesus. The sun was at its height, and heat radiated off the rocks. Surely that would add to the agony of any injury. Overhead, she could see the birds of prey circling, as they always did, hopeful of finding something. But that they were still circling aimlessly was a good sign.

The smell of the baking rocks and the wild thyme between them seemed overwhelming. Where was Jesus? She held her breath and strained to hear the slightest sound of breathing or movement. But there was nothing; only silence greeted her.

At midday, there were no shadows, and nothing to see but the sunlit stones and the loose dirt and the occasional wildflower that bloomed happily in the crevices. There was no Jesus, anywhere.

He had fallen where she could not find him. She leaned against a large rock and wept.

It was all over; all over before it had really begun. Jesus had cured her, but beyond that he had not been permitted to do anything, even to open his ministry. No one had heard his message, beyond those few in a synagogue in a little village. What he was would forever remain a mystery.

"Mary."

From up above her came a voice. She turned to see who was speaking to her and could see only a black outline of someone on the cliff.

"Mary." Again her name was called. "Why are you crying?"

Who could be asking her this? Who even knew her? Was it one of Jesus's brothers? But they would know why she was crying. And why were they not crying themselves? She had known Jesus for only a little while, they had known him all their lives.

"I am crying because I am looking for Jesus, who was attacked and flung down here, and I cannot find him." She cried the words out like a challenge: Help me find him, then!

"Mary."

The voice was familiar. She shaded her eyes and looked up at him. But all she could see was his outline against the light. She moved to the right, and suddenly she could see his face.

"Jesus!"

It was Jesus standing on the cliff, looking down at her.

"So you have been searching for me," he said. He gestured to all the empty rocks. "You alone."

She began to climb up to him. How had he escaped? How could it be that he was standing there, calm and untouched? "The others fled . . ." she murmured. "They were in danger. . . ." That may have been true, but it was not the reason they had fled.

Jesus held out his hand to her and pulled her up the rest of the way. She looked deep into his face. He seemed untouched, completely unharmed by any of the people who had attacked him. Even his new cloak bore no stains. "But how did you—I saw them bear you here—"

"It was not my hour," he said, as if that explained it. "I simply passed through the crowd and left them there."

But how? It was impossible. She had been here, and had seen it. He had not emerged from the crowd on the other side.

"What . . . what will you do now?" she asked.

"Clearly I must leave Nazareth," he said. "But I always knew that. Do we not have a journey to make to Magdala?" His eyes were kind, even as his voice was light.

"Your mother," she said. "I promised to return and tell her—"

"She will know," said Jesus. "You must not return. It is over here."

Was he not sad? He seemed so accepting of it all.

"I do not wish to grieve them," he said, answering her thoughts. "But I also do not wish to grieve my heavenly Father by delaying. I have two loyalties, but one must take precedence."

"How can you be so sure of the order of these loyalties?" she asked. How could one truly know?

"Loyalty to God must always be first. And God does not wish to cause pain."

"But choosing him often does!" Mary could see that, already.

"Then it is a pain he will comfort," said Jesus. He looked up at the sky. "Shall we set out? We can be there by sunset."

She looked up at him. At least he would be with her in Magdala. But would that confuse her more? He had a message from his heavenly Father; all she had was a calling to help Jesus in his ministry. And there was a vast difference.

The sun that had shone so fiercely at noon on the cliff rocks softened into a glow the color of old amber, bathing them in a kindly light. From where they stood at the foot of the mountain, the entire fertile plain of Galilee lay before them, and beyond that, the lake burned like a bronze mirror in the distance. By pushing themselves, they could certainly reach Magdala. But not by sunset. And it had already been a day draining beyond her strength.

The wide fields and the gentle plain seemed a welcoming carpet spread out for them in their hour of need.

"I suggest we stop and spend the night somewhere here," said Jesus. "Then, in the morning, you can return to your family and let them first see you when you are rested, not exhausted as you are now."

Now they were back among the olive trees and orderly fields, a perfect place to stop and rest. Jesus found a grove of olive trees on the right side of the road and beckoned for her to follow. All around them were gnarled old trees. He sat down at the base of one trunk.

She nodded. Yes, that would be better. She wanted them to see the marvelous thing Jesus had done for her, wanted them to see her at her best. "When I return to my home . . ." she began, hesitantly. "They are well off. They will reward you for what you have done."

Immediately she regretted the words. Jesus looked at her—not with anger, but with sadness.

"Please do not even speak of such a thing," he said. He paused so long that she thought he had said everything. "I am disappointed that you would think it."

"I am sorry—I only thought—"

"Of course you thought it," said Jesus. "But you, and all the others I have called, must understand: from now on I will be poor, and those who join me will be poor." He drew a breath. "As poor as those who throng around synagogues waiting for charity. It is worth considering. That is why I sent everyone back to his original home. If they do not wish to do this . . . they should be honest with themselves."

"But why must we be poor?" Mary asked him. "Moses was not, David was not, certainly Solomon was not! Why is it a condition that we must be poor?"

Jesus did not answer immediately. "We must leave Solomon out of it," he finally said. "Solomon's riches contributed to his abandonment of God. David . . ." He seemed to be thinking out loud. "David was certainly closer to God in his early years than in his later ones. And Moses . . . Moses left his palace in Egypt and went out into the desert. It is true, later he had wealth in livestock. But even that he left behind when God commanded him to return to Egypt and confront Pharaoh."

"But he did not leave his family behind forever, or his wealth," said Mary. "Later, his father-in-law joined him, near Mount Sinai."

Jesus smiled. "I see you know the scriptures well!" He seemed pleased. "But surely Moses did not take that wealth with him into the wilderness. And he himself sent Jethro, his father-in-law, back to Midian."

"Must a person strip himself of everything?" said Mary. "Is that truly what God requires of us?"

"We must be *willing* to strip ourselves of everything," said Jesus. "You make it sound like a hardship. But sometimes the greatest hardship is to continue to live in the world and serve all those masters." He laughed. "And Satan is out there among those things to keep you company. Cut away these things and he has fewer places to hide."

Satan . . . But it was the poverty part that was disturbing her. She did not want to be poor. And was it truly necessary?

∞ XXVII ∞

In the dull early-morning light, Mary awakened. Jesus was still sitting propped up against the tree trunk, his eyes closed. She raised herself up on one elbow and looked at him carefully.

The gathered cloak, so beautifully made of the finest white wool, had fallen back off his head, revealing his thick, dark hair. It was neatly trimmed, not wild or matted like John the Baptist's. Although he had passed a time in the desert, he did not look like a holy man who shunned cities and people. He dressed simply, as an ordinary man, looked like an ordinary man, associated with ordinary men. It allowed people to drop their guard, come near, and listen. It was his message he wanted them to hear.

He had awakened. He looked over at her.

"Ah!" he said. "How good to see you here." He stood up and stretched. The sun, already up, caught his face. His eyes were bright and alert. "We will go on to Magdala. Come." Before them stretched the open green plain with its fields, and already the lake was gleaming ahead.

Spring is here—the time of planting and rejoicing, thought Mary. And the fishermen—the fishermen will be out in their boats, with no special wintertime or storm conditions to worry about. How familiar it all is! How wonderful to see all this again.

It was after midday when they approached Magdala. They had stopped along the way for some figs from a vendor. They had sat down beside the lakeside path and shared the meager booty. After a short rest, they set out on the path—the path so familiar to Mary. On the way, they passed Seven Springs, and the bobbing and busy fishing boats there. But Jesus paid them no mind.

Then, suddenly, they were there. At Magdala.

She felt his hand on her elbow, steadying her. They made their way through the streets of the town, passing the warehouse where her family's life centered, where Joel and her father practically lived, passing the familiar old buildings and side streets. Somehow it seemed different because Jesus was here. They turned down her street. Her heart was racing. Her home was just a moment's walk away.

And then the house was there before them, blocky and stolid, familiar and yet strange. She could hardly breathe for excitement. She was back, free of the demons, a new person.

She stood before its wooden door. She pushed on it. Let them be home, she prayed. Oh, let everyone be there! Before she could push any farther, the door creaked open, and two suspicious eyes looked out at them.

"Yes?"

"I am Mary, the wife of Joel."

The eyes narrowed. "Gone for many weeks?"

The door did not move.

"Yes. I was ill. I know it is a long time—"

"Yes. A long time." The voice was tight.

"Who are you?" asked Mary.

There was a pause. "I was hired to take care of Elisheba."

Still the door did not move.

"Whom you left untended," the voice continued. "Because of your illness."

"I am cured," Mary said loudly. Let the whole town hear her! "Now let me in!"

Silently, the door swung open. She and Jesus stepped inside and found themselves facing a young woman who glared at them. She was very well favored, and looked at them appraisingly. Her eyes flitted over Mary, but lingered on Jesus.

"Where is Joel?" Mary asked.

The woman shrugged dismissively. "Do you not remember?" Clearly the woman thought Mary deficient in wits. "He is at work. Where did you expect him to be?"

Mary ignored her and stood looking, longingly, at her home. Here was the entranceway—here the gathering space—here the hearth. My dear home. My place.

"And where is Elisheba?" she asked.

"Asleep," said the woman. "Have you forgotten that, too? She is only two years old. She naps during the afternoon."

Impatient, Mary pushed past her and made her way to Elisheba's room. Every niche and shadow was familiar to her, like part of her own body.

The dimness in the room caused her to pause for a moment. Then she made her way to the bed. The little girl was fast asleep. Her face had changed in the time Mary had been gone. Mary reached down and encircled her within her arms. Oh, Elisheba, she thought. My heart! An enormous feeling of relief, of homecoming, flooded through her. She held her tightly, feeling the warm little back, the arms, the heavy, curly-haired head lying against her shoulder.

As she caressed Elisheba's neck, she felt a cord encircling it. With one hand she drew it off, over Elisheba's head, and looked at the little token dangling from it. It was a common enough one, used to keep away the Evil Eye, but it seemed as precious as gold to Mary. It had been around her daughter's neck all the while Mary had been away. It had protected her when her mother could not.

She laid the child back down, reluctant to let her go.

"Yes. Let her sleep." The voice was stern. It was that woman. "Do not disturb her any further."

"What is your name?" Mary demanded.

"Sarah." The woman stared back at her. She would obviously give no more than this.

"I must find Joel," Mary said to Jesus, turning from the woman.

She needed to see him, to give him this wonderful gift, her restoration. Then they would hurry back together, to Elisheba. And they would dismiss Sarah. And Jesus would stay the night, and tell Joel of his plans. Her home would serve as Jesus's. And then, later, she would go to help him for a short while.

They hurried through the crowded streets, Mary bumping others aside in her haste to get to Joel, until Jesus embarrassed her by asking the jostled people for pardon. She had to find the man who loved her and had already sacrificed for her beyond what most men would. She drew a deep breath and tried to calm herself.

She found she still had Elisheba's necklace clutched tight in her hand. No matter, she would remember to put it back after she returned home.

They reached the warehouse and pushed open its doors. Instantly a wave of humid air, tinctured with the old familiar smell of the curing garum, hit her. It was dim inside, given the high ceiling and stone vaults. For a moment she could see nothing; then, slowly, shapes resolved themselves. Men rolling barrels. Other men shouting orders. Rows of wooden drying racks. Vats filled with brine.

But everything stopped when she stepped in, as if a spirit force had seized the workers. She did not see Joel anywhere.

"Mary!" a worker totting a basket said, gasping. "Mary!"

"Yes, Timaeus," she assured him. "It is I."

Instead of smiling and greeting her, he bolted off.

She and Jesus looked at one another. "Help me," she said, simply.

"I will be here, beside you," he said.

Just then another worker, wearing a stained apron, edged hesitantly forward. "I will find Joel and tell him you are here," he offered.

They waited in the enveloping, artificial gloom. Then, suddenly, Joel was striding out of the dark, rushing toward her.

"Mary." He wrapped her in his arms. Jesus stepped back.

His embrace was warm and certain. "Oh, Mary, you have returned," he said, joyfully. "When I left you there in Capernaum, I did not know—oh, dear one, you are saved!" He bent his head down to her shoulder and wept.

After a long time he released her and stood back. "Is it really true? They are *gone*?" He searched her face, as if looking for little telltale signs of something yet lingering. "Gone?"

"Gone," she assured him. "Gone instantly, without a trace, and I am free." She took his hands, held them tightly. "Oh, Joel, you cannot imagine what it is for me to be free, delivered from them, restored to the person I was!" She turned to Jesus. "Here he is, the man who delivered me!"

Only then did Joel look at Jesus, puzzled. "It was you? What, my friend, did you *do*? We were in such despair—they seemed so strong—"

Jesus did not answer immediately; he waited a moment, as if weighing his words. "I commanded them, and they obeyed," he finally said.

"But others had commanded them," said Joel. "A very holy man had confronted them, the sacred scriptures had confronted them, all to no avail. What could you do, what secret did you have?"

Mary took Joel's hand in hers again. How good it felt to hold it once more! "Dearest, he was more powerful than the evil spirits. They had to obey him."

She felt Joel's hand stiffen. "Mary, do you know what that means?" He drew himself up, and she could feel him stepping back, putting a distance between himself and Jesus, although he barely moved. "He may be in league with them himself," he whispered, close to her ear.

"What?" Mary was shocked. Jesus merely shook his head, sadly. Somehow he had heard Joel's accusation.

"That is not true" was all Jesus said to defend himself.

"Isn't it?" Joel made Mary look at him. "Think of it! All our holy men could not budge the evil spirits. Even the words of the Torah could not. But a stranger comes in and has power over them. And who has power over the lesser demons? Satan himself, and anyone in league with Satan."

"Satan does not cast out his own spirits," said Jesus. "He does not make war on himself." His voice was still calm, reasoning. "A kingdom divided against itself cannot stand." He paused. "If Satan is fighting himself, he is doing the work of God, and that cannot be."

Joel stared at him, shaking his head, as if to clear it. "You confuse me with your words, your clever words." He paused. "I should thank you, reward you, for having helped my wife. But I cannot reward anyone in league with demons!" His face reflected his fear. He held up his hands as if to silence Jesus in advance, preparing himself. "And do not threaten to have them return! That is beneath even Satan himself!"

This could not be happening! Mary could not believe it—that Joel would turn on Jesus and accuse him of being in league with Satan. It was a bad dream. But everything connected with the evil spirits was a bad dream, and had been from the beginning. It was merely continuing. And now the evil had taken a new victim.

"It's him!" she said. "It's Satan who is entering your thoughts, Joel. If he cannot possess me any longer, he'll get control of you. He'll turn you against me, and against Jesus. He'll make black white, and white black, so that a kind man who ridded me of evil is now painted as evil himself. Stop it! Don't let him do this to you!"

"Satan is the father of lies, Mary. Don't you know that?" Joel said. "But it's you who've been deceived!"

"Deceived? I'm free of the demons, Joel. I'm free of them! And no one can know what that means except me! Not you, not my family, no one! And the man who drove them out, he's here, standing in front of you. Any reward you could give him—the warehouse, the business, all the gold we own—would not be enough. But instead you insult him, and make the worst accusation anyone can of a holy man: that he is in league with evil!"

"What did you say his name was?" Joel asked abruptly, ignoring her plea. "Jesus? A common name. Jesus of who, of where?"

"I come from Nazareth."

Joel stared back at him. Then he began to laugh, a nervous, braying laugh that was not his normal one. "Nazareth! Nazareth! Oh, Mary, you *are* a fool. This man is dangerous, and may be possessed himself. Yesterday he made outlandish claims for his . . . his . . . powers in the synagogue there, and was run out of town. What do you say now?" He had dropped her hand, and crossed his arms firmly, in an authoritative stance.

Mary looked at Joel, astounded. Could these truly be the words of kind, reasonable Joel? "What do I say? Or what does Jesus say?" she asked. "To which of us are you speaking?"

Joel looked a bit surprised by the question, but he quickly said, "You, of course," to Mary.

"Very well," she said. She realized that her answer would confuse Joel even more. "I was there. I saw it all for myself."

Now Joel looked truly shocked. "You were there? You went there with . . . *him* instead of coming here first?"

"Yes. I did. I needed to—to spend more time with him, before—before—"

"Mary!" Joel looked as if she had struck him.

"You ask who he is, and what he is, and make horrible accusations about him." Her words tumbled out, and she was trembling with emotion. "I know he came from Nazareth. I know his family. I have known them for many years. I cannot answer your questions as a rabbi or priest could. All I can do is stand before you and let you look at me and see that I am cured. You ask me what happened? The only thing I am sure of is that I was tormented and possessed by demons, and now they are gone, because *he* cast them out. Because he cared enough for me to return me to the glorious world of good and God. If that is evil, then let everyone be as evil!" She stopped to catch her breath. "I saw what happened at Nazareth. I saw people turn on him, as you have. They tried to kill him! Yes, actually kill him! And that is evil working, wanting to stop him, eliminate him."

"Mary, come away from all that! Leave that ugly world of demons, and exorcisers, and curses, behind." Joel was pleading with her, his face white. "Let her go!" he ordered Jesus. "Don't involve her in your dangers!"

"Joel," she cried, "I went away to keep from harming you further, and to do anything possible to regain my health. But I also owe my life to Jesus. Without him we would have no life. Just let me repay him, help him as he's helped me—"

"Mary!" Joel stepped back as if he had been physically struck. "Mary! This madness is worse than the demons!"

Now, at last, Jesus spoke. "Do not say that, friend. It is a blasphemy against the Holy Spirit." He extended his arm, but Joel swatted it away.

"Get away from me!" he yelled. The workers in the warehouse stopped what they were doing to look. Within a moment, Nathan was rushing toward them, pushing through the workers.

"Daughter!" he cried. Joel blocked him.

"Don't go near them!" said Joel. "This strange man—he's cast some kind of spell over her."

Nathan's eyes narrowed. Then he lurched forward and began to tear at his robe in a ceremonial act of mourning. "Jonah told me about him. His own sons, Simon and Andrew, were taken in by him. Out in the desert. And the stories they told . . ." He was choking on his tears. "Mary, my daughter and your wife, alone with all those men for a month. Waiting on *this* man. She's shamed, and dishonored, and we cannot take her back." Again he grasped his robe and ripped. "She must be dead to us."

"But . . ." Joel's face was rigid. "But I—"

"She's dead to us!" yelled Nathan, grabbing Joel's shoulder. "Shamed, shamed! To live with men in the desert is a disgrace, a sin! You *cannot* take her back. You cannot, or I'll cast you out of our family, legally dismiss you from the business, and remove Elisheba from your care. I'll ruin you, as she is ruined!"

"Father!" Eli shoved his way toward them. "Mary? What is this? Are you home at last?" For an instant he sounded pleased.

"She has no home!" shouted Nathan. "I have no daughter, and you have no sister!"

"And I have no wife," Joel mumbled.

Mary was so stunned at his surrender she could find no words, beyond repeating his name. "Joel! Joel! Joel!"

But he turned away rather than look at her.

"She's a whore!" said Nathan. "People will account her one. The mother of your child will be called a whore, and Elisheba will suffer for it, unless you banish her now. Now!"

Joel burst into tears.

"Oh, God, think of it!" said Nathan. "Think of Elisheba! Oh, God . . ." Now he bent over double, sobbing. "No! No!"

"It does not have to be this way, Joel," Mary cried. "Don't listen to Father! He's blind with hate. But you—you must know better. Look, look at Jesus. You can take the evil, hasty words back. You can say, 'Dear friend, you must be a holy man. You were able to defeat these powers of darkness, which even the holiest men in our community could not. I honor you, and I wish to know more about you.' Say it, Joel. Your whole life, and mine, will be different if you do. Do not pass this by."

But it was not Joel who answered.

"Go!" Nathan commanded her. "Why did you even come back? We had already given you up for dead!"

"I *was* dead," she said. "And you could not really expect that I would return to life. And, if so, whether I would ever be the same. And I am not. Your worst fears are realized."

"This Jesus!" cried Joel. "Why all this, just because of him?" His voice rose to an anguished howl. "Why? Why? I cannot bear it, what you have become!"

"How do you know what I have become?" she said. "Because Father has decided to imagine things that never happened, told third-hand? For that you would abandon me?"

"You've abandoned *me*," he cried. "You've never really been my wife. You always had secrets—first the demons, now this sojourn in the desert with this . . . madman and his followers." He started crying again.

Strangely, she felt as if she must try to be the strong one. I can no longer live as I have before, she thought. How foolish I have been to think that just casting the demons out would solve everything. I have started on the path that takes me far away from what I have known.

"So you will cast me out," she said slowly, stating the fact. She tried very hard not to cry, or to clutch at Joel. He would push her away, recoil from her touch, and that would be more than she could endure now. "We will go on to Capernaum," she added, telling herself not to break down, not to do anything that would anger Joel further or set him and the others off. "If you wish to find me, that is where I shall be. Other followers will gather there." When she heard Joel make a choking noise, she went on. "Leave room in your heart for me. I have not gone. This is something that you may join, too."

"Never!" He looked revolted. "I can only pray that you will come to your senses, pray, purify yourself, redeem your sin. And as for you"—he turned on Jesus—"get out of here, get away, take yourself to hell!"

Together she and Jesus stumbled out of the warehouse and into the bright sunlight. They stood blinking for a moment. Mary half expected Joel and the others to follow them out and chase them, make sure they left the town. But the door remained resolutely shut.

"I did not expect that," Mary finally said. She could barely speak. "I expected . . . a sweeter reunion."

Jesus nodded. "So did I, in Nazareth." Together they laughed a bitter laugh; there was a strange camaraderie between them.

"Your family was at least welcoming," said Mary.

"Yes, but then the villagers tried to kill me."

Now they both laughed in earnest.

The door flew open, and Nathan, Eli, and Joel stood there, glaring at them, looking both betrayed and disgusted.

"Who laughs together like that but lovers or conspirators? I think you are both!" Nathan yelled.

"We are neither," said Jesus. "But I understand if you can think only in those terms."

"You understand! You understand!" mocked Joel. "How noble of you! Now let you understand this: I am within my rights to have you killed. You have dishonored my wife and my house. Only my love for my wife will prevent it. But leave! Leave!" He glared at Mary. "And let me never see your face again! I cannot bear it!"

He stepped back inside and slammed the door.

Mary understood the restraint it had taken for Joel to say what he had but then to retreat. "Jesus," she said, "Joel is a good man. He is."

"Yes. I know that. It is hardest for people like him. I shall pray for him. We do not wish to lose him."

Lose him? How? To the demons? To the world? To them?

"It seems we have both lost our families," said Mary, drawing her breath slowly.

"It should not have to be that way," said Jesus. "But perhaps they will change. Not tomorrow, or even the day after, but . . . in time."

They were standing down near the busy waterfront. By now, the catches had been delivered and sorted, and even the fish-brokers had gone home. Workers were scrubbing the docks, readying them for to-morrow's early-morning catches.

"You were brave," said Jesus.

"I do not want this," she said quietly. "I do not want to lose my daughter, or have my husband cast me aside. I do not think I could bear it if I did not believe, as you said, that they would change." Her voice trailed off. "Why does it have to be this way?"

"I do not know," he said, slowly. "It is part of the sorrow of living on this earth, with Satan still free to afflict our daily lives."

"Jesus," she suddenly said, "I have another brother. A brother who is not like Eli or my father. . . ." But, of course, Joel had not been like them—or so she had thought. "Let us go, seek him out, before the oth-ers tell him their lies!"

Jesus looked doubtful that this was a wise choice, but he said, "Very well. But be prepared that he, too, may say hateful things. My mother did not follow us, after all."

"But she did not know what had happened," said Mary. Someone should have told her. Suddenly Mary felt very guilty for not return-ing, not doing so.

I am a mother, she thought. How could I have done that to another mother? Left her in such cruel, unspeakable doubt?

From her wrist still dangled the necklace of Elisheba.

"I must see my daughter again! I must take my daughter!" She gasped. "Yes, let us return to the house, and take her. I am her mother, who else should have her? Then we will go to my brother Silvanus, and he will give us provisions, even hide us . . ." She turned and rushed away, back through the streets, and Jesus had no choice but to follow.

Quickly she reached her house. This time she did not knock politely but shoved the door open and hurried back into Elisheba's room. When the caretaker tried to block her way, Mary hit her and pushed her down with the strength of a man. Then she grabbed Elisheba in her arms, yanking her out of the bed, and fled toward the house of Silvanus. Elisheba wailed in fear.

"Silvanus! Naomi!" Mary cried as she beat on the door. They must be home, someone must be!

Naomi, a puzzled look on her face, opened the door and stared.

"Mary!" she said, and then smiled in genuine welcome. "Oh, I am so happy that you have returned! But"—her eyes darted to the screaming child in Mary's arms, and then to the stranger behind her—"what—?"

"Is Silvanus here? Is he here?" Mary cried, hysterically. "I must see him!"

"He is out, but returning at any moment," said Naomi. "Please, come in—"

Before Mary and Jesus could enter, Nathan and Eli and a group of workmen rounded the corner and came pouring forward like a wave.

"She's stolen her!" cried Eli. "Stop her!"

"She has no shame, no shame!" The quavering voice of Mary's father sounded in the air like a summoning trumpet.

Naomi stepped to one side, frightened, as the group came between her and Mary, cutting them apart.

"Give us the child!" Nathan demanded, advancing toward Mary.

She clutched Elisheba tighter against her. The child was struggling, screaming. "No. No. I am her mother; if you banish me, I must have her with me. I will not be separated from her again."

"You are not fit to be her mother!" Eli strode forward and tried to wrench Elisheba out of Mary's arms. She held on tightly, until it seemed the child would be torn in half.

"Stop this!" said Jesus. "Leave the child with her mother!" He tried to stand between Eli and Mary, to break Eli's grasp on the terrified child.

"Who are you?" yelled Eli, shoving Jesus. "You have no rights here!"

Jesus came forward again, and now Eli and Nathan together turned on him and shoved him, so that he fell, although he immediately leapt up. His quick movements made them draw back. This man was obviously strong and fast, and would be a good fighter.

"I say, release this child to her mother," Jesus repeated. But he made no move to attack either adversary.

Now Nathan shoved at Jesus again, and he fell back. Then Eli hit him, and Jesus went down on one knee. At a signal, the other men in the group fell on him, kicking him and raining blows on him. Jesus made no move against them.

"So this is the man you follow!" said Eli. "What kind of a man is this, who won't defend himself but lies there like a weak woman and lets us hit him?"

"Those who practice violence will die of the violence," said Jesus, faintly.

"A nice cover for your cowardice!"

Eli and Nathan together grabbed Mary, and one of them forced her arms open and the other took Elisheba. Naomi started screaming.

"Hush, woman!" said Eli.

The men withdrew, carrying their prize, leaving Mary, Jesus, and Naomi alone.

"Come," Jesus finally said to Mary. "Come. Let us go to Capernaum." He drew in his breath with a harsh sound.

∽ XXVIII ∽

Mary had traveled that path to Capernaum so many times, but now it seemed a nightmare path muffled in infinite pain—pain behind it, pain ahead, and, most horribly, pain surrounding it on all sides. She stumbled against Jesus as she tried to walk, her eyes almost sightless with shock and tears. By the time they had reached the outskirts of Magdala, she was shaking so uncontrollably she could not go on. Her knees buckled, and Jesus led her carefully off the path and to a welcoming tree where they could stop unobserved.

Once they were away from the other travelers, Mary bent to the ground and began sobbing. She felt that she would never be able to stop, never reach the bottom of her grief. The tears and gasping sobs did nothing to alleviate her pain, but seemed to have a life of their own, standing apart from their cause.

Jesus sank down beside her. Through the curtain of her tears she could see the weedy green stalks growing from the rough ground, and the pattern of stitches in his cloak. The cloak that his mother had made, had given him before . . . Now, to her, the cloak itself, and every tiny stitch in it, represented the ties of family that had now cast them out. The care of the weaving, the joy of presenting a gift to a favorite son, the welcome of a homecoming—all gone now, all turned inside out. They were expelled, like Adam and Eve from the Garden, and their families seemed less saddened by it than God had been. The family, suddenly forbidden to them, now seemed to take on aspects of paradise.

"My daughter," she whimpered. She was clutching the token, somehow still in her hand all this time. She had meant to drape it back over Elisheba's head. "This is all I have of her!" She unclenched her fist and showed Jesus the little ceramic circle on its thong.

"Mary, you are always her mother," Jesus said. "It is not over."

Her heaving sobs slowly died away, and she struggled to catch her breath.

Jesus took the necklace from her sweating hand and passed it over her head. "You must wear this now," he said.

He dropped his hands to rest over his knees, and she watched those hands in grateful appreciation. They were not big, but they were strong and finely made. They had calluses from—she supposed—his work in the carpentry shop and his sojourn in the desert.

"Mary," he said, his voice coaxing, "Mary, do not grieve."

"How can I help it?" she said. He had to answer her, convince her. If anyone had the answer, it was he.

"Grief is for final things," he said. "This is not final."

This is not final. This is not final. Could that be true? "How do you . . . how do you know?" She finally choked the words out. If only he did know! If only he knew and could promise it.

"Because there is still love there, and the most ancient thing of all: a mother and her child."

"But the love is only on one side! Elisheba is too young—she cannot feel this. Others will replace me—she will forget—"

"Love will not fade," he insisted.

She looked into his face, saw the expression in his eyes; he was so sure of what he was telling her. He cared about her, understood her confusion and fears. His voice was strong and reassuring, like his hands. She lowered her eyes.

It cannot be! Her innate caution whispered in her mind. You are dangerously close to falling in love with this man. Just because he is kind and comforts you when your husband has turned you out. That is not enough. You are weak, and not in control of your own senses.

"We must go on," she mumbled, trying to stand up once more.

"In time," said Jesus, putting his hand on her arm and indicating that she should wait a bit. He did not attempt to speak further, however. They sat in silence and kept their own thoughts.

When they rose to journey further, it was midafternoon. The lake was still filled with fishing boats, busy with commerce. The cruelty of witnessing others' everyday life when your own life is destroyed brought fresh tears to Mary. But she walked on, thinking for the first time how sadness would someday visit each of the occupants of those boats; how someday the sparkling sun on the water would be unendurable for each of them.

As they rounded the bend and came upon the site of Seven Springs, they saw many boats bobbing in the water, heard the usual babble of voices exclaiming over nothing—in Mary's state of mind, fishing grounds and catches and nets were unimportant, as insignificant as the down flying from the thistles by the lake banks.

A loud, blustering man was yelling orders to a fishing boat out in the water. Mary winced; she did not want to hear him; his voice was as unpleasant as the whine of spoiled children on an outing, only louder.

"You fool!" he was shouting. "How many times do I have to tell you, haul the net in so it doesn't catch on the boat sides! How old are you? Thirty? How can a man who's lived thirty years already be so dumb?"

"Yes, Father," said a familiar voice. Mary looked at the man in the boat. It was Peter.

Jesus saw him at the same time. But he made no move of recognition. Instead he stopped walking and stood still and watched.

"Look at that net!" the landside man was saying. "It's half empty."

"There were many others out today," said Peter. "The grounds were crowded."

"Why did you let the others crowd you out, then? You should have pushed them away. Now come in, and let us count this pitiful catch before the day closes!"

Peter—and Andrew, Mary now saw—began paddling in. Soon they came near the shore; they flung the mooring rope toward their father, who secured the boat to a drilled stone. The men stepped out of the boat, wading in waist-deep water, and beached the boat. Then they began tugging the net after them.

"This is embarrassing," their father said, inspecting the net like an angry overseer. "You must be the worst fishermen on the lake!"

Peter bristled. "We know what we're doing!" He indicated the net, moving and bulging with flopping fish. "If you think otherwise, just compare the other catches from these grounds."

"How can I? They haven't come in yet."

"Yes, and you'd criticize us for that, too, if we were still out." Andrew had finally spoken. "You'd say we were irresponsible, waiting too late to come in."

"Stop arguing with me!" the man snapped. "I'm fed up with you! First you go off forever, taking some crazy woman into the desert to hear the mad preacher, then you stay on for days and days and days. Anything to avoid work."

"We didn't stay to avoid work," said Peter.

"Well, why did you stay? You never told me."

Mary was shocked. Peter had never told his father, or anyone else, about Jesus?

"I—I—" Peter shrugged.

Beside her Jesus moved. She saw the white robe from the corner of her eye, and then it had left her and moved onto the path, and then directly in front of Peter, Andrew, and their father.

Jesus threw back his hood. "Peter!" he said in a loud voice, louder than the father's, deeper, filled with authority.

Peter recognized him with a jolt. Then the horror of knowing Jesus had heard everything flooded his face. "Oh!" he stammered. "Oh. Oh!" He stood rooted.

"Who is this?" his father demanded.

Jesus ignored him. "Simon, called Peter. My rock!" he called to Peter. "Leave this. Come with me, and I will make you a fisher of men." He indicated the net, still squirming with its fish. "Of men. Follow me. We have other, larger catches awaiting us."

"Yes!" said Peter, dropping the net and stumbling forward. Joy flooded his face.

"You, too," said Jesus, pointing at Andrew.

"Master!" cried Andrew, kicking the net aside and coming to Jesus.

"What is this?" their father demanded. "What about the boats? What about this catch?"

"You see to it," said Peter. "You know so much about it." He stepped around his father and embraced Jesus.

"What, are you taking tomorrow off?" his father said. "We can't afford it, not now, not with the best fishing days starting—"

"Tomorrow, and the next day, and the next, and beyond that," said Peter. "I have a new master now."

Mary was astounded to see Peter standing there so resolute, and all at once. But perhaps he had been waiting for Jesus to reappear and rescue him.

"Come." Jesus turned and began walking away, and they followed him. The father started bellowing after them.

"Hold your peace, Jonah," said Jesus.

"How do you know my name?" he yelled.

"I heard it many times from the lips of your sons," said Jesus.

As soon as they were out of earshot of Jonah, they began talking excitedly. Peter gave a whoop of recognition when he saw Mary, but his greeting died when he saw her tear-stained, ravaged face.

"That bad, eh?" he said, shaking his head.

"Beyond what you could imagine," said Jesus. "Her family has turned her out."

"Joel?" Peter's voice was small with disbelief.

"Yes," said Jesus. "They thought she was bewitched, or I was possessed."

"That's absurd!" said Andrew. "Do they not have eyes? Or understanding?"

"They thought she had forfeited her reputation because she spent time alone in the desert with you men," said Jesus.

Peter gave a rueful laugh. "If only they had known . . ."

"Perhaps they were envisioning what *they* would have done in a similar situation," said Mary. Yes, perhaps sanctimonious Eli would have availed himself of vulnerable women, perhaps her own father, perhaps even Joel . . . Oh, hateful, vile accusations! But why else would those have been their very first thoughts?

"Out of the abundance of the heart the mouth speaks," said Jesus. He had evidently been thinking the same thing. "Come," he said, shepherding them forward, toward Capernaum.

They were still not beyond the limits of the fishing grounds when they encountered more boats in a congested area where the fishermen were almost bumping up against one another.

"Everyone fights for those warm currents," said Peter to Jesus. Jesus, after all, was not a fisherman, nor was he familiar with the intricacies of these grounds. Peter was nervously ebullient, beside himself at his daring rebellion against his father. Now he pressed close to Jesus, talking all the while. Mary could hear little of what he said, nor did she care to. It was very hard to care about anything beyond just staying on her feet and keeping herself from weeping. She kept touching the necklace around her neck.

Suddenly she heard an all-too-familiar voice on the path ahead. It was that unpleasant fisherman Zebedee, the red-faced one who always acted as though he owned the lake. Her initial encounter with his blustering, during her first walk with Joel, had made such an impression on her that she never forgot him. He had some sort of connections in Jerusalem, at the high priest's, she recalled, and that explained his overbearing manner but did not excuse it.

Oh, not now! Not *him*! was her first thought. Then her second: Jesus can take care of him.

Zebedee was scolding his sons, who were still out in the boat. Evidently they had not caught anything at all.

Peter turned and grinned at his company, as if to say, You see, you see how well *we* did!

The men in the boat did not look anything alike. One was burly, broad-faced, and broad-shouldered, and the other so delicate and fine-featured he could be mistaken for a girl.

"Father, we have done out best," the slight one said, pleading.

"Your best! Your best! Your best is my worst! We own all this"—he swept his wide-sleeved arm out across the water—"and now you fail!"

He didn't own the lake, no one did, but his conceit told him he did, thought Mary.

"My name rings across the waters!" he said. "All the way from Bethsaida to Susita. From Tiberias to Gergesa. Zebedee of Bethsaida is renowned all the way to Jerusalem!"

"Yes, and I am known also!" the brawny son now trumpeted. "Yes, the name of James is already famous!"

"No, it isn't, nor is it likely to be!" his father countered.

Once again Jesus detached himself and made his way down to the water, stepping carefully over the rocks that lined the shore.

"Friends," he said to the men in the boat, "row farther out, and then let down your nets."

"We've fished all night and come back with nothing," the big one said. "And now the best hours for fishing are over."

"Row farther out and let down your nets," Jesus repeated.

Astounded, Zebedee just stared at Jesus.

"Don't listen to him," he finally ordered his sons. "You're right, the hours for fishing are over for today."

Suddenly the big one snorted and, giving his father a scornful look, turned and began to row the boat out.

Jesus and his companions waited, watching as the boat reached the middle of the lake, paused, and let down its nets. Zebedee approached Jesus to challenge him, but when Jesus did not answer his questions he stalked away and took up his post at the water's edge.

A shout came from the lake. "The nets! The nets are breaking! Help! Help!" The men were straining to pull in the nets, and they were so full they were about to burst.

"Go!" Zebedee ordered another of his boats out to the rescue. Soon the two boats were making their way back to shore, moving slowly because of the weight of the catch. As they came closer, the vessels started to sink from the burden of the cargo. Zebedee jumped in the water and waded out to help guide the craft onto the pebbled shore. The boats were listing. Inside were nets so full they looked like huge wineskins.

In his glee, Zebedee almost jumped up and down. He was already calculating the profit from this extraordinary catch. "Oh, fine! Oh, fine!"

Jesus stood quietly watching as the father and his sons rejoiced over their good fortune.

"Right onto Caiaphas's table," Zebedee said, nodding. "Yes, these will grace the table of the high priest himself! And my name will resound in the highest quarters of Jerusalem!"

"Put *our* names on the shipment," the handsome, slight one said. "We are the ones who caught it."

"No, everything is in my name, the company's name," Zebedee said. "As it always is. One catch does not qualify *you* to claim it."

"His name should share credit with you. He told us where to go," said the heavier man, noticing Jesus again. "What is your name, friend?"

"Jesus. Of Nazareth. And yours?"

"I am James," said the big man.

"I am John," said his brother.

"You are Boanerges, Sons of Thunder," said Jesus. "Follow me, you Sons of Thunder, and I will make your names known far beyond these shores. Those who follow me will have names that endure beyond even these times and these years."

"What about Caiaphas? Are you known to him? Will we be known to him if we switch from Father's establishment to yours?" asked John.

Jesus laughed. "Caiaphas. When Caiaphas is forgotten, you will be remembered. In truth, Caiaphas will be remembered only because of us."

"He's crazy," said Zebedee. "Look, sons, perhaps I was too harsh. I'll give you a bigger percentage of the catch from now on. And as for him—"

"Follow me," said Jesus, "and I will make you fishers of men. No longer will you pull in catches from the lake, but from the villages. And instead of bringing them death, you will bring them life."

"Don't listen to him," ordered Zebedee.

James and John stood for a long moment beside the nets and their boat. James quietly secured the net over the side of the boat and waded ashore.

"I come," he said.

"And I also," said John, following his brother.

"Stop!" yelled Zebedee.

Only as Jesus led them away, Zebedee still yelling in the background, did they see the others.

"Simon!" James said. "You are with him, too?"

"Yes," he said. "But I have a new name. He calls me Peter, as he called you Boanerges, Sons of Thunder."

"Does he give everyone a new name?" asked James.

"No," said Peter. "Andrew here and Mary are still waiting for their new names."

James and John stared. "A woman?" they murmured.

"Yes," said Jesus. "And there will be others. She is the first."

"But she is a married woman. Where is her husband? How can he permit her to go free?" John asked.

"In the new Kingdom, everyone will be free," said Jesus. "No person will own another person. Each person will belong only to God. And this is the beginning of the new Kingdom."

In Peter's house, once again. How different from the first time, Mary thought. Or is it? The demons are gone, but I am still an outcast, and now others have joined me in exile.

Peter's wife, Mara, and her mother welcomed them warmly and bade them settle themselves.

"Dearest wife," Peter said, embracing her tenderly as the others took their places, "things will be different for us from now on."

She drew back, suspiciously. "How so?"

"I have left the fishing trade. So has my brother, Andrew." He broke away from his wife and put his arm around Andrew's shoulders. "We did not do this lightly."

"What?" Mara's voice was very quiet. "But you had just made an arrangement for this season with Zebedee, and your father—"

"Father is angry," Peter admitted. Then he grinned. "And so is Zebedee!" He indicated James and John with a flourish. "His sons have joined with us."

"Joined with you . . . in what?"

"We follow this man, Jesus of Nazareth," said Peter. But his voice had grown softer and more hesitant.

"To do what?" Mara turned, frowning, to look at Jesus. "I don't understand."

Peter looked imploringly at Jesus. "Master, you must tell her."

Instead of answering, Jesus said, "Thank you for allowing me under your roof, and for your hospitality."

"I'm not sure I want to give it, until you explain what you're all about. Our family needs to eat; we are a fishing family. If my husband leaves that trade, he knows no other."

"I have called your husband, and these others here, to join me in my mission."

"Yes, yes, but what *is* this mission?" Mara looked at him sharply.

"I announce the Kingdom, and in some mysterious way—which I myself do not yet understand—I also bring it about."

Mara snorted. She looked at her husband. "This is ridiculous. There are fifty people like him all over our countryside. All crying for reform, a new kingdom, uprising against Rome, the end of the age . . . How can you have become involved with this? If you follow him, we're ruined. Ruined! No money, the authorities punishing us . . . No!" She whirled and faced Jesus. "Leave him alone! I command you, leave him alone!"

Gently, Peter came over to her and separated her from Jesus. "My days of obeying you, or my father, are past."

Mary was amazed at his courage. Jesus had somehow given it to him. That in itself was a miracle.

"And what's to become of us?" she demanded. "I suppose your new master has thought of that!"

"If you seek God's Kingdom, all the rest will come to you," said Jesus. "That is a promise."

"Really! From you?" She almost spat at him.

"No. It is a promise from God himself."

"And I suppose you speak for God. How can you make promises on his behalf?"

"Because I know his character," said Jesus. "I know it very well."

"Oh, you know his character!" She turned back to her husband. "Is this the sort of man you follow? I suppose he's spent time with God, so he knows all about what he thinks! Even the wisest scribes don't know that, nor do they pretend to. Pretense. That is what this man is all about."

"Woman, we shall see!" said Peter, loudly. "And now we will rest here in our home, and I trust that you will behave with manners and decency. Otherwise, we shall leave, and take ourselves to the fields." He glared at her. "We are not afraid of the scandal, but perhaps you are."

With a gasp, she withdrew from the room, pulling her mother with her. Mary understood how they must feel. This was so sudden, so unexpected, and had no explanation. They had not seen Jesus do anything but stand quietly in the middle of the room. And yet their lives were to be turned upside down for him.

I had thought that, had the *women* seen me in Magdala, Mary thought, they would never have punished me and banished me. But perhaps I was wrong. Perhaps they would have turned on me just as the men did.

Jesus looked at his followers, now alone with him in the room. "Dear friends," he said, "I thank God for you. And yet you should know that a man's own household holds his worst enemies. I am afraid that, in the time to come, the divisions will be between a father and his son, between a daughter and her mother-in-law, between a husband and wife. I am afraid that, by my coming, I have brought not peace but division."

Yes, already . . . My husband, Joel; Peter's wife, Mara; and Zebedee and Jonah; and Jesus's own family, his dear mother, Mary, and his brother James and the others . . . Mary's thoughts were heavy. Why must this be? Jesus, tell us why this must be!

She blurted out the question, directly.

"Because, in this world, Satan blinds and divides people. And the pain is not only in the people who are blinded and cannot understand, but in those who see but cannot make others share their vision." He paused. "For most people, there is comfort in following the same old ways. Now you have become a different way."

❧ XXIX ❧

Rabbi Hanina's synagogue was filled the following Sabbath. Mary and Mara were among the women crowded into the back, forced to stand while the men sat comfortably on benches. Mary did not feel at ease with Mara; not only was she made to feel, as a follower of Jesus, a subversive influence, but Mara probably remembered her as the pitiful possessed woman who had sought shelter at her home. Jesus and the demons seemed to be one and the same in her eyes.

Rabbi Hanina was holding forth, leading the service. Mary wondered if she ought to seek him out afterward and tell him what had happened to her, but she felt that he would not want to hear about Jesus. His instructions on withdrawing and praying and confronting the demons had only resulted in her defeat and in her desperation and attempt to die; surely he would not welcome that news.

When the open invitation to stand up, read, and expostulate on a passage from the prophets came, Jesus stood up and once again read the passage from Isaiah that he had read in Nazareth. Once again his quiet comment at the end, "Today this scripture is fulfilled in your hearing," caused a stir.

But before the congregation could do more than murmur, a man stumbled forward. "What do you want with us, Jesus of Nazareth?" he cried in a low, guttural voice. "Have you come to destroy us?" He clutched at his arms and fell down in a heap.

Mara grabbed Mary's sleeve. "That man—he's possessed!" She then looked at Mary. "Oh, much worse than you were."

As if anyone could have been worse than I was, Mary thought. The poor woman does not know, cannot begin to understand.

"Be quiet!" said Jesus, standing before the man. "Come out of him!"

The man began to shake and scream, and then uttered a loud, hideous shriek before he went limp.

Now the murmurs in the congregation rose even louder. Mary heard, "What's this?" and "He orders evil spirits—and they obey him?"

"He has authority over them?"

Jesus had bent down and was speaking softly to the man when Rabbi Hanina came over and said, "This is not allowed on the Sabbath."

Jesus looked at him and said, "What is not allowed on the Sabbath?"

"Healings. Exorcisms. They are considered work, and no work is allowed on the Sabbath. You know that, surely."

"Rabbi," said Jesus, "suppose your ox or your donkey fell into a pit on the Sabbath. Would you wait another day to pull him out?"

"No, of course not, the Law allows for an animal to be rescued."

"Is not a person more important than a donkey?"

"Sir," said Rabbi Hanina quietly, "leave my synagogue. You are not welcome here again."

"Your synagogue? Is this not the gathering place of the children of Israel? And if I act within the Law, why am I prevented from coming here again?"

"Healing on the Sabbath is *not* within the Law, friend, and you know that. The donkey in a pit is an emergency. There is no emergency about this man and his condition. He has been possessed a long time; another day would have been time enough for him."

"If you had ever been possessed, you would not feel that way," said Jesus.

"Yes!" said Mary. Without being truly aware of what she was doing, she rushed forward. "Rabbi Hanina. You remember me. Mary of Magdala." She pulled off her headscarf, revealing her short growth of hair. "You shaved this head yourself. You know the state I was in—possessed, like this man. You sent me away in hope of my recovery. This man here drove them out—yes, when all else failed. And I can tell you, one day is an eternity when you are tormented by demons. The possessed cannot wait an extra day."

"Silence!" he said, holding up his hands. His face was white from the shock of seeing Mary again, so unexpectedly. "Women are not permitted to speak in the congregation." He said quietly, "But I am thankful that you were healed. That is the important thing."

"It may well have been on the Sabbath," Mary said, loudly enough that others could hear. "If so, God smiled on it."

"Woman," Rabbi Hanina said, "where is your husband? Why does he permit you to speak in public like this?"

The Rabbi could not have chosen a better weapon to silence her. Stunned, she turned away and stumbled down the aisle and out into the street. *Where is your husband?*

"And you must leave, too!" Rabbi Hanina told Jesus. "You have desecrated the Sabbath!"

"As long as it is day," said Jesus, "I must do the work of him who sent me. Night is coming, when no one can work."

"What are you talking about?" the rabbi said.

"My Father is always at his work to this very day, and I, too, am working."

"What? Your father? Who is he? Does he break the Sabbath, too?"

"He's from Nazareth," someone volunteered. "And his father is dead."

"I mean my Father in heaven—and yours, too," said Jesus.

"Are you saying that God works on the Sabbath? Blasphemy! The scriptures say that he rested."

"From creating the world," said Jesus, "not in doing good."

The rabbi actually clapped his hands over his ears. "Enough! How dare you speak this way? You cannot pronounce about what God is doing, or not doing. Especially to excuse your own actions. Stop it, or I'll have you arrested."

"It is not in your power to have me arrested," said Jesus. "I have broken no laws."

He turned and followed Mary out of the synagogue, bringing the healed man with him.

"Come," he said. "He needs help." He smiled at Mara, who was just emerging from the synagogue. "May we take him to your home?"

Later that night, huge crowds who had heard Jesus at the synagogue began to gather in front of Peter's house. They all seemed to suffer from some physical ailment—there were cripples on mats, blind people, and more who seemed possessed. As dusk fell, Mary and those inside Peter's house were able to look out and see a swaying sea of faces, muttering and calling for Jesus, begging him to come out.

"Help us!" they cried. "You say you can restore the sight of the blind, set captives free! Here we are—free us! Free us!"

Mary watched as Jesus listened intently and then bent forward, praying. Bracing himself, he stepped outside. Mary and Peter followed him.

At once a great cry went up, but he warned the people to stay where they were. Only then could he move among them. Astoundingly, they obeyed.

Mary saw him move out into the first group, speaking to them and laying his hands on them. Then he moved farther away, and the darkness enveloped him.

There were stirs and cries in the crowd. At once there seemed to be a multiplication of the people, as if they were converging from all points, even emerging from the waters of the lake. Jesus was swallowed up by them. He could not work, or speak to people, in such a situation. He battled his way back toward the door of Peter's house, hurried in, and slammed the door shut.

"There are too many," he said. "Too many. I cannot help them all."

He looked at the shocked faces of his followers. "That is why I need you," he finally said. "I cannot do it all alone."

"We cannot cure anyone!" said Peter, quickly. "We do not have that power!"

"You will," said Jesus. "You will."

Just then a scraping and pounding noise from the roof caught their attention. Plaster began to fall on their shoulders.

"What is this?" cried Peter's mother-in-law. "What is this?" She rushed outside to inspect, yelling, waving her arms. "Away from my house! Away from my house!"

Before she could come back inside, a large hole appeared in the ceiling, and four eager, apologetic faces peered down at them.

"Our friend here—he could not come close because of the crowds," they said. "He is paralyzed. So we have brought him to you!" And they began to lower a stretcher down through the roof.

For a moment Jesus seemed taken aback. Then he put out a hand to steady the litter as it descended. A weak man, who could barely raise his head above his pillow, looked back at him.

"The faith of your friends has made you well," Jesus finally said. "Son, your sins are forgiven," he said.

A voice sounded from the window. "Who are you to forgive sins?" said a man looking in. "Shut your mouth! Blasphemy!"

Jesus looked out at the man at the window. "Let me answer you," he said. "Tell me—is it easier to forgive sins, or to restore life to lifeless limbs?"

The man in the window frowned. "Neither is easy," he finally said. "And both are the province of God."

"Look!" said Jesus, and it was a command, not an invitation.

"Look! Friend, stand up on your feet and walk home!" He focused his gaze on the man lying on the mat. Slowly the man, scrabbling and hesitant, managed to raise himself up on his elbows.

"You can do better than that!" said Jesus. "You can stand up. You can even carry this whole litter and mat!"

Now every eye was riveted on him. Painfully the man continued to raise himself, then swung his withered legs up over the side of the litter. Trembling, he clutched the sides of the poles and pulled himself up. He put one leg out cautiously, then the next. He seemed so astonished, Mary was afraid he was going to faint.

"Pick up this mat," said Jesus. "Pick it up, and carry it out." His arms shaking, the man did so.

A deep silence filled the entire assembly as the man emerged from the doorway, until someone cried out, "Praise be to God, who has shown men his power!"

Still they kept vigil, surrounding the house, calling for Jesus to come out.

"Stay inside," said Peter. He was as shaken as all the rest, and leaned against a table for support. The wails and voices outside kept rising, loud and demanding. Outside, the darkness was broken only by flaring torches held aloft over the close-packed crowd, painting the faces red. There were so many of them, jostling and shifting against one another.

Jesus seemed torn. Then, before anyone could stop him, he yanked open the door and stepped outside. Mary could hear a deafening cry, a frightening, hungry roar, as if they were a lion ready to devour him, and their needs were so ravenous it was almost the same.

Before the door closed, she rushed outside, too. She pressed herself against the doorframe and tried to see what Jesus was facing. The crowd seemed to extend all the way to the waterfront.

But now that he was actually out and facing them, their cries faded away. He stood and looked at them, then finally said, "It is late, friends. Night is the time to rest. God worked during the daylight, did he not? Then even he rested. Let us follow his example. He established rest to replenish us, and he rested himself. Tomorrow will come. We will work together then."

At the assurance of another day, the crowds were soothed. They began to murmur and drift away. But then a disheveled woman fought her way to the front of the crowd and fell down at his feet.

"Help me! Help me!" she screamed, clawing at his sandals.

A companion rushed forward and put his hand on her shoulder. "Oh, teacher," he said, "she cannot wait until morning."

Jesus bent down and tried to see her face, but it was hidden under long, unkempt hair. "Daughter," he finally said, "you must look up."

The man shook his head. "They will not let her speak," he said.

"Who?" asked Jesus.

Swiftly the kneeling woman jumped up, and out of her mouth came the low, guttural words, "Jesus of Nazareth, have you come to destroy us? I know who you are—the Holy One of God!"

Is this truly what I was like? Mary thought. It was chilling to witness it in another. And yet . . . and yet . . . it is necessary that I see it. I can never understand otherwise.

"Be quiet!" Jesus commanded in a loud voice. "Come out of her!"

The woman collapsed in a writhing heap, and then a wild, inhuman shriek issued from her. A trace of its presence was briefly felt, cold and caressing, by the onlookers, before it disappeared.

An enormous silence descended on the crowd. Then, suddenly, Mary heard one man say, "We must tell everyone! Everyone!" Like a storm cloud running before the wind, the crowd broke up, scattering in every direction.

But Jesus had ceased even to see them. He had bent down over the quivering woman, and drawn her up to her feet. Mary, who could understand exactly what she was experiencing, came and put her arms around her.

"They are gone," said Jesus in a quiet voice. "They are gone."

"But . . . I have felt them leave before. It never lasted." The woman's voice was faint.

"They will not come back," said Jesus, his words definite and final. "Tell me, what is your name? Where is your home?" He motioned Mary to help open the door and guide her into Peter's house. Leaning on both of them, she stumbled across the threshold. Inside, she sank down onto a bench.

Peter and Andrew came over to her, and Mara as well. "We welcome you to our home," they said. "Wherever your original home was, this is also your home now." Mara handed her a cup of wine, and Peter a platter of figs. But she waved them away. She seemed barely able to speak. Mary remembered that feeling. She knelt down in front of her.

"I was beset with demons, also," said Mary. "Jesus sent them away. And as he said, they have not returned. You are safe."

"At last," she whispered. "You cannot know—"

"I can," said Mary. "I can."

The woman raised her head. "I am Joanna," she said. "The wife of Chuza."

The wife of Herod Antipas's steward—the possessed woman they had talked about in Tiberias! Peter and Andrew looked at one another. Someone from the royal household, now hiding in theirs!

"Your husband . . . ?" Mary did not want to ask directly. But they needed to know.

"He has despaired of me," said Joanna. "I was . . . incompatible with his royal duties. Herod Antipas began to look on him with disfavor because of me. My husband lost his trust; I all but cost him his livelihood. I did not want that. I had to go away. But I did not know where to go. And so I have been wandering, going from one friend's house to the next, but my friends are dwindling. Demons tend to drive away friends!" She gave a small laugh and pushed back her hair, and Mary began to see her true face. "They have stripped me of everything, taken everything away from me."

"Do you have children?" Mary asked.

"Yes. A grown son, and a daughter whose marriage prospects were ruined because of me. Now, perhaps, now that I am gone . . ." She sighed, a sigh torn with anguish. "It is just one of many sacrifices a mother makes without hesitation. If my absence can help her, then I gladly grant it."

She made it sound so simple. But of course she has already had all those years with her daughter, thought Mary. Not like me!

"There is nothing you surrender to God that you do not get back a hundred—no, a thousand times," Jesus said, looking at Mary, as if to reassure her about Elisheba.

But that could not be. Some things surrendered were gone forever, like the burnt sacrifices at the altar. God did not give them back.

Mary looked at Jesus. He knew such things. He knew things that he should not know, that there was no reasonable way he could have known.

"Will I ever know you?" she asked, reaching out to touch his sleeve as they left to go up to the rooftop.

"I have nothing to hide," he assured her. "Anyone can know me."

"Come. You need to sleep," said Mary, taking charge of Joanna. Together they climbed the stairs to the rooftop to rest. They avoided the hole in the roof and made little beds for themselves on the other side.

Lying on her back, gazing at the vast spangle of stars, Mary felt the brooding presence of God even if he did not speak to her. And in those few moments, it was as if she was lifted up a little way to meet him.

⁓ X X X ⁓

My dearest brother Samuel, also Silvanus, also whatever you please—

Oh, my sweetest Silvanus, has Naomi told you what happened when I returned to Magdala and sought you? Right before her eyes they took Elisheba from me. My own father—your father!—called me shamed and turned me out, and Eli joined with him, and then they turned on Joel and threatened to deprive him of all livelihood if he did not stand with them.

I had returned and thought to make my home once again with my family, thought they would welcome me and thank God that I had been delivered from my cruel oppression. But instead they turned on the man who had driven out the demons, and accused me of shameful things with the other men who follow him. I have been as chaste as the Artemis you read about in your Greek, as faithful as Penelope to her Odysseus, and yet this is how I was treated. Silvanus, they drove me away and took my daughter! You were my only hope, but you were not there when I rushed to you, and there was no rescue for me.

Only help me now! Please read my letters, and please somehow give the little letters I shall compose to Elisheba. No, don't give them to her, they will just take them away. Read them to her in private. Surely you can have her to your home to play with your children without suspicion. My heart cries every day that I am separated from her, and sometimes my arms actually ache with longing to hold her.

Now, because I know you care about me, even if all the rest of my family has cast me out, I must tell you where I am and what has happened. The man who delivered me from the demons, Jesus, has come to Capernaum, where he has been preaching, teaching, and healing. Perhaps you have already heard of him. His works of mercy have brought him great fame and also brought people from all around to seek help. He cannot enter the synagogue any longer, because of arguments with the authorities and disputes about the Law, and so he is preaching in the open fields. Huge crowds come to hear him. Silvanus, come yourself! Hear him, come to see me. I am one of his helpers. Every day more people come to join us, but four of his earliest followers were some fishermen you know who used to supply the ware-house—the sons of Jonah and Zebedee.

There is so much to do now, so much more than I have ever been asked to do before. I am busy all the hours of the day, and fall down exhausted at night, but I sleep soundly knowing I have spent the day doing good and helping people—people who are as desperate as I once was.

Who is he? No one knows. Even I do not know. I know where he came from, and I even know his mother and his brothers and sisters, but still I do not really know where he came from. He is a great mystery, and yet being with him does not seem mysterious at all.

We are all caught up in the excitement of this new life, one so different from anything we had ever expected. Our strength is constantly renewed, and each day we rush out to see what is waiting for us. I never knew such a life was possible.

But I will never be truly at peace until I am back with Elisheba, and until Joel understands. Jesus says that in time this can happen. I must trust that he is right.

Oh, come and hear him for yourself! Come and see me!

Your loving sister, Mary

∞ X X 1 ∞

To my dearest daughter, Elisheba, from her loving mother—

Your uncle Silvanus will read this to you, since you cannot read yet. But someday you will read (just as I learned to), and someday soon we will see each other again. I know that you will be as determined to learn to read and know what is in books as I was, and that you will ignore anyone who tells you a little girl should not read.

I think of you every day. No, I think of you many, many times each day. And what do I think of? I think of your laugh, and how you liked it when I made puppets out of my hands by throwing shadows on the wall. Once I made a rabbit with long ears. They were really my fingers, but they looked like rabbit ears. You held up your fingers and made other things, and I could never guess what they were. Do you still like to do that?

I remember the funny words you made up. You called flies "lauws" and shoes "szzzzz." Soon you won't remember that, and you will use the regular words, but I'll always remember and I'll remind you. Sometimes when we talk in secret we can use those words and no one else will understand. Then we can fool people and have our own secrets.

I remember how you loved the fig cakes made from the new figs when they were just gathered, even though they made a mess on your face. It's almost time for them again. Are you having them now?

I love you, my dearest, and I'm coming back to you soon. Soon. Kisses and hugs for you—your Mother

⁓ X X X I I ⁓

The news about Jesus and his night of healing spread quicker than a runner throughout the entire area. Soon enormous crowds streamed into Capernaum, paralyzing the town. Peter and his family tried to repair the hole in the roof and to put boards over the windows so they could have some privacy, but it was hopeless. They were so besieged within their own house, the headquarters of Jesus's ministry, that they could barely manage to feed themselves.

For the first few days, Mary stayed inside with Joanna, looking after her and hearing her story. It was good to have a woman like herself join them; now she did not feel so alone.

Jesus took to leaving the house before dawn, hoping to draw the crowds away. One morning, after Jesus, Peter, and Andrew had gone, Mary and Joanna followed, emerging onto the thronged streets of Capernaum. They made their way along the promenade, inquiring about the prophet—the teacher—the healer, and each person pointed them in a different direction. Frustrated, they wandered through most of the town, all the way to the demarcation line between the two Herods' territory. There sat the hated customs house.

Joanna laughed. "Well, they won't be *there*!"

But suddenly Mary saw them, right at the corner of the customs house. "Look!" She pointed. "They *are* there!" But why? Together they hurried toward the building, just in time to see Peter's back disappearing around a portico on the other side. That was the entrance for the collection of fees, where the despicable sons of Alphaeus robbed their countrymen by technically legal means—legal under Roman custom, that is. Little tables were set up where the assistants could answer questions and calculate the sums owed, while their masters were seated on rug-draped chairs just inside, reaping the benefits. But something had caused a crowd to gather and stare in at the seated tax collectors. Peter and Andrew were standing just outside the door.

"Peter!" Mary yanked at his sleeve, and Peter, startled, turned around. To Mary's surprise, instead of greeting her, Peter made a gesture for silence.

She saw that inside the building Jesus was talking to the man sitting in the opulent chair, and from the looks of them, the discussion had grown heated. The man was gesturing and pointing to his books. Mary noticed that, even though his gestures were florid, his face was wooden and fixed.

Then she heard Jesus say, "You don't really like this master, do you? I mean, money." Jesus reached down and picked up a silver coin from a stack near the man's books. "It's so . . . small." He held it up and looked at it as if it had a bad odor.

"Its strength has nothing to do with its size," the man said. Even his voice sounded wooden, as if coming through a hollowed-out tube. He retrieved the coin from Jesus.

"Levi, this is no calling for a Levite," said Jesus, leaning forward to speak more closely to the man. "It's true that God promised to provide for all Levites at their countrymen's expense, but I don't think this is what he had in mind. He meant that your tribe would then be free to dedicate yourselves to him without worrying about supporting yourselves."

Levi laughed, a sort of sad echo. "Well, I've no mind to minister at the Temple in Jerusalem."

"So you minister to Mammon instead?"

Now a louder laugh came from Levi's mouth. "What quaint words you use. Mammon!" He laughed again.

"I suppose you prefer 'ill-gotten gains'?"

"Another quaint phrase. Where do you *come* from, friend?"

"He comes from Nazareth." A familiar voice sounded right beside Mary, and she saw a tall, elegant figure step past her and into the room. "But he frequents odd places, like Bethabara and . . . Capernaum. Tell me, Levi, what *have* you done to attract his attention?"

Now the stiff man smiled. "Judas! What brings you up here?"

"Oh, the usual." Judas shrugged. "It's the season for making—what was it?—ill-gotten gains."

"Greetings, Judas," said Jesus.

Levi looked from one to the other. "You know each other?"

"I've heard of him, yes," said Judas. He nodded to Jesus. "I am pleased to meet you at last. I am eager to hear you speak."

Levi shook his head. "You always surprise me, Judas. With the things you know."

Judas made a gesture of dismissal. "Oh, next to Jesus I'm sure I'm quite ordinary." He pointed to the pile of coins. "Well, if you plan to abandon them, please leave them to *me*."

"Leave them, Levi, and follow me." Jesus said, ignoring Judas.

Levi just stared back at him, then looked at Judas, standing beside the money table. Then he looked back at Jesus.

"What did you say?"

"I said, leave all this." He looked directly in Levi's eyes. "Follow me."

Someone in the crowd outside guffawed, but Levi did not seem to hear it. Instead, he stood up. "All right," he said.

Now it was Judas's face that turned stiff. But before he could say anything, Jesus turned to the man sitting in the other chair, a smaller man with a mass of curly hair. "And you also, James!"

James just looked frightened. How did Jesus know his name?

"Would I call one brother without the other?" said Jesus. "I need you both."

"To . . . do what?" asked James in a thin voice.

"To leave your life of sin," said Jesus. "And you know in what ways you have sinned."

"I—I have many friends in the sinner category," said Levi. "So I will invite them all to my home tonight. James and I will announce our . . . resignation, and you can . . . talk to more sinners."

Was he testing Jesus? Mary wondered.

"Good," said Jesus. "I like sinners."

"May I come, too?" asked Judas. "I like them a great deal myself."

Nighttime, and the lanterns in the grand courtyard of Levi's mansion were glowing, attracting clouds of white-winged moths, fluttering in the soft evening air. The ornamental trees rustled in the slight shivers of breeze. Under their branches, crowds of people, some with silk head-scarves fluttering like the moth wings around them, were streaming toward the house. Levi's banquets were always spectacular. Rich people were usually invited, and condescendingly attended, but this time they were puzzled to see many unfamiliar people entering the grounds along with them. They noticed some Romans attending, and assumed Levi had to mix with them as part of his business.

Levi had issued invitations to people only that afternoon, and in a highly peculiar manner. "Friends! Friends!" he had actually shouted at people, walking along the docks. "I invite you to come to my home tonight! Yes, I know it's sudden, but—yes! Come anyway! Come soon!" Then he had dashed down another street to call out to more people. And so big crowds were coming out of curiosity. It was well known that Levi always entertained lavishly, setting out imported delicacies for everyone. Guests usually felt justified in stuffing themselves at his expense, since "at his expense" really meant "at *your* expense"—all the money the cheating tax collector had extracted from their pockets anyway.

At the entrance, a line of servants knelt to wash people's feet with scented water and dry them with linen towels. Inside the mansion, carved wooden screens had been drawn back to let in the evening air, and servers were circulating with pitchers of wine—Pramnian, of course, the best. Everywhere were platters of Jericho dates and the best figs from Syria, bowls of pistachios and almonds, and the delicious smell of roasted kid wafting in. Soon it would be carried in on its platter, heaped high and sliced, little pieces of apple decorating it.

In the center of the room, greeting guests, was Levi, flanked by his brother James, and Jesus. Levi introduced everyone who came past them to Jesus and announced, "I've quit my post. I'm going with him."

"Oh, yes! I believe that!" was the first response, followed by laughter.

"But I mean it," Levi would say, and then the people would start arguing or questioning him. Some just kept laughing and headed for the food.

Mary and Joanna had come with Peter and Andrew, and Mary saw that not only was Judas present, but also Philip had managed to get there. It was good to see him again; their little original band was coming back together.

Levi had engaged musicians, but soon their music was drowned out by the voices of the company. What were Jesus and Levi talking about? They were speaking animatedly. Only when she let her eyes wander to other corners of the room did Mary notice several men dressed very formally and observing, rocking back and forth on their heels, sipping the wine.

They all made their way closer to Levi, just in time to hear Jesus say, "I think you need a new name for your new life. From now on I will call you Matthew. It means 'gift of God.'"

The new Matthew looked uncomfortable with that choice. "I don't think it fits," he said stiffly. "You know what a tax collector is. We cannot serve as a legal witness, or as a judge. And we cannot even attend public worship. Some 'gift of God'!"

"You must use the past tense, Matthew," said Jesus. "You *could* not. That was when you were a tax collector."

Matthew looked around the room, at all his noisy, laughing guests. "To them, I will always be a tax collector," he said. "Nothing will change."

Jesus smiled. "I think you will find that to be wrong." He motioned to Simon. "Here's Peter—my rock. You see, I like to bestow new names on people. Simon says he does not feel much like a rock, either. But I tell him he will grow into one."

"A big boulder," said Peter, slapping his belly. He laughed. "I think I'm well on my way!"

Many fellow agents from Matthew's customs house came over to them, clearly eager to hear what had happened. "Well?" one of them said. "Are you really leaving the business?"

"It's true," Levi, now suddenly Matthew, assured them.

"Just like that?"

Jesus put a hand on Matthew's shoulder, sensing that he needed it. "Yes," he said. "But it had been coming for a long time."

Then it occurred to Mary that Matthew must have already heard Jesus speak elsewhere. Or perhaps he had personally known someone Jesus had healed. His first encounter with Jesus could not have been just the brief exchange about the coin.

"Can you afford to?" The other agent's question was pointed. "What does your wife say?" He looked around the richly appointed room, eyebrows raised.

"She says that she is relieved that we will no longer be ostracized because of my profession," said Matthew, bluntly. "It is hard to enjoy your wealth when others consider even the coins you have touched to be tainted. Sometimes they won't even accept them. And then it's the same as being poor, only worse."

"There is nothing worse than being poor."

"Ah! Judas! You tell him." The fellow tax collector nodded toward Matthew.

Judas greeted them all. "So this is your farewell banquet, Levi! Or must I call you Matthew? A splendid send-off, I must say. You might as well spend it all now, if it's so tainted. Get rid of it." He leaned forward conspiratorially. "Does your wife *really* say that?"

Before Matthew could answer, his brother James made him look across the room, where a group of notoriously dishonest merchants—who were always being fined for using false weights—were standing, eating and drinking together.

"The effrontery!" James said. "How dare they come in here!"

Then the other tax collector guest said, "They aren't the only ones. Look! Over there!"

Three of Capernaum's best-known drunks had cornered an entire wine jar and were drinking straight from it. Keeping them company were several obvious prostitutes in their regular working attire—loudly colored scarves, exposed arms, painted faces, and neckloads of jewelry. Their friends, a group of cutpurses, were sharing in the fun.

The religious elders seemed to see them at the same time, and made a straight line over to Matthew and Jesus. They marched up, their stiff robes rustling, and stared at Jesus.

"So this is the man who claims to be a prophet and a teacher," they said to Matthew, as if Jesus could not speak.

"He is one," said Matthew. "If you heard him teach—"

"We've heard *about* his teaching. That's why we're here—to investigate it. But tell us, why have you invited these sinners into your home? Have you gone mad?" They delicately avoided stating the obvious: tax collectors were different kind of sinner; they smelled better.

"I invited them," said Jesus. "I told them all to come." He looked over at Matthew. "You invited your friends, and I invited mine."

They glared at him. "Why? Tell us, teacher, why would you associate with such garbage? You know that uncleanness spreads to whatever it touches. That is the principle underlying our bathing and eating rituals. Surely you must know it will discredit your . . . your ministry, whatever it may be."

"I invited them because I have come to call sinners, not the righteous. It is the sick who need a doctor, not the healthy."

They looked at him with distaste. "It's you who need a doctor," one of them finally said. "A doctor of Torah! Of the Law!"

A Roman approached, a centurion who dealt with Matthew and counted him a friend. The religious leaders all but gathered their skirts and edged away, giving Matthew and Jesus baleful looks, irritated that their rebuke would have to be cut short.

"How will we survive at the customs house without you—and you?" the Roman asked Matthew, nodding to James as well.

"You'll have plenty of bidders to fill our places," said Matthew. The position was usually awarded by public auction.

"None as good as you," the Roman assured him.

"You say that to everyone, Claudius," said Matthew, but not sarcastically. "Well, I shall miss you—especially your compliments."

"You are getting a clever man," Claudius told Jesus. "He's hardworking, has a formidable memory, a genius for details—say, what *is* it you have recruited him to do? I don't understand exactly what . . . er . . . your organization is."

"I don't have an organization," said Jesus.

"Well, Levi will help you set one up. Really, he's cut out for it." He turned to Matthew. "You didn't have enough scope at the customs booth, that's the problem. Now you can really move ahead. Something to get your teeth into."

"You know, it's very ironic," said Matthew to Jesus. "I was not allowed to attend the synagogue, but Claudius was."

"'That is the principle underlying our bathing and eating rituals,'" Jesus repeated the words of the leaders. "But the religious leaders have it backward. A pagan, outside our laws—begging your pardon, Claudius—cannot be judged by the Law and is granted access to our services, whereas a son of Israel is denied it if he has been branded a sinner by those same laws. In fact, it's the sinner who most needs to come closer to the holy. They are so misguided!"

"Begging *your* pardon," said Claudius, "I don't think you have the authority to make such pronouncements. You know they are a closed society, those scribes and scholars, and don't recognize outsiders." He laughed. "I suppose that makes us brothers, in a way—both of us outsiders."

People were pressing around them on all sides. The crush of people shouldered Mary and Joanna aside, so they lost the rest of the conversation.

"You must have attended many such functions," Mary said to Joanna. After all, Herod Antipas was constantly having to entertain lavishly. "Were you—did you see the marriage take place?" Antipas had gone ahead with his marriage to Herodias, in spite of the Baptist's warnings.

"No," said Joanna. "By that I mean—I was present, but I did not really see it."

Mary understood exactly what she meant. The demons did not let you see. "Perhaps, in this case, it's just as well," she said.

Idly she wondered if Antipas and his bride had sampled her family's garum and whether they liked it. Did they notice the special amphora seal?

Once all that was so vitally important to me, Mary thought. And now—now the only thing from my old life constantly in my thoughts is my daughter. Oh, Elisheba! The very name wounded her like a knife, and at that moment she would have traded almost anything to be able to hold her daughter.

She was so sunk in her own dark thoughts here in the crowded and glittering room that the quick movement to her left did not disrupt her brooding. But suddenly loud cries rang out, and she stared as three hooded men ducked and feinted around Claudius to get close to Matthew, then attacked the obstructing Roman and pulled him down, striking as suddenly as a lion pouncing after waiting in stillness for hours. With a swirl of his cape, Claudius fell heavily on his back, and the assailants jumped on him, knives flashing. One—two—three— bright shiny curved blades arced in the air. *Sicarii.*

Now everyone in the room was yelling and screaming, some joining the fight and others shrinking back. Mary saw a tangle of legs and arms, heard an ugly *thunk! thunk!* as the knives kept hitting something. Claudius struggled to his feet, his training as a soldier overcoming the element of surprise. Now the enemies would fight as equals, matching skills.

"Death! Death!" one of the attackers was yelling. "Kill him now!"

As Claudius rose up, one of the men clung to his back like a rider on a wild horse. Another of the assailants rushed forward to stab his chest, but Claudius expertly fended him off by kicking the knife out of his hand. Then he spun around and threw off the attacker on his back with such force that the man hit his head against a wall and was knocked unconscious. He sprawled out, and his hand uncurled and released his knife. Claudius stamped on his wrist and broke all the bones in his hand. Mary could hear them snap and crunch like rotten wood.

The last man now attacked Claudius from behind, locking one arm around his neck and attempting to stab him in the back. But his hand got tangled in Claudius's cloak. His hood fell back and revealed his face, a lean ferretlike face, a face Mary had seen before.

That man who had forced his way into Silvanus's house! The man who had murdered someone in Tiberias. Simon. That was his name, Simon.

"Simon!" Mary heard herself crying out. "Simon! Stop! Stop!"

Simon was so startled to hear his name called that for a moment he hesitated, and that was all the time Claudius needed. He reached up and broke Simon's stranglehold on his neck, breaking his arm in the process. It, too, made an ugly noise, but duller than the other man's hand. Simon yelled out in pain and protest, as though he had been unfairly attacked, and crumpled to the ground.

Mary ran up to him and stared. Yes, it was the very same man.

"It's your fault!" Simon accused her, his eyes bulging with pain from the broken arm. He still stubbornly clutched his curved knife. "You yelled, and caused this!"

"Caused what?" Mary yelled back at him. "You couldn't have escaped. If you had killed this Roman, you would have been crucified. And for what?"

"If you don't understand, then you are one of the enemy." His eyes narrowed. "You already were, anyway. I remember now. I remember being asked to leave that house, and you just standing by, smiling and nodding. A collaborator!" Even in his pain, he mustered the indignation to spit.

Claudius was shaking his head and rubbing his forearms, stunned at his narrow escape. "He'll be crucified now," he said. "An attempt is the same as success. As far as the criminal is concerned, of course, not the victim." He looked at them. "All three of you." By that time, his fellow Roman soldiers had ringed the men and laid hands on them. They hauled the unconscious man to his feet and held him up. Simon they tied up, seeming to enjoy his pain as they forced his broken arm behind his back. The third man, whom Claudius had unarmed by a kick, was apprehended and held immobile, his arms pinioned.

"Take them away," Claudius ordered the soldiers.

"Simon!" It was Jesus speaking. He had said nothing during the entire altercation; now he spoke loudly.

The ferretlike assassin turned his head to look at his addresser.

"Simon!" Jesus repeated.

Claudius looked puzzled, but he signaled to the soldiers to wait a moment.

"What is it?" Simon snarled. "Let's get this over with! Let me die for my people! No lectures from you, no trials by the Romans, no mercy from the conniving, cowardly government! I don't want any of it!"

"Simon!"

There was something in Jesus's voice that made Simon stop talking. He closed his mouth and waited.

"Simon. Join me."

"What?" said Matthew, his face going pale.

"No!" said Claudius. "He's attacked a representative of Rome, and that's treason. He must die."

"Traitors die all the time," said Jesus. "What was that you asked, Mary? What for? What is his death for? A very deep question. Simon, would you not like to do something to bring about the Kingdom? That is what you have been working for, isn't it?"

"I don't know anything about a Kingdom," said Simon. His face was beginning to register the shock of his broken arm.

"I think you do," said Jesus. "Would you like to join us and learn more about it?"

Simon just glared back at him.

"It does not involve knives and assassinations," said Jesus. "You must understand that from the start. But, then, you've had your fill of them, I would assume."

"This man is under arrest," Claudius said. "He has to be taken away."

"Yes! Yes! I'll go with you!" Simon suddenly said to Jesus. His eyes gleamed; any escape would serve.

"You can't take him," said Claudius. "Not on your own authority—whatever that is."

"What if I promise his good behavior?" Jesus said.

"You can't do that, legally. He's got a history of these attacks. This time, we were lucky enough to catch him."

"You can punish me in his place if he causes any more trouble."

"I'm not even tempted. After all, you haven't caused us any trouble, so punishing you in his stead doesn't help us."

"Simon, do you swear to leave all violence behind?" Jesus said.

Simon hesitated. Finally, he nodded. But he did not look Jesus in the eye.

"You can start by handing over that knife you are trying to hide," said Claudius.

Simon dropped it on the floor.

"What about you, Dismas?" Jesus asked the silent third man, whom Claudius had kicked.

The man looked so shocked to hear his name that he just stared.

"I said, what about you, Dismas?" Jesus repeated. "Will you join me?"

"No!" Dismas looked frightened. "No, you're crazy!"

With no more ado, the Romans hauled him away before he could change his mind.

The second man with the broken arm was just regaining consciousness. He also looked oddly familiar to Mary. Perhaps he had been the second *sicarii* in Tiberias. He opened his eyes to find himself a prisoner.

"And you?" Jesus asked.

"What? Who are you?" The man glanced at Simon, now a prisoner, and the Roman not only alive but issuing orders. He groaned and shut his eyes.

"My name is Jesus," he said. "I invite you to join me and my mission."

The prisoner shook his head. "The only mission I know is fighting Rome and her friends," he said. "No thanks."

"Simon has said yes."

The man looked disgusted. Then he shrugged. "People are full of surprises."

"Surprise yourself and join us."

He thought for a moment and said, "No."

"Take him away, too," said Claudius.

Now only Simon was left. He looked around in disbelief. "I should go with them," he finally said.

Jesus shook his head. "Your choice has been made, has it not?" He looked at Claudius. "I pledge to you that you have nothing more to fear from him."

Claudius just stood there eyeing them.

"I swear it, too," said Matthew. "I will stand surety for him as well."

Simon turned on him. "It was you, who betray your own people, that I wanted to kill. The Roman just got in the way. I hate collaborators worse than the Romans themselves."

"I know," said Matthew. "I had been watching for your knife for a long time. But I am no longer a tax collector."

"Oh? Well, I hold with the prophet Jeremiah. Can a leopard change his spots? Never." Simon looked smug.

"But Isaiah says that the leopard shall lie down with the goat, and scripture does not lie. Now, how to explain that? Something must change for that to happen," said Jesus. "Therefore, it is entirely possible."

"For the fighters against the occupation to lie down with the Romans?" asked Simon. "That is even more difficult."

"Will you release him?" Jesus asked Claudius.

"I cannot," he said stubbornly.

"I guarantee your safety," said Jesus.

Claudius opened his mouth to argue, but his words died away. "Very well. But you are exchanging your life for his." He looked sternly at Simon. "Can you appreciate that? Any misdeeds on your part will kill this man."

Simon looked away, as if he could not bear even to look on the face of a Roman. "Yes," he finally muttered. "Yes, I know."

"Release him." Claudius gave the order reluctantly. "Don't make me regret this," he warned Jesus. "Or all of you will die."

༜ XXXIII ༜

My dearest Keziah—

I had written pages and pages of things for you when I thought I would be seeing you soon and they would explain everything. But I had no chance to deliver them to you, and now I am away from Magdala for a little while. But if you would come and see me . . . somehow. Then I could hand you the explanation I had written out, and you would know all. I cannot repeat it here, again—I do not want to recount it, it was too painful. If I saw you, then I could talk about it, face to face. Only know that I was ill and had to leave Magdala for a time, and that now I am in the Capernaum area, where I hope and pray you can come to meet me.

Have you heard of this man named Jesus who is from Nazareth? He is a prophet. I have never met a prophet before, but I know he is one. He has now formed a family that is serving as a new family for me. It is made up of people he has helped or called to join him in his mission. I told you all about it in the earlier writings, which of course you have yet to see.

It is far from the life I had imagined for myself when we used to daydream together. In fact, I did not know such a life existed. The only religious lives I knew of were fiery prophets like John the Baptist, who lived in polit-

ical danger, or people who withdrew to the desert to escape the corruption of everyday life, or scribes who spent their time studying scripture. I did not know it was possible to be holy any other way. But this man, Jesus—he doesn't quote texts, he interprets them; he doesn't withdraw from ordinary people, he seeks them out; and it is not dangerous to be associated with him, for he's no threat to any ruler. Oh, Keziah, he will be preaching out in the open fields just north of Capernaum in three days' time. Please come to hear him, and to see me, and let us embrace once more. How I have missed you, dearest friend. How I want to see you!

Your companion, Mary

৩ XXXIV ৩

The hawks flew high in the bright summer day, wheeling and search-ing for prey on the ground. Usually they found what they were look-ing for between rows of flax, or in the open fields, where the wind blew across the browning grasses. But this day they were thwarted, because the open fields were black with crowds of people. They were converg-ing from all around, thickest in the meadows near the water's edge. Any potential meal for the hawks had scurried away from the tramp-ing human feet.

Mary and Joanna stood together in the field, shaking their heads. The word had gone out that Jesus was going to be preaching on this day—had not she herself tried to alert Silvanus and Keziah?—but the numbers were overwhelming.

"Who would have thought so many would come?" said Mary. "And where are they coming from?"

"From places far away," said Joanna. "There are not enough people around the lake to create such a crowd."

"If only we had these numbers in our movement, we could easily overthrow the Romans," said Simon, standing beside them.

"You must forget about that," said Mary, sternly. She and Joanna had been assigned to help Simon, to welcome him into the fellowship. But he was difficult, and it was obvious that he had joined Jesus just to save his neck.

Simon looked over at Jesus, who was talking to Peter and Big James. Mary and the others had assigned him that nickname, since the other James, Matthew's brother, was small. It seemed more polite to call the larger one "Big" than the smaller one "Little."

Simon shook his head. "He was a fool to stand surety for me. When this arm is healed"—he held up his bandaged arm—"it will strike again."

"Simon, then you are the fool," said Mary. But she knew that, though he would not admit it to himself, Jesus's daring had unarmed him.

Simon shrugged. "Perhaps," he said. "Perhaps. But the country is groaning for deliverance."

"You said it yourself," said Joanna. "If you had these numbers, perhaps." She indicated the huge crowds with a sweep of her hand. "But you do not. And you have proved that you have no wish to die."

"So you call me a coward?"

"No, Simon," Mary hastened to assure him. Let him not seek to prove otherwise! "We know well enough that you have not come to Jesus, and us, because you wished to. But we hope, in time, that you will see it was the right thing for you to do." He was glowering. "Simon, I have known you longer than anyone else here. And I know your courage and dedication. I just believe that it can be better served by hearing what Jesus says. He, too, wants deliverance."

Simon grunted. "Not the right kind." He winced as he tried to cross his arms.

"Well, it remains to be seen who will convert who," said Joanna, with a broad smile.

Mary noted how robust Joanna looked, how competent and healthy. Thank God for another person rescued from the demons! She reached out and put her arm around Joanna's waist. Perhaps my real sisters are those who have been enslaved by the demons and then set free, she thought.

"Jesus is ready to speak," Joanna said, and the three of them left the waterside and joined his other followers at his side. It was going to be a hot day, Mary thought, noting how stifling the air already was.

The sea of listeners was vast, almost as vast as the lake beyond them. Some were healthy in body but obviously needful of hearing something that would speak to their secret, hidden, shameful sins. Some seemed to belong to the strict religious Pharisee sect, like

Mary's family. Some hobbled on crutches, some took slow and hesitant steps. There were peasants, obviously poor—their thin frames, faded homespun tunics, and battered sandals betrayed their station. There were lepers, grotesquely bent over, whether in despair or in disease, it was impossible to tell. Some were lying on stretchers, their thin, ragged bodies beseeching help.

"Just let your shadow fall across my father, and he will be healed," cried one young man, pointing to a motionless mound on a litter.

"You have come here because you are hungry for the word of God!" Jesus called out. "And God has words for you, words he wants you to hear!"

Amazingly, the noise of the crowd died down, and Jesus's words carried across them.

"My friends, I have so much to tell you!" Jesus said. "The most important thing is, you are precious to your heavenly Father. And he *is* your Father, and he wants you to think of him in just that way. He wants you to come into his presence just as a child runs to its father, crying, '*Abu!* Daddy!' No ceremony, just a joyous race into his arms!"

The people stirred and murmured, shaking their heads.

"You do not approach God, your Father, your *abu*, with ceremony," said Jesus. "Ritual cleanliness, offerings—none of these is sufficient. God wants your *heart*, that is all."

"Blasphemy!" A lone, reedy voice rose.

"Blasphemy? No!" replied Jesus. "Did not the prophet Hosea say, 'I desire mercy, not sacrifices'? Now let me tell you of the Kingdom of heaven. It is coming, and yet it is already here, among you, this very instant. You can enter into it today, this hour! It is impossible to describe it directly in words, it must be felt by the heart."

"How? How!?" cried a thin middle-aged man very near the front.

"There are two ways," said Jesus. "The first is very simple. At the end of this age—which is coming, and sooner than you expect—people will be divided up. One group will be taken up to be with their heavenly Father, and he will explain why. He will say, 'I was thirsty and you gave me water, I was hungry and you fed me, I was naked and you clothed me, I was in prison and you visited me.' When they protest that they had never seen God hungry or thirsty or in prison, he will say, 'If you helped another person in need, you did it to me.'"

"But what of keeping the Law? What of the cleanliness?" a woman called out.

Jesus thought a moment. "Daughter, keeping the law is praiseworthy, and no one can take it from you. But more is required. Have you helped those brothers and sisters of yours?" He indicated the crowd.

But who has time if she must spend so many hours with the rituals? thought Mary. And what woman is free to help strangers directly? She did not think Jesus was being fair to the woman.

"And the second?" someone demanded. "The second way to the Kingdom?"

"It is to grasp the meaning of it, its great mystery, so that you can live your life according to it," said Jesus.

"How?" A rotund man in expensive clothes shot the question out.

"Ah, my friend," said Jesus, "you know how to savor and appreciate the fine things of life." He went over to the man and fingered his cloak. "You are a man of taste."

The man snatched back his cloak, afraid Jesus was going to order him to give it to the poor, now crowding up toward the front.

Jesus laughed and let the material drop. He seemed to find the man's confusion amusing. "The Kingdom of heaven is far more precious than this piece of material, even if it came from Arabia, even if it was made from the finest wool! The Kingdom of heaven is so precious, it is like a pearl. A pearl that you should spend every last bit of your money on. Exchange everything for it!"

He then whirled, spun around to face a different group. "Yes, it is a pearl! A pearl of overwhelming price. And once you have it, you must treasure it. Let me tell you something: not everyone can understand. Not everyone can appreciate it. So, when you have this pearl, do not throw it in front of people who cannot honor it. They are like pigs. Would you give what is holy to swine? Do not offer your pearl to a pig. It will just trample it underfoot in the mud. And do you know what else? The pig will then turn on you and attempt to gore you. It will hate you for it and want to grind you into the mud and destroy you."

Was that what inspired all that hate when I went back to Magdala? Mary thought. Perhaps it was the pearl that was the enemy, not me. Perhaps they saw it in us, shining, when I could not.

"But the best news for you today is that the Kingdom of heaven is already here, and is already within you, within your very being! You need wait no longer. It is here, and you are part of it!" Jesus's voice rose.

"But how?" a young woman asked. "How can that be?"

It was Keziah! Mary's heart seemed to stand still. Keziah had come, she had received the letter Mary had sent by a willing but very inexperienced messenger. Or perhaps she had never received the letter, but had come on her own. Mary bit the back of her hand. She would wait until Jesus's answer, then she would rush to her friend.

"Because you had ears to hear, and a seeking heart," said Jesus. "Let me tell you something: no one comes to me but that my Father draws him. If you are here, then you are surely part of the Kingdom."

Mary saw Keziah frown. She knew so well what that frown meant.

"Keziah!" She hurried to her. "Keziah!" She embraced the confused young woman, who tried to push her away, at first weakly, then angrily.

"How dare you?" Keziah was saying, shoving Mary away.

"Keziah! Keziah! It is I, Mary!"

Keziah stopped struggling and stared at her. "Mary?"

"Did you get my letter? Have you come because of it?"

"I—I—" Keziah caught her breath. "Yes. I received it. But, Mary"—she pulled away—"I did not recognize you."

Mary yanked off her scarf, revealing her stubbly head. Keziah gasped.

"Yes, my dearest vanity is gone," said Mary. "I had to sacrifice it. But—oh, my friend, you are here!" She took her hands. "Let us find a private place."

The crowds were thick around them, but Mary led them away toward the pebbled beach, where it would be cooler and a few trees offered shade. A few boats were rocking back and forth nearby, anchored so that their occupants could hear Jesus, but other than that they were alone.

"Here—here—" Mary pulled out the bulky pages she had thrust into her belt to give to Keziah should she come. "This will tell you everything."

"Must I read it now?" asked Keziah.

"Yes," said Mary. "Otherwise you will wait until you return home, and then there will be a thousand questions you wish to ask, and I will not be there to answer."

"Very well." She shot a look at her friend, took the pages, and went off to a rock to read them. When she returned, she was not smiling. She took her place beside Mary, and together they leaned against the boulder, their elbows touching.

"I do not know what to say," Keziah ventured.

"I did not know how to write it," said Mary.

"You have been utterly turned out? Joel drove you away?"

"Not only Joel, but my father and my brother," said Mary.

"Did they not rejoice that you were healed? Oh, Mary, what a dreadful affliction you suffered alone!"

"They did not care about that," said Mary. As she spoke the words, she realized how damning they were. "All they cared about was my reputation. No, not my reputation, but theirs. Mine merely reflected on theirs."

"But that is terrible!"

"It is the truth." Mary paused before adding, "The truth is, they do not care about me. No, not even Joel! They care more for their standing, their reputation in Magdala." As she said the words, they struck at her like hammer blows.

"What of Elisheba?"

Mary sighed. "I tried to kidnap her."

"You didn't!"

"Yes, I did. I wanted to take her away from them, from all of them, to keep her with me. But they were stronger, and took her away." She clutched Keziah's sleeve. "Will you watch her for me?"

"Mary," said Keziah, gently, "I am not known to your family. There is no way I can watch her or help take care of her."

Mary fought back tears. "Yes, of course."

"What of Joel?" Keziah asked. "Is he—will he divorce you?"

She had not allowed herself even to consider that. "I—he did not mention it when I saw him."

"But the others will work on him, try to persuade him," said Keziah.

"But I—what can I do? If I return—"

Keziah looked toward Jesus, who was talking, and sweeping his arms out over the crowd to emphasize his words. "It would seem you have work to do here," she said.

"Yes," said Mary. "What—what do you think? Can you see what draws people to him?"

"Can I see what drew *you* to him?" replied Keziah. "Yes, I could see that. But it does not speak to me. I will not fall in behind your Jesus. I must return to my home."

You have no need of him, Mary thought, sadly. And without a pressing need, no one comes to Jesus. Perhaps the ones truly to be pitied are the ones with no deep needs, she thought.

"Thank you for coming," she said. "It has meant more to me than I can say." She embraced her old friend with sadness.

It has meant that I know I can never return, she thought. She waited until Keziah had gone before she put her hands over her eyes and wept. I cannot go back. That way is lost to me.

She sat alone for a long time, trying to get control of her tears. Finally, drained, she rose and made her way back to Jesus. Jesus—the only thing left to me, she thought.

Just as she approached, a group of hideously disfigured people—seven men and three women, although it was hard to distinguish one from another—made their way toward him. Lepers. Their skin was blanched and peeling off in sections, and their feet were twisted knobs. "Help us, then!" they cried. "If you know of the Kingdom of God!"

Jesus looked at them and then asked an unexpected question. "Do you wish to be made well?"

How odd. Who would not wish to be made well in such a condition?

They nodded, and cried out to him once more. "Jesus, master, have pity on us!"

"Go, show yourselves to the priest and offer the sacrifice Moses commanded," he said. There was a ritual for the cleansing of lepers prescribed in the Law.

They looked disappointed, but rose and bowed respectfully. Nothing happened in that instant, but as they rose, it seemed to Mary that they stood up a tiny bit straighter. Painfully they turned to make their way back toward Capernaum, swaying in the waves of heat.

Jesus had almost finished speaking when a blind man staggered over to him and cried out, "Help me!" He clutched Jesus's robe.

Jesus stopped speaking and took the man's face in his hands. He looked long and deep at him, before finally saying, "What do you wish me to do for you?"

Why did he always ask that? Mary wondered. It was so obvious what the man wished him to do!

"I want to see!" he cried.

Jesus prayed, then touched his eyelids, gently. "Your trust has restored your sight," he said.

The man stood blinking, squinting, rubbing his eyes.

"Can you see?" asked Jesus. "What do you see?"

"I see . . . shapes. Colors moving. And . . ." He put out his hand and touched Jesus's face. ". . . A face. Your face." The man moved closer and his cloudy eyes looked into Jesus's clear ones. "I see your face." He fell on his knees and grasped Jesus's hands. "Thank you," he murmured.

"Do you behold these healings?" Jesus asked the crowd. "They are just a sign, a sign that the Kingdom is dawning, is already here, as I told you. As Isaiah promised, the blind will see, the prisoner be set free, the brokenhearted comforted. I am just its instrument—I am only God's instrument to proclaim it."

The day was drawing to a close; soon the last warm slants of sunlight would fade away.

"My friends, go in peace," Jesus called to them. "Return to your homes and tell others of what God is doing."

"They will never leave," Joanna said to Mary in a low voice.

But, surprisingly, they did. The vast company began to melt away, walking slowly up the footpaths around the lake. By the time twilight came, Jesus and his followers were alone.

The fire crackled and sputtered, sending sparks out into the night like little stars. They were sitting in a circle around it, drained from the day, although it was Jesus who had done the work. But in a mysterious way they felt they had participated as well.

"You will do these things, and greater ones as well," Jesus told them. "There is much to do, and I cannot do it all alone. I need you to help."

"We don't—we don't know how," Philip said, shaking his head.

"Is it possible for us to learn?" asked Peter. "Can you teach us your secrets?"

Jesus smiled. "The secret is one that is open to all but that few want to use: obedience to God. Do what he requires of you, and you will be granted great power."

The fire hissed like a snake; Simon looked behind him, thinking one might be there.

"All I know about is keeping the commandments," said Philip.

"That is a start," Jesus told him. "It is a foundation. Most people want their special instructions first thing, and the truth is, they come last. God gives you the simple tasks first. He who is faithful in small things will be given big things."

"Master, I do not wish to seem—disrespectful, or preoccupied with such things, but—how are we to live?" asked Matthew. "Forgive me, I'm a practical man, I deal in money and tabulations, that's all I know, and . . . we must eat. Or are we to beg?" He held up his hands. "I don't mind that, it's not my pride I'm concerned about, even if all my former colleagues passed by and saw my outstretched hand, but . . . it would consume all our time. I mean, begging is a full-time job. And surely you have other jobs for us." He cleared his throat. "From what you say, that is."

"I am grateful that I have a man of business with me," said Jesus, touching Matthew's arm. "You are quite right, we have pressing matters that we should give all our attention to. When I told the people not to worry, I was also well aware that, yes, we all have to eat."

"I have money," said Joanna, suddenly. "I have a great deal of money." She leaned over and untied the sack she carried around her waist. "Take it. I gladly give it to us, to feed us so that we can attend to the important things."

Jesus reached out, took hold of the pouch, opened it, and looked into it. "This is generous," he said. "It will free us to do the task God most wants us to do."

"When my husband set me free . . ." Joanna's voice faltered a little. "No, let me be honest, when he cast me out because I was hopeless, he wanted to soothe his own conscience, so he gave me all this money. He of course thought I would be robbed of it right away, not being able to take care of myself, but it bought him peace of mind. Even though I was possessed, I was not stupid. I knew well enough how to protect the money. And now it is yours." She seemed relieved to be rid of it, and pleased that she could do something for Jesus.

"Thank you, Joanna," he said.

Mary looked at the faces around the fire. They were each other's family now; there was no one else to rely on. "Will there be others joining us?" she asked Jesus.

"Perhaps," he said. "It depends on who the Father draws. If he has others he wishes to come . . . then we must welcome them. Men and women."

"Master," said Mary, unable to stop herself, "men leave their homes all the time. But women—that is different. It places unnatural demands on them."

"Perhaps the price is too high for you," said Jesus. "But I sensed that you were different, and that my mission needed you. Had you been a man, I would have called you without hesitation. Was I wrong to treat you in the same manner?"

"No!" she quickly answered. "You were not."

"I wish I knew where God was leading us," Andrew said, looking around at his companions.

Jesus did not answer right away. Finally, he said, "Even Abraham was not told that. When God commanded him to leave Ur, he did not reveal anything further. But, after all, if Abraham had not left Ur, the other things would never come to pass, so why reveal them?"

"Because if Abraham had known everything he would have been better able to decide what to do?" asked the smaller James, Matthew's brother.

"Because he would have been inspired by the promises and better able to endure hardship?" Peter suggested.

"The second answer is better," said Jesus. "It is true that God sometimes gives promises to sustain us through the bad times. But it seems he does not reveal his will to curiosity-seekers, only to those he knows will obey his will. And for those who will obey, he does not need to reveal it."

"This is a hard saying!" cried Philip. "Who can endure it? Or understand it?"

"I think we are expected to endure it *without* understanding it," said Jesus. "One thing I can promise: stepping out on this journey is a great adventure. A life with God is never dull."

Nor are you, thought Mary. But where are *you* taking us? she silently questioned him.

∽ X X X V ∽

Another scorching day, and the crowds began to gather before dawn. Mary heard them before she was fully awake, and they broke into her dream, which was just as well: in it she was seeing Joel pushing her away and Elisheba running after her, arms outstretched, and she awakened crying.

Keziah . . . Keziah was here, she thought. Then, as she slowly came awake, she remembered that Keziah had come but could not help her, and that Keziah had not understood Jesus. And Silvanus had not come at all, in spite of her letter. Perhaps he had not gotten it. Or . . . had he sided with the rest of her family? They must have told him about her brief visit to Magdala, painting it in lurid tones.

The murmur of the crowd roused her, and she quickly made herself ready for the day. Each day . . . each day I do not know what awaits. How long will Jesus remain here in the fields, teaching?

The crowds were still large, but now the front was filled with Pharisees. They were meticulously dressed in their talliths, prayer shawls with extra-long ritual fringes, which identified them, and in this attire they looked oddly out of place in the hot, open fields. No sooner had Jesus left his private place of prayer to address them than they began flinging questions at him.

"Rule on this, teacher!" One of the Pharisees pushed his fellows away and stood in front of Jesus. "We are under Rome, are we not? So—is it lawful to pay taxes then, knowing they use our very money to oppress us?"

The question was a burning one throughout the country. Zealots said no, which made them traitors in the eyes of Rome. Compromisers said yes, which made them cowards to their countrymen. Either answer would discredit Jesus in many eyes and harm his ministry.

"As if we should ever aid them!" Simon hissed to Mary and Joanna. "How can he answer otherwise?"

Jesus asked, "Show me a coin."

An obliging man held up a Roman denarius.

Jesus took it and studied it. "What image is on this coin?" He handed it to the Pharisee.

The man eyed it as a tainted graven image. He glanced at the profile on the silver coin. "Tiberius Caesar's," he finally said.

"Then pay Caesar in his own coin, and pay God in his," Jesus said.

Beside Mary, Simon shook his head. "Pay taxes to Caesar!" he muttered. "How can he say that?"

"All these laws are passing away," said Jesus. "The coming Kingdom will render them all meaningless. To make more of them than they deserve is a mistake."

"Our Law is eternal!" one of the other Pharisees cried. "It is part of our convenant with God."

Just then a young man rushed forward, running toward Jesus, his clothes flying behind him. "Praise God! Praise God!" he cried. He even leapt up and did a little turn in the air, landing gracefully and flinging his arms out like a dancer. He threw himself at Jesus's feet. "Thank you! Thank you! When you only sent us to the priest, I didn't know— I didn't understand—" His accent marked him as a Samaritan, a dreaded, heretical Samaritan.

Jesus took his hand and made him stand up. He looked at the man carefully. "This man came to me in a group of lepers. But there were ten of them! Where are the other nine? Is there no one among them to return and give praise to God but a foreigner, a Samaritan?" He touched the man's head. "Go. It was your trust that made you well."

The man bowed and then took his way out through the crowd.

"A Samaritan!" someone said. "You touched a leper, and a Samaritan in the bargain!"

"That is what I meant about the misinterpretation of the Law," said Jesus. "Sometimes a foreigner, a pagan, can be more right with God than someone who manages to count out his mint and his thyme and make a proper tithe—sacrificing ten leaves out of a hundred. God told the prophet Samuel, 'The Lord sees not as man sees. Man looks at the outward appearance, but the Lord looks at the heart.'"

"But all we can see is the outward appearance," said one of the religious men, a short, stocky one, who also happened to be handsome. "That is all we can go by. We do not have the mind of God. Are you saying that we should pretend we do? That would also displease God." With his looks, he probably knew firsthand about being judged on appearance, although it must usually have worked in his favor, Mary thought.

Jesus thought for a moment. "You have spoken well. God does not want us to pretend to knowledge that is reserved for him alone. But he does desire mercy, so we should strive for that whenever a question arises."

It was past noon, and people should have been thinking of home and food, but they did not move. They stood there in the sunlight and kept asking Jesus questions, giving him no ground.

Suddenly Mary saw a familiar face in this crowd, a pretty woman with reddish hair standing with a man she was also sure she had seen before. James! Jesus's dour brother! What was he doing here? And behind them—yes, it was Mary, Jesus's mother, her face a mirror of worry. They were gesturing to some muscular men on either side of them, and the men shoved through the crowd and marched toward Jesus, followed by Jesus's mother and the others.

The men pushed everyone aside to reach Jesus, and immediately attempted to grab him, but he pushed them away. "Mother," he said, ignoring the men and addressing only his mother. "Mother." He sounded shocked and very sad.

"My son, you have—you have—" She burst into tears. "You have gone mad! Your behavior in Nazareth—and now these things you are saying—please, you must give yourself into our hands, and let us take you back home, where you can rest and recover."

James pushed toward him with a scowl. "So this is what you abandoned our carpentry shop for? This heresy? How dare you demand that I take your place for *this*?" He tried to grab Jesus by the shoulder.

Then Mary recognized the other woman. It was Leah, Jesus's sister. Yes, of course. She had married and lived in Capernaum.

"Jesus, Jesus!" Leah was begging. "Please, abandon this! All these things we have heard about you, we've now seen for ourselves! You have truly lost your way! What has happened to you? Return to Nazareth, rest, come back to yourself!" Her head covering fell off, revealing her luxuriant and lovely hair.

He recoiled from them. "No," he said. He looked so sorrowful that Mary thought he might burst into tears. But he regained control of himself.

"We are your mother, your sister, and your brother!" cried Leah. "Think of it. Your mother, sister, and brother!" She came closer, till she stood only an arm's length away from Jesus. But she made no move to reach out for him. The strongmen stood waiting for a signal to move in.

Jesus stepped back. Instead of addressing them, he looked around at Mary, at Peter, Simon, and all his other chosen followers. The deep affection on his face would seem rightly to belong to his own family. Instead, he raised his voice and addressed all the people present. "My mother, my sister, and my brother? Who are my mother, my sister, and my brother?" He looked over at Mary, his mother; at Leah, and at James. "My mother, my sister, and my brother is the person who hears the word of God and does it."

"We do," said James, stoutly. "We do listen for the word of God!"

"But you think I am mad," said Jesus. "These two things cannot be reconciled."

"Jesus, Jesus!" His mother began weeping, crying out in anguish. "My son, my son!"

"No, Mother, he isn't your son!" said James, encircling her protectively with his arms. "He isn't your son at all. Nor is he my brother!" He forced her to turn around and all but dragged her through the crowd, away from Jesus, who stood still and watched them depart.

After that there was only silence, and the crowd stared. What had this Jesus just done? He had rejected family loyalty, the bedrock of everything their tradition honored. It made no sense. Without a family, what was a man? Everyone was identified by a family. "Of the house and lineage of David." "A Benjamite." The family was all. And Jesus had repudiated its importance, saying—what? That a man could make his own family, choose his own closest relatives?

The crowd, as shocked as Jesus's family, drifted away. Only a few remained, and among them Mary saw Judas. He was standing, staring, elegantly dressed and alone.

"Come, Judas!" Jesus called out. "Come, and join us! Become my brother!"

Judas just backed away, horrified to be singled out and called. And why? He had said nothing, only watched.

"Judas! Come! We depart for another place. Come with us," Jesus called.

Judas turned and hurried away, disappearing into the remnants of the crowd.

"Come, let us cross to the other side of the lake," Jesus said to his companions. "We need to go to a private place to rest."

It did not take long to procure boats to carry them. They pushed off into the water. Mary felt a great relief. She looked out at the hillside where the crowds had been. So many of them! As the boats made their way out into the deeper parts of the lake, she felt safer. All these people—how could Jesus possibly answer them? He had healed her when he was almost alone and had no other claims on him, but now . . . how could he ever do for so many others what he had done for her?

As the shore receded farther into the distance, Mary could hear the calls of those left behind on the hillside.

They landed on the eastern shore of the lake, in the separate territory of Herod Philip, Antipas's brother. They beached the boats, and Jesus made his way ashore, picking his way among the boulders. The terrain here was severe; the sandy-colored rocks and ground were not welcoming. But at least they could withdraw in privacy.

Jesus gestured to all of them. "Come!" he called, leading them along the rugged beach. The sun would sink soon. They had seen it rise. What a long time it had seemed in between; how Jesus had stretched the hours.

Mary watched as Jesus made his way among the boulders, throwing his own long, thin shadow alongside their bulging ones. His head was lowered; he was clearly saddened by what had happened with his family. But suddenly a curdling cry arose from—where? They could not tell.

Jesus stopped and looked around.

A naked man approached him, appearing from behind one of the rocks. He was so filthy that he looked more like an ape than a human, and he brandished a sharp stone in each of his hands. While they watched, he took one of them and slashed himself across the chest. A diagonal line appeared on his dirt-encrusted skin and dripped dark blood. Manacles were on his wrists and ankles, but only a link or two of iron chain remained on them.

They were back in that dreadful stretch of territory where Mary, Peter, and Andrew had been attacked once before. This man would be far stronger than his size indicated.

"Run!" Peter told Jesus, taking his hand.

But Jesus just stood still. Peter tried to drag him away.

"Master! This man is dangerous!" Still Jesus did not move, and Peter fell back, protecting himself.

The possessed man snarled and circled around Jesus on all fours like a beast. He drew back his lips and growled.

Another man appeared, also possessed, but less severely. "Don't let him near!" he warned Jesus. "He has broken all his chains, and no one can subdue him! He will kill anyone who approaches!"

The man with the broken chains continued to circle them. Mary grasped Joanna's hand. The poor man! she thought.

The man-beast was now within close range of Jesus. He was crouching, bent low, muttering. His back was so covered with scabs and scratches that it looked like a badly tanned hide, and his hair was standing in filthy tufts.

Without waiting for him to say a word, Jesus said, "Come out of this man, you evil spirit!"

In reply the man rushed toward Jesus, yelling, "What do you want with me, Jesus? Swear to God that you won't torture me!" The voice was a shriek.

Jesus did not move or give ground. The dangerous man was crouched right at his feet. "What is your name?" he asked, coldly.

The man raised his head and bared his teeth. "My name is Legion," he said, "for we are many."

"Leave this man!" Jesus then commanded the legion of demons.

The man jerked his head. "Don't send us away from here!" the voice—not his own—said. "Don't send us away!"

"Away to your master, away to hell," Jesus said.

"No! No!" Ugly shrieks rent the air.

"Leave him!" Jesus repeated his order, loudly.

"Send us into the pigs!" the voices begged, whining.

Only then did Mary notice the large herd of pigs grazing on the slopes of the hill, near the steep drop-off bordering the lake.

"Very well," Jesus finally said. "I give you permission."

The man was racked with spasms, and pitched forward to the ground, writhing. Ghastly wailing sounds came from his slack mouth, and then he lay still, as if dead.

At the same time, an intense noise rumbled from the hillside nearby. The pigs were suddenly agitated, as if something had frightened them, or as if the ground under them had given way, as in an earthquake. They began churning, then running frantically, snorting and uttering high-pitched cries. The ground shook as they rushed down the hillside in a herd. Mary almost gagged from the unfamiliar pig-odor, warm and musty, that carried in the air. And their eyes—she could see their tiny eyes, glowing red where the setting sun hit them, and the saliva drooling from their quivering snouts. They thundered past the shore and plunged into the water, where they thrashed and flailed and drowned.

Then, from the cliff above them, the rest of the herd—a waterfall of swine—poured over the lip of the cliff, pig after pig, falling in a cascade toward the ground below, hitting with a sickening noise. The first ones smacked on the rocks and burst, and the others fell on the bodies, making thick, ugly sounds. They piled up as high as a man's shoulder, hundreds of them. Terrified squeals filled the air.

Mary saw Simon standing nearby, his mouth hanging open. "Here is your secret word," she said. "Pigs. Is that not symbolic to you?"

He only nodded, dumbly. "It was just a password," he said. "Chosen at random. I did not mean—"

Pearls before swine, Mary thought. Do not throw your pearls before the swine. . . . Are my family in Magdala like these swine, dull of understanding, hopeless? They turned on me like this pack of pigs.

The swine continued to hit the ground, bursting open, crying out in terror. The man lay as if dead, not moving, at Jesus's feet.

The sun had sunk behind the hills when the last of the pigs stampeded over the cliff. An entire, immense herd had perished. They lay heaped on the beach and bobbing in the water.

Mary and Joanna were wiping the man's forehead with wet cloths and attempting to revive him when he finally opened his eyes. He was utterly limp. They understood, and cradled his head.

"Give him some food," they said, "and clothes. We must have something—a mantle, a tunic." Oh, this was all too familiar. Mary remembered the kind woman who had given her her mantle. "Anything."

Peter contributed a mantle, and Philip had an extra tunic. Simon took off his own sandals. Andrew was able to offer some figs and unleavened bread.

The man slowly sat up. He was dazed, unable to remember anything. Again, Mary and Joanna understood.

"Who are you?" he asked, moving his head weakly.

"This is Jesus," said Mary, "a holy man who has the power to banish demons. He did the same for me. And for her." She indicated Joanna.

"God has made you well," said Jesus. He did not seem to care about the pile of dead swine.

The man kept looking around. "You saved me!" he finally said.

"God saved you," Jesus insisted.

"No one could do this," the man said. "I have been afflicted for so many years, and every holy man here was called upon, to no avail." He looked down at his body, in wonder. "I have been like a beast for so long. Clothes! What a miracle!" He stroked the tunic and cloak. Suddenly he grasped Jesus's arm. "Let me come with you! Let me stay with you! I want to be with all these others, your followers!"

"No," said Jesus, softly.

Mary was shocked. Did he not always take in those he had delivered?

"But—this is where I belong. I feel it! I do not want to leave you! Until now I have—"

"No," Jesus repeated.

"You cannot do this! I must be with you! There is nothing else for me!" The man began to cry. "Do not deliver me only to abandon me!"

"Do you not have a family?" asked Jesus, kindly.

"I did," the man said. "But I do not know—it has been so long— and I am so changed. It cannot be as it was."

Jesus looked at him, and Mary could tell that he was torn. He could see the man's anguish, but knew what was best for each person. "True. It cannot be as it was. But you are a living witness of what God has done. You have a task, and that task is a hard one: you must return to your home and tell everyone what God has done for you, and his great mercy toward you."

"But I don't want to be in my home! I wasn't welcome there before, and I won't be welcome there now!"

"That is why I said it was the harder task," said Jesus. "To return to those who look down on you, just to witness to God—he has indeed given you a difficult task. But it is God who has given it, not I."

Just then the swineherds came rushing down the cliff path, breathless, and stood before their dead swine. They set up a wail. Close behind them came the townspeople, drawn out of their homes by the noise and commotion. They looked around at the mound of dead pigs, out at the floating bodies in the lake, and then at the little group around Jesus.

"What is going on?" one of the men demanded. He stared at Jesus and then, in recognition, at the possessed man. "What has happened here?" It was hard to tell which frightened him more, the dead animals or the restored man.

"This man has been delivered from his demons," Jesus said. He put his hands on the man's shoulders and turned him around to face his audience.

"Joshua!" the man cried. "Is it really you?"

"Indeed it is," the possessed man said. "The very same, the one you have known all your life."

But instead of welcoming him, the man shrank back. "This isn't possible! He's been mad for years! He even ripped off his chains!"

The others in the group pointed to the pigs. "What's the meaning of this? Who is responsible for this?"

"The demons went into the pigs," said Peter, "when this man was delivered."

"Who's going to pay for them?" one of the men asked. "This is a huge loss! Hundreds of drachmas!" He turned on Jesus. "Are you going to pay for it? Are you?"

Jesus looked surprised. "It was the price of deliverance for your brother here." He indicated Joshua.

"He's not *my* brother," said the man. "Who's going to pay for the pigs? Who? Who?"

Joshua gave a final begging look toward Jesus. But Jesus shook his head. "No," he said. "You must stay here."

"Get out of here!" one of the men in the crowd yelled at Jesus. "Get out! Get out! Don't ever touch these shores again!"

They picked up stones to hurl at Jesus and his followers. Quickly they made their way back to the boats, even though the light was failing.

The boats rocked slowly, as they plied their way back across the lake. Mary clutched the side of the boat, weak with the realization that Jesus could have sent her back, as he had Joshua. He did not have to choose her. And all this time she had thought that he had had to, that anyone he healed was welcome to come and join him.

The words he had said back at Bethabara—which she had not paid particular attention to—"you do not choose me, but I chose you"—now roared in her ears.

Why me and not Joshua? She wanted to reach out and insist he come with them. But Jesus had spoken decisively. Perhaps there was something Joshua must do in Gergesa before he would truly be free, that only he and Jesus knew.

It was late before they returned safely to the spot where they had camped the night before. Another night in the open fields. Mary was growing used to them. It no longer felt so odd to be outside, sleeping directly under the sky. Houses were on their way to becoming a memory.

"Foxes have holes, and the birds of the air have nests, but the Son of Man has nowhere to lay his head," Jesus said as they readied themselves to settle down for the night.

"Master," said Peter, "in the summer that is all very well, but what shall we do in the winter?"

Jesus continued to spread out his cloak on the ground. "When the time comes, we will see."

The thought of lying outside in the lashing rains was so distressing that Mary winced. She could almost feel the cold fingers of the raindrops, the sting of the wind on her face.

"My friends, we shall—" Suddenly Jesus broke off. He looked around in the direction where he had heard something.

Two lanterns were swinging in the darkness, seemingly hanging there in the air. Mary saw hands clutching the handles, and in the dim light she saw the face of Judas and, above the second lantern, the handsome religious man. "Ah. My Father has drawn two more." Jesus stood up. "Welcome."

Judas came forward nervously. "I don't know exactly what I am doing here," he said.

"God does," said Jesus. "Trust him."

Judas laughed. "He's never spoken to me before. I don't know why he would now."

"He had never spoken to Moses, either, but Moses recognized it."

"I am no Moses."

"God knows that." Jesus turned his attention to the other man.

"I found your answers to be . . . satisfying," the man said. "Rational. Persuasive." He paused and finally said, "Impressive."

Jesus laughed. "It is flattering that you thought so. Who are you?"

"My name is Thomas," he said. "We want to join you."

"You do not know what that means," said Jesus.

"None of these other people did, either," said Judas, looking around. "From what I can see, they are just people who have taken a chance in faith."

"Faith," said Jesus. "Yes, that is the most important thing. Do you have faith?"

"I—yes, yes, I do!" Judas seemed flustered in defending himself. "I have long been searching for someone whose integrity is absolute. I said to myself, when I find that honest man, someone whose answers I can trust—"

"God will tell you right away there is no honest man," said Jesus. "As the Psalmist says, 'There is not one who does good, not even one.' All are sinners in God's eyes."

"No, I did not mean—I seek only what is good within human reason. Look, I am a realist! I do not seek perfection!"

"Surely you will not settle for less in yourself?" Jesus asked.

"You are a hard taskmaster! Allow others leeway, tolerate nothing less than perfection in yourself? I will try, but—"

To Mary's surprise, Jesus said, "'I will try'? I hate those words! Say, rather, 'I will.'" He glared at Judas. "If your child is drowning, do you say, 'I will try to rescue him'? No, indeed! So with the Kingdom. We do not need the fainthearted. Go take your 'I will try' elsewhere."

"All right, then. I *will.*"

"That is better." Jesus turned to Thomas and indicated that he should sit down with the group. Then he nodded to Judas. "Sit. Join us." He looked around and said, "You are the ones I have chosen to open my heart to. But there are many others who wish to follow at a farther distance. And so they shall. They shall come with us, and listen, and as they feel moved to do so, can come forward to us."

"But . . . where are we going?" asked Peter.

"I think it is time we left this area and went farther afield. Let us go out to the other towns of Galilee, to Korazin and Bethsaida. For this was I sent."

Judas leaned forward. "I am honored that you selected me and have allowed me to enter this circle. But you must know what is happening in the world outside. Things worsen—in the realms of men," he hastily added. "Pilate has just attacked a group of Galilean pilgrims who came to Jerusalem in peace. They were at the Temple when he ordered his soldiers to cut them down. For what reason I do not know."

Then followed a deep silence. "We must pray for them," Jesus said. "Our poor countrymen!"

"Some were from Tiberias, some from Capernaum, some from Magdala," said Judas. "I heard it from my father."

Magdala! Who? Was it anyone she knew? Mary felt cold in wondering. Oh, let it not be so!

"With Pilate, we serve under a cruel master," said Philip.

"All human masters are cruel, in one way or another," said Jesus. "That is what I seek to change."

At that moment, another man approached in the darkness. Peter leapt up to see who it was.

"Peter!" said the voice. "Don't you recognize me?"

Peter opened the door wider. "I—" He faltered, searching his mind for the name.

"Nathanael!" said the man. "We were together at Bethabara! John the Baptist! Remember?" The man stepped in, lean and dark and nervous.

Jesus rose to meet him, clasped his hands. He kissed both his cheeks. "It has been some time since you left us."

"But I have come," Nathanael said. "It is a long story."

Nathanael! So, after great soul-searching, he had decided to return. Mary was pleased.

"But you are here!" said Jesus. "I think we all have long stories. I think we will hear them around the campfires night after night. But I thank God that you have come," he said. "I had given up looking for you."

"Welcome. I am Thomas. I came only a few moments ago. Now I am not the latest one." Thomas nodded to Nathanael.

Thomas: one of the religious. A rigorous questioner, a skeptic. He was the only one so far recruited from the ranks of the Orthodox. It was good that they had won over one of the strict religious. But as Mary looked at Thomas, she wondered if this was wise. What if he fell away and denounced them to his colleagues?

Can the leopard change its spots?

The sudden suspicion made her feel ashamed that she dared to look into another's soul.

ༀ XXXVI ༀ

The next morning, they set out, walking along the dusty pathways that served as the roads in the region.

"Will we go as far as Dan?" asked Peter, loudly enough that everyone heard him.

"Do you wish to?" asked Jesus.

"Yes! Yes! I always loved the phrase "from Dan to Beersheba" that meant the entire glorious kingdom of Israel!" he said. "From the north to south, in one great sweep!"

Jesus laughed. "Well, Peter, we will surely go to Dan. If not now, then someday."

Mary, too, had always loved the phrase "from Dan to Beersheba." It conjured up images in her mind of Solomon's kingdom, and she could almost see the chariots with their gallant charioteers, could picture the mighty armies that marched across the land, see the camel caravans coming from the north and the east, all racing to lay their goods at Solomon's feet. And then there were the fleets of ships docking, bringing their cargoes of ivory, apes, precious jewels, and perfumes. That was when Israel was mighty, when she was the envy of other nations, not the shrunken nation she was now, the slave of a greater political power, Rome.

As they made their way higher into the hills, with each step they could see more and more of the Sea of Galilee spreading out below them. By the time they reached a shaded spot where they would rest and eat, they could see almost the entire way to the far southern shore of the lake.

They took out their food and shared it: wine and some cheese and bread. The wine, poor to begin with, had worsened in the heat and from being bounced about in the wineskins; the cheese had begun to dry out, and the bread was tasteless: poor persons' fare.

Our fare from now on, Mary thought. This will be new to all of us. James and John surely have had the finest wine from their father's household whenever they wished. Judas—he must be well-to-do; his education reveals that. Joanna is used to palace fare. Peter and Andrew, respected citizens of Capernaum, have never had to do without. And Jesus, Jesus himself, was at least comfortable when he lived in Nazareth.

She bit into a piece of cheese, and it brought trailing with it memories of the cheeses she had always had at home: the goat cheese and the smoked cheese of ewes and the white curds of cheese they ate with parsley and onions on thick pieces of bread. When it was there, she had taken it for granted. But no more, no more. Now the remembrance of those cheeses would serve as a tantalizing reminder of her past, dancing before her as a temptation, making her taste them in her dreams.

Far below her she could see Magdala, or what she thought was Magdala. She could make out the thick grove of trees that marked the northern border of it. All day she had worried about the people from Magdala Judas said had been injured by Pilate. Who were they? And why had Pilate attacked them?

Surely it was not Joel. Joel would not have been in Jerusalem. He would never have gone to make a pilgrimage. The Joel she knew was not inclined to do such things. And her family, Silvanus and Eli and Nathan . . .

Yes, they might have gone. It had been many years since Eli had gone, and doubtless he wanted to return. Oh, let it not be that they have been injured by Pilate's soldiers!

"You look troubled." Judas was watching her.

"No, it is nothing."

"I sense that there is something. Tell me." His eyes held deep interest.

Finally, Mary said, "I—I was worrying about my family in Magdala. I hope they have not been among the Galileans injured by Pilate."

Judas nodded. He moved over closer to her and reached out as if to touch her arm, but hesitated. "There is no shame in caring for those whom we love, even if they have cast us out."

Was this Judas? It did not sound like him. "No, I know there is not," she said after a pause.

Bowing her head in shadow, she said a quick, personal prayer that Eli and Nathan were safe. She felt that God answered and reassured her.

They kept walking upward, toward the rocky plateau that spread out high above the lake. They passed groves of olive trees, clinging to the slopes, and a few twisted fig trees with their broad leaves offered up to the sun like palms, but the lushness of the Galilee and its valley had been left behind.

"We'll stop here," Jesus announced at sunset, as they approached the outskirts of a very small village that had a well nearby. Far below them, the lake had put on another of its hues, this time becoming as red as brick.

For the first time, there were no throngs of people clamoring for Jesus's attention, no lines of stretchers with invalids waiting for him, no teachers of the Law wanting to ask him questions.

"We have you all to ourselves," commented Philip. "I don't think that has happened since—since we were all in the desert with John the Baptist."

As he spoke those words, suddenly a most disturbing idea . . . or thought . . . . or vision . . . came into Mary's mind. It concerned John.

But they had heard nothing about John recently. The last news they had of him said he had gone to Samaria and was baptizing and preaching there, out of Herod Antipas's reach.

John had not actually been as shockingly unorthodox as Jesus, Mary thought, in spite of his wild appearance and fiery language. His message of repentance was of the more traditional kind: do good works and be kind. He did not require that someone repudiate his family or his normal way of life. Whereas Jesus . . .

She and Joanna had made themselves beds from wayside brush and covered them over with their mantles. She thought it would be difficult to sleep, but it was not. The exhaustion of the days just past, and then the effort in making the climb, had tired her.

And then, in the darkest time of the night, she awoke. She was fully, startlingly awake. She pulled herself up on her elbows and looked around at the lumps of sleeping figures by the fire, or what was left of it. Her heart was pounding. Right before her eyes was another figure: John the Baptist. He was gesturing and yelling, but she could not hear him. He was being assaulted, grabbed by soldiers, and dragged away. She could see him receding in the distance, still flailing out at his captors, kicking and twisting.

For an instant there was nothing. Then another picture snapped into place: John the Baptist imprisoned in a dark stone room, shackled in chains. He was bent over, as if he had been beaten or starved, his thin arms draped over his knees, no sign of any resistance or vitality. His hair was stringy and lank, and it looked as if whole hunks had been torn out, leaving places where his skull gleamed bald.

John raised his head and saw her. Yes, he was staring right at her.

"Tell Jesus!" he whispered. "Tell Jesus!" He stretched out one hand imploringly.

"Tell Jesus what?" she asked, out loud. "I know nothing."

"You can see me," said John. "Here in prison. Tell Jesus. It is Herod Antipas's doing. It is his evil. He will silence me."

But where are you? she started to ask. Even as her mind framed the question, John and the prison cell seemed to collapse and shrink, and she could see where the cell was: in a great fortress crowning a hill, high on a summit in the desert, rearing up over bare flanks of sand and stone. She did not recognize it. There were no landmarks around it. Except . . . She commanded the picture to expand itself. There was water at a distance, with a lakeshore. But not the Sea of Galilee. It was a long, narrow body of water surrounded by utter desert, and no plants or trees grew on its shore, nor were there any houses.

Mary had never seen it before, but she realized it must be the Dead Sea, the Salt Sea, far to the south.

Then, once again, she saw John in his cell. He seemed simultaneously to see her, too. He lurched up to his feet, staring at her.

At once he vanished, and there was nothing left but the sleeping figures by the campfire, utterly silent except for sleep-breathing.

"Tell Jesus." Tell him what? Surely it had all been just a dream, no matter how urgent and realistic it had seemed.

But the pictures . . . seeing pictures . . . I saw them once before, when I saw Bilhah my ancestor in my own kitchen.

No, that was just make-believe, imagination. I did not actually *see* her, except in my mind. I *thought* about her, and then painted a picture, as a child would do of a tree or a cloud, her own sensible voice lectured her.

Or . . . can the demons have returned? Can they be back in my mind again? Utter terror took hold of her. No, no!

But this feels entirely different. This is a message of some sort, it is not something to torture me.

When am I supposed to tell Jesus? she asked the John the Baptist figure. But he did not reappear to answer her.

Surely I can wait until morning, she thought. John did not ask for anything. He did not request that Jesus do anything, only be told. She would obey his wish.

.   .   .

Long before true dawn came, Mary heard someone getting up. She must have slept again after all; the night had passed away like a smooth-running stream. Beside her Joanna slept peacefully.

Mary rose. It was good to be alone for a few minutes. The lake appeared far below like a ghostly purple blur.

Here I am, she prayed. God, please listen to me. So much has happened since this strange man, Jesus, drove out my demons. I follow him because I believe he is acting in your name. But if he is not—please tell me, and then give me the courage to leave him. I am drawn to him, moving as if in a dream. But I have had so many pulls in my life—the demons, and the love of home and my family, and the desire to be well, and the desire to be loved, and the desire truly to be your daughter and serve you—that I may be confused. Help my confusion! She squeezed her eyes closed, as if that would clarify her inner vision.

As she held herself still, she seemed to retreat into a little hollow that was reserved just for her, set out for her by God since the beginning of the world.

There was nothing in there that warned her against Jesus, nothing that sounded any sort of alarm. The feeling was calm there, infinitely kind and ministering, and seemed to encircle her with care and tenderness. The stings of the loss of Joel and of Elisheba were soothed—not forgotten, not dismissed, but accepted and borne.

"Just as Moses's mother had to relinquish Moses, and Hannah had to relinquish Samuel, and even Jesus's mother has had to surrender him, sometimes a mother must offer up her child to the care of God," came the assurance.

But it is not Elisheba I am offering up, she protested. Elisheba is just a baby. It is myself—the mother. There is nothing in scripture about that.

"True. It is new. The prophet Jeremiah said each person's sins were his own, and would not be visited on his children. But he never dared to say that a mother must find her own way, regardless of what her family may want."

The last voice seemed to be Jesus's, breaking into her solitude. It continued what he had once said about having come to bring enmity—this time between a mother and a daughter.

"But will she ever understand?" Mary whispered to the invisible presence. "Will she ever understand, and forgive?" It seemed unbearable to her that Elisheba would not, that she would lose her daughter forever.

"If it is given her to understand," a voice said. "That is up to God. But he is a God of mercy."

It had been a real voice. Mary looked around to see where it had come from. Jesus was nearby; he had risen early and left the sleeping group, and in the growing light she could see him near one of the larger rocks. But he seemed lost in his own thoughts and prayer. Surely it could not have been his voice she had heard.

Shaking her head, she brought herself back into the world around her, the world of growing light and rocks and rustling olive trees. She had something to tell him, something urgent. How could she have delayed?

She approached slowly. Jesus was sitting still, his eyes closed. His hands were folded within his mantle.

"Jesus." She reached out her hand and touched his shoulder lightly. Instantly he opened his eyes, as if he had been waiting for her. "I have a message for you. It came to me in the night, in a dream—or a vision."

"Is it about John?" he asked.

"Yes." How did he know that? "I saw him taken away by force by soldiers, then in shackles in a prison. It was horrible! He was thin and looked ill. He said, 'Tell Jesus.'"

Jesus bowed his head. "John," was all he said, with deep sorrow in the one word, weighing it down.

"It was in a fortress near the Dead Sea," said Mary. "High on a mountain."

Jesus looked up at her. "How do you know it was at the Dead Sea?"

"I saw it. Not immediately, but I asked the vision to show me what lay near the mountain. It showed me a long, thin body of water in the midst of a desert. Nothing grew near it, and there seemed to be no life about it at all. Thus I knew it was the Dead Sea."

Jesus closed his eyes for a moment. "Which side was the fortress on?"

Now she had to close her own eyes and try to conjure up the vision again. "I believe on the east side. From where the sun was rising, I think it was located on the east side."

"Machaerus," said Jesus. "One of Herod Antipas's strongholds." He stood up. "You saw it all?"

"Yes. John told me to tell you."

Jesus smiled. "So your visions have survived. They were part of you, not just the curse of the demons."

Visions of any sort were a curse, she thought. "I wish they had disappeared with them!" she said.

"Perhaps it is this part of you that the demons wished to destroy or pervert," said Jesus. "Demons do not attack people unless they perceive them as a threat."

Mary almost laughed. How could she be a threat to anyone or anything? She had just been an ordinary person, trying to live an ordinary life.

"I want to be ordinary," she insisted. "I don't want visions."

"God has decided otherwise," said Jesus. "Who are we to argue?"

Mary grabbed his arm. "But—"

"Mary, be happy in whatever life God has called you to," he said.

She felt disappointed in his answer. But she must forget her own concerns now. "John! What is he trying to tell us?" she asked.

"That he has been imprisoned by Herod Antipas to silence him. But his true message is to warn me and call me to action. From this moment on, my true ministry must begin. John cannot speak, and I must. I have no choice."

When they rejoined the awakening group, Jesus said, "I have had sad news about John the Baptist. He is imprisoned at Machaerus. Herod Antipas has taken him."

Peter, struggling to sit up, rubbed his eyes. "Who told you? Has there been a messenger?"

"Someone came in here and we did not hear them?" Thomas sounded indignant. He jumped up, flinging off his covering.

"It was a vision," said Jesus. "Granted to Mary in the night." He nodded toward her. "Mary has the gift of prophecy, I think," said Jesus. "We must trust it."

"Tell us! Tell us what you saw!" Nathanael insisted.

"We cannot help John in any way other than to pray for him," said Jesus, after she had described it. "No one can storm that prison, certainly not us. Our way is not with swords."

Together they bowed their heads and prayed fervently that God would protect John even in his loathsome prison.

"God said to Moses, 'Is the Lord's arm too short?'" Jesus said. "No, it is not. There is no dungeon beyond its reach. We must have faith."

After the group made ready, they set off, climbing higher.

At length the slope leveled off, and they were high on the stony, windswept plateau that overlooked the land on both sides. Far to the north, in the valley below, they could see the marshy area around Lake Huleh, the first lake formed by the Jordan on its way to the Sea of Galilee. It was small and marshy, but rich in wildlife and fish.

The land around them was boulder-strewn, except in the few places where people had, with great labor, hauled the stones away and stacked them in piles at a corner of the fields: a difficult, demanding country, so different from the green and welcoming Galilee. A few stunted junipers stood like sentinels in the fields, their branches twisted and bent from the winds and harsh winters.

Mary was relieved when they reached a little village in the late afternoon. But as they approached the outskirts of the village, they heard wailing and moaning. A large group of people, camped nearby, were mourning noisily. The men were sitting on the ground throwing dust on their heads, and some others were wandering around dazed, ripping at their robes. The women were crying and singing dirges. As they came nearer, three men stood up to block their way.

"Go around the other way!" they ordered. "Do not come near! Leave us in peace!" One tall man brandished a staff and waved it threateningly.

But Jesus strode up to him and took hold of the staff, forcing it down. "Who are you?" he asked gently. "What are you mourning?"

"Who are *you*?" the man asked. His face was streaked with the dirt of mourning.

"Jesus of Nazareth," he replied.

At once the man's demeanor changed. "Jesus? Of Nazareth, you say?"

"Of Capernaum until recently," Jesus said. "But originally of Nazareth."

"John the Baptist told us about you," the man said. "He said there was this man he had baptized, who had now gone out on his own and was a rival. You had even dared to take some of John's disciples! Why did you do it?" he asked angrily. "Why did you leave John?"

"God had different demands for me. But I respect John, as a true prophet and man of God. And, yes, some of John's followers came with me"—he indicated Peter, Andrew, Nathanael, Philip, and Mary—"but it was of their own free will. I teach nothing contrary to John."

"John the Baptist has been imprisoned, is that not true?" Mary asked, coming over to the mourning man. She had to know; she had to know about the dream, the vision.

"Yes," said the man. "He told us to seek our safety here in the northern hills of Galilee. He knew he would soon be arrested."

"And he is in Machaerus, isn't he? That fortress on the eastern shore of the Dead Sea," asked Mary.

"Yes."

"Is that why you are mourning?"

"Yes. He is doomed. His mission is over," said the man. "But we, his disciples, will remain true forever. They cannot kill all of us." His eyes glowed with intensity.

"Join us," said Jesus. "We also honor John."

The man frowned. "No. We will follow no one but John. If your teachings were the same, you would not have left him."

"True," said Jesus. "John announced that the Kingdom of God was coming. I announce that it is already here."

The man laughed, but it was not a real laugh. "Oh, yes. Already here. That is why Antipas has the power to imprison John!"

"Antipas has only the power granted to him from above. But already that power is on the wane. The signs that the Kingdom is dawning are to be seen everywhere, in the healings that I have been able to bring—"

"Healings are all very well and good, but they do not mean the Kingdom is here," said the man stubbornly.

"I do not think John would agree," said Jesus.

"Well, we can't ask him, can we?" replied the man. He turned away and went back into his tent, where he sank down and closed his eyes.

Jesus led his own group to a site on the other side of the village. "Here we will rest for the night," he said.

Mary went to him as soon as the primitive camp had been made. Andrew and Philip had gone into the little village to buy whatever provisions they could find, and had come back with lentils, some dried lamb, and a few fresh leeks. From that they would make a stew to feed them all.

"So it was true," she said to Jesus. "My dream. About John and the prison."

"Yes," he said. "I told you it was."

"I wish it had not been," she said.

"I am grieved that it turned out to be true, but you should be thankful that your visions, purged now of Satan, will let God speak to you. He will tell you things he wishes others to know, through you."

"I hate the visions! Ask God to remove them!"

"God has decided that you shall not be ordinary, Mary of Magdala." Jesus smiled. "Rest in his sovereign wisdom. He gives you the gift not for yourself, but to help others. Accept it gratefully!"

After dinner, he led them in prayer, then asked them just to sit quietly and meditate. They sat, eyes closed, feeling the close of day in the calls of birds at twilight and the rising wind.

"Friends," said Jesus finally, "I had meant for us to withdraw and spend quiet time apart, here in the north country, before our true mission begins. But now that John is imprisoned, I see that we must return. The voice of challenge, the voice of the prophet, must not cease for one instant. His is silenced: so I must speak all the louder. Tomorrow we must start back. Back into Herod Antipas's territory. We must not be afraid."

They sat quietly, heads bowed.

"It is in the world of men that we are called to move," Jesus said suddenly. "The heights are only for refreshment, for exaltation, not for permanent dwelling."

Lying down beside her that night, Joanna whispered, "I don't want to go back there. I want to put it all behind me, go somewhere else."

Yes, anything connected with Herod Antipas must be painful for her.

"I wish we could just go to a foreign place and start with no memories at all," agreed Mary. "Truly to start anew."

As soon as she said it, she realized that Jesus would rebuke her for that thought. He would say that once you have been touched by the Kingdom the things of the past cease to have a hold on you.

⋙ XXXVII ⋘

This night, Mary thought, I will sleep well. I am so tired. The twilight deepened, the campfire burned down, and the stillness of the heights enveloped them.

And at first sleep came easily. She drifted away, lulled by the tranquillity surrounding her, and the fatigue in her body. But halfway through the night, vivid dreams came to her, so vivid that they made her sit bolt upright. They were worse than the one she had had about John the Baptist, much worse.

She saw Joel lying on a bed, his body crushed. His chest was covered by a blood-soaked bandage, and he was gesturing feebly toward someone—or something—across the room. His arm seemed to be bandaged, his hand protruding from the binding like the claw of a sea creature.

"Help me," he was whispering. "I cannot bear it."

Someone was hovering over him, wiping his brow, and taking care of him. Mary implored the vision to pull back, reveal more.

The person bending over Joel was Eli. Beside him Joel's mother and father were standing by, holding each other. Her own mother, Zebidah, was standing nearby, holding Elisheba.

Joel was on his deathbed. Joel, so young and healthy. What had happened to him?

Mary sat up, her dream fading, her vision lost. Her heart was pounding. She gasped and clutched at her own throat. All around her everyone was sleeping. The night sky was clear, and the stars were bright and far away.

Was it a dream or a vision? If a vision, she had to know more.

For a few long moments, there was nothing. And then the pictures came back. Joel at the Temple, entering the inner courts. Joel and a group of fellow Galileans approaching the heights, where they could see the massive stone altar spattered with the blood of sacrificial animals. Suddenly a contingent of Pilate's Roman soldiers converging on them, yelling, shooting arrows. Confusion. No one knowing where to go. They run, they duck, they fall to the ground. There are screams, shouts from Pilate's men, blood. People fall back. The dead and the injured topple into the crowd behind them. The great mass of people crowding into the court collapse backward against the ceremonial bronze doors, and then Pilate's soldiers begin beating whoever they encounter. A club lands on Joel's head, then his stomach, and finally his legs, almost breaking them. He crumples and falls.

Another vision appeared: a heap of injured, dead, and dying people, an ugly mound of moving, bleeding flesh in the court of the Temple. Soldiers come with litters and drag them out, beyond the Temple precincts, so that the outer Temple doors can be closed for the night. The injured and dying lie in the street just beyond those gates. Someone else's problem. Not Pilate's.

Somehow Joel gets home, carried slowly by his fellow Galileans. It takes them many days. But now he lies in a darkened room, dying.

Joel! No, it cannot be. He has never gone to Jerusalem before.

Surely God cannot have been so cruel as to strike him down for seeking the Temple, trying to fulfill the obligations of visiting it for the first time.

Again she sat up, panting for breath. But the vision was so clear. It seemed so certain. She must return there, immediately. And Jesus! Jesus must come to Joel, must cure him. Jesus could save him.

There is no case impossible unless Jesus is not permitted to treat it, she tried to calm herself by repeating.

The night went on forever. The dark-blue sky, the stars were ugly to her, because they were not dawn. When light finally came, she leapt up from her makeshift bed.

At the sight of Jesus walking along the edge of the cliff in the dim light, she could wait no longer. She rushed toward him, grasped his arm.

"Jesus!" she said. "I have had another vision. A terrible one. The Galileans that Pilate attacked in the very grounds of the Temple, that Judas told us about—my husband was among them! He lies on his deathbed, dying of injuries from Pilate's attack. We must go to him in Magdala, you must save him!"

To her surprise, Jesus shook his head. "I must save him? You can go to him, you can pray over him. God will listen to you."

"God, yes," she said. "But not Joel. Did you yourself not say, 'A prophet is not without honor except in his native place and among his own kin'? Joel will never hearken to me, or believe in my prayers."

"But he is not a believer in my message," said Jesus. "I learned in Nazareth that if someone does not believe, I can work no healings there."

"He had not had an opportunity to believe!" said Mary. "It is true, he turned against you when we came to Magdala, but he had not heard what you had to say, nor had he himself witnessed any of your works. Oh, you must go to him!"

"We will go together," said Jesus. "But I beg you, do not expect too much. If he does not consent, then—"

"But he cannot die, he cannot!" cried Mary. "It would be wrong, everything about it would be wrong!"

"It is wrong for John the Baptist to die," said Jesus. "And yet he will."

"But John is holy!" said Mary. "He has made his life that of serving God and speaking out as a prophet. He knew death was always near. Joel was just an ordinary man, not deeply observant, but a good man."

"I will go," Jesus said. "I will do what I can. But it is up to Joel what he allows God to perform."

Jesus and Mary set out immediately, after Jesus gave the others instructions to wait a few days and then to set out for the town of Bethsaida.

They spoke little, although Mary longed to talk to Jesus about her life with Joel, what he had meant to her, how he had loved her—and she him—and how she had still believed that their separation was only for a short time, and therefore bearable. Surely Joel would have come to understand what Jesus had done for her, would somehow allow Jesus and his followers to become part of his own life, would reunite her with Elisheba.

But as she walked along in grim silence in the ever-hotter sun, the most dreadful feelings of loss took hold of her. She began to shake with fear. At this very moment, Joel was lying hurt, surrounded by all the family except his wife. Does he even think of me? she wondered. Or am I dead to him?

Oh, let Joel be alive when we get there! Let him even have begun to recover! she prayed.

The familiar streets of Magdala, the lakeside path and the open market square, known to her all the days of her life, were before her once again. The houses seemed so comforting and familiar, as if their very familiarity could stave off disaster. But there was no more time to think; they turned the corner of one street and came upon her own house. As soon as they saw the large crowd gathered outside, Mary knew that the vision had been true. When they were making their way toward the door, people suddenly recognized her and gasped as if she had been dead and just risen from a grave. They did not hinder her entrance, however, and she and Jesus slipped past them and went into the house.

It was just as she had seen it in her dream: darkened, shuttered, and so close and airless that every smell was magnified. A ring of relatives were standing about in the largest room, some of them mourning already. They barely looked up as Mary and Jesus passed through and into the bedroom.

The smell of illness was so pervasive that Mary choked. Standing beside the bed was—just as in the dream—her mother holding Elisheba, who was whimpering and staring mournfully at the person on the bed.

Mary could not look, not yet, at what was on the bed. Instead she flung herself upon her mother, clasping both her and Elisheba to herself so tightly her arms ached. "Mother! Mother!" she whispered.

"Mary?" Her mother pulled back and stared at her in disbelief. "Oh, Mary, can it truly be you?" Her eyes filled with tears. "You are back, oh, my daughter, and just in time." She did not see Jesus; she thought Mary had come alone.

Elisheba merely looked puzzled at this vaguely familiar stranger, then gave a weak smile. The dark eyes seemed enormous, warily measuring what they saw.

"Elisheba . . ." Elisheba reached out her chubby arms and encircled her, and Mary's heart raced with joy.

"Mother . . . I was told of Joel's accident. . . ." No need to explain who told her, or how. "And now I see that it is true!" She summoned up the strength to look at the bed.

Joel lay flat on his back, his splinted arms crossed over his bandaged stomach, his bruised legs propped up on a folded blanket. He was so sunk in pain and weakness that he did not even open his eyes or seem to hear anything happening around him.

Mary knelt beside him. This was Joel, his dear, familiar profile looking as it always had. But the dark circles under his eyes, the sunken cheekbones, and the cracked and bloodless lips—this was the image of impending death. With each breath Joel drew, his labored wheezing forced little bloody bubbles of froth out between those thin lips. She touched his forehead. She expected to find it hot, burning with fever. Instead, to her shock, it was cold. He was so near death that already the chill of it was on him.

"Joel," she whispered, stroking his forehead, his cheeks—also cool. "It is I, Mary, your wife." She took his hands and began rubbing them.

He did not stir or give any sign that he felt anything.

"Joel," she kept saying. "Joel, open your eyes! Joel, open your eyes!"

Only then did Eli, standing off to one side, recognize her. He jerked his head and gave a sudden start.

"You!" he cried. "You! How dare you come here?" He moved swiftly and grabbed her arm, yanking her away from the bed. "Don't touch him! How dare you touch him?"

"I am his wife!" she said. She pulled down her head covering so that all could see. Yes, let them all see who she was, even down to the cut hair. No matter what had happened to her, she was still Joel's wife, and belonged here more than any of them.

"Not any longer!" said Eli. "He was divorcing you." He lowered his voice so that no one but they could hear.

She twisted her arm free of Eli's strong grip. "He had no cause!" she said, keeping her voice loud.

"Cause enough," said Eli. "You have been a shame and a scandal, blackening the name of the family."

"Why?" she challenged him. Everyone in the room was staring. "Because I was ill? Or because I was cured? There is no sin in either!"

"The Law clearly states that a man may divorce his wife if he finds something 'indecent' about her. What better word for you?"

"Illness is not indecent, nor is seeking a cure," she argued. "You have always been a cruel man, using the Law as something to hide behind to justify your own cruelty. Now tell the truth: did Joel actually go through the prescribed ritual of divorce?"

"No," admitted Eli, glaring at her. "But he had announced that he would, upon his return from Jerusalem."

Mary had turned away from him and was bent down again to tend to Joel. "Joel—dearest husband—please open your eyes. I need you to open your eyes. It is not over. You can be helped. There is someone here, someone I have brought, who can help." She kept rubbing his temples.

One of Joel's eyes—the less swollen one—opened partway. He could not turn his head to see her, but he seemed to recognize her voice. "Help," he said. "Help." Then he stretched out one of his arms, just as he had done in the dream.

"I am here," she said. "I am here. Try. Open your other eye. Speak to me. Joel, there is help."

Slowly the other eye opened, although it could not be wider than a slit. His lips parted and he whispered, "Mary?"

She grasped his hands. "Yes! Yes! I am here!" She leaned over and kissed his cheek. "It is all right now. It is all right now."

He gave a long, deep sigh. "Here now," he repeated. "Here now."

She seemed to sense a slight squeezing of her hand, but it was so weak she could not be sure. The family was crowding all around her now, pushing up to be near the bed. She felt as if she could not breathe. And if she could not, then what of Joel?

"Please," she said. "Stand back. This is too close." She leaned over right near Joel's ear. "Joel. I have someone here who can help. You saw him before. You know that he cured me. He is a special man, sent by God. He has helped people much worse than you. I have seen it with my own eyes. Lepers—whose skin has gone from white to glowing health. Men whose legs would not work, now able to walk and even jump and run. What you have is small in comparison. Here, let him help!" She stood up and held out her hand to Jesus. "Come. Here is Joel. He needs you."

Jesus, who had been overlooked by everyone as he stood in the shadows, now stepped forward. He took his place at Joel's bedside and looked down at him where he lay, his breathing labored.

Mary could not tell anything from Jesus's expression. Did he think it possible to save Joel? Did he despair of it? He was concentrating so hard on Joel's face that he seemed unaware of anyone else in the room.

"Joel!" he said. "Can you hear me?"

There was a long, slow moment when Joel gave no response.

Oh, God! Mary thought. He is going, leaving us! We got here too late, in spite of our best efforts!

But Joel finally gave a response that was more like a croak. "Yes," he said. "Yes."

Jesus then took both his hands. He held them and closed his own eyes and prayed. Finally, he said, "Joel, your bodily injuries can be healed. But only if you completely trust in me, and believe that I can ask God for this favor, and that he will grant it. And that with God nothing is impossible."

Joel just lay quietly. At long last he said, "With God nothing . . . is impossible, that I know." It took a great effort for him to speak, and he had to wait a while before he could continue. Then he whispered, "But you—no, I cannot trust you." He coughed and brought up blood. "I have . . . seen you. You delivered my wife, only to enslave her. To keep her with you." He gasped again, and his voice grew soft. "You can . . . perhaps work mighty works, but only because Satan has allowed you to. You are . . . his agent." His words were very faint.

Mary gasped. "No, Joel. No, you are wrong! He is Satan's enemy; do not help Satan! It is he who whispers those words into your ear now!"

Somehow, Joel managed to struggle and lift his head off the pillow. His eyes opened wider, and although he looked at Mary with a softness she remembered, his stare at Jesus was hostile.

Jesus moved closer to him and tried to take his hands again. "Put your trust in God!" he begged him. "Pray with all your heart!"

But Joel pulled his hands away and shook his head, feebly. "Don't touch me!" he finally rasped. "You evil man!"

Mary fell forward, crying, laying her head on his chest. "No, Joel! No! It is your only hope!" She wiped his face tenderly. "Oh, Joel, don't leave me! Don't leave Elisheba! Let Jesus help you!"

He shook his head again, slowly, letting it sink back down. "No. And to think . . . you only came to my deathbed . . . like a vulture! You will get nothing, nothing, I tell you! That's really what you . . . came for!"

"Joel, forget me!" she begged. "Give me nothing. That is your right. But please, please, let Jesus intercede for you!"

"No!" he cried, with a loud voice that shocked everyone. Where had it come from? Then he fell back against the pillow with a thud.

"Pray for him anyway!" Mary ordered Jesus. "Cure him anyway! Later he can repent. Later he will see that he was wrong! Later . . . later is a luxury only the living have. Give that to him!"

Jesus was praying, his eyes closed, his hands clasped. He alone seemed oblivious to everyone else in the room.

"It is too late," he said, in great sorrow. "It is too late. Without trust . . . it was too late."

Even as he said it, Mary looked down to see that Joel's eyes had closed and his chest did not seem to be moving. A feeble rattling sigh came from his throat, then silence.

He was dead. Joel was dead. She slumped down by the bedside and wept, with her head by his arm.

The rest of the people in the room set up a wail, but she did not hear it. All she felt was Joel's absence, all she heard was the silence from his lips.

It had been near sunset when Joel died, which meant that there could be no funeral, no burial, until the sun rose the next day. The women must prepare him for burial. That included Mary, although she did not think she could bear it.

"Jesus," she said, clinging to him, "why could you not save him?"

Jesus looked sadder than anyone else there. "Because he would not let me," he said. Then he turned aside and wept for a moment. After a little while, he said to Mary, "Do what you must. Be with the women, prepare your husband. I will wait."

Sorrowing, Joel's father, Ezekiel, and Mary's father, Nathan, lifted Joel's inert body off the bed and bore him to a room to prepare him for burial. The women helped lay him on an alabaster slab. After the men departed, Joel's mother, Judith, reverently removed his clothes and prepared to wash him. Standing over him was his sister, Deborah, and ringing them were her brothers' wives, Naomi and Dinah, and several cousins whom Mary remotely recognized but could not think about now. She winced as she saw his injuries. His ribs were black and blue and his arms were broken in several places.

Joel! Beautiful, well-formed Joel had been beaten and murdered. He had been killed like one of the sacrifices on the high altar—like a ram or a bull. But not by a priest—by Pilate, the representative of Rome!

Now the women poured water from clay pitchers over his body, washing him clean of the old blood on his wounds. It was so strange to see the water pouring over him and yet to see no movement from him. Mary reached out a trembling hand and gently closed his eyes and then smoothed his hair. She stroked his cheek. Already the flesh did not feel like that of a living person, but was cooler and harder, and the color had fled from him, making him pale. Through their tears they sang Psalms as they rubbed his body with aloe oil and myrrh, and together they held him so that the shroud could be wound around him, the white linen shroud that would enfold him. His legs and arms were bound, and a special cloth was put over his face before the last pieces of the shroud were fastened on his head. Then they lifted him onto the litter that would carry him to his grave in the morning, and cleaned and dried the alabaster where he had lain.

The women beckoned for Mary to come with them to the special room that would be set aside for them to pass the night, since they were now ceremonially unclean from having touched a dead body. Numbly she followed, walking with them in silence. They re-entered the main floor of Mary's house (was it ever *my* house? she wondered; it does not seem so any longer), already stripped of the deathbed cloths, the windows opened to let in fresh air, and the floor swept. Mary sank down on a stool. There were other women waiting in the room, relatives who had not participated in the actual burial preparation. Dully Mary looked at them. Who were they?

They clustered together, whispering, as if Joel still lay there and could be disturbed. They embraced and comforted one another, but no one embraced Mary. For a few moments she did not care; she did not want to be touched or talk to anyone; she was too distraught.

Then, gradually, she began to hear the low murmurs.

"*She's* here, she actually came, she left that crazy man she's with—"

"No, no, she brought him with her, didn't you see him? He dared to come forward and take Joel's hands."

"Some people have no shame."

"Which one? Mary or this . . . man?"

I am the widow, thought Mary. My husband just died. Here are the women of my family. But no one acknowledges me.

There was Eve, her aunt, the woman who had winked and given her the love potion to make her a good wife at her betrothal gathering. And another aunt, Anna, who had the potion for Joel to make him "like a male camel." And the cousins, who had squealed and giggled at the gathering. And Zebidah, her own mother, and her own sisters-in-law . . .

Mary stood up, weak on her feet but needing to look them in the face.

"Are there no words of comfort for me?" she cried.

The women, as a united group, stopped speaking and looked at her. "Comfort? For you?" Deborah, Joel's sister, finally asked. She was now a grown woman, this girl who looked so like Joel and had been close to her brother.

"Yes, for me," Mary said. "I have lost my husband."

Zebidah came over to her and took her hand. "Yes. That is tragic."

"Will no one tell me of his journey to Jerusalem? Of how he came to be on this pilgrimage?" Mary cried. "He had never gone before!"

Joel's mother, Judith, shook her head. "He said a number of families were going and he felt called to join them."

Joel? Joel felt called?

"He had changed his mind about many things," she said, pointedly.

"My husband was on the pilgrimage," said a woman, someone Mary did not recognize. "There was no premonition of danger. Then . . . Pilate grew agitated about something—perhaps he had had a scare about an uprising, there are so many of them, and most start in Galilee—and when he saw all those pilgrims, something they did must have set him off. After the attack, after the others found Joel, they brought him back here, but it was a long trip. The jouncing of the don‑

key caused him such pain. . . . By the time they reached Magdala, he was already delirious and hot with fever, and we could see that the wounds were angry and festering. It took too long to get here."

"Thank you," said Mary. "Thank you for telling me." Poor Joel! How terrible must have been those long-drawn-out days of travel from Jerusalem to Magdala.

"And what of you?" one of the cousins finally asked. "Why are you gone from us?"

Gone from us . . . gone from us . . . They make me sound as if I am dead! thought Mary.

"I—"

"Mary was possessed." Her own mother's harsh voice, forgoing any whispering, rang out. "Yes. Demons took her over, and she was forced to seek treatment. But, unfortunately, the man treating her was evil and tainted her. Joel recognized this, and put her aside as his wife. So," she said, standing directly in front of Mary, "you are not truly his widow."

"For now and forever I am always his wife," said Mary. "And I did not leave you, I have never left you."

"Unless you repent, and purify yourself, you are no longer my daughter," her mother said. Never had she seen such a look on her mother's face, such utter condemnation.

"Mother, I have done nothing wrong!" she said, reaching out to her. Her mother stepped back.

"Mother!"

Her mother retreated into the shadows.

"You say you are the widow," said Deborah. "You were *not* a wife to my brother!"

Deborah had always been her friend, claiming that she wanted to be like her, that she admired her. Mary felt as if she had been struck. "I—I was always—" she started to defend herself, then turned aside in confusion.

"Oh, you'll come back here, to live in Joel's house and count his money," said Deborah. "But you should know this: until seven years have passed, no one will trust you. You must live quietly and under our guidance. Your daughter will be raised by Dinah, who has already taken her to her home."

Dinah? Taken Elisheba away? Mary gave a cry of grief.

"You should have thought of that before . . . before you started all this," her mother said. "Dinah knew this would fall to her, and that is why she stood apart from preparing Joel, from actually touching the dead body. She had to remain ritually clean. And so must Elisheba. Yes, she will take the child, and care for her."

"But we want you here," said Joel's mother, Judith, quickly. "We want you to return to normal life. Seven years . . . it is not so long. It will quickly pass."

"Of course, as a widow, you will have certain restrictions." Her mother spoke again. "Widows do not enjoy the freedoms of wives."

"And your probationary years . . . There are many things you will have to give up," said Deborah, a self-righteous smile on her face. "Then, when you have proved yourself . . ."

"Is there no one to come forward and hold me as a fellow sufferer, to comfort me?" Mary looked at the sea of hard, set faces before her.

Naomi, Silvanus's wife, broke ranks and embraced her. In her ear she whispered, "Do not despair. Do not despair. I and your dear brother will never let you go, or turn our backs on you. We will help you get through the seven years."

This circle of women, so tightly woven, so like a sisterhood, now seemed an evil net to entrap her and kill her.

"I must return to Joel!" she suddenly said. "I must be with him!" She stood up and quickly left the room, fleeing back to him.

Even a dead man is more kind to me! she thought, stumbling into the chamber. Several lanterns burned on each side of the bier, but the rest of the chamber was very dark. And cold—no need for warmth there. She took her place on a stool beside the bier and kept her own lonely vigil, staring at the white-wrapped figure lying so long and so still on the litter. She could not even think any special thoughts, she was so stunned and shaken. She forgot the women. All she could do was stare, and weep, and then go back to staring. The women and what they had said faded into nothingness.

"Oh, Joel," was all she said. "Oh, Joel."

She barely heard Jesus come in and sit down beside her. He said nothing at all, just closed his eyes and prayed silently. She felt that Jesus understood more than all the women put together, experienced more than they, and perhaps, perhaps, could impart to her some of his understanding of death and pain. All that mattered was Joel.

She wanted to say something worthy of the tragedy, but what came out was "I don't want to leave him!"

"The pain of separation is very great," said Jesus. "It is the deepest hurt. Nothing I or anyone else can say can take away that hurt."

"I left him, and now . . . now I will never see him again. And he died angry at me. And nothing can change that."

Jesus reached out and took her hand, encircling it with both of his. "He was angry because he did not understand. That did not change his love for you."

"They have cast me out," she finally murmured. "The women . . . they are crueler than the men!"

While they talked in low voices, the lanterns set around Joel's bier flickered and waved, making patterns of shadows on his white shroud. How odd it was to be speaking of such deep personal matters in front of him this way.

She looked at the still, shrouded body. Joel had sent her away to Jesus. Now he had given her an opportunity to start all over and choose once again, this time by herself. She could rejoin the family, submit herself to their strictures, accept the punishment for straying from whatever they condemned.

She ached with the loss of Joel and the idea of a final loss of her family, but the thought of abandoning Jesus was even worse. "For then I shall be truly lost," she murmured, so low that Jesus could not possibly hear her. Yes, that was the dilemma: the conviction that somehow Jesus, above all else, had become necessary for her life.

The funeral procession was forming outside the house. Joel's body lay on its litter, held by his weeping father, Ezekiel, by Nathan, by Jacob and Ezra from the warehouse. The ritual signs were all observed: There were ceremonial rips in the clothes, and the prescribed dirt on their heads. Tears ran down the men's faces as they made these formal signs.

Behind the litter, the townspeople were gathering, and the musicians to play the funeral pipes, the women who would sing the age-old songs of lamentation. There were professional mourners there, too, hired by someone in the family, who would sound their ululating, piercing cries all the way to the tomb.

The women were expected to lead the procession, and already Judith, Zebidah, Deborah, Naomi, and the cousins had taken their places. They had drawn up in ranks when Mary tried to take her place at their head.

She did not see Elisheba anywhere. In spite of the still, mounded form of Joel on the litter, she looked frantically for Elisheba. She should be here, in my arms, Mary thought. I must hold her, she must be carried in the forefront of her father's funeral procession.

Farther back, she saw Dinah clutching a child with a hooded wrap. She broke away from where she was standing and sought her out.

"Elisheba!" she said, pulling back the head covering. The dark eyes of her daughter stared back at her, but the little girl did not smile or give any sign of recognition.

"You!" Dinah hit her hand. "How dare you touch her, and render her ceremonially unclean?" She looked at her own hand. "Now I am unclean as well!"

"To be unclean from her father's death is an honor," said Mary. "And one she would regret as she grew older had she not acquired it."

Elisheba held out her arms, tentatively. Mary reached out and tried to take her. For an instant she felt the warmth of her daughter, held her close.

"Help!" Dinah called out. "She's trying to take her!"

Instantly a large group of men and women from the village, who were making up the rear of the funeral procession, surrounded her.

"Drop her! Drop the child!"

One of them clutched Mary's arm and twisted it. Another grabbed Elisheba.

"Stop this!" Jesus came forward and tried to take Elisheba back. "Let her mother hold her."

One of the men—not too overcome with sorrow to strike—hit Jesus in the face and wrenched Elisheba out of his arms.

"This woman has no right!" he said. Triumphantly he marched over to Dinah and put Elisheba, who had started to wail, back in her arms.

"Elisheba—!" cried Mary.

A woman beside Dinah shoved her. "Take your place in the procession!" she ordered her.

Everyone had assembled, and a long tail of townspeople snaked out behind the official mourners. The sun was shining, and the lake was sparkling. The mourners would lament and cry, and the flutes would play, and Joel would be borne to his tomb, carved out somewhere in the hillside beside Magdala.

"We never selected a tomb site," Mary said to Jesus, her voice shaking. "We thought we had many years."

She looked at the long procession. She had no place in it; she had lost that place when she went out into the desert.

"Let the dead bury the dead," Jesus said to her, indicating the entire funeral procession.

And, indeed, they did look dead; strange how she would never have thought of those words, but they were true.

"Come, let us go," said Jesus. "We are neither wanted nor needed. Leave the dead to one another."

She should have protested, but she only longed to get away. This was no longer home to her. "But my daughter is with the dead people!" she said.

"She will grow up among them, but God will provide opportunities for her to listen to other voices," said Jesus. "And if she says yes to them, then she can have another life as well."

"I want to bring that other voice to her! I want her to hear my voice," said Mary.

Jesus guided her away from town, to walk beside the water. Fishing boats were bobbing up and down, nets were being hauled in, and life was going on as it always had. The tasks of daily life drowned out the wails and the dirges only a little distance away.

"Your voice is not yet clear," said Jesus. "You have much to learn and much to experience before you can speak with the voice that God intends, with the voice that Elisheba will listen to."

But I will speak to her, somehow, Mary thought. I will not abandon her. She will hear my voice, even now, even before I grow wise! A mother does not need to be wise, only to love as a mother.

෨ XXXVIII ෨

Peter's house, but without Peter. Mary was too devastated to journey all the way to Bethsaida, some eight Roman miles away. This was a different kind of depletion from the demons, different even from the first time she had been driven from Magdala. It was too much for her to comprehend. She would never accept it, never. But now she was too stunned to fight it further.

Mara was kind but guarded. Jesus and Mary were the people, after all, who had lured her husband into a strange and unknown life, leaving her behind. Simon—she refused to call him Peter—had left her, and she did not even know where he was.

At this time, Mary did not care what Mara or her mother thought. She was only grateful to sink down on the pallet they offered her and try to obliterate all feeling, all memory. She even drank all the watered wine they provided in a clay pitcher near her bed, hoping it would send her into a dreamless sleep.

But her sleep was not dreamless. Joel came to her, accusing her, shaking his head, and saying cruel things. Elisheba tried to walk to her but was held back by a barrier, a marble fence like the one in the Temple dividing Jews from unclean Gentiles.

In the clear light of morning, the horror did not go away. Joel was dead. Elisheba was gone. It had not been a dream, it had not been vanquished by the passage of the night. Mara was laying out food for them, and Mary tried to eat it, knowing that her body needed it, but tasting nothing. Mara was asking questions about Simon, about Jesus's mission, but she could barely hear them.

"Your husband is not gone, just called away to other duties." Were those Jesus's words? Was that what he was telling her? Could she, Mary, really care?

There was a noise at the door, and Mara excused herself. Only then did Mary look at Jesus, trying to signal him with her eyes. Before he could respond, a tall stranger walked into the room, wearing a headdress and a lower-face covering that obscured his face. He must be a Nabatean, a desert tradesman.

"Yes, sir? Who are you, and what do you want?" Mara asked the stranger.

He peeled off his head covering, and Mary saw to her shock that it was Silvanus. "I needed to see you," he said, simply. "I was able to find out where Jesus stays in Capernaum. I only hoped that you would stop here on your way back to—wherever it is you are going." In disbelief, Mary rose to her feet, stepped forward to embrace him.

"Oh, Silvanus!" was all she could say, clasping him to her. "You have come. I have seen you at last!" She stepped back, releasing him. "Since my first return, to Magdala—and then, at the funeral . . . did you receive my letter?"

"Yes," he said. "I did."

"And so you know. You understand."

"I know. But I do not understand."

"But I have not had a chance to explain," she said. "When you hear—when you talk to Jesus—" She indicated him, and the two men nodded to one another.

"I am not interested in his message," said Silvanus, flatly. "I long ago disregarded all messages from self-appointed messengers, either now or in the past. But I am deeply concerned about you." He embraced her again. "You are my dear sister, and what you have gone through—oh, how can I help you?"

So he would not listen to Jesus. So be it. What was it Jesus had said? It depends on who the Father draws . . . But he had shown kindness regardless. That was the important thing.

"Elisheba has been taken away, by Dinah," she said. "Dinah! It was Father's doing, and Eli's, and . . . perhaps the women in the family as well. But I must know that she is safe, that she will be watched over by someone who loves her and loves me. I asked you in my letter—please be my go-between! Without you, I am lost! And she is lost to me!"

"I . . ." Silvanus looked tormented. "I will do what I can. But you must understand, that may not be enough."

Mary asked Mara if they might excuse themselves and talk privately. When she nodded yes, they went into the little courtyard and stood under the tree that shaded its center.

They talked, quietly and eagerly, about all that had happened since they had last met. Silvanus told her of Joel's anger and bitterness, of Eli's condemnation, of their own parents' bewilderment. "We had reports of this man, this Jesus. His fame is spreading. We heard about what he had done in Capernaum, until the crowds got so large he had to leave. And the pigs in Gergesa! Oh, everyone was talking about that!"

"Silvanus, you'll never believe this, but remember the Zealot who broke into your house and used the word 'pig' as a code? He's joined Jesus as well."

"No!" Silvanus laughed. "And that notorious tax collector, too. We heard about him, and the attack on the Roman soldier in his house. How can they get along together?"

"I don't know," Mary said, "but somehow they are different now."

"Jesus is attracting attention from people higher up than that," said Silvanus. "I heard that Herod Antipas was most interested in him." He paused. "So, my sister, you seem to be involved in a great adventure. People talk about Jesus all the time now." He sounded curious, but not envious. "Tramping about with Jesus is no place for Elisheba," he said. "She's too young. Surely you know that." He looked at her, as if to ascertain whether she had taken total leave of her senses.

"Yes," she admitted. "I know that."

"They would have taken her from you in any case," he said. "They had already prepared a legal document, saying that until seven years had passed and you were healthy it was not safe for her to be in your keeping. They had convinced the authorities to sign it, making it binding. They would not have even let you see her, except in the presence of Eli."

"But after seven years—"

"These questions can be answered differently. Now, here is what I have brought you: they wanted to take your inheritance away as well. In his weakness, they tried to persuade Joel to do it, to sign over his property to Eli. But he refused, and when he died, there was no such document. I have spoken to Joel's father, Ezekiel, and he agrees: the money, Joel's share of the family business, all goes to you. He knew Joel's heart, and that he did not mean those bitter last words. When Ezekiel saw you at the house, saw how you were cured and still faithful to Joel, he was moved. He wants you provided for. If you wish, I can sell your portion and give you the proceeds. Whatever you wish, I will do. But it is all rightfully yours." He held out a box, within which were documents and a bag of gold coins.

Mary almost gasped when she saw it.

"We know that is what he wanted, since he refused to sign papers altering the inheritance."

"Thank you, Silvanus," she said. "Thank you for still being my brother."

"I will always be your brother," he said.

Dear Silvanus. "Remember that I am always thinking of you," she said, "and pray that you and Naomi will be well and can convey my love to Elisheba. Know I hold her in my heart. Tell her so."

"When Eli is not listening," said Silvanus.

On his way out, Silvanus stopped and talked briefly to Jesus. Mary could see how closely he was studying him under the cover of friendly and casual greetings. His eyes were searching Jesus's face, trying to see what it was that made people leave their nets and fishing boats and families for him, what was his reputed power.

Mary followed Silvanus outside and bade him goodbye.

"What is it about this man?" asked Silvanus.

"Can't you feel it?" asked Mary. "That he has a great power?"

"No," admitted Silvanus. "He seems personable enough, but not so outstandingly so as to draw people the way he does." Silvanus embraced her, holding her close to him. The solid feel of him, the familiar family closeness, brought back a thousand memories. She squeezed her eyes to keep the tears inside, but she could not.

"Dear sister," he said, "I release you into his care. But I will worry about you all the time, for it cannot be safe to be in the company of anyone being watched by Herod Antipas."

"Protect Elisheba for me," she said, letting him go.

"I promise," said Silvanus, as he took his leave. "I promise. . . ."

Early the next morning, although they were hardly rested, Mary and Jesus set out from Capernaum. The freshness of the coming day with its promised clear sky and sweet breezes seemed mocking. Joel would not be seeing this day or enjoying any breezes. The horror of the tomb, with its darkness and stillness, was made more horrible by contrast with what was going on just outside it. How was it possible that Joel was there—Joel, who had been as alive as she? And if he could be there, then she, too . . . No, no, it was impossible to comprehend, one's own death and stillness and the not-caring and not-seeing. . . .

"Jesus," she suddenly said, "did you ever play funeral?"

He slowed his step and looked at her. "I beg your pardon?"

"I mean—when I was a little girl, once a group of us played funeral."

"How in the world did you do that?" he asked, shaking his head. Then he laughed and added, "And why?"

"Someone in the village had died," she said. "It wasn't anyone we knew well, but we had watched the funeral procession and seen the mourners and heard the dirges. I remember seeing the body on its litter, with its graveclothes and flowers, lying like a statue. And I suppose we children were looking for a new game, so that afternoon I got sick and 'died' and my friends wrapped me up in a mantle and put me on a homemade stretcher—a blanket on two poles—and then took me to a place in a garden. And here was the frightening part. I was covered with heaps of blankets, like being buried in the ground. And from far above me I could hear my friends reciting verses and saying farewell to me, and how they would miss me, and I could feel a slight bump as they dropped flowers on top of the mound of blankets."

He had stopped walking and was just listening, watching her face intently. "And then?"

"And then it was quiet. Very quiet. I felt the movement in the ground from their footsteps as they walked away. And I was alone. Alone in that dark, hot place. I tried to sit up—the game was over! But I found I couldn't move. The blankets were very heavy. I started screaming, but I could barely breathe, and the blankets were muffling my voice. Now I felt dead, truly dead, and it was so unbearable"—she paused and gulped for air—"I have been terrified of death ever since."

He took both her hands in his and turned her to face him. "Mary," he finally said, "death is not like that."

He sounded so reassuring. But, Mary thought, how does he know? How can anyone know? Joel knows now. But he cannot tell me. "What is it like, then?" she asked in a small voice.

"It is not the end," he said. "You do not remain in that dark, hot place. The spirit cannot be kept there. God wants it." Then, as if he had said too much, he asked, "How did you escape?"

"My friends came back. They had only gone a little way when they realized I wasn't following. They pulled off the blankets and . . . brought me back to life." Now she laughed. "Yes, we pretended that was what happened."

"You will grieve for Joel for many days," said Jesus, discerning her true question. "You must allow yourself to. You will think of graves, and spirits, and guilt, but in the end you will walk away from that, just as you did from the pile of blankets." He looked at her. "That I promise you."

It was late afternoon when they reached Bethsaida, crossing once more beyond Herod Antipas's territory and into his brother Philip's. Beyond the walls were the usual fishing docks and promenade, although these were not set directly on the lake itself but on a lagoon. The town looked very peaceful, glowing in the warmth of the fading sunlight.

"I think we should go to the marketplace," said Jesus. "Even though it will be empty now, it's still the natural gathering place. Anyone we wish to find will come there."

The streets were filled with prosperous-looking people shutting up their shops, carrying food and water for their suppers, leading their pack animals to rest. Magdala had been prosperous, too, but it had a different feeling to it, more bustle and commerce.

As Jesus and Mary passed along the small streets, they noticed that many of the colonnaded buildings gleamed with clean new limestone façades, and down one vista they saw a palace under construction.

"They must want to make this a miniature Athens," said Mary.

Jesus nodded. "Perhaps someday we should visit the real Athens and compare," he said. Then they both laughed at the unlikelihood of that.

Eventually, they came to the market square, passing the last of the merchants guiding their donkeys home, baskets bulging with unsold goods. The square itself had the forlorn look of a place just abandoned. Debris from dismantled stalls littered the ground—squashed fruit, trampled beans and leeks, pigeon feathers. A few bored unemployed laborers were lounging against doorways, casting disdainful looks at anything passing by. They looked up when Mary and Jesus approached from the other side of the square, but quickly lost interest in them.

It looked to be a long wait, thought Mary.

"They will find us," Jesus assured her. "Or we will find them."

The idlers finally drifted away—obviously no one was going to hire them at this late hour—and there remained a lone energetic soul at the other side of the square who was sweeping the piles of trash into heaps. He whistled as he swung his twig broom at the lumps of fly-swarming garbage, seeming not to mind as the insects enveloped him with each sweep. He worked his way around the perimeter tirelessly. It was nearly dark when he reached the side where Mary and Jesus were standing, and they retreated before the onslaught of his fly-raising broom.

"Oh, I beg your pardon!" the sweeper called.

He waved the flies from around his own head, where they formed a buzzing halo.

"What is your name?" asked Jesus.

"You can call me Beelzebub," he said.

Instead of laughing, Jesus replied, "I would never call anyone that but the one whose real name it is."

"I just meant . . . that I'm the Lord of the Flies," said the man—a boy, actually—indicating the cloud around him. "Right now, anyway."

"If you were the Lord of the Flies, then you could command them," said Jesus. "Do they obey you?"

The boy laughed. "Does it look like it?"

"No, and for that you should be thankful," said Jesus. "Now tell me your real name."

"Thaddeus," he said. He rested his broom, as if puzzled by this stranger's interest in him.

"Are you Greek?" Mary asked.

"No," he said, "I just had parents who wanted to be."

Now Mary laughed. "A common affliction." She thought of Silvanus.

"Good," said Jesus. "Because, if you were not a son of Abraham, then I could not invite you to join us." He turned to Mary to explain, rather than to Thaddeus. "Others are welcome to listen, but I am seeking the children of Israel."

"What? Join you? What do you mean?" Thaddeus looked alarmed. This was what happened when you dropped caution and talked to strangers. He gripped his broom handle and drew back.

Instead of answering, Jesus asked, "What do you do? When you are not sweeping the market, I mean."

"I sell painted pots and jugs and, when anyone wants them, I copy frescoes. Sometimes"—he said this defiantly—"I even copy statuettes of Artemis and Aphrodite and Heracles for clients."

"So your parents are not the only ones who like Greek things?"

"No," he said, "I love them as well."

"I am not surprised," said Jesus. "Here you grew up around them. You would have to be blind not to appreciate their beauty." He paused. "But if you would join me, I would give you other eyes to see the beauty in different things."

"Like what?" he asked. He gripped his broom handle tighter.

"Like those unemployed laborers who waited here until sundown."

"What? Those bums? They just hang around the market and irritate people," he said.

"People, yes, but not God," said Jesus. "He sees them differently." Jesus left Mary's side and stepped closer to Thaddeus. "Let me tell you what the Kingdom of God is like. It is like a rich man who hired some laborers early in the day, as is usual. But as the day wore on he found he needed more laborers, so he went back to the town square and hired some more. By midafternoon, he found the work needed still more, so he returned and hired others. Finally, very late in the day—about the time our friends here were leaving the square in failure—he went back and hired some more. In the evening, he paid them all the same wage. The ones hired first complained, but the rich man said, 'Have I not paid you what we agreed? If I want to be generous with my money and overpay someone else, what business is it of yours?' And so it is in the Kingdom of God. God is generous and will reward us in surprising ways, and he will choose surprising people. Like those irritating men."

"This doesn't make any sense," said Thaddeus.

"Join me and learn how it does make sense."

Suddenly Thaddeus's face registered recognition. "I know who you are. That Nazareth man. That famous Nazareth man who talks so strangely. And performs healings and exorcisms. Yes! Don't deny it!" He pointed a finger at Jesus. "But you disappeared after the pigs went over the cliffs. Where have you been? What have you been doing?"

"Recruiting workers to bring in the harvest of the Kingdom of God," said Jesus. "Soon the training will begin, and then the mission. Will you not join us?"

"I—I'll think about it," Thaddeus said, backing off. "My parents— what would they think?"

"Ask them," said Jesus.

"They would say it is too dangerous," said Thaddeus. "My name-sake, a local prophet some forty years ago, claimed he would divide the Jordan River and lead his followers across it, like Joshua. His head ended up on a stake in Jerusalem. His followers were slain. The mem-ories of that are too fresh. And then there's John the Baptist."

"Arrested," said Mary. And I have seen him in his cell.

"Dead," corrected Thaddeus.

Jesus seemed to step back, as if from a blow. "Dead?" he said.

"Beheaded," said Thaddeus, solemnly.

"When?" asked Jesus. His voice was very quiet.

"Let us sit down here," said Thaddeus. "I don't like to say it so loud." He indicated one of the makeshift benches set up by a departed merchant. The three of them sat down, and then Thaddeus turned to Jesus. He had a very young, appealing face, and hair so light he looked like a foreigner from one of those northern lands. "It was just two days ago."

The same day Joel died, thought Mary. That is why we did not know. And that day I would not have cared, either.

"Herod Antipas had him executed?" Jesus asked sadly. "From the moment he was arrested, this ending was certain."

"But Antipas seemed afraid of him," said Thaddeus. "He probably would have kept him imprisoned forever. But he did it to please his new stepdaughter, Salome. She danced before Herod at his birthday banquet after he promised to give her whatever she wished—'even unto half my kingdom,' he said. So she demanded John's head on a platter."

Mary looked from Thaddeus's agitated face to Jesus's expression of horror.

"A platter?" he said.

"A big silver one," said Thaddeus.

Mary thought she was going to be sick as she pictured John's severed head presented in that manner. Were the angry, accusing eyes closed, or did they stare up from the platter?

"To please a dancing girl," Jesus said. "Such evil is . . ." He seemed overcome with it.

"So this is not the time to join a prophet," said Thaddeus. "Begging your pardon. I know they are after you, too. I heard people say that Antipas was looking for you. And so are the Zealots. They are convinced you are the one to lead them. They want to proclaim you king."

"King," said Jesus. "King of what?"

"King of . . . king of . . . the land of Israel, I suppose. They'll find a proper title. Fighting Son of David, Son of Man, Son of the Star, Messiah, I don't know. Any name will do, I suppose."

Jesus stood up. "Stay a few moments with Mary," he said. "I need to . . . Forgive me, I must take a moment alone." He walked stiffly around the corner and out of sight.

Thaddeus and Mary turned to each other awkwardly.

"I am sure he will not be long," said Mary. "He is just overwhelmed by this terrible news."

"I am sorry I was the one to bring it to him," said Thaddeus. "What are you—why are you both here?"

"Some members of our group are meeting us here. We had separated when . . . for personal reasons," said Mary. She could not bear to talk about Joel now. "We agreed to meet here in Bethsaida. One of our group, Philip, is from here."

Thaddeus looked perplexed, but did not ask any more questions.

Mary was thankful for the silence. Her heart was so heavy that talking was hard for her. Just sitting or walking required all her strength. Deep inside was a pain that sometimes felt like a weight and sometimes like a hollow space. Even listening to Jesus was a great effort, and his words of comfort did not penetrate far enough into the realm that hurt so much.

After what seemed a long time, Jesus returned. He looked so shaken and weighted with sorrow that Mary wished she could comfort him. But her own loss was too great.

It was now growing dark, and Thaddeus got up to go home. Just as he was shouldering his broom, John and the other disciples reached the square, searching. In the deepening gloom, they could barely see across the square, but then John spotted Jesus.

"Master!" he cried. "Master!" He ran over to him, the others following. His fair face was flushed, and his head covering had slipped off his curly hair. He reached Jesus and grasped his hands. "We saw some-one casting out demons in your name, right on the outskirts of town! What nerve! So we stopped him, since we didn't know him!" He crowed with pride. "You should have seen his face!"

"You should see yours," said Jesus. "It is not a pretty sight."

"That's not something John is used to hearing," said his brother, catching up. "Too many people have told him he's pretty, all his life." He laughed as if it pleased him. "But, master, that man—he deserved to be stopped!" Big James nodded his head emphatically.

"You don't understand," said Jesus. "He who is not against us is for us. You should have left him alone."

"But—" Big James looked defiant. "That just—we just—"

"James, are you not going to ask about Mary's husband?" Jesus looked sadly at him.

"Oh, yes, of course, I meant to. . . ." Clearly he had either forgot-ten or just taken it for granted that Jesus would cure Joel.

"He died," said Jesus.

Now a stunned silence hit all the disciples. Jesus had gone to Mag-dala, and yet . . .

Judas was the first to speak. "Mary, I am deeply sorry. I offer you all my sympathy." He stepped forward to come closer to her.

The others crowded around as well, extending their arms to enfold her, as if that would blanket the sorrow.

Mary pulled her mantle closer around her. All these murmured words of sympathy seemed like foam on the sea, floating on the sur-face but unable to do more than decorate the depths of pain beneath.

The wind came up, reminding them that night had come and they had no place to go.

"Where are we going tonight?" The question came from practical Andrew.

"I don't dare ask my wife to house these . . . these rivals. That's how she sees all of you, I'm afraid," said Philip.

"You can come to my house," said Thaddeus, who had not left the square yet.

"Who's this?" asked Simon, ever suspicious.

"A friend," said Jesus. "Someone we just met while waiting for you."

"Is he to join our group?" Simon said.

"No," said Jesus. "I invited him, but he declined. However, Thad-deus, it is kind of you to offer. And we will say yes."

Thaddeus's parents' house lay in the upper part of town. From there they had a fine view of the half-finished palace of Herod Philip. Pointing it out, Thaddeus said that the ruler liked Bethsaida so much he was building this luxury palace to pamper himself here.

"There's talk that he even plans to change the town's name to Livia-Julias, after the late emperor's wife," said Simon, who thrived on gossip.

"Is she still alive?" asked John, surprised. "The old emperor died so long ago."

"Oh, she's very much alive," said Simon, almost chortling with the joy of talking politics again. "And still the power behind her son the Emperor Tiberius. She's enjoying it, so they say. After all, she killed so many people to make him emperor, she ought to enjoy the results. Pity if she did not."

"How old is she?" asked Peter. "She must be a mummy by now."

"Seventy," said Simon, who had all such facts at his fingertips. "There's another political struggle in Rome," continued Simon. "Sejanus has persuaded Tiberius—"

"That's enough, Simon," said Jesus unexpectedly. "There are more important matters here. Antipas has had John the Baptist executed."

"What?" Simon cried. "When?"

"In celebration of Antipas's birthday," said Thaddeus. "There was a banquet, and . . ." He recounted the whole sorry story while the disciples listened in silence.

At last Nathanael said, "Let us pray for him." There was nothing but intense sorrow in his voice, as he put the human culprits—Antipas, Herodias, and her daughter Salome—behind him and thought only of John and his martyrdom.

"Father, hear us on John's behalf," said Philip. "Take him to yourself, let him be safe with you."

"You are the God of righteousness," said Big James. "Do not let this evil go unpunished! Avenge your servant John."

"Protect his soul and console us," said Judas, quietly.

"We now stand alone," said Jesus. "It is up to us to carry on John's work."

They all looked around uneasily. To carry on John's work at this point was to be a political target.

"Is that . . . wise?" asked Matthew. Even his stolidness seemed to be shaken. "Could we not accomplish more by working quietly, teaching and studying and—"

"Hiding? Is that the word you are looking for?" asked Judas, suddenly. "Hiding has much to recommend it. Some of the most noted people have hidden—Elijah, and David, and Moses. There is no shame in it."

Now Thomas, a Torah expert, spoke up. "Really, Judas! Why hide your own cowardice behind scripture? All three of those people were ready enough to step out when God told them to."

Judas bristled. "I'm no coward, and I stand by what I say. All three of those men were hiding from a tyrant, like Antipas, who wanted to destroy them. The pharaoh wanted to kill Moses, Saul wanted to kill David, and Ahab and Jezebel wanted to kill Elijah—all for unjust reasons. They had an obligation to hide and protect themselves."

"God does not want us to hide right now," said Jesus flatly. "He wants us to get about our ministry, and out in plain sight. The time is short and the people need to hear. So . . ." He paused to order his thoughts. "All this has happened so much faster than I had expected. I thought we would have more time. . . ." He sighed. "But we do not. So be it. I want you to go out on missions, two by two, into the countryside and to the towns and villages."

Peter looked shocked. "And do what?"

"Preach the news of the Kingdom of God, heal the sick, and cast out demons."

"How?" Peter's normally booming voice was very small.

"I will give you the power."

"So easily?"

"Along with prayer," said Jesus. "That is the important part."

"How can we know it has happened?"

"You have to trust," said Jesus. "And then be brave and make promises in public with everyone watching."

"But if . . . if it fails?"

"You have to believe that it won't," said Jesus.

"But—but—"

"I don't want the brothers to go out together," said Jesus, his mind moving quickly. "I want different pairings. Simon, I want you and Little James together."

The Zealot and the tax collector! Mary was shocked.

"Peter, you go with Nathanael."

The impulsive man with the contemplative. How could they work together?

"Judas, you go with Big James."

The refined with the unimaginative—how irritating for them both.

"Matthew, you and Thomas will work together."

This is the first pairing that makes sense, thought Mary. They are both practical. Then she thought, But no! The Orthodox Thomas will be offended by the tax collector, who is unclean.

"Joanna, you will go with Philip."

Mary and Joanna looked at one another. He was going to call them, just as he was calling the men. They weren't simply to stay behind and tend the camp.

"And, Mary, you and John will work together."

John. The pretty and mercurial John. Am I the opposite—plain and leaden? Oh, we can never see our own traits. Whatever they are, Jesus thinks mine make a foil to John's.

"There will be no leader," Jesus said. "I give you all equal authority."

Mary felt she was going to faint. She could barely bring herself to stand and talk, her heart was so heavy, but even had she felt free and powerful, she could never do this. How could she ever go out to the people now, with this demanding mission?

"No, master," she finally said. "I cannot—I do not know enough—I am a woman—I have nothing to give anyone, no wisdom—"

"You are right," said Jesus. "You do not know enough, and you have no wisdom."

Oh, thanks be to God! He realizes his mistake, thought Mary. She felt dizzy with relief.

"That is why you must rely on God," Jesus continued. "And remember, God gave you the gift of spiritual visions. You are a prophet. Perhaps the only one in the group."

"But she's a woman," Peter blurted out.

Jesus looked at him sternly. "And were not the prophetesses Huldah and Noadiah from ancient times also women?"

Peter opened his mouth to say something else and then thought better of it.

"Now," continued Jesus, speaking carefully, "your instructions are very simple. You will take nothing with you—no money, no extra clothing, no bread. When you get to a village, you may stay with whoever welcomes you. In entering a household, first say, 'Peace be unto this house.' If a man of peace is there, your peace will rest on him; if not, you may take it back."

Jesus looked around, giving them a chance to question him. But there were no questions, just frightened looks. "Heal the sick who are in the town, and tell them, 'The Kingdom of God is near you.' But when you are not welcomed, go into the streets of that town and say, 'Even the dust of your town that sticks to our feet we wipe off in testimony against you. Yet be sure of this: the Kingdom of God is near.' I tell you, it will be more bearable on that day for Sodom than for that town."

"But . . . sir . . . in the village . . . how do we proceed? How do we introduce ourselves and begin?" asked Philip.

"You heal the sick by laying on your hands and praying. You drive out demons by commanding them to depart. You preach of the Kingdom, what you have already experienced of it." He shook his head, as if he found them very slow. "He who listens to you listens to me; he who rejects you rejects me; but he who rejects me rejects the one who sent me." He paused. "I am sending you out like sheep among wolves. Therefore be as wise as serpents and as harmless as doves. The time is short, so much shorter than I thought. So we must speak, and work, now. The harvest is ready, and you must bring it in. The night is coming, when no one can work. So we must work while daylight lingers."

There was a long and very profound silence. Finally, Nathanael said, "Sir . . . when do we begin?"

"Tomorrow," said Jesus.

✿ XXXIX ✿

The worn wooden doors of the hillside village of Korazin were shut tight in the noonday heat when Mary and John arrived there. With their dusty robes and heads shielded against the fierce sun, the pair looked like nomad traders. Or, rather, traders who had been robbed of their goods, for they carried nothing except a drinking gourd to use at wells. They moved slowly and with the fatigue of travelers who had been on the road a long time.

Before the journey, as the disciples had left the house in Bethsaida,

Thaddeus had suddenly grabbed Jesus's sleeve and said, "I've changed my mind! Can I come with you?"

Jesus looked around the room, at its shelf lined with painted jugs and statuettes. "Are you sure you are ready to leave this?" he asked.

"Yes, oh, yes!" Thaddeus went across the room and grabbed a statuette, one with long, flowing hair that looked like Aphrodite. He lifted it high as if to smash it, but Jesus stopped him. "If this belongs to your parents, then they should be the ones to destroy it. We cannot repay their hospitality by attacking their house. Come. I have reserved Andrew for you as a companion in the mission."

Andrew had had no partner, Mary suddenly realized; he had been assigned to make a threesome with Matthew and Thomas. Jesus must somehow have known that Thaddeus would be joining them.

When the disciples had separated on the road outside Bethsaida, Mary and John had chosen to go to Korazin.

Peter announced that he was going northward, to Dan. "I've always wanted to see it, and Jesus was going to take us there, before we turned around," he said.

"Peter, don't be overambitious," said Jesus. "Dan is a long way from here."

"All the better!" said Peter.

The rest headed in other directions—farther west toward Gennesaret, across the lake to Gergesa, north to the villages along the Jordan.

Outside of town, Jesus had gathered them together under the shade of a large oak tree. Standing side by side, they made a large circle; as a group, they looked strong. Jesus stood in their midst, closed his eyes, and prayed.

"Father, I know you hear me. I know you have chosen these people and given them to me. Now clothe them in your power, so that others can see you in them, and they may also be drawn. Open the eyes of those who look upon them and their works—the works you will give them to do."

One at a time he touched their shoulders. "Receive that power. Know that you have it."

When he touched her shoulders, resting his hands on each one, and spoke his words, Mary closed her eyes and tried to discern special strength entering her. But she felt no different.

"We will meet by the banks of the Jordan after forty days' time," said Jesus. "At the place it flows near Bethsaida. Now go."

Mary had chosen Korazin because she had known the name since childhood but had never visited it, and because, as a lively Galilean town in the hills, it was not a fishing village. Right now, in the wake of her time in Magdala, anything connected with fishing was too painful for her. Let me have farmers and weavers and traders and stonemasons, she thought. Anything but fishermen.

As she and John turned westward toward Korazin along the dusty footpath above the lake, she felt truly as if her old self was buried with Joel in the tomb and she was embarking on a new life. Jesus should have given me a new name, she thought, as he did the others.

Now, as Mary and John entered the town of Korazin, high in the hills overlooking the lake, she wondered if it had been a wise choice. The town looked deserted or hostile. The volcanic black basalt out of which the entire town was built gave it a forbidding look. All the houses lining the streets were of the same dark color, although many had decorative geometric carvings over the lintels to give them a more pleasing aspect. Inside the dwellings it must be ferociously hot, since they absorbed the sunlight rather than reflecting it back. The windows were small and did not admit the breezes that were, mercifully, playing over the hills.

They made their way into the very center of town, where they hoped to find a well; they were not disappointed. A large one awaited them, and they were able to draw water from its depths, water that tasted deliciously cool and almost magically refreshing. For Mary it was especially restorative. She was still greatly oppressed by the sorrow and heaviness that blanketed her like the hot air of this Galilean noonday.

"Oh, Mary," John said, as they rested on the wall around the well, "where do we begin?" He sounded lost.

"What would Jesus do now?" she wondered. She wiped the trickling sweat off her forehead. "We must do likewise."

"He always waited until the Sabbath, went into the synagogue, preached, and then got thrown out," said John, with a wicked smile. "Then, afterward, other people came to him, people who were desperate and didn't care what the authorities thought of him."

"I suppose we could attempt it," said Mary. "Shall I get up to read and speak?" The thought of a woman's trying that was amusing.

"The entire congregation would faint," said John. "Come, let's look for the synagogue. It's a place to start."

Wearily they rose and wandered through the streets of the town.

Mary had to admit it was an attractive place; with everything built from the same material, all the buildings matched, making the town seem more planned than it must truly have been.

"Oh!" John said, as they approached a lovely building with rising steps, an imposing porch, and lintels carved with pictures of the Ark and with twining vines above the portal. "This is very impressive." They stopped to admire it.

"This must be the synagogue," said Mary.

John was lost in admiration of it. "It's really beautiful," he said.

Mary looked sharply at him. She had thought him a superficial person, someone with wealth and good looks who had been spoiled all his life. Now she saw that he had another side, a contemplative side that had been overshadowed by the demands of his life of fishing and his family's social position. "Yes, it is," she answered softly. "Perhaps we should start here. But what day is it? How long until the Sabbath?" They had lost track of days.

"I don't know," admitted John. "But it cannot be longer than two or three days. Our last Sabbath was before we met at Bethsaida."

How odd, the way the days flowed away. How long since Joel had died? Surely this would be only the second Sabbath. Or was it the third? She had not been able to bring herself to think of religious services, let alone attend any. She clutched the amulet of Elisheba's necklace, still around her own neck. The feel of the stone comforted her.

"We have two or three days, then, to meet the people and get to know a bit about Korazin," said Mary.

Korazin did not seem anxious to meet them. Its doors remained resolutely shut, and as they wandered up and down the streets they occupied themselves looking at the various types of doors on both sides of the street. Some were painted a brilliant blue, others a dark red, some had carvings, and others were of natural wood color. With the black background, they made a pleasing mosaic.

The two were hungry. They had followed Jesus's instructions not to take anything with them, and now they were paying for it. Mary had left her box of money and business papers in the safekeeping of Thaddeus's family, and they had not cheated by buying anything along the way. So far, no kind soul had seen fit to treat them to anything, and they were famished. All they had had was the food they had brought along from Thaddeus's.

"How can anyone invite us in or provide for us if all the doors are shut?" asked John. "I don't understand how we are to survive."

But Jesus had ordered them to do this, thought Mary. Surely he had thought it all out.

"We can't just knock on someone's door and ask to be fed," said John.

"No," agreed Mary, "we cannot. Jesus did not tell us to beg."

The heat of the noonday had passed, and people were starting to open their doors again and venture out. As Mary and John stumbled by, a tiny figure tottered out of her house and saw them.

"Are you visitors?" she asked. Her voice was so faint they could barely hear her.

"Yes," said Mary, "we are from the lake region. We have never been here before."

"Ah." She came out to them. "Why are you here?"

"We came because we were told—" started John.

"We came because we wished to meet you, and others of Korazin," Mary cut in quickly.

"Why?" The old woman was suspicious.

"We have some important news for those living here," said Mary.

"What kind of news?" she asked. "We've had only bad news here. John the Baptist has been executed, and that leaves us without hope. We thought he was the Messiah. We hoped he would lead us . . ." Her voice trailed off. "But all that was a dream. He failed."

"Yes, John died," said Mary. "But the Kingdom of God has not." The strength of her voice, and her conviction, surprised her.

The curious woman invited them into her house, which was very dark inside and, as Mary had imagined, very hot. But she wanted to hear more. In fact, as it turned out, she had heard about Jesus—"that fellow who caused such an upheaval in Capernaum"—but she knew nothing specific about him. Mary and John tried to explain their relationship with him, all the time commanding their stomachs to stop rumbling and their heads to stop spinning. At long last, the woman set out some food for them—dried figs and hard dried bread and some very unpleasant wine. They tried not to bolt it down. Mary wished she had some coins with which to repay her. Why did Jesus forbid it?

"Thank you," they said before commencing the meal, and never had they meant it more.

The woman explained that she had been alone since the death of her husband ten years earlier, and that she had been childless, so she relied on help from her cousins.

"And I can tell you it's little enough, and grudgingly given," she said. "If only God had seen fit to give me children." She paused. "But he knows all. And I *do* eat every day."

Her unquestioning trust and gratitude struck Mary to the heart. "I, too, am a widow," said Mary. "My husband died from injuries in the attack on Galilean pilgrims in the Temple." She did not add that she had a child, or that she was estranged from the rest of her family. "This is my brother," she said, indicating John.

I've lied, she thought. But this woman won't understand about Jesus, and how men and women there are all brothers and sisters.

In the end, the widow offered them a place to rest and sleep. She also ended their confusion over what day of the week it was. "Sabbath is the day after tomorrow," she told them.

The beautiful synagogue was well attended. Evidently everyone was proud of it and no one liked to miss a service. The inside was worthy of the outside: the Torah resided in a niche with a finely carved arch above it, and the seats and benches were of sycamore wood, which was expensive, being worm-proof, but beautifully decorative.

In the service, the Torah readings followed a liturgical year, but anyone was free to come up and choose a portion of the writings of the prophets to read in the second part of the worship.

"Shall we use the same reading as Jesus?" asked Mary, leaning over to John. "I cannot think of a better one."

When the time came, he rose from his seat and read the same portion of Isaiah as Jesus had, and then proclaimed, "Our master, Jesus of Nazareth, read this scripture and then said, 'Today this scripture is fulfilled in your hearing.' And we, his loyal followers, seek to bring these wonders to you."

There was the same stunned silence, the same murmurs. The same stirrings and calls of "Blasphemy." But the rabbi treated them gently.

"My son," he said, "I fear you are misled and mistaken; your master cannot be the promised deliverer. All the signs we are to look for are not there; he does not come from the right place. But if you wish to expound further"—he graciously indicated the porch of the synagogue—"I am sure there are some who have questions."

Mary and John were allowed to proceed normally out of the synagogue; since they did not claim to fulfill the prophecy themselves, they were not borne out by shouting hordes of angry worshipers, and, once standing outside, were asked polite questions.

This master of yours . . . Who does he claim to be? . . . We've heard of him. . . . Didn't he run those pigs over the cliffs in Gergesa? . . . How exactly does he claim to fulfill that reading in Isaiah? Where is he now? What did he think about John the Baptist?

But answering questions was not what Jesus had ordered them to do. He had ordered them to act as he had, not to explain about him.

Suddenly Mary felt compelled to cry, "Bring me a person who is imprisoned by sin and its suffering! God will cure such afflictions; through Jesus he indeed sets the prisoner free, as the scripture says. And he has given us his power, as his disciples."

Could she really be saying this? Did she herself truly believe it? She did not know what she could actually do, but only treating someone would impress the townspeople; talk about Jesus and his mission changed no hearts.

After a long time with no movement from the crowd, a crippled woman came forward, slowly moving sideways like a crab. Her back was bent so low that she could only move by swinging her arms and thrusting herself on a diagonal from the direction she wished to go in.

She knelt in front of Mary and John. "I counted ninety years last Passover," she said, "and I have been afflicted since Tiberius first became emperor." To spare them doing the calculations, she said, "That is almost fifteen years ago, when I was seventy-five."

"Why have you come to us?" asked John. He sounded frightened, as if he wished the woman would say something to disqualify herself.

"I have nowhere else to turn." She raised her withered face and stared defiantly at Mary and John. "If you truly have been granted power by God, then show it now!"

Mary watched as John screwed up his face. "Very well," he said. He began praying, silently. Next he reached out his hands and put them on the old woman's head. He clasped the curve of her skull and prayed fervently. Then, abruptly, he released her.

"In the name of Jesus of Nazareth, stand straight!"

She fell to the ground and tried to pick herself up. Agonizingly, she shuffled her hands in front of her and drew herself up once more. But her back was still bowed.

The crowd began muttering impatiently. One or two people jeered.

This will never do, thought Mary. This is actually discrediting Jesus. She closed her eyes and desperately called out to him, Tell us what to do. We are hindering you, not helping you!

Without even consciously waiting for a response, Mary moved

forward and took the crippled woman's hand. Slowly, cautiously, she drew her up to her full height.

"Jesus of Nazareth has made you well," she said. She had no idea how it had come about. But it had happened.

The woman ran her hands over her side and back, and she stood tall and straight. She was overcome, speechless.

"Praise be to God and to Jesus, his prophet!" said Mary, loudly. She reached out to the woman again. "Your sins are forgiven!"

Now there was a loud murmur. Mary looked out at the gathering. It was growing larger as more people poured out of the synagogue and filled the platform.

"*I* do not forgive sins," she said. "Nor do I have the power to. But by releasing his daughter from her bondage, God has clearly proclaimed that her sins are forgiven."

Then, just as had happened with Jesus, the people converged on John and, especially, on Mary. They wanted to be cured. Never mind about the message, the scripture prophecies. They showed a remote curiosity about Jesus, but what they greedily wanted was physical cures and physical miracles.

"Help me! Help me!" The cries turned into a cacophony, shrill and ugly. A pale young man with watering eyes clutched John's robe and tugged at him. Someone behind Mary yanked at her mantle, and as it slid down, her head was revealed.

"The hair of a harlot!" a voice cried. Shorn hair was a public disgrace and often decreed for notorious wantons. "Look!"

"Ooh," people chorused, "perhaps she's a witch, and that's how she cured the cripple!"

"Moses said you shall not suffer a witch to live!" The voices rose. Now the crowd surrounding Mary and John was dangerous. They were helpless to fend off any attackers. Jesus had not even allowed them a staff—not that that would have been of use against so many.

Mary felt stunned by the rapid sequence of events—from the menace of the crowd, to the courage it had required to attempt to carry out Jesus's instructions in the first place, to the swift answer to her request, and then this sudden unmasking of her past condition.

Oh, God! she prayed, almost wordlessly. Help me. I cannot know what to do now.

The muttering crowd was closing in tightly all around. She could feel its pressure, like the coils of a giant snake encircling her and John.

"I am no harlot!" she cried, so loudly that everyone could hear her. "My hair was cut as a Nazirite, when I took a vow. Now let me tell you about that!"

This bold preaching by a woman was as shocking as the cripple's cure. The people stepped back a bit. Mary felt the coils loosening. She took a deep breath.

"I was afflicted with demons!" she pronounced without shame. "I was tortured, and everyone in my family was tormented as well by my illness. I tried all known cures, including the Nazirite vow. But only one thing was more powerful than the demons: Jesus of Nazareth, a mighty prophet who follows in the path of John the Baptist, commanded them to leave, and they obeyed. Since then I have followed him and seen much mightier things than this. My hair is growing, but while it remains short, it is a sign of what failed: the old ways, the old cures. Take notice of it! Do not waste time on those old ways, those old cures! The same prophet Isaiah says, 'Remember not the events of the past, the things of long ago consider not. See, I am doing something new!' Submit yourselves to the new way, the signs of the opening of the very Kingdom of God!" Her voice had grown louder and louder as she spoke, until it was ringing, and she herself was tingling with whatever power had given these words to her.

"Where is this Jesus?" someone finally asked.

"Now he is preaching and healing near Bethsaida. He sent us out to do his work."

She stopped to catch her breath. She had publicly preached, openly witnessed, something she would never have believed herself capable of doing. She nodded toward John. Let him speak now. He needed to.

"Let us tell you more about the message," he began.

"Prove you're not a witch!" a loud voice rang out. Mary saw that it belonged to a short, dark man in dun-colored robes.

"How can I do that?" Mary answered. She was disappointed that John was not to be given an opportunity to speak.

"Drive the demons out of someone else!" he challenged. "Show that you have been truly cured, and don't harbor any yourself."

"Very well." Mary spoke calmly, but she felt close to collapsing. This was asking too much of her. She feared confronting any demons. What if they turned on her and sought her out again? And what if she tried, in front of all these people, and failed?

Someone shoved a young woman down in front of Mary. She lay

in a bundle at Mary's feet, huddled up in her mantle, looking hardly human. Only the slight trembling of the material betrayed any life within.

Mary bent down and tried to see her face. There was nothing but the rounded shape of her head covered with coarse rust-colored material. Mary took the material and drew it slowly back.

I can't do this! she thought. I am going to disgrace myself and Jesus and open myself up to another demon attack.

As her trembling fingers drew the headdress back, the woman suddenly leapt to her feet and revealed her face, distorted with both pain and anger. "Leave me!" she ordered. One of her hands moved swiftly and caught Mary's in a nasty grip. Pain shot through her wrist and arm.

"No!" said Mary. "I will not leave you. I will not leave you until you are restored to yourself. No matter how long it takes." Where did those words come from? How can I possibly mean them? Mary thought, in one corner of her mind. With her free hand, she touched the top of the woman's head. "In the name of Jesus of Nazareth, whom even the demons obey, I command you to leave her!" she cried, in a ringing voice.

Just as had happened in other cases, the demon flung the victim down on the ground. The woman released Mary's hand and began clawing at herself, trying to rip her clothes open. Foul words poured from her mouth in a different voice, and the woman seemed to be choking, while being torn apart inside.

Mary bent down, took one of her arms, and motioned to John to take the other. "Now rise up!" she said, and together they dragged the woman to her feet, forcing her to stand upright, while she writhed in agony. "Depart!" she ordered the demons.

The woman twisted and fought where they held her, pulling at her wrists.

"Depart!" Mary kept commanding the demons. She could feel their presence, heavy and stultifying nearby, ready to attack her again. She braced herself.

Then one of the demons spoke clearly and coldly. "Jesus I know and respect, but why should I obey *you*?"

"I am a follower of Jesus and commanded by him to vanquish you."

"Ah, yes, we recognize you. We have known you well. Too well." The demon laughed.

In spite of her fear and the dreadful memories aroused by the voice, Mary repeated her order for the demons to leave their victim.

Forcing her voice not to betray her fear, Mary cried, "Leave this woman! Jesus commands you to leave."

"And go to *you*?" The cunning deep voice welled up from the woman's throat.

It could feel her fear, Mary knew that. "To go to your master, by the command of my master!"

The demon in the woman's body resisted, lunging and feinting with such strength that Mary and John felt their arms were about to be ripped off. Around them the crowd had grown. Only the demon had a voice, taunting and whining, and Mary answered that voice.

"Depart forever!" she cried. "Depart forever, and return to the realms of hell!"

And then there was a loosening in the struggle, and the woman slumped down. With several shudders, she seemed to shrink farther into herself. Mary thought she saw shadows of forms departing, but she could not be sure. And suddenly there was nothing but her, and John, and the woman clinging together.

Mary felt herself crying, since the exhausted victim could not. From deep inside, tears welled up, tears that seemed unstoppable.

"So—you are not possessed," the man who had challenged her finally said. His voice was hushed. "Such a demonstration of God's power I have never seen."

Mary turned to him, her eyes still swimming with tears. "You should not have mocked God, but he was gracious and turned it to good." She put her arm around the woman. "What is your name?" she asked.

"Susanna," the woman replied in so quiet a voice she could barely be heard.

"A lily," said Mary. "Susanna means a lily of the field. Now your colors will no longer be dimmed by Satan." She paused. "You must have family here."

"She is my wife!" responded the challenger.

"Will you let us take her home with us for this evening?" asked Mary. "Having had the same experience myself, I know how to treat her."

The man looked simultaneously relieved and disappointed. "Very well," he finally said.

Together she and John led Susanna down the steps of the synagogue and steered her toward the widow's house, the house they now presumed to call their own. Susanna was so weak she felt like a hollow gourd as she leaned on them for support. She had gone utterly silent, borne along by her saviors.

When they arrived, the widow was not there. Perhaps she had gone to the synagogue herself and witnessed all of it. Mary hoped that she would understand and would not be at one with the skeptics in the crowd. Mary felt a bit guilty using her house and goods for Jesus . . . but had not Jesus told them to do that very thing?

Susanna lay down on a pallet in the dim, dark, cool house. The shutters were drawn against the afternoon heat, and the door was shut, as Mary and John had experienced when they first arrived. They wiped Susanna's brow, but other than that did not attempt to rouse her. Mary know how debilitated she would be.

As they watched her, Mary and John cautiously exchanged thoughts. They were sitting on the floor, the cool, hardened dirt soothing to their limbs and feet.

"I was frightened," John admitted. "I secretly hoped no opportunity would present itself for us to speak."

"I was frightened, too," said Mary. "And to be put to the test not once but twice—had I known that, would I have dared to go?"

"I don't know where you found the courage to speak about our mission like that."

"Nor do I," said Mary. "The words just seemed to come to me. I felt that Jesus knew what we were doing, and was urging us on. But even then . . ." She shook her head. "To actually say the words in front of people . . ."

"I wonder how many people heard the words?" said John. "All they seemed to care about, or to see, was what happened when we touched those people."

"But they had to hear the words," said Mary.

"I'm not so sure."

Susanna cried out and stirred, and they were instantly by her side.

"Help," she murmured. "Help, they are here. . . ." She turned over.

"She will be like this for a while," said Mary. "When Jesus touched me, my deliverance was instant, but I am not Jesus."

"But you had the power." John's voice was full of admiration.

"Jesus must have willed it," she finally said. In truth, she was baffled. All she knew was that Jesus had told her to act thus, she had done it, and these cures and miracles had happened. She could not explain it.

Just then the widow came slowly in the door, each movement seeming to take forever. She shuffled in and stood looking at her three guests.

"So that's why you're here," she finally said. "To cause a sensation, to make trouble. I shall have to ask you to leave." Seeing how limp Susanna was, she added, "Tomorrow will be time enough. But you must be gone by morning."

"But why?" asked John. Mary shot a look at him. There was no point in protesting. The widow had not had to take them in at all, and she was the only one in the town who had shown any hospitality. If she now withdrew it, that was her right.

"The Sabbath," she said. "You did this healing on the Sabbath!"

So she chose to focus only on what day it was, thought Mary, not on what was done. A crippled person stood straight, demons had been sent away, but it had been done on the wrong day. This made Mary angry, but she tried not to show it.

John, however, snapped back at the old woman: "That's so stupid. That's a stupid, stupid thing to say!"

The widow, with her pinched little face and black eyes, drew back as if she had been slapped. "How dare you speak to me like that? You can get out now. Now!"

Mary stood up and went over to her. "Please," she said. "Let this recovering woman rest here just tonight. You may punish us all you like, but spare her." Seeing how hard the widow's expression was, she added, "Out of the love of God, be merciful."

The widow snorted and backed away. "Help yourselves to the little food that's here, drink the water, lie down where you are, but by morning you must go." She turned her back on them, went into another room, and shut the door.

"She fears for her reputation." Susanna spoke for the first time, her voice very faint. "She has to be careful with everything she says and does. To harbor you two, and then me—she *is* being generous." Mary and John bent over her to hear her words. "I don't know who you are, but I am grateful to you."

While they passed the hours in the widow's house, they tended to Susanna and told her about their lives and the teacher they followed. "I don't know if I have the right to invite anyone else to join us. Only Jesus can do that. But if you can, come with us to meet him. It's really him you have to thank for healing you," Mary said.

"If my husband will let me," Susanna said.

It had struck Mary that he was quite a bit older than Susanna, and seemed bossy and demanding. Susanna must have been married to him when she was quite young.

"Would you like something to eat?" Mary asked. Juicy grapes filled with sweet nectar would have been exactly right, but the widow had no grapes and Mary and John had no money to buy any. Besides, it was the Sabbath, when nothing could be bought or sold. She reached over and examined the platter to see what it offered. "A dried fig cake?"

Susanna shook her head.

"Some bread?"

Although it was as dry and hard to chew as the fig cake, it would have to do. They broke off some small pieces and gave them to Susanna, then handed her a cup of the watered wine, which really was just sour pink water at this point.

Susanna fell back on her pallet. "I feel so light, with them gone. I feel as if I am going to float away." Then she fell asleep.

That night, as they all lay in the room, they heard voices outside, people demanding to speak with them. But the widow remained in her room with the door closed and did not answer the crowd. Susanna slept peacefully, and John finally stopped turning on his mat, and Mary found that she, too, felt as light as air. Gone was the stifling oppression that had followed her and smothered her since Joel's death; in casting out the demons and acting as a healer for the crippled woman, she had been delivered from her own shadows. She felt exalted, that God had lifted her up and breathed on her and held her in the palm of his hand. And she heard him whisper her name. "Mary," he said. "Mary."

Before there was even a hint of light in the sky, Mary was awake—if indeed she had ever been asleep. She had lain down, but her memory of flying, of being carried high above the heavens and caught up with God and spinning in the air, was not a dream.

In the night, she had seen the dazzling heavenly side of the clouds, the way the spiritual creatures saw them, and there she had glimpsed the shining faces of other—what?—people? angels? Some she almost recognized, but their features were transformed and glowing with a brilliant radiance that changed them. Jesus was there, of course, but also those who looked somewhat like Peter and Big James, and a man who was clothed in Roman official garb, and Jesus's mother and his brother James, who strangely enough seemed to be the same age, and her companion-disciple, John, as an old man. Then there were hosts of people in odd costumes—a man with a long beard that hung down like a waterfall and dark, narrow eyes, wearing something that looked black with a white collar with two prongs and a woman dressed all in metal. And everywhere was an unearthly light, more golden than pure gold, and beneath was a sea of glittering sapphires.

She had not awoken so much as slid into the room again, marveling at what she had seen, cherishing the feeling of God's warm wings over her: God's wings, covering over her weaknesses and failings, protecting her, loving her anyway.

As they rose and made ready to leave, *those* movements seemed like a dream. The true reality was what she had seen while she, to all appearances, slept. But the fleeting glimpse of God's glory made the room and everything in it dim.

The door to the widow's room remained resolutely shut, but Mary and John wrote a short note to thank her. Susanna turned to them and said, "I must come with you! I must meet Jesus!"

"But your husband—" John began.

"Write him a note also!" she said. "You have the means at hand. Leave it here; the widow will deliver it."

"Are you strong enough?" Mary asked her gently. "Our way will not be easy. And it is many days until we rejoin Jesus."

"I am strong enough to search for Jesus. I am just not strong enough to face my husband and the townspeople!"

She feels exactly as I did, Mary thought.

"We will help you," Mary said.

They left Korazin, which was only just stirring in the early-morning light. A fresh breeze blew through its empty streets, whispering down between houses and then out over the hills plunging to the lake.

But at its outskirts, John turned and started to shake his sandals ceremoniously. "I cast your dust from my feet—"

"John!" Mary cried.

"They rejected us! They rejected the message!" He lifted his right foot high and shook it ominously from side to side. Particles of dirt flew off.

Mary grabbed his arm. "They did not reject us. Many listened. Susanna was healed. If they did not listen, it is because we did not deliver the message clearly. We did not explain."

"They did not give us a chance to." John's handsome face was clouded with anger.

"Perhaps we did not try hard enough," Mary said. "I don't think Jesus meant us to condemn those who had not heard."

"I disagree." John kept shaking his foot, but more slowly.

Susanna, who was standing quietly beside them, said, "Why is it that you cannot agree on what this Jesus said—or wants?"

Now John lowered his foot. He looked puzzled, deflated. "An excellent question," he finally said. "I can't answer it. I suppose we hear him differently."

"Doesn't he speak plainly?" Susanna asked.

"He speaks plainly to each of us," Mary said. "But we seem to hear different words."

"Oh." Susanna's face fell. "That makes it difficult to follow him, doesn't it?"

ಬಃ X L ಬಃ

My dearest brother—my Silvanus,

How I have longed to speak further to you. That short time that you came to Capernaum, precious as it was, should have only been a start, rather than an ending. Thank you for your words, thank you for coming, thank you with all my heart.

I am writing this from the mouth of a cave. Yes, a cave, high in the hills. When we descend, I will find someone to carry this to you.

After we left you, we received the terrible news of the murder of John the Baptist. Jesus now feels that he must carry on that mission, and he then sent us out to train as his helpers. He sent us out two by two, and I was paired with John, Zebedee's son. He said, "I am sending you out like sheep among wolves. Therefore be as wise as serpents and as harmless as doves." And do you know what else? We were to take nothing with us. Oh, it is very hard to be a beggar, to accept charity. (Do not worry, I have not thrown away the moneys you gave me, they are safe and awaiting a proper usage.)

Now there are three of us, for another woman joined us in Korazin. Like me, she had been possessed. Like me, she was also married. Like me, she has left to meet Jesus. What her husband will do we do not know, but he will probably behave like Joel. She is having difficulty believing that she is truly well, and for that reason needs some time apart. Perhaps—it would be a miracle—perhaps her husband will understand.

The hermit who lives in the cave gave John some writing materials, and so he is writing as well. He is not at all what I had thought him. He has a volatile temper, as you already know, but he also has a dreamy side. He even told us that he used to like the bad weather when they couldn't go out fishing, because then he could stay inside and daydream. He liked to make up stories to tell himself. He used to write them down so he could remember them; I told him he ought to be writing down everything that has happened since we met Jesus. He said perhaps someday he would, but so far Jesus had not given us enough time. I am afraid that when we finally have the time we will have forgotten.

But I am off the subject. You see, Silvanus, it's just like when we are talking!

Korazin was the first place we went. But since then we have been all over Galilee—up in its heights, where the air is thin and cool; down on the plains, where the main highway passes—speaking to whomever we could about our mission. Dear Silvanus, I must be honest—most of them, like you, listened but did not alter their journey.

No, we have not become rebels. As we were climbing up a narrow path, we chanced upon a very ferocious hermit, one of those religious ascetics who withdraw from the world. He was as cross as a hibernating bear about being disturbed in his 'lair. But of all the people we had encountered, he seemed the most interested in Jesus, once we had told him who we were and why we were trespassing on his hillside. He immediately beckoned us to come into his cave, which I was not eager to do. I had hoped never to enter a cave again after my experience in the desert.

Unlike my cave, his was dank and smelled of mold. Inside, he had one guttering lamp that burned rancid tallow, and the foul foodstuffs I could see on a flat rock explained why he looked skeletal. But there were piles of scrolls, and a great deal of paper. It is his paper that I am using now, a kind gift from him.

Immediately he began questioning us about Jesus, trying to ascertain if he fulfilled all the predictions about the Messiah. You will be relieved, Silvanus, to know that he did not. (I should, rather, say it would be Eli who would be pleased; I think you do not care one way or the other.)

To begin with, he asked if Jesus claimed to be the Messiah. When we said not in our hearing, he nodded. Then he asked if he was from the line of David. We said we did not know. He said that surely Jesus would have told us. (If I ever see his mother again, I will ask her. Jesus would just smile and refuse to answer.)

"Is he anointed?" the hermit asked, his eyes reflecting the dancing flame of his little lamp.

"I don't see how he could have been," John said. "Only the high priest in Jerusalem is."

"He should—let's see"—he hastily shoved one scroll out of the way and unrolled another—"the prophet Micah says he should come from Bethlehem. Does he?" His dark eyes fastened on us, and I could not tell whether he wanted us to give the correct answers or the wrong ones.

"Not that I know of," I said. "His family is from Nazareth."

"Oh." Now he looked disappointed. He pointed to another scroll. "There's something here in Zechariah about riding into Jerusalem on a donkey." He paused. "In fact, there are other prophecies about Jerusalem and the Messiah." He scrutinized the scroll of Zechariah. "It says here that there will be many things happening in Jerusalem. 'And I will pour out on the house of David and the inhabitants of Jerusalem a spirit of grace and supplication. They will look on me, the one they have pierced, and they will mourn for him as one mourns for an only child, and grieve bitterly for him as one grieves for a firstborn son. On that day the weeping in Jerusalem will be great.' Then he goes on to say, 'On that day a fountain will be opened to the house of David and the inhabitants of Jerusalem, to cleanse them from sin and iniquity.' "Well, I don't know what this tells you about your Jesus, since he isn't in Jerusalem." He rolled up the scroll as noisily as possible.

"But, then," he suddenly said, "the book of Daniel tells us that someone called the son of man is going to reign and then judge us. I believe the exact wording is, 'There was before me one like a son of man, coming with the clouds of heaven. He approached the Ancient of Days and was led into his presence. He was given authority, glory and sovereign power, all peoples, nations and men of every language worshiped him. His dominion is an everlasting dominion that will not pass away, and his kingdom is one that will never be destroyed.' "

When we just shook our heads, he tried another tack. "There are the references in Isaiah about a suffering servant who is beaten and mistreated, for our sakes," he offered.

"Jesus is hale and hearty," John replied.

"Well, then . . ." The hermit shrugged. "He does not seem to fit any of the scriptural references." He paused. "I had heard of his good works in Galilee. Of course, nothing is predicted for Galilee, except—wait—yes! In Isaiah"— he consulted the scroll—"it does say, 'In the future he will honor Galilee of the Gentiles, by way of the sea, along the Jordan—the people walking in darkness have seen a great light.' But that's about all." He sighed.

In truth, although it may have troubled him whether Jesus was or was not the Messiah, it did not trouble me. Jesus is Jesus; that is enough.

"Of course," he said, "perhaps it is just as well this man doesn't claim to be the Messiah, for you know the Law of Moses says a false prophet must be put to death."

No, I had not known that. It is a law that has seldom been applied, unlike the one about witches and mediums.

After we helped him roll up the scrolls—he had made a terrible mess, and the damp cave would surely damage the texts—he gave me this paper and told me I should set down my thoughts. He was setting down his. He indicated a pile of scrolls on the other side of the cave. "Yes, all my thoughts, since I have been here," he said proudly. I wondered who he had in mind to read them. But, then, writers do not think about that, they only want to write. The audience can find them later, they—we—hope.

Dearest brother, I send my love to you and ask you, as you knew I would, to read the little letter I will enclose to Elisheba, and then keep it for her to have later. Go to Joel's tomb some early morning and tell him I loved him, for me and in my words. You will know them.

Your sister, Mary

My dearest little one,

I think of you every day, and every day I see something I want to tell you about. Today it was a big tortoise, hiding under some brush on a hill. I could hardly see him, he kept so still and his colors were that of the soil and leaves around him. If I could have, I would have taken him right to you, so you could have him as a pet. Tortoises are gentle, in spite of their strange scaly skin and big claws. But if you ever have one for a pet, do not make the mistake of thinking they are slow. If you turn your back and look elsewhere for very long, they can escape and you will never find them!

My sweet Elisheba, tomorrow I will find something else I think you should know about this wonderful world you live in. And when we are together again, we'll go out and look at everything I have written about, from *morning to night. May the God of Abraham and Isaac, Jacob and Joseph, Sarah, Rebekah, Rachel and Leah hold you in his arms, until I can.*

Your loving mother

ଓଉ X L 1 ଓଉ

The forty days passed, snatched away every sunset after an exhausting day, and too soon Mary and her companions had to turn their faces toward Bethsaida—too soon because this journey together was still changing them, and they did not feel ready to call a halt to their pilgrimage.

They found Joanna and Philip by a well on the outskirts of Bethsaida.

"We've seen no one else," said Philip, "so we must be the first. We may as well wait here." He leaned against the stone wall of the well, shaded his eyes, and looked at Susanna.

"We brought someone to meet Jesus," said Mary. It was good to see Philip again, and Joanna. They seemed like true family now. "I cured her!" she said excitedly. "Of demons!"

"You mean God cured her," John corrected.

"Yes. Yes, of course. It was God. In Korazin. I called on God, and he answered."

"You sound surprised," said Philip.

Mary nodded. "I suppose I was." Surprised that he would answer the request of a person like her. Perhaps it confirmed at last what she had so much trouble believing, that she was truly well and the demons were gone for good. In some secret part of herself, she imagined that everyone could see what she had once been. Now that was gone. Who, then, had cured whom?

"Don't worry, we were surprised, too," said Joanna. "The first town we came to—Endor—we were so nervous we hoped no one would seek us out." She came over to Susanna. "Welcome. It is a joy to have another woman join us."

Susanna looked uncomfortable, and Mary explained, "I do not think she can permanently join us. Her husband is expecting her return."

"But I do so want to meet Jesus," Susanna said in a low voice. "I must stay at least until then."

As they waited, townspeople came out to the well at sunset to draw water, milling around them and tethering their donkeys to the palm trees ringing the well. They filled their jugs and seemed very lighthearted, greeting the disciples easily and talking about the grape harvest now being gathered.

"The women are dancing in the vineyards," one bulky man said, with a knowing nod. "By torchlight. Better join them!"

John just smiled. No need to explain why they could not.

"Where did you go?" asked Philip, after the crowd had left the well.

"Into the hills of upper Galilee," said Mary. "We started out in Korazin, but then went farther up into the hills, where there were very few people. We saw wild mountains and ravines, and thick cedar and cypress forests on the heights, but no villages. Then we came down and visited the road to Tyre and Damascus, and then some other villages, nearer the lake. We had our greatest success at our first place, Korazin. What about you?"

Philip and Joanna recounted their experience in Endor, where they had been chased out of the synagogue, and then the better experience of being able to heal some people who were greatly afflicted with crippling illnesses.

"No demons?" asked Mary.

"There were some people who seemed to be oppressed, but we saw no genuine cases of possession," said Joanna. "And believe me, I would know!" she said with a laugh.

They were all tired; the strain of the mission had taxed them to the utmost, and now they drew strength and restoration from resting and talking together. That evening, they pooled their food and then took an early night, sleeping out in one of the harvested fields. There were no vineyard festivities for them, nor could they have kept awake had they gone.

The next morning, Matthew and Thomas appeared before daybreak, followed by Judas and Big James. Matthew looked markedly thinner, as if the walking and poverty had taken their toll on his thick frame. In fact, he looked near collapse, and as soon as he reached the well he drew up several dippers of water and drank it all. Thomas looked, not thinner, but sterner, as if he had seen things that had left a mark on him.

"So, friends, where have we all been?" Judas asked. Even he, usually so jaunty, sounded tired.

"We went back to Gergesa," said Matthew.

"No!" Big James looked surprised. He alone did not seem to have been sapped by the demands of the mission; his voice was as loud as ever. "By yourselves?"

"Yes," said Matthew. His usually flat tone had changed, and betrayed excitement.

"But why?" asked Judas.

"Obviously the people there were so desperately needy," said Thomas.

"But so few who could understand the mission," said Philip. "Did you cure any?"

"One or two," said Matthew. "But it was not so easy as it was for Jesus. And two of them attacked us." He held up his arm and bared it, showing an ugly bruise and a mass of scabs. "Those poor, poor creatures," he said.

"Did any of you have to shake the dust off your feet?" asked John.

"No one out-and-out refused to listen to us," said Thomas. He sounded disappointed, as though he really wished he could have carried out the rejection ceremony.

"John tried to," said Mary. "In Korazin. I think he just wanted the experience."

"The townspeople were almost hostile," said John.

"But not all of them," Mary said. "We were able to preach there, to heal many, and even acquired a companion." She paused. "So I told John to lower his foot!"

"Well, we've been to Jerusalem!" announced Judas. "After all, my family lives near there, and Big James's family had a connection with the high priest's household—something to do with supplying fish. Anyway, we were able to get into the high priest's mansion, up near the Temple, and spy around a bit."

"James!" said John. "You didn't! We left all that behind, all those connections, when we turned our backs on Father."

"I just wanted to pay a courtesy call, that's all," said James gruffly. "It never hurts to have influential people on your side." He stopped, his face growing red. "I tell you, I didn't betray our mission!"

"You didn't explain anything, either, I'll warrant," his brother said.

• • •

That night, they went down to the banks of the Jordan, where Jesus had said he would meet them. The sound of the water flowing deep in its channel soothed them, and they let it sing them to sleep as they lay nearby. The next day, Simon and Little James found them. Simon started waving his arms and running toward them, and Little James trotted after him.

After they all embraced one another, Simon explained that they had gone westward, to the cliffs of Arbel and then down to Magdala.

"The leopard hasn't changed his spots after all," said Philip, shaking his head. "You went back to that place, to the hideout of the Zealots."

"I wanted to see some of my old friends," Simon admitted. Then he narrowed his eyes and looked around defensively. "And I wanted them to see me. I wanted to tell them what had happened to me."

"Yes?" asked Matthew. "And what did they say?" Clearly he remembered all too well the knife-wielding man who had caused pandemonium at his party, and still saw Simon that way.

"They were disappointed in me," Simon admitted. "They said I had lost my nerve, become a coward."

"Did any show interest in joining us? Or even coming to listen to Jesus?" Matthew asked.

"One," said Simon. "He was young. The older ones—no, they said they would rather die by the sword."

"But then we left those cliffs and the caves and went down to Magdala," said Little James. His hair was wilder than ever, and he seemed lost in his enveloping robes.

"And what—what happened there?" Mary asked. But she was afraid to know.

"We made some converts!" Little James proclaimed. "Yes! In that busy town, with all the boats and fishermen and merchants, we went down to the harbor promenade itself, in the heart of the town, and began to preach. To tell them about Jesus, and his mission." He paused, and pushed the tangle of hair out of his eyes. "Oh, there were plenty of mockers. But there were also people who were curious. Two crippled men came forward, and I—and we—we prayed, and laid our hands on them, and they—they walked away. Upright, and not limping. And then more came. And we talked, and talked. . . ."

Who could these people be? Mary wondered. Were they my friends, my neighbors? Could my mother and father have heard them speak? Might their minds have been changed about Jesus?

"Some of them said they would come here, to see Jesus for themselves," Little James finished. He was out of breath, he was so excited.

"Good work, James."

The voice was unmistakable. It was Jesus.

They turned to see him standing just a little way away, his feet planted between two reaped furrows near the riverbank, the sun behind him and edging his robe.

"You have done well," Jesus said, coming over to them. He greeted them all by name, individually. "Was it difficult?"

They all began talking at once, telling him about their experiences in the desert, the mountains, the cliffs, the caves. Mary and John were especially excited to report their success in driving the demons out of Susanna. And then Matthew and Thomas recounted their encounters with the demons in Gergesa.

"We saw Satan fall like lightning from the sky!" they said.

"Yes!" said Mary, reliving the exalted moment when she had ordered the demon out of Susanna. "The demons obey us!" Again she had that little tickling of pride, of feeling special. She, who had been demon-ridden, now had demons obeying her.

Jesus looked at them, one by one. "Are you pleased that the demons submitted to you?" he said, as if they were entirely misled. "Be pleased, rather, that you are written in the book of life."

What did that mean? Mary wondered. But she needed to introduce Susanna, and now she led her forward, taking her hand. "Teacher, here is one who was beset with demons, as I was. And she wishes to thank you for releasing her."

Susanna knelt in front of Jesus, bowing her head. "I can never thank you enough for restoring my life to me," she murmured.

Jesus took her hand and pulled her up. "It was God who restored your life to you," he said. "And we must thank him for his power."

He looked around at all the gathered disciples, still dusty and recovering from their mission. "Never forget that it is God who gives you the power to combat evil in his name," he said. "It is never you."

But God must select his agents! thought Mary.

"Any glory you receive is due to God," Jesus said. "It is not of yourself."

He looked closely at Susanna. "Will you join us?" he asked, searching her face.

"I—I only left for a short period—my husband—yes, for a time I can—" All the words came tumbling out, the hesitations along with the acceptances, like water rolling over rocks.

"Good," said Jesus. "For whatever time you can give us, I am grateful."

He never said that to *me*, thought Mary. Does he prefer *her*? Oh, the ugliness of competition, of wishing to be preferred!

I helped her, and now I am jealous of her, Mary chided herself. Oh, what a vicious creature I am! But I met Jesus first, I knew him longer—

"Mary, don't trouble yourself with such thoughts." Jesus was addressing her, touching her arm. She looked into his eyes and found it impossible to believe that anyone could be more precious to him.

"I don't know what you mean," she said, stiffly. She pulled her arm away.

"Do not trouble yourself," Jesus repeated.

Later in the day, Peter and Nathanael found them, and close on their heels came Thaddeus and Andrew, filled with excitement.

"We went to Nain," said Thaddeus. "And people there—they just couldn't hear enough of what we had to say!"

Nain! Where Joel's family lived, Mary thought. Were they there? Did they hear?

"Did you do more than just talk?" asked Jesus. But he said it gently, not accusingly.

"We laid our hands on a few people," said Andrew. "But we don't know if they were truly cured, cured forever. They seemed better, that is all I know."

Jesus nodded. "Peter, did you get up to Dan?" he asked.

"I almost got up there," he said. "I got as far as Thella. But—"

"The marshes of the Huleh stopped us," said Nathanael. "Nevertheless, we threw down some pagan shrines that we saw on the way."

"What about the people?" Jesus asked. "Statues, after all, cannot change their ways."

"Oh, we did talk to them, and—"

"Did any of them listen?" asked Jesus.

"Well . . ." Peter looked around, confused. "Some of them, yes. But most of them drifted away."

"And where did they go?" asked Jesus.

"I don't know," Peter said. "I just know I looked about and saw that the numbers were smaller."

"It is difficult," said Jesus. "You cannot know who truly hears and will remember, and who will forget."

As they spoke, the sun was sinking behind the hills of Galilee. A few last rays shone down on the surface of the lake, making it seem touched by a sacred presence.

"I have been preaching and teaching as well," said Jesus, "and have been received much like you. Some are ready for the message, others not." Around them the empty fields stretched out. Soon the rains of autumn would come, restoring the land, banishing the drought, and letting the farmers sow their crops. "When a farmer sows his grain, he cannot know where the seeds will fall," Jesus continued. "He has to cast them widely, scattering them as far as his arm will allow. Some fall on hard rock, and are doomed from the start. Others fall on shallow soil. They can spring up for a little while, but then they run out of substance and die back. Others fall on such fertile ground that they are soon competing with the weeds and other voracious plants just to survive." He looked around at them. "Do you understand what that means?"

Peter started to speak. "A farmer has to prepare his soil!" he blurted out.

Jesus laughed. "You are truly a fisherman. You have never watched a farmer at work. Are there any farmers here?"

The Zealot, the tax-collector brothers, the fishing brothers, the rabbinical scholar, the Jerusalemite, the palace matron, the fresco-painter, Mary the housewife, all shook their heads.

"How can I have started in Galilee and not found a farmer?" Jesus laughed. "Here is what I meant: The seed is the word of God. It can fall on rocky ground—ground that is either hostile to it—or Satan keeps watch and snatches God's word away so it reaches no ears. The shallow ground—that is someone who is excited about anything he hears, but his enthusiasm is short-lived. The fertile ground—why, it's the world: the world that offers so many riches, worries, and diversions that the word of God is soon choked off."

He paused. "But there is a fourth place the word can fall. It can fall on receptive soil. And there it can bring forth an abundant crop. When we sow, we are only responsible for using all our strength to cast that seed far from us. We cannot know where it will fall. You all have done well. I am proud of you. Let God take care of the crop.

"Can you see these barley fields?" Jesus asked. "They are bare now, but in harvest time they are white with grain and produce. I will need your help in bringing in that harvest when it ripens."

"You want us to bring in grain?" Peter looked disappointed.

"Not grain, but souls," said Jesus. "But look now—see the people at the far side of the fields? They are preparing for the Festival of Booths; let us make our own booth here, and spend the holiday with them." He looked at them fondly. "But first let us go back to the Jordan. There is something that must be done."

He turned and led them toward the reedy banks of the river. It was low now; the rains of winter, the melting snows of spring were not feeding it, and it gurgled and flowed placidly in its bed. "Come," Jesus said, motioning for them to descend the steep banks and stand by the water's very edge. When they all stood side by side, Jesus bent down and, cupping his hands, brought up a handful of water.

"John baptized in the Jordan, a baptism of repentance. I baptize no one, but later I will baptize with fire; you will see. Now you must baptize one another, not for repentance but in brotherhood and sisterhood—although, for those who follow me, there is neither male nor female, slave nor free, Greek nor Jew."

They looked at one another. In this fellowship there were no slaves, nor were there any Greeks. Not yet?

"John, take a handful of water and pour it out upon the head of one of your brothers or sisters," Jesus said.

John took some water, then turned around, the water streaming from his fingers, as he tried to select someone. He lifted his hands over Mary's head, and she felt the cold water splash upon her, heard John say, "We bind ourselves to Jesus and to one another."

The water dripping around her face, she bent and took the Jordan water and poured it over Joanna's head, saying, "With this water we pledge ourselves to Jesus and to one another."

One by one the rite was repeated, down the line of the waiting disciples. The words varied, but at the end of it they turned their shining faces to Jesus, who was smiling at them.

"Who are my brothers and my sisters?" he said. "It is all of you."

Around them, in the falling light, the Jordan's deep green darkened into brown, and it kept flowing past, ever past.

At the Festival of Booths, all Israelites were to abandon their secure homes for seven days and live outdoors in "booths" made of palm and willow branches, in order to re-enact the years their ancestors had spent living in tents in the desert with Moses. It was a joyous festival, coming at the end of the olive-and-date harvest, and just before the winter rains. Since the simple instructions of Moses, the scholars had defined exactly what these structures should look like. They must be both detached and temporary. They must be between twenty cubits and ten palms high. There must be at least three walls to them, and they must provide a view of the sky and the stars. The furniture within them must be of the absolutely simplest sort, and the cele-brants were to live in the shelter for the entire seven days, unless there were violent rains. Inside, the booths should be decorated with leaves and fruit.

The Pharisees and the Sadducees differed in their interpretation of the correct use of the prescribed plants. The Sadducees, who believed only in the written words of the Law, said the citron and myrtle, the palm and the willow, were to be used to make the booth itself. The Pharisees, who claimed that there was an oral law of tradition as well as the written law, said those plants should be used only for a ceremo-nial sheath to be carried in ritual. These schools of interpretation, and their followers, did not set up booths near one another.

"Well, master, which is it to be?" asked Judas. "Walls, or wands?"

Jesus thought for a moment and then said, "Why not both? After all, if we do not use these things for walls and wands, what shall we use? We can hardly build of cypress."

The hills surrounding Bethsaida were rich in woods and orchards, and the disciples dispersed to gather the branches. The woods were filled with people collecting myrtle and palm, the youths laughing and chasing one another through the brakes. Although the long, intense blast of summer sun had long since dried up the wildflowers, within the woods itself it was still cool and green, and oaks and poplars whis-pered overhead while Mary and her companions scoured the area for their branches.

As she heard the teasing calls of the young men and women, something ached within her. She was glad for them, but felt a great hollow within herself. Was that sort of joy over for her, forever? She was not yet thirty years old. How quickly it had come, and then fled.

But you are not young, she told herself sternly. Almost thirty . . . that is not young. Many widows are your age, and they content themselves with what was, with their memories.

But Jesus . . . She glanced over at her companions hacking away at the branches. Could it be—does he regard me differently from them?

And what would it mean if he did? I regard him differently from any other man I have ever known, but he is still a man.

He will marry someday. He must. He needs a companion.

Her hands had stopped moving and gathering the branches. The sky seemed to wheel around her.

Why am I even thinking these things? she cried to herself. I must stop it. It's wrong!

But why is it wrong? a quiet little voice asked insistently within her. Why?

That voice . . . her own, or Satan's? But why Satan? Jesus was a man. Men married. That was the truth of it.

On the edge of the field, Peter was wielding a heavy stone to pound the posts into the ground, the posts that would serve as the four corners of the house. They were of the requisite palm, and were high enough that even Peter, Nathanael, and Judas, the three tallest, could comfortably move about under the ceiling. They roofed it with more palm branches, being sure to leave a portion uncovered to show the open sky, but not more than was covered, as the Law stated. They dragged in stones to allow them to sit, since they did not want to construct furniture just for this occasion.

The hum of excitement, with so many people working to set up their booths, made the field more bustling than the Magdala docks at midmorning. Shelters of all sizes and designs were taking shape around them, and the workers were singing, some in competition with their neighbors to see who could finish first and start festooning the outside with the fruits and leaves.

Little James and Simon, two of the smallest men, were straining to drag a big, flat rock into the shelter, which would serve as a perfect table for them. Peter laid aside his hammer and gave them a hand, shoving as they pulled. Soon the rock resided in its place of honor inside the booth. Joanna and Mary scrubbed it off, then went back to hanging dried gourds, pomegranates, and apples on the inner walls.

Feeling sure that Thaddeus's family had probably left for their booth, Mary dispatched Thaddeus to return to his home and retrieve her inheritance box, and she instructed him to buy some lanterns.

A long slow sunset warmed the fields, casting rich red light over the empty furrows. Up in the hills, they could just make out the walls and watchtowers of vineyards, and imagine the owners recently bringing in the harvest. Tonight, perhaps, they would sleep out among the shorn vines, still dancing by torchlight between the neatly planted rows.

The light faded. The hut was finished, and Thaddeus proudly hung the new lanterns on the walls. The ground, serving as a floor, had been swept as level and clean as they could make it, and everyone had gathered around the rock-table. In Jerusalem, of course, there would be elaborate ceremonies at the Temple, but here they could be simple. As simple as the rituals Moses himself doubtless had performed. They had prepared a meal, cooking lentils in one of their small pots, preparing bread by baking it in the hot coals in the ground, and there were chopped apples and some of the new grapes and olives from the surrounding groves. Mary's money—brought safely back by Thaddeus—had provided all this, as well as some good wine for the entire company.

It felt good to be able to provide, Mary thought, very good to contribute, to be not just a perpetual guest and beggar.

Jesus poured out cups of wine for them all, then filled one for himself. The wine shone a deep red as it poured from the jug into the cups, catching the lantern light. He blessed it and thanked God for it, and then broke the burnt flatbread and passed it around as well. People ladled the lentils into their small earthenware bowls and waited expectantly.

"Will one of you say the prayers, and recite the proper texts?" asked Jesus.

Thomas immediately volunteered. "From the book of Leviticus, Moses instructed us: 'As to the Feast of Booths—on the first day you are to take choice fruit from the trees, and palm fronds, leafy branches and poplars, and rejoice before the Lord your God for seven days. Live in booths for seven days. All native-born Israelites are to live in booths, so that your descendants will know that I had the Israelites live in booths when I brought them out of Egypt.'"

Jesus nodded. "Thank you, Thomas. A good Torah student like you would surely have known this. And for the rest?"

"There's also Deuteronomy," said Nathanael, the other student. "It adds that we are supposed to truly celebrate. It says, 'Celebrate the Feast of Booths for seven days after you have gathered in the produce of your threshing floor and your winepress. Be joyful at your feast— you, your sons and daughters, your menservants and maidservants, and the Levites, the aliens, the fatherless and the widows who live in your towns.'"

"The fatherless." Poor Elisheba, now fatherless. "The widows." That is I, thought Mary. God had thought of us, wanted us included.

"We're Levites," said Matthew, turning his head toward his brother.

"All we need to complete the commandment is to find an alien," said Judas. "Perhaps that's me. I'm the only one here who is not from Galilee."

"We don't have any maidservants and menservants," corrected Andrew.

"Yes, we do," said Jesus. "That's what we all are now. Maidservants and menservants to God's people."

Peter looked confused. "I'm sorry, I don't understand," he finally said.

Jesus just smiled at him. "You will. All of you are on the way to understanding, but you have made great progress, Peter." He held out his cup and asked if Peter would refill it.

Why did Jesus feel Peter had made progress? Peter's placid face looked so contented and so bland as he sat there chewing his bread that Mary could not ascribe any depth to him at all. She tried to put him out of her mind, to think only about this moment as they sat gathered together. The warmth of the circle, the feeling of closeness with them all, was comforting, especially in the midst of her feelings of loneliness and confusion about Jesus. She felt a great surge of love as she looked around at all the faces.

After supper, they strolled through the fields. The light had faded to a dim purplish twilight, and everywhere children had left their booths to run and play hide-and-seek behind the other shelters and the last cropped rows of stubble in the furrows. Older boys and girls were ready to venture out and use the coming darkness and festivity as an excuse for mingling and flirting. The night was ripe with joy and cele-bration.

Just to her right, a young woman—a girl—danced past, her anklets

jingling and her hair flying. Behind her, a laughing youth was following, trying to catch the folds of her garment. Together they vanished
behind one of the booths, and Mary heard their voices no more.

Mary thought of Joel and his tomb. The laughter and the chasing
were so fleeting, the tomb and its stone so long.

"We should call ourselves the Delivered Daughters of the Demons,"
said Joanna, linking arms with Mary and Susanna, scattering Mary's
thoughts abruptly. She was laughing.

"Another demon-possessed person, a man, once wanted to join us,
after Jesus cured him," Mary told Susanna. "But Jesus wouldn't allow
him to. So we are doubly fortunate—to have been delivered, and then
to start a new life with one another."

Susanna stopped walking and turned her head, first to Mary and
then to Joanna. "Should I stay?" she asked. "I don't know what to do."

How well Mary understood!

"First," said Joanna, "you should decide if you want to stay or feel
called to stay—which are not necessarily the same thing. And then
you will have to ask Jesus."

"My husband," Susanna said. "Is there any way I can talk to him
or explain it to him?"

"You can write him a letter, pour out your heart," said Mary.

"I cannot write," she said.

"I can," Mary said. "I will help you. I will write down whatever
words you tell me, and we shall find a messenger to take the letter
to him."

Letters, letters—how they can carry our soul, Mary thought. Is
Silvanus keeping my letters safe for Elisheba?

Gradually the noise and playing in the fields abated; parents called
their sleepy children in and shut the flimsy wooden doors of their
huts. Sleeping outdoors in the makeshift booths seemed like play.
There was more than enough room for all in Jesus's group to lie down
and still see up into the night sky from their pallets.

"Think of our ancestors in the desert," Jesus said, after they were
all quiet. His voice sounded soft and drowsy. "They were slaves in
Egypt, and were used to living in their mud-brick houses with the low
ceilings, and collapsing in exhaustion at the end of their days. Then,
suddenly, they were out in the desert. There were no houses, but there
were no slaves, either. It was empty, except for God."

Except for God . . . except for God . . . Mary lay on her back and looked up at the stars. It got cold in the desert, although it was not very cold here. God knew his people would forget about their sojourn in the wilderness with Moses in times to come. God had cherished his time with us, having us all to himself. But he knew we would quickly forget. So he instituted this festival. And every year, we must remember. We must be back in the desert, alone with God, once again.

Under those stars, with their cold white radiance still burning into her mind, Mary dreamed again. This time the dreams were a parade of silent pictures, and she could not hear anything the people were saying. She saw Magdala, saw armies fighting in it, saw boats filled with armed men battling out on the lake, then saw the lake turning red with blood, and the shoreline near her home heaped high with bloated bodies. And close on the heels of this picture, so dreadful, she saw Jerusalem itself enveloped with fighters, and then—could it be?—no, it could not. . . .

She sat bolt upright, her heart pounding and rivulets of sweat streaming off her, although it was not hot in the booth.

The Temple was in flames. It was caving in on itself, buckling, stones flying everywhere, rivers of blood running down the steps, far from the altar where the animals were sacrificed and channels were provided for draining off the blood. This was—it had to be—human blood. All was silent in her vision, no cries, no sound of orders, no identifying language. Who was fighting whom? Who was dying? In the melee, she could not even separate Romans from anyone else.

As if a hand had knocked her flat, she fell back onto the mat and was forced to endure more visions. The rest of Jerusalem was in flames. The houses high on the hill nearest the Temple—where the high priest and the wealthy lived—were a conflagration. People were running away like panic-stricken cattle. The walls of Jerusalem were gone.

She turned over, choking. She could smell the thick black smoke, could hardly breathe. Clouds of it were rolling up into the sky. The entire city was aflame.

Mercifully, she awoke. She was sweating, panting. She crawled toward the door, seeking the cool night air.

Outside, she rocked on hands and knees and gasped for breath. As far as she could see, the palm-frond booths of the celebrants spread out on all sides. It was a picture of peace.

Take these visions from me! she cried out to God. I cannot bear it, I cannot! Tears were streaming down her face.

She could still smell the burning wood, the flesh, the plaster. And the ugly red, the deep red of the flames, lapping like a demented animal. . . . She was going to be sick. She fought to regain control.

Send me some other vision, she cried. Something good, something blessed. Do not torment me with only cruel visions!

At last, her breathing slowed and, seeing that the fields around her were quiet and safe, she crawled slowly back into the booth and fumbled for her mat. Everyone seemed to be sleeping soundly.

She found the edges of the mat and lay back down on it. The night sky overhead, visible from where she lay, seemed benign once more.

She closed her eyes, afraid of what she might see.

I'll stay awake! she promised herself. Yes, I'll stay wide awake.

But once again she slipped away into sleep, and this time she saw other things. A peaceful group of people were gathered, the peace among them itself palpable. She could not see any of their faces, she could only experience the feelings. And then—this was very odd—she saw Jesus with all his clothes gleaming, and his face radiant. And then she felt the radiant light on her eyelids, and awoke, and it was the sun.

During the day, Jesus walked among the booths, falling into conversations with families, particularly with the elderly and the children, who were less shy about talking to him. He seemed especially to enjoy their candor; the old people fussed and cursed the Romans, and the children asked whether he had any children, and if not, why not.

The disciples, trailing behind him, tried to observe his behavior.

"Perhaps we should have talked to more people on our mission," John said to Mary in a worried tone. "And listened more."

Peter had muscled his way up front and was trying to get Jesus's attention. He is always so pushy, Mary thought. She heard him asking something about sending the children away, for they surely were bothering Jesus. He even tried to push one back. She saw Jesus scold him, and heard him say, "The Kingdom of God is like one of these little children. Let them come!" as he scooped up a little boy, swinging him so he squealed with delight.

By the time the drowsy yellow heat of midday had settled on the reaped fields, so that even the butterflies had ceased to flutter, a larger crowd converged on Jesus. From their clothing, Mary recognized them as a group of Pharisees, religious experts and authorities, come from the city to spoil the open fields for him by harassing him.

"Teacher," one portly magistrate said, appearing at the head of a group that marched resolutely across the furrows up to Jesus, "we need your interpretation of a difficult matter of the Law."

Jesus looked around at the wide fields surrounding them. "So you have come all this way to seek my opinion?"

"Indeed," the man said. "For, although we are from Jerusalem, we have family here. . . ."

"Yes, of course." Jesus nodded. "Of course that is why you have come." He paused. "So, friend, what is it you would ask my opinion on?"

"Teacher," he said, "is it lawful for a man to divorce his wife?"

"Well," said Jesus, "what did Moses command?"

"You know that Moses permitted a man to write a bill of divorce and send her away. What he said was—"

" 'If a man marries a woman who becomes displeasing to him because he finds something indecent about her, and he writes her a certificate of divorce, gives it to her and sends her from his house' "—Jesus finished for him—"and in the rest of the passage, Moses specifies whether or not he is allowed to remarry her if he changes his mind. But Moses only gave you this permission because your hearts were hard. God does not permit divorce. Earlier, in Genesis, it says, 'For this reason a man will leave his father and mother and be united to his wife, and they will become one flesh.' "

Instead of looking dashed, the Pharisee looked vindicated. "So you say Moses erred."

"Even our last prophet, Malachi, says, ' "I hate divorce," says the Lord God of Israel,' " Jesus said. "That is how God feels on the subject. It is plainly stated. We are concerned here not with Moses, but with God."

The Pharisee just nodded and made as if to move off, but then he came closer to Jesus. "Herod Antipas is looking for you," he whispered, so low that only those standing close to Jesus could hear his words. "I come to warn you." His tone had changed from challenge to concern. Perhaps this had been his real reason for coming, Mary thought, and the question about divorce just a ruse.

"Antipas?" said Jesus loudly. "Tell that fox that I drive out demons and heal people today and tomorrow, and on the third day I will reach my goal."

The Pharisee just stared at him, baffled. "I've done my duty. I've warned you." He turned away.

Jesus's statement made no sense to Mary, either. The third day? They would still be here on the third day.

Only as he and his followers left did another group come into view, led by a well-dressed middle-aged man. They approached Jesus authoritatively.

"Teacher," this man said, "I have heard of your great wisdom and knowledge. So I and my students here would like to put before you a thorny question." He gave a mock bow and indicated the men surrounding him. "You know how the Law commands that if a man dies without an heir his brother must marry his widow and give her a son, so the family line does not die out. So our question is this—and forgive us, but we must know—what if a man dies and each of his successive six brothers marries her, in turn, and none of them leaves any heirs. So altogether she had seven husbands."

Jesus laughed. "She had an interesting life, I would say."

The man frowned. "That is not the question. The point is, in the last days, at the great general resurrection of the dead, whose wife will she be?"

Jesus looked carefully at the man's clothing—creamy-white wool mantle, gold embroidery on the tunic sleeves, sandals with brass studs.

"Are you from Jerusalem, too?" he asked.

"Yes, we are," the man said.

They had to be Sadducees, then: men from the Temple establishment who did not believe in a resurrection and mocked the idea of spiritual beings like angels or heaven. Their question was an elaborate joke.

"I am sure this question is of great personal concern to you," said Jesus, his smile fading and his eyes boring into the man. "However, it is simple. You are in error, because you do not know the scriptures and the power of God."

He might as well have slapped the man as to accuse a Temple authority of not knowing the scriptures or the power of God. The man pulled back, making an audible grunt.

"When the dead rise," said Jesus, "they will neither marry nor be given in marriage; they will be like the angels in heaven."

"Angels!" puffed the man. "Angels?" He shook his head. With a snort, he turned away.

Jesus ignored him, instead turning to the disciples and the others. "In the account of the burning bush, God said to Moses, 'I am the God of Abraham, the God of Isaac, and the God of Jacob.' He is not the God of the dead—that is impossible—but the God of the living," he explained. "Therefore, you are badly mistaken!" he called after the man.

"Now you've made an enemy," said Big James.

Jesus looked at him as though he were as ignorant as the Sadducee. "He was already my enemy," said Jesus.

"But shouldn't we be trying to win them over?" Judas asked.

"Yes, but they refuse to hear the truth," said Jesus, sadly. "Come." He wanted to return to the booth and to rest during the heat of the day.

Before they could get there, a finely dressed, handsome young man crossed their path. He swallowed as if gathering his nerve to speak to Jesus, then finally blurted out, falling on his knees, "Good teacher! What must I do to inherit eternal life?" He looked desperate. This was no ruse, no test.

"Why do you call me good?" Jesus finally answered. "No one is good but God alone. And you know the commandments. You know what to do. They say, 'Do not murder, do not commit adultery, do not steal, do not give false testimony, do not defraud, honor your father and your mother.'"

The young, honest face stared up at him with a look of disappointment. "Teacher," he said, "I have kept all these commandments since I was a boy."

Jesus stood absolutely still for a long moment, just looking at him. Finally, he stepped forward and said tenderly, "Then there is only one last thing you need to do. Sell everything you have and give to the poor, and you will have treasure in heaven. Then come, and follow me." He indicated the disciples with him. "Join us. We want you."

The man's face looked as though a shadow had actually passed over it, darkening it and settling in the curves and hollows of his cheeks and eyes. His mouth was working, but no words came out. He started to move his arms and reach out, but they fell back to his sides, and painfully he drew himself up, looked longingly at Jesus, and then turned away.

Jesus watched him go, and Mary saw tears gleaming in his eyes.

"He looked very rich," said Big James. "Obviously he can't just leave it." He sounded smug, as if to remind Jesus that he and John had made a different choice.

Jesus was so grieved he could barely speak, but when he did, all he said was, "How hard it is for the rich to enter the Kingdom of God!"

Peter grabbed his arm and said, "*We* have left everything to follow you!"

"And you will be repaid," said Jesus. "I tell you the truth, no one who has left home or brothers or sisters or mother or father or children or fields for me and my message will fail to receive a hundred times as much in this present age—homes, brothers, sisters, mothers, children, and fields, and with them persecutions, and, in the age to come, eternal life."

I don't want any other children, Mary thought, I only want Elisheba! Nothing else can satisfy me, not a hundred substitutes. Not if all the children here were given to me . . .

Before they could reach their own booth, another man crossed before them and halted them. He also looked like a Pharisee. Mary winced. How many more of these were going to crop up, like a field of thistles, before Jesus could rest?

"I heard you speak," the man said. "I've heard you in Capernaum, and I've heard you in the countryside. Your words are wise. Now tell me what, in your opinion, is the most important commandment?" His manner was humble, and he seemed merely curious.

Jesus answered quickly, "It is 'Hear, O Israel, the Lord our God, the Lord is One. Love the Lord your God with all your heart, with all your soul, with all your mind and with all your strength.' And the second one is 'You shall love your neighbor as yourself.' There is no commandment greater than these."

The man looked awed. "Oh!" he said. "You are right in saying that God is one and there is no other but him. To love him with all your heart, with all your understanding, with all your strength, and to love your neighbor as yourself, is more important than all burnt offerings and sacrifices."

Jesus smiled. "You are not far from the Kingdom of God," he said.

Although people had been listening breathlessly on all sides, they fell silent at that, and no one put any further questions to him. Slowly Jesus and his disciples made their way back toward their booth, the only sound the crunching of dry field stubble under their sandals.

A group of women stood to one side, head coverings shading their faces from the midday sun. They seemed to be of all ages—several were bent in the telltale curve of age, others were stout and solid in the middle of life, others were slender with the smooth skin of youth. Mary noticed them as she passed, wondering idly if it was one enormous family clan, and thinking how blessed they were to all be together for this festival.

Something seemed to slow her, and she turned and looked carefully at each face. She looked directly into each woman's eyes, although usually she felt it was impolite to do so. Dark-brown eyes, so deep they looked black; eyes fringed with such heavy lashes they threw shadows on the woman's cheeks; eyes the tawny yellow of the shells of tortoises; even one pair of startlingly blue eyes, as blue as any Macedonian's: Mary saw all these, and felt a surge of gratitude to God for creating such wonderful little variations, as precise as a jeweler's art. Then, suddenly, her eyes locked into a pair of brown eyes and she knew them. She had seen the woman before.

The brown eyes were perfectly shaped, neither rounded nor almond-shaped, and within them there resided an understanding and quietness that Mary had seen only in Jesus.

How fortunate to have such peace! was Mary's only thought. If only someday someone would see something like that in my eyes, in the eyes of John, and Peter, and Judas, and Joanna . . . but now that is not true. Our eyes do not show peace or wisdom or anything but very human struggles.

She looked again at the quiet eyes of the woman, smiled wanly at her, and passed on. Then she felt a tug on her mantle. "Mary! Mary! Is that you? Are you still with him?" a voice said.

She turned to see the woman with the beautiful eyes, her hand still clutching the wool of Mary's mantle. The woman pulled her head covering back so that the sunlight fell on her face.

"Oh!" Mary felt a jolt of final recognition. It was Jesus's mother.

"You have been with him all this time?" the woman kept asking.

Mary stopped and let the others go ahead. She clasped Jesus's mother's hand. "Yes, I have," she said. "Here, let us draw aside." She took her hand and together they stepped back.

The hot sun beat down on their heads as Mary uncovered hers as well, so that they could truly see one another. "When I last saw you," she said, "you and James were in Capernaum to take Jesus away. You felt he was a danger to himself. What has happened since then, to bring you here?"

"I have prayed a great deal," said Jesus's mother. "I have asked God to show me what is true, what is right. And I came to hear him speak, as others hear him, to see him as if for the first time." She paused, then said humbly, "God has shown me my confusion and error, and has brought me here to his side."

"God has truly brought you at the right time," said Mary. "But we have had so many things happen since we left you in Capernaum. . . ."

They withdrew farther, to the shade of the lone oak tree in the fields, and there they sat down. She told his mother of the exorcism in Gergesa, of the commissioning of the disciples, of their mission.

"A practice mission, to be sure," Mary said. "Yet we did progress—we did feel a power, and were able to heal and drive out demons." She paused. "I think his vision is coming true."

His mother looked thoughtful, lost in her memories. "There were signs," she said. "I had messages from God, or so I believed . . . many years ago. These . . . voices . . . told me Jesus was not an ordinary child. And it is true, I received no such messages regarding my other children. But for so long, Jesus *was* ordinary! He was a happy, playful child. A popular young man. True, he had a passion for the Torah, but many people do . . . and he left us once to stay in Jerusalem, at the Temple." She shook her head. "But for so many years, he lived a quiet life. And then, suddenly, he went off to hear John the Baptist, and . . ." She smiled at Mary. "You know everything that has happened since then. You saw him when he went to John. You know more than I do!" Her voice betrayed how hard it was for her to admit this.

"He truly is inspired," said Mary. "He . . . he has powers. . . ." She paused. "Did you never see them?"

"No," said his mother. "As he grew up, he seemed such a normal young man, I questioned the voices and the vision I had had. Perhaps they had been sent by Satan. But when he returned from the pilgrimage to John the Baptist, and gave that reading at the synagogue . . . it was so shocking, how it began . . . not what I had expected."

"Come," Mary said. "I will bring you to him. He is waiting for you."

∽ XLIII ∽

Inside the booth, it was dim and surprisingly cool. The pounding heat and light did not penetrate the palm fronds, and when Mary first stepped within, it took her a moment to see anything. The reedy walls gave off a dry, sweet scent.

Several people were lying down, stretched out on their mats with their arms over their eyes. Where was Jesus? Should she disturb him? But as her vision grew clearer, she saw that he was at the very end of the hut, sitting cross-legged, his head bent. He was praying.

Mary approached him and waited respectfully. But as the moments passed, and he did not raise his head, she knelt beside him.

Immediately he raised his eyes to hers. "What is it?" he asked softly.

"Teacher, I have brought . . . Your dear mother has come," Mary finally said, pulling gently on the hand of the elder Mary, who bent down and looked into the face of Jesus.

It was hard to tell who was the most affected, Jesus or his mother. Jesus looked astonished but happy, and his mother looked as if she could not believe she was with him again. She bent farther down and they embraced; then Jesus rose and drew her to her feet with him.

"Mother," he said, and infinite satisfaction seemed to lie in that word, "you are here at last."

"I finally came to see . . ." Her voice was faint, and Mary could not hear the rest. All she could see were the two of them clasping one another.

They remained that way for several long moments. Then they relaxed their embrace, and Jesus turned to face his followers.

"Friends," he said—and only Mary could detect the slight difference in his voice, could sense the change in it—"my mother has come all the way from Nazareth to join us." He turned to her, and suddenly laughed. "Or perhaps I speak too soon? Have you come to visit, or to join?"

She looked around at all of them. Mary was once again struck by her beauty. "I . . . I came to visit, but I remain to join," she slowly said. Her voice had the same richness Mary remembered as so distinctive; the years had not dimmed it.

"You are his mother?" asked Peter. He stood up and spread out his hands. "He has a mother?" He laughed at his own joke.

"Everyone has a mother," said Jesus. He sounded disappointed in Peter.

Judas stood up. "Welcome!" He gestured toward the elder Mary. "Would that all our mothers would come to us again."

"Where is your mother?" asked Mary.

"I am afraid she cannot come to us," said Judas. "She died several years ago."

"That is hard," said Andrew. "Very hard."

"Yes, it is." Judas seemed embarrassed to have mentioned it. "But it is common. So many people lose their mothers, it is unusual for an adult still to have one. I envy you," he said to Jesus. Then he dropped down onto his mat.

"I heard you speak to the Pharisees and the Sadducee," said the elder Mary. "So they have come all this way to bait you?"

Jesus smiled. "To test me, I would say."

"I would say bait you."

"Perhaps it is the same thing." He sighed. "Forgive me, Mother, but I am truly very tired from all their testing." He knelt and took his place on his mat. "I must sleep a little while. Stay here with me."

He made a sleeping place for his mother, and in the hush of the hot afternoon, they all lay down to take their rest.

But Mary was afraid to fall asleep, afraid that she would dream more ugly visions. The hideous war-images she had seen had stayed with her all day, through all the strolling and the questioning of Jesus. She would simply close her eyes, but sleep was another matter. Overhead, in the fronds, she could hear a loud fly buzzing.

We are here now, all together. What do we do next, where do we go? The questions drummed like a heavy autumn rain in her mind. All this seems to be leading up to something, but Jesus has given no indication that he intends ever to do anything different. Are we to have a lifetime of what we have been doing?

And what would be wrong with that? she asked herself sternly. It is a hard life, but even one healing makes it worthwhile. And yet I wish he would teach us more, explain things to us, open up his heart to us. . . .

She jerked herself up. She had started to fall asleep in the thick, hot air. No! She raised herself up on one elbow and shook her head. All around her, no one was stirring.

How lucky you are to be able to sleep and not dread the dreams! she told them silently.

In the cool of the evening, Jesus and some of his group ventured out again; Peter and Andrew went into town to buy food with money from Mary and Joanna. They returned with leeks, lentils, and raisins, as well as barley for bread. The two Marys did most of the cooking, and they said little, both glad to have a chance for reflection. It was good to be working side by side, good to be making an offering of labor to their fellows. When the rest of the group returned, they had grilled leeks, a lentil-and-raisin stew, and thick crusty barley bread waiting for them. Peter held up the wine he had selected and claimed that it was from the very slopes near Nazareth.

"In honor of you," he said to Jesus's mother.

"I hope it is from one of the good vineyards," she said. "We have some that are better left unsampled." She smiled as she said it, however, as if to let him know she had had her share of the bad kind.

The evening being fair and warm, they ate cross-legged outside, forming a circle. Before beginning, Jesus said a long prayer of thanks for the food and the companions around him, and asked God's blessings on both. Then he said, "And I thank God, too, for bringing my mother here." He nodded toward her and held out his hand to her. She came and sat beside him.

"It is indeed a special evening for us," Jesus said. "The two families join together, my earthly one and my heavenly one." He put his arm around his mother. "And everyone's family is welcome to come and join us."

If only they would, thought Mary. If only they could.

The evening breeze was sweet, whispering of the joys of harvest, of homecoming. They savored the fare from the countryside: the freshly gathered grapes, the rich slippery olives from groves nearby, and the dark, thick fig paste. Cucumbers and melons had never seemed so refreshing. They could taste the very goodness and bounty of God reaching out to them through the land and its produce.

The fields seemed to breathe warm around them, peaceful and protective.

"We will be staying here the whole seven days?" asked Judas, the first of the disciples to speak.

"Yes, that is the prescribed length of the festival," said Jesus.

"Then why did you say that on the third day you would reach your goal, if we are staying here?"

"I can reach my goal without moving," said Jesus.

"I wish you would stop talking in riddles!" said Peter. "Just say it out, plain, what you mean. Or at least explain it to *us* later, in private." He sounded more hurt than angry.

"What do you want to know, Peter?" Jesus asked.

"All right—what did you mean by asking that man why he called you good? Why did you say only God was good? You knew what he meant. And you *are* good. So it made no sense!"

"I meant, was he asking me if I was in God's place."

"Now, why would he have done that? He was just asking a simple question, and calling you good was a term of respect."

"I want him to think about what he calls someone before he does it to flatter," Jesus said after a pause.

"Well, I'm sure he will from now on!"

"What did you mean about receiving new brothers and sisters to replace those we've left?" Mary asked.

Jesus indicated those around the circle. "Don't you think you have?" he answered quietly. "And there will be more than these. Did I not say a hundred times as much?"

"But you also said there would be persecutions, along with the brothers and sisters. And you said 'in this present age.'"

"You have seen the beginnings of them already," said Jesus. "You have seen people turn on us. The disciple is not above his master, nor the servant above his lord. If they have called the master of the house Beelzebub, how much more those of his household?" Jesus gave a sigh. "But that is not tonight. Let us enjoy this night, free of all persecution and want. Later on, we will want to remember it."

"'In this present age' . . . you keep using that phrase, instead of saying 'now.' Why do you do that?" Once the questions had started, they kept pouring out.

"When we go inside, then I will tell you," said Jesus. "And it will be, as you wish, for yourselves alone. But here, where so many people are wandering about and listening"—he stopped speaking just to make his point, and suddenly they could hear voices and movement very close to them—"is not the suitable place." Still, he seemed to want to linger outside, and so his disciples sat quietly in the night air with him.

At length, when they were gathered inside, Jesus set their lantern in the middle of the floor and said, "You have asked me where I am leading you, and it is fair and right that you should know, for you have risked much to follow me. So now I will tell you what I have touched on in every message I have delivered, in every prayer I have prayed, and in all my thoughts."

They all waited, not knowing what to expect. Mary felt her mouth go dry. It fell so silent she could hear people breathing.

"The present age as we know it is due to end soon," he finally said. "I can say it no plainer than that. We do not have much time left. The end will come suddenly, like a thief in the night. And when it does, all earthly order, all the things we have known, will vanish. God's new Kingdom will dawn, and those who have not prepared for it will be swept aside like chaff to be burned."

They all just stared at him. Yes, everyone knew that a day of judgment was coming, and perhaps had something to do with the Messiah or a mysterious Son of Man, but the portents for it were vague.

"Now?" Peter was the first to speak.

"It could be tomorrow," Jesus said. "That is why it has been so urgent that we speak the message to as many as we could. We had to warn them."

"Well . . . warn them of what?" asked Judas. But he was somber, not challenging. "What can anyone do?"

"Warn them that the coming order will be completely different, and that, if they do not wish to be destroyed in the upheaval, they must repent and change their lives," said Jesus. "Everything will be different, *everything!* That is the message. If I had to choose only one phrase, I would say, 'The first shall be last and the last shall be first.' The poor will be blessed, the rich fall, the powerful will be feeble, and the meek and weak will be the ones to inherit the coming age." He looked around, and suddenly his face lost its gentleness and became fierce, something Mary had never seen before.

"Can't you see it? Can't you feel it? What do you think the healings and the exorcisms meant? They didn't exist by themselves, they existed as signs that the Kingdom was already dawning. Satan's power was being challenged, and already he was loosening his grip on the world. The demons we drove out acknowledged as much." Now, as he spoke, his face changed again, and he seemed transcendent, elated by what was going to happen.

An utter, deep silence fell on the circle. No one wished to speak.

But I don't want all this to end! Mary thought. I don't want it all to vanish, I can't let it all go. . . .

"But we can't reach everyone," Thomas finally said. "There is no way that we can warn them all."

"So . . . this is why you do not think the efforts of people like me to free us from the Romans are worthy?" asked Simon, considering it for the first time.

"Now you understand," said Jesus. "Fighting for some small political cause, when all is going to end and people will be doomed if they have not prepared, is a disgrace. It doesn't matter who rules whom, or how high the taxes are, or whether it's unfair that a Roman can force someone to carry his gear a mile. Carry it two miles, what's the difference? The Roman and his pack are soon going to vanish."

"Will anything remain?" asked Peter, hesitantly.

"Good deeds remain, which is why you should carry the pack an extra mile. Your good deed will endure, the Roman and his pack will not. It is hard to understand, but it is part of God's mystery."

Mary hesitantly said, "This may be an unworthy question, teacher, but . . . will it hurt?"

Jesus nodded sadly. "For those who are not right with God, yes. There will be weeping and gnashing of teeth, all too late. Great lamentation, worse than for the fall of Jerusalem in the time of Jeremiah."

The fall of Jerusalem . . . that dreadful dream . . . Oh, dear God, that was what it had meant! Mary felt a cold sweat creeping over her. And it must be soon; that must be what the dream implied.

"But . . . how will we know when it is coming?" asked his mother. "How can we prepare ourselves?"

He looked over at her, as though relieved that she was there with him and he could warn her himself. "There cannot be any preparation, except always to be ready. I tell you, it will swoop down so quickly that no one can do anything. If there are two people in a bed, one may be saved and the other not. If there are two people working at a mill, one may be saved and the other not. One person may look up to see his partner snatched away. It will be a terrible day, and worse to follow— signs in the sky, cataclysms as the earth ends. I know this. I have received this knowledge. You must believe me."

"But, teacher, you did not tell us to preach this to anyone," Peter said. "You instructed us only to tell people to repent and believe in God's coming Kingdom, and ally themselves on that side."

"What more did they need to know?" asked Jesus. "If they would not respond to that message, do you think they would believe a more detailed one? I tell you, it will be as in the days of Noah. People continued eating and drinking and enjoying themselves right up until the rain fell, although they, too, had been warned. They kept on with their regular lives until Noah had entered the ark and the door was closed."

"But, then . . . what use is it to tell them?" asked Matthew.

"Because God has ordered us to," said Jesus. "All the prophets—he told them to speak, to deliver the message, because the guilt would be on their souls if they did not." He paused. "If someone hears the message and does not respond, then he is guilty. If the message is not delivered, then the person who fails to deliver it is guilty."

"Should we not tell them directly that we know it is coming? Warn them more strongly?" asked Matthew's brother, James, joining in. His legalistic mind thought that all situations should be covered.

"Let me tell you a story," said Jesus. "And its meaning is not secret. Once there was a rich man who refused to give even a crumb to a poor beggar at his gates named Lazarus. When both men died, Lazarus went to Abraham's side, while the rich man went down into hell. The rich man was parched and desperate for even a drop of water, and he begged Abraham to let Lazarus dip his finger in water and cool his tongue. Even though Lazarus was kindhearted and would have given what the rich man had refused to him, he could not comply. There was a great gulf fixed between paradise and hell. So the rich man begged Abraham, 'Please, then, send Lazarus back to my five brothers to warn them, so that they may avoid my fate.' Abraham replied, 'They have Moses and the prophets. And if they do not listen to Moses and the prophets, they will not be convinced even if someone comes back from the dead to speak to them.'" Jesus looked around at them. "Is that not clear?"

"Teacher, with all due respect, I must disagree," Judas said. "General warnings are easy to ignore, as are general admonitions. Keep tidy. Pay debts on time. Be kind to widows. People brush those aside. But if someone came to them and said, 'You must die tonight!' they would pay attention. Perhaps we need to speak more directly."

Before Jesus could answer, Thaddeus asked in distress, "When is all this to happen?"

"The day and the hour no one knows," said Jesus. "But it will be soon. Very soon." He looked around at them. "But you should rejoice. Rejoice that you are already in the Kingdom. And have the privilege of bringing the message to others."

They crept off to sleep. The jovial good spirits of the celebration had vanished like the world Jesus predicted was due to end. It all seemed trivial now—gathering branches, eating meals, observing the instructions to build booths and remember the desert.

Mary lay restlessly on her mat. What would happen to her? And Magdala? That dreadful vision of Magdala—was that its final hours she had seen in the dream? How could she abandon her daughter to that fate?

When she heard Jesus get up and leave the booth, she hurriedly rose and followed him. She had to tell him about the dreams.

A half-moon was just rising, coating the clusters of booths in a bluish tinge. Mary could see Jesus walking toward the wooded slopes above the fields. He was alone; only a few people were still up, their songs and laughter floating across the fields. Clutching her robe around her, she tried to catch up with him. He was taking very long strides. But she ran, and just before he came to the woods, she reached him and touched his sleeve.

"Jesus—I had another vision. Last night. I'm afraid it is about the end that you were telling us about. I had to let you know." Her words all came out in a gasp.

"Why did you not tell me when we were all together?" He turned to face her, and she saw how resolute his expression was. The cold moonlight made him look stern, judgmental.

"I . . ." She felt as if he was accusing her of being secretive. "I do not always trust these visions, and I did not want to alarm others." Did he think she wanted an excuse to be alone with him? She had thought he would be pleased to see her. She was disappointed. "The visions were ugly."

"Tell me." He seemed a bit more welcoming now.

Around them, a small breeze blew across the furrows, warm and earth-scented, before it disappeared into the woods. This world was not ready to end.

"There were three of them," she said in a low voice, as if the earth might overhear and despair. "The first was of Magdala. There was a terrible war there, fighting—I could see mounted Roman soldiers sweeping into the town, fighting the townspeople. But worse than that was a sight of the lake filled with boats at war with one another."

"Boats? At war?" He questioned her sharply. "Not fishing boats?"

"Some of them may once have been fishing boats, but now they were filled with desperate, ragged fighting men, and other boats were filled with Roman soldiers. As I watched, I saw some of the fighters throwing stones at the Romans, which caused them no harm at all, while the Romans fired arrows at them, which hit their targets all too well. Some of the boats were sunk, and when the men tried to swim away, the Romans cut off either their heads or their hands. They all drowned, and the sea was bright red."

He gave a groan, as if he could see it, too. "The water all red?"

"As red as if buckets and buckets of dye had spilled into it. And then I saw the shore all lined with bodies, and wrecked boats, and while I watched the bodies swelled and . . . I could smell the stench. It was overpowering. When I awoke I could still smell it."

He was silent for so long that she had to ask him, "Can it be true? Is this to happen? Is this what you meant?"

"Romans . . . God can use any agent as his scourge," Jesus said thoughtfully. "He used the Babylonians and the Assyrians. And so now it is to be the Romans."

"My home!" Mary said. "I can't bear to think of this happening to my home. And the children. At the end of time, are they spared? They do not need a new world in order to start all over; the world is already new to them, they haven't soiled it by their own evil."

Now Jesus looked as though he would weep. The sternness in his face had changed into softness and sorrow. "Were the children spared when Jerusalem fell? No. And it was not the Babylonians who killed them, but their own families."

"No. I cannot let it happen. I will go there and rescue my child."

"It will not be possible."

"Yes, it will. I must leave you."

"You can leave me, but you cannot prevent what is to happen." He took her trembling hands. "It is not in your power." He clasped her and held her to quiet her shaking fear. "You said there were three dreams. What was the second?"

The second. The Jerusalem one. Quickly she told him about it, speaking the words very low, not wanting him to release her. But at length he did.

"The Temple, you say?" he cried. "Then the knowledge I was granted is true. Oh, Father, would that it were not!" He stood still, and started trembling himself. Now it was Mary's turn to reach out her hand to steady him.

"When will this happen?" she asked. "Do the visions mean it will be very soon?"

"We can't know," he said. "That it was Romans, yes, that could mean soon." He paused. "The third?" He looked as though he expected this would be the most dreadful of all.

"It was of you. You in a shining white robe, with a large group of people gathered around you. But where you were, and who they were . . . I do not know. It was the last dream, and it faded quickly."

"Ah." Instead of smiling, as she had expected, he looked as though this vision was as troubling as the others. "So it must be. It is coming, and it will await me, if—" He broke off. "Thank you for telling me of your revelations. I can trust them. I can trust you."

"I could never hide anything from you." As she spoke, she wanted to cry out, "Stay with me! Stay with me always!" But even if he should promise that, what did it mean if the apocalypse was near?

"For in the days before the flood, people were marrying and giving in marriage . . . up until the day Noah entered the ark."

The sun still shone the next morning, bright and warm, with no hint that soon it might shrivel up or darken. In the friendliness of the gentle dawn, Jesus's stern words in the darkness faded away. Even he did not seem concerned, as he went about his normal actions and asked his mother how James was surviving in the carpentry shop. And how were Simon and Joses faring? She told him that James was as sour as ever but proving a shrewd manager of the business, and that Simon was a talented assistant. Neither of them had so far shown any interest in where Jesus's teachings had led him, although it was impossible not to hear about the crowds at Capernaum and the incident of the swine at Gergesa.

Jesus was able to console her for their lack of concern, although he surely suffered the same hurt as she did from their indifference.

"I will come and seek James someday," he promised her.

This time when they went out, people were waiting for Jesus. As usual, some were afflicted with illness, some were poor, some were curious. But this time, as the day before, there were also the Pharisees, the strictly observant, the scribes and scholars. Stationed at the far edge of the crowds were a sprinkling of Antipas's police. As Jesus moved out among them, suddenly a stocky, bald man approached him from behind and touched his sleeve. Instantly he turned around to see who it was, although the touch was feather-light. Confronted with Jesus's stare, the man hesitantly admitted that he had come to ask Jesus's further help.

"You restored my sight, but I am having trouble. . . . I can't get used to it. . . . I thought all my troubles came from being blind, but I am so confused. I see things, and they don't look like . . . like anything I can name. I have to smell and touch them first before I know what they are!" The man looked so distressed that one would have thought he was in bodily pain.

Jesus took his hand and talked to him as if they were the only ones present. "So nothing looks as you expected?" he asked.

"I did not expect anything, except to be able to see where I was going so I would no longer have to be led or tap along with a cane. There would be no more falling and no more fear of being hit by something

I could not detect. And now I have more trouble walking. Steps, barriers, hills—I can't tell a real step from a shadow. I can't tell what's real."

He stopped, aware that everyone was listening. But he plunged on. "And the brightness, all those colors . . . they seem so . . . pointless. Before, when I held an apple, I knew it by how firm and how heavy it was, and especially how it smelled. I could predict its taste by its smell. But now the color! What has that to do with anything? Red, and . . . I just stare at it. And there are other red, round things, too, pomegranates and persimmons, and I have to take them and hold them and smell them, to tell which is which, just as if I were still blind."

"But are not the colors beautiful?" asked Mary.

"No! They are just confusing!" said the man. "I don't like them, they hurt my head!"

Jesus laughed. "Too much richness can indeed be confusing. And a scarcity of things—whether it's color or possessions—can focus the mind mightily. But light is one of the first things God created, and he wants us to live in it." Here he had been speaking so that everyone could hear. But then he lowered his voice so only those nearby could hear. "You are blinded now in a different way. You are dazzled by the glory of God's world. You will have to accustom yourself to it little by little. Take that apple and stare at it, look at every shading on its skin, and ask someone to name each tint, so you can learn them, and gradually you will come to recognize all the things that surround you. But you will always see them differently from others, because you had to choose to see them."

"I don't understand what the colors add!" the man cried. "I don't want them!"

Jesus then turned to the others. "That's what we do to God every day. He gives us sight, he presents things to us, and we wail, 'I don't want them!' Friend, you now have the blessing of sight, and there is no going back."

"Maybe you should not restore sight," said Judas, catching up to Jesus. "I never would have thought it would cause more difficulty to the person."

"It's always easier to live at a lower level than you could," said Jesus. "That is why I ask people, 'Do you want to be made well?' Some are wise enough to admit they do not."

His mother now came closer and said, "Why would anyone not want to be made well? I cannot believe that they would choose otherwise."

"They think they want to, but they do not realize the demands it will place on them," said Jesus.

"It can't possibly be easier to be blind than to see," said Thomas. "I just cannot accept that!"

Jesus looked at him and shook his head. "You heard what he said, and he knows what it is like both to be blind and to see. We know only one, and cannot imagine the other."

"Perhaps you ought to stop all this healing, then," said a man looking on.

"God is a god of light, and he wants us to live in the light," said Jesus. "No matter how difficult it is. The darkness is always easier."

Then a young man came toward Jesus and said, "I was afflicted with demons, and you drove them out. Do you remember me? But, like the blind man, I find that it's very difficult. For one thing, people continue to treat me as if I had the demons. They don't trust me to do anything, and I can see them testing every word I speak and watching me all the time."

He was standing straight and he was well dressed. There was nothing about him to indicate any weakness.

"It is hard when people remember only what you were," Jesus said. He paused. "But there is something else troubling you."

"Yes . . . I'm afraid they will come back. Perhaps that's what people sense. That they may come back!"

"Have you amended your life?" asked Jesus. "Whatever it was that invited the demon in, have you banished it? Because, if you have merely breathed a sigh of relief and done a bit of tidying up, then the demon indeed will come back. And he will bring his fellows. And you will end up worse than you began!"

The young man fell to his knees. "I think I have . . . but there has been so much to do, so many repairs to make."

"Pray to keep the demons away, and continue in your efforts to salvage the damage they have done, and God will surely protect you."

As he walked on, the enemies on the edge of the crowd seemed to draw closer in. Mary could see a veritable wall of Pharisees clad in their severe robes, and a milling group that could only be scribes, clutching their bundles of writing materials to their sides. And beyond that, staring impassively as any implacable pagan god, were the soldiers of Herod Antipas. They wore their distinctive blue uniforms and kept their right hands on their sword scabbards. Gone was the celebratory mood of their gathering, replaced now by spying and tension.

Suddenly someone cried out, "A sign! Give us a miraculous sign!"

Jesus stopped and looked to see who was calling. All around was a sea of faces; it was impossible to tell who had spoken.

"A sign?" Jesus repeated. "And what will you do with a sign?"

"Then we will believe that you are a true prophet!" the voice came again, and now they could see it belonged to a tall, commanding young Pharisee in the back.

Instead of replying gently, Jesus shouted back, "You are a wicked and adulterous generation! You'll get no sign, no sign at all!"

Stunned, the people drew back.

"Only the sign of Jonah, that's all you will get!" Jesus cried. "For Jonah preached to the people of Nineveh, and they repented. Now these very men of Nineveh will condemn you at the time of judgment, for a greater prophet than Jonah is here, and you do not listen!" He turned to the other side of the crowd. "And the queen of Sheba will likewise condemn you at the judgment, for she came from the ends of the earth to hear Solomon's wisdom, and now one greater than Solomon is here!"

"You are insane!" cried the questioner. "Do you mean yourself? That you are greater than Solomon? What nonsense!"

The crowd began to make rumbling noises, and Antipas's soldiers moved in to quiet them, brandishing their spears and shoving people aside. They shouldered their way down to Jesus, and their captain stretched out his hand to take hold of him. "You'd best come with us," he said.

But Jesus pulled his arm back and stared at the soldier so intently that he seemed unable to move. For several long, wordless moments, they looked at one another, and then the soldier stepped back. "You've been warned," he muttered. Then he barked at the crowd, "Disperse! Back to your booths, your quarters! Leave this man alone! Cease following him, provoking him, and questioning him!" He pointed at the Pharisee who had asked for a sign. "I mean you! If you ignored him, he would soon disappear! You create the attention that allows him to flourish!"

The Pharisee looked back at the soldier with the utmost disdain, as if he were an oozing mound of offal on a cobblestone—and, indeed, to the strictly observant, the minions of Antipas or Rome were just that unclean. He did not condescend to answer, but he did obey. He spoke no more to Jesus.

•   •   •

For the remainder of the festival, with the soldiers patrolling, Jesus and his company stayed quietly in their booth. They used the time to ask him questions, and to rest and think. Mary kept turning the visions over and over in her mind, trying to recall tiny details about them, the better to know what to expect when the events occurred. The vivid colors and sounds remained, indelibly splashed with the tint and smell of blood, and the figures moved, over and over again, slashing and falling and crying out.

She also found herself watching Jesus carefully, trying to discern what he felt for each of the disciples. Did he prefer Thaddeus to Judas? Did he seem more eager to answer the questions of Thomas than those of Peter? How did he speak to Susanna? She was still with them. Had Jesus especially welcomed her? She tried to compare his expressions and his behavior toward each of them with that toward his mother.

At the same time, she disliked herself for having these thoughts—for the unspoken competition for his approval that she sensed.

She kept wondering whether there was any special place for her in Jesus's affections, or whether the understanding she sensed between them had been only her imagination.

Am I just a lonely widow, who tries to make something I need out of something that is not there? The answer varied from day to day, depending on what Jesus said or did.

That I still mourn Joel, and feel bereft, is true, she admitted. That I feel different and no longer alone when I am with Jesus, that is true. But what he feels, I cannot know. He and I share my visions, and I am able to help him, but beyond that there may be nothing—nothing of the things between a man and a woman.

Will I ever know? she asked herself. And do I dare to find out?

After the festival was over, Jesus led them away from Bethsaida and up into the hills. His mother stayed with them, as did Susanna. Joanna and Mary had exchanged some more of their personal treasure in Bethsaida, so that the group's needs could be met on the next leg of their journey.

As they walked along the path in twos, sometimes Mary was near Jesus and sometimes she was not. It was always a privilege to walk near him and be able to talk to him, or even just to walk beside him and keep silent. Once, as she fell back to allow the Zebedee brothers to be in the forefront with Jesus, she overheard an exchange that wiped from her all the guilt about her wish to be preferred by Jesus.

Jesus had motioned them to come up to him, and when they took Mary's place, he said, "What was it you were talking about back there?"

"Nothing in particular," said Big James.

When Jesus remained silent and continued looking at him, he shrugged. "We were talking about Antipas, and what it meant that those soldiers were watching us."

"But you were arguing," said Jesus. "You, and John, and four or five others."

"We were arguing about who is to be the greatest in the new Kingdom, when as you said everything is to be turned upside down," Big James admitted. "John and I—we want to ask your permission to be allowed to sit on either side of you. To be your special helpers."

So! They are all plotting to be advanced; they all want to be Jesus's favorites! thought Mary. And I only want his affection and esteem, whereas they want prestige and a special position. That realization made her feel superior.

"They have no right!" said Philip, who had come up on the path. "I knew you first."

"I was there from the beginning, too," said Peter.

"I brought you to Jesus," corrected his brother. "I was the first."

"Jesus had a vision of me under the fig tree," said Nathanael. "I was one of the original people he called."

Jesus stopped walking, and the rest of the company halted, too. The dust they had raised on the path now enveloped them, hanging in the air like a mist.

"My Sons of Thunder! You don't know what you are asking," he said to Big James and John. "Can you drink the cup I am going to drink?"

"We can," they answered stoutly.

Jesus shook his head. "You will indeed drink from my cup, but sitting at my right or left is not for me to grant. These places belong to those for whom they have been prepared by my Father."

"They should not go behind our backs like that!" said Peter. "Sneaking around, trying to secure—"

"Peter!" Jesus raised his voice. "All of you! Listen!" He turned around, slowly, to make sure everyone could hear him. "Do you want to be like Antipas and his soldiers? Like the Romans? They live according to rank, and love to lord it over one another. It must be the opposite with you. The greatest among you must be a servant, no, a slave to the others. Just as I serve others."

"A slave?" Peter looked insulted. "A slave? You say we are God's children, and God's children cannot be slaves!"

"You must be slaves to God's Kingdom." Jesus said the words plainly. "There is no place for ambition in God's Kingdom."

John and James, disgruntled, fell back and let Mary and Joanna take their places.

"Master," said Mary, "I have no ambition."

Jesus looked at her, turning his eyes full upon her, and in that moment she felt he could see into her mind. "Mary, I fear you do," was all he said.

She was thunderstruck to hear those words. This was *not* true—was it? Yet he was right about the others. . . . She felt her cheeks flushing with shame.

Then Joanna began to talk about what she knew of Antipas and what he was likely to do. He would have them followed, she warned. From now on he would always be watching. The slightest misstep, and they would all end up like John the Baptist—imprisoned, if not executed.

"Even Antipas has to follow *some* law," said Mary. "He cannot just lock us up." She was grateful for the chance to continue talking with Jesus, but on a safer subject. Antipas was certainly preferable to her own feelings about him.

"He will find an excuse," said Joanna. "I know him. I know how he thinks."

"You are right, Joanna," said Jesus. "But we will not hide from him, or change our behavior. What we do, we do openly. Let Antipas do his worst."

"Yes!" said John, who was right behind them, his handsome face aglow. "Let us go boldly about, even unto death!"

"If it comes to that, John," Jesus said slowly. "But there is no shame in seeking to preserve your life. When I am gone, I expect you to flee from persecution, as long as you do not deny me."

What was he talking about? When he was gone? Mary suddenly felt very frightened. The white robe, and his saying, "It is coming, and it will await me. . . ."

"You must not say such things!" Mary cried, pushing John aside and clutching Jesus. "Please!"

"Mary, Mary," he said, "what will be, we cannot deny. We must be prepared."

"But your message—if you are silenced, then what of those who have not yet heard the message?" Thomas insisted.

"That is why I must keep speaking, keep moving, as long as I am allowed to. And afterward, you must speak for me."

"Afterward . . . When I am gone . . ."

He had not spoken thus before. Now, as the words rang out, Mary almost felt a shadow passing over the bright day, as if the wings of a giant eagle had blotted out the sun in flying by. If he vanished, then there would never be warmth again. A genuine chill crept over her skin.

It could not be. She had not had a vision of it. If there was no vision, how could it be true? My visions tell me everything. It was the first time she had allowed this admission, had dropped her guard against their revelations.

The vision showed him in the dazzling robe, ennobled, glorious. But the robe of martyrdom—is that not said to be glorious? Could that be what I saw?

Behind her, the disciples were tramping up a rough incline, some of them using staffs to propel themselves along, others, in the rear, grumbling. John and James had fallen back, embarrassed by their exchange with Jesus. Beside them, the other ambitious disciples were still arguing.

As they climbed, the cooler air of the heights was beginning to touch them, and the pine trees, now forest-tall, were rustling in the breeze. Mary was hardly aware of Judas as he came alongside her until he spoke, so lost was she in her own thoughts.

"Jesus can choose only young people to follow him," he said. He was stabbing his staff into the ground, as if he needed it to anchor himself for the next step.

"His mother seems to keep up," said Mary, watching her as she walked sturdily alongside Peter.

"She isn't very old," said Judas. "She can't be any older than her late forties. Matthew is close to that. Also Simon. He's been a zealot for a long time. That's why he's so jaded. Being a zealot for a long time and having nothing happen—that has to age you."

"He seems younger since he joined us."

"Yes," Judas agreed. "Jesus has that effect."

"And now Jesus is talking about his mission being cut short by Antipas. We can't let that happen!" Judas would be a likely ally in any plan to outsmart Antipas. He was clever and resourceful and more worldly than the others. Mary remembered a phrase of Jesus's, that the children of this world were wiser than the children of light, at least in regard to certain things. Judas seemed a very competent child of this world.

Judas thought for a moment, and all Mary heard was his staff thumping. Finally, he said, "No, we cannot allow it." Then he said a startling thing. "We must stop Jesus, if he tries anything too provocative."

Stop Jesus? The idea seemed disloyal. But should he not be prevented from a dangerous action? "How?"

"By persuasion," Judas said. "I am sure his mother would help us. And if all else fails . . . there are more of us than of him."

The idea of forcibly preventing Jesus from any course of action he was set on seemed not only abhorrent but somehow impossible. But to save his life . . .

"Yes. Yes, if it comes to that." Mary felt both relieved and conspiratorial, low. The shadow left the sky, but the chill remained.

Judas walked silently beside her for a bit, then said, "I understand that you and Joanna have been contributing to our livelihood. Do you need someone to oversee the finances? I am very good at it."

Was this why he had come alongside her? "Have you training in it? I would have thought Matthew—"

"He wishes no reminders of his former life," said Judas. "The same for his brother, James. And who else is there? The five fishermen? A Torah scholar? These men have no experience in handling money. Jesus doubtless admires their salt-of-the-earth, homely virtues, but that isn't what's needed here. We have our own money from members; we have contributions from outsiders; we have expenses for food and drink. Someone has to manage it. I have the experience. Or do you wish to?" he asked politely.

"No," she said. She wanted to be free to direct her attention to Jesus and his message, to help him whenever she could.

"Then I offer my services," he said.

They rested that night within a forest, a protective enclave of pines and oaks. Such forests were survivors from ancient times, from the days of Joshua and the conquest of the promised land. They had waited and watched while David, Solomon, Josiah, and Elijah had guarded the land. Now they guarded Jesus and his companions. Farther down the slope were other followers, those who trailed him at a distance, or who did not know him well but were drawn to him.

Under the pines, the disciples built a fire and gathered around it. They could hear the crowd a bit below them, eager to adhere to Jesus, seeking a powerful leader.

But as they arranged themselves around the fire, they saw that Jesus looked sad and distracted, not like a mighty leader. The flames leapt when pine branches fell into the fire, spitting as they swallowed up green needles. The fire lit the faces of Jesus and those beside him, showing every line and muscle on their faces and necks.

If we are young, Mary thought, tonight we do not look it. These are not the eyes of young people.

Jesus was looking at them, his gaze passing over each of their faces.

"My friends," he finally said. "And Mother, a friend above all." He nodded toward her. "I feel that we have entered another phase of our journey." He looked around. "Not only because we are in a part of Galilee unfamiliar to most of us, but because we have now attracted the attention of the Romans, of Antipas, and of the religious authorities. Soon we must go to Jerusalem to confront them."

Jerusalem!

"Not Jerusalem," whispered Mary. "No, master!" Bad things were waiting there.

Jesus lowered his head and closed his eyes for a moment. "I thank God for all of you," he said. His face grew anguished. "But so few, out of so many!"

Below them they could hear the throngs that followed at a distance, milling around on the slope beneath.

"We are completely yours," Mary assured him.

"And now we are threatened by the Romans and by Antipas before we have even completed our journey all through the land. We must keep going. I ask you: Are you willing? Will you persevere? It will be difficult."

They all murmured assent, but their voices were low.

"You have heard me speak of the end," he said. "But it is not given to us to know the times. We can only do what we have been given to do, up until the very last hour."

"My son," said his mother, "how can you speak of the last hour? Your hours have barely begun!"

He laughed, but it was a quiet laugh. "We always feel that way about someone we love. But the truth, my dear mother, is that it has been many years since you first held me. And for those we love, the hours are always too swift." He turned his head from his mother and looked as fiercely as an eagle at the rest of them. Then his gaze sought out James and John. "He assigns the last hours. Not I."

"We are willing," they all chorused. "We are willing." Their voices were deep and mournful.

During the night, it began to rain. Suddenly the winter had come. Only a year ago, I was drenched by the winter rains as I sought deliverance—any deliverance—from my demons, Mary thought. I did not even know Jesus. His mission had not yet begun. And now, already, he feels that it is threatened.

She pulled her head covering up over herself, grateful that she had made her bed underneath a sheltering pine. She could hear the drops splattering all around her, heavy and cold.

So many people have heard him speak. But so many have yet to hear. He cannot reach them all, she thought, as the rains hit the branches above her.

She heard others moving their pallets nearer to escape the rain.

"Mary?" It was the voice of Judas. Had he been near the entire time?

"Yes?" She felt uneasy. What if he thought . . . if he imagined that she might . . . ?

I belong only to Jesus. Those words, unexpected and final, flashed through her mind.

"I do not understand what lies before us," he was saying. "I am confused. Jesus has never really answered my questions, the ones I wished to set before him in the desert from the very beginning." His voice was low and confiding.

What questions were those? Mary could remember only challenges.

"Perhaps he did not think you truly wanted them answered," she finally said. She inched her pallet a bit farther away from him.

"He should have been able to tell that they were real," Judas insisted. She heard a rustle as he moved his pallet farther under the tree.

Perhaps he was not sidling up to her. Perhaps he only wanted to stay dry. She chided herself for always thinking the worst of someone. Jesus would not like that, she thought. He expects the best of us, and takes chances on people like Simon and Matthew. But how can I learn to think like that?

"I was honest in my searching," Judas continued. "I've been searching, I fear, all my life."

She sat up so she could hear him better, and answer without disturbing others. "Your search must have been satisfied," she whispered. "You joined him."

"I joined him, yes, and there are days when the search seems over, but . . ." His voice grew even fainter, like smoke trailing away from a dying fire. "Perhaps the fault lies in me, but there are other days when I am overwhelmed by the unanswered questions."

She bowed her head and closed her eyes. She knew so well what he meant. "At some point you must rely on deep trust," she finally said. That was what she had done: blind trust, fervent commitment. Wall everything else out. Stamp on it.

"You know some of the followers—the ones back there, lower on the hillside—have left," Judas said. His voice was very soft in the dark. "I heard Jesus asking Peter about it. It bothers Jesus when anyone departs. He said—and very sadly—'Will you go also?' And Peter answered, 'To whom shall we go? You have the words of eternal life.' And that is how I feel. I want to hear his words, hoping that one of them— one miraculous one—will answer all those questions. If I left, I would never hear them."

It was a negative reason for staying with Jesus, but Mary could not fault it. What was important stood firm: they were here with him, not scattered elsewhere. And perhaps one elusive word would win Judas completely over, if he remained near enough to hear.

ᓂ X L V ᓂ

My dearest brother, my Silvanus—

This may be the last time I can write anything to you. I hope I can find a messenger to take it to Magdala; we are in the hills far from the lake and heading north. Yes, I know, that is not the place to be in the winter.

Everything has changed. I remember now that you warned me that Jesus was attracting attention—the wrong sort of attention. You were right. The religious authorities have come down from Jerusalem, Antipas's soldiers have harassed us, and I have had the most dreadful premonitions of destruction and terror. And a strange mood has overtaken Jesus; he talks about the end of this age, says it is coming soon, says he must go to Jerusalem and face "it" there. We are all oppressed, feeling threatened, even though we can see no enemies on either side as we make our way up the steep hills.

Jesus's mother is here with us, and that is some comfort, for she has her own quiet strength—different from his, but no less sustaining. There is another follower here, a Judaean named Judas, who feels with me that Jesus is in danger, and wants somehow to stave it off. I do not know if that is possible: cannot foresee from what direction the danger is coming.

Oh, Silvanus, treasure your quiet life by the sea! And please give Elisheba this little note from me, your loving sister.

My own sweet Elisheba—

It's raining and cold, and although most people don't like that, I always do, because you were born in the winter, and so it means your birthday will soon be here, and that you will be three years old. Three! When people ask you how old you are, you can hold up your three middle fingers, and only them. That may be hard until you practice a few times. Fingers can be tricky to manage!

If I were there, I would give you a special gift. But instead, you gave me one. I am wearing it now. I wear it always. It is a necklace with a little amulet on it that you wore first. I think it helps keep our spirits together, and when I see you again I will take it off and put it back around your neck, and then my joy will be complete.

All my love, my most precious daughter,
Your own mother, Mary

∾ XLVI ∾

The season was turning nasty. The rain of the night before had soaked the ground; the dormant land would spring back to life, and the rains would fill waiting cisterns and barrels. But for those forced to live outdoors, it was a dismal and chilly time.

Jesus and his party trudged on. Mary wondered why Jesus had

chosen this area; there were so few people, and the terrain was so difficult, made more so by the rains, which turned the slopes slippery.

At last they came out upon a plateau, farther north than the region where Mary and John had gone. It was bleak and windswept, and as they struggled up, one by one, they saw the valleys spread out before them, and the hills, and could see almost to the ocean. A wide, flat region was just visible, stretching out between them and the sea.

"The great plain of Megiddo," Jesus said, as they gathered around him, trying to catch their breath. "It is where they say the last great battle will take place."

Mary stared at the flat plain, which did indeed look large enough to accommodate several armies. But now it lay tranquil.

"At the end of time . . . at the last days . . ." He looked intently at it. "This is where they will all meet. The armies of the just, and the armies of the evil. And there it will all be decided."

"But . . . you said the world would change, come to an end as we know it," she said. "Perhaps tomorrow. So how can this battle be fought?" It did not add up; both were all destruction and finality, but the two pictures did not fit together.

Jesus turned to look at her, and his face seemed radiant—almost like that in her vision. But not quite. "This will be the final battle of the ages, before all ages end." He was seeing things, things beyond their understanding and imagination. "But first the Son of Man must come and judge, and there will be great tribulation on the earth."

"When?" The anguished question burst forth from her. "When, Lord?"

"Mary, Mary." He stepped over to her. The double calling of her name was thrilling. "You need only step out day by day. This will not happen in your lifetime."

"But you said it would come soon!" Judas protested.

"Something will come soon," Jesus said. "Something momentous. I feel it is the dawning of God's Kingdom. But there is a long stretch between the dawn and the midday, when the final battle will be fought."

Nathanael came up to him and said, "I see none of this. All I see is quiet farming lands. I cannot envision these things you tell us about."

"That is all you need to see," said Jesus. "We need to proclaim the message while it is still quiet, and people can listen. Now hear me!" He stepped away and raised his hands. "Those end times I spoke of—no one but the Father knows when they will truly happen. We must speak, and act, as if we had all the time in the world, bearing in mind that we may not. You must live as if you already are in eternity, where time itself has disappeared."

For him it may be simple, but for us that will be almost impossible, thought Mary.

"We will continue to proclaim the message as we know it, day after day, for as many days as we are granted." He turned to look at the great valley stretching before and below him, brown and hazy. "*I* see those armies. But when they will clash, I know not. We may have ample time."

He turned away from the sight of the broad valley and led them on.

There seemed to be no people anywhere. The windswept hills and plateaux spread out on all sides, but they saw only goats and empty olive groves and a few flocks of sheep on the steep hillsides. It appeared to be the very edge of the world.

Rain began to fall again, drenching them. As they sloshed across one muddy field ringed by gentle inclines on all sides, Jesus suddenly said, "Here. We stop here."

It was a dismal place. There were no trees, and the wind tore through it, whipping raindrops at them like javelins.

"Master," said Peter, "shall I make shelters?" But it was a foolish question: there was nothing to make them out of.

"No," said Jesus. "Then we could not be seen." He put down his pack, took his mother's, and led her to the only shelter available—a low gorse bush, bristling with thorns. He spread out a blanket over its top and indicated that she should take refuge by it.

The larger group of followers struggled up onto the level field and milled about in confusion. The sound of all their feet stepping in and out of the mud sounded like a mass of oxen trampling a riverbank, with loud sucking noises.

"Friends!" Jesus called out in a ringing voice, one that carried even to the rim of the field, where more and more people were spilling out. "Let me speak to you! You have journeyed far without hearing, and thus you have proved that you truly wish to hear!"

The people drew closer, and as they gathered closer in knots, most of the field remained empty.

"Blessed are you all, for what you shall hear!" Jesus cried. "For I tell you, the prophets themselves wished to see what you see but did not see it, and to hear what you hear and did not hear it."

Was he to unveil his final plans? Was that why he had brought them to this remote place? Mary wondered, looking around. Then, from one corner of her eye, she saw others coming up over the rim. New people. Where had they come from? As she watched, more and more came, filling up the empty spaces on the field, until the crowd was vast.

"Do you think I have come to abolish the Law or the prophets?" he cried. "No, I have come not to abolish them but to fulfill them. But you must do more than obey them, you must go further. You have heard the commandment 'Do not murder.' But I tell you that anyone who is angry with his brother will also face judgment. As will anyone who calls his brother a fool. He will be in danger of hellfire."

Mary looked out over the sea of faces, upturned and listening intently. He is telling us to curb our thoughts; he is saying that thoughts are as real as actions.

"You have heard the commandment 'Do not commit adultery.' But I tell you, anyone who looks at a woman lustfully has already committed adultery with her in his heart."

There was a low chuckle of amusement among the company.

"Do you find this a hard saying?" Jesus quickly said. "Then let me assure you that if your right eye causes you to sin, you must gouge it out and throw it away. It is better for you to lose your eye than to let it drag your whole body to hell."

The chuckling died away, replaced by uneasy sideward glances.

"And if your very right hand causes you to sin, cut it off! Yes, cut it off!"

He was pacing back and forth through the mud, his robe hem trailing like a ruler's train, but instead of jewels, it was covered with mire and weeds. His voice rose over the wind and rain.

"You have heard that Moses said, 'Eye for eye, and tooth for tooth.' But I tell you, do not resist an evil person. If someone strikes you on the right cheek, turn to him the other also. If someone sues you and wants to take your tunic, let him have your cloak as well." He started to take off his cloak. He stepped forward to give it away, but people drew back.

Simon nudged Mary. "Is he mad?" he whispered. "He's gone too far this time."

"Love your enemies!" Jesus cried. "Pray for those who persecute you!"

"I'll never pray for the Romans!" muttered Simon. "It's enough that I don't kill them any longer."

"If you do so," said Jesus, "that makes you like your Father in heaven. He sends the rain upon the deserving and the undeserving alike." He held out his hands to catch the rain. "If you love only those who love you, what credit is that to you? And if you greet only your brothers, how are you different from anyone else? Even the pagans do as much. Be perfect, therefore, as your heavenly Father is perfect."

Even though he had not raised his voice louder, the stunned quiet of the crowd made it seem he was shouting. "When you pray, do not be like the hypocrites, who love to pray standing in the synagogues and on street corners for everyone to see. But go into your room, close the door, and pray to God, who is unseen. And he, who sees everything done in secret, will listen. Let me tell you of two prayers. One righteous man went to the Temple and said, 'God, I thank you that I am not like other men—robbers, evildoers, adulterers—or even like this tax collector here. I fast twice a week and give a tenth of all I get.' But the tax collector stood at a distance. He would not even look up to heaven, but beat his breast and said, 'God have mercy on me, a sinner.' This man was the one justified before God. For everyone who exalts himself will be humbled, and he who humbles himself will be exalted."

The wind picked up, and gusts of rain blew in everyone's faces. Some people stumbled up and fought their way to the edge of the field to seek shelter. Jesus, by contrast, pulled back his covering and bared his head to the rain. He watched the people trudging away, and on his face Mary saw a fleeting expression of deep sorrow.

"Do not judge others!" he yelled—for himself as much as for others, as he watched them slinking away? "For, in the same way you judge others, you will be judged. Why look at the mote of sawdust in your brother's eye? First take the beam from your own eye and then you will see clearly to remove the mote from your brother's!"

He stood for a moment, solitary and tall, like a monument in a field, watching their backs as they retreated, out of earshot. Then he squared his shoulders and continued.

"I tell you, do not worry about your life, what you will eat or drink, or about your body, what you will wear. Look at the birds of the air; they do not sow or reap or store away in barns, and yet your heavenly Father feeds them. Are you not much more precious than they?"

Mary thought of her family's great warehouses storing the dried, smoked, and salted fish. How could they not rely on these stores? Without them, they could not prosper in their business. And yet . . . how freeing it was to leave it all behind.

"And why do you worry about clothes? See how the lilies of the field grow. They do not labor or spin. Yet I tell you that not even Solomon in all his splendor was arrayed as one of these. If that is how God clothes the grass of the field, which is here today and tomorrow is thrown into the fire, will he not much more clothe you, oh, you of little faith?"

He looked around at them, seemingly at every one, before continuing. "So do not worry, saying, 'What shall we eat?,' 'What shall we drink?,' or 'What shall we wear?' The pagans run after such things, and your heavenly Father knows you need them. But seek first his Kingdom and his righteousness. Then all these things will be given to you as well." He paused. "Therefore, do not worry about tomorrow!" Jesus commanded everyone. "For tomorrow will worry about itself. I tell you, each day has enough trouble of its own."

He began to walk around to the various groups, huddled miserably against the rain. Mary strained to hear him as he got farther away.

"Which of you, if his son asks him for bread, will give him a stone? If you, then, know how to give good gifts to your children, how much more will your Father in heaven give good gifts to those who ask him. So, in everything, do to others what you will have them do to you."

Now he turned around and repeated it. "If you hear nothing else, remember this: do to others what you will have them do to you, for this sums up the Law and the prophets. Follow me, and hear more!" He paused. "There are many here who mourn, and I say you are blessed, for you will be comforted. There are others here who hunger and thirst after righteousness, and I say you are blessed, for you shall be filled. Those of you who are meek, you are blessed, for you will inherit the earth. And for those who are merciful, you are blessed, for you will be shown mercy. And those who are peacemakers, you shall be called the children of God. And blessed are those who are persecuted because of righteousness, for yours is the Kingdom of God."

Then he left the listeners in the field and came over to his own disciples. "And for you, my chosen ones—blessed are you when people insult you, persecute you, and falsely say all kinds of evil against you because of me. Rejoice and be glad, because great is your reward in heaven, for in the same way they persecuted the prophets who were before you." As he spoke, he looked at each face in turn, and when he said "persecute you," his eyes were upon Mary's face.

She just stood shaking and shivering in the cold, and the sound of the word "persecute" had such depth, it was like staring into an abyss. Persecute. There were so many ways to be persecuted: quick attacks, long slow imprisonments or wastings, isolation, torture. The cistern that Jeremiah was thrown into, the pit Joseph was flung into . . . Losing Elisheba is supreme persecution for me. Yes, indeed, I've lost her because people "falsely say all kinds of evil" about me because of Jesus. So for me the persecution has already begun.

His eyes leaving her, Jesus passed before all the others, calling them one by one to the dreadful possibility of persecution. They looked back at him, their faces perplexed and frightened.

Then, abruptly, Jesus turned back to the vast company of people on the field. As her eyes took them all in, Mary could not explain to herself how the crowd had suddenly grown so large.

Now her shivers were not just from the cold. Jesus had somehow drawn them out of nowhere.

The daylight was fading. Andrew came up to Jesus and spoke softly.

"Sir, night will be coming soon, and we are in a remote place. We must send these people on their way in time for them to get safely home. They are wet and cold, and will be hungry."

As we are, thought Mary. Yes, I am ready to make a shelter and crawl into it, to eat the bread and dates I have carried, to try to get dry.

"Perhaps we should give them something to eat," said Jesus.

Andrew just stared at him. The rain had flattened his head covering so it was plastered against his forehead like a cap. "What? Even if we took all our treasury, everything that Mary and Joanna have brought, we could not feed all these people! And there is no place to buy anything. We are in a wilderness!"

"Well, what do we have?"

Andrew, flustered, looked into his pouch. "Stale bread, salted fish—that's all I have."

"And the rest of you?"

Startled, the disciples began pawing through their sacks to see what they had.

"Let us offer that," said Jesus. "We can only offer what we have." Then he added, in a manner unusual for him, "Remember that. You can never offer more than you have, but you should never apologize for it."

They heaped up their food in a common pile—dates, dried figs, flatbread, salted fish—and it was small indeed, compared with the horde that surrounded them.

"Let us offer it," said Jesus.

Each taking an armful of food, the disciples spread out and approached the waiting people. "This is all we have," they said.

As Mary held out her bundle, people snatched it away and it vanished. She expected people to start fighting over it, but they did not.

"Bless you!" one woman called. She shoved toward the front of the crowd and touched Mary's head. "Bless you!" Her touch seemed actually to confer the blessing her words spoke.

When they had finished distributing the little they had, the disciples gathered again near Jesus. As they watched, the crowds seemed satisfied—how, Mary could not imagine.

"We cared for them," said Andrew, in amazement. "That alone seemed to fill them."

Jesus just nodded. "The offering of the food means more than the food itself," he said. "People are dying for lack of interest, and the spirit is hungrier than the body. A word can mean more than a loaf of bread."

From the appreciative murmurs reaching Mary's ears, she knew he was right. The sincere gesture had spoken loudly; more loudly than the rumbling of stomachs.

The pounding rain and the cloud-veiled sky made darkness come down early. A few torches were lit in the crowd, but the rain quickly doused them. Instead of dispersing, however, the people gathered in knots, drew together, and then, suddenly, marched toward Jesus, resolute, unstoppable.

And now came the words, the startling words: "Our king!" they cried. "You are our king!"

Still they did not rush, but marched in orderly fashion across the oozing, dark field. "Our king!" they chanted. "Our king!"

Jesus seemed taken by surprise. He backed away. Still they kept coming, chanting, "Our king! Our king!"

Jesus faltered and drew farther back. He took refuge behind Mary and Andrew, as if he needed to collect his thoughts.

"They proclaim you," Mary said, faintly. She thought, fleetingly, No, no, do not leave us! Do not go to them!

"They do not know what they do," said Jesus. Still he stood rooted in indecision.

"You are our king, our promised Messiah!" they cried. "You must lead us! We have waited so long!"

The foremost of them were getting close to Jesus. These were earnest faces, men and women, brave enough to be in the front.

"Are you not of the house of David? We know you, we know you are the one! You will smash Rome, set us free!"

"We can wait no longer!" some young men near the forefront cried. "We came here to see, and we are satisfied! Yes, you are our warrior! You care for us! We will unite behind you, drive them out!" Their tramping footsteps grew nearer. "The day is here! The day is yours!"

Mary looked at Jesus and saw that his face was wooden, fixed, carved. But the carving was one of horror and repulsion.

Still the crowd kept coming. Only when they were dangerously near did Jesus step out to confront them.

Standing by himself in their path, he held up his hands. "Friends! Followers! You are mistaken! I will not lead you against Rome!" His voice was all but swallowed up in their chanting, "Our king our king our king."

"The Messiah!" they cried. "The Messiah! He will break the bonds of Rome, make us great again!"

"I cannot break the bonds of Rome," said Jesus. "Nor can any Messiah. There is earthly power, and heavenly power. The grip of the Romans on earthly power is supreme."

"We are promised a Messiah!" they yelled. "We want a Messiah!"

"Such a Messiah is impossible," said Jesus.

The crowd kept coming, but now it slowed. His word "impossible" had stunned them.

"Yes, impossible!" he cried. "Such a Messiah as you long for will never come. God is always the God of the present. The military Messiah is of the past." He watched them come to a halt. The failing light showed their robes and their figures but not their faces.

"The Messiah is God's anointed," said Jesus. "When he comes, he will be different from what you are looking for. God will use him for a new thing."

"You! You! You are that new thing!" they cried, advancing once again. They reached Jesus and attempted to lay hands on him. But he drew back to stand beside Mary and Andrew.

"Do not touch me," he said sternly, and somehow the force of his words stopped them.

"You must lead us!" they cried. "You must! Israel cries out for you!"

"No man can serve two masters," Jesus said. "For he will love the one and hate the other. I cannot serve as Israel's earthly leader and also serve God."

Even as he spoke, a dark line appeared at the edge of the gathering. Men in uniforms. Helmets. Armor. Antipas's men. On and on they came, pouring over the rim like water flowing.

Jesus looked up and saw them. "Ah. They are here. The forces of this world."

The crowd that had been advancing on Jesus to proclaim him Messiah now whirled to face the newcomers. Antipas's soldiers were coming, their spears horizontal, ready to attack.

They turned on the company, feinting and thrusting with their weapons. The people scattered and ran for cover, screaming in surprise as much as pain. This was supposed to be a secret place. Antipas's invasion here was an outrage, a shock; people believed his reach did not extend to these remote regions.

"Scum! Vermin!" the soldiers cried. "Do not think to escape us! All traitors must die!"

As they tramped forward, Jesus stood patiently waiting. When they drew close enough for him to speak, he said, "We have done nothing to merit this. I spoke to my followers, I distributed food, I told them I was no king."

Antipas's soldiers halted in front of him, their legs planted in the mud. "We heard that. But such gatherings are dangerous. King Antipas does not like them. It is not what is said, but the expectations people harbor."

"I cannot help that," said Jesus.

"Antipas thinks otherwise," the captain said. "He thinks you fan these expectations. If you do not desist, he will arrest you."

"On what grounds?" Jesus seemed unconcerned.

"Agitation," they said. "It makes no difference that you rejected the Messiah business. Any crowd-gathering is subversive."

"Even crowds gathered for charity?" asked Jesus.

"That above all," the captain said. "That criticizes Antipas. He has been generous with his charity, and to have people asking for more and turning to someone else—no, it cannot be permitted!"

"Am I free to go?" asked Jesus pointedly.

"Yes," the captain said reluctantly. "But we will be watching. And the first wrong thing you do"—he jerked his head southward—"you will go straight to Antipas." He gave the order, and the soldiers left the field, with a few backward glances, their feet making ugly slopping noises as they went.

The people, too, deflated by Jesus's rebuff of their offer to proclaim him king, soon followed the soldiers and left the field. The night was closing in, and the rain-washed steep paths would be dangerous in the dark. So they hurried away, and soon the vast field was empty, and the crowds were only a dream.

Jesus and his followers huddled under a makeshift tent set up to take advantage of a large oak on the edge of the field. There the ground was less wet. The disciples with the best cloaks stripped them off and used them to make the tent awning, draping one end over a low branch. Inside, the number of people generated enough heat to keep themselves warm, and Jesus, wearing his lighter wool mantle, spread it across the shoulders of John and James on either side of him.

"Now I have granted your wish," he said. "One at my right hand and one at my left." He laughed softly, but he seemed drained. "You got so angry, my dear Sons of Thunder, I thought the captain was in danger from you."

Big James just shook his head. "If I'd had a spear—"

"I wonder if you have heard anything I've said?" Jesus asked. "Violence is the way of *this* world, and we are not interested in this world."

"I don't think the people hear you clearly, either," said Mary. "Or Antipas. But how can they understand?"

Jesus nodded and spoke directly to her. "It is difficult. What is easy for you to grasp is not within reach of everyone."

"I suppose that means us!" Big James snapped. "So we're just too stupid to understand?"

"Why *do* you favor her?" Peter suddenly said. "What does she know and understand that the rest of us can't? Look, master. I've known her for years, and she's a good person, but she had the demons, and so now she has visions instead, but why does that give her wisdom? She seems . . . well, just like the rest of us!" He stopped to pause for breath. The pelting of the rain on the flimsy tent sounded like a tribal drum, thumping to emphasize his words.

No one spoke, which told Mary that they all agreed with Peter. He had voiced what they all felt. She felt deeply embarrassed, as if she had willfully tried to best all her fellows.

It isn't true! she thought. The visions and the voices weren't a ploy for me to gain attention and position. Jesus, tell them!

But Jesus just sat and looked from one face to another, as if he was waiting for someone else to speak. The rain was the only voice in the tent.

But . . . I did think that, since only I had the visions, I offered Jesus something the others did not, she admitted silently. And I did not want any of the others to have them. If someone else suddenly had started to have them, it would have threatened me.

"Prophets have visions," said Jesus at long last. "True visions are the mark of a true prophet. Peter, have you had any visions?"

"No," he admitted. "But visions alone do not signify greatness. Are not ordinary people sometimes granted visions?"

"Yes," said Jesus's mother, brushing her wet hair back off her cheek. "Even I have had visions. When I was younger—visions about you, my son. Faint ones, ones I never told you about, but they were visions. Does that make me a prophet, or someone holy?"

Jesus nodded. "*I* think you are holy," he said. "But I do believe that Mary has been granted some special spiritual gifts, not because of her own worthiness or wisdom but because that was God's own mysterious choice. He chooses someone, often someone who seems very ordinary. Moses complained that he was slow of speech. Gideon said he was the least in his tribe and within his whole family. Does God not pronounce, 'I will have mercy on whom I will have mercy, and I will have compassion on whom I will have compassion'?"

"Yes, but mercy and compassion are not the same as special privileges," said Peter. "After all, I might have compassion for a raven, but I don't dote on him."

Has it been that obvious that I wanted God to dote on me? Mary thought. She was acutely uncomfortable.

Jesus took what seemed forever before he answered. "In the coming Kingdom, we will all be God's treasures, as it was in Eden. But Mary has had more of what shapes a soul in her lifetime than you. What shapes a soul? Suffering. It is a sad fact that without suffering our spiritual eyes are often never opened. And Mary has had the demons, has been vilified, has lost her husband—both in his affections and in life. She has had her daughter taken away from her. Such things change a person, just as cut and seasoned wood is different from green. And so it is not just the visions."

"Are you saying we are green wood?" Peter looked hurt. He stood up and looked around the group.

"Comparatively, yes," said Jesus.

"Like this stupid fire we have outside, which just smolders and stinks because the wood is green?" Peter sounded incredulous.

"You should stop questioning Mary." Judas's controlled voice cut in. "You have no right to do so."

"Can't you see what's going on?" said Peter. "There should be no favorites!"

"Peter!" said Jesus. "I am a carpenter. Don't you think I understand about wood—green as well as aged? To call green wood useless makes no sense. All wood starts out green."

"Must I wait and wait until a long time passes and the green fades? I want to be useful now!" Peter begged him.

Jesus looked at him, a sadness crossing his face. "Oh, Peter," he said. "Now, when you are young, you dress yourself and go wherever you wish. But when you grow old, you will stretch out your hands, and someone else will dress you and lead you where you do not want to go."

Peter had opened his mouth to answer, but now he was left without words. This vision that Jesus described—whatever it predicted, Peter wished he had not heard it. Heavily, he sat back down.

A deep silence fell upon their company. Mary could hear everyone's breathing; she felt so uncomfortable that she wished she could get away instead of being imprisoned in this tent with these people who disliked her.

But they don't all dislike me, she told herself. Even Peter does not dislike me; he just dislikes what he thinks is my special position. She looked at Jesus's mother and at stout Joanna and hesitant Susanna. They don't dislike me; I have always felt close to them. Andrew, Philip, Nathanael—they have always been friendly. Even Simon seems fond of me and the others. Matthew and Little James and Thaddeus—I don't know them well, they keep to themselves. But I've never sensed any hostility from them. It's Peter, then. Just Peter, who is jealous of the visions. I should not feel awkward with all the others because of him.

But I do. The feelings of any one person affect the atmosphere of the whole. Just as . . . a little green wood causes a great deal of smoke.

"Now we should have our own meal," Jesus said, moving slightly on his crossed legs, as if he did not sense anything amiss. "I believe there may be some food left over. Does anyone have something to offer?"

Peter quickly began to rummage in his pack, keeping his head down. Everyone else followed suit, and to their surprise they found an assortment of food still there. One by one they crept up to Jesus and laid the food out for him to see. There were some small flat loaves of bread, some fig cakes, some grapes, and pieces of dried fish.

"Our own feast," Jesus said, smiling, and the warmth of his voice banished the awkwardness hanging over them. Faults and all, they were somehow still equally dear to him; he made them feel it.

"Friends, let us give thanks." He picked up a small piece of bread and broke it further. "For this, God our Father, we are grateful that you provided." He then held out the two small pieces, in his left and right hands, his strong carpenter's hands, and they were passed down to the waiting company. Each person tore the piece he received in half, and although there should have been nothing left by the time the bread reached Mary at the end of the line, she clasped a sizable piece. She looked up and down at the others and saw that they were trying hard not to react.

"Blessed be God, who always answers our needs," said Jesus. He was smiling, watching the expressions on their faces. It was as if he was teaching them: You can trust God to remember you. And he has no favorites. If he feeds the crowd, he will also feed you. "As for the ravens, they do not farm or store their food, but God feeds them. How much more will he feed you—Peter."

When Peter jerked his head at the sound of his name—almost cringing, as if he expected to be rebuked—Jesus said, "There is no need to worry. God loves you as much as the ravens. The hard part is remembering the opposite—he loves the ravens as much as you." He paused. "God reprimanded Job, saying, 'Who provides food for the raven when its young cry out to God and wander about for lack of food?' It wasn't Job."

Now the feeling in the miserable little tent changed to that of a royal banquet, as if they were reclining on the most exquisite couches, with gilded feet and silken cushions, in an exclusive company—as if this gathering were the most privileged one on earth. A strong sense of loving all of them swept over Mary, who had just felt so excluded. She looked over at Jesus, laughing and leaning against Big James and John on either side of him. Up and down the line everyone was smiling, and she saw Judas trying to catch her eye. Even he seemed relaxed and tolerant now.

As she turned to look at Jesus again, she saw that his face suddenly seemed to glow, like a rainbow in a dark cloud, and that his garments were shining. It hurt her eyes to look at them.

Without thinking, she moved her head and saw that most of the others were eating peacefully, their eyes on their food. But Peter was staring at Jesus, as was Big James and John. They were seeing what she had seen.

That is what her dream had foretold—the dazzling robe, the shining face. It had unfolded, and so soon.

Ꭷᏽ X L V 11 Ꭷᏽ

The gloom of the wintry sky hung over them as they walked briskly north. They were to journey to the upper reaches of the territory of Herod Philip, Antipas's brother, near Mount Hermon, withdrawing from Antipas's and the crowds' harassment.

This wild and hilly country, where the Jordan arose, was rich in trees, and streams tumbled down the slopes, sending spray as they fell. It was cool here, and far in the distance they could see the outline of Mount Hermon, already covered with snow. In spring, enough of it melted to swell the Jordan and raise the water levels in the Sea of Galilee.

I wish I could remember exactly what the scriptures said about Dan and Jeroboam, she thought. But there is one here who knows all those things—besides Jesus—and that is Thomas. Yes, I'll ask Thomas.

She sought him out to question him, noting how pleased he seemed that she thought him knowledgeable.

"It is a great blessing to know so much," she told him. "You can answer questions without needing outside help."

"It is not the pure blessing you imagine," he assured her. "It makes me too sure of my own interpretation sometimes. There can be a hundred—no, a thousand—ways of looking at a particular text. When you become set on only one, it is dangerous."

"Still, I wish I knew more." Now she had the chance to ask him. "What do you think of Jesus's interpretations? You must agree with them, but do you not feel some of them are surprising?" She wanted to say "shocking" but did not.

He thought for a moment before answering; Thomas was always

cautious. "As someone trained from boyhood in studying scriptures, I sometimes have to bite my tongue when he speaks. But he has an authority . . . and later, when I can turn over the text carefully in my mind, I realize that he has either seen more in it or gone beyond it to its true intention. And so I am always eager to hear what he says about a text. I wish he could speak on every single word." He gave a wistful sigh. "He would have to live a thousand years to do that."

His melancholy words touched her.

"Sometimes the texts share our yearning for things that we know can never be but that we hope for," Thomas went on. "As when, in Ezekiel, God says, 'I will put my Spirit in you and you will live.'" He paused. "I must trust that God will do this. I think Jesus can help show us how this can happen. I can't explain it! I just think he knows things . . ." His voice trailed off. "More than I know, with all my studies." Another pause. "That is why I joined him. To learn. And every day I do."

We all have our own reasons for being in this group, Mary thought.

"What are you two talking about so earnestly?" Judas strode up alongside them. He looked eager to join the conversation.

Thomas moved over to give Judas room. "We were just talking about why we were here. Why we came, and why we stayed. Why did you?"

Judas shrugged. "As if we could truly answer that." He glanced at both of them, trying to read their faces so he could gauge his answer. "We all heard what we needed to," he finally said.

"And what was that for you?" Thomas asked.

"He seemed to have all the answers," said Judas, so quickly the response was obviously rehearsed. "But where do you think he is taking us? I don't like this, it has a bad feeling, as if he is wandering aimlessly, hoping to attract more attention from the authorities. Why?"

"I don't know," said Thomas. "I agree, it feels dangerous."

"As a woman," Judas said, "surely you must be concerned for your safety." He moved closer to Mary, implying his protection.

"No more so than the men," she said. And that was true; the threat seemed indiscriminate. If anything, women would be more likely to be spared in an attack.

Judas moved yet nearer to her. "I've put the books in order," he said. "The contributions . . ."

As they walked farther north, they passed into pagan territory. An occasional shrine was visible from their path, rearing up amid the leaves, honoring Apollo or Aphrodite or who knew what god? What had once been the territory of an Israelite tribe, the tribe of Dan, now irrevocably belonged to the Greek world. It was part of the overall loss of glory after the invasions of the Assyrians and the Babylonians and the Greeks and the Romans. The prophets said that was the punishment for the Israelites' worshiping idols. Now, when they no longer wanted the idols in their land, they were forced to endure them against their will.

On the third day, they reached the site of the ancient city of Dan. A newer Roman settlement spread out to one side, but the hill itself was overgrown.

"We are here, Peter!" Jesus said, embracing his shoulders. "The place you wanted to reach."

"It was farther away than I thought," Peter said. "But my dream is fulfilled! To come to the northern extent of Israel in Solomon's times . . ." He looked around, his eyes taking it all in. "So this was it. The boundary of the land."

"Yes," Jesus said. "In those days, when we were mighty, foreign kings would halt here and tremble in wonder."

All around them, the woods waited, silent except for birdcalls. A silver tongue of a stream—soon to join the Jordan—gushed out of the thickets.

"We may need swords to hack our way through," Jesus said. And it was true, the woods seemed to present a solid wall before them.

"We have them!" said Simon, raising his at arm's length.

"Yes!" Judas echoed him, brandishing his.

They pressed forward, Simon and Judas clearing the way before them. The quiet all around seemed profound, as if the woods had captured the old site and guarded it for a great long time, and were determined not to yield it up. As they cleared the path, they were going uphill, ever uphill.

The sun was setting as they finally emerged into a clearing. Someone had been here recently. Mary could see the signs of a campfire, even some footprints in the damp soil. So people still came here in stealth, compelled by something on this hilltop.

Cautiously, they emerged onto a large paved area. It was of stunning size. Mary could see—almost, in her mind, not quite a true vision, not yet—the people from long ago who had thronged this place, holy to them. At the far end of the pavement was a flight of broad stairs leading up to what clearly was a "high place," an altar.

The light was fading, caressing the steps and the empty platform. The trees and shrubs surrounding the place rustled their leaves, shivering as if a goddess had directed them to move in unison; they danced and obeyed.

Jesus stood at the lowest step.

"We will rest here," he said. "In this place that was part of the great sin of Jeroboam." His light wool mantle, the one his mother had given him back in Nazareth, glowed a rich rose in the dying light.

"Thomas, you know the scriptures," Jesus said. "After supper, you can tell us about this place."

After they had eaten, they hunched around their campfire, which did little to illuminate the dark, featureless platform nearby.

"Tell us," said Jesus. He nodded toward Thomas.

"It is a sordid tale," Thomas said. One that he had already recounted to Mary on the path here.

"Tell it anyway," said Jesus. "Perhaps the evil that still lingers here needs to hear it."

Thomas related the whole sorry history of this site, of its idolatry and apostasy. In the generation after Solomon, the kingdom had split. Rehoboam, Solomon's son, ruled the southern land of Judah, and Jeroboam, an overseer of Solomon's building projects, ruled the northern one, Israel.

"Since the Temple and the legitimate priesthood were all in Rehoboam's land, Jeroboam had to invent his own rival ones," he explained. "He did so in Dan and Bethel, making worship centers with golden calves, and he created his own priests and rituals.

"He had defied God and his Law, and as a result, the entire northern kingdom was destroyed, and along with it, ten of the twelve tribes of Israel."

"Thus Jeroboam and his kingdom perished," said Jesus.

"Not soon enough!" cried Thomas. "It took two hundred years! And in the meantime, the kings who succeeded him became more and more wicked. Did not Ahab also build an altar here?"

"God tried to warn them through his prophets, but they would not listen," said Jesus. "Nor do we. Now such means are not enough. That is why he will bring this present age to an end. When the wickedness has finally reached its height. As it has."

The wind was rising, making the treetops murmur. All around them were great oaks with wide-spreading branches, very low to the ground. It was as if the spirits of the idols were lingering, listening, warning them: We are still here, this is our place, be careful what you say.

Over and over the prophets preached against sacrificing to idols "under every spreading oak," Mary remembered. Now it seemed all too real—the low branches inviting altars and intimacy, bidding you to come in under their shelter. The false gods and their idols fancied high places, staking out a claim on them. She shivered, feeling the animosity of the old gods brushing her cheek as they passed in the night, and remembering Ashara.

They bedded down, the men keeping together, the women likewise. This time they huddled a little closer, feeling the need to do so in this alien place. Mary had little trouble falling asleep, for the faint echoes of any gods remaining here were nothing compared to the ferocious demons that she had once grappled with. But her dreams were disturbing: There was a fleeting image of Jesus being attacked and beaten and bleeding. And then, out of the darkness and silence, came some figures, grandly dressed in antique costumes. They took their places on the platform, which now had an altar upon it, and one man, more richly attired than the others, in a green-and-gold-embroidered gown, began addressing the company. The way he spoke, using many words Mary did not recognize, with others pronounced oddly, made it difficult to understand him. He gestured toward a covered object, and someone whisked off the covering, and it was a glittering animal, partly kneeling and partly rising on its forelegs. It had horns and the familiar snout of a bull. It must be the golden calf, and the figure must be Jeroboam himself, somehow taking form again in her mind and manifesting himself. He was still here, then. Mary sat up, gasping, and opened her eyes to rid herself of him. She looked at the empty platform, calfless now, silent except for the scurrying of small animals and the whisper of the weeds growing nearby.

He's gone, he's gone, he's gone to dust and powder, Mary reassured herself, and his golden calf along with him. He does not exist.

Later, in the very early morning, she saw Peter pacing back and forth by himself down on the pagan platform, appearing almost to float in the blue-purple shadows of the high place. The mists from the surrounding woods and the floor of the platform made it look as if incense were streaming from hidden censers.

She rose and went to him. He looked so agitated, and this ominous, oppressive place made her feel protective of him. He did not notice her approach until she was right behind him and touched his shoulder. The mist swirled around her, as high as her knees. "Peter, what is it? May I help?" Somehow she sensed he, too, had had a dream, or a vision.

"Help?" He turned around to face her. His face showed anguish and sorrow. "I do not know . . ."

"Did you have a dream? A vision? Even a voice or a feeling?" Had Jeroboam come to him, too?

Now he seemed to awaken, revert to his old self. "Yes," he finally said. He paused a long time. "But I cannot reveal it to you. I know you think you have a special insight or wisdom or vision. But I cannot trust it. I cannot forget the time when you were so weak and afflicted with demons—and the truth is, if Andrew and I had not taken you safely to the desert, you would have died! So I cannot believe—forgive me, but I cannot—that you are above us all in spiritual wisdom!"

"Of course you cannot," she said. "But let me try to help, in whatever way—"

"So I will set you a task," he said. He did not seem in need of comfort after all, and she regretted seeking him out. "Tell me what the vision or dream I had was. Then I shall believe you are favored with spiritual knowledge."

"Only God can do that," she said.

"Then ask God to reveal it to you," said Peter. "He will surely do that, if you are in his confidence." He looked at her challengingly.

"Peter, I only came to help," she said.

"Then help! Tell me what the vision was!"

"How can that help? You already know what it was. My telling you can add nothing to it. Better that we should interpret it."

"No! I cannot trust your interpretation, unless you can convince me that God *does* reveal things to you. So you must describe to me my vision."

He had set a test for God, not for her. She did not care whether she could see Peter's vision. She did not care if she could see any visions at all; in fact, she would rather not have this gift. So let me fail this test! she cried to God. Yes, let me fail it, and set me free!

"I will ask God to reveal it," she finally said. "I cannot know when he will choose to do so—if indeed he does choose to. He may not."

Peter nodded at the last sentence. "That is the most likely out-come," he said pointedly.

Gathering her robe around her, she left Peter. She should have felt insulted, but she did not.

Peter distrusts me, she thought. But why should he not? What if I were as he thinks me—an impostor, an inspired guesser? I hate this gift I have! Let it vanish, as suddenly as it came! She found a half-overgrown path that led away, to the brow of the hill that fell sharply and overlooked a wide level place, and there she rested.

My Father, God, she finally prayed, Peter has had a vision, perhaps sent by you. He wishes me to see it, to test me and know whether you truly reveal things to me. If it is your will, show it to me. I do not re-quest this or want this except to glorify you.

She sighed with relief. God would not reveal it, and she could fi-nally shrug off all these strange revelations that had been granted to her. She was ready for them to stop. Perhaps they were after all just an aftermath of the demons, of her heightened sensibility, and as she re-turned to her normal life and way of thought, they would fade away.

But before these thoughts could even finish, she was suddenly vis-ited with pictures: pictures of Peter in . . . it must be Rome, the clothes looked Roman . . . being chased and captured and then tied to some crossbar. But he was much older. His hair was gray and sparse, and his big frame was pale and weak. And there was something else, a rotund man wearing a laurel wreath . . . a Roman emperor, but it was not Tiberius. She knew Tiberius from his coins, and this was not Tiberius.

But what needed interpretation? It was all so clear. Was Peter say-ing anything? She willed the picture to return, and listened very care-fully to the voices. "Another way," he was saying, "I am not worthy." That was when they—the Roman soldiers—turned him around and upside down on that big beam of wood.

I can tell him that, she thought. I can tell him those words. "An-other way. I am not worthy." Perhaps he will know what they mean.

She sat for a long time in that place, savoring her aloneness with God, disappointed that he had not removed the burden of the visions from her. Yet, if that was the price of being called to him . . . ?

∞∞∞

Back in the camp, people were up, dressed, and ready for the day. Peter was busy rolling his blanket up and talking loudly to Andrew, as if nothing had happened. Time enough to speak to him later.

Jesus was nowhere to be seen. Perhaps he had stolen away, taken private moments to pray or gather his thoughts. The rest of the group were milling, awaiting his direction.

The mist had rolled away, and now the woods and the pagan altar did not seem so mysterious or threatening. The morning brought reassurance and safety.

Finally, Jesus returned, and he seemed refreshed and invigorated. "What do you speak of?" he asked them.

"Master," said Peter, voicing the question they had all been asking in their minds, "why have you brought us here?"

Jesus thought for a long moment. "Because it is far away from everything. Even Galilee is too connected to the powers in Jerusalem and Rome. I needed to think—to think about what I must do, and where I am needed."

"And have you decided that?" Judas's voice was clear.

"Yes, I fear I have." Jesus's voice was low. "Would that I had not."

"And what have you decided?" Judas asked.

"I must go to Jerusalem," Jesus said, quickly. "And what will happen there . . . You know that Jerusalem kills its prophets." He waited a moment. "I can expect no less."

"No, master!" Peter rose and rushed over to him, laying hands on him as if that would prevent it. "No, you must not! We will not permit that!"

Jesus pulled away. A look of utter horror passed over his face. "Go away, Satan!" he commanded, in the same tone he used in exorcisms.

Stunned, Peter fell back.

"Satan, be silent!" Jesus cried. "You see as men see, not as God wishes!"

Peter had fallen to one knee and put his hands up as if to ward off a blow. "But, master," he said at last, "I *am* a man. I cannot see as God sees. I only know that I wish to protect you from anything or anyone that would harm you."

Jesus shut his eyes, clenched his fists, and seemed to be praying. After a long silence, he uncurled his fingers and let his hands hang down by his side. "Peter," he said. "Who do men say that I am?"

"Some say John the Baptist restored to life!" cried Thomas, out of turn.

"Some say Elijah!" said Andrew, unbidden.

"But who do you say I am?" Jesus looked into Peter's eyes.

"I say . . . I say . . ." He groped for words. "I say you are the one we have been awaiting, the anointed one, the one who ushers in the Kingdom of God. . . ." He knelt at Jesus's feet. "Perhaps, even, you are chosen by God, as his son, in that you understand him, understand his mind better than anyone else now living. . . ."

Jesus stared back at Peter and grasped his shoulders. "Ah," he said. "This has been revealed to you by God, my Father in heaven." He bent down and drew Peter up. "Now arise." He looked around at everyone. "I must tell you all, I am unsettled about this. There is yet more to be revealed."

They shuffled about on the platform, looking all around them, at the trees and the paving stones and their own feet, anywhere rather than at Jesus. They could not bear to see the uncertainty in his eyes. He had always been so rock-solid, so sure of his actions. If Jesus faltered now, what would become of them?

"I will await direction," Jesus finally announced. "I will not move until I have it."

"But—in this place?" Judas sounded alarmed. He, too, had felt its evil influence. In fact, this morning his eyes looked clouded, different.

"It is good to face the enemy," Jesus said. "If Satan is powerful here, then we need to make our plans in his shadow, not in innocent sunshine."

Had they been there only for scenery or rest, the beautiful area would have been ideal. The hill where the high place had been established almost a thousand years ago commanded a magnificent view of Mount Hermon, and in the days they spent there, the winter rains held back, sparing them. The trees on the slopes were remnants of the original forests covering the land—oaks, terebinths, cypresses, rearing their crowns majestically, casting their shadows over the entire forest.

As they waited on Jesus, Mary sought out Peter to tell him that she had received an insight into his dream. His face changed when she described the Roman soldiers and the thick beam of wood. And when she repeated his words, he seemed to falter and needed to reach out to a nearby tree trunk to steady himself.

"You heard those words?" he whispered.

"I do not know what they mean," she said. "But, yes, I did hear them."

"What alarms me is, I do not know what they mean, either. And the soldiers . . . the binding . . ." He shuddered. "But, whatever it was, it is far in the future. I was old." He tried to reassure himself.

"Did not Jesus say something about your future? 'When you grow old, you will stretch out your hands, and someone else will dress you and lead you where you do not want to go'? Could this be what he meant?" Mary asked.

"Oh, God!" cried Peter. "Could it be . . . Were they executioners?" His voice grew thin with fear. "I merely thought it meant I would be a senile old man, led around by my family." He looked as if he was about to cry. "Not to be executed! By Romans!"

"Peter," said Mary, "these are just shadows that we saw." What, then, did her sight of Jesus being beaten mean? "It is beyond us to know anything more about them."

"Except . . . God revealed it to you," Peter said. "So it is proved to me: your visions and insights are real. I must respect them. I will not question you again. Forgive me, I had to be sure."

"And I honor you for that. The scriptures are full of false prophets. I do not wish to be among them. The truth is, I do not wish to be among the prophets at all—true or otherwise!"

"God has chosen otherwise," said Peter. "He is a strange companion." Then he burst out laughing. "How disrespectful that sounds!"

Mary laughed, too. "No. It only means that you know him well enough to be on familiar terms with him."

She needed to speak with Jesus. She needed to tell him of her dream about him. He had been rising early and stealing away before any of them awakened, and only returning in the late evening, speaking gently to them as they sat for the last few minutes around the campfire. His thoughts and conclusions he kept to himself, but each night he seemed more preoccupied and sorrowful. They dreaded hearing his message, whenever he would finally decide to share it.

Hastily she flung off her coverings, strapped on her sandals, and followed him. She rushed across the ancient platform, stumbling slightly on some of the weed clumps. It was he, she thought, observing his distinctive walk. She followed him onto the pathway leading through the woods.

He was moving slowly along the path, picking his way carefully in the dark. With a burst, she caught up to him, grasped his arm.

"Mary."

"Master." She dropped her hand. "I have been wanting to speak to you alone." Now that she had seized the opportunity, she felt tongue-tied.

Jesus just waited. He did not say, "What is it?" or "Speak up!"

"I know this is a difficult time for you . . . a turning point . . ."

"Yes."

"I needed to tell you that I had another of those dreams, or visions, or whatever they are. You were in it. I must tell you what I saw."

He sighed. "Yes. I must know." In the darkness she could not see his face, only hear his voice.

She quickly recounted her impressions—Jesus in someone's hands, beaten, bleeding. Being attacked.

"Could you see where this was?" he asked. That was all he said.

"From the background . . . it was in a city someplace. It was crowded. There were buildings all around."

"Jerusalem." Jesus pronounced the word almost exultantly. "Jerusalem."

"Master," she said, "I do not know that. I cannot identify the place, or what was truly happening as I watched."

"It was Jerusalem," he said. "I know that. And I will die there."

She knew better than to contradict him. She could not bear it if he turned on her and said, "Go away, Satan!" as he had to Peter. But with all her being she wished to argue against him. And so she merely said, "You were not being killed, only . . . hurt."

"You saw only the beginning of it," he said. "You were spared the hideous ending." The slowly growing light made his face recognizable. "More and more has been revealed to me in these last days," he said. "Some things so ugly I can barely force myself to confront them. But I see now . . . I grasp . . . that my first understanding was—was incomplete. There will indeed be an ending, and God will act to usher in a new age, but it will not be as simple as I thought. I am an integral part of it, not just an announcer of it, as John was. Somehow, my going to Jerusalem, to the heart of the kingdom, where the Temple is—the place sacred to God—is necessary. I don't quite understand it, but this is what God has unveiled to me."

"But why? What must happen there?"

"I cannot answer that," he said. Now she could see his face clearly. His eyes were troubled, confused. "I only know I must obey."

"Obey what?"

"God has told me I must go to Jerusalem during the Passover. Do you remember when you went there as a child?" His tone changed abruptly, and the question seemed a superficial, social one.

"Yes," she said. "But I only remember the crowds, the size of the Temple, the blinding white stone, and the gold decoration."

"Did you feel nothing holy?"

"If I did, it has not remained with me," she said. "Forgive me."

"If you did not, perhaps you sensed what was coming." His voice grew distressed. "Or perhaps a child can sense better than others if true holiness is present."

"But I was very young."

"All the more reason." He sounded resolute. "The Temple and its corrupt priesthood have been rejected by God," he said. "In a few years, not one stone of it will stand upon another."

In spite of herself, she gasped. The Temple was an enormous structure, it seemed as solid as a mountain. "No!" But the vision she had had . . .

"Yes. There will be nothing left of it." He turned and took her by the shoulders, gently. "I told you, this present age is coming to an end. And the reckoning will begin in Jerusalem and spread from there."

"The Temple—we were told it was God's own dwelling place. Does that mean he will flee and desert us?"

"He will never desert us," said Jesus, authoritatively. "But what it means, I do not know. Only that I must obey the summons and go to it. And when I am there, I must act as God directs me."

"The vision I had—"

"It was real. We just do not know the frame that surrounds it." He took her hands in his. "Thank you for revealing it to me. And thank God for letting you see these things." He tightened his grip on her hands. "And thank God for letting you come to me and speak freely."

She felt a deep excitement and honor at his words, as if a pure spring were welling up and bubbling over inside her.

He recognized whatever it was that bound them. He was acknowledging it, even thanking God for it. She could not name what it was, it was too special for any name, it just *was*, and—oh!—God had led her here, had created her just for this.

When the words did come to her mind, "Jesus is mine!" was the form they took.

The exultation of possession surged through her. He was hers, he regarded her differently from everyone else, he honored her above the others, they were both of like minds. The revelations were granted to them alike, different but completing each other. She was able to offer him something no one else could.

He loved her. Now she knew that. Why could she still not speak? She put her hand up to her throat as if it could force words out. She needed to speak, to say something. But she just kept looking at him, at his long face with the deep-set eyes. Everything she ever was or had ever wanted seemed to be in that face.

"Mary, not that way." It was Jesus who spoke. "Do not listen to Satan." He sounded almost defeated. "I expected his opposition. Yes, I expected it. But not in this form. And from both you and Peter. He spoke to you, and you listened." He paused, then said gently, "But, Mary, listen to *me* now, and not Satan. You know he attacks us through our gifts, and you have many gifts. He is using them as a source of pride for you."

Pride? she thought. I am not proud!

But as she looked into his eyes, she felt ashamed. He could see the secret joy she had when she knew more than the others, or was granted a revelation that was barred to them, even though she pretended to herself she did not want it.

"Forgive me," she finally said, feeling shrunken. All excitement had fled now, and she wanted to slink away.

"I do not mean to be harsh," Jesus said. "It is always easier to see Satan working in others than in ourselves. Mary, remember that he only attacks those who are trying to do good. It is no indictment of you."

But it was, of course. He disliked her pride; he had seen it; he had unmasked it. It would make it impossible for him to love her—that way.

"But it is not your pride that Satan is most concerned with," said Jesus.

No! Let there not be more, let him not see any further into me! Mary begged.

"His bigger aim is to take that which is most natural and make it a stumbling block for us." Jesus paused, as if reluctant to go on. "That is, the love of a man for a woman and a woman for a man. Mary, I know that you love me."

She was mortified. For what was clearly going to follow was not, "And I love you, too." She wanted to run away from him, flee from this shame. If he could not return them, why did he have to expose her feelings like this?

But why deny it? He knew everything anyway. What could be worse than what he had already said? "Yes, I do," she said. "And you love me as well. I know it!" she added defiantly, although she no longer believed it.

"Yes, I do love you," he said. "I love your courage and your integrity, your insights and your quietness, and if I were going to have a life that went in another direction, I would choose you to be beside me on that path. As it is, I still choose you to walk the path with me. But it will be a unique path, not the one open to others of marriage, children, home. I cannot belong to anyone that way. But Satan knows how difficult it is for me, and he constantly reminds me of what I must forgo."

"I don't understand! Why can't you take that path?"

"Because the path that has been chosen for me is one I must walk alone; at a certain branching of the path, there is only a foothold for one."

"Chosen for you! You've chosen it for yourself." She wanted to strike back at him now, cover up her own confused feelings. "You just tease us all, with all your mysterious allusions and hints, and we keep following, but we don't know where we're going or even why we're here!"

"It isn't easy for me, either. At least you have each other."

"If you have no companion, it's because you—it's not as if—"

"It is what I have chosen, as you said. It does not mean I do not value the companionship I am allowed."

"I don't—I don't understand." She fought to keep her voice from breaking.

"It will all become clear to you. Then my words will come back to you, and you will understand. For now, understand that I *do* love you. But not as Joel did. Don't desert me! I will need your strength. Please!"

She tried to turn away. She wanted to run away, to run far, far away.

"Please, Mary, please stay with me! Without you—the rest cannot endure."

"The rest—the rest—what are they to me, truly?" All that bound them together was Jesus. And without him . . .

"You were baptized into brotherhood together. They need you. They *will* need you."

She didn't want to be needed, she wanted someone to fulfill her needs. She did not reply, and started to move back toward the camp. The others would be getting up now, looking for them.

"I have to go to Jerusalem. That is where I must speak, in the heart of God's sacred place. I must go, even if I must go alone." He sounded plaintive, as if he were begging her to understand, to promise to stay the course.

She turned away and left him standing on the platform. Her crushed feelings were so great she could not bear to look upon him another moment.

ᴔ X L V I I I ᴔ

As they prepared to leave Dan, Mary kept silent. She felt that her face must be bright red—from anger? shame?—and so she tried not to look at anyone, lest someone read her countenance. The stinging sensation of being rejected smarted like a slap. Rejection? Of course that was what it was, in spite of Jesus's bland and soothing words. She had exposed herself to him, revealed her deepest longing to be his alone, for him to also be hers. He had backed away, said it could never be. Now he knew her need, and neither of them could ever forget it. It would always be between them.

No one else even noticed her mood. They were all busy talking and gathering things up, wondering aloud where they would go next. Everyone wished to leave this haunted place. But to go where?

Jesus seemed distracted, distant. "We will stay here in Philip's territory until Passover," he said. "Let us go on to the vicinity of his city. It is quite near here."

"Do you mean Caesarea Philippi?" Peter asked. "Surely we won't go into the city itself!"

"Why not?" asked Jesus. His face was unreadable, and for that instant Mary hated it. That was his way: lead people on, get them to blurt out something; say nothing himself, just let others expose themselves, parade out their ideas. It suddenly occurred to her that he never instigated an encounter with anyone; people always had to seek him out first. The sick, the poor, the needy, they have to come to him, throw themselves on his mercy. *As I did!*

"It's large, it's teeming with foreigners, and we don't belong there!" answered Peter, resolutely.

"Perhaps that's exactly where we belong," said Jesus.

"But . . . it's expensive!" Peter said. "The rooms—the food—"

"We have means," said Jesus.

I suppose he means me! thought Mary.

"I think it is a misuse of funds." The distinctive voice of Judas rang out. "True, we may have means, but is this how we should spend them? The poor—"

"So you're concerned for the poor, Judas?" Simon spoke. "This is the first time I've heard of it."

"I think going into Caesarea Philippi is a waste of money," Judas said to Jesus, ignoring Simon. "We can camp outside and save ourselves this expense. Unless"—he nodded—"you wish to speak to people in Caesarea Philippi. In that case—"

"But they are Gentiles!" cried Thomas. "Why speak to them? Is not your message to Israel only? What meaning can your message have to them?"

"The Messiah is only for the children of Israel!" said Peter, stoutly. "It can have no meaning to outsiders. It is part of our tradition, no one else's."

Jesus stood on the uneven ground above the haunted pagan platform. "Perhaps . . . but the reckoning will come for them as well. Should they not be warned? The prophets included all the other nations in their indictment, but they also offered repentance. Perhaps we have been too limited."

"What are you saying? That Gentiles are also to be called?" Thomas looked indignant. "They are filthy, unclean peoples!"

"But when God condemns a people, he also offers them salvation," said Jesus slowly. "He sent Jonah to preach to the people of Nineveh. Amos warned the surrounding nations. I must ask God."

So now he is concerned about this, thought Mary. Now he will forget about me, and the things we talked about in the early dawn.

Should I be thankful for this, or feel slighted?

She chose—or, rather, could not help choosing—the latter. I know it is beneath me, she told herself. He has a lofty mission. He should address himself to that. I must not hinder it. She knew all that, but she burned with disappointment and envy—even of the Gentiles, about whom he now seemed suddenly concerned.

They set out walking, trudging along toward Caesarea Philippi. Coming down off the mound that had once been the city of Dan, denounced by Amos eight hundred years ago, took the better part of the morning.

When they emerged onto the flat ground, they all felt better, relieved to leave the memories and spirits of that cursed place behind.

Along the path there were numerous pagan shrines, and Mary saw some of the disciples tugging at Jesus's sleeve and asking about them. For herself, she kept well in the back, away from Jesus.

"What troubles you?" Mary heard the unmistakable low voice of Jesus's mother.

She could never tell her!

"Nothing troubles me except the uncertainty," Mary replied evasively.

"Yes . . . the uncertainty." The elder Mary pulled up alongside her. "I fear something. Something coming." She was breathing heavily. Mary realized that, for Jesus's mother, this trip was a physical challenge as well as a spiritual one. She had probably never undertaken such a long journey.

"Why did you leave your home and seek to join him?" Mary had to ask. It was the supreme question they all had to ask, and each answer would be different.

Jesus's mother thought for a moment, turning the words over in her mind. "I knew from the time he was born that he had a special calling or mission. And when he embarked on it, I needed to be there, to see it. I came a little late to it, but I am here." She paused, catching her breath. Mary slowed down, to allow the older woman to walk comfortably with her.

"You are blessed. Your son allowed you to join him. There are not many grown sons who would do that."

"I know." Jesus's mother looked at her. Mary was struck once again by her subdued beauty as well as her forthrightness. She walked resolutely behind her son, asking nothing but to share his fortune, whatever it might be.

What a difference from the women in *my* family, she thought, enviously. They have kept me even from my daughter, whom they do not love.

They spent the winter on the outskirts of Caesarea Philippi, a city of great beauty, with its Roman-style forum, its wide streets, and its fountains and marble statues. In spite of its worldliness, they were captivated by the place, and were beginning to feel more at home in it when Jesus suddenly announced that he was taking them to the springs nearby, where water gushed out of underground caves and formed the beginning of the Jordan, an area the Greeks called sacred to Pan.

They now knew better than to question or argue, but it seemed a very strange place to lead them. As they walked obediently along behind him, they talked quietly with one another, asking the question that was turning into a refrain: what did this mean?

The rains of winter had finally abated, and signs of spring were everywhere—a softness in the air, skies as blue as faience, and wild almond trees, the earliest to bloom, showing their white blossoms in the woods, set off by the tender green of new leaves. Farther south, back in Galilee, the season would be ahead of them. And in Judaea, in the area that surrounded Jerusalem, the winds might already be hot, blowing in from the desert. As they walked the path toward the springs, birds were calling, knowing nothing but delight in the season that lay ahead.

But for us, what lies ahead? Mary was apprehensive. She did not want them to go to Jerusalem, did not want any of the visions to have a chance of coming true.

It was noon when they came to an open area under a craggy cliff face. The sun was caressing the face of the cliff, throwing its light deep into a myriad of niches carved into the stone that housed idol after idol. Each arch was shaped like a seashell, opening to reveal its treasure.

The statues were beautiful. Exquisitely carved, their graceful hands held cornucopias, staffs, spears, and bows, and their perfect faces smiled out at their worshipers, who were thronging toward them and milling in front of a large grotto with a mawlike opening.

"Let us stand here and look," said Jesus, leading them to where they could see the niches, the devotees before them, and the small temple to one side, where goats were tethered. Their thin bleats sounded like an arcane musical instrument, something to signal initiates of a secret sect.

"Here it is—their temple. Remember it when we come to our own Temple in Jerusalem," said Jesus. "Look. There are the goats ready for sacrifice. Here are the pilgrims, come to see and feel something holy. Here are the gods, looking down with approval. Things made out of stone and carved with human hands, which they then pray to—as if idols have power beyond the hands that created them."

"Yes!" Thomas suddenly interrupted. "Like Isaiah said—people who make idols take a piece of wood, carve half of it, bow down to it, and then throw the other half onto the fire to bake bread with. Fools!"

"They would claim that they aren't worshiping the wood itself, but just a representation of a god who lives elsewhere," said Judas. "They are not that simple-minded. Isaiah was very witty, but he underestimated them. And it is never wise to underestimate your enemies."

"Well said, Judas," said Jesus. "And as for our differences, although we have no statues in the Temple, we have a sanctuary that represents the presence of God. It is hard to distinguish the goats at our Temple from the ones here. Or the pilgrims who come partly for the journey and partly for religious reasons. I wonder, could an outsider detect any difference between us and them?" With a sweep of his arm, he indicated the entire setting before them.

The golden color of the cliff, its niches, the tawny flagstones on the gathering place before them—all emitted a feeling of deep, dozing peace, warm in the sun, requiring nothing beyond appreciation and an indulgence of the senses. This Greek religion was sophisticated in every sense, refined and pleasing and undemanding.

"Zeus, Athena, Hera, Aphrodite, Artemis—they are all happy in their niches," said Judas, nodding.

"I'd like to smash them!" said Simon, his old Zealotry flaring. "Yes, take a club and smash them!"

"But the main god here is Pan," said Jesus, ignoring him. "It's in this grotto that they sacrifice goats to Pan. And out of the grotto flows a spring that goes on into the Jordan. And the Jordan is holy to us."

"They pollute our holy water with these obscene rites!" said Thomas.

"Is that what it means?" said Jesus. "Or is it the other way around? Does the fact that the Jordan has been sanctified to us in our history, from Joshua to John the Baptist, wipe out the pagan rites at its source? Does holiness spread, or does iniquity contaminate? Think carefully on it."

So he was not going to tell them. Mary wondered why he did this, teasing them with questions and then refusing to deliver the answers, which he surely knew.

"My friends—and now I must call you friends, not followers or disciples, but friends, for so you all truly are—we are ready to set out for our journey, like the Jordan itself," Jesus went on. "As the Jordan flows from its source into the great Salt Sea, through thickets and desolate wastes out of which there is no outlet, so for me there will be no outlet from Jerusalem. Like the Jordan, I will end in the place I seek from here."

"Then let us also go, there to die with you!" said Thomas.

Jęsus, strangely enough, did not contradict him.

Were they all to die? Is that what Jesus was telling them? Mary did not know if she would have the courage. Or, more than that, whether she would even want to have it.

Jesus beckoned for them to follow him to a more private place, away from the temple site. A grove of willows formed an arbor where they could gather.

"Judas, do you have the pens and paper you use in keeping the accounts?" Jesus asked him.

Judas nodded. He began fumbling in his sack. As he looked up, Mary saw, once again, the dark, veiled sense of something in his eyes.

"I think, my friends, that it might be wise if you addressed a few words to those you left behind," Jesus said. "Judas has the blank paper for you. If there is anything you wish to say to anyone elsewhere, now is the time to do so."

He means our last words! Mary's hand instinctively sought the talisman from Elisheba around her neck.

"But, master," said Peter, "you said we were to leave all behind us."

"Yes, Peter, I did say that the old life must be abandoned when you begin the new. But many did not have a chance to say a proper farewell, and that is what you should do now."

A final farewell! Because later we cannot. Because . . . "Then let us also go, there to die with you!"

"I have no one to write to," said Judas. "But I will be pleased to take dictation for anyone who wishes to write but cannot."

"I will also," said Mary. They spoke quickly to smooth over the embarrassment anyone might feel at being unable to write.

Jesus withdrew to the banks of the little stream, leaving them alone with one another.

"I—I need to write to Mara," said Peter. "Can you help me?" He sat down next to Mary. She was surprised that he would seek her, a woman, rather than Judas. But, then, he had known her longer, and better.

"Of course." She smoothed out the ragged piece of papyrus—not the best grade, just the kind used for routine bookkeeping—and nodded to him to begin.

"Write, 'My dear wife,'" he whispered. "Say, 'I trust that you and your mother have been well. Since we left Capernaum, we have traveled a great deal, preaching to large crowds and healing many. Now we are on our way to Jerusalem, where we will celebrate Passover.'" He paused, letting her catch up with him. "Oh, this is hard!" he said. "It seems I must either tell everything, or tell nothing."

"There isn't space to tell everything," Mary said, wistfully.

"No, of course not. Well, then. 'I will pray for you at the Temple, and please know I am thinking of you all the while. Your husband, Simon bar-Jonah.' This does not even sound like me, I'm afraid," he said. "But I just—I don't know what to say. I don't want to alarm her with talk of danger."

"I think just the greeting, coming from you, is enough. That is all she will want."

John had his head down and was scribbling furiously on his paper. His brother, Big James, stood beside him, muttering, "One of us writing to Mother is enough. I won't write Father!"

The elder Mary came and sat next to Mary. "Would you look at this for me? I can read so much better than I can write." She held out the small piece of paper.

To my dear son James—

I found Jesus near Capernaum and have been with him ever since. I rejoice in my heart that I made the journey and joined him, and I pray that you can find it in yours to put aside the anger you have for both of us. God loves you no less than Jesus, nor do I love you less than Jesus. There are no words to say how much you mean to me. We are going to Jerusalem for Passover, and I will pray for your peace and health there.

Your loving mother

"This would melt the heart of anyone who breathes," said Mary, handing her back the paper.

"I do not seek to melt it, only reach it," said his mother, with a sigh.

Susanna took her place and asked Mary if she would help her write to her husband. "I want so much to explain it to him," she said.

Mary smiled, but it was a sad smile. Susanna sounds the way I did when I tried so hard to reach Joel, she thought. "Yes, of course," she said. "It can be short. Remember, I helped you write one already."

"But we don't know if he ever received it," said Susanna.

"No. As Jesus says, we deliver the message, but we cannot know where it goes."

Mary felt her eyes pricking as she thought of the right words to leave with Elisheba. Her sadness hung over her like a cloud, robbing her of both thought and feeling. Consumed by the thought that she would never see her beloved daughter again, she concentrated on writing a short note directly to Eli, enclosing a few lines for Elisheba. She had stopped being afraid of Eli.

✜✜✜

They set out a day later, heading for Jerusalem through Samaria. It was quicker, and Jesus seemed to be in a hurry, after his long winter of deliberate waiting. They saw none of Antipas's soldiers about as they went through Galilee, although they kept a constant lookout. But they passed unhindered to the border of Samaria, leaving the jurisdiction of Antipas behind for that of Rome. Mary wondered if exchanging Antipas for Rome was an improvement. Antipas might be more petty and active in pursuing enemies, but Rome was impersonal and implacable and offered no escape or appeal.

They continued their journey southward, making their way through the valleys bounded on either side by the high hills. As they passed, the Samaritans sometimes stood jeering at them and other times just stared sullenly. Feelings between Jew and Samaritan had not improved in the years since Mary had first made that journey; if anything, they had deteriorated. But it was different to be walking these roads with Jesus and the other disciples, not cowering before the roadside taunts or dreading what the next encounter might be, as she and her family had done.

The day grew warm, and by noon it was quite hot. By the time they approached Shechem, the ancient chief city of Samaria, they were ready to stop and rest. They found a convenient well, and Jesus sat down on its rim. He sent his male followers into town to buy some food, while he and his mother and the other women waited. All around, the stillness of noonday seemed to hold them motionless, but they could see little puffs of dust rising along the path to Shechem as someone approached them. Soon a woman came into view, carrying an empty water jar. She neared the well, and as she did so, Jesus spoke to her and asked her if she might get him a drink.

She looked at him warily. She was a middle-aged woman, with traces of beauty still upon her face.

"What?" she finally answered. "You, a Jew, ask a drink from a Samaritan?"

"I do," said Jesus. "Will you dip down into the well and give me some?"

She did so, lowering her gourd far down and then hauling it up with swift, strong motions. She handed it to Jesus, still eyeing him as if he must be dangerous. He thanked her and drank. Then he handed the gourd back.

"We are not supposed to speak to one another," she said. "Or drink from one another's cups."

Then Jesus laughed. "Woman," he said, "if you knew the gift of God and who it was who was asking you for a drink, you would have asked him for a drink instead, and he would have given you living water."

Now she drew back. This man must be insane. "Sir," she finally said, "you have nothing to draw water with, and this well is very deep. Just how can you get this living water? Even our common ancestor Jacob, great as he was, had to dig this well to get water."

"Yes, and everyone who drinks from it will get thirsty again. But whoever drinks the water *I* give him will never thirst. It will become in him a spring of water welling up to eternal life."

"Then give it to me, so I won't have to come back here and keep drawing the water!" she cried.

Jesus said. "Go, call your husband and come back, and I will show you."

"I have no husband."

"You speak true! For you have had five husbands, and the man you are now living with is not your husband."

She was so stunned she forgot to be frightened. Instead she just blurted out, "I can see that you are a prophet!" She turned to go into town, leaving her unfilled water jar in her haste. She walked a few steps, then halted. "Sir," she said, "we Samaritans have always worshiped God on our mountain here"—she pointed to Mount Gerizim nearby—"but you Jews claim the true place to worship him is in Jerusalem. Why?"

Jesus shook his head. "Believe me, woman, the time is coming when he will be worshiped neither place, but in spirit and in truth everywhere. God is spirit, and his true worshipers must also worship in spirit."

"I know a Messiah is coming," the woman said, "and when he does, he will explain all these things to us."

"Woman," said Jesus very slowly, "I who speak to you am he."

Clapping her hands over her mouth, the woman rushed off to town, and Mary heard her cry to the first person she encountered on the path, "Come, see a man who told me everything I ever did! Can this be the Messiah?" She bumped into the returning disciples, and then hurried past them into the town. Soon townspeople were streaming out, running to hear Jesus, and once again he and his followers were surrounded by crowds.

He had said he was the Messiah! He had said it! Mary was as stunned as the Samaritan woman. She turned to Jesus's mother and saw that she was smiling.

"You knew." Mary touched her arm and spoke softly, only to her. "You have always known?"

The elder Mary turned to look directly at the younger one. Her eyes, soft brown and filled with knowledge, searched Mary of Magdala's. "I have known," she said. "But he had to come to this understanding on his own." She took Mary's hand and held it fast.

"Come!" Jesus said. "Let us go into Shechem and teach there." To the disciples' astonishment, he rose and beckoned for them to follow.

They spent several days there in Shechem, where they listened eagerly to Jesus's teachings, and many embraced them and hailed him as the Messiah. "Now that we've heard him for ourselves," they told the woman, "we can believe everything!"

Peter, Thomas, and Simon were especially appalled. Jesus was eating with these people, the same group that had been declared unfit to help rebuild the Temple centuries ago, and who had been a thorn in the side of the Jews ever since. Jesus was welcoming them as followers and believers! What would it be next—Egyptians? Romans? They kept to themselves and refused to sit down with the Samaritans or eat any of their food. When it was time to continue the journey, they packed up so eagerly and early they were waiting for Jesus at the outskirts of town.

The word "Messiah" hung over them as they marched south, but no one dared to speak it aloud.

Jerusalem! There she was, over the horizon, gleaming far before them. They halted on the first ridge that allowed them to glimpse the city. For some of them, it was their first. It was midday, and in that light the city gleamed white, as if clad in purity and sculpted out of marble.

As they came closer and began to descend steep paths, Jesus suddenly halted once again. He looked at each of his followers and then toward the city, and began to weep quietly. He stood alone; no one knew what to do. Then Peter awkwardly stepped forward and embraced him, patting his shoulders and trying to comfort him. John also stepped up, putting one arm around him.

They all crowded closer to see what was causing him such pain, and Mary heard him say—his voice was muffled against Peter's shoulder—"Jerusalem! If you, even you, had only known on this day what would bring you peace—but now it is hidden from your eyes." He turned to look at the city again. "The days will come upon you when your enemies will build an embankment against you and encircle you and then hem you in on every side. They will dash you to the ground, you and the children within your walls. They will not leave one stone on another, because you did not recognize the time of God's coming to you."

"An embankment . . . encircle you"—was that part of the vision she had seen earlier? Was that how the Romans would get into the city to defile the Temple? Now Jesus was seeing it, too.

His mother joined Peter and John, and she embraced Jesus as well, her head bowed. How her heart must have been torn to see him so tormented. The city was now spread out fair before them, rejoicing in its celebrations and in its beauty, but he saw it as it would be.

At last, Jesus was quiet, comforted. Giving a great sigh of acceptance, he motioned for everyone to continue the journey.

There were crowds converging now, streams of people coming from all directions to ascend to the holy city, and they were singing, as pilgrims had always done, the special Psalms that celebrated going up to Jerusalem. The joy and the pride that all Jews felt in Jerusalem was not lessened by the political tension there. Whenever there was a holiday, but especially Passover, with its theme of deliverance from oppression, the Romans brought in extra troops, and Pontius Pilate came from his headquarters in Caesarea to keep an eye on things. This time, even Herod Antipas was coming. They must have heard rumors of some impending trouble, thought Mary.

As they climbed up the hill called the Mount of Olives, which was closest to Jerusalem, they stopped at a village called Bethany, where Jesus apparently had followers. Perhaps they had heard him preach in Galilee. Mary was surprised to find that there were people here who followed Jesus. They had been warned many times that he had "come to the attention of the authorities," but that was not the same thing as having actual followers among ordinary people so far from home.

He surprised them even further by telling Mary and Judas, "I want you to go into the next village and look for a donkey colt tethered just outside it. It's young enough that no one has ever ridden it. Untie it and bring it here."

Judas said, "You mean . . . steal it?"

"If anyone questions you about it, just tell him, 'The Lord needs it and will send it back here shortly.'"

There was no point in arguing, for their circumstances now were extraordinary. They all sensed this. They took their leave and headed for the village.

As they walked, Judas glanced over at Mary and seemed about to speak, then stopped himself. Finally, he said, "Would you like to meet my father?"

"Your father?"

"Yes. You know he lives near Jerusalem. When we arrive—when we have a moment—I would like very much to introduce you to one another."

"But . . . but . . . why?" Jesus would surely frown on their visiting their old homes.

"Passover is coming in a few days. Although I know we are supposed to celebrate it with Jesus and our fellows—as well we should—perhaps we could at least stop and meet my relatives, who will be gathered at my home."

"But . . . I cannot think why I, a stranger, would belong there," said Mary. The thought made her acutely uncomfortable. At the same time, she yearned to see somehow, if just for a moment, how her own family in Magdala would be sitting down to the celebration.

"I cannot help believing—hoping—that perhaps you might consider joining my family."

No! Not this! She felt shocked at his words and averted her eyes from his intense scrutiny.

"I believe that if we are partners in being disciples, wherever Jesus sees fit to send us, we could be together, work together," he was saying. "As husband and wife."

What have I done to encourage such ideas in him? I should have spoken more firmly that night we were camped. . . . Mary sought desperately for words as they trudged along the path, not daring to look at him. "I—I do not know what to say," she finally mumbled. "I think perhaps this is . . . is too soon."

"No, it has been a long time coming. I have known you for an entire year now, have watched you and admired you, and—I am certain of my feelings."

Once again she was walking a path with a suitor. Once again the surroundings were peaceful and lovely—one by the lakeside, the other on the gentle hill outside Jerusalem. But everything was different, too. With Joel she had been young and had no other path than marriage.

I am past that now, she thought. I am free, beyond marriage and ties to that life. Outside of Jesus, I cannot imagine committing myself to another person in that manner.

And Jesus has made it plain that he does not seek that.

In an instant, she relived the fierce pain of rejection that she had had to swallow when Jesus had turned aside from her desires, and the distance that still separated them as a result of it. Oh, let me not inflict any such similar pain on another person! she begged.

They were still walking. They should at least stand still. Mary halted, and waited until Judas did, too. "I think we are to put such things aside now," she said, as gently as she could. "Remember what Jesus said, 'In the Kingdom there is neither marriage nor giving in marriage.' And if everything is to end soon, we must not think of creating new complications."

"Complications? You call the love and commitment between a man and woman 'complications'? Two believers would be a very special, blessed union!" He seemed angry, as if she did not understand, or insisted on pretending she did not. She would have to speak more plainly. But, oh, dear God, she did not wish to wound!

"Judas—this cannot be. I cannot be your wife. The true reason is that my own feelings do not permit it." Disguise it, give him some comfort, some face-saving: "I am so recently a widow. I am still so unsure of my own mind. It will be many years before I—"

"I will wait," he said, his face solemn.

"There may be no future," Mary said. "We cannot think in those ways."

Stung, he turned away and resumed the walking. For many moments he was silent. Finally, he said in a low, determined voice, "Very well. You must forget what I have said. I wish to forget it. It is now a source of shame to me."

Mary knew so well what he felt. "No, it should not be!" she said, quickly. "My own situation—"

"I said we will forget it!" His voice was harsh and ugly. "It did not happen, I did not speak those words!"

"Very well," she said. His sudden reversal was startling. "If you choose not to remember, neither do I." If these were his moods, she was doubly glad she would not be bound to them, subject to his violent temperament.

They kept silent as they walked. Mary felt so uncomfortable that she wished she could disappear. But after a little while, Judas began talking as though nothing had happened. She stole a sideways look at him and saw his eyes narrowed, even though his voice sounded even.

They reached the outskirts of a town shortly thereafter, none too soon. And tied to a fence post was a white donkey colt. Judas untied it, and as he did so, a boy appeared and said, "What are you doing?"

"The Lord has need of it and will return it shortly!" Judas barked. No one would have dared argue with him.

They turned around and led the donkey back to Bethany, and only the sound of the donkey's hooves on the dirt path broke the silence between them.

Jesus greeted them with pleasure as they presented him with the beast. "Now, my friends, we must continue to Jerusalem," he said. "Just for a look. We will return here in the evening to sleep."

It was midafternoon. They had a few hours before the city gates closed. Jesus threw a cloak over the donkey and mounted him, and they set out down the steep path from the Mount of Olives.

They were now in the midst of hordes of other pilgrims making their way to the holy city, singing and jostling. Mary expected to be invisible, one of many in this sea of people. But suddenly all eyes were on Jesus as he trotted along on his donkey—which, oddly enough, did not seem to mind being ridden for the first time. Peter was leading him by a bridle, since he was not trained for a rider's commands. The

crowds drew back and made a path for him. Then, as Jesus and his followers approached the city gates of Jerusalem, they began to lay down
their cloaks for the donkey to walk over, and they waved cut palm
branches and began crying out the words of Psalm 118, "Blessed is he
who comes in the name of the Lord!"

Then others took up the chorus, shouting, "Hosanna to the Son of
David!"

"Blessed is the coming Kingdom of our father David!"

"Blessed is the king who comes in the name of the Lord!"

"Peace in heaven and glory in the highest."

Then one loud, hoarse cry: "Blessed is the king of Israel!"

"The prophet Zechariah foretold this!" one man shouted. "He
said, 'Your king shall come to you, righteous and having salvation,
gentle and riding on a donkey.'"

"So it's all staged." A familiar voice spoke directly into Mary's ear.
Judas's. "Jesus knows and read all these prophecies and decided to act
them out."

She turned to look at him. His face was dark and angry. He looked
betrayed—not only by her, but by Jesus as well.

"He has arranged it all," he hissed. "The donkey. The crowds.
Clearly the donkey was arranged—we know that. And what next? What
need he do when he reaches Jerusalem? Let me see—there are so many
prophecies. Of course, he does not have to fulfill them all. Just a few. So
people can . . . . marvel." He made the word "marvel" sound like a curse.

She did not know how to reply, because what he said was true. The
donkey *was* arranged. It could still have an innocent explanation, although she was unable to supply it. But he had never felt the need to
ride a donkey before. That fact was indeed troubling.

She chose not to answer, and walked quietly beside Jesus as he was
hailed by the crowds. She saw soldiers and officials on the walls of the
city, staring down at them. Doubtless they would be asking one another, "Who *is* this?" and perhaps that was Jesus's only aim—to pro-
voke people into asking that supreme question, "Who *is* this?" The
disciples had already answered it, but now others must.

A group of frowning teachers of the Law were watching them.
"Teacher, rebuke your students!" they ordered Jesus when the crowds
cried out again, "Hosanna! Blessed is he who comes in the name of the
Lord."

Instead of arguing with them, or ignoring them, Jesus cried, "I tell
you, if I silence them, the very stones will cry out!"

They stared at him, annoyed.

Jesus and the disciples entered the gate of the city and were allowed to pass through, leaving their enthusiastic greeters behind. Now they were just common pilgrims. As they walked through the narrow streets, Mary noticed large numbers of Roman soldiers stationed on each corner. She did not remember such a presence from her childhood, but she could not be certain. They looked poised for trouble, ready to intervene at a moment's notice. In their stern gaze Mary felt their disdain and hostility.

They really hate us, she thought. They hate our festivals and our religion, and they hate being stationed here in Jerusalem. All we are to them is trouble.

At length they reached the precincts of the Temple, approaching the great gate that separated the common streets from the holy grounds. Only the bored soldiers standing guard, their feet planted at a wide stance, seemed unmoved by its glory.

The opulence and size of the building were overwhelming. It seemed godlike in itself, a fitting home for the supreme God of heaven.

Others had the same thoughts. Peter, still holding the bridle, turned to Jesus and said, "Master! What huge stones! What a magnificent building!"

"Are you impressed with this?" Jesus's voice was sharp. "I tell you, not one stone will remain upon another in a short time."

He dismounted from the donkey and strode into the outer court of the Temple, where animals were sold and the money-changers had their booths. He just stared at it for many long moments, then silently turned away, remounted the donkey, and said, "Come. Evening is falling, and we must find a place to sleep for the night."

As sunset stained the skies, they left through the same gate they had entered and made their way back across the ravine and to the Mount of Olives, where many pilgrims were camping.

At the foot of the mount was a garden, neatly fenced off, that held an ancient olive grove and oil press. It looks most inviting, Mary thought. I wish we could stop here.

One either side of their path were groups of people spreading out blankets and settling in, heedless of the discomfort of the sloped site. At holiday time the population of Jerusalem swelled so enormously that there was no place for the pilgrims to sleep but beyond the city walls.

As they passed, Mary noticed that many eyes were trained on Jesus, as though they knew who he was and were watching him. But how did all these pilgrims know him? And why did so many hail him earlier?

Jesus selected the place where they would rest, but then withdrew and did not invite any conversation. Even his mother sought the company of the other women. He sent John and James to return the donkey, but his manner forbade any discussion of it.

All around them the disciples could hear the drowsy murmur of hundreds of voices as many others drifted off to sleep, surrounding them like an army.

The next morning, the entire mountain seemed to be stirring as all the pilgrims awoke and made ready for the day. There was much to do: people had to reserve their lambs to be slaughtered according to protocol at the Temple on Passover Eve, had to procure the requisite herbs and wine. But Jesus seemed unconcerned with this. Instead, he said abruptly, "Let us return to Jerusalem. We must go to the Temple."

Barely giving them time to gather their possessions, he set a brisk pace toward the city. As they passed a gnarled old fig tree leaning over a stone wall, Jesus grasped one of its branches and pulled it down. He quickly examined its leaves and their undersides and then said, "No figs, although there was a promise of them!" He shook the branch and released it. "No one will ever eat figs from you again!" he cried.

What was troubling him? Mary had never seen him behave so irrationally. Surely he knew it was the wrong season for figs. What was he thinking?

She glanced at John, who was walking beside her, and saw the puzzled look in his eyes, too.

Loyal as always, they walked quietly behind him, not questioning.

A huge crowd was pressing against the gates of Jerusalem, waiting for them to open. When they did, the people poured in like a river, surging toward the Temple. Already it was bustling and ready for business: the gates were open and welcoming, and the din of noise from the outer courts showed that the citizens of Jerusalem had come here early to beat the crowd of outsiders.

The entire periphery of the Court of the Gentiles was lined with animals and money-changers. There were cages of pigeons, stalls with sheep and goats, and endless tables, so it seemed, for changing money.

All this was necessary, for the Law specified that certain animals must be sacrificed. But since it was impractical for people to bring the

animals from a long distance, there had to be some means of their ob-
taining animals once they were in Jerusalem.

As for the money-changers, the only acceptable Temple payments
were in Tyrian silver, which was purer than the Roman standard. So all
other currencies must be converted. And if the money-changers were
offering the public a convenience, should they not be allowed to make
a profit? So the argument went. They had to live, after all, and this was
not a charitable operation.

All around them rose the din of the transactions, an offering of
noise as thick as the incense that rose from altars, or the chanting of
Levites.

"Goats! Goats! Buy your goats here! The best!" This call was the
first to greet them.

"Unblemished! My animals are unblemished! Remember the words
of Malachi: 'When you bring blind animals for sacrifice, is that not
wrong? When you sacrifice crippled or diseased animals, is that not wrong?
Cursed is the cheat who sacrifices a blemished animal to the Lord!'
God spits on blemished offerings. But mine are perfect!" one loud,
red-faced vendor yelled. He was trying to manage a leash of disobedient goats, bleating and straining to escape.

"Lambs are best!" another man called. "Lambs! Pure and docile,
acceptable to the Lord!"

"Have you unclean currency?" A man grabbed Mary's right sleeve.
"You cannot bring it into the Temple precincts! You must exchange it
here!"

"His rates are robbery!" Someone else grabbed her left sleeve. "He
lies, cheats! Look, examine mine!" He shoved a handful of coins under
her nose. "You can search all you like, but you'll not find a single coun-
terfeit here! Not a one!"

Suddenly Jesus turned on one of the tables. "You robber!" he
yelled. "You thief!"

The vendor looked stricken, then glanced around to see if anyone
had heard. This was not an accusation to be borne lightly. "I beg your
pardon!" he cried. "I do not cheat! How dare you say that! You'll have
to answer me, sir, in a court of law, for defaming me—"

"You are all thieves!" shouted Jesus. "All of you!" He rushed at
the tables and started heaving them over, upending the money piles
and books. Before anyone could react or stop him, he had overturned
an entire row, scattering their contents all over the ground. "You
vipers, you bloodsuckers! It is written in Isaiah, 'My house shall be

called a house of prayer for all nations.' But you have made it into a den of robbers, as Jeremiah said!" he screamed.

The coins were rolling around his feet, and the merchants were scrambling to retrieve them. One dignified merchant grabbed Jesus's shoulder and said, "Shall we disobey the Law of Moses? How else can people adhere to the regulations? We are just providing a public service!"

"A public service! Making the outer courts of the Temple into a common marketplace!" Jesus cried.

"The Law of Moses has left us no other choice," the man insisted, refusing to lose his temper. "I admit, it leads to this ugly scene of tables and animals and piles of coins. But what would you have us do? Break the Law? We are bound to it."

Ignoring him, Jesus suddenly grasped a whip from a passing man who had a donkey-goad in his hand and began attacking the money-changers and animal-sellers, beating them with the whip—which had painful knotted cords on it—and shouting at them about the desecration. Frightened and angry, they scattered. Jesus strode through the mess on the ground, brandishing his whip and yelling, chasing them. Roman soldiers were watching on the sides, keeping silent, but surely storing up information to report to Pilate.

During all this, the disciples were too stunned even to ask him, "What are you doing?" This was an unknown Jesus, a Jesus in some ways a stranger to them.

Mary had never seen Jesus display such a temper, seemingly triggered by such a small thing. She had wished to talk to him, to settle the unfinished matters between them. Now she wondered if it were even possible. The man she thought she knew, believed she loved, had only been a part of this prophet, this person who suddenly seemed very far away from them all. Instinctively she turned toward his mother, and beheld a similar shocked expression.

Now the Temple authorities came rushing down, angry and boiling over with words. "What's the meaning of this?" one man called. "How dare you cause such a disturbance in a holy place?"

"A holy place?" cried Jesus. "This commerce desecrates the holiness of the site. And it does so with *your* permission and connivance!"

"They are but providing a necessary service," the man said. "You owe us damages!"

"You owe God damages!" Jesus yelled.

"We know who you are," the man said, "that Galilean rabbi who has whipped people up with his rhetoric and Messianic teasing. Jesus of Nazareth, aren't you? Staged a big entrance to Jerusalem yesterday. A lot of people bowing and waving palms. You just feed the people's hopes that a Messiah is in the wings—leading them on for your own glory."

"You know nothing," Jesus said.

"We know enough to constrain you. Stop this now, before you end up in serious trouble. Look, friend"—the man moved closer to him—"there has been a lot of damage here already, and the Roman authorities are braced for more. A rebel named Barabbas tried to waylay a whole contingent of soldiers yesterday. He killed two, but then was captured. Now his followers threaten more violence. So you'd best lie low if you don't want to be confused with those characters."

"I have warned such rebels," said Jesus. "I told them to stop."

"Well, you're not much of an example," the man said. "Why in the world would they listen to you?" He swept his hand to indicate the overthrown tables and the escaped animals.

Strangely, they were allowed to leave with no hindrance. The soldiers lining the sides of the portico stood stolidly, woodenly, and did not lay a hand on them. The muttering merchants gathered up their goods and looked around, wondering how long it would take them to set up once again. Jesus was a nuisance but, they hoped, a one-time nuisance, like an unseasonable hailstorm or an onslaught of locusts.

As the disciples left the city under the silent leadership of Jesus, they passed the fig tree and saw that its branch and leaves were withered, as if they had shriveled up under Jesus's curse. The tiny new spring leaves were blasted and black, and the branch drooped.

"Master!" cried Peter, in alarm. "What is this? How has this happened?" He held up the limp branch. His face showed fear and confusion.

"Does this amaze you?" Jesus said. "If you have faith, you can tell a mountain to move and throw itself into the sea. This is nothing!" He took the branch, examined it, and let it drop. "Whatever you ask for in prayer with faith, you will receive."

What did that have to do with faith?

It was so mysterious and dark; this had nothing to do with faith, or helping people, or preaching, or casting out demons, all the things she thought defined Jesus's mission. That was the reason why she had followed him, why they had all followed him.

At supper that night, they were all quiet, keeping their heads bowed. Mary noticed that Jesus's mother also looked miserable, keeping her head down as well. Jesus said little beyond the prayers, and right after supper Judas hurried away. She saw him heading down the steep path. Was he going back home to see his father? Jesus would not approve, but perhaps Judas did not care. Perhaps Judas disliked the nasty demonstration in the Temple, and the punishment of the fig tree.

Mary sought out Jesus's mother where she leaned against one of the scrubby pine trees struggling to grow upright on the slope. Her head was buried in the crook of her arm, but Mary touched her shoulder softly. Jesus's mother raised her head, and Mary could see that her eyes were filled with tears. Wordlessly, Mary took her in her arms. The older woman wept.

"He was always so respectful of the Temple, so observant," she whispered. "When he was a child, he loved to spend time there, and he asked the scribes and scholars so many questions they grew weary. . . ." She shook her head. "And now, to do this—"

"Clearly what he saw outraged him. Perhaps he felt he had to redeem the Temple," Mary said. But she said it only to make his mother feel better.

"What would James say?" Jesus's mother asked.

"Neither of them said anything," said Mary. Big and Little James had stood there, as dumbfounded as the rest of them.

"Not them. My son—Jesus's brother! He's so pious! He'd die— he'd be so ashamed! I hope no one in Nazareth will hear about it!"

"Nazareth is a long way away," said Mary. "Come, let's sit in a comfortable place and talk. . . ."

Finally, Mary asked the question that had been nagging at her: *was* their family descended from David? It shouldn't matter to her, but it did. Another prophecy . . .

"Yes," said Jesus's mother. "We always were told it was so. Such a thing made us feel good, gave us a strength on days when things were going badly. It was a special sort of spur to do your best. But there are many families who claim kinship with David's line; it is not uncommon."

So it was true: this one prophecy, at least, could fit him. And it was one he couldn't control, unlike the one about the donkey.

Later, with the elder Mary lying down for the night, Mary stood up and walked restlessly. She saw Thomas hunched over a small scroll, writing something by firelight. She stooped down to try to see what he was doing.

He looked up and said, "I'm writing down some of the things Jesus has said. You know, here and there. I'm afraid I'll forget them otherwise. I've already forgotten so many."

She bent over the writing surface and read a few lines:

Jesus said, "I will give you what no eye has seen, what no ear has heard, what no hand has touched, what has not arisen in the human heart."

Jesus said, "One who seeks will find, and for one who knocks, it will be opened."

"I never heard him say any of those things," said Mary.

"He says different things to each of us," said Thomas. "It depends on whether you were standing near at the time. You could compile your own list, I'm sure."

"You ought to explain when and why he said these things," said Mary. "It's hard to understand otherwise."

"It's only for me," said Thomas. "I won't forget."

I suppose he does speak to each of us differently, thought Mary. But some of the things he said to me, not only will I never write them down, I wish I could forget them!

From a distance, she could hear Jesus speaking to someone, speaking in a gentle and friendly tone. The sound of his voice as it used to be aroused a great yearning in her. Why had he changed? And was the change permanent?

He's as mercurial as Judas, she thought.

And where was Judas, and why had he stolen away?

ೞ **L** ೞ

The Temple, again. Jesus had led them there, and now they stood in the outer courts, watching him ready himself to speak. Something about his very stance and bearing seemed to gather people around him.

Anyone could teach in the porticoes of the Temple, and many rabbis gathered their followers there. But in this crowded holiday time, few would attempt it. Nonetheless, Jesus stationed himself near one of the pillars and stood, a rock in the midst of a swirling mass of people surging into the Temple to pay respects, sightsee, and reserve animals.

The booths of money-changers and animal-sellers were back in their places. The proprietors glanced warily at Jesus as he passed, but he paid them no mind this time, which was curious. Why did he overlook their effrontery today and not yesterday? The soldiers noted him and perhaps stood a little more at attention, but only their eyes followed him. This time, however, Mary noted a large contingent of Pharisees and scribes on the periphery of the crowd.

As soon as Jesus raised his arms and said, "My people, I welcome your questions about the Law and the scriptures"—a standard invitation for students and followers—an enormous crowd gathered. They fired question after question at him, some of them simple—"What did Moses say about gathering wood on the Sabbath?"—and others more complicated—"Does honoring one's mother and father mean you must obey their wishes about who you marry if you are forty years old?" Jesus answered them all, seemingly without hesitation, as if he had always had the answers stored up and waiting.

"By what authority do you teach these things?" A clear ringing question from a Pharisee. A stocky man strode forward and confronted Jesus. "You talk as if you had some special license or privilege."

Jesus abruptly stopped talking and looked at the man. "I will answer your question if you answer mine. Is that not fair?"

The man looked confused. He had asked the first question. This was out of order. But he nodded.

"The baptism of John," Jesus said. "Was it of God, or of men?"

The man frowned. He turned aside to consult with this colleagues. Mary could supply the argument herself, without even overhearing them. If they say it is of God, then Jesus will ask them why they did not submit to it. If they say it was only of man, then the crowd will react and turn on the Pharisees, for they believe John was a holy man.

"We cannot tell you," the Pharisee finally said—as Mary could have predicted.

"Neither, then, will I tell you by what authority I do these things," Jesus said.

Beside her, Mary heard Jesus's mother give a stifled cry. She turned to her and said, "What is it?"

"I am afraid," she said. "These people he is baiting—they have great power. And he is making enemies of them. Open enemies, where others can see, and therefore they cannot ignore the insult." She looked up at him and pushed her fist into her mouth. "Oh, my son!"

"Their power is limited," said Mary, trying to reassure her. "Rome restrains their hand."

"But they will enlist Rome in their cause," Jesus's mother said. "They will call upon Rome, and then . . ."

"But he has done nothing to offend Rome," Mary assured her. "Rome is bound by her laws."

The Pharisees and Sadducees repeated many of the old questions about marriage, Sabbath restrictions, purity regulations, and they received the same replies, challenging and answering them, that they had earlier, in other places. But this was more serious: he had unmasked them before their peers, in the very seat where they held sway—here in Jerusalem, not far away in unorthodox, forgettable, Galilee.

"Come." Jesus suddenly signaled to his group. "Let us go closer to the sanctuary." He led them up and into the Court of the Women. He would go no farther, since he did not wish to exclude his women followers.

Here, in this smaller area, only someone who followed the Law could enter—no Romans, no Phoenicians, no foreign merchants. Here were the famous thirteen wide-mouthed offering boxes, here were the four corner-chambers for priests, purified lepers, Nazirites, and oil and wine offerings.

A number of people were lined up before the offering boxes, putting their money in. Jesus looked at them, then said, "When you give alms, do not let your right hand know what your left hand is doing." He nodded at one contributor, who snatched back his right hand and stared at it. Directly behind him was a stooped old lady, who tremblingly stuck her hand into the opening and then stood staring at it for a moment as the coin made a little *ping!* in joining the heap of others in the bottom of the box. She looked ill when she heard it.

"She has just given all she has!" Jesus pronounced. "More than these rich people lined up behind her." He indicated some well-dressed men waiting their turn. "They are giving but a portion, but she has given all she has!"

"Then she's a fool." Judas spoke, right behind Mary. "Now she'll be a public nuisance, begging or throwing herself on her children. Oh, it's showy, but stupid."

Where had he come from? Mary had not seen him since his disappearance the night before. He had not been with them this morning.

"How cynical," was all she could manage.

"Practical," he answered, not apologizing. "You cannot just accept every pronouncement Jesus makes," he said. "Some of them don't make sense."

Now Jesus seemed to be seeing something else. He looked over the heads of the crowd and addressed only the authorities and Pharisees, who had followed him.

"Woe to you!" he cried, pointing directly at a group of Pharisees. "Yes, woe to you! Oh, you sit in Moses's seat. But you tie heavy loads on people, loads they cannot bear. Everything you do is done for an outward show: the long fringes on your prayer shawls, the place of honor at banquets, the most important seats in the synagogue."

There was a rustling among them, but no one answered him. "Woe to you, teachers of the Law and Pharisees, you hypocrites! You shut the kingdom of heaven in men's faces!"

The religious elite looked at one another, smugly, shrugging.

"Woe to you, teachers of the Law and Pharisees, you hypocrites!" he repeated. "You give a tenth of your spices—mint, dill, and cumin. But you have neglected the more important matters of the Law—justice, mercy, and faithfulness. You blind guides! You strain at a gnat but swallow a camel!" Jesus's voice rose to anguished breaking point. But his listeners kept bland faces.

"Woe to you, teachers of the Law and Pharisees, you hypocrites! You build tombs for the prophets and decorate the graves of the righteous. And you say, 'If we had lived in the days of our forefathers, we would not have taken part with them in shedding the blood of the prophets.' So you testify against yourselves that you are the descendants of those who murdered the prophets. Fill up, then, the measure of the sin of your forefathers!" he cried. Now the crowd murmured angrily, insulted.

"You snakes! You brood of vipers! How will you escape being condemned to hell? Therefore you are sent prophets and wise men and teachers. Some of them you will kill and crucify; others you will flog in your synagogues and pursue from town to town. And so upon you will come all the righteous blood that has been shed on earth, from the blood of righteous Abel to the blood of Zechariah the son of Berechiah, whom you murdered between the Temple and the altar. I tell you the truth, all this will come upon this generation!"

Beside her, Mary heard his mother gasp. "No, no," she was murmuring. "Now they will destroy him!"

Mary turned to see her lovely face contorted with fear and pain. "They cannot punish him just for words," she said. But she was not so certain. Words had mighty power.

"When we brought him here—oh, many, many years ago—to make the customary offering for a firstborn son," the elder Mary said, "there was an old man here in the Temple courts—I thought he was somewhat age-befuddled, that is how I explained it to myself—who looked at us and said, 'This child is destined to cause the falling and rising of many in Israel, and to be a sign that will be spoken against, so the thoughts of many hearts will be revealed. And a sword will pierce your own soul, too.' And, oh, my soul *is* pierced! I see what is coming!" She clutched Mary's arm. "Can you not see it, too?"

In spite of all my visions, I see nothing now, Mary thought. Although there was one of Jesus beaten, attacked . . . but nothing since. And if it is imminent, should I not see it now?

"No, I see nothing," Mary reassured her.

"Oh, you are wrong!" his mother said. "I feel it, I know it. Oh, my son!" She tore free of Mary's restraint and pushed forward toward him in the crowd. But she was unable to pass through and reach his side.

Now Mary looked around, carefully; she saw that there were more soldiers arriving. Some wore the livery of Antipas, others that of Pilate.

They are here to arrest us or to report. The authorities are indeed interested in us. Afraid of us. No. We are nothing to be afraid of; we have no power, she thought.

She noticed that the only person near Jesus was John. John was standing resolutely by his side, ready to be arrested along with him.

But there were no arrests. The soldiers merely stood at their posts looking down determinedly. They had been given no orders to act.

Jesus stepped down off the platform and went out among the crowd, answering individual questions and ignoring the soldiers ringing them.

"You don't see the chief priests, do you?" Again the voice of Judas. "The high priest Caiaphas himself, or Eleazar, or Jonathan. They're not here. They know all they need to."

"I would not recognize them. And what exactly *do* they know, if they have never seen Jesus in person?"

Judas shrugged. "*I* think they know they have a problem on their hands. And if they do not already, a report of the 'Woe to you!' sermon will convince them."

"You sound as if you are on their side. Why have you turned against him?" she demanded.

Judas gave something that could have been mistaken for a laugh. "Turned against him? I don't know what you mean. I merely question: is that so wrong?"

"You told me once that you were seeking, seeking desperately, and that you thought he had the answers. Not answers you would have foreseen, but answers that were so compelling you were forced to consider them. Oh, Judas, what has happened?"

"I did consider those answers. They did not hold up. I am, I am afraid, once again on the seeker's high road."

So he had rejected Jesus. The full import of that hovered, waiting for her to understand it. "So you feel . . . his answers were inadequate? They did not satisfy you?"

"They were absurd," said Judas. He was angry. "I thought he knew things none of us did, but he has become bogged down in all those arcane prophecies and in fighting the authorities." He stopped to gather his thoughts. "The authorities! What are they? And now for Jesus to waste his time with them, become embroiled with them—tithes of cumin and mint! What philosopher, what leader, what Messiah would bother with this? He's a politician, like all the rest. I have no interest in politicians. They have nothing to give me."

"But we are part of the age we live in, and politicians rule our age, and every age," she said. "Moses had to confront Pharaoh. Esther had to come before Xerxes. We wish we could be distinct from the petty powers that rule our times, but we are not."

"A great man transcends it," Judas said.

"Only later, in the judgment of history," said Mary. "Moses could not become a leader *without* Pharaoh's opposition."

Judas gave a dismissive grunt and turned away. But before he did, Mary grabbed his sleeve. "Do you think Jesus is in danger?" she asked.

Judas looked at her with a mixture of pity and condescension. "Yes. I know he is."

Those eyes. Different since we were in Dan, in the place of Jeroboam, the place where evil walked among us.

How did he know?

"Where do you hear these things?"

"From various people. Outsiders to our cause."

People he should have repudiated once he joined Jesus. So he had given nothing up!

"But Jesus does not threaten Rome or the high priest."

"Jesus is more of a threat than you seem to realize," Judas said. "You are so naïve."

Naïve. No one had ever used that word to describe her. But, politically, perhaps she was. There was no shame in that. "I cannot think of him as a threat," she repeated.

"That is because what you are is not threatened by him."

They all left the city unhindered, despite the scrutiny of the soldiers. Once again they camped on the Mount of Olives, amid all the other pilgrims. This time, however, after they had settled themselves, Jesus suddenly announced, "A man I cured from leprosy some time ago has invited us to come to his house in Bethany for a dinner. I am going. Who will come with me?"

It was late and quite dark. They were all tired, and already settled for the night. The thought of going elsewhere, making conversation with strangers, then returning at midnight—it was too much. Several of them declined, saying they would remain, to keep the spot. "After all," said Matthew, "if we all leave, there will be no place to return to."

I suppose I should go, Mary told herself. She looked around at the other women, silently asking them with her eyes. Jesus's mother? Tired as she was, the elder Mary nodded. Joanna? Yes. Susanna? Yes. Then, if they are going . . . I must.

It was not a long walk to Bethany, but it meant they must cross the crest of the hill and then descend on the other side. With this small number of companions, Jesus was more accessible, talking readily to whoever came alongside him. Mary wanted to; she wanted badly to speak to him, but something held her back. She wanted to be alone with him, with no threat of interruptions, such as an unexpected "Jesus, I have been wanting to ask you . . ." from one of the others. And so she held back, waiting.

The old matter between them still hung unresolved. Now, at last, she was ready to speak of it. Sometime there must be an opportunity, she thought. Sometime. And when it comes, I will claim it.

The village of Bethany was small, the main path cutting through its market space and trading area. Beyond that, the larger houses of the well-to-do bordered the path, looking down at them.

Wanting to make sure that his guests found their way, their host had stationed boys with lanterns at the main crossroads of the village, and they beckoned and asked, "Jesus? Jesus of Nazareth?" to everyone passing by. When Jesus indicated that he was the one they sought, they turned and led the party to an imposing house away from the main area.

This house was not as large as Matthew's, nor were there as many torches and servants in the courtyard, but it was still an impressive dwelling, especially for one who had recently been leprous.

Once they were inside, their feet washed by servants and their cloaks removed, Simon came forward and greeted Jesus effusively.

"My dearest rabbi! Perhaps you do not remember—but I was one of the lepers who sought you out by the lake. I regret that I was unable to return then and render thanks. But my heart is deeply grateful, and I do so now."

"I did not know who you were," Jesus said. "I was only concerned that you—and all others—afflicted with illness should take your place in the midst of life again, rather than be relegated to a graveyard." He suddenly turned his head and addressed everyone in the room in a loud voice. "For, make no mistake, I have come that everyone should have life, and have it more abundantly!"

Now Mary could see a large company in the room ahead of them. All the people inside rose and saluted Jesus.

"Yes!" they cried. "More abundant life! That is what we all wish!"

"I mean the life of the soul," said Jesus. "Not . . ." He indicated the cushions and the inlaid mother-of-pearl tables.

The disciples, behind Jesus, filed into the room and saw that the tables had been set for a large company.

"Please," Simon said, indicating Jesus's place with pride. Jesus took it. He selected John to be on one side, and his mother on the other. Simon would be on the next couch.

"Simon," said Jesus, "how have you been received since your healing?"

"At first it was difficult," his host admitted. "People did not want to believe I was well."

Mary understood completely.

"And even I had trouble accepting it. That the condition would not return. I had lived with it so long—"

"It seems as if your family kept your business, so that you had something to return to," said Jesus. Again he looked around at the rich surroundings.

"Yes. For that I am grateful. I did not have to rely on the begging bowl."

Mary noticed that Judas was reclining near her, munching on a piece of parsley and listening with an intent expression. Peter and Andrew were eating heartily; after all, the disciples seldom got a full meal. Big James was likewise engaged in his food. None of them noticed a woman who stole in with an alabaster jar until she was standing just behind Jesus.

An assassin! thought Mary. She threw her napkin down and stood up, ready to protect Jesus. This person was standing at his left shoulder, at the perfect place to drive a dagger into his back. Beside her, Big James also stood up.

But neither Jesus's mother nor John paid attention to the stranger. They just kept eating, until the loud noise of a stopper being removed caught their attention. Jesus then turned around and confronted the woman, who fell to his feet and started kissing them.

Who was this? Another secret disciple—secret from the others, but known to Jesus? He did not seem surprised by it. The woman stood up and solemnly and reverently began to pour the contents of the jar onto Jesus's head, even as he was eating. The overwhelming and unmistakable perfume of the rare ointment nard filled the room. As it dripped around Jesus's head and began to run down his face, she tenderly took a cloth and wiped it away. Then she took what was left in the jar and anointed his feet, rubbing the ointment all over, on the soles and between the toes.

A profound silence filled the room, her hands making the only sound as she massaged the nard into his skin. Then she unbound her hair and began wiping the ointment off with it, with little circling motions. A very small sound of crying escaped from her, but no one could see her face; it was hidden by her hair.

Finally, she arose and, covering her face with her hands, turned to leave. She had not addressed Jesus or asked him for anything; she had only rendered this gift.

"Spikenard!" Peter's voice was the first to be heard. "Spikenard! The most expensive perfume there is! This must be three hundred denarii's worth!"

"A whole year's wages for a soldier, not to mention a poor craftsman!" Judas was indignant. "What a waste!" He turned on Jesus. "Master, how can you have permitted this?"

Jesus looked at Judas. "Leave her alone," he said. He turned to the woman and took her hand. "She has done a beautiful thing; she has anointed me beforehand to prepare my body for burial."

At that, his mother cried out.

"Yes, it is a good deed she has done, and as long as the world lasts, she will be remembered for it."

"Son—" His mother reached out to touch his shoulder, but he did not turn to her. He continued dividing his glance between Judas and the woman.

"As long as the world lasts"—did he mean people would talk about this on and on, beyond just their own times? Mary wondered. But why? It made no sense, like so much he had said recently.

"Judas," he finally said, "if you are so concerned about the poor, remember that they are always waiting, always ready to have a kindness done to them. It is never too late. But me—me you will not always have."

The woman slipped away, but as she departed, Jesus called after her, "I thank you. This will be my only anointing; when the time comes, there will not be an opportunity."

With that, his mother moaned. The rest of the company stood up; it was impossible to continue with the meal now. In spite of Simon's murmurings and assurances, they quickly took their leave.

Outside the house, a large curious crowd was waiting, even at this late hour and in this private place, to glimpse Jesus. Mary did not wish to look at any of them; she was concerned only with Jesus's mother. Surely Jesus would take her to his side and explain what he meant, and comfort her. To have made those statements about his death so matter-of-factly—how could a son have done that? And she was relieved to see that he did so; the elder Mary and Jesus were walking together, his head bent down as he talked to her.

Suddenly Joanna gasped, "It's *him!*" and stiffened, grabbing Mary's arm. Her fingernails dug into Mary's flesh.

"Who?"

"Eliud! Antipas's spymaster." She ducked her head so he could not see her face. "I thought never to see that ugly face again. But it means that Antipas is having Jesus followed. That incident with the money-changers—although he wasn't arrested, it means he will be kept under surveillance from now on."

They hurried past, holding their veils over their faces. Mary could just glimpse, through the thin material, the outline of the man's features: big blunt ones, with thick lips. His eyes took in every person passing.

"Antipas had Jesus marked long before this," said Joanna. "Now he will see his chance. He and the Temple priests with their religious police can pool forces, make their case. . . . Jesus has walked into their trap."

That made Jesus seem like a blundering, unaware victim. But to Mary, it was Jesus who had set up a trap, using himself as bait. She did not understand why, but that was the truth of it.

"I do not think anything will happen to Jesus that he does not wish," she finally said. It seemed to her that Judas was right when he noted Jesus seemed to be carefully arranging a series of events. His interpretation—that Jesus was therefore an impostor—did not ring true, but his initial observation was shrewd. Jesus might stage actions with a certain end in mind—primarily to convince others of something—but he was incapable of dishonesty. That Mary knew to the very core of her soul.

"Perhaps he has foreseen only so far," said Joanna. "And things can take unexpected turns. I think I can find out what Antipas has planned." She lowered her head and spoke even more quietly, so that Mary had to strain to hear her. "Antipas is in his Jerusalem palace," she said. "I know all the ways in and out; I can easily gain entrance and do my own spying."

"No! It is too dangerous!"

"Of course it's dangerous," said Joanna. "But our whole group is in danger. I am willing to risk myself to help the rest."

"Jesus would never permit it!"

"Yes, he's all too willing to bear the brunt of the trouble. But why else was I cured? Perhaps for this very task. No one else among us has access to Antipas's quarters. I must do it."

"I will come with you."

"Now *I* must say to *you:* no."

"And again I can say to you: why else was I cured? Two will be more invisible in this case than one. I insist on coming."

It did not take more than that to persuade Joanna. She was grateful for the support. "Then tomorrow, after we have entered the city, we'll—"

"What are you women talking about so earnestly?" Judas was beside them. How much had he heard?

"We were saying how much longer the way back seems," said Mary quickly.

"Yes, it is always so when you are eager to get there," said Judas. He seemed pleasant enough, no longer perturbed or sarcastic. "And I for one am certainly ready to rest."

The next morning, they went once again to the Temple, where Jesus intended to teach, but this time only the common people. His encounters with the authorities were over; he had said everything to them he wished to say.

She and Joanna had decided to let Jesus get engaged with the crowds and his teaching before they slipped away. It would be simple to do in this vast throng. Every day more pilgrims had arrived in the city, adding to the confusion.

It was easy to overhear many snatches of conversation, for people talked too freely. Amid the innocent chatter—"We bought our lamb from the vendor right by the gate"; "All our cousins are here, and we're squeezing into my uncle's tiny house"— there were the low political mutters: "So Antipas is here. . . . Does he mean to have it out with Pilate?"; "Annas, that old fool, he's trying to run the priesthood, like he was still high priest"; "That man people are following . . ."

More ominous were the rumors of *sicarii* on the loose, roaming the streets ready to strike. Barabbas was locked up, but there were many others with eager knives and nothing to lose except their lives, which they were glad to offer. The tension, fear, and excitement blended in the air.

"Now!" Joanna tugged at Mary's sleeve. Jesus was holding forth, laughing, and some children surrounded him, asking eager questions. They turned and left the Temple courtyard and hurried through the vast gates and out into the streets, where they were immediately swallowed up by the surging crowds. There were only two days until Passover, and the crowds had almost reached their peak.

"He's staying at the old palace," said Joanna. "When Pilate is in the city, he takes over the modern one Antipas built near the wall. Poor Antipas! He has to make do with colored marble instead of white, and with some drafty halls. But it's all worth it, I suppose, to placate his Roman master."

The palace, known as "the old Hasmonean palace," was quite close to the Temple Mount: a convenient place for conspirators to gather and then slip away.

"There is a small door back here that only the servants know," said Joanna, leading Mary down a close alley. A half-sized door was tucked into the vast wall before them. Before entering, Joanna bit her lip to steel herself. Now she did not seem so self-possessed, so certain of her ability to penetrate this enemy fortress. "If I did not feel that there was something of vital concern to Jesus going on here, I would not have the courage to go inside." She stopped and swallowed. "I am not sure even so that I have the courage."

"Yes! Yes, you do!" Mary urged her. Perhaps that was why there needed to be two of them: to buoy up one another.

With a surge of resolution, Joanna turned the door handle and entered. Mary followed.

It was dark in the passageway; no oil lamps or lanterns lighted the way. Evidently it was seldom used. "Come, I know the way," said Joanna. "Is your veil ready?"

Mary nodded. She had a large one that would hide her face.

They stole down the corridor, and then Joanna led them out into the light, past another hallway and then into a high-vaulted white-washed chamber. It looked like a simple storeroom: pots and linens were lying on wooden shelves.

"This way!" Joanna knew exactly where to go. They emerged into an antechamber that divided into two hallways. Then she halted and looked around the corner. "No guards. Down here is the dining chamber. And it is almost time for the midday dinner. We can serve them, and observe."

What if someone saw Joanna and recognized her? If the guests did not know about her disgrace, that would be good, part of the disguise. But what if they knew she was no longer in the entourage?

Several servants were carrying large trays down the corridor toward the dining chamber, hustling along. Mary and Joanna fell in with them.

The smell of the food almost undid them. There was cooked cucumber with fennel and almonds and grapes in wine sauce—something neither of them had tasted for a long time. But they commanded themselves to stop thinking about it, and their mouths stopped watering. They entered the dining chamber and saw a few couches drawn up around marble serving tables, glittering with inlaid gems.

Antipas was there, reclining on the couch: Antipas and his forbidden wife, Herodias. Joanna clasped Mary's forearm in a tight grip. "There they are," she whispered. Her hand was trembling, and she pulled her veil down farther over her forehead. They watched as the servers set platters down on the little tables before the rulers.

Antipas was only about fifty, but he looked much older—worn away with his cares and constant vigilance. His bride—his Herodias—was attractive in a nervous, overpainted sort of way, but was her love worth killing John the Baptist for? Mary wondered. And how much love did they have now? Both were older, and passion must have ebbed. Ebbed too late for John the Baptist.

Antipas lifted the lid of one of the dishes and shook his head. The server whisked it away and hurried back toward the door. Mary and Joanna fell in behind her.

This palace, this life, as well as her husband, Chuza, was what Joanna had left behind, Mary thought. Did she miss it? Was it arousing strange feelings? How could it not?

In the kitchen, the cooks were busy with the next course. The fish was to be laid on a platter of Sumerian watercress and garnished with leeks and sour onions, to be served neither too hot nor too cool. No one seemed to question why these two women were there. Joanna was so confident and knowledgeable about where everything was that it would have been presumptuous to ask her what she was doing. Antipas was known for setting traps and planting spies, and perhaps this was one. So they smiled and handed her and Mary the trays when they were ready.

Mary watched Joanna to see how to present it to the rulers. There was a certain set protocol. Uncover. Smile. Bow. Ladle. Then retreat. But they did not leave the chamber. Instead, they stationed themselves in discreet shadows at one end.

An old man in a russet robe hurried in, followed by a middle-aged one with thick black eyebrows. They joined Antipas and Herodias at table and began gesturing, talking heatedly.

"It's the high priests!" whispered Joanna. "The present one, Caiaphas, and the former one, Annas. I recognize them. I have seen them both too many times."

"The high priest, here?" Somehow she had thought he spent all his time in the Temple.

Joanna gave a low laugh, quickly stifled. "They both need to bow to their master. Of course, he isn't their ultimate master. Pilate is that." She thought a moment. "Old Annas is Caiaphas's father-in-law. The whole office is governed by family politics. But Annas is the brains.

Caiaphas is stupid. He does whatever old Annas tells him. He always has."

"We need to get closer," said Mary. They could hear nothing.

"We will," said Joanna. "After the dinner, they will retire to a receiving chamber. Come." She led Mary to it.

The receiving chamber was high-vaulted and boasted timbers inlaid with gold. The windows opened onto two vistas: one the Temple Mount itself, and the other onto wide streets of this opulent section of Jerusalem.

Mary and Joanna stood like obedient servants along the back wall of the chamber. Sure enough, Antipas and Herodias entered with stately measured steps, trailing their royal robes, followed by Caiaphas and testy old Annas. But when Judas stepped in, it was all they could do to keep their posts and not rush forward.

Another servant entered and proffered goblets. All the party took them.

Judas! There he was, dressed in a fine blue robe Mary knew he had never worn while with Jesus, smiling and talking to Antipas, to Herodias, to Annas, and to Caiaphas. He nodded and seemed perfectly at home. They welcomed him. They seemed to know him already.

Mary felt sick. She watched him—she could not take her eyes away—in disbelief. Judas! One of Jesus's own disciples, here with these people.

They were talking, and smiling, and saying things Mary and Joanna could not hear. The women had to get closer. Silently, they nodded to one another, pulled their veils tighter, and approached.

Mary glided over to the party, holding a pitcher she had snatched from a waiting tray. "More wine?" she murmured, keeping her head down and changing her voice. She was trembling with fear that she would be caught, and it was hard not to spill the wine.

Judas turned a smiling, blank face toward her. He showed no recognition. "Indeed," he said, nodding, and she refilled his goblet, her arm shaking.

Let him get drunk! she thought. Let him get drunk and babble, so that I may know what he is thinking! She dared not look directly in his eyes—those oddly changed eyes now—lest he recognize her, but she longed to see what was in them.

"We've had enough of him," Annas pronounced, in a querulous voice. "This has to end."

"More wine?" Joanna asked, delicately refilling his goblet. He turned grateful eyes to her and nodded with approval.

"That's easy," said Caiaphas, raising his bushy eyebrows. "Arrest him."

"On what grounds? You lost your grounds when you let the ruckus at the Temple two days ago pass unchecked." Judas sounded disgusted. "Now you have no excuse." He leaned forward. "He'll give you none. He's clever. He knows exactly what to do, how far to go."

"Well, we'll create one," said Caiaphas.

"You ass," said his father-in-law. "It has to hold up for the Romans. If they sense anything underhanded, they'll turn on *us*."

"Don't worry, it will hold up," said Caiaphas stubbornly. "This man endangers our nation, he endangers the compromise we have worked out with the Romans. He'll incite a rebellion. He cannot be allowed to continue."

"Caiaphas, you surprise me," said Annas. "You actually *think* sometimes." He turned to Judas. "But he is too popular. That's the problem. Afterward people will be content, they always forget sooner or later, we can count on it, but now . . . if we arrest him, in front of all those crowds—you saw him up at the Temple, you saw that motley mess hail him when he first entered Jerusalem—there will be trouble. We have to do it quietly. Away from the crowds. That's why we need you."

"And that's what I offer you." Only his foot-shuffling betrayed any nervousness. "I can lead you to him when he's alone. I know all his movements. I guarantee a quick, clean arrest, away from his adoring crowds." He ran the words together.

Annas nodded. "Very good."

"But I expect to be well paid. After all, no one else can offer you this." His voice was getting thinner and more brittle.

"Ten pieces of silver." Caiaphas spoke, in his sonorous priest-voice. Judas laughed.

"Twenty." Caiaphas raised his hands, palms up, to show benevolence. "Shekels. *Tyrian* shekels."

Judas shook his head ruefully. "You disappoint me, gentlemen," he said. "I offer you something priceless, and you try to cheat me."

"Thirty." Old Annas spoke with authority. "That's final."

Judas turned his head this way and that, hedging. "Too low," he said.

"Take it or leave it. After all, what you are offering is a private arrest. We can make a public arrest for free."

"And get into trouble."

"We can manage that. We plan to have a Roman cohort, and what problem can Roman soldiers not handle? A few legionaries, a few killings—they have no qualms about that. They do it every day. Of course, we would *prefer* a quiet arrest, but we are quite prepared to proceed without it."

"Very well," Judas said. "Thirty pieces it is."

"See me in my office," said Caiaphas. "I will pay you there."

"No. Surely you have that much money with you—a trifling sum, as I said. I prefer to be paid now. I do not want to explain to some clerk what this is all about."

Grumbling, Caiaphas scratched around in his money bag and withdrew individual pieces of silver reluctantly. "Five . . . ten . . . here's another two . . ."

Judas stuck out his palm and accepted them. "But our agreement—you will not harm him in any way—this stands?"

"If you don't wish him harmed, why are you turning on him?" Annas asked.

"I think he should be protected from himself," said Judas, slowly. Mary had heard him speak that way before, choosing his words carefully to give a certain impression, to protect himself. But earlier, he *had* spoken to her of trying to prevent Jesus from coming to harm. Did he now truly believe that was what he was doing? Was he just using the Temple authorities as he had thought of using Jesus's mother to achieve this? "He has raised enormous expectations that he can never fulfill. When he cannot, people will turn on him. This should give him a chance to think, before it is too late."

"And enrich you in the process."

"Thirty pieces of Tyrian silver? Gentlemen, you must think I am some farmer from Galilee. It is not much money. But I rest content," he hurriedly added. There were still eighteen pieces of silver to be delivered. One by one they clinked into his palm, hitting the pile already there.

"You joined him," said Caiaphas. "You must have seen something in him. What is it people are following? I am baffled."

Three, four, five, six. The last of the coins joined the others in Judas's hand.

"I did believe in him," said Judas, his real voice back. "I thought he had the answers I sought. He had answers, but not answers I wanted. Or needed. They are not the same. I was ready to accept what I need, even if painful. But he cannot supply it. And so"—he spread his hands, and the staged voice returned—"the least I can do is protect him from harm. Isn't that so, gentlemen?"

Mary felt as though she would become sick that instant, have to dash outside and vomit. Judas had not asked them for any reassurance or particulars about how they would protect Jesus from harm.

It is up to us to warn him! Me, and Joanna. We must tell him about Judas. We must let him know what is waiting.

Judas. She looked at him, so trim and sophisticated, swaying in his expensive robes. Oh, Judas . . . you were almost there. You almost understood. And she surprised herself by weeping for him, stifling her cries before Joanna heard her. She wept for him rather than for Jesus. She did not understand why, but it was Judas who rent her heart.

Judas took his leave, slipping away like a shadow. The remaining plotters continued to discuss the Jesus problem. When Mary got control of her tears, she drew Joanna to one side and said, trying to steady her trembling voice, "Shall we stay? There may be more to hear."

Joanna cast a doubtful look at the huddled conspirators. It would be hard to penetrate their circle. The meal was over, and they had been served with all the wine and sweetmeats they could eat. All the servers would have withdrawn except the rulers' own attendants, and strangers would be obvious.

"It's too dangerous," whispered Joanna. She glanced over at them. "One more pass through. We can pretend we are looking for used goblets or spilled food."

They approached the remaining four and tried to act natural, looking anywhere but at them. They kept their eyes down.

". . . not sure I trust him," one was saying. "It's tricky to rely on disillusioned disciples. They are notoriously changeable. All this Jesus has to do is suddenly say something that appeals to Judas, and then—"

Mary bent down and scooped up a wine goblet, bobbing obsequiously.

"It's a chance we'll have to take," another said. "He sounded disgusted. Rather cynical."

"What's a cynic?" A woman speaking. Herodias. "A cynic is only someone who has loved deeply and feels betrayed. Such a person is easy to win back. I agree with Caiaphas."

So it was Caiaphas who had the reservations. Perhaps he was not so stupid after all.

"And when he's arrested, then what? What do we do with him? Lock him up, like Barabbas?"

"No, we have to hand him over to the Romans for a trial. Right away. Barabbas can rot in prison. The Romans have to hear this case before they leave Jerusalem and scurry back to Caesarea for their banquets and chariot-racing. Once they do that, it will be years before the case is heard. As soon as we have him, we'll turn him over. And press charges against him."

Joanna had found one overturned goblet, and she made a show of collecting it. But then she nodded to Mary. They must go. It was over.

Just then, one of the guests turned and looked at these servants. Fortunately, the glance fell on Mary, the stranger, rather than Joanna, whom Antipas might have recognized.

They retreated from the room and threw down the goblet. "We can't go back to the kitchen," said Joanna. "Let's go! Now!"

They walked down the corridor and, making several quick turns, ran out the servants' door and into the safety of the little alley. They hurried away until they reached a main street. Then Mary slumped against a wall.

"Oh, God in his heaven!" she cried, invoking the Sacred Name. She was dizzy, overcome by what she had seen and heard.

Joanna steadied her. "God favored us. He meant us to hear. But what must we do? Warn Jesus, of course . . . but shall we confront Judas?"

Confront Judas. If they did, would he just change his plans?

"No, we mustn't let him know we have heard," said Mary. She was absolutely sure of this. "We must pretend everything is normal. But we must tell Jesus. And his mother."

"Not his mother," said Joanna. "Why grieve her? And she will not be able to persuade him. We have seen that he loves her but he keeps his own counsel."

"Joanna," Mary said, "I am so troubled. All of us came to Jesus with questions, some of which have never been resolved. But we trust him—how can another follower like us do this? Why not just fall away, desert? Many have. We have seen other curious followers leave, drift away. Why is Judas doing this?"

"For revenge," said Joanna without hesitation. "He is like a slighted lover. Such people do not slink away but want to exact pain on the one who caused them pain, so that person will acknowledge their power and existence. It is a way of getting recognition, as well as punishing."

"But Jesus has not caused him pain."

"You don't know what Judas asked of him, what he expected, or what Jesus's response was."

That was true. She knew nothing about the others' relationships with Jesus. They were private, and each was unique, unlike other teachers' relationships with students.

"I hate him!" Mary burst out. And to think this man, Judas, thought she might become his life companion.

"Don't hate him," said Joanna. "That only confuses your thinking."

"You sound like Jesus!" she said. "Love your enemies—"

"Isn't that what we are supposed to do? Sound like Jesus? Jesus told us to pray for him—for all our enemies."

"I'll do that, but . . ." The anger at Judas, the lost disciple, was overwhelming, as well as the sorrow, that had caused her to weep.

"We still must combat Judas," said Joanna. "Pray for his soul, but stop his plans."

As they pushed their way through the streets, packed with people, they looked around anxiously. The crowds were full of exotically attired pilgrims, Jerusalemites, Roman soldiers, and mysterious people whose origins could not be guessed. The sun was sinking, and those who had to leave the city surged toward the gates. Passover was coming.

"Why is this night different from all other nights?" was the traditional question.

Would this Passover be different from others? the pilgrims were wondering. Would the Messiah come? Each year there was that possibility. That was why Passover was always in the present and never in the past.

ᔕᖺᓂ **L 1** ᔕᖺᓂ

It was too late to go back to the Temple. Jesus would have left by now; the day was done. They had to find him on the slope of the Mount of Olives. So many pilgrims were packed on the little path leading up to its heights that Mary and Joanna decided to turn aside and go into the olive grove at the foot of the mountain and wait for the mass of people to pass.

Inside the garden, called Gethsemane because of its olive press, they found a quiet and green retreat. The olive trees around them were ancient and whispered of lost secrets, of a time even before Jerusalem was restored. What had they seen? The rebuilding under Nehemiah and Ezra? Had they waited and waited through the five hundred years while Israel reconstituted herself and fought first the Greeks and now the Romans? Had Maccabee leaders conferred under their bent branches? Had the soldiers of Antiochus rallied here?

"This place is haunted," said Joanna. "I hear too many voices." She had settled herself under a particularly thick-trunked olive tree.

"Not as loud as the pilgrims outside," said Mary. She was still reeling from what she had heard in the palace. All very well and good for Joanna to say they could just warn Jesus and prevent it. What if they could not? Judas—the defection, the bold betrayal—troubled her so greatly she felt as if she had been physically struck. She welcomed the little quiet pause between the hearing of the plot and falling in again with Jesus.

She sank down under the tree beside Joanna. Her thoughts were whirling, noisier than the tumult of the crowds streaming past them. Their many languages blended into a whole; innocent conversations about food and shelter sound ominous, like a roar. For the first time, Mary questioned the Law requiring people to gather for the three festivals in Jerusalem. And, for the first time, she questioned Jesus's motives in choosing to come here now.

The greatest number of people all gathered together . . . the Romans and Antipas's partisans and the Temple authorities, all looking . . . Jesus wanted to be scrutinized, wanted the attention that only this time and this place could give him. He wanted to go beyond Galilee and thrust himself into the very heart of the nation. It was all part of his plan, a larger design than involved him in the divine dawning of the Kingdom of God.

And now Judas would try to stop all that. Judas would see that he was arrested, hustled away before whatever climax Jesus had hoped for came to pass. He would be silenced and set aside.

She and Joanna had to warn him so he could protect himself. But what if Jesus did not choose to do so?

The olive grove was so peaceful and protected that they sat drinking in its benevolent, gentle air. The trees around them seemed to whisper and console, murmuring, Quiet yourselves. . . . This is but the moment. . . . Think clearly. . . . All things pass. . . . How tempting just to stay here, breathe deeply, and have faith that everything would sort itself out, that things would happen as they were meant to.

At length, Joanna stirred and said, "We must go up. It is getting late."

And Mary broke her intense reverie to see that the crowds had thinned and that they now had no reason not to set out on the path. Reluctantly she stood up and prepared herself, and they left the tranquillity of the garden-grove and got onto the common path.

They easily found the others, who were still in the same spot and had already lit the fire for the evening meal. Jesus was not with them, but was standing apart, looking down at Jerusalem, now barely visible in the growing gloom. The walls could be seen, and the white reflection of the Temple, but the dark was fast coming down.

I must tell him! Mary thought. Before the evening meal, before the gathering with the others. It must be now.

She approached him, feeling very apprehensive. She reached out a hand and touched his shoulder, gently, as he was gazing at the barely visible outline of Jerusalem. Immediately he swung around and looked at her. But his expression was not welcoming.

"Yes?" he said.

"Master," she said. Suddenly she was acutely aware of the last time she had sought him out to be alone with him, and what had passed between them. Oh, do not let that discredit this message! she begged.

"Yes?" he repeated. He was looking at her—not coldly, but almost without recognition.

"Master, Joanna and I were able to get into Herod Antipas's palace today. We spied on them—and quite well, I must say. The high priest Caiaphas was there, and old Annas, and Antipas and Herodias—"

"Quite a gathering," said Jesus. "Were you impressed by them?"

His question stung her. "No," she said. "Why would I be? They are hardly enviable."

"Many people would envy them," he said.

"I am not one of them," she said, wishing he would not test her so. "And if riches impressed me, remember that I left them behind in Magdala."

He kept looking at her. He said nothing. Finally, she came yet closer to him and said quietly, "We heard their conversation. They consider you dangerous. They want to silence you."

Instead of making a comment, Jesus just continued to look at her, his eyes boring into hers until she turned away.

"The most shocking thing is . . ." She paused. Did she have the courage to tell it? ". . . Judas has sought them out. Judas . . . Judas was there. He told them things about you. He agreed to lead them to you, secretly."

Now at last Jesus seemed to be listening. "Judas." He raised one hand to his forehead and began to stroke it. "Judas."

"Yes, Judas!" She took a breath. "*Judas.* He even . . . he even let them pay him. Yes, he accepted money from them to lead them to you."

"Then they have wasted their money. My whereabouts are not secret."

Was that all he had to say?

"They want to arrest you in private! When the people—the crowds—cannot see," she cried.

"Judas," he suddenly said. "Judas. Oh, my dear Judas! No, no!"

"It *was* Judas. I saw him and heard him. I, too, grieve. He was so close . . . he understood so much of what you said . . . he seemed sincere . . . but, master, you must protect yourself against him!" She took a deep breath. "He is evil! He is our enemy!"

"There is no way to avert evil," said Jesus, after a pause. "What must come, will come, but woe to that man through whom it comes."

"Jesus—" She reached out her hand toward him. I have to say it. I have to tell him how sorry I am about what was said at Dan, how I now understand, how I am now content to—

"I can bear to hear no more." He cut her off. "I thank you for what you have told me. It took courage. Now go and say no more. I must prepare myself, and the others."

But I must tell you of my feelings, of all these things that are troubling me. . . .

"Yes, master," she said, turning away, obeying him.

The rest of the party were busy; Simon had put himself in charge of the fire and was barking out orders about the skewers to be roasted over it. Susanna was organizing the dishes, and Matthew had arranged for the wine—soon to come, he assured them. Watching them concern themselves with these trifles only made Mary and Joanna's secret knowledge more painful.

Now Jesus joined them, smiling and laughing, as if he had no other matters on his mind. Was he showing that these forgettable everyday actions were significant? Yet he himself had indicted them, ordering his followers to leave everyday life behind.

Perhaps he himself is not sure what is meaningful, thought Mary. Perhaps . . . oh, perhaps we have all followed a man who is only a learner himself!

They were all seated, all eating together. Jesus broke the bread and gave thanks, as always, holding the bread in his strong, able hands. His light wool mantle draped easily on his shoulders. There was nothing in his demeanor to indicate that this would not go on forever. A gathering . . . breaking bread . . . a peaceful night . . . preaching in the morning . . . on and on, for all the days before them.

"Tomorrow night is the Passover," Jesus said at length. "It will be our last time to eat together as we have always done." He looked around at them one by one. No one asked him what he meant by "the last time." When his eyes rested on Mary, she felt that he understood all her anguish but that they would never actually speak of it.

"Passover in Jerusalem!" said Thomas. "I've always dreamed of it."

"We will have a fine feast," said Jesus. "I have made arrangements. Peter and John, tomorrow you must go into the city early by way of the Sheep Gate, and a man carrying a water jar will meet you. It should be easy to find him, for men rarely carry water jars. Follow him through the streets; he will enter a certain house. When you meet the master of the house, tell him that the Teacher needs a place to celebrate Passover with his friends. He will show you a large upper room, furnished and appropriate. You shall make preparations for us there."

So he has followers here in the city as well, secret ones that we will never know about, Mary thought. How many of them are there, scattered all about, who have come to join him one by one, and whom he recognizes but we will never know about? I am surrounded by an invisible cocoon of secrets, so many mysteries. . . .

"My sheep hear my voice," said Jesus, answering her unspoken question. "And other sheep I have, who are not of this fold."

The wind rose, and the pine branches above them shivered. The other sheep—who were they? And then the forbidden, petty thought: does he love them more than us?

Jesus was almost directly opposite her, the flickering firelight giving his face a ruddy glow. And all the others . . . John, as always, keeping near him, his pale features now given a bit of color; Big James, his wide jaw clenched; Thomas, his handsome face clouded with thought, as usual; Peter, laughing and talking to Simon beside him—Simon, his old fierce scowl traded for a smile; Susanna, smiling and relaxed, no hint of torment . . . Why, I love them all, Mary realized with surprise. These people, so difficult at times . . . but under it all, I love them fiercely. Our loyalty to Jesus has bound us all together.

Eli and Silvanus seemed a mist; her mother and father, vanished; Joel, a distant if still painful memory. Only Elisheba was still real; looking at Jesus and his mother, she now knew that that bond of motherhood could never be truly broken. Someday, someday . . . we will come together again, and all will be understood and forgiven, and somehow it will all be mediated by Jesus, whom Elisheba will come to know. Somehow . . .

"As we set out for Jerusalem, I called you friends, and so you are," Jesus was saying. "And there are many things I wish to tell you, as friends. Later you will look back on them and remember them and search my meaning."

No one said anything. They were afraid that to do so would keep Jesus from saying what he truly wished to say, for he always answered questions, no matter how extraneous. So they held silent as all around them their neighbors were noisily bedding down for the night.

"You know that there are signs that this age will soon be ending," Jesus said, as if he were announcing a mere water shortage or trade disruption. "Soon all will end. God will act to bring this about. We can only bow to his will, submit ourselves to serve the cause as best we can, sacrifice ourselves to his purpose. I am entirely ready to do this. Are you?"

No one said anything, until Matthew finally asked, "How will we know that this is coming to pass?"

"There will be signs—unmistakable signs in the heavens and on earth. Until then, do not be deceived. Do not be misled. Stand firm. My friends," Jesus was saying, "you were all given to me by my Father. And I have promised him that I will not lose one of you—except the son of perdition, the one doomed to destruction—no matter what happens. So do not fear."

Judas, who had said absolutely nothing during the entire meal, gave a jerk when Jesus said "the one doomed to destruction," and turned his head toward Mary. His face was stiff, and his eyes did not meet hers directly, but again there was that dark, almost empty look in them that gave her a chill of recognition. Mary noticed that his fancy blue robe was missing. Had he hidden it in a nearby tree trunk, to be put on again when he rejoined his Temple friends?

The face of Jesus's mother was illuminated by the dying fire. She alone looked apprehensive, bracing herself. But she held herself still.

They lingered by the fire for a long time, savoring its slow dying and warmth. Then, one by one, they stood up, making their way to their pallets. Jesus again went toward a ridge, away from the others. Mary followed him.

This time he faced the ugly valley called Gehenna, south of Jerusalem, where rubbish fires burned continually and all the city's filth was thrown. An acrid smoke drifted up, stinging their nostrils when it was blown their way. Mary remembered the pit where she and Joel had thrown the shattered idols, so long ago.

"Foulness," Jesus was muttering. "All filth and degradation is smoldering there." He turned to Mary as she approached, as if he had been waiting. "Do you know why the eternal fires burn there?"

"No, I do not," she admitted.

"This was the place where human sacrifices were made to Molech," Jesus said. "Even the kings of Israel, the very same that worshiped in the Temple, sacrificed their sons and daughters to the god Molech. When Josiah became king and instigated his reforms, he consigned the site of Molech's altars to be a rubbish dump. And so they are, to this day. But still the evil is not expunged." He sighed. "Something more is needed. Evil does not disappear just because time passes."

"There is too much foulness and evil here," she agreed, pointing to Gehenna and its smoke far below. "But Joanna and I found a peaceful, quiet place near the foot of this mount. It is an old olive grove, and was deserted even when crowds surged around it. Perhaps you would find it restorative."

"Peaceful," said Jesus, in wonder. "In the midst of all this?"

"Yes. Just to the left of the main path at the bottom. There is a gate, but it can be opened."

"I must go see it, then," said Jesus. "Perhaps early tomorrow."

A rustle behind them betrayed another presence.

"A nasty sight." Judas was standing just beyond their reach. Had he heard them? Heard about the private olive grove?

"It is the manifestation of sin," said Jesus. "If we could always see sin, it would look just like this."

"Unfortunately, we cannot," said Judas, his voice sad.

"Satan does not wish us to see it," said Jesus, "lest we flee from it in horror." He turned and left Mary and Judas standing together, making his way toward his sleeping place.

Judas kept looking down into the ravine.

"Yes, evil is very ugly," said Mary. "And sometimes it shows its face boldly. Judas, what must be done about it?".

"Why, set fire to it," he said, offhandedly. "As Josiah did."

"People do not burn so easily."

Judas now turned and stared at her. "People?"

"People who have gone over to Satan, listened to him." There was a mighty pause. "Judas . . ." She hated him, but he could still abandon the path he had started out on, could choose to betray Caiaphas rather than Jesus. "You know what I mean."

There was a very long pause. Judas looked as though he was going to confess; a series of expressions raced across his face. But then his old mask came back to him. "No, I'm afraid I don't," he said. "But perhaps you should look to yourself, and make sure your demons have really gone. It seems they may once again be speaking to you, misleading you."

Oh, he is clever. He knows just where to attack, how to render his foe helpless . . . or so he thinks. Like Satan himself, as Jesus warned me. "I am sorry for you, Judas," she finally said, in a strong voice. "You are wrong."

"About your demons? We shall see."

"No, not about my demons. It's yours I am concerned about." Could Satan have entered into him back at that dreadful, haunted altar at Dan?

Satan tried to get Jesus in the desert; he failed, but he got Judas instead at Dan.

"It grieves me to see you slipping back into madness," he said, his voice full of concern. "It really does." He paused. "Come, it's time for rest." He tried to steer her back toward the sleeping area, putting his arm around her solicitously.

Did he plan to wait until they were all asleep, so he could slip away again?

The feel of his arm was repulsive. People thought snakes were dreadful to touch, but Mary had once had to pick up a small snake that had invaded her room, to take it outside, and she had found its skin to be smooth and dry and cool, pleasurable to the touch. Even chameleons—she had had one as a pet once—had a whimsical bumpiness that she found appealing when she patted its head. But the arm of this man—who had been unable to accept what he perceived as rejection by Jesus, or his disappointment in him—or whatever it was, even Satan's whispers—felt more of an abomination than Ashara ever had.

She shook it off and moved away with a shudder that he caught. "I am not mad, but it pleases you to claim I am: more lies, like everything about you lately. Don't you get tired of lying and pretending to be something other than you are?" She stopped herself from saying any more, for fear that Satan would know he had been found out.

In the brightness of the almost-full moon, his handsome, lean features were illuminated as if the moonlight itself loved him. He had a rueful smile on his lips. "Ah, Mary. I have never done that. I have always been a questioner, and everyone knew it."

But now you're a liar and betrayer as well, she wanted to say. She ached to say it, to fling it at his posturing, smug self, but that would give him information he must not have.

"You will take your questions and your falsehoods to your grave," was all she could manage.

"Many worthier persons than I have done that," he said. "It will be an honor to join their company."

"Don't cast yourself with famous philosophers and rebels," she choked out. "They will not welcome you. Put yourself, rather, with"— she wanted to say the disobedient sons of Aaron, and the rebellion of Korah against Moses—"those who stumble and condemn themselves."

Again the wry chuckle. "You need rest," he repeated. But he did not attempt to touch her again.

"You need repentance," she retorted. "But who will give it to you?"

Lying on her makeshift pallet, she took a long time to dismiss Judas from her thoughts. His downfall tore at her. Caiaphas and Antipas she did not blame. They did not even know Jesus; they just viewed him as a troublemaker from Galilee, in a time when not attracting Roman attention was very important. But in so many ways, Judas had seemed the most informed, the most aware, of all the disciples.

Perhaps that was the problem. Could it be that the more perceptive a person was, the more troubling he would find Jesus and his message?

For a movement to endure, it needed to win the Judases. It needed the questioners to explain why their questions were answered, and not in simple terms, but in complicated reasoning.

Judas's defection was not simply the loss of a disciple for Jesus but, far more troubling, the loss of a surer footing for the movement as a whole.

∽ L11 ∽

The moon shone on Jerusalem, touching it with blue-silver light. The Temple gleamed like a submerged pearl, and throughout the city the marble palaces and buildings glowed like jewels beside their ordinary limestone sisters. Mary could see it all from where she lay, vainly trying to sleep. The walls of the city were so clearly visible that they stood like knife blades guarding the buildings and houses within, a stark demarcation line. Soon the dawn would come, and the priests would throw open the great doors of the Temple, and the guards would order the gates of the city to be pulled back. It all seemed so comfortingly eternal. This sacred place would always be with them.

She saw Jesus standing nearby, looking out at the city. His back was to her, and she could not read the expression on his face, but from his stance she guessed it was sorrowful. Just looking at Jerusalem seemed to summon up some deep grief within him.

His watchfulness meant that Judas could not slip away, she gratefully concluded. Judas was trapped here on the mountainside. Whatever he had planned for that night, he would now be prevented from doing. She would be able to rest.

But sleep, when it finally came, was not peaceful. The bright, searching moonlight seemed to assault even her eyelids. It probed her dreams, which were troubled with violent scenes. But only one of them remained with her when she awakened.

There were pictures of Jesus bleeding and reeling. She had had this dream before, but never so explicitly. This time, besides seeing him beaten and hurt, she saw buildings around him, landmarks she recognized: the outer courts of Antipas's palace and a city gate of Jerusalem, but not the north or east gate through which they had already entered. She saw the face of Pilate—she had never seen him before, but she knew who he was by his attire, a formal Roman toga—and she saw Antipas, floating somewhere on the periphery. And Dismas, the dagger-man she had glimpsed so briefly, so long ago, at Matthew's banquet. He was dying. But what did that have to do with Jesus? She had forgotten his name until she heard it murmured in her dream. "Dismas. Dismas."

She came slowly awake. Others were stirring. Dawn was here, the entire sky was a delicate rosy pink, and in the tender light the city was almost pulsating with ethereal beauty. At a distance, it seemed to fulfill every high-minded desire for beauty and holiness.

They gathered around the early-morning fire, hearing the roosters crow far below announcing the day. Jesus spoke in gentle words, as if he was entirely satisfied with what the day would lay before them.

"We will gather for the Passover feast in the place that has been prepared," he said. "I think you will find it a godly and fine table. You will be led there by the disciples who will help prepare it." He nodded toward the women and toward Peter and John. "We will celebrate the Passover together. I long for this evening." His voice rose, and Mary heard a joyful note in his voice.

But the beatings . . . the whippings and the bleeding . . . should I not tell him of this? Mary thought. I must tell him! I must confide whatever my visions have revealed to me!

He was coming toward her. Now she must tell him.

He smiled. "Mary, I am going to withdraw to the garden you told me about," he said, "the olive garden at the foot of the mount."

"It is secluded, and if you need to be alone, you will be," she said. "But I must tell you of something I have seen—"

"I have seen it, too," he said quickly. "No need to tell me." He paused. "Mary, I go forward to take my place in these visions. That is only the beginning. There is more, much more besides, that the visions, being limited, cannot show us. But I see them. My Father tells me. He reveals it to me." He took her hands. "But your sight is precious to me. Thank you for sharing it with me, as you have all along."

"Judas—" she began.

"He has gone the way he must," said Jesus. "You tried. You tried your best."

She was startled. How did he know? Had he overheard?

"Don't you know the scriptures? It was destined. 'Even the friend

490

who had my trust, who shared my table, has scorned me.' And: 'If an enemy had reviled me, that I could bear; if my foe had viewed me with contempt, from that I could hide. But it was you, my other self, my comrade and friend, you, whose company I enjoyed, at whose side I walked. . . .' It is difficult for you to understand this, I know."

"To understand, no," she finally said. "But to believe—yes, it is. How could anyone who has known you—"

"Knowledge and belief are not the same thing," he said. "In days to come, you must remember this."

They set out down the steep path toward the city. The excitement of the coming evening was already in the air; the ancient holy day seemed to create an incense of its own.

Mary glanced over at Judas, who was walking along with a fixed smile, but she found the sight of him so revolting she wanted to wrench a stone from the path and fling it at his head, sending him careening to the bottom, where he would lie so broken and injured he would never walk again.

The intensity of her hatred startled her. And Jesus speaks of loving our enemies and praying for them, she thought. Sometimes, it's impossible!

As they approached the final bit of descent, right before the path would level out and cross the Kidron ravine, Mary pushed her way up to where Jesus was walking with Peter and John.

She slipped alongside them and then said to Jesus, "Here is the garden—to the left."

The silvery olive trees—some so high that they reared to the sky like oaks—were easily seen from outside. Jesus stopped and looked at them.

"I shall go in and pray," he said.

"Are you not going to the Temple?" Peter looked surprised.

"Not today," said Jesus. "I will not be teaching today, except to all of you."

"But will we not see you today?"

"In the evening, yes," said Jesus. "We will all gather at the place I told you of."

He turned aside and went toward the gate, and he invited none of them to accompany him.

Now they went on without him, making their way into the city, each with an assigned task. They climbed up the steep sides of the

Kidron ravine to the Sheep Gate and entered with flocks of bleating sheep being driven by their herdsmen toward the Temple. The disciples stationed themselves by the gate, watching intently for a man with a water jar. It was not long before a stocky man sidled into sight, awkwardly balancing his jar on his head.

Peter rushed up to him. "Are you the one?" he blurted out.

The man turned suspicious eyes on Peter. "The one who will lead you to a house?" he asked.

"The very one," said Peter, loudly.

The man winced at the booming voice, then motioned to Peter. John joined them. "Let me show you," said the man.

They followed him through the twisting and climbing streets of Jerusalem until they emerged into the Upper City, which was the well-to-do area that Joanna and Judas knew all too well. He pointed toward a doorway and then slipped away, as if he did not want to enter.

Peter turned to the others and said, "Here it must be. We will make the arrangements. Those of you who are procuring the food, this is where we will gather later." He looked around at them. "Remember we must buy a lamb. We should have done it earlier. But there will still be plenty to choose from."

Yes, the flocks of late-arriving lambs they had just passed would assure that, Mary thought. No reason to chide themselves.

"Come, let us go to the Upper Market," said Judas. "They have the best selection."

"No, let us choose a lamb first!" said Mary. "That is the most important thing." She turned to the others. "We need the lamb. We cannot have Passover without it. And in only a few hours it must be slaughtered, and we must arrange for the preparation—"

"Shouldn't we first inspect the place where we will gather?" asked Judas.

"No," said Mary. "There is no time to waste." She did not want to hear any of his suggestions.

The Temple was seething with people. It was good that Jesus had not come here today. No one would have heard him had he spoken or tried to teach. The latecomers were converging on the lamb merchants, the others were surging toward the sacrificial altar and the offering trumpets. Confusion reigned.

The disciples pushed toward the lamb vendors. Hundreds of bleating and tethered animals were milling and bucking. There was no memory here of Jesus and his attack on the merchants: people were lined up ten deep in front of the money-changers' stall. How futile Jesus's actions had been; how little anyone had heeded them, thought Mary. She felt weighted with sadness.

It would have been best to take time choosing an animal, but as it was, all they could do was point to a reasonably well-proportioned lamb and say, "That one! That one!"

"Very well, sir," said the merchant. "And will you wish to make arrangements for the preparations? I have here an associate with a fine kitchen, still able to take reservations. . . ." He pointed to a grinning man next to him.

In the end, they contracted with the merchant to provide the lamb and roast it in accordance with Mosaic Law. But Philip and Matthew said they would take the lamb themselves to have it slain in the proper manner on the Temple grounds; they would not hire an agent.

Judas reached into his money bag. "You will need money to purchase all the goods," he said..

No, no! Mary almost dashed the money from his hand. But she remembered that most of the money came from others, including herself. That was not tainted.

Judas counted out the money coin by coin.

"I myself will see to other things," he said. "You do not need me to buy food." He smiled and bowed.

Why did no one else ask him what things? Mary thought. When you trust someone, everything is unquestioned.

"Come," said Nathanael, suspecting nothing.

"Nathanael," Mary began, "Judas is—Judas is—" She wanted to break her promise to Joanna, tell the others about Judas. But if they knew, Peter or Simon or Big James might bluster and threaten and give Judas the warning he needed to make timely changes in his plans.

"Follow him!" she said. "See where he goes!"

Nathanael looked around. "He's gone already. We have lost him. Why did you say that?"

Mary could not answer; the words froze in her throat.

A field of baskets stretched before them in the Upper Market, each filled to the brim with succulent produce. They had to buy so much: bitter greens, and horseradish, and barley and wheat flour for the unleavened bread, and apples and almonds and dates and raisins for the *charoseth*, and eggs and olives and vinegar, and of course the wine, the finest they could afford. And mustard and honey and grapes for the lamb sauce. Each vendor beckoned, each promised the very finest wheat from the fields of Zanoah and figs from Galilee and wine from the vineyards of Zeredah, and dates from Jericho, and lettuces from farms near Jerusalem.

Mary did not wish to be the leader of this expedition. She could think of nothing but Judas and how to thwart him. But everyone seemed to be looking to her.

"Dearest Mary," she finally said to Jesus's mother, "you have much experience. You have presided over many a Passover dinner. I believe you should select the bitter herbs and the ingredients for the *charoseth*."

The elder Mary nodded to her. That in itself was disconcerting. It made her uneasy that Jesus's mother should defer to her.

"And as for the rest—perhaps each of us should select something. Joanna, you choose the flour for the unleavened bread; Susanna, you choose the ingredients for the lamb sauce." She hated issuing these orders. But someone had to, so that they could proceed. "Men, choose something you long to eat, not ritually designated things, but something you have missed. I will choose the eggs," she said, deliberately selecting a lowly task for herself.

Wandering by herself in the market, she could overhear much, and she made it her business to: there was mention of Barabbas, talk of two Roman soldiers who had been stabbed, murmurs about the coming days with Antipas and Pilate bracing for an uprising of some sort. Stationed around the market, at corners and behind stalls, Roman soldiers, hands on their swords, looked around warily.

The pungent odor of fresh blood wafted down; the lambs were being slaughtered up at the Temple—hundreds, no, thousands of them. The head of each household passed a knife across his chosen animal's throat, and then the entire ritual of catching the blood was enacted, and finally the priests threw the blood at the foot of the altar, where it drained away. She could hear the squeals and cries of the doomed animals on the mount, even from where she stood.

Does God really want this? she asked herself. It is true that long ago he told Moses to do this, but that was for a small number of people. This crowd—the provisions they have to make to accommodate thousands of animals—could Moses have foreseen this? It is ugly, it is nauseating. She choked as a strong wave of blood-odor drifted down to her. And as for celebrating only at the Temple—does that not produce a hardship for many devout families? To come here is not easy, and once you are here . . . the endless expenses!

She looked about her and had to admit that the atmosphere was anything but holy. Crowds fighting over bargains for lambs and food . . . no place for people to sleep or live . . . no privacy or opportunity to meditate—it all obliterated holiness rather than encouraging it.

Mass pilgrimages have nothing to do with holiness, she suddenly realized. They may serve to let people see that there are fellow Jews from far away, to help them feel a surge of brotherhood, but that is all man-to-man, not man-to-God.

How can I get close to God? It's God I care about, it's God I need, not a throng of pilgrims!

She made her way back to the house reserved for them to celebrate the Passover. She needed respite. She wished Jesus would be there and would tell her something that would make her feel better.

But there was no Jesus. Only the other women, busy already with preparations for the dinner.

The place set aside for them was a spacious upper room that overlooked the rooftops of the city. Low tables, and reclining couches, were already set up. At midday, the chamber was very bright.

"So we are to dine Roman-style," said Mary, looking at the arrangement.

"It fits in with the ceremony," said Susanna. "It does not conflict with the ancient instructions."

"But do we have the proper number?" asked Mary. Roman-style dining always involved multiples of nine—three couches around one table, three diners to a couch.

"Oh, we are not going to be purists," said Joanna. "We are having several serving tables in the middle, and placing couches along all the sides. There are almost twenty of us, and should we not all be at the same table?" She laughed. "Moses said nothing about it, and I daresay the Pharisees would not object."

There were to be the thirteen men and the four women. Joanna was singing as she arranged the tables and couches. In the kitchen, Jesus's mother was busy making the charoseth, chopping apples and grinding the costly cinnamon to flavor the wine. Susanna was kneading the barley and wheat flour to make the flat, unleavened bread; it must be baked this afternoon and allowed to cool in the oven so it would be crisp. Mary would have to add the eggs to be roasted, and shred the horseradish to make the bitter dip, along with vinegar, for the herbs. As the women worked, they imagined the coming dinner.

"There will be a fine gathering," said Susanna. Mary could detect a tone of sadness in her voice. Her thoughts were back in Korazin; perhaps she was wondering what her husband was doing, where he would be having the seder.

"Put these cups on the table," Jesus's mother was telling her, handing her a tray laden with pottery cups. There were not enough of them. But Mary arranged them and then went back for more.

"How kind of the owner to provide even cups and trays," Jesus's mother said. "Where is he, that we may thank him?"

"Only Peter and John have seen him, and they are still busy with the lamb," said Joanna. "Our mystery host seems very shy."

Or perhaps he does not wish to be identified, thought Mary. It is dangerous to know Jesus or be seen openly with him now.

The kitchen on the ground floor, though small, was quite adequate and well provided. There were chopping boards and mortars and pestles and an array of knives available to them and waiting. But it still felt awkward to make themselves at home in a stranger's kitchen.

The small indoor oven—a luxury—was already heated and ready for the unleavened-bread dough, which Susanna was patting out into flat circles.

"Hurry, Susanna!" said Joanna. "Work faster! You'll not pass muster with the Pharisees otherwise." She turned to the two Marys and said, "They have worked out exactly the amount of time between the mixing and the baking—it must be no longer than the time it takes to walk slowly a Roman mile."

"And if we exceed that?" Jesus's mother asked.

"Then our unleavened bread is not fit for the feast," Joanna said. "But, luckily for us, no Pharisees will be present, nor are any watching now. Go on, put it in the oven."

"It is these things my son criticizes so harshly," said the elder Mary. "And in the end, it may be for these things that the religious authorities are his enemies and condemn him." She was close to tears. "He deserves to be opposed for a noble dispute, not the length of time it takes to make unleavened bread."

"Like one of the prophets," agreed Joanna. "Elijah challenging the priests of Baal, Nathan confronting David, Moses and Pharaoh—all are a long way from the Pharisees and their tithes and cooking rules. Such is the diminution of the times."

Mary set down her basket of eggs and selected some to be roasted along with the bread. Moses told us to do this, she thought, and we are still doing it. Almost reverently, she placed the eggs on a tray to go into the oven. Perhaps in the end that is all we know, all we can understand. Simple rules and simple instructions. God can trust us with that.

Dusk settled upon the city. From the windows in the upper room, they could see the sunlight withdrawing from the roofs and fading, to be replaced by a warm glow upon the limestone buildings. Then it, too, faded, and a blue tint washed over everything. A full moon, pale against the sky, rose. The Passover was beginning.

One by one, the disciples mounted the stairs and entered the room. Philip and Nathanael arrived first, and looked about in admiration.

"What a fine place!" Philip said. "Whose is it?"

"We don't know that yet," said Jesus's mother. "We must wait for him to reveal himself."

Andrew and Matthew followed close behind, and then several others—Thaddeus and Big James and Thomas. They were puffing as they ran up the stairs. Then they stopped and stared at the room, so beautifully appointed and waiting.

It was growing quite dark outside when Judas appeared at the top of the stairs. He was still not wearing his fine blue robe, in spite of the formality of the occasion. Perhaps he imagined that only it, not himself, was tainted. He, too, seemed impressed with the tables.

"This is magnificent," he said, to no one in particular. "Who do we have to thank for this?"

"A secret but loyal disciple," said Joanna, watching his face as she spoke.

"I see," said Judas. "He chooses his own." He turned away abruptly.

As the dark deepened, Peter and John arrived, bearing the roasted lamb on a covered tray. "We've got a fine one!" they said. "He roasted well, better than the others in the common kitchen! He was so fat, he took longer than the others!" And, indeed, the smell of the meat was delicious. They very seldom had meat these days.

The only one missing was Jesus. After what seemed a very long time, he appeared on the stairs and entered the room.

He looked rested and at peace, was Mary's immediate thought.

Gethsemane had been restorative for him. Oh, thank God I knew about it and could tell him!

"Greetings, friends," he said. "I am thankful that we can all gather here."

His mother came over to him and said something in private. Mary saw him nodding. Then he said, "Let us take our places."

Mary secured a place for herself on the second couch from the main one, but she and all the other women would be serving a great deal of the time and not always in their assigned places. John was beside Jesus, where he could lean over against him.

But instead of taking his place and proceeding with the time-honored ritual, Jesus stood up and removed his outer garments, including the fine cloak his mother had made for him. "You are all to be servants," he said, looking at each of them. "The greatest shall serve the least. I have come to set an example for you." He wrapped a towel around himself, draped another over his arm, and called for a basin of water. Mary rose and went to the kitchen to bring it to him.

Taking it, he said, "It is necessary that I wash you. You must serve one another this way." Bending down, he took Thomas's feet and began to wash them, then dried them with the towel. It was utterly silent in the room, except for the sound of Jesus's hands in the water.

When he got to Peter, Peter jumped up. "No, you shall not do this!" he said, drawing away.

"Unless I wash you, you have no part of me," Jesus said.

Peter stared for an instant. "Then—not my feet only, but all of me!" he cried, sitting back down and holding up the hem of his robe.

"Those of you who are clean, you need only the feet washed," said Jesus. "Others, who are unclean . . ." He looked at Judas. Judas quickly uncovered his feet and stuck them out to be washed.

Leaving Judas, Jesus then came to Big James, and enacted the rite with solemn quiet. Next he took his place at Mary's feet, and she could hardly bear to have him touch her feet and kneel like a servant before her. It seemed all wrong. Never had a man performed such a menial service for her, and that it was Jesus made it seem even more inappropriate. Yet, at the same time, she could not help feeling bound to him by this gesture in a way that nothing else could have come close to doing.

When he had finished washing everyone, he said, "Remember this. You are to be servants of one another, just so." He robed himself and took his place at the head couch.

The little serving tables held plates, with the first course—lettuce and shallots and sesame seeds. There was honeycomb, and apples and pistachios. These were the foods selected by the men who had missed them so sorely as they ate simple fare day after day.

"I recognize the figs of Galilee," said Mary. "I know you have missed them, Simon. But the dried fish from Magdala—who besides me has longed for it?" That it was on this table seemed a mystical benediction for her. All that the fish symbolized—the routines and rituals of her old life—seemed to be there still, neither forgotten nor dead.

"I have also longed for it," said Peter. "Don't you think there are things I regret having left behind? You aren't the only one."

Of course that was true. They had all left things. Mary nodded at Peter.

Everyone ate, slowly. There was chicory dipped in vinegar and a raisin sauce Joanna had made. Mary and the women rose to fill the wine cups for the entire company, returning to their places before Jesus raised the cup and initiated the dinner proper. Then the main meal was presented—again, the women rose and brought in the platters of roast lamb, date paste, baked onions, and coriander relish. They had already prepared a tray of the ritual foods: the lamb shank, the roasted egg, the watercress, the salted water, the unleavened bread. They placed it on the little table directly in front of Jesus.

The meal proceeded in its time-honored way, and Thaddeus, the youngest, asked the ritual questions.

After the traditional questions, Jesus poured out some wine and held it up in his cup. "I will not drink the fruit of the vine again until I drink it anew in the Kingdom of God," he said. He took a sip. "This is my blood of the new covenant, which is to be poured out for many as an offering for sins. As often as you drink it, you show forth my death." Then he suddenly said, "One of you here will betray me."

They all stared at him, then at each other.

"Is it—is it I?" asked Thomas. Fear trembled in his question.

"Is it I?" asked Thaddeus, apprehensively.

All the others were mumbling and soul-searching. Each of them had doubts. Each feared that he or she might, inadvertently, be the one. Mary saw John, prompted by Peter, lean over and whisper something in Jesus's ear.

"Surely not I, teacher?" asked Judas, his voice so low it got lost in the other murmurs.

"It is one whose hand is with mine on the table." Jesus's voice was even quieter; Mary could discern his words only by watching his lips.

There were only two hands on the table: Jesus's and Judas's. Judas snatched his back. No one else but Mary seemed to have caught Judas's question or heard Jesus's answer.

Jesus proceeded calmly with the rest of the ritual meal. He took a piece of the unleavened bread, slowly broke it in pieces, and said, "This is my body, which is given for you." He then distributed the pieces. After they had all eaten the pieces, quietly and thoughtfully, Jesus dipped a piece into the remaining food bowl and its juices and handed it to Judas. "What you are about to do, do quickly," he told him.

Judas rose precipitously. He all but shoved away the little table before him. The others looked at him, assuming that he was going out to give money to the poor as an offering—after all, he had sole charge of the finances.

Mary rose as well. She had to stop him. Jesus made a motion to her. "No, Mary," he said. It was a command. She sank back down, stunned.

Judas disappeared down the stairs and out into the night.

Now the faithful were alone in the upper room. "I have wished so ardently to celebrate this Passover with you," Jesus said. "You are my chosen ones. And I must speak to you now.

"My children, I will be with you only a little while longer," said Jesus. "You will look for me, but where I go you cannot come. I give you a new commandment: love one another. As I have loved you, so you should love one another. This is how all will know that you are my disciples, if you have love for one another."

Peter spoke up. "Master, where are you going? Why can't I follow you now?"

Jesus looked at him sadly. "Simon, Simon," he said.

"No, call me Peter!" Peter objected.

"Satan has demanded to sift you like wheat," Jesus said starkly. "But I have prayed that your own faith may not fail. And once you have turned back, you must strengthen your brothers and sisters."

So Satan had asked for Peter as well as Judas!

Peter cried, "Lord, I am prepared to go to prison and to die with you!"

Jesus shook his head. "I tell you, Peter, before the cock crows this day, you will deny three times that you know me." He then turned to the others, and his face was like flint. "When I sent you forth without a money bag or a sack or sandals, were you in need of anything?"

"No, nothing," Thaddeus and all the others replied. Mary nodded.

"But now it is different. Take a money bag, take a sack; and if you have not a sword, sell your cloak and buy one. For the scripture must be fulfilled: 'He was counted among the wicked.'"

Simon and Peter produced two swords and waved them. "Lord, look, there are two swords here already!"

Jesus seemed satisfied. "It is enough," he said. "Come. I must speak to you, speak as friends and not as servants." He indicated that they should retire to the other part of the room, where there were pillows and places to sit.

"Sit, my dearests," said Jesus, speaking to all of them as to a lover. "I have so much to tell you—my heart is breaking."

They sank down on the pillows and resting places around him. He continued standing.

"I must leave you," he said. "But you knew that. What you did not know was that it is better for you if I go, for after I go I will send the Comforter, the Holy Spirit, to you. I will not leave you orphans; I will come to you. And I go to prepare a place for you."

They all just looked at him. They did not know what to say.

"Peace I leave to you; my peace I give to you. Not as the world gives do I give it to you. Do not let your hearts be troubled or afraid."

He spoke more, but it was confusing. All Mary could hear was that he was going away. "You would rejoice that I am going to the Father," he said.

Then he spoke about his being a vine and their being the branches. But none of it made sense, not now, not tonight. "By this is my Father glorified, that you bear much fruit and become my disciples. As the Father loves me, so I also love you."

The word "love"—how I longed for that! Mary thought. But in the particular, not in the general. Not to share with all these others, parceled out like an equal ration.

"You will weep and mourn," Jesus was saying, "while the world rejoices; you will grieve, but your grief will become joy." He looked at them one by one, lingering on each face. "But I will see you again, and your hearts will rejoice, and no one will take your joy away from you."

What could he possibly mean? Everything he said tonight was so mysterious. The foot-washing. Calling the wine his blood and the bread his flesh. The swords. And now this. Only the part about Judas was clear.

But it is clear only to me and Joanna, thought Mary. Perhaps the rest of it is equally clear, but we cannot see it. We cannot understand.

She wanted to go and fling herself at Jesus's feet and cry out, "Explain things! Please, explain things so that we might understand!"

"Shall we sing the traditional Passover Psalms?" Jesus was saying. "Let us begin with 'I love the Lord': 'I love the Lord, because he has heard my voice and my supplications. Because he has inclined his ear to me, therefore will I call upon him as long as I live.'"

His face seemed distant and his thoughts far away. He was already gone from them.

Come back! she wanted to say. She reached out to him, but he looked at her sternly, as if warning her not to touch him, and she dropped her hands. He continued intoning the Psalm: "'O Lord, truly I am thy servant; I am thy servant, and the son of thine handmaid.'"

His voice rose, long and plaintive, out into the night, beyond their walls.

∞ LIII ∞

As they joined him in the Psalm, their combined voices made familiar words comforting in an unfamiliar situation. Then Jesus bowed his head and said, "I must speak to my Father about you, my dear ones."

They fell silent and waited. "Dear Father, I revealed your name to those you gave me out of the world. They belonged to you, and you gave them to me, and they have kept your word. Now they know that everything you gave me is from you, because the words you gave to me I have given to them, and they accepted them. I pray for them.

"And now I will no longer be in the world, but they are in the world, while I am coming to you. Holy Father, keep them in your name that you have given me, so that they may be one just as we are. When I was with them, I protected them in your name that you gave me, and I guarded them.

"But now I am coming to you. I speak this in the world so that they share my joy completely. I gave them your word, and the world hated them, because they do not belong to the world any more than I belong to the world. I do not ask that you take them out of the world but that you keep them from the Evil One. As you sent me into the world, so I sent them into the world."

"I pray not only for them, but also for those who will believe in me through their word, so that they may all be one, as you, Father, are in me and I in you. Father, they are your gift to me. I wish that where I am they also may be with me, that they may see my glory that you gave me, because you loved me before the foundation of the world.

"Righteous Father, the world also does not know you, but I know you, and they know you sent me. I made known to them your name and I will make it known, that the love with which you loved me may be in them and I in them."

Though Jesus spoke softly, there was not another sound in the room as they all listened intently to his astonishing words. Mary could not understand what he meant, but she felt he was commissioning them for a much greater mission than the one he had sent them out on earlier. It seemed too grand for them. "They are your gift to me. . . . They do not belong to the world. . . . They have kept your word. . . ." Did we really do that well? No. We were a constant disappointment— weak and vacillating. But he has faith in us. In us . . . Truly, I do not understand. But I must trust him. If I believe other things he says, he is also asking that I believe this.

"Come, my chosen ones, my loved ones. I do not call you servants, but friends," he said, holding out his arms to embrace them one by one. "Now let us go out."

They left the room and emerged onto the street with the elite houses of the Upper City, a section the older aristocracy favored. The spacious, handsome homes lining the broad-paved streets in the area exuded an air of luxury and peace. Nearby lay the palace of Annas, and a little beyond that, the palace where Pilate was residing. The moonlight washed over them, intensifying the white of their façades. Within, Mary assumed, people were celebrating Passover with all due ritual and sumptuous appointments. Jesus's enemies were observing the feast with what they believed were clean hands. Was Judas with them? Had he gone to their table and taken his place?

They followed Jesus down the stepped streets through the Lower City, where the houses quickly grew smaller and closely packed together. But the soft yellow glow of oil lamps shone from tiny windows where the Passover was being celebrated with the same words and ritual as that of the richer houses in the Upper City, for on this night, all Jews were one.

Now they passed through the part of the Lower City that formed the original City of David, a long spur extending from the Temple Mount and dipping down almost to the depths of the Kidron Valley. It had long since ceased to be the center of the city, but its associations with David were timeless. From there, they exited through a small eastern gate and found themselves in the Kidron Valley.

As they trailed behind Jesus, none of them dared to speak. What they had heard him say in the upper room was so disturbing yet so ennobling that no one wanted to spoil it by discussing it with others. So in silence they walked behind him, not looking at one another.

The path up the Mount of Olives was before them. Jesus continued on it, but when he reached the gate to the garden of Gethsemane he halted. "Come with me. I want to pray here." Then he turned into it, holding the gate open.

Inside, as Mary had seen earlier, a grove of ancient olive trees stretched before them. They were neatly planted in rows, and some of their trunks were the size of Peter's waist. The moon looked as though it were caught on one of the high cypresses bordering the garden.

Jesus halted and gathered them all around him. These were the men minus Judas, and the women who had faithfully followed him from Galilee. "I need to pray," he said. "If any of you wish to return to our site on the mount, you are free to leave. I will join you later. I cannot say how long I will remain here, and so you are free to go."

Finally, Thomas spoke, but his voice was tremblingly soft. "Master . . . you have made all these references to something momentous happening. We do not understand. But if we leave you now, how will we ever understand? We will not see what is to occur."

Jesus sighed. "My love and my trust in you will abide, even if you do not see and are not here."

Some of them—Little James, Matthew, Thaddeus, and Nathanael—decided to return to the campsite and wait there. The rest stood still in the quiet, dry-scented grove and looked to Jesus for further instructions.

He beckoned to Peter, to Big James, and to John. "Come with me," he said. The four of them made their way among the trees till they were seen no more.

Now all the rest looked at one another.

"We must all wait here, and say our own prayers," said Thomas finally. He turned aside and went to be by himself.

Even in the dim light Mary could see that Jesus's mother was crying. She went over to her and said, "Please do not weep. We simply do not understand what he meant, or what will happen."

The elder Mary turned to her and said, "He spoke of his betrayal. He has already spoken of his death. He spoke of returning to God. How can you say we do not know what will happen?" She almost gave a shrill cry but stifled it. "Oh, I do not think I can bear it!"

Mary put her arm around her. "He expects us to bear it," she said, not realizing until she said it that that was part of what his prayer was about. The rest she still did not understand. "He knows it will be hard—no, agonizing. But he is saying it must be." She waited a moment to marshal her thoughts. "But we do not know exactly what must be. Perhaps even he does not. That is part of the test."

"I am tired of the tests. I have had one after another. I cannot . . . No more tests! No more tests!" Jesus's mother cried out.

"God knows what you can bear and what you cannot," Mary said. "He must have confidence in you." She did not know where those words came from, but she knew they reflected what she believed of God, what had been revealed to her—however darkly and strangely—until now. "Here, let us sit together." They found a place at the base of one of the huge olives.

The moon climbed higher, escaping from the cypress branches. Now it shone openly, illuminating the entire olive grove, turning the massive trees into silver beasts in rows, like war elephants.

Just then Mary saw the flickers of torches and heard, ever so faintly, the march of feet. She stood quickly—Jesus's mother now slept restlessly on the ground beside her—and trained her eyes on the area just beyond the gate.

An enormous company was suddenly at the gate, with lanterns and loud cries. They broke it down, not bothering with the latch, and poured into the grove. All the sleeping disciples awoke and leapt to their feet, dazedly confused. Simon, the first to react, rushed forward and tried to prevent their approach.

"Stop! Come no closer!" he yelled, waving his arms. He reached for his sword, but one of the soldiers struck it from his hand and pushed him aside like a child, and the former Zealot, weaponless, had to yield. Now Mary could see that the people in front had staffs and clubs, but behind them were soldiers of the Temple, armed with swords, shields, and pikes. There may even have been Roman soldiers farther back, not clearly visible yet. Only an official order could have legally commissioned them.

The soldiers kept pouring in, an enormous number of them. Mary and the other women stood to one side, marveling at the size of the force sent out against Jesus. His mother was standing rigidly, watching, but her tears had ceased.

Suddenly Jesus appeared from one side of the grove.

"Whom do you seek?" he asked, his voice loud.

"Jesus of Nazareth," several of them answered in unison. Some others grabbed the watching apostles and held them fast.

"I am he," said Jesus. "Let these men go!"

Oddly, they obeyed, releasing the disciples.

Just then, behind him, Peter, Big James, and John appeared. With a swift movement, Peter reached under his cloak.

But Mary's attention was diverted by the arrival of yet more people, a company of well-dressed men, and in their midst—Judas!

Judas made his way over to Jesus, his face all friendliness and full of happy greeting. "Rabbi!" he said, as if he had not seen him in weeks. "Teacher!" He approached deferentially and took Jesus's hand, as a good student should, to show submission and respect.

Jesus raised his hand. "Friend, do what you came for." Judas kissed it.

Jesus looked down at him. "Judas. Do you betray the Son of Man with a kiss?"

Judas snatched his hand away.

Then Jesus turned to the accompanying crowd, ignoring Judas. "Why have you come out armed against me as if I were a robber or leading a rebellion? I was with you every day in the Temple, and you did not arrest me then. But this is your hour—the hour of the power of darkness." He took his time searching each face; many of them he had already seen in the crowds when he preached.

Peter suddenly leapt forward, pulling the hidden sword out and slashing a man near Jesus who looked threatening. He nicked the man's ear, and blood spurted out. The man drew back with a cry.

"Stop!" Jesus cried to Peter. "All who live by the sword will die by the sword. Shall I not drink of the cup my Father has given me?"

Then he went over to the stricken man and touched his ear, praying that it should be healed.

"Take that man! Seize him!" the captain of the guard ordered, and a contingent of soldiers moved forward, rushed toward Jesus, and grabbed him.

There was a scramble, a sound of scuffling, and Mary watched, amazed, as all the male disciples fled. Peter threw down his sword and ran, and so did Big James, rushing toward the gate. John followed, and all those whom Jesus had just shared the Passover with and prayed for: Andrew and Philip and Simon and Thomas. They left Jesus to his fate and ran for their safety. Only the women stayed behind, witnessing it all.

The soldiers moved to surround Jesus, and Mary lost sight of him. So many sent to take him—so many, as if they needed an army. *"But this is your hour—the hour of the power of darkness."* She reached out and embraced Jesus's mother beside her, who was trembling but speechless. Joanna and Susanna hurried to them.

Ugly shouts filled the night, shouts of men who had run prey to ground and had it cornered. The flaring torches and swinging lanterns gave the garden the grotesque look of a wild party that had gone horribly awry. Then the mob was moving toward the gap where once there had been a gate, bearing Jesus away with them. On the fringes of the moving mass, Mary saw the one person she knew: Judas. He was trying to force his way back into the center of the group.

"Wait! Wait!" he was crying.

She could not help herself; overwhelming hatred consumed her, and she abandoned the elder Mary and tore toward Judas, covering the ground so fast he never saw her approaching. On her way she overtook a boy who held a torch, shoved him onto the ground, and wrenched his torch away before he knew what had happened. In three swift steps she was upon Judas, who had turned to see someone behind him. His face just had time to register recognition before she swung the torch back and struck him in the face with sufficient force to knock him to the ground. The burning torch had singed his hair—she could see it smoking—and, she hoped, burned his face badly.

He rolled over to shield his face, but that just left his neck and hands exposed, and she ground the red-hot stump of the torch into both his hands, feeling it digging into his flesh.

"Die! Die!" she screamed, pure liquid hatred surging through her entire being.

He groaned and somehow managed to grab the torch handle and tried to yank it away, pulling her down with it. She fell on him and started clawing his blistered face, feeling the burnt layer peeling off and soft, bloody flesh underneath ripping open.

"Die, die!" she kept saying, almost unaware of what she was doing. Only the urge to beat and claw and rip stayed with her; all else had fled, like the disciples who had run away.

He managed to get hold of her wrists and pull her hands away, then to twist and throw her off and onto the ground. He struggled to his feet, his face puffed and bleeding. His knees were shaking, and he reeled, trying to steady himself.

"You are damned," said Mary. "Why don't you die? Or can't you die?"

Judas, his burnt face covered in blood, just stared at her, unable to believe what had just happened. He kept trying to touch his face but could not stand the pain.

"I know why you can't die," she panted, regaining her feet. "It's exactly what Jesus said. This is your hour, the power of darkness."

"And what do you think Jesus would say if he had seen this?" Judas finally spoke, his voice high with pain and shock. "He would know he has failed. You have proved that it's impossible to follow what he preached. Turn the other cheek. I did, and you have injured both of them."

"Would that I had ripped them both off!"

"You see? With Jesus since the beginning, but now, when you are angry, you act as if you had never heard of him."

"You are wrong. Only for Jesus would I ever have attacked anyone as I attacked you."

"You only think that. Jesus provided you with an excuse, that's all." He paused, trying to steady his voice, stop his trembling. "We really want the same thing, you know. To protect Jesus. We just did it in different ways."

The mob was fading away in the night.

"They're getting away," sneered Mary. "You'll lose them."

"I know where they are going," said Judas. "I will not lose them."

"And where is that?"

"To the house of Annas, and thence to Caiaphas's palace. Jesus will be examined and questioned there, and detained until after the crowds have left Jerusalem. Then he can go back to Galilee with his faithful, peaceful"—he touched his burnt hand—"brave, loyal"—he looked around pointedly at the empty garden, bereft of the men—"followers."

"Go, join your masters," said Mary. She did not want to be in his presence for another moment, since she had not succeeded in killing him. She still wanted to kill him.

Angry and ashamed—whether of her loss of control or her earlier failure to stop him, she did not know—she turned back to the other women. They had been staring in disbelief at her attack.

"Mary!" cried Joanna. "What . . . How could you have done that?"

"I had to do something for Jesus," she gasped, still catching her breath. "I could not let Judas walk away."

"Well, he certainly isn't walking well now—you've seen to that."

Far down on the other side of the Kidron, they could see the moving lights that signaled where the mob was going; they were climbing up toward one of the city gates.

"Annas—they are going to the house of Annas," Mary said. "Where is it? Joanna, you must know. We must follow them." She looked at Jesus's mother, who was very quiet and still. "Are you up to coming? If you would rather stay here, some of us will stay with you."

"I am ready to follow," the elder Mary said. "Though it take me to Rome or even the ends of the earth."

"So are we all," the women said together.

The house of Annas was in the Upper City. But at Annas's house— which was large enough to be called a palace—an unruly mob was gathered before the gates, milling and muttering. It was the mob who had captured Jesus in the garden and delivered him here. Now they waited, like hungry dogs before a slaughterhouse, hoping to slip in. The gates were shut tight, however, and scowling guards glared out at them. The women disciples—the only women in this crowd—stood at its edges and watched. Mary did not see Judas. Had he slunk away? Or had he been allowed to join the inner circle inside, braving his condition?

Suddenly there was a stirring. Someone was coming out into the courtyard.

"Clear out!" a loud voice yelled. It belonged to a man in the uniform of a Temple soldier. "Make way!" Even as he spoke, a procession was coming across the courtyard. "Open that gate! Stand back!"

The gate was flung open, and a contingent of Temple guards emerged, their eyes darting back and forth for possible trouble in the crowd. Then followed a small group of priests and scribes, all bundled up against the chill. And in their midst, Jesus: bound, captive, looking straight ahead. He did not look for them, nor did he see them, and the soldiers on either side blocked their view.

The party with its prisoner set out down the street leading to Caiaphas's residence. The women followed, silent, not speaking even to one another, hurrying to keep up.

Caiaphas's palace was an enormous residence lying quite near Antipas's palace—which was occupied for the moment by Pontius Pilate himself—with two-story buildings, a gigantic courtyard, fountains, porticoes, and outlying and adjoining courtyards. In the moonlight the columned porticoes threw sharp-edged shadows like long fingers out into the huge courtyard.

Now the gates were opened, and Jesus and his captors were ushered through, quickly. Just as quickly, the gates shut, keeping the mob with its torches and staffs and lanterns outside.

"Go away!" the guard shouted at the crowd. "Go away! They'll be here all night. Go home!"

Some of them obeyed. It was late, past midnight. But others stayed on, keeping watch. Mary still did not see any sign of Judas. Perhaps she had really injured him. She hoped so.

People kept pressing up against the gate, trying to convince the guards to let them in. The soldiers were kindling a fire in the courtyard, and the people begged to be let in to warm themselves. But the guards ignored them.

Then someone succeeded in getting the gatekeepers to open the doors a crack. Mary saw that two men were standing there, speaking earnestly to the guards. Then, in the brightness of the moonlight, she saw one man's features. It was John!

Before John and the other man could slip inside, Mary and the women boldly pushed through the crowd to their side.

"John! John! Oh, you are here!" Mary was overjoyed to see that another of Jesus's disciples had also followed him. Then the other man turned. It was Peter.

John motioned to her, silencing her. Then she realized that John was known to the guard, and not suspected of being a disciple. Vaguely she remembered something about John's father, Zebedee, having connections with the high priest, but she could not recall exactly what it was. They could pass inside; they could get closer to Jesus, no matter the means.

Her old mission partner looked at her sadly. "Mary, go back. It is dangerous to be here. You must not witness it. The Sanhedrin is meeting here, late at night. They are having a preliminary trial. It is most irregular. No legal trial can be conducted at night."

"No, we must be with Jesus," she insisted. "We cannot turn back. We have come too far." She pressed herself up beside John, so that they could all pass in with him.

Inside the courtyard, fires were blazing. The cold of the spring night had deepened, and the high priest's servants—required to be on duty no matter the hour—were standing by. A large number of soldiers were also there, pacing about and rubbing their hands to keep warm. It was a quieter and more orderly group than the mob outside, but more menacing in its anonymous authority and official uniforms.

Mary saw Jesus and his captors entering the palace. The moon was still high but had started downward, signaling that the night was more than half over. But many hours of darkness yet remained.

Jesus vanished inside, and the door shut with a bang. There was nothing to do now but wait, wait in the courtyard. John and Peter were making their way over to the fire; never once did they look at the women or indicate that they knew them, for everyone's safety.

It was so cold! The fire was beckoning. Mary guided Jesus's mother toward it, being careful to stay away from the side where John and Peter were standing, warming their hands.

How good it felt! She held out her palms and let the heat from the snapping wood warm them. Only then did she examine her hands for injuries. Yes, there were a few, but far fewer than Judas had sustained. That pleased her.

"Oh, Mary, what do you think will happen?" Jesus's mother whispered. She did not sound afraid so much as resolute, as if she were bracing herself.

The dreams . . . Jesus's bloody predictions, his insistence that something momentous would happen . . . How could his mother not remember his words?

"I do not know," she had to answer. "We must pray that, whatever this examination and trial are, they will be fair, and if that is so, then as Judas said, they will release him to return to Galilee." She took the elder Mary's hands. "They are afraid of him. We must understand that. We must remember the political situation and how his message may have made him seem dangerous. But when they are assured that he is not, when they are satisfied that he poses no threat—" She broke off as she heard Peter saying something.

Standing beside the fire, Peter had his cloak pulled up around his face, shielding most of his features. He extended his hands, which looked bloodless and white in the moonlight.

"You are one of his followers!" the voice of a servant woman near the fire rang out, unnaturally loud. "Yes, you! You are one of his disciples!"

Peter jerked around, clutching his hood. Had it slipped? "What?" he said. "Woman, I don't know what you are talking about!" His voice was choked.

"You!" Now one of the Temple guards came forward and pointed directly at Peter. "I saw you there in the olive grove! You struck my uncle. You cut his ear with your sword! You *are* one of that Jesus man's followers!"

"No!" cried Peter, clenching his fists. "I tell you, I don't know the man!!"

"But you're a Galilean! I can tell by your accent! It gives you away. Obviously you're one of them! You have to be!" the servant girl cried.

Peter turned away, ignoring her. John stepped back, trying to hide in the shadows.

Then another man, one of the high priest's servants, pointed at Peter, saying, "I swear, I saw you! You are a follower of that Jesus!"

Peter stared at him. Angrily, he cried, "May Yahweh curse me, may he strike me dead and cut all my family off from the land of the living, if I know that man—that Jesus—"

In the still night, a rooster crowed from somewhere just beyond the nearby city walls. Its raucous, jarring call filled the courtyard.

Peter suddenly stopped speaking. The rooster crowed again, its cry even louder than the first time.

Just then there was a commotion, and one of the doors opened across the far courtyard. A group emerged; and there was Jesus, bound and flanked by guards.

Peter stood dumbstruck, as did John and Mary and all the soldiers and onlookers. Jesus passed very close to them, and he turned and looked at Peter sadly. Peter gave a stifled cry. Then Jesus swept past, marched away by Caiaphas's guards and the Temple soldiers and, behind them, a large group of tired, official-looking men: the Sanhedrin. They, and the soldiers, took Jesus to the porticoes.

"Oh, God!" cried Peter, and he fled, sobbing, out the gate. "Oh, God!" The rooster crowed again, and the gate clanged shut.

Some of the people warming themselves in the courtyard stayed where they were; others sauntered over to the portico to see what was happening, what amusement they might be offered to lighten this tedious, cold night. Jesus's women followers rushed over along with John and reached the shadowed portico before the others.

Jesus was standing, still bound, surrounded by his enemies. All pretense of their being unbiased examiners had been abandoned, and now there were only openly proclaimed torturers and jailers around him. Caiaphas was circling him like an animal, his bushy beard, along with his wild hair and eyebrows, making a frame for his face that looked leonine. One of the councilmen was chanting, "Death! Death! You are sentenced to death for your foul blasphemy!"

Two others spat at him, then laughed. One of the soldiers stepped forward and, whipping out a rag, blindfolded him. Then a soldier struck him in the face, and another pounded him from behind with his fists.

"Prophesy!" cried one of the councilmen. "Tell us who hit you!"

"Yes, yes! You can see things, tell us what you see!" A blow followed, sending Jesus to his knees. Then another guard hit him over the head with a staff. Now he fell forward onto all fours.

"Can't you tell us who it was? What's wrong with you?"

A howl of laughter went up.

"False prophet, false prophet!"

Mary, who had so easily attacked Judas, was now paralyzed. All the power that had flowed through her was drained away, and she could not move, although she felt as though the blows were falling on her as well. She had seen that picture of Jesus bleeding and beaten. But that had been hazy, and this was horribly, brilliantly clear.

Move, move! Her mind was shouting. Move, help him! But she stood rooted and helpless. All she could do was reach out to his mother and take her hand.

"Get up!" One of the soldiers threw a thick rope around Jesus and yanked him up. "Stand up, like a man!"

Another soldier beat him with his fists, and then Caiaphas said, "Enough. You have an appearance to make. You must show yourself to Pontius Pilate, our gracious governor. Now." He flicked the blindfold off. Jesus turned his eyes on him, but Caiaphas looked away.

One of the soldiers prodded Jesus with his pike. "Go!"

Stumbling along the street, barely able to see because of their tears and shock, the women and John followed the thinned-out crowd to the palace where Pilate was in residence. It was the dim, murky time when night was just yielding to day, the day the rooster had heralded so loudly. The moon had sunk behind the buildings, and the only light came from the few guttering torches in the crowd and the smudge hinting of dawn in the eastern sky.

The streets were still; Passover celebrations were long over, and people inside the houses slept. The most observant of them had already cleared out the trash from the dinners, and there were little piles of it along the street.

Pilate's borrowed palace was not far from Caiaphas's. It seemed to cover an area larger than the Temple; its enormous walls, fortified with guard towers like a military stronghold, made it look impregnable. Inside, Mary supposed, were all the accoutrements of pleasure, doubled and then tripled to satisfy every appetite. Dazzling white walls, towers, gates, all shouted that Herod Antipas of Galilee was a mighty king and all his subjects must recognize his greatness and bow before it. Now Pilate had challenged all that by appropriating it for himself. Rome is greater, he was pronouncing. Rear all your towers, build all your walls, but when Rome is ready, we will either lay it low or take it over at our pleasure.

By the time Mary and the others arrived, Jesus and his captors were nowhere to be seen. The crowd around the gates consisted of the curious and the religious, the latter wearing their prayer shawls and tefillin. Then there were the tough-looking rebels, ready for a fight. Jesus's assured enemies, the polished members of the Sanhedrin, remained outside the gates as well, on call to help prosecute him further if need be.

Mary and the others fought their way through the crowd and up to the very front, where they clutched the bars of the gate, trying to see inside.

In Mary's mind, the sight of Jesus, beaten, would not fade; she would never leave following him. "John, what does this mean?" she said. "Why have they taken him to Pilate?"

"Because they want him condemned," John answered quietly.

"The Sanhedrin, with its illegal nighttime trial, has found him guilty of blasphemy. That's an offense that calls for death by stoning, but only the Romans can execute people under their jurisdiction. So they hope to convince the Romans to do just that."

"Execute?"

"Execute," said John, slowly. "They want Jesus to perish, like John the Baptist."

"But—but he's guilty of nothing!" Mary said, as if John had pronounced the judgment himself. It could not be. What had Jesus ever done that was illegal?

"Blasphemy is considered high treason against God, the most heinous of all crimes possible."

Suddenly the elder Mary was standing beside him. "Blasphemy! But my son was of all people respectful of the Holy Name." Her voice shook.

"There's a member of the Sanhedrin—Joseph, he comes from Arimathea—who's a secret disciple. He told me out in the courtyard, quietly in passing, that, although Jesus wouldn't answer most of the questions, they tricked him into saying something they could interpret as blasphemous."

Another hidden disciple. How many secret disciples did Jesus have? And could anyone really trick Jesus? Had he not foreseen all this in his blood-soaked predictions?

"I was known to Joseph because of my father's connection with Caiaphas's household, so he trusted me and confided in me," said John. "But we mustn't betray him."

Never mind about Joseph. "Pilate! He killed my husband!" To think that now Jesus was before him. "He's known to be cruel," whispered Mary.

"He's known to be *arbitrary*," said John. "He may disappoint the accusers and not go along with them. He has no use for the Sanhedrin, he's made that clear. He may side with Jesus just to thwart them."

The elder Mary looked on rigidly. She seemed drained of all emotion and strength, yet she still stood upright and did not even put out her hand for support. "So my son must appeal to the Roman governor? Is Pilate our only hope?"

"No," said John. "He must *defend* himself before the Roman governor. The Sanhedrin has already found him guilty. But can they persuade Pilate that Jesus has committed a crime that would threaten the Roman emperor?"

"Jesus has committed no crime!" cried his mother. "Why is he on trial at all?"

"Jesus himself said it. He said it was the time of the power of darkness," said Mary. That was the only true explanation.

Dawn was just breaking. Would the forces of darkness now retreat? "Will Pilate even be hearing cases this early?" asked Jesus's mother. It seemed unrealistic to expect him to address this now.

"They are demanding that Pilate hear the case before he attends his usual amusements," John said. "They are determined to force through some resolution by midday."

"Oh, God!"

All around them they could hear scattered conversations: Yes, this man—this disgraceful apostate, Jesus—has been presented to Pilate. As well he should be. And Pilate will know the truth, that all this Messiah talk and coming-Kingdom talk and predictions of the end of the world is subversive and threatens the public order. Pilate will make short work of him.

For what seemed forever, they waited before the gates of the palace, where they could see officials entering and leaving, but nothing more than that. Then, suddenly, a knot of people burst from the palace, led by a magistrate in a crimson-bordered robe.

"Pilate!" murmured John, recognizing him. Roman soldiers flanked him, as well as scribes and lawyers. And in their midst, a bloody Jesus, still bound. They all mounted a tribunal platform that overlooked the wall.

Pilate came to the edge of the tribunal and looked down at the crowd. His gaze rested on the contingent of the Sanhedrin, who were standing together near the front.

"In order to accommodate your . . . peculiar religious rituals, I have come out to you," said Pilate. His voice was shrill and unpleasant. "I do not need to do this, but I do it in order to please you, my people." He gave a mocking smile. "Since setting foot in my quarters will apparently render you ritually unclean, I address you here." He made it clear that just addressing them made *him* feel unclean. "So listen." He then nodded to his soldiers, and they prodded Jesus forward.

"This man here, this Jesus of Nazareth. Why have you brought him to me at all? If he's insulted your god, that is your own matter. I certainly don't care about it, and neither does the law of Rome." Pilate looked out at them accusingly.

With each spat-out word, with each tilt of his head, Pilate registered his disdain. And Mary stared, dumbly, at this man who had killed Joel and now would decide the very life of Jesus by his whim.

He was medium height, and middle-aged, and had a head of dark hair, close-cropped. His shoulders were broad and showed well beneath his official robe, but he held himself stiffly. In fact, there was something very statuelike about him, as if he did not have enough human energy to give his movements smoothness, as if it took all his effort just to stand there and make abrupt, jerky gestures.

Then Caiaphas called back, "We have found this man guilty both of blasphemy, and of misleading our people; he opposes the payment of taxes to Caesar and maintains that he is the Messiah, a king."

Pilate turned to inspect Jesus, looking carefully at him, barely suppressing a smirk. "Are you the king of the Jews?" he asked.

"You say so," Jesus replied.

Pilate laughed.

Then Caiaphas shouted, "He is subverting our nation!"

Another Sanhedrin member cried, "He has stirred up the people of Judaea by his teachings!"

Pilate looked first at the accusers and then at Jesus. "Aren't you going to answer them? Don't you hear the testimony they are bringing against you?"

Jesus just stood silently, while Pilate stared at him in amazement. Finally, Pilate laughed. He turned back to the crowd and shouted, "I find this man not guilty."

Mary felt a great wave of relief. It was over. Pilate had spoken. Jesus's enemies had failed. "Thank you, thank you," she murmured to God.

"No! No! He's a criminal!"

"Execute him!"

The crowd screamed, a thousand voices all calling on Pilate to punish him. The roar of their voices shocked Mary. Jesus's enemies must have put agents out in the crowd, to lead the others in cries for his doom.

"He began by causing trouble in Galilee," cried Caiaphas, from the forefront of the crowd, "and has come all the way here just to continue his agitation!"

"Galilee?" Pilate sounded surprised. "Galilee? You are from Galilee?"

Jesus gave no answer but a slight nod.

"Then you fall under Herod Antipas's jurisdiction in that region," said Pilate. "Antipas must judge you!" He sounded gleeful, as if it was revenge on Antipas.

At a signal, the soldiers grabbed Jesus's arms and dragged him from the platform, down the steps, and through the gate. Other soldiers held the crowds back.

As Jesus passed them, he seemed to see them, and Mary felt that he knew they were there and was strengthening them by his deep awareness of their presence. But could they not, somehow, also strengthen him? Was there no way they could help him?

Again they followed, along the narrow streets and through the public square with its market, busy trading now in the first flush of morning. The familiar palace soon loomed ahead, the massive buildings linked by their porticoes and walkways, sitting majestically at the head of a wide flight of steps. When Mary and Joanna had come here, they had not approached this way, and Mary was seeing for the first time the formal entrance of the palace. Jesus and his captors mounted the steps and vanished inside, followed by Caiaphas and his party, and guards quickly closed the doors. There would be no secret entrance today.

After what seemed a very long time, Jesus emerged again, now wearing a rich scarlet-embroidered robe, but with his hands still bound. The blood from the earlier beating had dried on his face, appearing dark and streaked.

"Where are you taking him?" cried one of the waiting Sanhedrin. "What were the findings?"

The captain of the soldiers said, "Nothing. No verdict. He refused to answer his accusers. He wouldn't even accommodate Antipas when he requested a miracle. So it's back to Pilate." Behind him, Caiaphas looked frustrated and angry.

Pilate had already gone inside, but the stirring of the crowd and its shouts as Jesus was marched back brought him out again. He motioned for Jesus to be hauled up before him on the platform once more. Then he made a show of admiring the new robe hanging lopsided from Jesus's shoulders, put there in mockery.

"*Ecce homo!*" he cried, with a flourish. "Behold the man!"

The crowd roared with laughter. Some clapped and whistled.

"A gift from Antipas?" Pilate asked. "But you'll have to take it off and stand here without borrowed clothes." The soldiers stripped off the robe and handed it to Pilate, who tossed it onto a chair on the platform. "So he's sent you back. A pity." He motioned to Caiaphas.

"Come here, you. And all your fellows from your religious court, or whatever you call it."

Caiaphas came to the gate of the palace but stopped short of the entrance line, lest he contaminate himself. His followers did likewise.

"Now, you listen!" yelled Pilate, his voice reaching as high as a crow's cry. "You brought this man to me and accused him of inciting revolution. I have conducted my investigation of the charges and have not found him guilty. Nor did Antipas, obviously. So he has committed no capital crime. Therefore, I shall have him flogged and released."

Oh, thanks be to God! The silent words poured from Mary as she heard the pronouncement. The charges had not stuck; Jesus would be free! God, you are so merciful! She reached out and took Jesus's mother's hand in hers, and Joanna's on the other side.

"No! No!" the crowd shouted. "No, away with this man! If you release anyone, we choose Barabbas!"

"Release Barabbas to us!" More cries from the other side of the crowd.

"I tell you, I shall release Jesus!" Pilate yelled back at them.

"No! No! Crucify him, crucify him!" Their voices rose to a roar, like a thundering waterfall, drowning out the protests of Jesus's supporters.

"Shall I crucify your king?" Pilate asked.

"We have no king but Caesar!" the chief priests screamed, again and again, and the crowd repeated it.

"I find no guilt in him, and I will not crucify him!" Pilate cried stubbornly. "What evil has he done?" Pilate raised his voice until it almost broke. Jesus stood by, looking not at Pilate or at Caiaphas but at his followers in the crowd, who were vainly trying to outshout the others.

"If you release him, you are not a friend of Caesar. Anyone who makes himself a king opposes Caesar," Caiaphas's deep voice boomed out.

The crowd then began surging, swelling, as if a riot was imminent. "We will report you to Rome!" they cried. "We will make sure that Caesar hears of your disloyalty!"

Pilate's demeanor changed. He hesitated for a moment, then signaled for a servant and gave him instructions; soon the servant returned with a basin of water.

Pilate turned to the people, raising his hands. "I am innocent of this man's blood. Innocent!" The basin of water was held out before him, and he dipped his hands in the basin and washed them slowly, splashing the water over his wrists. Then he held them out for a towel, which another servant handed him.

"Release Barabbas to them," said Pilate, dully, to the centurion on duty. While he waited the few moments for Barabbas to be brought out, Pilate looked back and forth between the crowd and Jesus. Jesus gave no sign that he had even heard the verdict, let alone contested it. Then, as Barabbas was pushed out on the platform, Jesus looked hard at him. Jesus leaned toward him and said something. Barabbas, his face prison-white and strained, looked stricken.

Whatever the words, they were inaudible from Mary's distance.

Barabbas stumbled down the steps; at the gate, the guard cut his bound hands apart. He reeled out into the crowd, greeted by raucous cries from his fellows. He looked back at Jesus just once before vanishing into the mob.

"Flog him!" Pilate ordered, pointing to Jesus. "Then take him outside the city to be crucified. Let it be done!"

Just then there was a violent motion near Caiaphas, and Mary saw him: Judas. Judas, with his blistered and bruised face, was grabbing the high priest's robes and shaking him. Caiaphas's teeth were rattling, and his jaw snapped open and shut, but his colleagues quickly grabbed Judas and pulled him away.

"Take them! Take them!" he was yelling, beating at Caiaphas with a leather money bag. "Take them back! Oh, God, you lied! I have sinned, sinned in betraying innocent blood!"

Caiaphas shrugged, and straightened his collar. "What is that to us?" he said. "Look to it yourself."

With a strangled cry, a shriek of torture, Judas fled. Mary saw him darting away down the street, pushing people out of his way, running toward the Temple.

So Judas had realized the masters he served were liars. But too late to save Jesus, the master whom he had betrayed. Let him be the one crucified, Mary begged God. He has killed Jesus! No. She looked at Caiaphas, at the other Sanhedrin members, at Pilate, at the crowd itself. They have all killed Jesus.

And Peter . . . Peter denied him, and Jesus heard him. And he saw all the men disciples flee from Gethsemane. How could he have borne it?

At that instant there was a scuffle and some movement, and Mary saw Jesus being pushed down the steps and into the paved courtyard of the palace, shoved into the midst of a ring of jeering Roman soldiers.

Pilate ceremoniously dismounted from the platform, saluted his approval to the soldiers, and disappeared inside his palace.

Jesus's remaining disciples fought their way up to the front of the gate, straining to see. But everything was a blur, with only the words "crucify" . . . "crucify" being whispered, shouted, ringing in their minds. Mary gripped the bars of the locked gate and stared in at the milling soldiers, heard their laughter and catcalls. Then, abruptly, Jesus was revealed in their circle, his hands still bound, and his bloodied face looking past them and out into the crowd.

He sees us! He sees us! Mary saw his eyes lock into hers, then slide over to his mother's, and Joanna's, and Susanna's, and John's. He was not seeing the crowd or his enemies, he was seeing only them.

I want to tell you . . . I want to tell you . . . Mary broke into stifled sobs. I must tell you, I must beg your forgiveness. . . . I did not mean to say . . . Oh, please . . . Absurdly, even now, she wanted to kneel at his feet and talk about these inconsequential things that were bothering her. She wanted him to know how she felt about him. That she finally understood.

Two soldiers were bringing out a purple robe, holding it up reverentially, its great size making it fly out behind them like a sail. They draped it over Jesus's shoulders and fastened it with great care. Another soldier wove a crown that had projecting thorns like those radiate crowns Roman emperors fancied, indicating divinity.

"There!" The soldier waved it proudly, and with a flourish set it on Jesus's head. Some of the thorns curved inward, piercing his forehead and causing little trails of blood at each point. They trickled downward over his cheeks. He could not reach up to wipe them away.

"Hail, king of the Jews!" Some of the soldiers bowed.

"Wait, he needs a scepter!" A soldier offered a reed and stuck it in Jesus's bound hand. "There, that's it!" He fell to his knees in facetious adoration. "I am blinded by your splendor!" he said, hiding his eyes.

"King of the Jews, king of the Jews!" they choroused. One by one they bowed. "And how shall we serve you, Your Majesty?"

Jesus stood stock-still and gave no indication that he had even heard any of them.

"Shall we run to Syria and get snow to cool your drinks?" a young soldier asked.

"Perhaps you would like a dish of quails, or melons out of season?"

"Or shall we smite your enemies? Kill those Edomites or Jebusites or Canaanites or whoever your people fought? Oh, I forgot—they don't exist anymore. Well, we can find a substitute."

They continued bowing and mocking, but when Jesus did not respond they started spitting at him, crying, "Do something, you weak coward!"

When he still did nothing but stare at them, one man snatched the reed out of his hand and began beating him over the head. "Say something, you fool!" he screamed.

"Enough of this," their captain said. "Strip him. Let's get on with it."

They whisked off the borrowed purple robe and dragged Jesus over to a post at the far end of the courtyard. They cut the ropes binding his hands and quickly positioned his wrists around the wide post, then bound them again. "Let's have it!" With Jesus bent over, the captain yanked his clothing down to expose his upper body to the whip, which one of the soldiers brandished with glee. It had multiple strips, weighed down by lead pellets that would bite into flesh like a dog's teeth.

Thirty-nine blows were allowed by Jewish Law, but the Romans were not bound by these rules. Few men could survive forty; hence the Law limited it to thirty-nine. But a vigorous flogging was considered a mercy before a crucifixion. It rendered a man half dead before he got to the worst death a prisoner could face, a death limited to foreigners and the criminal classes and other scum; no Roman citizen could be crucified. Conquered peoples like the Jews, slaves, enemies—those merited crucifixion.

Mary could not think; she could not even feel. She had seen all this beforehand, the bleeding and the buffeting, but not Jesus dead. She had never seen him dead, not in any vision at all. She turned to his mother. She must think of Mary, his mother. Yes. All she could do now was to help his mother.

The elder Mary was staring into the courtyard where Jesus was being brutally flogged. The expression on her face was of sheer agony. The sweetness, the depth of understanding that had always shone on her face, had vanished. Now there was nothing but pain. Her face was so contorted that it seemed it must actually duplicate her son's, as if they were one.

"Stop! That's enough! Now out! Out to Golgotha!" A burly soldier was waving his arms. "Get back! Get back!" He moved menacingly toward the crowd as the armed soldiers prepared to open the gates. Another soldier plucked Jesus's own crumpled cloak from the ground and threw it back over him.

When Mary and the other disciples did not give way, the soldiers flung open the gates and swept them aside.

Jesus staggered out, carrying a huge beam of wood across his shoulders. Although he was a strong man, he was now so weakened that he reeled under the weight. It was a crossbeam; it would be fastened to an upright once they got to the execution site.

"Where are they going?" Mary cried. "Where is this place?"

"We can only follow," said John.

Mary and his mother pushed themselves—with the strength of big men, which had somehow been granted them—through the knotted crowd of Jesus's enemies. Pressed in tightly together, people were already sweating, and the smell was rank. The jostling and the shoving were vicious, as if the small space had turned people into animals being herded down a chute. At the same time, they were yelling and laughing, enjoying being part of the ghoulish procession.

Fighting their way through them, twining and twisting around bodies, Mary and his mother were finally able to reach him, coming up behind his bent back, and to grasp his mantle, then touch his shoulder.

"My son, my son," said the elder Mary. "Oh, Jesus!"

Jesus looked directly into her eyes. His own were not dimmed by the pain; they seemed more riveting than ever before. "Mother," he said. His voice was very low. "Do not grieve. I was born for this hour. I choose it."

"Son!" With a sob, his mother reached out to him. But the soldiers prodded him forward.

Mary pushed herself in front of him. "Dearest! I must tell you—I must—oh—I was wrong—what I said—what I thought—"

He paused for only a moment. His enemies were all about, pushing him forward.

"I know," he said. "I know your heart. My best heart." He looked directly into her eyes, but only for an instant. "I know it all." Then, as he was shoved forward, "I count on your love."

For years to come, Mary was to remember those words, try to recall the exact tone in which he said them, try to fathom what he meant. But now she felt only an immense release and benediction. He understood. He forgave.

A contingent of Roman soldiers led the way. All executions must take place beyond the city walls, lest death contaminate the city. Crowds lined the streets, eagerly watching what to them was a mere entertainment and spectacle. It was only midmorning. Was it possible that at this time yesterday they were buying the Passover foods?

Mary could not remember. It all seemed a swirl. Yesterday Jesus could just have walked away. Had he chosen to eat his dinner and then leave for Galilee, Judas could never have found him. None of this would have happened.

And yet . . . Judas knew where we came from. The authorities could have followed us back to Galilee. Would they have?

And what was it Jesus had said? She strove to remember. Something about his having to die. That he would go to Jerusalem and be killed. He seemed to have willed it. Had there not been a Judas, would he have gone to the chief priests himself?

None of that mattered now. Now there was only the sun shining over the streets of the city, making it seem a happy, normal day; there were the crowds, a mix of the curious, the hostile, the bored. And Jesus, struggling under his burden. Behind him—although she had no time to think about that now—straggled the other men to be crucified along with him, lurching along the streets, dragging their crossbeams, having come from other trials, other prisons.

With all their strength, Mary and his mother kept their places right behind Jesus. He was bent under his burden; only his innate strength, forged over the years of carpentry and of walking throughout Galilee, sustained him now. His beautiful robe was soiled and trailing; his sandals—strange how Mary noticed his feet and his sandals—were poorly fastened and hindering his walk. Then, while she watched, he suddenly lost his footing on the slippery pavement and fell forward.

He fell to his knees, and the beam swayed to one side, off one shoulder. Though he tried to regain his footing, he could not summon the strength to rise with the beam. No one helped him, and the soldiers pushed back anyone who tried. They shoved Mary and his mother away roughly. At last, one of the soldiers jerked him up and gave him a push forward. He staggered a few paces, lurching down the street.

The crowd surged in close again, and then halted abruptly as Jesus fell again. This time his mother rushed forward, weaving through the knot of soldiers, and reached his side. She did not try to help him rise, but cradled his head and wiped his face. She did not want him to rise or proceed another step further.

"Get off him!" A burly soldier yanked her up and almost flung her back into the crowd. For the first time, a groan of pain came from Jesus's lips.

"And get *up!*" Two soldiers each hauled him up and set him on his feet, then shoved him to propel him forward.

"Oh, my dear one!" Mary held Jesus's mother tightly, although it seemed useless as a comfort. There could be no comfort, only horror, for her. Only horror, fear, and deepest pain for them both.

Jesus fell again.

"You! You there!" The soldiers halted the procession. They pointed at a man who, clearly unaware of the events of the day, had just entered one of the gates to trade in the city. "Come here!"

The bewildered man obeyed and came to the captain of the soldiers. He was young and had enormous shoulders.

"Carry this beam!" the captain ordered him. "This man isn't able."

Before either Jesus or the stranger could protest, they removed the beam from Jesus's shoulders and fastened it on the stranger's.

"Don't worry," the captain said. "We won't crucify *you!*" He laughed.

As Jesus relinquished his crossbeam, a group of wailing women approached him, their voices lamenting the sorrow of the times, of this time.

"Do you weep for me, women of Jerusalem?" Jesus whispered, his voice soft with exhaustion. "Weep, rather, for yourselves and your children. For if men do these things in the time of green wood, what will they do in the time of dry?"

Green wood—dry—Once before he had spoken of green wood, Mary remembered.

Jesus passed on, and they followed, pressing by the weeping women, weeping with them. But Mary and Jesus's mother were not weeping for Jerusalem, or for themselves, only for Jesus, for the bent back ahead of them, trudging over the smooth paving stones.

Now the two men walked together, treading the streets between Pilate's quarters and the execution place.

Mary leaned toward Jesus's mother, suddenly struck by the idea that the five of them—herself, the elder Mary, Joanna, Susanna, and John—could help Jesus escape. They could together cause enough confusion to make it possible for Jesus to slip away. "Mary, when we get near this place—wherever it may be—will you help him escape? We can create such a disturbance that we may be able to do this."

"I—I do not—" His mother, deep in stunned sorrow, was unable to respond.

Mary turned to John, Joanna, and Susanna. "We can stop this. There is a chance. We must do this. We must!" She looked around. "We are all he has now!"

"But will he follow us?" John asked. "I feel—from what he has told us—that he accepts this, if he does not actually welcome it."

Was there no help for him? No earthly thing they could do for him?

The throngs were swelling now, more coming from their houses and markets to witness this procession. People hurried to do their business before sundown and the beginning of the Sabbath. The Sabbath shoppers, jamming the narrow street, squeezed the executioners and their victims and followers into a long thin line moving past the curious faces of the onlookers.

"We must keep close to him!" Joanna said, forging ahead, pushing aside others. They had somehow fallen back. Just ahead of them Mary could see the back of the man carrying the crossbeam, as he struggled to keep moving forward—even though he was young and healthy. Jesus walked in front, flanked by two centurions who kept a wary eye on the crowds for any would-be rescuers. There were none, however, just apathetic crowds. One woman broke from the ranks and rushed forward to wipe Jesus's sweating face with her handkerchief, but the centurion flung her aside. Others held out cups of water, but Jesus could not reach them.

All this time, they were still skirting the high outer walls of the palace, which looked like another city wall. The smooth white stones, cut so precisely, looked down upon them. But jammed up against them were the spectators, gaping to see the bloodied men staggering under their burdens, following them like dogs hoping to lap up some blood at the execution site. Back behind them came a grisly parade of the other condemned men; how many, Mary did not know.

When Jesus stumbled, one of the soldiers grabbed his shoulder and yanked him up. "Not much longer now!" he said.

When Jesus stumbled again, a little farther on, and fell to his knees, the centurion kicked him. "Get up! Get up!" Jesus, now on all fours, crawled a little and finally got to his feet again. He was swaying, unable to stand straight.

Mary tried to reach out to him, but one of the soldiers turned on her and hit her straight across the face, slamming her backward. "Stay away!" he yelled.

Her face stinging from the blow, she fell back.

"We must do something, John! We must!" she begged him. But now she knew the soldiers would not hesitate to cut them down.

I'd give my life if it would free Jesus! she thought, and, knowing that she truly meant it, she marveled at it. She, who had always feared death.

Now they were coming to two of the enormous guard towers of the palace, which flanked one of the city gates. Mary could see the Roman soldiers poised on top with their bows and spears, ready to suppress any disturbance.

And then they were through the gate and outside the city walls. That was bad. As long as they were inside the city, they were still a distance from the execution site. Now it might be upon them. They were on rocky ground, on the northwestern side of the city, where stones were quarried. It was bleak and dull, the only variation in color the different shades of stone: gray, brown, white.

Mary saw them: tall standing beams affixed to the crest of a hill, their dark stakes pointing skyward. This was the place. This was the other half of the cross, waiting for Jesus.

The spectators broke ranks and ran toward the hill, fighting for the best spots from which to view the executions. Only the condemned men themselves, their guards, and their followers trudged on slowly.

Now. If they were to do anything, it must be now. Mary looked at John. "Are you still willing?" she whispered. "If I divert them by throwing myself at the guard, can you move quickly and lead Jesus away? Look, over there—there are some cliffs, some hiding places, and if we can get there—"

"Mary, I would do anything, but this is foolish. They will see us running over the open ground and can easily catch us. How fast do you think Jesus can run now?" He was gripping her arm. "Think, Mary, think!"

He was trying to stop her. But, no, he could not. She must do this, or hate herself forever afterward. She had to try.

Wrenching herself away, she flew toward the head of the procession, circling around Jesus and confronting the centurion. Taken by surprise, Jesus only stared as she threw her cloak over the guard's head and then shoved him; he fell heavily down on his knee.

"Jesus! Jesus!" She reached out and touched his arm. "Run! That way! That way!" She pointed to the rocky ground to one side.

But Jesus just shook his bloodied head. "Shall I not drink of the cup my Father has given me?" he said with a finality that silenced her.

"Mary, your bravery will always remain with me." He turned to continue toward the upright stakes.

"Get that woman!" said the guard, disentangling himself from the cloak, but the centurion only shrugged. Her assault was of no moment to him, just a diversion from this unpleasant duty.

Mary was already making for the rocky area, trying to hide, for she did not yet realize she was not being followed. Panting, she reached the incline, clambered up it, and slid down in safety to the other side. Here a few straggly pines were growing, anchored in the thin soil. White, stony ground, boulders, pines, ravines—that was all she saw. Then everything converged onto an orchard, a thick orchard that would shelter her.

She stopped, still panting. There was no one around, no one following her. From a distance she could hear the shouts of the crowd on the execution site.

I must go back, she thought. I must stay with Jesus. She pulled herself to her feet and turned back toward the quarry.

∽ LV ∾

The ugly, gaping hole of the quarry formed an empty, upturned bowl. On its summit the crowds had gathered, dark as ants, swarming under the upright beams that reached into the sky.

Mary forced her way through the crowd, searching for the other disciples. She heard the ugly chorus of offhanded remarks all around her: "Who do we have today?" "Some rebel leader from Galilee, a couple of minor thieves." "After the holiday they have better ones." "I heard one of them claimed to be the Messiah." "No, he was a revolutionary." It was a crescendo of insults.

At last Mary found the others, as near the foot of the cross as possible, staring helplessly as Jesus was flung on his back at its foot and two soldiers came forward with mallets and nails to fasten him to the crossbeam.

Crucifixion was a long, nasty business. A person might hang on a cross for days, depending on how strong he had been when he was fastened to it, gradually losing the ability to breathe, his whole body weight sagging and borne by his bound arms. Some of the crosses provided footrests, but since these only prolonged the agony, they were hardly merciful. Sometimes, near the end, the condemned person's legs were broken to hurry the process: then no weight could be supported by the lower body.

Jesus said nothing, did not protest, and offered his arms without resistance. The soldiers, one on each side, took them and positioned them, then drove huge nails through his wrists with only two blows. His strong hands curled and uncurled with the pain of the strikes. The sound was terrible, the unmistakable noise of flesh and bone being smashed.

"Now," they said. They looped ropes around the crossbeam and hauled it, slowly, up the length of the upright beam. Finally, the crossbeam settled into its waiting notch with a loud *clunk!* One of the soldiers threw up a ladder and secured the two parts of the cross with sturdy ropes. Then they brought out the mallets and nails, to secure his feet to the lower beam. Mary shielded her eyes when they leaned over to nail his feet; it could not be looked upon, she could not bear it. They removed Jesus's clothes, leaving him with only the barest strip of cloth still on his body, and the crown of thorns.

"Here—here—" the soldier called out, as he tossed down Jesus's cloak, his belt, his sandals, his tunic. The soldiers below caught them.

During all this, the disciples could not speak or move. They watched in horror; even Jesus's mother stood like a statue. Mary reached out to hold her closer, but it was like holding something as stolid and dead as the wood of the cross.

Under the cross, the soldiers assigned to the execution sat down and began dividing up Jesus's clothes. The burly one—one of the men who had driven in the nails—set aside the cloak: the cloak that Mary and the others had seen draped over Jesus's shoulders in so many places—in the boats, out in the fields, in the synagogues. It was a soft, light color that was easy to see from a distance. The soldier who had driven the nail in his right hand took the belt. One of the others took the sandals, and another the tunic. Then the burly one held up the cloak.

"It's all in one piece," he said. "A fine job of weaving!"

Jesus's mother—who had woven it—now moved slightly, but only slightly, as she stared ahead. She clutched Mary's hand.

"So I say, let's cast lots for it!" the captain said. "No need to destroy it by dividing it up into four pieces." He pulled out a small leather bag and extracted dice. The soldiers squatted down while they cast lots.

A small sound came from the cross. Jesus was speaking, looking down at the soldiers as they gambled for his clothes.

The murmuring of the crowd made his voice almost impossible to hear. Mary strained hard, shutting her eyes as if that would help her hear better.

"Father . . . forgive them, for they know not what they do."

That could not possibly be what he meant! Their actions were deliberate, not accidental, not ignorant. Mary listened harder, hoping he would repeat his words. But he did not.

The captain, the happy winner of the cloak, now climbed up the ladder again, with a cup of wine vinegar. "Here, drink!" he said, shoving the cup at Jesus. But Jesus turned his head away. The soldier then fastened a sign above Jesus that said in Greek, Latin, and Hebrew: THE KING OF THE JEWS.

Nearby, the other two condemned men were being nailed to their crossbeams and then hoisted into place on either side of Jesus.

"What are you looking at?" A soldier caught Mary staring and walked toward her menacingly. "Next maybe it will be you. We have a special way with women—they're crucified with their backs to the crowd. After all, a woman must be modest!" He laughed and, making a little feint toward Mary and her companions, turned aside to the other crosses to fasten the charges against the men. Both those signs said CRIMINAL AND REVOLUTIONARY. With a flourish, he indicated that the public was now invited to come close. The crowd rushed forward.

Milling around the feet of all three crosses, they taunted the men hanging on them.

"You should have stuck with Barabbas; now, there's a man who knows how to use his knife!"

"How many of you are still hiding up in the caves? Got any women up there? Anyone going to be missing you tonight?"

"At least these two are good Jews. Too good, too Jewish for their own skins! But what about him—this failed, pathetic Messiah? An executed Messiah—what a joke!"

"Hey, you—Jesus, is it? Aren't you the one who said you would destroy the Temple and rebuild it in three days? Go ahead—show us how powerful you are!" Screams of laughter.

"Come down off the cross, then we'll believe in you!"

"He said he saved others, but he can't even save himself!"

"He trusted in God. So let God rescue him now if he wants him!"

Then a stir as a contingent of religious authorities mounted the steep sides of the quarry. Caiaphas and his party had arrived. With slow, deliberate movements, as if to emphasize its official nature, the group halted at the foot of the cross and read the sign above Jesus.

"'King of the Jews!' Well, well! Actually, it should say, 'He *claimed* to be king of the Jews,' for it's certainly a delusion," said Caiaphas. "And at my house, you even claimed to be God's son. So you should have no trouble coming down off this cross. Come on down. Astound us!"

Jesus just looked at them.

"Come down and we'll believe. Bargain?" one of the scribes said.

"If you can do it, why refuse? We will all be converted. Isn't that what God wants, if it's true? He wants everyone to believe."

Then one of the revolutionaries joined in. "Aren't you the Messiah? Aren't you? Then save yourself and us!"

"Shut up!" A loud, resounding cry came from the other cross. "Have you no fear of God? You are condemned along with him! And we both deserve it. We did what we were accused of. But this man is innocent."

Jesus turned his head toward the man who had spoken. "Dismas," he said.

The man's face registered surprise and thankfulness at the same time. "Yes," he said. Clearly he wondered how Jesus could remember his name, but his gratitude overwhelmed his curiosity. "Oh, yes, Lord."

"Dismas," Jesus repeated, his words slow from his cracked lips, "that time at Matthew's . . . you chose this way."

"Yes. Would I had chosen another. I deserve this death. But yours . . . Lord, oh, Lord! Remember me when you come into your Kingdom."

Jesus answered him, "Truly I assure you, today you will be with me in paradise."

"Paradise!" yelled one of the onlookers. "They'll be in a tomb today, that's all!"

"No, they'll be thrown to the dogs!" someone else called. "Tombs are for rich people!"

At this horrible prediction, Mary flinched. Oh, why did his mother have to hear this? It was beyond cruelty, beyond what anyone should have to endure.

The sky was darkening, swift-moving clouds suddenly obscuring the sun. The wind rose, lifting dust, blowing it into their faces, swirling it around the crosses. The two revolutionaries vanished from sight.

"A storm!" one of the soldiers said, grabbing for his cloak.

But it was more than a storm. The sun itself seemed to dim, and darkness fell swiftly upon them.

"Eclipse!" cried someone. But solar eclipses did not occur when the moon was full; everyone knew that. And no eclipse had been predicted by astronomers.

In the confusion caused by the darkness, the disciples were able to come closer, to the very foot of the cross. Jesus looked down at them, recognizing them one by one; they could feel it. They felt him reaching out to them, trying to strengthen and sustain them.

Without being able to move his arms, Jesus indicated by a movement of his head that he was addressing the elder Mary.

"Dear woman," he said, "behold your son!"

And with another slight movement, he was able to signal John. "Behold your mother."

John reached out and embraced the elder Mary. Jesus nodded, almost imperceptibly.

The darkness deepened. Now it almost seemed like night, and there were ominous rumbling sounds. Did they come from the sky or from the ground? Mary could not tell.

"I thirst," Jesus's voice came from above, and one of the soldiers heard him. He scrambled up a ladder and offered a sponge soaked in vinegar to moisten Jesus's lips.

Standing below the cross, only the faithful disciples and the soldiers were left. But many more disciples—nearly all women—had emerged from the crowd and now found their way to the others. Some were women who had followed from Galilee, others the hidden disciples of Jerusalem. It was safer for women to be seen publicly. Of the male disciples, only John had been brave enough to stand by. No wonder Jesus loved him.

John . . . Who would have predicted it would be John, the hot-tempered, pretty-faced John, who would be the beloved disciple? Mary thought. In the beginning, he did not seem very promising. He was petulant and dreamy at the same time, overshadowed by the blustering Peter and the clever Judas. A man's mettle was not easily discerned. I am fortunate, she thought, that I was paired with him on the mission.

But all thoughts of John or the Galilean women or even Jesus's mother vanished as she suddenly heard Jesus cry out, "My God, my God, why have you forsaken me?" It rent the air, louder than the rumbling thunder and the strange sounds coming from under the earth.

He was twisting on the cross, turning as if in agony. His mouth was open, and his eyes stared out at the sky.

"He's calling on Elijah!" someone said. "He expects Elijah. Let's wait and see if Elijah comes to rescue him."

But there was no movement except the swirling clouds and the restless stirrings of the onlookers. Jesus himself was still.

"Father, into your hands I commend my spirit." Mary heard those words, surprisingly loud. Jesus had bowed his head, and it rested on his breast. The crown of thorns fell off, tumbling to the ground, rolling along until it stopped against a rock.

"It is finished." Jesus spoke. Then his head drooped down, no strength in it at all.

The women fell on their faces, groveling on the ground.

God had deserted them.

God had fled or turned away, everything had collapsed, Jesus was dead, and only she and his stunned and crushed followers were left.

Mary picked herself up off the ground. What did they matter? Jesus was dead. None of them could do anything to save him. And now he was just a dead body that must be attended to. And no one had thought of that.

A tomb was needed. Rites were needed. Preparation of the body was needed. And they had none of these things. They were visitors in a strange city, far from their homes, utterly dependent on others for even the smallest things. And now they were outlaws, associated with an executed criminal.

The crowds . . . they had melted away, vanished like specks of dust. The unknown disciples from Jerusalem might help, but they stood like stunned animals, staring.

It was late afternoon, and the Law expressly forbade leaving an executed criminal exposed after sundown.

The soldiers roused themselves from where they had been squatting. Another officer joined them, and then two of them went to Dismas's cross, where he hung, wheezing but still breathing. Suddenly one of the soldiers raised a club and smashed Dismas's shinbones with two sharp blows. Immediately his body sagged forward.

Dismas gave a strangled cry of pain, but the soldiers had turned to the other insurrectionist, who was watching them approach with apprehensive eyes.

"No," he begged. "No, no, please—"

His plea ended in a scream as the soldier swung back and hit his legs a hard blow. The bones shattered, and his feet twitched where they were pinned by the nails, the toes curling up.

"They will be dead by nightfall," the soldier who had struck the blows assured his companion. He looked up at the sky to make sure, as he made his way to Jesus. He stopped at the foot of Jesus's cross.

"I think he's already dead," the second soldier said. "A mercy." He walked around the upright beam and looked at Jesus from several angles. "He's gone," he said at length.

"We must make sure." The first soldier thrust his spear into Jesus's side, and there was no movement. A gush of blood and clear fluid poured out.

Mary had to look away. In that moment, the horror, the finality of the end, could not have been more painfully clear.

"You were right," the soldier said. "We should get him down while we are waiting for the other two to die."

"We'll need a ladder." The soldier went to find one, returning quickly.

They leaned it against the cross. One of the soldiers cut the fastening ropes, but not before he had secured both ends of the crossbeam with more ropes, to lower it and its burden. It was too hard to pull the nails out from the upright angle; the men needed to work on the ground. Before proceeding, they managed to pry the nails out of the feet.

Slowly the heavy crossbeam was lowered, carefully, as if the weight on it were suddenly breakable. It came to rest at the foot of the cross, and the men got busy with Jesus's hands.

Already those hands and arms looked different, paler, the skin more translucent. Mary stared at them, remembering, suddenly and vividly, the vision she had had of Jesus being transfigured, and then, soon thereafter, seeing him look truly changed, somehow become gloriously paler and lighter. But that was nothing like this, nothing like this starkness. That was a living, shining transparency, and this was a flat and fading dullness.

"There!" The soldier wrested the hands free, tossed the nails aside. They were heavy and long and made a loud noise as they landed on the rocky ground. The soldiers lifted Jesus free of the crossbeam and laid him flat on the ground.

With a cry, Jesus's mother rushed forward. She threw herself on his chest and began to wail, loud, wavering cries, and wept and cradled his head, then raised her head again and cried to the skies. The soldiers stood back, abandoning the body to her.

"My son—my son—" His mother tried to raise him up, kept begging him to move, to respond. But he lay there limply in her arms, such a heavy weight that she could barely hold him.

John crept forward, inspired by Jesus's charge to care for his mother. But he stopped, helpless, before the sprawled dead body. Though he moved awkwardly to touch the elder Mary protectively, she did not even feel it.

With all her strength, Mary drew near to join them.

Once she was close enough to see the pale, still Jesus stretched out on the ground before her, she almost lost what little strength she had summoned.

Oh, he is dead, he is truly dead! Like Joel, he lay there inert, white, gone. And killed by Pilate.

I have done all this once before. I cannot do it again, I cannot. But she crawled to his head, cradled by the elder Mary, and kissed his cheek, covered in cold, dead sweat.

He accepted her kiss. She felt it. Unlike Joel, he had not died repudiating her, with even his corpse seeming hostile to her. It was different, after all. Joel's last words to her were "You will get nothing!" whereas Jesus had said, "Mary, your bravery will always remain with me."

"My son, my son," his mother was repeating, over and over, like a prayer, stroking his hair.

Mary leaned over and touched the woman's own hair, echoing her movements with her son. It was the only comfort she could think of bestowing.

Suddenly there was a stir, and a strange man in the robes of a religious elder was standing over them.

"Pilate has given me permission to take the body," he was saying. "Here." He offered a tablet; the soldiers took it and examined it.

"Irregular," one of them finally said. "We need to show this to our captain."

"I assure you, it's all in order," the man said calmly.

John got to his feet, but the man motioned to him to look away while he awaited the return of the soldier and his superior.

The centurion made his way over to them, looking down at Jesus. "I see—I see—well, if Pilate has signed it . . ." He shrugged. "Go ahead."

"Thank you," the man said. He motioned to other men he had brought with him. They stepped forward briskly. They even had a litter. Carefully, but with a practiced manner, they transferred Jesus to it.

"This way," said the first man, leading them.

John, Jesus's mother, Mary, and the others followed.

They left the crucifixion site and headed farther away from the city, out into the open country, and as they walked, the little procession was silent, utterly silent, stunned silent.

Everywhere there was nothing but gray. Gray ground, gray outcropping of rocks, gray sky rapidly darkening to evening, gray clouds scudding across the heavens. The abnormal darkness had disappeared, replaced by this disappointingly normal dullness. Normal dullness. How could that be? The darkness of the noontime, the sandstorm, whatever it had been, at least acknowledged this tragedy. But for it to be normal—oh, God had indeed forsaken them. He had made this day end normally, even the weather, so no one would remember it.

. They rounded another stony hill and suddenly saw greenery. Spread out before them was a garden—olive trees, a well, trellises and grapevines, fig trees and roses. It sprang out in its lushness like a mirage.

The man gave a signal for them to halt. "This is my tomb garden," he said. "I had prepared it for myself and my family, as a place that would be pleasant to visit. But it has never been used."

They were safely beyond the execution site, and the soldiers had been left behind. John went over to the man and said, "Thank you, Joseph. You have given us a great gift."

Joseph. Had not John spoken of a Joseph from Arimathea, who was a member of the Sanhedrin but was a secret disciple? He must be that man.

Whoever he was, he motioned for the bearers to proceed. They all followed over newly laid gravel pathways toward the cliff face, where three chiseled doorways faced them.

A rich person's tomb site: carved from a cliff face, with rock beds inside, and spacious—not unlike rooms of the living. But no suppers would ever be held here, except outside, when relatives came *in memoriam*, and no conversation would ever take place within the elegant space, as the bodies dried and the graveclothes moldered and the only thing they were awaiting was a transferral into a decorated pottery container to make room for more burials. A tomb was only on loan, even for the rich. In the rocky area around Jerusalem, no one had the luxury of a personal tomb that would remain his for eternity.

But it was a tomb, at least for the moment, unlike the ditch frequented by dogs where Dismas and his unnamed companion would lie.

"I have spices," Joseph said, indicating a box alongside one of the tombs. "Nicodemus helped provide them."

At the sound of his name, a man cautiously emerged from one side of the rock and came toward them.

"We thought they would be needed," he said. This man, too, was an elder, and well dressed. He must be yet another secret disciple.

Mary went over to the box, opened it, and stared: there were large alabaster containers of aloe and myrrh inside, extremely expensive spices. Nicodemus had stinted nothing. "This is most generous. And we are grateful," she said, her voice shaking.

She gave directions for the litter to be laid on the ground. Even as she was doing it, she wondered why it fell to her to give orders. Joseph was here; Nicodemus; John, whom Jesus had singled out; Jesus's mother; Joanna; Susanna; some others from Galilee. Yet they were all looking to her for direction. Perhaps their courage had failed them. Perhaps they had given all they had. Perhaps they simply needed to rest. In any case, there was no one but her to tell people what to do.

And it did not matter, not really. These hasty rites were not the final ones. She—and others, doubtless—would return and complete them properly. So it was important only to do the barest minimum here, before darkness fell.

"Do we have anything to wash him with?" she asked. But she knew already that they did not. So she continued, "Then let us proceed with the anointing."

Joseph opened the alabastrons containing the aloe and the myrrh, standing back while the first burst of the perfume permeated the air. Then Mary took handfuls of it and, bending down reverently, spread it all over the body of Jesus, as she had tended the body of Joel. The dull sheen of the ointment covered the bruises, the bleeding, the gaping wound in his side, disguised the stark, bloodless color of his feet. The oily substance served to make him look as if he had never been living, as if his life had been a pretense all along.

The linen grave-wrappings were wrapped around him by the men, and a special facecloth was placed upon his head and secured with more windings. Finally, a long shroud was fastened around his body.

Joseph told his men to take Jesus inside the middle tomb. They lifted him up with quiet respect and took him inside. Soon they emerged without their burden, and bowed their heads to Joseph.

"We have laid him on the lower rock-couch," they said.

"Very good," Joseph said.

They turned their attention to a round stone that was waiting beside the rock cliff, already positioned in a grove.

"Close it," Joseph said, and three of the men put their shoulders to it and shoved it along the groove. It took a moment to roll, but then it slid across the opening of the tomb, stopping at a carefully positioned barrier. When it stopped, it made a loud *thunk!* An echo came back from the depths of the tomb.

"It is done," said Joseph. "May he rest in peace. A truly good man, and perhaps more than that."

John, Mary, Jesus's mother, and all the others who had persevered thus far said nothing. The sound of the rolling tombstone had silenced them. It spoke so loudly that there was nothing they could utter.

"Thank you," John said at last, speaking for all of them. "Thank you, more than we can ever say, or repay you."

Joseph shook his head. "A pity, a great pity . . ."

Darkness was coming. They did not want to be here alone at night.

"I can offer you a house in Jerusalem," Joseph said. "A house where you can rest. Until you know what it is you wish to do . . ."

They sat, huddled, in the large room of the loaned house. A loaned tomb, a loaned house—Joseph was generous. But he had hurried away, afraid of his Sanhedrin colleagues. "Keep yourselves hidden," he advised the mourners. "They don't know you, and can't identify you—yet—but usually the followers are hunted down along with their master."

Pulling his garment up over most of his face, he slipped away.

So no wonder Peter denied knowing Jesus. Mary thought. And no wonder the others ran away. John is a brave man.

John was seeing to everyone else, settling them all, trying to comfort them. He led Jesus's mother to a couch and had her lie down, he asked Joanna and Susanna whether they could serve the food if any were to be found—he did all the things that should be done with a group of injured survivors of a war. But he was met by stony silence, drooping limbs, and sagging faces; they sat immobilized by grief.

"We must have light," he said, moving to light oil lamps around the room, which was almost completely dark. Full night had fallen, and the only light came from the almost-full moon that had just risen.

"We are not supposed to kindle lights on the Sabbath," said

Mary, automatically. "We were supposed to have kindled them before sunset."

"I don't care about the Sabbath." John pronounced the heretical words calmly. "I don't care about the Sabbath any longer." He held a flaming reed over a wick, lowering it slowly and deliberately. The fire caught, and light leapt into the dark space. "I mean, I don't care about the rules governing it. Jesus said the Sabbath was made for man, not man for the Sabbath. And I cannot believe that Moses would want us all sitting here in the dark for hours when our dearest family member has just died, even if he died at a time that ran afoul of the Sabbath."

"That's why they wanted to end the crucifixions," Joanna finally said. "The soldiers killed the men so that the Sabbath could be better observed."

The Sabbath, with its unyielding handclasp over their lives—Jesus had healed and worked on the Sabbath, and now how could they go back to the old way? And in the end, that was what they had killed him for. Too many people felt the same way, too many people were breaking away from the strictures, too many people were dancing along behind him. The iron grasp of the religious establishment, as well as the iron grasp of the Sabbath, in whose name they ruled, was being broken. And that could not be tolerated.

"And I'll kindle a light, too." Mary stood up and took the glowing reed from John, her eyes meeting his, partners in defiance. She bent down and lit another lamp, and the light in the room increased more than twofold.

"Here." She handed the reed to Joanna, who took it and lit another lamp. Joseph's room was abundantly supplied with them.

One by one they each rose and lit a lamp, and the room expanded with light.

When they wished to sleep, or rest, or whatever it was they felt might be granted to them that night, they extinguished the lamps, breaking another Sabbath stricture. And they lay down in the darkness, and each communed with God, by himself.

Lying on a hard, narrow bed beside Jesus's mother, Mary only waited until everyone was silent before casting herself directly at God's feet.

She lay rigid as the bed itself, fists clenched, sending her formless thoughts and feelings upward, praying that they be accepted. Sometime during the night, mercy drew a veil over her mind, blanking it out with sleep. No dreams, no answers came, but she escaped for a little while the torture that the world had become.

The natural daylight broke into the house, rolling back the scroll of darkness. Now the Sabbath stretched before them, a time of inactivity and prohibition. But that was past. It had died along with Jesus, Mary thought, as she woke up and saw the murky light stealing into the room, and remembered everything.

We have work to do, she thought. I must purchase the right anointing oils, and we all need something to eat, or will soon. We have not eaten since . . . since we ate with Jesus.

His death, the loss, struck her backward, and for a moment she was stunned as the pain flooded in, brighter and stronger than the sunlight.

I cannot bear it, she breathed. I cannot. I cannot go on. But as she lay there for many long moments, she heard the stirring of the others in the larger room, heard the breathing of Jesus's mother on the bed beside her.

After I have tended to their needs . . . after I have anointed Jesus as he should be anointed, after I have seen them all depart for Galilee and do—I don't know what—go back to fishing or studying or tax collecting . . . then I can think what to do, but now . . .

With an odd strength, she heaved herself out of bed. Her legs were steady, made strong by her new mission: complete what you have before you, complete it well, then . . .

The elder Mary still slept. Mary bent down and examined her face. Even in all her sorrow, in all her torment, her face was still peaceful and somehow beautiful.

I always drew strength from that face, from her calmness, Mary thought. But now everything is turned upside down, and my task is to provide strength for her.

She left the bedroom and stole out into the main chamber. More people were there—where had they come from? Slumped in a corner was one wrapped figure, a large one. She tiptoed over to it and lifted the covering mantle.

Peter!

She was so shocked she almost cried out. How had he come here, how had he found them?

The other hunched form—it was Simon. And the third one—Thomas.

Why were they all creeping back? What had happened to bring them here?

John was already up and looking about, worrying about practical details.

"John," she said, joining him in the private alcove, "how did they find us here?"

"Somehow they knew where we were. They came in the night, one by one," he said. "Perhaps, somehow, Joseph got word to them." He paused. "They seemed relieved to be here."

"What shall we do now?" Mary felt oddly brisk and efficient.

John thought a long moment before he answered. "We must wait," he finally said. "As Joseph said, we will be hunted. But it is likely to be a short hunt. We will not cause trouble, we will not be visible. The authorities have nothing to worry about."

"Why do you say that?" she cried, clutching his arm.

"Jesus is gone," he said. "There will never be another Jesus. No one else can speak like him, no one else can heal like him, no one else can do—well, anything he did!"

"But, John—we were together in our mission. Jesus sent us out. And, you know, by some mysterious power, we *did* heal people. We *did* preach to people. Susanna—I healed her!" Mary stood beside him, reminding him.

"But no one can speak the way he did. All we did was repeat what he said. We had nothing original to say." He spoke softly.

"Perhaps repeating what he said is enough."

"But people asked him questions, and he was able to answer each one, individually, and we cannot do that. We don't have the wisdom. We can't just quote from him. Then we would be like the Pharisees, always quoting their teachers." He shook his head.

"Jesus said he wanted us to reach out as he did. That the missions were just the beginning of our teaching. Otherwise—yes, it would all vanish with him. I do not think . . . I do not think he wanted that. I think that was what our mission—clumsy and unskilled as it was—was all about."

"It was certainly clumsy and unskilled," John agreed.

"But we are . . . different from him," Mary said. "He expected us to be awkward and nervous. He did not condemn us for it." She waited for him to speak. When he did not, she continued. "He knew we would learn. He knew we would be able to carry on."

"He was wrong," John said. "It's all over. There is nothing to carry on."

Peter and Simon and Thomas were stirring. Then Peter stood up and looked around, blinking. "My friends," he said, "I am so pleased to be among you once again—" He broke off and started to cry, bringing his face up into the crook of his elbow. "I thank God you will let me back into your fellowship. I betrayed him—I said I didn't know him—" He burst out into loud, heaving sobs.

"I know," said John.

"Oh, God!" Peter wailed.

"You were surprised, but Jesus was not," said John. "He foretold it."

"It is unforgivable," sobbed Peter.

"Jesus already forgave you," said John. "So you must accept it."

"I cannot."

"Then you betray him again." John looked sternly at him. "He has perished on a Roman cross, as Caiaphas and his supporters wished. It has all come true, as they ordained. Jesus has been vanquished by them, silenced, and executed. You know what happened?"

"I—I heard. But not the details." Peter slumped back onto a stool. "I do not think I can bear it."

"After you left," Mary said, trying to hold her voice steady, "and the Sanhedrin trial was over, he was rushed away to Pilate." She had to stop and wait for her voice to stop quavering. "Pilate was as cruel as his reputation—he just gave in to them—to the crowd yelling, even though a few minutes earlier he had pronounced him not guilty—"

"No!" Peter rose up, his bulk swaying. "Pilate set him free?"

"The crowd overcame Pilate—I mean in words—they threatened him—he was frightened—" Mary shook her head, unable to continue.

"Pilate gave in to them," said John. "And so Jesus was executed above a desolate quarry known as the Place of the Skull. And now he's dead, laid to rest in a borrowed tomb, thanks to the kindness of the same wealthy man who is lending us this house."

Mary saw Peter flinching at each revelation. He had fled like a coward. His fervor and resolutions had not prevented his flight to self-preservation.

"Oh, Lord, forgive me!" was Peter's only response, as he bent over in sobs.

Thomas said nothing. Simon seemed so stunned by the execution of Jesus and Dismas that he kept repeating over and over, "But one was innocent and the other not, did they not understand that?" The release of Barabbas had sent him into a frenzy of talk. "Barabbas—they let him go. All that killing. An enemy of the state. But Pilate did not care. Jesus killed no one. That means Jesus's message was wrong. He said those who live by the sword shall die by the sword, but just the opposite happened."

That is the question we are all grappling with, Mary thought. Trust Simon to state it baldly: Jesus was wrong. He told Simon to reject violence, but they let the murderous Barabbas go free and in his place executed Jesus, who had never killed anyone. Jesus had predicted the end of this age, but the sun rose and the moon shone the same as always. Jesus was wrong. And if he was wrong about these things, what else was he wrong about? He said he would be with us always, but now he is gone.

Perhaps we were fools for having followed him! It is all over.

It only remains that I must anoint him, thought Mary. Because I still love him. After sunset, and the darkness, pass away once again. And then it will be truly over.

⋙ LVI ⋘

The streets of Jerusalem were quiet, emptied of the holiday throngs. The markets were closed for the Sabbath, the stalls boarded up, and the awnings taken down.

In her strange heightened sense of discernment, Mary looked carefully at the buildings in this rich section of the city, noted their chiseled stone faces and the heavy wooden shutters, wondered how much they cost, then wondered why it mattered. None of it mattered. She and John hurried past them, past Pilate's palace, out the gate, retracing their route the day before. Nothing was stirring at Pilate's except a few soldiers on guard. The stones of the courtyard were clean. No blood, no trace of what had happened yesterday.

And then they were out the gate, following the path the doomed men had walked, out across the stony reaches. They had felt compelled to come back, to retrace the steps, as though somehow that would ease the mourning or bring them closer to Jesus. They could walk in his footsteps, participate in his journey in a way they could not when it was actually happening.

The day was gloomy, overcast. The bright, mocking sunshine of the day before had fled, as if knowing it was inappropriate. Cold winds whipped across the open field where they walked, their heads down. They said nothing, silent in their grief, but sharing it nonetheless.

They were approaching the site. Ahead they saw the three crosses, empty and waiting for their next guests.

Mary stopped. "I—I cannot face it after all," she said softly. "Not yet." She turned her head away. John halted beside her.

Across the bleak, stony field she saw the hill where she had fled after her brief, absurd attempt to rescue Jesus. "I—let's go over there," she said. She wanted to withdraw to its solitude, block out the sight of the ugly crosses, gather her courage before approaching again.

Together they walked over toward the hill. How she remembered the running; how she had panted, how her feet had slipped on the loose gravel. But then, then, if only she could go back, Jesus had been alive then, alive, she had only to turn her head and see him. When she turned and looked back now, there was only emptiness, a path with no one on it.

They climbed the hill, just as she had before, but more slowly, and crested it. Below was the orchard, the orchard that even then had seemed so out of place. She had not entered the orchard. At that point she had stopped and heard the cries of the crowd, and known she could not run away.

Down below, in the dull light, the trees were enveloped in a haze. She was still not ready to return to Golgotha, the Place of the Skull. She would stay in the orchard just a little while. They descended and made their way to the rows of trees, trees that shimmered in their new leaves, their branches shaking in the wind.

And one tree, whose branch did not move, but something hanging from it did. . . .

Mary gave a little cry as she saw the dark bundle hanging from a branch of one of the farther trees, and she knew it was not a bundle, not a bag, but something longer and heavier, something with a head, arms, and legs, and feet that were drooping, and the bundle turned very slowly, pushed by the wind. . . .

"Stay here," said John. He approached the tree cautiously, quietly, as if he was afraid he would startle it. Mary saw the bundle moving, twisting as John came near it.

"Oh, God!" he cried. "Oh, God!"

Disobeying him, Mary rushed to him, running over the rough ground, passing the other trees. She reached him and took his hand.

"Oh, God," he was still saying. The figure hanging in the tree turned toward them, and Mary saw the blackened, bloated face of Judas.

A cry died in her throat as she stared at him. His eyes were already gone, pecked out by birds. A red, swollen tongue protruded from his slack mouth, and his head was angled so far to the right it rested flat on his shoulder. A foul smell, stronger when the breeze picked up, came from him. She gagged and turned away.

He had killed himself because he had betrayed Jesus! As if that would bring him back!

"Too late, too late!" Mary shouted at him. "You're useless, useless, your remorse is useless, as useless as your life." Her hatred was still strong; death did nothing to vanquish it. "I'm glad you didn't repent, I'm glad you didn't follow him to Golgotha; if you had, he would have forgiven you, and you must never be forgiven, you must stay unforgiven, for eternity . . . eternity. . . ."

"Mary!" John sounded shocked.

"You don't know what he was, you don't understand, he was worse than possessed, he deserved to perish unforgiven; didn't Jesus call him the son of perdition? He said he was doomed to destruction—"

Creak . . . creak . . . the rope turned slowly with its weight, and the lifeless feet dangled, almost touching the ground.

"This is the only peace you will ever get, the peace of hanging from a rope!" she cried. "And, John—there's the money bag on him; we ought to take it, it's our money, he was the treasurer, and now we need it, and—"

"No," said John, sternly. "Leave him and his money. Would you really want to touch it?"

"No," she said, starting to sob. "No!"

"Then come. This place of death is worse than Golgotha." He steered her away, and they left the tree, groaning softly with its weight.

A few moments later, they were standing at the foot of the middle cross, bleak and silent except for the wind whistling through the low grass. So much noise and pain yesterday; today such quiet. As if the horror had vanished, sucked up somewhere into a void. They knelt and prayed, and Mary whispered, "The evil seems gone, but I know not where. Or how."

In the rooms of the borrowed house, people were moving about, but slowly, like stunned animals. Though more of them had gathered in the time Mary and John had been gone, their eyes looked empty, haunted. They spoke to one another in murmurs, as if they were afraid someone would overhear them. The men kept looking nervously out the windows. But the Sabbath stillness hung over the streets.

She and John stood together, and John said, "Friends, we must tell you of what we have seen. Judas is dead. He hanged himself."

The others gave cries of shock and pain. But they had not known about Judas, certainly not the full extent of it. Mary wanted to tell them, to expose him to all of them. But something stopped her. She could not bring herself to do it. Her most violent hatred seemed to have abated, purged by the visit to Golgotha.

"Let us pray for him," said Peter, rising. Mary stood silently while the others did so.

"We must—we must buy food for tonight," Mary said when they were finished. "And spices to . . . to anoint Jesus later."

Jesus's mother, sitting in the shadows at the far end of the room, said in a soft voice, "We do not want food."

"No, but we must force ourselves to eat." Surrounding her, the dispirited and weakened disciples sat where they were, drooping. "Jesus would demand that we do it." How she knew that, she could not say. But it was as if he were standing right beside her.

As the daylight faded, the markets reopened for business, and suddenly hordes of people appeared, eager to shop. Mary and John went to get the food and the spices, and on the way they talked further about what they had seen in the orchard.

"Judas had a father near Jerusalem," said John. "Should someone not tell him? We know his family name—Iscariot."

"When our other business is done," Mary said.

What did they owe Judas and his family? What would Jesus have told them to do? She did not know. Or, rather, she did. But she did not want to. Judas could wait. There was other, more important business.

Bread, wine, cheese, lentils, green onions, leeks, fig paste—it would be a simple meal. But nourishing. And that was what they needed now— just the simplest nourishment.

Forsaking the tables, and sitting on the hard floor to observe their mourning, the disciples formed an oval around the room. There was no head and no foot, so that all were equal. All the remaining disciples had reassembled, but Judas's absence seemed to loom over the room, larger than any one of them. The other missing person—their host, Joseph of Arimathea—also seemed to be there in a mysterious way.

A basket of bread was passed around, and they tore off pieces one by one. They leaned forward into the center to ladle out portions of the stewed lentils, helped themselves to the platter of fresh greens and the goat cheese, then settled into their places. Last, a pitcher of wine was passed around, and one by one they filled their cups.

It was time for the blessing. A meal, particularly one just after the departure of Sabbath, must have a blessing. But a dead silence hung over them, blanketing them. It was all they could do to fill their plates. They could not recite a blessing. Blessing? God had deserted them. He had abandoned Jesus in his direst hour, and now all his followers were likewise abandoned. God had looked at them all and shrugged or, worse yet, mocked.

Peter raised his portion of bread in both hands before his face. He held it reverently.

"Our master said this was his body," he said slowly. "He said this was the bread of the new covenant." He moved it slightly. "I don't understand, but this is what he said. And he said we must remember him when we eat it."

The lamplight on the bread, so like the light upon it the night Jesus had held it, jolted Mary. She could almost see his hands—strong, sunburnt—clutching the bread, instead of Peter's blunt fingers.

"This is my body," he had said. "This is my body."

In unison they all raised the bread to their lips. At once Jesus was there with them. The bread seemed no longer bread, but part of him.

But Jesus is dead and in that rock tomb, thought Mary. The tomb I must visit tomorrow.

They were all chewing the bread, looking puzzled. They all felt it, then.

The rest of the meager meal proceeded, and then the cup was raised. John said, "'This is my blood of the new covenant, which is to be poured out for many. As often as you drink it, you show forth my death.' This is what he told us." Together, slowly and thoughtfully, they raised their cups and drank.

By saying those words, Jesus had assured he would be with them at every meal, for as long as they lived. He was certainly with them tonight. The wine, dark and strong, seemed truly like blood.

"We are—we are still here," Peter finally said. "And we must remain together. We must never forget."

"But without Jesus"—Thomas's voice rose plaintively—"what must we do when together? He talked about love and being servants, but he must have meant what we all did by ourselves. There is no point in our going about as a band any longer. It's back to our homes, where we can recount our memories of Jesus."

"Memories fade." John spoke, surprisingly strongly. "I don't think Jesus had in mind memories."

"What else can there be?" Peter said. "It's all we have left. And he never even wrote anything down! We must rely on our own versions of what he said."

"I wrote some things down," said Thomas. "But of course they are incomplete."

"It's over, over," said Peter. "We will always remember, and honor, him, and perhaps we can gather for a dinner once a year, and drink the wine and break the bread, and talk about him. But . . ." He took another sip of the cup.

Outside, the dark deepened. The circle was broken, missing Jesus, but somehow Jesus was there anyway, in spite of Peter's words. Why could Peter not see it, feel it? Mary stared at the bread. Had Jesus's words over the bread that last night imbued it with a change that would hold for every other piece of bread that was offered in his name? The bread was different. She almost did not want to eat the rest of it, but knew it would be against his wishes not to. Slowly she lifted it to her mouth and took it in, again. She could see Jesus beside them all. Why could the others not?

Suddenly she felt safe, protected. They were all frightened, but this strange little ceremony—yes, it had brought Jesus back into their midst, if only for a moment. It would vanish, like all visions and exaltations, but if one could grasp it, use it for strength, then . . .

The brightness of Moses's face after talking with God had faded. The glory of the Lord hovering over the newly built Temple of Solomon had departed. The strange intensity of Jesus's person in the rain-spattered tent, following her vision of his exaltation, had been fleeting. But that did not make any of them less real.

Why does God not let us keep these things? she cried to herself. If we could just see them, grasp them, go back to them when we feel weak—then we would not falter. Why does God take them away?

She stared down at her cup, with its little bit of wine still at the bottom. The Jesus-wine, which made him present among them.

"I tell you, I will not drink of the fruit of the vine again, until I drink it anew in the Kingdom of God." That was what he had said. But now he would never drink anything again.

"We must rest," Peter was saying. Everyone agreed. They dutifully picked up their plates, gathered up the food, collected the leftover wine and bread.

And then it was over, and Jesus took his leave from their midst. But they had seen him.

They were sleeping—or trying to. The lights were all extinguished, and everyone had lain down. Mary could hear, in the stillness of the room, some muffled crying, and people turning this way and that, uttering sighs that were close to groans.

As soon as dawn is near, I will go to the tomb, Mary told herself. I could go now but . . .

The image of making her way out across the rock-strewn ground in total darkness was frightening. And the tomb itself: confronting the tomb in blackness would be horrible.

By her bedside she had three small jars of anointing spices: Ethiopian myrrh; galbanum, a waxy sweet gum from Syria; and, most expensive of all, fragrant spikenard oil in a salve from India. These were difficult to find, even in the large Jerusalem market, and so costly that she ended up with smaller jars than she would have liked, feeling fortunate to have them at all.

How slowly this night crept by! She was anxious to be on her way; now a sort of fever had taken hold of her, hurrying her to her last task. She wanted it to begin; she wanted it to be over.

Did she sleep? Did she dream? She did not know; everything was so confused since Jesus had died, even inside her head. She heard the roosters start to crow, but dawn could still be a long way off. More cries came, and then the very faintest rumble of a cart somewhere on a city street. The cart signaled the start of a new day.

Silently she rose and put on her shoes. She had slept fully clothed, so as not to fumble when she got up and wake the others. Now she drew on her mantle, folded neatly at the foot of the bed, and took the three jars in her hands. At the door, she turned and looked back at the dark room.

I love you, every one, she told them silently.

The city was still quiet; the cart she had heard must have been a lone one. It was cold, and the sky overhead was liberally sprinkled with stars. The waning moon was up; it would not set until well into the morning.

She could hear the birdsong, though, calling from the trees just beyond the city walls, a loud chorus. Of course. It was spring now in the world, time of mate-selection and nest-building—even though for the followers of Jesus it had become nothing but a mockery. The exuberant warbles and chirps punctuated the lingering night, singing her on her way as she crossed the stony field.

The lightness of the rocks, reflecting back the fading moonlight, helped her to see her way. She was relieved no one else had wanted to come; she had not invited them very openly, as if afraid they would accept. Particularly Jesus's mother.

Only as she approached the area where the tombs lay did she think about the stone sealing the entrance. It was large and heavy. She had thought of it poetically, of its shutting out the light, but not of its weight.

I can do it, she told herself. I can move it. It hasn't been there very long; it won't have settled into one spot. I am strong. If I want to move it, I will be able to. And I want to.

As she rounded the path and entered the garden area, the new green was discernible even in the dim light. The path to the garden was dull, uneven, and stony. Now, suddenly, like a little glimpse of Eden, there was a carpet of grass, and fruit trees in flower, and beds of roses, neatly cultivated, near the tomb wall. There were other beds of flowers, too, which she could not distinguish yet. And there was a stone bench to sit on, just beneath a flowering almond tree.

She sank down on it, setting the ointment jars by her feet, content to wait for the dawn. She was only thankful that she was here, near Jesus, in this beautiful garden. She bowed her head and prayed—prayed for Jesus, wherever his spirit now was, prayed for the disciples and family he had left behind, bewildered and grief-stricken; prayed for herself, that she would have the courage to enter the tomb; and prayed for Elisheba, that someday, somehow, they would meet again, and she would be forgiven, and in this life her child would be blessed.

Blessed beyond what I could offer her now, Mary thought. I do not know how or where I can live; I followed a master who has been declared a criminal; my very life may be in danger. I can still be no real mother to her, not yet.

Oh, Elisheba! I must give you to God, now more than ever. Now I relinquish you into his keeping, trusting him above all human beings.

But Jesus trusted God, and was abandoned at the cross. He deserted

Jesus, left him crying out in shame before people who taunted, "Let God rescue him!" and laughed when nothing happened.

But at the same time, it was as if Jesus wanted it, had planned it all. And last night, he was there with us . . . wasn't he? Or was it only memories? He said he would usher in the Kingdom, but it did not happen. Unless he meant something else, and we are not seeing it.

And I trusted Jesus, but he could not prevail against . . . *this*.

The tomb was beckoning.

She stood up and looked at the almond blossoms screening the tomb, white and full on their branches. She could make out the flower beds now, could see that they framed purple and yellow crocuses, and narcissuses, rearing their golden, sprightly blossoms. Along the borders, the white lilies had not opened yet, their heavy heads bending under the dew. Two doves flew overhead and called to one another.

If I linger any longer, I will be afraid, she thought. I must do the anointing.

She approached the rockcliff with the tombs. Only as she came closer did she see that the stone had already been rolled back. The door of the tomb was exposed. It yawned open, its mouth dark.

Her heart was pounding.

The stone is gone; surely not; surely I am mistaken. Is this the wrong tomb? Did I truly know my way back?

If I am lost, then, oh, how will I ever find the tomb again? I must go there! I must find him!

But the stone bench and its carvings were the same. This *was* the very tomb.

Grave-robbers! Her hand flew to her mouth. She had not thought of that. But this was a rich man's tomb site, and robbers would be attracted to it. And if the stone was taken away, then animals—

Stifling a cry, she plunged forward. I should have come yesterday, I am too late, I should have feared this!

The thought of animals entering the tomb was so terrible she was sobbing as she rushed to the doorway and tried to see inside. But it was too dark, and she could discern nothing. She fell on her knees and felt along the rock-cut funeral ledges inside; there was nothing there.

With a shriek, she fled the tomb. Frantically she looked all around the garden, and beyond the area where the tombs were laid out, but found nothing.

She could not believe what she had discovered. The utter loss of Jesus, to know that now he could never be found, stunned her.

That he should disappear . . . not have even a resting place . . . this last punishment was a final mockery from God. She cried out to God, but knew he was not listening.

Half blind with weeping, she returned to Joseph's house and stumbled in. Everyone was still asleep, but she went to John and Peter and shook them. When they roused, she motioned them to come outside.

"John . . . Peter . . ." It was hard to speak; these were the first words since she had awakened. "I—I went to the tomb—I took the spices to anoint Jesus—the moment the Sabbath was over—but I waited too long, it was too late—"

"Why did you go by yourself?" Peter demanded. "Don't you think we would have wanted to come?" It was as if he wanted to atone for his earlier desertion.

"I—I felt called to go, it was too early to wake you, I don't know—"

"What happened, Mary?" John asked.

"The tomb is empty!"

"What?" cried John. "Are you sure?"

"Yes, I went in there, it's true!"

Looking at one another, the men hitched up their gowns and began running to the tomb, leaving Mary behind. She followed as quickly as she could.

But by the time she arrived, they were leaving the garden, walking stiffly, their faces stunned.

"He's not here," John said. "Just as you told us."

"We must tell the others!" said Peter.

They looked at one another and rushed away, without even asking her to accompany them. It was just as well. She did not want to be the one to tell his mother what had happened.

The flower beds were now easily seen in all their spring beauty, not only yellows and purples but the fainter pinks and whites. The blossoms burst out of their sheaths like little stars.

Mary sank down on her knees before them, which, in their loveliness, somehow tore at her heart more than anything else. She pictured the robbers stepping on them on their way in. She bent her head into her hands and wept loudly, desperately.

Someone was moving near one of the rose beds. She looked and saw it was a gardener, shuffling and clipping and examining branches. Today, of all days! What an intrusion.

When I come to myself, I will question him about the stone, she thought. But not now. Not yet. She rose from the bench and sought more privacy as her tears flowed, unstopped and unstoppable.

"Woman, why are you crying?"

Those exact words! I have heard them before! She felt a wild chill. But where have I heard them?

"Whom are you looking for?" the gardener continued.

The gardener is speaking to me. How dare he? How dare he intrude upon my grief? Is he that stupid?

Brimming with anger, she stood and whirled to face him.

He was outlined dark against the light, as someone—who?—had been once before, long before. He was wearing a loose gardener's tunic, and a gigantic shade-hat, and leaned on his spade. He seemed very patient and only politely curious.

"The body of my master has disappeared from this tomb," she said, pointing toward its entrance. "Please, sir, if *you* have taken it, tell me where it is, and I will retrieve it. Or if you have seen anything, anything at all, tell me. You work here, you may have seen something." She wiped her tears away, trying to dry her eyes and steady her voice to speak clearly.

The man just dug his spade a little deeper into the soil, and rested his foot on it. She tried to see his face, but it was in shadow, like the rest of him. "Mary," he said.

It was the voice of Jesus. The very same.

She went cold and hot, and such jolts of temperature shot through her that she almost lost her voice. "Teacher," she finally croaked out. "Teacher."

He drew back his hat and cast it aside, and there was Jesus: alive and robust and filled with color, not corpse-white. "Mary."

The sound of her name was like a wind passing over tall reeds, whispering, calling her, enfolding her.

"Teacher!" She stumbled forward, rushing toward him.

He was alive. He was standing there in the garden, healthy and unharmed. She could not even think, but flung herself at his feet.

She clasped his feet, and only as she touched them—warm and fleshed—did she see the huge nail-wounds on them, now crusted over.

She expected him to reach down, touch her head, pull off her head covering, and stroke her hair, comfort her. She kept crying and feeling his feet, murmuring, "Lord, Lord, you are here."

Then his odd words, as he stepped back. "Do not touch me. Do not cling to me, for I have not yet ascended to my Father. But go and tell the others. Tell them what you have seen. Tell them I am going to my Father and your Father, to your God and my God." Her hands fell onto the grassy ground as his feet pulled back, beyond her touch.

She withdrew her empty fingers from the grass and looked up at his face as she rose.

He was there, but was remote. She dared not disobey and touch him, but she longed to. His familiar eyes looked at her tenderly.

What has happened? Why are you alive? Was the crucifixion all unreal? Were you put into the tomb alive? Did you not really die? And what will happen now? All her questions surged to the tip of her tongue, but the look in his eyes silenced them. She did not dare to speak, although her soul was singing. She turned and left him, knowing that he might no longer be there when she returned, yet obedient to his order.

Tell the others. Tell the others. That was all she remembered. Tell the others.

The day was well under way, and the streets were now crowded with animals and merchants and customers, but, running, she squeezed between them on the busy streets and arrived at the house out of breath. She burst through the door and found everyone gathered, watching, in the main room. Clearly John and Peter had already told their tale. They turned their eyes toward her.

The door flapped back, banging against the wall, acting as a trumpet to her announcement. They were all looking at her.

"I have seen Jesus," she said.

They sat staring, saying nothing.

"I have seen Jesus, and he is alive," she cried. "I met him in the garden. I saw his wounds, yet he lives. The tomb is empty. Ask them." She indicated Peter and John.

John turned to Mary. "Do you mean that, after we left, you saw him? Oh, we should have stayed! To see him! If he lives, I must see him. Is he coming here?"

"He said only to tell you that he has risen and is now going to his Father, God."

"We missed him!" cried John. "We missed him!" His anguish filled the room. "Oh, I cannot bear it!"

Jesus's mother came to Mary and took her hands. "He lives?"

"As sure as I stand here," she said. "And these very hands touched his feet." She let the elder Mary caress them.

His mother bowed her head over them, kissed them, and wept.

They stayed at Joseph's house; they did not know what else to do. Some of them wanted to return to the garden, but Mary knew Jesus would no longer be there.

"You will search in vain," she warned them.

Stubbornly, Peter and John went there, and returned to confirm her prediction.

"It was empty," they said. "And crawling with Roman and Temple soldiers. It was all we could do to escape from them. They are furious. They think it is some plot, but they are not sure what it means."

"Nor am I," Mary said. "I only know that he has escaped them forever. And as for us—Jesus never stays. He is always one step ahead of us. It is we who are slow to follow."

All day they talked about what Mary had seen, and kept questioning her about it, and she found, to her sorrow, that already the sight of Jesus in the garden was fading. When it had happened, everything was extraordinarily sharp, so that the smell of the cut hedges, the coolness of the dew on the grass, the deep, healthy voice of Jesus were clear, but now, as the others pressed her for details, she was grasping, floundering, trying desperately to remember.

How hard it will be to remember all his teachings, she thought. If only he had written down what he wanted us to cling to and pass on, for we will make mistakes, we will forget.

Nonetheless, when the questions ceased from the group, she found herself reliving those few precious, charged moments in the garden.

He lives. He is alive. He called me by name. And he said just what he said so long ago in Nazareth: "Why are you crying?" He must have remembered that time. That is why he said it. And just as I thought he was dead then, and searched frantically for him among the boulders, I was doing it again. And once again he was standing above me, safe on the rim, calling to me.

He lives. But what does this mean? He does not live as he did in Nazareth. This is different—profoundly, deeply different.

Darkness fell, again. It was the third night since the crucifixion. The first had been spent prostrate with grief, the second with the unexpected memorial meal. And now there was this one, following the astounding reports from John and Peter and Mary. They had kept the doors locked and bolted, and even posted a guard, since they feared the authorities might be after them for questioning.

This dinner they took together as a quiet affair, with no ceremony. They ate quickly and adjourned after brief prayer. They were clearing away the dishes when, suddenly, John stood stock-still and stared, frightened.

Jesus was standing there. Full-bodied and among them, despite the locked doors. "Peace be with you," he said.

"Lord!" said John, rushing toward him.

"Oh, my son!" His mother held out her hands.

Jesus smiled at them, and motioned them forward. They gathered around him, making a circle. "Oh, Lord," they were all murmuring.

Later, he parted his tunic, showing his wounded side, and held out his hands, stained with clotted blood. Curious, but stunned, they crowded around and took turns inspecting his wounds.

Then he said gently, "All this was foretold in the scriptures, had you the eyes to see it and the mind to understand. The Kingdom has indeed been inaugurated, the new age ushered in, by my new life. Death is vanquished and Satan conquered. You stand on its threshold, you open its doors."

He looked tenderly and possessively at each of them. "Now you must share this treasure. You are witnesses to all these things." He paused for a long moment. "I am sending the promise of my Father upon you. But stay here in Jerusalem until you are clothed with power from on high."

Then, taking them in turn, he held each face in his hands and, looking directly into the person's eyes, said, "Peace be with you. As the Father has sent me, so I send you." Then he took a breath and breathed directly on them, murmuring, "Receive the Holy Spirit."

When Mary took her turn and he clasped her face in his warm hands, she felt weak with joy and the mystery of it.

He blew his breath gently across her face and nostrils, saying in a low voice, "Mary, receive the Holy Spirit." He held her face in a tight grip, then let it go. He was telling her she must make way for the next in line.

PART THREE

Apostle

♋ LVII ♋

To the most honored lady, Elisheba of Magdala, patron and leader of the synagogue at Tiberias—

Greetings and blessings from Mary, called Magdalene, apostle and servant of Jesus in the church of Ephesus, mother of the lady Elisheba of Tiberias.

As your loving mother, I beg you to read this, not to throw it away as you have the other letters I have written you all these years. Have gracious pity on me, for I am now very old, having just passed the age of our ancestress Sarah—ninety. And you, not being young any longer yourself, must feel that the days when we might speak at last are growing short.

In all the reports I have heard of you, I take great pride in your accomplishments. For I know full well that you are a respected and powerful leader of the synagogue in Tiberias, well versed in scripture and tradition and renowned for charity. That is why I pray that your charity will extend to me, your mother.

Do not be hardhearted. I cannot wait much longer in hopes of ever seeing your face again. So much has happened since that day over sixty years ago when I was forced to leave you. And we must understand that day, for, without that understanding, we can never understand one another. Or forgive one another. There are failings on both sides to overcome. I write this with sorrow, and admit mine with all my heart.

I have in my hand the text of the curse to be read at prayers in all the synagogues against the "Nazareans," as you call us. Here is what this prayer says: "For apostates let there be no hope, and the kingdom of arrogance do Thou speedily uproot in our days; and let Nazarenes and heretics perish as in a moment; let them be blotted out of the book of life and not be enrolled with the righteous. Blessed art Thou, O Lord, who humbles the arrogant."

I heard that this was authorized by the Sanhedrin and adopted so that any person attending synagogue remaining silent during this prayer might give himself away and be cast out.

Why must you see us as the enemy? Why has this breach come about? How it would grieve Jesus. I know that very name is abhorrent to you. But I know you must also be curious about it, if only to know more about this man—this group of followers—who has caused you such personal loss. So I beg you, read the history that I will attach to this letter. I have labored on it for many years, as a testimony and safeguard against rapidly failing memories and vanishing records. In the fall of Jerusalem twenty years ago, so much was destroyed, lost forever from our history. The Temple—gone! The glory of our people, leveled and utterly demolished by the Romans. The records, burned to ashes, along with so much else. The flight of both Jews and Christians from that doomed city—we survived, but we have lost so much.

Only John and I are left. Peter died in Rome. James, son of Zebedee, was beheaded nine years after Jesus left us. The rest were scattered and must have died by now. There were many others, but they, too, are gone. Only John and I, old and with frail locust-bodies, live on.

People come to us, making pilgrimages to ask: What was it like? What was he like? What did he say, what did he look like? And we answer them with what little strength we have. But speaking to people one at a time is very laborious.

So I have written it all down—what I know, what I can remember, so that it will survive me.

This is what happened after Jesus returned to us, as I remember it.

ঙৎ LV111 ঙৎ

The Testament of Mary of Magdala, Called Magdalene

Jesus came back. Jesus stood among us once again. That is the foremost thing, the most important thing. He had died. I had seen him in the tomb. And then I saw him alive—the first person to do so. He appeared to me in the garden, and later that night he appeared to all the disciples. We were cowering behind locked doors, afraid we would be hunted down.

He came to us and assured us that all was well, that he lived. One of us, Thomas, was not there that first night. And when we told him, he scoffed at us—understandably. Jesus returned and convinced him that it was indeed him. Jesus, the same man crucified and now, mysteriously, restored to life. Thomas felt his wounds, touched his flesh, and then exclaimed, "My Lord and my God!"

Jesus just said gently, "Thomas, have you come to believe because you have seen me? Blessed are those who have not seen and have believed."

And that is why I write this history of what happened to us from that moment onward. So many will come after us, and none of them will have seen, and they must be assured of what we have seen.

Jesus did not stay with us very long. During what seemed such a brief time, but was actually forty days or so, he appeared among us, but never really walked with us again. He was not there constantly by our sides, eating with us, talking with us, resting with us. No, he would appear at startling and odd times, almost as if he were testing us. We would be doing something—fishing, or cooking, or walking—and suddenly he would be there.

He gave us a few further instructions. One was that he was commissioning us to spread his message farther—far beyond the borders of Israel—and the other that we were to remain in Jerusalem until something important happened to us, something he did not describe.

We loved those times with him, we basked in them, but we dared not question him. How much longer will you stay? How can we reach you? How can we carry on without you? These were all questions we were burning to have answered. He kept assuring us that "something" would come to answer all these things, and that he would always be with us, but we did not understand.

And then, one sunny day in early summer, he appeared among us. How odd that we had become used to this. It no longer startled us. He spoke of our mission, and how he would always be with us, and then we knew. He was leaving, saying farewell. And in a vastly different way from when he had died on the cross.

By then he had trained us well. None of us wept or protested. I did not clutch at him, although I wished to. We merely tried to behave as he would wish us to.

"Come, my children, my friends, my brothers and sisters," he said, leading us out beyond the city and once again to the Mount of Olives. We passed the olive grove of Gethsemane, we kept climbing, past our old resting place. Finally, we attained the very height of the mount.

Spread out before us, glorious like a work of art, was Jerusalem, trumpeting its beauty and its eternal existence.

Jesus gathered us around him, and said, "You are witnesses of all that has happened. You know my message, you have heard it from the beginning. Now I send you forth to teach others. But, first, remain in Jerusalem until you are clothed with power from on high." Then, one by one, he took us by the shoulders and embraced us. "Remember I am with you always, until the end of the age."

And then he vanished. He was taken away from us. Some of us thought he had been taken up into the clouds; others could not say what had happened, merely that he was gone. But surely he would come again! We remembered what he had told us since the crucifixion, when he was telling us he would leave once more and then return in glory. It concerned John. He said, "What if I want him to remain until I come? What is that to you? You follow me." We thought that meant that before John died, Jesus would return. He would come back and walk with us again. What else could he have meant?

We stood stupidly, staring all around us. And then there appeared two men, dressed in white, who seemed to come from nowhere.

"Galileans!" they said. "Why are you standing there looking at the sky? This Jesus who has been taken up from you into heaven will return in the same way as you have seen him going into heaven."

Crazy with excitement but also fearful, we went back to Jerusalem, singing and trying to convince ourselves we were filled with joy, when we felt bereft. We went straight to the Temple, as if it had answers for us. It was all we knew to do then.

But the moment I entered it, I knew I could never feel at home in it again. Despite my memories of Jesus there teaching, there were too many other ugly ones: Joel being attacked. Jesus and the money-changers. The face of the high priest, Caiaphas, shouting in the crowd for his death. Even that barrier for women was suddenly no longer tolerable. It made no sense.

But Jesus had foretold the fall of the Temple. He said not one stone would remain upon another. We did not understand, nor did we believe it. Only later, like so much else, would we come to comprehend. And even now there is much that remains veiled from us.

We were still using Joseph of Arimathea's house, and gathered nightly in the upper room, where so much had passed. To me, that was the true holy place, not the Temple, for Jesus had returned and first stood among us there. Once before, we had shared a meal when he was absent from us, eating in sorrow and yet still in fellowship. Now we must eat again, when he had left us in a different way.

We women left the Temple early and returned to the house, carrying the food we would need for the evening meal. We were astounded to find Jesus's brother James waiting for us there. His mother gave a little muffled cry of happiness and came forward hesitantly to grasp the hands of James, her next-eldest after Jesus. He was shorter than his brother, more stocky. No one would mistake one for the other. Yet there was a slight resemblance in their deep eyes.

"My son!" she said. "Oh, my dear son!" She did not ask, "Why have you come?" Mothers know better than to ask that; we only accept as a gracious gift that our children *have* come.

"I saw him!" James said, his dark face registering confusion and puzzlement. "I tell you, I saw him!"

"You knew about—"

"Yes, of course I knew about it, who does not? I had come here for the Passover—"

"You were here? The entire time?" The elder Mary's voice shook.

"I was staying in rented lodgings," James said. When his mother raised her eyebrows at the expense, he said, "The carpentry shop has done well in the past year. But, Mother—he suddenly came and stood in my room. Yes, in my room. And he told me such things—he explained so many things—and I . . . It is all astounding. So many prophecies he opened from the scriptures. But it was my brother! And yet not my brother, but someone else—"

"He promised me he would come and seek you someday," his mother said. "He has kept that promise, kept it gloriously." She reached out and touched his cheek. "But now he has left us. He has returned to his Father, also as he said. And now we must find our own way. He made it clear he had work for us to do. A great deal of work."

"Yes, in fulfilling and perfecting the Law," said James. He knitted his thick dark brows. "We must be more zealous than ever in pursuing it."

"Is that truly what he said to you?" asked Peter, coming forward.

"Why, what else could it be? He came to fulfill the prophecies and the Law and the scriptures, and nothing can be done apart from them." James looked surprised that anyone would even question it.

"But he himself did not keep the Law rigorously," said Peter. "Did he actually say this to you?"

"What matter the exact words?" asked James. "We are here to

show that he was a dutiful son of Israel, nay, the most dutiful of all! Any religious authority who criticized him was wrong!"

"You are welcome," said Peter. "All brothers in Jesus are welcome." Peter extended his arms, but did not move to embrace James. "And all brothers are equal here. Jesus told us once that we are the same to him as a blood brother or sister."

"Did he say that?" James looked perplexed.

"Nonetheless," I said, "certainly to have his blood brother join us is a special privilege." I smiled at James, remembering the other, less pleasant conversations with him. Perhaps he had changed. Jesus did change people.

Peter raised his eyebrows and moved away.

We had the memorial supper again, the breaking of the bread and the special words over it, and the passing of the cup of the covenant. This time we were not broken in sorrow but bound in a mission, although we were not sure what it was. We were waiting for directions, and knew that they would come.

As we each sipped the cup, it seemed that Jesus himself had offered it to us, and then nodded in approval as we drank it.

Our group kept returning to the Temple, praying and trying to observe all the rites. As I said, we did not know what else to do, although I myself was not drawn there. Jesus was gone—what else did we have to cling to? And so the men went dutifully to the Temple, as if trying to prove that they were more pious than any Pharisee, so that people would point at them and say, "There's a follower of that Jesus, but see how traditional they are! Jesus was a true son of Abraham!"

They gathered at noon regularly at Solomon's Portico to pray, not only the inner circle of disciples but many others: disciples from Jerusalem, followers from Galilee, both men and women. We, the women, and Jesus's brother sometimes joined them. This particular day was the beginning of the Feast of Weeks, also called Pentecost, the one I had attended so long ago as a child. This time, I passed into the Temple grounds free of any secret sin, nothing hidden or shameful upon me, questioning the Temple rather than myself.

I tried not to think of Caiaphas, knowing that if I saw him, I could not answer for my own actions. I hated him with an indescribable depth of hatred.

Even in that confused and milling court, we were able to withdraw and pray as a group. I tried to concentrate only on the words of the prayers, tried to blot out my feeling of loss without Jesus among us. It was impossible not to see him here in the Temple, and yet this was not where he belonged. The Temple had cast him out, turned on him, destroyed him.

As I was standing there, my head veiled and bowed—how shall I describe this? for it is impossible—I heard a loud sound, a sound like the whirring of wings when a flock of birds is startled and flies away. Yes, like a flock of marsh birds. The beating of the wings stirred up the air, so that a wind rushed over us. I looked up, but there were no birds. There was nothing, but a wind was now blowing. I saw it move my headscarf, I saw it stir the hems of the others' garments.

And then I saw something red and glowing appear in the air, dancing like a flame. Like several flames, like tongues of fire, as they parted and came to rest on our heads. I saw the points of the flames resting on the heads of the others, but they did not cry out in pain, and their head coverings were not scorched. Then I saw a circle of light and flame surrounding me; I beheld it out of the corners of my eyes. I put out my hand to touch it, but I felt nothing; my hand passed through it. The noise had passed away, and now only the flames remained around us.

John the Baptist . . . John the Baptist had said, "One more powerful than I will come. . . . I baptize you with water, he will baptize you with the holy spirit and with fire." And Jesus—what was it he had said, on that first day when he returned to us? "But stay here in Jerusalem until you are clothed with power from on high."

And—as I warned you, I cannot adequately describe it—I felt a deep presence hovering, but not one I had ever known before. It seemed to speak, it seemed to whisper, it seemed to penetrate the very depths of my mind.

I was not aware of speaking, though I heard the others do so. Andrew suddenly began speaking in a foreign tongue, and so did Simon, and so did Matthew, and so did . . . all of us. But what were we saying? The words were tumbling out, and we did not know what they meant.

The pilgrims in the outer court with us suddenly grew quiet, eerily quiet. Now, had there been any wind elsewhere, we would all have heard it. But it was utterly still, except where we stood.

"Aren't you Galileans?" One man finally approached and challenged us. "Why are you speaking all these languages?"

But we just continued speaking, unable to control ourselves, words pouring out.

"Listen! We are from every land under the sun, united only by our common descent from Abraham!" the man cried. He flung his arms open to indicate the entire crowd. "We are Parthians, Medes, and Elamites, inhabitants of Mesopotamia, Judaea, and Cappadocia, Pontus and Asia, Phrygia and Pamphylia, Egypt and districts of Libya near Cyrene, as well as travelers from Rome. Converts to Judaism as well as born Jews, Cretans, and Arabs, yet we hear these Galileans speaking in our own tongues!"

Were we truly speaking all these languages? But we knew none of them!

"They are just drunk!" A loud voice cut across all the crowd. "They have had too much new wine!"

Then Peter began behaving in a way utterly unlike himself. It was at this point that I realized something had indeed come upon us and changed us. I could not see it in myself, but I saw it instantly in Peter.

He stood up boldly before the crowd, walking over to a raised stone where he could address the crowd—Peter, a man now strengthened beyond recognition.

Raising his voice, he cried out, "Listen to me, all of you!" His words had a startling authority. "We aren't drunk! It's still midmorning! No, it is what the prophet Joel predicted. He said, 'It will come to pass in the last days, God says "that I will pour out a portion of my spirit upon all flesh. Your sons and your daughters shall prophesy, your young men shall see visions, your old men shall dream dreams. Indeed, upon my servants and my handmaids I will pour out a portion of my spirit in those days, and they shall prophesy. And I will work wonders in the heavens above and signs on the earth below: blood, fire, and a cloud of smoke. The sun shall be turned to darkness, and the moon to blood, before the coming of the great and splendid day of the Lord, and it shall be that everyone shall be saved who calls upon the name of the Lord."'"

Where did Peter remember all this from? Jesus had promised that we would remember things, but . . .

"You who are Israelites, hear these words!" Peter was crying. "Jesus the Nazarean was a man commended to you by God with mighty deeds. . . ."

And he went on to tell them the entire story of Jesus. There was not a single sound in the courtyard. They were transfixed. Peter! Wavering, hesitant, denying Peter!

Cautiously, I felt above me, wondering if I could detect warmth there, something to show this deep change. For, if Peter had it, might I not also? All the flames had looked alike.

"Therefore let the whole house of Israel know for certain that God has made Jesus both Lord and Messiah, the Christ, the anointed one, this Jesus whom you crucified."

Another long silence. Then one lone voice cried, "What are we to do, my brother?"

Without hesitation, Peter declared, "Repent and be baptized, every one of you, in the name of Jesus the Christ for the forgiveness of your sins; and you will receive the gift of the Holy Spirit."

Where had this definitive answer come from? Jesus had never told us such things. But these flames, this mysterious presence inside— could it be that comforter, that advocate that Jesus had promised?

He had said it would be another version of himself. But this did not seem the same. Would Jesus have said these things? Should we trust this newfound companion? Even if Jesus had introduced it?

And then the entire courtyard rushed forward, crying, "Baptize us! Baptize us!" and I stood looking in amazement.

We were compelled to keep records, and find a site with running water that could accommodate this vast group: some three thousand. Peter's spontaneous sermon had made three thousand converts. Three thousand people who were willing to stand up in public and declare themselves followers of Jesus—more than had dared to do so in his own lifetime.

But *was* this the same as following Jesus himself? Peter was Peter, not Jesus, and this odd accompaniment by a spirit was still not Jesus. True, sometimes in the scriptures people had been given God's Spirit temporarily as a measure of strength for service in extraordinary times. Now it seemed that this Holy Spirit was to be our lifelong companion, and it was somehow supposed to substitute for Jesus.

But—oh!—I would rather have had Jesus himself, Jesus in all his confounding perplexity. Yet, gradually, I was forced to accept that this was what he had decreed for me. And I could only bow my head and say yes to it. What choice did I have? "Do not cling to me." Those words would ring forever in my ears, his holding me at a distance. Yet he had spoken to me first, before all others.

The three thousand were duly baptized, and now our fellowship swelled. What were we to do? We were Galileans, strangers and pilgrims in this Jerusalem area. Yet we had been granted a house and headquarters, and many converts were coming to us. Were we to remain here?

Now, with our newfound companion, we prayed to the Spirit and trusted that he—or she, or Wisdom, or whatever this presence was—would lead us where Jesus wished us to go.

Two things happened almost immediately. The first was that Peter and John began to perform the same acts as Jesus in healing and preaching. In fact, Peter became so famous that people laid out their sick in hopes that his mere shadow would fall across their litters and cure them!

The other was that we, as disciples and apostles and converts, began to organize. We needed another house to serve as our center, for Joseph's was only lent to us. But many in Jerusalem began to follow the Way (as we were first known), including even some Temple priests, and they made houses and meeting places available to us. And since some were better off than others, people pooled their resources and shared, so that no one would go hungry. This spontaneous charity caught the attention of the public, and that is how we first became widely known.

But much more than that went on in our gathering places. We broke bread and consecrated the wine cup in Jesus's name, we prayed, we pored over the scriptures to find all the references of long ago to Jesus, as he had told us. We distributed food and clothing to the poor among us.

Oh, we were very busy. From dawn until midnight there were tasks to be done. We had little time for grieving, little time for reflection, only time for action and the dashed-off prayer.

As one of the very earliest disciples, and someone who had known Jesus throughout his entire ministry, I was called upon time and again to tell new converts about him, to try to make him alive to them.

How hungry they were to know about him. I know now that this hunger, this thirst, is going to continue, and there is no way I can meet it. I am trying, in this little testimony, but I humbly realize how inadequate it is.

Postscriptum, to my daughter:

And now, Elisheba, I send this on to you. I will be sending more, for the testimony is hardly complete. But I wanted you to have this beginning, the part that may puzzle you the most.

My blessings on you, and I pray that you may find it in your heart to respond. I have tried to recount all things honestly, but one thing I left out. I said the coming of the Holy Spirit was indescribable. But so is my yearning love for you, unextinguished after all these years. I pray you, listen to your heart. Surely it speaks to you of me. God would not be so cruel as to silence it forever.

∞ LIX ∞

To the widow of Joel of Nain, sometime known as Mary of Magdala, now as Mary of Ephesus—

My mistress, the lady Elisheba of Tiberias, widow of Joram of Magdala, has requested that I answer your correspondence. She wishes to tell you that she has read the strange witness-account of your life—or what you claim is the beginning of such a document—and found it only troubling. That after more than sixty years you lay such a self-serving defense at her feet, asking that she recognize you as her mother, to have some sort of reconciliation, is overly bold and presumptive.

She says that, during all the years when she was growing up as an orphan, with a mother who was known to have been possessed, deserting her family and joining a band of wandering prophets and rebels, you never attempted to see her or contact her. She grew up with great shame over her mother, a scandal to the town. In her childish way she wrote you many letters, but they were never answered, and finally she gave up. Had it not been for the kindness of her uncle Eli and his family, she would never have known a home. Uncle Eli taught her everything and gave her a reason for pride in her family.

Over the years, she had thought of you as dead, as dead as that rabbi you had followed. So many of his band were hunted down and executed. The name of the hated rabbi has become even more odious among the faithful of Israel since his death, and the subsequent vile heresy and perversion of the Law of Moses that his followers practice only grows more abominable to the observant.

She says that, in the hour of need of the Jewish people, after the Temple fell and everyone was scattered, you and the followers of the discredited rabbi still persisted in your heresy. Even the sufferings of fellow Jews today have not brought you back, and that makes you worse than the Edomites, those former blood-brothers of the Jews who turned their backs when we were in need.

So now, after all these years, you appear in her life, and ask her to read a defense of the heresy! As if she would be converted!

My mistress says to tell you, with greatest sorrow, that she still does not have a mother.

Salutations and peace, Tirzah of the household of the Honorable Elisheba

∽ LX ∽

To my dearest and only daughter, Elisheba, purchased at a price and loved always.

From Mary, apostle in the church of Ephesus—

When I received the letter from your assistant, I cannot tell you of my great transports of joy. At long last to have heard your voice, if only at second hand, and so filled with anger. So many things you said that I wish to answer, to explain. So many things you said that have revealed much to me. I never received those childish letters you sent; I suspect your "kind" uncle Eli set them aside. And now I suspect that you never received mine, either, although I entrusted some to Silvanus and sent others directly to Eli. Again, kind Uncle Eli probably deemed it best that we never reach one another.

I did come to Magdala after the death of my master, but Eli did not permit me to see you or speak to you. He told me they had told you I was dead and, as far as they were concerned, I was. I remember telling him that not only was I not dead, I was more alive than I had ever dreamed possible. But he was not interested in knowing what had happened to me.

Now think about that. These people purported to be kind, charitable, religious people, but they were uninterested in what had become of their sister, who they knew had suffered from a grave illness. Ask yourself what kind of charity that is. I think it merely shows that the best of human "goodness" is still riddled with selfishness and blindness, and that is why we can never please God with our attempts at holiness. Isaiah says it best: all "our righteousnesses are as filthy rags."

Whenever I met anyone from Magdala all down the years, I would ask about you. I tried so hard to know what had happened to you. I had heard of your marriage to Joram, a leader of the Jewish community in Tiberias. I did not know of his death, and I extend my deepest sympathy to you, for I know what it is to be widowed. I have never heard whether you have children; my meager bits of information have been so lacking. But I have been grateful for whatever I was given.

Whatever has gone before, it is here no longer. The events, the people, the barriers that kept us estranged, have vanished. You are no longer a child, dependent on an adult to withhold or pass on a letter. I am no longer part of a wandering band, but have been settled here in Ephesus for many years. I am even respectable now! Yes, among my own group I am now an honorable elder, esteemed and revered. My group of heretics has now been accorded recognition as a genuine religion. There are thousands of us, spread out all over the world now, from Spain to Babylon. We started as a tiny group of frightened people, grieving the death of our master in Jerusalem, and now you can go to almost any city in the empire and find fellow believers. Even as early as seven or eight years after Jesus, there were believers in Damascus and elsewhere. So the stigma of belonging to an unknown heresy has disappeared.

So—let us cross over the last of the remaining barriers, which are only in our own minds, with outstretched arms. There is no one to stop us, and we can follow our hearts.

I respect the feelings that made you respond in such a detached fashion, and even use a surrogate to write, but I pray that they may soften. In any case, just receiving the letter was an answer to earlier prayers.

I am continuing, at the urging of the congregation here in Ephesus, to write about the history of Jesus and the early believers, and I will send you copies of those portions as I write them. I want you to have them. Even if you destroy them unread, they belong to you.

Your loving mother,
Mary of Magdala and Ephesus

The Testament of Mary of Magdala, Called Magdalene, in its continuation

As I recounted, my brothers and sisters in the Lord, our early days were filled with one astounding happening after another. Indeed, we love to return to it in memory, for, looking back, it was like the days immediately after a wedding, when the bride and groom are so caught up in one another and have eyes for nothing else as they spend their allotted time in the bride chamber, away from the rest of the world. We were in that bride chamber, too, having been selected by Jesus as his companions for eternity—we knew that for a certainty now—and more than companions, as sharers in his very Spirit.

For we were changed. I could see the changes in others, in Peter's sudden authority, in John's deep understanding, in the elder Mary's complete acceptance and happiness, and in the stern James, who now held his brother in fiery reverence rather than in disdain.

But I did not, then, see changes in myself.

It did not take long before our activities came to the attention of the same people who had attacked Jesus—and, as they thought, silenced him. Peter and John had been, as usual, at the Temple worshiping. On their way up the steps, they had passed a crippled beggar, who held out his hand for money. To his surprise—and that of those around him—Peter cried out, "Gold and silver have I none. But what I do have I give you." He bent down and held out his hand. "In the name of Jesus the Christ from Nazareth, walk!" Then he took the man's right hand and pulled him up. Not only did the man stand on his own, but his ankles and legs stopped trembling, and he bounded up the steps, praising God.

Naturally, this attracted attention, for the beggar was well known to everyone who passed up through the Beautiful Gate of the Temple. He held on to Peter and John, and as soon as a curious crowd had gathered, Peter began preaching about Jesus.

The captain of the Temple guard, flanked by Sadducee priests, hurried out and arrested Peter and John, but not before many people had heard them and been converted in their hearts. They put Peter, John, and the healed man in prison until they could schedule a hearing the next day. I watched them being taken away. Just so had Jesus been taken away, and by the same authorities.

But, unlike Jesus, Peter and John returned to us, freed. And they told us of the interrogation, which Jesus had never had an opportunity to do.

"It was all the same people," said John. "We were honored to be interrogated and threatened by Caiaphas and by Annas."

It was then that I got the first, tickling hint that perhaps I, too, had been changed by the coming of that Spirit. Until now, I would have pictured myself leaping at Caiaphas and tearing at his eyes. I would even have wanted a *sica* to pull from my belt and slash at Annas. Now I just felt sadness for their blindness, their own violence.

The loss of my own violence felt odd, as if I were missing a limb.

But they are evil! I thought. They deserve to be punished! Yet, somehow, the old picture of revenge had lost its savor and zest.

"They questioned us and threatened us, and finally agreed to let us go if only we would agree to speak no longer to anyone in this name," said Peter.

"They could not bring themselves to say the name 'Jesus,'" said John. "It was as if the name itself had power."

"It does," said Peter. "I healed the beggar by saying, 'In the name of Jesus the Christ from Nazareth, walk.'

"Then all of us held hands and prayed," he said. "The words came to me and I said, 'Now, Lord, take note of their threats and enable your servants to speak your word with all boldness, as you stretch forth your hand to heal, and signs and wonders are done in the name of your holy servant Jesus.'"

Of course, that was not the end of it. We were arrested again—yes, the women as well as the men. We were taken off to the public jail. It was my first glimpse inside a jail, and I was immediately filled with compassion for prisoners, whom I had never truly thought about before. The jail was a dark, cavelike place, even though it was not actually beneath the ground. We huddled together and tried to keep our spirits up, but I was frightened.

Although I cannot explain this, somehow the door was opened in the middle of the night and we stumbled blindly out. Peter claimed it was an angel who charged him with the mission: "Go, stand in the Temple courts, and tell the people the full message of the new life"; I cannot attest to this. Perhaps it was only a careless, or sympathetic, jailer, who had not locked the door, and when we tried it, it swung open. Even if it was the jailer, God must have influenced him; God does work through people. Indeed, I believe that is his preferred way.

The next morning, we went right back up to the Temple and began teaching and preaching—yes, I as well. I felt then that I could teach, if not preach. And swiftly the guards came out and arrested us all again.

Arrested again! Mary of Magdala, respectable woman. (Thanks be to Jesus for restoring me to that state.) This time I would be privileged to stand trial myself and not hear of it secondhand from Peter and John.

We stood before the mighty Sanhedrin, that august body of priests, scribes, and elders that had condemned Jesus. We were bound and trussed and roughly turned to face our accusers. There were supposed to be seventy of them, but I did not see seventy staring back at us. I looked for the faces of Nicodemus and Joseph of Arimathea, Jesus's secret followers. I thought I saw them in the farthest row back. But I could not be sure.

Caiaphas stepped forward, his face strained. Caiaphas. My utmost enemy. Once, as I said, I would have taken this opportunity to rush forward with a cry and a knife. Now I found, unexpectedly, nothing but regret and resignation for this misguided man. I did not love him, no, but I grieved for him.

"We gave you strict orders—did we not?" The deep, booming voice of Caiaphas rang out. "We ordered you to stop teaching in that name. Yet you have filled Jerusalem with your teaching and want to bring that man's blood upon us."

But suddenly I heard myself answering, "We must obey God rather than men!"

Then Peter added, "We are witnesses of these things, as is the Holy Spirit whom God gives to those who obey him."

The Sanhedrin, after a brief murmur, burst out in accusations.

"More blasphemy! Put them to death!" one man cried. Others seconded it, crying out for our blood.

"This foul false prophet that led them has made them as mad as he was!"

"Silence them!"

"Just a moment." One member stepped forward and confronted Caiaphas. I was to learn later that his name was Gamaliel, and he was a revered Pharisee and teacher of the Law. "Fellow Israelites, be careful what you decree. As you know, other impostors have appeared: Theudas, with his four hundred men, and Judas the Galilean. All of them claimed to have some special revelation, or to be the leader Israel sought. But they all perished, and their movements along with them."

Caiaphas stared at him. "We know this. What of it? All impostors and heretics and their followers must be destroyed."

"Just this: leave these people alone. Let them go. If their movement is from God, he will defend it and there is nothing you can do to uproot it. If it is not from God, it will perish. It is very simple. You need do nothing." He paused. "Should it be from God, surely you would not want to be found fighting against him?"

Caiaphas stood rigid, anger making his face a mask. Finally, he said, "Very well. But surely even you will admit that they deserve punishment for their public disturbances. They should be flogged."

Like Jesus! was my first thought. Then my second: Oh, God, it is so brutal and painful.

The Temple guards dragged us off and took us to a private courtyard, where they had us bound and flogged with the same sort of whip that had been used on Jesus.

It was painful beyond my imagining, although I had seen Jesus flogged. Childbirth is very painful, but childbirth brings forth a gift of God, and afterward, although a woman remembers the pain, it is unimportant. I suppose this also followed that pattern. We were brutally beaten, hit with sticks and staffs as well as whipped, the whips feeling like red-hot wires lashing my skin, but because enduring it proclaimed our loyalty to Jesus, we were able to bear it.

At last they loosened our bindings and released us. As we were stumbling about, they commanded us, "Now stop speaking in the name of Jesus!"

Peter, reeling against one of the posts, mumbled a prayer for strength.

As we found our way out, Andrew suddenly turned and cried out, "Let us rejoice that we are found worthy to suffer dishonor for the name—of JESUS!" back at his tormentors.

Then, before they could act, we ran as best we could through the gates. We could not move very fast; we limped in pain. But no one followed us.

We had been found worthy to suffer like Jesus, punished by the very same men. Later, we were to hear someone named Paul witness that Jesus had appeared to him, charging him with a mission. He claimed to be an apostle of Jesus equal with us.

At first, the claim seemed outlandish. But this Paul, a Jew from Tarsus, who had never even seen Jesus in his lifetime, said that Jesus had appeared to him—more than appeared, had overwhelmed him and given him a commission.

Paul may never have seen Jesus, but he had seen us—and persecuted us. As a zealous agent of Caiaphas and his own religious urgings, he had hunted down our brothers and sisters mercilessly, even pursuing people beyond the borders of Israel in his missions of punishment.

He was hated and feared everywhere. So, when he suddenly disappeared on a Christian-hunting mission to Damascus, we all rejoiced.

Then . . . he appeared at our headquarters in Jerusalem, claiming Jesus had changed his life. He was here, not because he needed our approval in any way—he was adamant about that—but just to learn more about what Jesus had said and done in his earthly life. He wished to talk only to Peter and to Jesus's brother.

What were we to make of him? If we truly believed that Jesus yet lived, why could he not appear to others, unknown to us? we reasoned. But how could we welcome them? How could we even understand them? Their experiences of Jesus would be so different from ours. Yet it was not up to us to judge them, much less to discredit them.

In those early days, as I said, we were first like a bride and groom, then like a new small family, and then like a big clan. We all knew one another, we trusted one another, we eagerly compared our experiences and the special things the Holy Spirit had revealed to each of us, discussing them late into the night in rooms all over Jerusalem. We pooled our money and resources, and offered up all decisions, by prayer and petition, to divine guidance.

And we waited for Jesus to return. We expected him at any moment. Had the messengers on the Mount of Olives not said he would return in the same way as we had seen him leave us? He had returned from the grave to stand unexpectedly among us, and we fully believed he would do so once again. We were sure our separation was temporary—very temporary.

There were days when I arose and felt that this was the day. I knew it. I had the unmistakable certainty that this was to be no ordinary day. Jesus would appear—perhaps when we gathered for our meal, perhaps only to one of us, but he would appear.

And I would go about my tasks that day alert and constantly looking to one side. And the day would end with my seeing nothing.

Paul—whom I still have reservations about, but who said some
very deep things—wrote that once he had begged God to relieve him of
some tormenting "thorn" in his flesh. God's only answer was, "My
grace is sufficient, for power is made perfect in weakness." In a sense, I
had gotten the same answer: My grace is sufficient. And so I stopped
looking for his momentary return, long before anyone else did.

Our group in Jerusalem continued to grow, and soon we had factions
among us—Greek-speaking Jews and Aramaic-speaking ones. It was
inevitable, but the fracture lines began to appear in our fellowship,
which in any case had grown too large to gather in one place. Once that
happened, we began to develop rival factions and quarrels. Soon there
were "Peter's people," "Mary's people," "the Greek Jews of the Synagogue
of Freedmen," and many others.

If I were asked what one persistent memory of that time is, I would
honestly have to answer: the quarrels. The accusations of favoritism—
were the Greek widows slighted at the expense of the Hebrew ones?—
and other such things tore us in pieces, long before Nero's wild beasts.
And so the wonderful, heady, ecstatic early days came to an end.

Another thing that divided us, very early, was whether it was permis-
sible to allow a Gentile to join our company. The Greek-speaking Jews
were, after all, still Jews. And yet the hunger of outsiders to hear about
Jesus was much greater than that of his fellow Israelites. That was the
shame and the scandal. We had constant inquiries from those outside
our tradition, and hostility from those within it. What must we do?

It was Peter who was granted the vision, the guidance, this time. He
was staying in Joppa at the time, and had gone up to the rooftop at
midday to pray. And as he was doing so, a strange dream—or vision—
filled him. He saw a great sheet descending from the sky, and it lowered
itself and opened before his eyes, and it was crawling with all the unclean beasts that the Law of Moses forbids us to eat. There were snakes
and tortoises and those shelled creatures of the sea, and rabbits, and,
most foul of all, swine. Even to look upon them was repugnant, and
when a voice commanded Peter, "Arise, and eat!" he recoiled.

Even against the voice of what seemed to be God—but might be
Satan—he protested. "I have never eaten such things, have never
transgressed the Law that declares these animals utterly unclean."

The voice overruled him, and said, "What God has declared clean, you must not declare unclean."

Still he argued, and repeated his protest two more times, to be met with the same answer twice more.

Then the vision, the cloth and the animals, faded away. Some Gentiles from Caesarea—who, during prayer, had received a puzzling command from God to seek Peter out—knocked at his door. Their Roman master, Cornelius, had been commanded in a vision to send for Peter.

How could he refuse? He went to the household of Cornelius, told them of Jesus, and ended up baptizing them. They were now in our fellowship—Gentiles. Romans. We were supposed to eat with them, welcome them as brothers.

And there were others, even more forbidden. There was an Ethiopian eunuch who was baptized by one of our number. A eunuch, when the Law of Moses clearly stated: "No one who has been emasculated by crushing or cutting may enter the assembly of the Lord."

"Forget the former things, do not dwell in the past. Behold, I will do a new thing; now it shall spring forth; shall you not know it?" Had not the scriptures themselves predicted this? But how were we to implement it?

And, yes, there were so many different opinions and interpretations of what we must do. One party of us—led by Jesus's brother James—thought that only by strict adherence to the Law of Moses could we find our direction in this new territory we traversed. He, and others of his persuasion, held that we must continue to worship at the Temple and fulfill all the requirements of the Law, and, in effect, be holier than the Pharisees. They were insulted at the charges that Jesus had somehow flouted the Law and were determined to prove that he, and his followers, were utterly obedient sons of the ancient traditions.

Others said, James, it is over, and we must go forward.

James ignored them, and maintained his iron grasp over the church in Jerusalem. It was strange how even Peter deferred to him, but I think it can be explained by the feeling at that time that somehow Jesus could be understood by assuming he had royal, or special, blood, and that therefore his family shared it and should be accorded honor and privileges. We could not help it. How many times had we heard of the royal line of David, the special promises attached to that blood? Even the sacred covenants of our people were couched in the language of bloodlines, starting with Abraham, who must have a son of his own body.

So now there was to be a Holy Family, as sacred as David's, that would set itself up as leaders among us. Jesus had brothers, and surely they must take precedence over everyone else. But it was an old way of thinking, and Jesus and the Spirit he had sent among us overturned it, although not immediately. Even as late as today, Symeon, a cousin of Jesus, is considered a leader in the church. But he is under suspicion by the Romans, not as a Christian, but because of his descent from David, where the Romans are still expecting popular leaders to emerge.

James, with all his Mosaic and rabbinic rules and restrictions, was so oppressive many of us drifted away and met on our own. I did not care to attend his meetings or give heed to his lecturings. I was gratified that he had belatedly recognized his brother, but his practices were stifling.

Far worse than James and his strict legalism within our fellowship were the persecutions from the Jewish religious authorities outside our group; they put Stephen, one of our Greek-speaking converts on trial and stoned him, then unleashed their fury on any "apostate" Jew they could find. Their persecutions scattered us. Some of us went to Samaria, where we found people ready to listen, and made many converts. Others went farther afield, and so, by the time ten years had passed since that crucifixion on the hill of the Skull, followers of Jesus could be found as far away as Ethiopia, Rome, Cyprus, and Damascus.

The dreadful request of Big James—as well as John—to sit at Jesus' right hand and drink of his cup was answered by our other enemy, the secular authority of King Agrippa, who had followed Antipas on the throne.

At that time, several of us were still in Jerusalem, attempting to steer the church away from the misguided vision of James; in particular, Big James was outspoken in opposing him and in preaching directly to the crowds. This did not sway the other James, but it did bring Big James to the attention of Agrippa, who made it his business to boost his sagging popularity by cracking down on the Christians. Big James was an obvious target, and easy to arrest. I watched as Agrippa's soldiers apprehended him while he was speaking in the Upper Market, coming up behind him and grasping him in a hammerlock.

We were used to being arrested, but not by the secular authorities. This sent fear through us, and we prayed for Big James's release, never imagining God would refuse us.

But on a windy summer day, the word went out from the palace: James bar-Zebedee was sentenced to death by beheading, to be carried out in the courtyard of the palace. Beheading . . . in token of his family's high social standing, no doubt. Their long-standing connections with the high priest's household had served only to determine what manner of execution he would undergo.

John was so stunned and unmanned at the news that he sat in his house in Jerusalem and rocked, his head in his hands, when we came to him and told him.

"James—no, no," he kept repeating, rhythmically. "No, no, no."

At that time, Jesus's mother was living with him, as he had promised Jesus, and she bent over him, trying to comfort him, while we gathered around him.

"John, my dear son—my true son now, as Jesus asked—please do not tear yourself apart with grief. It was what your brother wanted, what he requested, long ago. Do you not remember Jesus's answer?"

John raised his head to her. "I can never forget it. 'You will indeed drink from my cup.' But we did not know what we were asking! As Jesus told us."

"But now you do," said the elder Mary. "Would you now take it back?"

"No," he said. "Not for myself. I am ready. But for my brother . . ." He turned away. "It is too high a price. To die that way . . ."

"It was a more merciful death than his master's," Jesus's mother reminded him.

"Yes, of course, I know, but . . ." John bent his head and wept.

He could not bring himself to watch the execution, although it could be seen through the palace gates. Nor could any of us; we had seen one execution, and that was all we could bear. We waited together in John's spacious house, so cool and light, and prayed while Big James went to his death—bravely, we were told, proclaiming his faith.

It was too shocking, the first of our loyal band to die. Until then, we had felt protected by God himself. Had not the jail been opened for Peter and the rest of us? Had we not walked freely about the streets of Jerusalem, defying the chief priests and our enemies? We believed that our urgent mission made us safe.

With hushed breath and weeping, we laid James to rest, in a rock tomb not far from Nicodemus's garden, in the presence of all the church members of Jerusalem. John could barely stand up, and had to be supported by the others.

"James, James," he was calling, "oh, James!"

"Jesus is with him now," said Peter. "Jesus was waiting."

"But Jesus is with us as well," whispered John. "We do not need to die to see him." He continued weeping.

Agrippa, striving for popularity, saw that his action pleased certain segments of the people. So he launched a manhunt for the rest of us, and captured Peter at Passover time, flinging him into jail, while we hid in various houses friendly to us, shielding us from the authorities.

Although we feared for our lives, there was never any question of our ceasing our mission. We could not be silenced; Peter had once said to Caiaphas, "It is impossible for us not to speak about what we have seen and heard." And so we only plotted about how we would survive, not how we would abandon our cause.

To our joy and surprise, Peter escaped! He came to us where we were meeting at a house, and the woman watching at the door was so startled that she thought it was a ghost. She came staggering into the main room to tell us—but when we rushed to the door, we found a very alive Peter standing there.

We led him in. He was foggy and shaken himself. He had thought it all a dream.

"I—I found myself wandering about in an alley," he said. He looked dreadful: his hair disordered and his clothes tattered. "I thought it was all a dream. I don't know how I got out. I think—I thought—an angel led me. But the night air, and the smells in the alley, told me it was no dream."

Someone had pressed a cup into his hands and insisted he drink. Bread and cheese were handed to him, and he ate ravenously.

"It's too dangerous here," Peter said. "I can stay no longer."

"I don't think this house is watched," said its owner, the mother of another follower, Mark.

"I mean Jerusalem," said Peter. "I must leave. I urge all of us known to the authorities to do so as well."

"But—where will you go?" asked John.

"Where they will never look for me. Rome."

"Rome!" Jesus's mother cried.

"Yes. I will go directly to Rome. There are Jewish brothers there who need to hear my story."

"But Caligula hated our people—"

"They say Claudius is more amenable to us. The new emperor does not claim to be a god, unlike his predecessor. But we must establish the church in Rome; it is, after all, the headquarters of the world."

"Rome! But our enemy—"

"It's hard to think of a Messiah who came not to destroy the Romans but to die for them, isn't it?" said Peter quietly. "But if we admit that Gentiles are welcome, then that includes Romans, even the ones in Rome itself."

"Romans. We have some in our fellowship here, but actually to go there—oh, Peter, you mustn't." John reached out to him, gently.

"I'm afraid Jesus told me to." Peter looked directly at John. "And so I must. And I must say farewell, knowing I may never see any of you again."

Peter gone, too! One by one we would all disperse, fall away, die. Suddenly I felt very alone.

∞ LX11 ∞

The Testament of Mary Magdalene, in its continuation

What were we to do now? How did we know where to go? Should we just huddle together and pray? Should we look for signs? How had Jesus decided what to do? We had never known. He had only announced what he planned to do, not how he had been led to that decision. We knew he spent much time in prayer.

Somehow it came to me that we might all be asked to do that which was most in opposition to our nature. Did Peter feel uneasy with non-Jews? Then to Rome he must go. Did Matthew long to return to Galilee? Then he must remain here. Did John feel called to go abroad, like Paul? His commitment to Jesus's mother meant that he was tethered. Mary, his mother, was no longer young, and she had other children here in Jerusalem, especially James, such an important figure in the church. As long as Mary lived, John must stay here.

And I? What must I do? What was Jesus telling me to do? Could I ask him directly? (Paul talked about the Spirit of Jesus telling him this and that, indicating where he was to go. Could this also happen to me?)

I wanted, above all, to return to Magdala. To see my family again. To search out and hold my daughter again. She would be seventeen now. A woman. The age I had been when I was betrothed to Joel. My child— no longer a child. My need to see her, at last and in person, gathered into an ache that rose like a wave.

I secluded myself—not easily done, for I was now living in the large household that John had established on Mount Zion—and begged Jesus to tell me what to do. But, in truth, I already knew what I wanted to do. I only wanted him to give permission.

I knew he would say no. I knew he would tell me to stay in Jerusalem, to attend to the needs of the persecuted believers there.

As I knelt, my eyes squeezed shut and my mind racing, my forty-two-year-old knees all too keenly aware of the hard stone floor where I knelt, I began by presenting my case, item by item. First, I needed to ascertain if there were any followers of the Way in Magdala. Second, I needed to see the state of the brotherhood in wider Galilee, so I could prepare a report. Third, it was dangerous in Jerusalem, so it was best I go elsewhere for now.

I expected silence. I expected a nagging feeling of knowing that all my good reasons were just selfish disguises. I expected to be asked to surrender them.

Before I could finish laying them out, an unmistakable answer came. Go. Go to Magdala. It requires more courage than any of the other choices.

"Before they call, I will answer: while they are yet speaking, I will hearken to them."

The affirmation of this promise of Isaiah almost took my breath away.

Sometimes Jesus lets us follow our heart's desires, even though he knows it will not lead us where we wish. As the Psalmist said, "And he gave them their request; but sent leanness into their soul."

And—oh!—what leanness was waiting for me there. I approached the city wall and passed through easily in midday, although I was trembling. The sight of the most harmless buildings sent me into a shaking, and I had to reach out my hand to steady myself. The market square—the long street running alongside the lake, where my old house was—my father's warehouse—all the cobblestones, the quays, the gutters, the lakeside path—all this had formed me, was still part of me. And it was all still here. And somewhere, somewhere, was Elisheba. These streets held her, these waters dashed against a breakwater where she walked.

I did not know then that she was no longer there. She had married and gone to Tiberias, so when I walked the streets looking for her, she was not to be found. But—oh!—how I stared at every face, trying to see if it might be hers. How would she look as a young woman? Like me or like Joel, or like neither? Was she tall or short, was her face round or long, her mouth thin or full? What was she, this daughter of mine, what had God brought her to be?

I reached the lake. The light was fading. Had the glory fled? This was where it had all begun. But did people here now follow him? Joel . . . and Jesus . . . and Elisheba . . . and all I have is this floating, empty present, detached from my beginnings, not led yet to my ending, and yearning all the time for one human face above all, my daughter's. And I cannot find her.

I bent my head and listened to the waves.

"Remember, I am with you always, until the end of the age." Jesus had said that, just before he departed forever.

Departed forever. Those melancholy words are at such odds with what he actually said: that he is here, this very moment. At this quay. Why, then, does it feel so empty? I am the only one here. He is not here, despite what he said. And neither is Elisheba. I am just a misled and foolish woman, sitting by myself on a deserted quay.

Elisheba! Jesus! Come to me!

Weak and dispirited, I was prepared to spend the night there, just huddled in self-pity and sadness, but someone—as it turned out, a follower of Jesus—saw me there. He would not be put off—though I actually preferred to stay there by myself—and took me off to a harbormaster's house.

He was the son of the harbormaster I had known in my youth, and he was a believer. When I confessed who I was, I had my first experience of being revered.

"You were with Jesus? Jesus himself?" His face registered such excitement as I had never seen—not even when people had first met Jesus, the real Jesus. He rushed to his door and whispered something to his servant, moving his arms wildly.

He had summoned the church people who met at his house, and soon they all swarmed in to meet me. They asked me question after question, touched my garments, made requests.

"You were the first to see him, after he rose," one young man said. "He must have favored you above all others." He knelt reverently.

Here was irony indeed—the people of Magdala bowing before a woman deemed unworthy by others in Magdala to see her own daughter.

"You are mistaken," I said. "Jesus does not favor anyone. All are equal with him."

"But you were with him! You were chosen to be one of his inner circle. We heard him speak, but only from a distance. Tell us, tell us, what it was like. Tell us everything he said!"

I remember what Jesus told us, that last night at our dinner, how the Holy Spirit would come and later remind us of everything he had said to us. Now it seems to me that I should record even the most minor things Jesus said as I recall them, for they may be significant to someone else, someone I will never know.

I spent all that night trying to answer their questions; none of us slept, until our tongues grew thick and our heads were drooping. I had as many questions for them as they had for me: How had the church in Magdala started? Was it founded by someone who had been overwhelmed by the presence of Jesus when he passed through? Had any Gentiles tried to join? How many members did they have? Had they adhered to ritual and worshiped at the synagogue?

That last question caused a snort of laughter.

"With Eli and his party in charge?" one man said, shaking his head. "You can imagine the reception we got."

"Eli bar-Nathan?" I asked. "His wife is Dinah?"

"The very same," the man said. "Your brother. He's so pious and stiff and righteous, he might as well just turn himself into a pillar of salt, like Lot's wife. All he does is look back."

"We tried to expound on the scriptures and explain about Jesus," another man said, "but Eli made sure we were silenced and evicted from the synagogue. We were never allowed in again."

"He hates us," the first man said. "If the Roman authorities came looking, he would be the first to turn us in."

"I am the one he hates," I said, realizing that our private family rift had caused great hardship to others. "He was so angry at me for following Jesus that he evicted me from the family as surely as he evicted you from the synagogue. He never let me explain, never gave me a chance to speak."

"That's Eli," one of the women said, shrugging.

"Tell me—is he still living in the same house?"

"No. He's moved to finer quarters. He now lives near the western edge of the market square. I think he made a big profit when your old home was sold."

"And the girl they took in—my daughter—does anyone know her? Have you seen her?" My heart stopped, waiting for the answer.

"They had a big brood of their own," one woman said. "Several boys, I think."

"And a daughter," I added, hoping to prod their memory.

"Yes, that's right. Her name was Hannah. She grew up to be quite beautiful—and willful." The woman laughed. "She ran off with a merchant from Tyre. They say she liked his brocades!" Shrill laughter all around.

"Was he a—a—pagan?" I could not picture this. What a blow for Eli and Dinah.

"He wasn't Jewish," said the man. "I suppose they don't worship Baal anymore, but he worshiped whatever they worship up there."

"The other girl," I persisted. "Do you remember anything about her?"

The woman shrugged. "It has been many years since we have seen her. Remember, we were expelled from the synagogue some time ago."

"I need to find out," I said. "Please direct me to Eli's house tomorrow."

Then they plied me with more questions about Jesus and the church in Jerusalem, until I could no longer speak.

Now I stood in front of the house, a large stone one, quite imposing. He must have done well with the sale of Joel's house, I thought. Yes, indeed, he must have.

I could hardly breathe. Behind that door lay the earthly thing most dear to me, but perhaps barred to me forever.

When the door was opened by a servant, I found myself just staring dumbly.

So Eli and Dinah had servants now. "I wish to see the master or the mistress of the house," I said firmly. I felt oddly strong at the same time

as I felt weak. The strength came from Jesus, who seemed to be standing there beside me. The weakness was all my own.

"Very well." Rather than bid me enter, she shut the door in my face
and left me standing there.

Eventually it opened again, and Eli was on the other side, glaring
at me.

"You!" was his first word.

"Yes. It is I, your sister, Mary." He continued to glare at me, and the
door remained only half open. "May I come in?"

Grudgingly he opened the door, and I stepped in. My first impression was of a spacious atrium, and beyond that, gracious rooms.

He was staring at me, looking me up and down. I was forty-two
and had not seen him in many years. He was fifty-three, still handsome, his face little changed save for some weathering. His sons were
grown men, his daughter married and gone away. Surely it was right
now for us to approach one another again.

"The years have been kind to you," he said, sounding as if he was
forcing the words out.

Had they? I did not know. I could not say when I had last looked at
my image in a glass or a basin of water. I had been so concerned with
that invisible part of myself, I had not hearkened to the other.

"How are you, Eli?" And I truly wanted to know. I felt a strange
concern and—yes—care for him. This was my brother, and time was
running, faster than we would have liked. We no longer had the luxury
of hate and misunderstandings.

"Well enough," he said. Still he did not move to usher me into his
house proper. He left me standing in the atrium like a tradesman.

"And Dinah?"

"Well enough," he repeated.

He stood stock-still staring at me. This was the way it must be,
then. "And my daughter, Elisheba?"

"No longer here," he said.

"Where is she?"

"She has married. A fine man from Tiberias, called Joram."

Married. My daughter was married. And I had not been consulted, or even informed.

"She is only seventeen!" I cried.

"Time enough," said Eli. "It was a good marriage."

"And she lives there?"

"Yes. But I shall never tell you where!" He might as well have thumped a staff on the ground.

"Why not?" Before he could respond, I said, "If you do not tell me, I shall employ someone to find out."

"Then employ him," said Eli, crossing his arms over his chest.

"I shall," I said. "But it would be much simpler if you would tell me."

"That I shall not."

"I see." I took a deep breath. "What about the letters I sent? I never had a reply."

"She did not wish to speak to you, either in writing or in person." He held himself rigidly, his eyes wide and unblinking.

"Is that true? Or did you withhold the letters and never give her a choice?"

"Are you accusing me of lying?" His eyes bulged at the insult.

"Yes, Eli, that is exactly what I am doing," I said. "Did you, in fact, give her my letters?"

"No," he admitted. "I knew they were filthy tracts, filled with heresy, and should be destroyed." He made a dismissive gesture.

"Thank you for admitting that," I said. "So my daughter never knew I tried to write to her?"

"No, but what difference does that make? She would not have wished to hear or read your words. She is devout, and knows the truth. The truth that you wish to distort." He shook his head.

I stood looking at him, feeling both oddly relieved and infinitely sad. She had not rejected me, but she had never even seen the letters I had laboriously composed to her over the years. And to answer Eli's question: the difference it made was the eternal difference between truth and lies.

"I see." I looked around. "I see that I am not invited to enter your home, even now."

"You are an apostate, a disgrace," said Eli. "Never would I allow you to pass into my home." He guided me firmly back toward the door.

"Where is Silvanus?" I asked. I needed to see him, needed him badly.

"I assume you mean Samuel. Do you think you will have better luck with him?" said Eli. "Samuel has passed away. He has been gathered to our ancestors. You may visit his tomb outside the city wall."

My hand flew to my mouth. "No! Oh, when, and how?"

Eli scowled. "Of a wasting disease," he said curtly. "At least ten years ago. His Greek ways did not help him in the end, nor did his Greek physician!"

"Oh, Eli," I said, "did you ever stop to think that your hatred is the true wasting disease?"

He snorted. "Let all heretics perish." He pronounced my sentence, and closed the door on me.

And so now you know, Elisheba. That is what happened when I returned to Magdala, looking for you.

I set out on foot to Tiberias. After spending a day inquiring of many people where a man named Joram, a native of the city, might lodge, and being directed to a one-story stone house in the section of rising ground, I stood in front of it and knocked, but there was no answer.

No answer. Were you out shopping? Away on a journey? I would never know. All I knew was that I stood and knocked, and the door never opened, although within that house lay you, my dearest daughter.

Was that your house? I knew no other name but Joram to inquire of, and there must have been many a Joram in Tiberias, but from Eli's words, this Joram was a well-known citizen.

Over the years I returned several times, always to find the door shut. Over the years I asked about you, but only silence was returned to me.

෴ LX111 ෴

To the woman known as Mary of Magdala and lately of Ephesus—
My mistress, the lady Elisheba, has read the apologias that you insist on sending her, and continues to find them strange and embarrassing. She is especially disturbed by your recounting of your meeting with Eli and your subsequent hunting for her in Tiberias. Over the years she has noticed people inspecting the house, creeping about, and peeking into the courtyard. She has had a feeling of being spied upon, and now she knows why. You have had her watched, you have sent out people to make reports of her to you.

Again, we ask that you cease this. If you fear God and want to honor his commandments, you will stop sending these disturbing letters to a lady who only wants to live a righteous life in peace.
Tirzah, a servant of Elisheba

To my mother—

I cannot help adding my own words, although I had sworn not to. Tirzah speaks for me, but not with the words I would choose.

For all my life you have been a mystery to me. Now, finally, I know you. I appreciate your courage in making that possible.

But to meet—no, I think it is better that it remain as it is.

Your daughter, Elisheba

✣ LXIV ✣

The Testament of Mary Magdalene, in its continuation

I returned to Magdala and spent many days with the believers there, trying to answer their questions and recount for them everything I thought they should know. But they seemed already to have a firm foundation, and that was reassuring. I told them that even now others besides me were compiling records of the sayings and deeds of Jesus, so that as human memories faded these of Jesus would not be compromised or lost.

"You are famous here in Galilee, you know," one of the elders said. "You had something that no one will ever have again, the opportunity to walk beside the living Jesus."

And to think, at one time everyone had had that opportunity!

"Will you stay here with us for a while?" they asked. "Guide us, instruct us?"

I felt an obligation to return to Jerusalem, where the mother church was, but I had promised that I would try to be responsive to the Spirit's direction, and now I felt a strong urge to remain longer with these people.

"Yes, yes, I will," I assured them. And I let them find a small room for me, a flimsy frame draped with blankets up on someone's roof. From that rooftop I could look everywhere across the lake and up into the hills, and sit out by myself at night, when the sweetest breezes were coming down from the heights.

Every night, as I stood there, just before I went inside the makeshift room, I would look toward Tiberias and send prayers and love toward that house where I knew my daughter lived. I even sent a basket of the choicest fruits there as a gift, with a letter, but the boy had to leave it at the door, for once again no one was home—or answering the door.

Why did I not return myself at this time, when I was so close? I have asked myself that so many times since. I think I was unnerved by Eli's cruel words and feared they might be true. And in that way I was a coward. I was forever rehearsing the fine words I would say when I stood face to face with my lost daughter, and they were never fine or persuasive or loving enough. So I said none of them, which was much worse.

While I struggled with these disheartening thoughts about my estranged family, I was at the same time being adored by the small Christian—I shall use that term, since it is coming into widespread use now—group in Magdala. They met in various houses, where they would gather in the evenings. They had begun meeting, as had other believers, on the day the empty tomb had been discovered, rather than on the Sabbath. So it was always a regular workday, and the meetings had to take place at night.

Tired from their work, nonetheless the people seemed full of strength and spirit, eager to see one another and to talk about Jesus. The men brought wine, and the women fish, bread, grapes, olives, figs, and honey. Having a meal together was part of their worship; as they ate together, they re-enacted a meal with Jesus and his followers, and recalled his pronouncement about his body and blood. Just as had happened to us our first night without him, when suddenly he was present, so now it was with these people, this night.

Afterward we sang Psalms and read scripture, as well as portions of letters from Christians who were traveling and wanted to report about churches they had visited. Paul was famous for writing such letters, but there were many others; this particular church had a correspondent named Justus, who was concerned about the protocol of the service. He did not want it to be too much like a synagogue.

"As if it could be," said a woman sitting beside me. "The moment Jesus is mentioned, we will be evicted!" She gave a hearty laugh, and I could not help smiling, imagining Eli doing the honors.

A man got up to prophesy, feeling led by the Holy Spirit. He wished to speak about the presence of Jesus in everyday things. After a concluding prayer, the group then addressed the needs of the community. They also wondered about how customs varied from one church to another. Aside from the few letters they received, they were ignorant of what others did.

"We have no way of knowing," one man said. "Sometimes we have visitors, like you, and that helps, but since we are more or less a secret group, how do we recognize and reach out to fellow believers?"

"It seems that you have informal leaders," I said. "But perhaps you should elect some permanent leaders, elders or servers, so that they could contact other churches in the name of your church. I know in the Jerusalem church, which has to be considered the mother church, we have certain officers, people who serve on councils or select missionaries to go to a new church and instruct it. I remember Peter and John had to go to Samaria to talk to the converts there."

"We don't want officers!" one young man said. "We are supposed to be all equal. The moment you make someone an elder, a hierarchy starts. And how are we supposed to rank people? Are teachers below the charity people? What about the people who prophesy? Now, you tell us—weren't all the followers of Jesus equal?"

Before I could answer, he just continued talking. "There's a lot of talk about how Peter got a special commission from Jesus. Well, is it true? You were there. Is it true?"

"I don't think so," I answered, trying very hard to remember whatever Jesus had said about Peter in front of us. And it would have to be in front of us, if he was supposed to have primacy. I remembered Jesus's predicting the end of Peter's life, about his being led where he did not wish to go. I remembered his telling Peter to "feed my sheep." But that was not specific, nor did it give him any authority.

"Some of Peter's people are saying that," the youth said. "There are a lot of them around here—we're close to Capernaum, where his family lives—and they claim that Jesus made Peter his . . . his . . . representative, or something. That he gave Peter his own powers."

I could not help laughing. "It's true, Peter has been able to heal people. And he is a powerful speaker. But we were all given the power to heal people by Jesus, when he sent us out on a mission."

"The Peter people claim he is able to forgive sins," the youth persisted.

"I have never heard Peter say that," I said. "And I have spent a great deal of time in his presence. I don't think Jesus designated a successor. He knew we were all unworthy—or all equally worthy."

"The Peter people claim that unless Peter or one of his deputies visits a church and lays hands on the people, they can't be true Christians or have the Holy Spirit given to them."

"Why, that simply isn't true," I said. "What is true is that sometimes the original disciples have to go and correct false teachings. There are so many teachers about now, all preaching about Jesus, and some of them are just not well informed. Their understanding is incomplete. There were some disciples calling themselves Christians who had been baptized only according to the rite of John the Baptist, for example, whereas our baptism is of initiation, not repentance."

Even as I said the words, I realized that perhaps some regulation of practices was necessary, after all. But how could this be managed? Already there were groups in Alexandria and Damascus and even Rome. How could we in Jerusalem force everyone to follow the same rules, the same wording?

"What do you do there in the church in Jerusalem?" one woman asked.

"Why, we . . ." What a challenging question. "We," I began again, "we worship at the Temple, we also have meetings where we re-enact Jesus's last meal with us, we attend to the needy, we send out missionaries to daughter churches."

"What about sending out missionaries into hostile territories?"

"There are such missionaries, but they are sent by the Holy Spirit, not by us." I thought of Paul and his ventures in the hinterlands beyond Ephesus. Unknown Greek Jews from Crete and Cyprus had proselytized in Antioch. And who had gone first to Alexandria? Or to Spain?

"But people still consult with you, as if they have to get permission for things," the older man said.

"Yes, I suppose so. But only because the largest concentration of the original disciples is there, as well as Jesus's mother and brothers." I shook my head. It was all very confusing and contradictory. Why had Jesus not carefully prepared us for this? Told us what to do?

"But it's impractical to expect people to consult with Jerusalem," the woman objected.

"It's equally impractical to assume that everyone, by some miracle, will come to the same conclusions," the youth said.

"We've had miracles before," I reminded them. "We just have to trust to the guiding of the Spirit."

"That will lead to chaos," said another woman. "Already we've heard that the group in Bethsaida has taken in pagans. And then tried to get them to go through the entire conversion process. Circumcision and all! Not easy for a grown man; I don't care if Abraham did it at the age of ninety-nine."

"Never mind all that!" a loud-voiced woman overrode all their murmurings. "Just tell us about Jesus. Tell us what it was like to be with him. Tell us, tell us!"

Describing him was almost impossible. ("He was of medium height . . . dark hair, dark eyes, deep-set, firm mouth . . . pleasant voice that could be soft or rise to address hundreds of people . . . strong and able to tramp long distances"—what did that reveal? It could describe a thousand people.) The special things, if one attempted to describe them, made the recounter sound daft. "He always looked directly at you, and you felt he knew everything about you." (The woman in Samaria: "Come, see a man who told me everything I ever did.")

"He never put you on probation, but knew what you were capable of long before you did. The future and the present were one with him."

"He seemed ancient, possessed of knowledge not available to the rest of us, and yet entirely of this time and place."

It was no use. These descriptions did not capture him. But the last one—the problem of his being of this time and place—meant events were now rushing forward, past the time he had lived.

After the religious authorities targeted the Jerusalem church for persecution, killing Big James and arresting Peter, things had become very dangerous for Christians, but also for Jewish moderates. A growing movement of Jewish extremists was now gearing up for a fight with Rome, a fight to the death. They looked back at the divine intervention with the Maccabees and Pharaoh, and were ready to throw themselves on the mercy of God once again. The moderates said that this was stupid, that Rome was not Antiochus or Pharaoh, and that it was foolhardy—no, certain destruction—to defy Rome. The Jewish world had become divided, with the extremists provoking the Romans at every turn, hoping to spur a response and ignite the war, a war that only they wanted, but which would engulf everyone.

Now this put the Christians to a test: were Christians still Jews? If the Zealots fought Rome, should Christians join them? Or was this war beyond their concern?

Why, why did Jesus not give us a hint of direction for all these problems?

I bent my head down and closed my eyes, trying to shut out all the voices.

Because—the answer came to me—he trusted us. And . . . because there will be many other questions as time goes on, and he could not have guided us specifically in them all.

He meant this group to go on and on, long past the problems of Jerusalem or the Temple or the Romans. Way into a time we cannot even picture, with peoples whose names we can never know.

That answer—and the image it brought, of a line of believers descending from us through the ages to come—was so startling that I began to shake.

I made my way back to Jerusalem. I must confess that I took the long way, savoring the journey. I did go into Tiberias and stood once again before the house that would not admit me. I knocked, but upon getting no answer did not linger.

I passed through the towns of Arbel and Nain, and by the time I reached Jezreel I was tired. I was still strong and in good health, but it was a long journey for anyone. And so I sat for a few moments, and then made my way to the synagogue, not to worship but to inquire, quietly and cautiously, if there were any Jesus followers in the town.

There was an old caretaker sweeping the aisles, and he said, "Oh, those crazy people!" He shook his head. "Why would you want them?"

"Because I am one of them," I said. I was surprised at how easy it was now for me to say it.

"They meet at Caleb's house, down by the market," he said, giving me explicit instructions. "But they are all insane!"

I was used to this. We were always called insane. After all, we believed that an executed carpenter was the Messiah. And that he had been restored to life by God. Was anything more insane than that?

"I thank you," I said.

"Woman, you seem sensible! Don't seek them out!" he cried after me, as I set out toward the address.

Now I was getting bolder about knocking on strange doors. I did so without a second thought. (Elisheba, would I have been so bold without having first tried yours? Now I can stand before any door in the world and knock. And even today, old as I am, I am willing to go anywhere, undertake any journey, in order to knock at long last at that door I long above all others to have open for me.)

A man flung the door open, and I stepped in. The first thing I saw was crates and sacks piled up to the ceiling. They made the atrium look like a warehouse.

"Caleb?" I asked.

"Who are you?" The doorkeeper looked me up and down.

"I am Mary, of Magdala," I said.

"Oh, God!" was his response. He drew back and then fell to his knees.

"One of *his*! One of his very own! Oh, God; oh, God!" He started bowing, and then took my right hand and began kissing it all over.

"Stop!" I said, snatching my hand away. "I am an ordinary person, like you."

"You knew Jesus!" he kept repeating. "Jesus, Jesus!" Then he looked up and blinked. "You truly are Mary of Magdala? The woman cured of demons! Oh, yes, we know your story!"

How did he know my story? How accurate was it? But after I died, how could I go about correcting all the false stories? Even now, it would be an impossible task. The false stories about Jesus, about Peter, about James, about John, about Jesus's mother, about me . . . No, already it was not humanly possible.

"I seek to spend some time with believers here," I said. "I am on my way back to Jerusalem."

"The mother church? The true church, where all truth resides?" The man started bowing again. I smacked his back as I would a child's, and that brought him upright with a start.

"We aren't the keepers of all truth," I said. "That is absurd. There is not any doctrine. Did not Jesus say that where two or more are gathered, he is there? We aren't like the priests in the Temple. There will be no Temple, no central authority, no pronouncements from us!"

The man came to his feet and looked directly into my eyes. "Oh, you are wrong. If the world endured, then this would surely come about. There would be a central authority, and everything would be as codified as the Law of Moses now is for devout Jews. But praise be to Jesus, this world will end before any of these things comes about!" He swept his arm out to indicate the array of chests and sacks.

"It's all ending soon," he continued. "As Jesus said. And we are prepared. We have the supplies. We won't be extinguished all at once. We'll last here. For a while, at least. We've quit our jobs, given away our possessions, made our peace with the outside world. What delicious freedom!"

"But . . ." I was at a loss for words. I kept looking at the stockpile in the atrium.

Another attempt to control the unforeseeable. Another attempt to predict our own ending. But Jesus had expressly warned against this. He had said that the time and the place no one knew.

"Friend," I finally said, "I fear you are misled."

Our endings can be sudden, as sudden as in Jesus's parables, or they may take years, but they are always a surprise in some way, as also in his parables.

"But Jesus said the time was almost out!" the man insisted. "I heard him. I was in that field outside Capernaum, that day he spoke and the ten lepers came to him—"

Yes, that day. I remembered it so well, but I had heard different things. "I know," I said. "I was there, too."

"Then how can you possibly be walking about so unconcerned?" he demanded. "If *it* comes upon you suddenly, then . . ." He looked so concerned that I realized that my coming here had not been happenstance, that I was badly needed to free these people.

"Then I will be greatly surprised," I said. "But there may be no way to prevent that." I looked up and down the atrium, at the piles of supplies: there were sacks of grain, grinders, baskets of dried fish giving off their characteristic salt-smoke smell. "When do the other believers gather here? Is it tonight?" For it was the day after the Sabbath, the resurrection day.

"Yes," he said. "They will arrive shortly after sunset. There are some twenty of us. Now, in the meantime, would you like some refreshment? And could you keep me company while I sort these pistachios and bag them?"

"I will do better than that," I said. "I can help you sort them."

"I'd rather you told me everything you know and remember about Jesus," he said.

That request again! How could I, or any of us, fulfill it? And even if we attempted to write it all down, we never could recount everything.

"I think I can do both," I said. And we went into his attached storeroom and bent down together to divide up the pistachios, setting them in separate heaps and then scooping them into the rough bags, while I answered his questions and told him what I could.

The believers came in the evening gloom, each bearing an oil lamp to be placed on a ledge in the main room, and as the numbers increased, so did the light. Soon the whole room was glowing with the yellow light of the lamps, and it seemed to take on a golden softness.

Caleb introduced me with an embarrassing deference that I was then forced to deny. Yes, it is true I was an original disciple, I said, with Jesus from the beginning. Yes, it is true I was one of his first cures. Yes, I was the first to see him alive again, and, yes, I still speak to him—and he still speaks to me. But I am still just a person, no different from any of the rest of you.

"You are wrong," one woman said. "Your face shows a glory ours do not."

Did it? It was most likely the golden oil-light that was imparting this glow, I told myself.

"Moses's face shone when he had talked to God, and so does yours," the woman insisted.

Oh, how tempting it would have been to believe that! To think I had somehow earned a divine glow so obvious that others could behold it. Truly the snares of Satan are subtle. The more spiritual he can make us feel, the higher our pride swells.

I forced myself to laugh, although for a moment I succumbed to a jolt of excitement. "Yours glows, too," I assured her. And in some way, it did. Little by little, inner transformation begins to show on the face.

As Caleb had said, there were about twenty that came to the house, and they seemed to be of all ages, equally divided between men and women. In addition to the oil lamps, each had brought a provision of some sort, not only for the meal they would share after the prayer service, but also to be donated to the growing stacks in the atrium.

Their prayer service was different from the one in Magdala and different yet again from ours in Jerusalem, but that was not surprising. Theirs favored texts about people in olden times, like Enoch and Elijah, being suddenly taken up to heaven, and their favorite Psalm seemed to be the one that promised, "God will shoot arrows at them and strike them unawares. . . . The just will rejoice and take refuge in the Lord."

Afterward, at the meal and the sacred words recalling Jesus's supper, I found that, although the order and the choice of phrases were different, the same feeling of his being present pervaded the table. I was grateful to bow my head and take the hands of the unknown man and woman on each side of me, feeling in them a link to whatever mysterious fellowship Jesus had left behind, marveling at it.

When the meal and remembrance concluded, we began talking, and I had to ask them why they were so certain the end of time was upon us. "For Jesus told us the time and the circumstance no one knows," I reminded them. "He said even he did not know it; only God did."

"Yes, but he made it clear it was coming soon," Caleb insisted. "At least from the words we have been given, about how we should be prepared and how all is passing away."

I had to think and try to recall his exact words. But they had faded, and I could remember only the ideas. "It is passing away, but that is the old order of things. The Kingdom has already begun, and is present this moment."

"That makes no sense!" said the young man sitting on my left. "It all looks the same to me. When I first believed, I expected to walk out my door and have everything look different."

"Doesn't it?" I asked.

"No. The same old streets, the same merchants in them, the same signs hanging over the same shops." He looked profoundly disappointed.

"But do you see them differently—the merchants in those stalls, the traders in the streets?"

"I don't understand," he said.

"I mean their faces, their eyes. When you look in them, do you see someone different? Do you, perhaps, see Jesus?"

"I don't know what Jesus looked like," he said.

"Oh, I think you do," I said. "I think you would recognize his eyes."

"I don't look in people's eyes. It's rude," he said.

"Jesus always looked in people's eyes," I said. "That I can tell you." I paused. Should I be sentimental, and tell an old story? Yes, I could do that. Jesus was never concerned with embarrassing himself, and neither should I be. "A rabbi told a story once that has always remained with me, and I think Jesus would say it applies here. You know the Sabbath begins—and ends—with sunset. And a new day begins with sunrise. So a wise man was asked how you can discern when night has passed into day. Was it when you could no longer see the stars against the lightening sky? Was it when you could discern the difference between a black thread and a white one? The wise man shook his head, although these were time-honored definitions. 'It is when you can look into the eyes of another person and see that he is your brother,' he said. And that is how, if you are of the new order, you know the old world has ended." I looked around at the growing stores of provisions, now creeping into the living quarters. "You are wrong, my friends. The world is not going to end tonight, or tomorrow, and even if it did, these provisions would do you no good."

"Granted," the woman on my left said. "But even so, we should abandon ordinary life and devote ourselves to prayer and meditation. In whatever time we have left, we need to purify ourselves and focus our minds on what is important. No more daily or worldly things, only that which is eternal."

They were all looking at me to give a learned answer. The awful responsibility of it—of attempting to convey what might have been in Jesus's mind—hung heavily on me as I answered them.

"I think . . . that Jesus always saw the eternal in the everyday. He did not divide the two, as we are prone to. Your last day on earth should be spent as you spent all your others—doing your daily tasks with love and honesty. I do not know what else you can do. An ordinary day is, perhaps, the most holy of all."

"He said we were to watch for him!" Caleb leaned over.

"I never heard him say that," I said. "All I ever heard him say was that many workers were needed for the harvest, and that we were to apply ourselves to that."

"Is there anyone whose life is so in tune with God that an ordinary day would be acceptable to them as a last day?" the woman cried out.

"No," I had to admit. For, if I knew it was my last day, I would rush to Tiberias and pound on that door and force my way inside and embrace my daughter, and with my last breath I would tell her I loved her.

∞ LXV ∞

When I returned to Jerusalem, I found it filled with angry political agitators and frightened citizens, with the church of the faithful caught up in the turmoil.

Suddenly the Emperor Claudius expelled all the Jews from Rome, because of fierce fighting and quarrels among them. He could not understand the issue, but the fighting was actually between Jewish Christians, who believed in Jesus, versus the Jews, who did not. It was the first time we came to the attention of a Roman emperor; would it had been the last!

Also, about this time a severe famine hit us in Judaea, and we had to rely on the churches of Syria for relief. So—another first: the mother church was dependent on the charity of her daughter churches.

Let me tell of the subsequent events that swirled around us until we left Jerusalem. I have already mentioned King Agrippa, who briefly—for three short years—acted as king of Judaea.

He was followed by his weakling son, Agrippa II, a tragedy for our people, since his main loyalty was to Rome. Although he tried to forestall the final confrontation and war, it was only to curry favor with his overlords. In any case, he was ignored on both sides, and the war went forward.

He was a great friend of the Emperor Nero, and even renamed Caesarea "Neronias" to flatter him. And evidently he embraced his idol's vices, for he was involved in an incestuous relationship with his sister Berenice. Unlike his subjects, he survived the war intact, and retired to Rome with an honored title.

It was during his reign that James, the brother of Jesus, was executed. James had been an irritant to the Sanhedrin for years, because he insisted on keeping the Law meticulously and worshiping ostentatiously at the Temple.

So, when an opportunity arose, they seized James and put him on trial. The sentence was no surprise: that he be stoned to death for blasphemy. Thus he died some thirty years after his brother at the hands of the same religious council.

None of us saw it. Not only did we not wish to, by this time we did not want to be seen in the Temple vicinity to remind the Sanhedrin of our existence. It was from the very Temple wall that they hurled him to his death in the Kidron ravine below. But we mourned him deeply; whatever our differences, he had been a leader and Jesus's dear brother.

Trembling, John and I carried the news to Mary, his mother. Frail now, in her mid-eighties, she spent most of her days in the sunny upper room of John's house, staring off into the distance of the Jerusalem hills from a window. Sometimes she still went to the market, other times she walked in the neighborhood, leaning on our arms, but it was clear her strength was failing. Now we had the most dreaded task of all, the task of telling a mother her child has died.

Her back was to us, a shawl draped around her shoulders—blue, her favorite color. Her hair was white now, but still thick, and in the noon sun it shone like pearls.

I knelt beside her. "Dearest Mother," I began. My throat closed and I could say nothing else. Dearest Mother . . . I clasped the arm of the woman who, for more than thirty years, *had* been my mother. When Jesus said to John, "Behold your mother," I think he meant both of us. Mary, more my mother than my own mother, right from the first time I ever beheld her, in my childhood.

"Oh, Mother," I said, starting to weep.

"I know," she said. "I know." And she bent over and held me, comforting me, still first a mother to those around her.

James's death hastened Mary's own. The sorrow of it pulled her down, although she did not falter in looking outward to others. She sent word to her other children, searching for them. Joses, Jude, and Simon came to her, old men now. Ruth and Leah were lost. Perhaps they had died by now. What had they done after Jesus had died, condemned as a criminal? Had they ever revealed their relationship with him? Had they ever come looking for their mother? So many things we would never know; so many sorrows Mary had had to live with.

And yet she had an adopted son, the faithful disciple John, who had been given to her by Jesus as he looked down from the cross. And she seemed closer to him than to any of her surviving children. So, again, the question arose in my mind: what is true family? For here were sons and sisters and brothers made closer through Jesus than those given to us by nature.

During those last days, she seemed equally dedicated to the followers of Jesus who were strangers. She spoke to many of them who made the pilgrimage to John's house, high in the Upper City section, to seek her out. The growing reverence paid to her seemed only to exasperate her. Many believers knelt at her feet and did not dare touch her hands, even when she extended them.

"Oh, blessed Mother," they would mumble, hardly looking at her.

"Come," she would say. "Take my hand. It is a comfort to me. It has been a long time since *he* grasped it. I miss him. I wish to see him again. I know you do, too." And she would stretch out her other hand and touch the person's head. "We will be together, and he will welcome us equally."

And when they would protest, bowing before her honor and seniority, she would say, "I do remember his saying, 'Who are my mother and my brothers? They who hear the word of God and do it.' You and I will stand together before him."

She died a year after James, and it was a slow slipping away. First she walked less; then she stopped walking beyond her chamber; then she stopped walking within her chamber; then she was confined to her couch. It was like a child's progress in reverse: her world grew smaller and smaller, until only her gestures remained, her graceful hands imparting a farewell blessing to all of us.

When her hands rested on my head, I felt her strength ebbing, and I prayed that a little of it might remain with me. I wanted to be her daughter, to carry on her life.

The Holy Spirit told us where she must be laid: in a cave at the foot of the Mount of Olives. In solemn procession we bore her litter down the steep slope out of Jerusalem and then a little way up the side of the mount.

I looked above me, at the dark cypresses waving in the brisk wind. The Spirit was right in leading us here; this place had a natural solemnity. And, as had been revealed, a grotto opened beyond the trees. The bearers set the litter down, and we gathered around it.

Over the shroud, Mary was covered with a blue pall-cloth, as bright as the morning sky above us. I stood near the bier; soon so many people had come streaming out from the city that they stretched into the olive grove near the grotto.

Her nephew Symeon stood at the foot of the bier and led the prayers. Symeon was the son of Clophas, Joseph's brother, and was himself in his fifties. I have heard it said that he was "elected" head of the church to replace James, but that is not so. He elected himself, and we acquiesced. He seemed a good man, and still some of us clung to the idea that there was something magical about sharing Jesus's earthly blood.

"Precious in the sight of the Lord is the death of his saints," he intoned the words from a Psalm. "And surely she was a great saint, and most precious to the Lord." He bent and kissed the pall.

Then the bearers took up the litter and bore it into the grotto, while the rest of us stood blinded with tears on this bright morning.

"Peter is dead."

Symeon announced it simply, after one of our gatherings, when we had finished eating and praying and singing. He stood up and made his way slowly to the front of the large room in John's house and spoke those dreadful words. Before we could burst out in a storm of questions, he held up his hands and drew out a crumpled paper.

"One of the brothers from Rome has sent word," he said. "And Peter was not the only one to die—although the one most dear to us. There has been the most cruel and sweeping persecution against our fellows, who are being blamed for the great fire that swept through Rome."

"I don't understand," old Matthew said. The disciple was now frail, but he had worked diligently in Jerusalem all these years, compiling texts and keeping our accounts. "How can this be?"

"The fire raged for days and destroyed large portions of Rome," said Symeon. "Nero is so hated, he was suspected of setting the fire himself so that he could embark on one of his building programs and rebuild the city. In truth, he was not even there at the time, and though he is clearly deranged, even he would not set fire to his own city. But he needed a scapegoat, and he chose us."

"Is there any evidence—even the slightest—to link any Christian with this?" asked Joanna. She, too, was now an old woman, but her mind was as penetrating as ever.

"Only that some eyewitnesses reported seeing people actually throwing things onto the flames to feed them," said Symeon. "So, from there, Nero—or his advisers—hit on the idea that it must be the Christians, because they believe the world is coming to its close and will end in flames. They wanted to bring it on, he said, rejoicing in that they were helping to bring about the final days."

"Perhaps some of us were that misguided," I said, remembering the people in Jezreel, who were so eager for the end. It was entirely possible.

"Nero may be insane, but he's clever," said Symeon. "He knew the difference between us and the rest of the Jewish community, and he knew we did not have the official protection of Rome that the Jews did to practice our religion. He knew many people are suspicious of us because we have secret rites and do not sacrifice to the emperor. We have no patrons or champions in high places; there are not enough of us to mount an effective defense. And so he attacked us, in the most gruesome manner."

We demanded to hear everything, and he recounted it all with a trembling voice. Christians were rounded up and killed for amusement—some were thrown out, dressed in animal skins, into the arena, to be torn apart by wild beasts; others were smeared with tar and, fastened to a stake, set on fire to act as human torches to illuminate Nero's pleasure gardens. The leaders were crucified, along with Peter.

"The brothers and sisters were at least able to take his body and bury it," Symeon said. "It's on the side of the hill where he died—near Nero's racetrack."

"And the rest?" Matthew asked, dreading the answer.

"Mass graves, if there were any graves at all," said Symeon. "They died bravely, as bravely as the Maccabees, and for that they will be honored forever."

"Are there any of us left in Rome?" another man asked. "Has the entire church there been wiped out?"

"We know this correspondent is still there," said Symeon. "But there may be very few survivors."

"The martyrs will make our numbers increase," said Joanna. "People will seek out this faith that creates such heroes."

"Not if it is illegal," said a young man on my left. "People are basically cowards."

"We don't want cowards," retorted Joanna. "Let those stay away!"

"No," I said, standing to address the company. "We are all cowards. Peter himself denied Jesus. The point is, we can become something beyond our natural selves. So I say, let the cowards come. I myself am a coward—under my own strength."

"And Paul has been executed." Symeon had saved that for last. "His long years of appeal have ended in a beheading in Rome. Under Nero, again."

"No!" Several voices rose.

Paul had cheated death so many times, it seemed impossible that at last it had claimed him. Ten years ago, he had been attacked by overzealous leaders in the Temple for suspected irregularities of worship at the sacred site. Using his Roman citizenship, he had eluded the Sanhedrin and the execution they had planned for him by appealing for a Roman trial. Eventually, he had gone before the emperor. And now it had ended like this.

"He always knew it might happen," Matthew said. "In his letter to Timothy, he wrote, 'I am already being poured out like a drink offering, and the time has come for my departure. I have fought the good fight, I have finished the race, I have kept the faith.'" He gave a wheezing cough. "A fitting epitaph. May we earn a like one."

One by one, our leaders were being stripped from us, and it frightened us. James the Just, Peter, Paul—who would be next?

And there was more yet, as Symeon delivered his last hammer-blow of ominous news. "The high priest at the Temple yesterday ordered the sacrifices for the emperor to be stopped," he said.

Daily sacrifices for—not to—the emperor had proclaimed Jerusalem's loyalty to Rome for over a hundred years. It was illegal in the Jewish religion to sacrifice to a human being, but they could honor him by sacrificing on his behalf. A nice compromise. And now . . .

"The altar is empty," said Symeon. "The fire is out. This morning, there was no sacrifice, no prayers."

"An act of war," said Matthew.

"Yes." Symeon nodded. "As of today, we—the province of Judaea—are at war with Rome."

"It can end only one way," I said. "Only one way."

We fell to our knees and began praying, but also lamenting, mourning for Peter and Paul and all our brothers and sisters in Rome, and for Jerusalem and its coming conflagration, which we knew would be much greater than that which had just swept through Rome.

Peter . . . gone, martyred. I sat quietly and thought of him. Spared so many times and now, at last, taken. What had Jesus said? "When you grow old, you will stretch out your hands, and someone else will dress you and lead you where you do not wish to go." And that had happened, just as in his dream so long ago. They had bound him and taken him out to the Vatican hill and crucified him. The letter said he had begged to be executed another way, since "he was not worthy to suffer the same death as his master." So the soldiers crucified him upside down.

Peter had been utterly changed from the loud fisherman I had known—oh, so long ago, in my youth and his. His belief had made him a man as brave as a Maccabee.

This was a greater miracle than the ones credulous people wanted to create for Jesus—walking on water, changing water into wine, multiplying food. Such things would be cheap magician's tricks, whereas the real magic was to take such weak and fallible human material and change it into a hero beyond our human limits.

That night, my mind all aswirl with the horrible images of Peter suffering, shuddering, on the cross, his limbs white because they were drained of blood as he hung upside down, his face red and flushed, his mouth open and panting, I tumbled into a strange sort of tunnel, a long black one.

My visions had ceased when Jesus left us. In some ways, I was relieved to be finished with them and the terrible obligations they placed upon me. For over thirty years now, I had relied only on my own ideas and insights.

Now, as I descended into the dark vortex of sleep, I found myself falling, not supported, clutching at the sides of wherever it was I was tumbling, and for the first time in years I knew in my utmost being that I was in another place, a protected, holy place.

"The place where you are standing is holy ground." And I knew it to be so.

And, like Samuel, I could answer—but silently, only in the secret recesses of my mind—"Speak, for your servant hears." I could wait in obedience. And so all those years must have changed me as well. Changes are always invisible in ourselves, yet so noticeable in others.

I fell, turning, weightless, until I reached a broad place that was lighted by a light beyond oil lamps, beyond even the sun. It was so dazzling I had to shield my eyes. There seemed to be a large gathering there, all looking toward a figure who was wreathed in even brighter light, so that I could not look at it.

"I was caught up into the third heaven, but whether in the body or out of it, I do not know—God knows." That was what Paul had written, and now I understood. "I was caught up into paradise and heard ineffable things, which no one may utter."

I had been given this gift—and this burden—so many years ago. And now there was no shirking it, there was no escape.

I saw all of Jerusalem spread out before me. It was as if I was soaring over it, had miraculous wings that bore me over the Temple, over the flat mount that Herod had created, over the modest houses in David's original city, over the sprawling palaces and opulent houses of the Upper City, over the three rings of city walls that guaranteed our safety. How beautiful it all was, glowing in the sunlight, crying out that this was David's city, our heritage and surety forever.

I dipped; I came up over banks of clouds. Jerusalem. And then, suddenly, beneath me, the city erupted in flames. In the vision I could fly anywhere, and I sought the outskirts of the city. And there I saw vast files of Roman soldiers, lined up outside the walls, their insignia proclaiming LEGION V, LEGION X, LEGION XII.

The walls were falling, one by one. I heard the wails and screams of the people inside the city. I saw smoke start to rise. And then—oh, hideous sight—I saw the Temple burst out in flames. I saw its walls crumple, saw its stones collapse inward like a worm-eaten barrel. I saw people streaming out, beating at the flames, and screaming. I saw a huge plume of fire and smoke ascending from the inner sanctuary.

Was the Temple not to stand? Yet once before I had had a glimpse of this vision. Just as God had repeated Pharaoh's dream so that he would know it would truly come to pass, and soon, so now with me.

Then the words of Jesus hammered in my ears, repeated in the dream, magnified. "I tell you, not one stone will remain upon another in a short time."

The Temple . . . I cried out, "It has been in our land for thousands of years, and it is where God dwells." And in the vision I was granted a body, made up of many souls, that was stronger and more forceful than mine.

And then I saw a group of priests entering the sanctuary, and as they saw it shake, I heard a voice saying, "Let us depart from here." By this God told them it was over, and from now on he would not be bound by walls built by man.

The Temple was to be destroyed, and God was ready to move else-where. His words to us all were: Do not defend it, I have already de-parted.

But the Temple . . . where I had come as a child . . . the place where Jesus had taught . . . where the Holy Spirit had come to us . . . where Peter had first preached and converted people to Jesus—how could it vanish, be cast aside? It was the capstone and cornerstone of our religion.

"It is gone," the vision said to me. "It exists no more.

"Jerusalem will perish. The Romans will prevail. There will be no last-minute reprieve, as there was when the Assyrians assaulted the walls seven hundred years ago. Those who rely on that are deceived. Get yourselves out of Jerusalem. You must cross the Jordan to a safe place. Leave no one behind. I will lead you. There you shall await my instructions.

"And above all: do not fear, for I am with you always, until the end of the world, as I promised."

The room swirled; I came gently back to earth as the brilliant light faded and resolved itself into a single small flickering flame of an oil lamp on a stand nearby. But the voices were ringing in my ears and I knew I would not forget a word.

When I recounted all I had seen and heard to the gathered church that evening, the usually talkative group was confused and quiet. They were still stunned by the news from Rome, and now this: a command to quit Jerusalem, where we had centered ourselves for more than thirty years, where Jesus had died and come back to us, and go else-where. And where was this elsewhere? And why should they trust my vision? It had been a long time since I had had one. Most people there had never even connected me with revelations or visions.

And I had to admit, to myself, that I had had an earlier vision that had not come to pass. There had been that horrid one—still vivid after all this time—of the Sea of Galilee red with blood, with a water battle between Romans and rebels.

"It was Jesus who revealed this to me," I said. "It was quite unmis-takable. And quite unequivocal. I do not want to leave, but I know I must obey."

And that was true. I was now in my mid-sixties (oh! but that seems young to me now) and settled in Jerusalem. I did not relish the hardship of setting out on a journey and trying to make a new home. And as they continued to question me, I realized that I would be cast in the role of leader. It was to me that Jesus would reveal the site.

"Some of us can't make the journey," an older man objected. "We haven't the strength. Or the means."

I thought of the stories about how Lot argued with God over flee-ing Sodom, delaying until it was almost too late, and then only follow-ing the instructions partway. It was human nature.

I looked around the room, at the upturned faces searching mine. How many of the original disciples were here? John; Matthew; Thad-deus, who had proved stalwart in tending to our charity cases; Simon the Zealot, little and bent now and barely able to lift a staff, let alone a sword. The others had been scattered abroad and were lost to us, and perhaps had died far from home. There were rumors that Thomas and Philip had gone to India, and Andrew to Greece. But no one knew.

"My instructions were that everyone must go," I said.

"Or what will happen?"

"You will perish." Certainly that had been my vision.

"Then perish I must." An old man with thin, shaking bowlegs rose. "I cannot make that journey."

"Then your martyrdom will show your love of the Lord," said Symeon, rising now and taking his stand beside me. "And perhaps act as a witness to draw others."

"And mine." An old woman rose, who was clearly incapable of making the journey.

Slowly, all over the room, old and trembling people rose and added their voices to the others who were ready to lay down their lives.

"We will not hinder the journey of the others and cause deadly delays," said a woman so ancient her skin was nothing but folds. "That would be a grave sin." She paused, and wheezed, bending over almost double. "We must make our martyrdom in this manner, and I do it gladly."

So I was to lead this group out into the wilderness, like Moses. It was an awesome task, even though my group was much smaller and more obedient. It meant utter trust in God that our journey would be guided by him, and that he would protect us.

Jerusalem was seething. The streets were filled with pushing, angry, frightened people, and suddenly there were many more Roman soldiers about. They seemed to be everywhere—guarding street corners and gateways and watching every person who passed into a market or through the Temple gates. The word was that Nero had not taken kindly to the insult from the Temple and had ordered reprisals. The Zealots were gathering, streaming into Jerusalem. Gallus, the Roman governor of the province of Syria, was bringing his Twelfth Legion down from Antioch, marching toward us. The Twelfth, whose insignia I had seen in my vision!

The day we went to pay our final respects to the Temple—and to look carefully and lovingly at each stone and at the splendid gates and mighty altars of sacrifice—it was not the Zealots but the priests who jeered at us.

"So you're here, you hypocritical traitors!" A loud voice rang out as Symeon and I led our group through the courts and to Solomon's Portico. I looked up to see a figure robed in embroidered silk, wearing a huge head covering that framed him against the sun, standing just beyond the wall that divided the Court of the Israelites from the Court of the Priests. "You! You who pretend to be still in accordance with the Law of your ancestors, but who trample them underfoot! Your leader Peter in Rome has met his just end! Would that all of you would suffer the same fate—the fate of James of Jerusalem as well. And that other James before him! May all such blasphemers perish so!"

The man's violent hatred struck us.

"We have as much right to be here as you," Symeon answered.

With a wave of his arm, the man signaled to the Temple police, and the uniformed soldiers left their posts around the walls and streamed toward us.

"Come, let us depart," said Symeon. "God will judge these men."

And thus our planned respectful, sentimental farewell to our ancient holy site was turned into a rout and a hasty retreat.

We made ourselves ready for the journey, gathering our possessions and selling those too bulky for transport, binding up the rest. Before leaving, we walked once again the places where Jesus had walked. We entered through the gate he had entered riding the donkey; we walked to the procurator's palace, and we looked into the high priest's courtyard; we lingered in the garden of Gethsemane. We did not go to the tomb, but instead to all the places where he had first appeared to us afterward. For me, the garden outside the tomb. For the others, the upper chamber in the borrowed house. And we went to pay our respects to the blessed Mary where she rested in her grotto tomb.

To leave the things that make your memories, that constitute your very self—oh, how hard. We had been born here as a group who knew Jesus beyond the grave, and it was the city so dear to Jesus himself. Now we must quit it. But our clinging to a special place would grieve Jesus, who had told us not to cling to him, let alone an earthly place.

And so we set out, a group of some hundreds, from Jerusalem, on a sunny day that showed the city at its most beguiling. Never had the Temple sparkled more, never had its gold trimmings flashed more bravely in the sun, never had its great bronze gates—opened now to allow the faithful to come inside—shown their carvings more elegantly. The pull was very strong.

But we marched out, prepared for our journey, and passed the contingents of Roman soldiers camped sullenly just outside the city gates. They were milling about, glaring at us as we passed.

"You must cross the Jordan to a safe place." But where was that?

We journeyed down toward the river, taking the Jericho road, the one haunted by thieves and bandits—the one Jesus had spoken of in the parable of the Samaritan. Then we began to trace the journey of the Jordan, keeping well out of its thorny thickets and its low places.

We passed the place where John had baptized, and where I had sought my deliverance—or, rather, we passed it from a distance. I saw its steep, barren banks, remembered its desolation when I was there, but I knew it was not where we were being led.

We kept tramping along the road, going north, ever north. Below us was the winding Jordan; across it was the brief low plain before the hills rose. Jesus had said we must *cross* the Jordan. He meant us to go to the other side.

Here were pagan cities, the league of the Decapolis—the Ten Cities—which were thoroughly Greek and formed a citizenry band of their own. Other than that, the terrain looked utterly bare.

We trudged on. I still received no message about where we should stop. Behind me were spread out all the faithful—those physically able to make the journey—and they were all waiting for divine direction as they walked along, the dust swirling up around them in a great cloud.

We were not yet up to the Sea of Galilee—which I longed to reach and look across, straining to see Tiberias and Magdala—when I felt a strong urge to pause.

"Stop! Rest!" The order went out, and the party halted.

We were still some leagues from the southernmost end of the sea, and the Jordan was meandering through thick brush to our right. But there was a path down toward the river and, beyond it, a road.

I sat, lowering my head and awaiting some direction.

Here in this bright midday, the most open time of day, I received instructions.

"Go across the river. Ford it. Then follow the road on the other side." Is that all? I asked. Will you still not tell us our destination?

But there was no further guidance.

We crossed the river, low at this time. We were able to wade across, holding our robes up around our shoulders. I could not help thinking of Joshua when he first crossed the Jordan and entered this land, and the stones from its bed he had heaped up in memory of it. It seemed that we should likewise make some memorial, but how? And so we crossed, leaving no marker of our journey behind.

We set out on the road leading away from the river, and as we crested the most immediate hill, we saw spread out before us a fair city.

"Here. Here is where you will wait." The words were loud and insistent in my mind's ear.

But . . . I could see from looking that this was a pagan city. On its outskirts were buildings with the evenly spaced columns that indicated a Greek temple.

"How can we live here?" I cried aloud. "This is a pagan place! Why have you led us here?"

"It is safe. It will not be crushed by Rome. And you will survive and go forth another time."

We climbed as the road made its way into the hills and the city, the city called Pella, and I said, "This is the place, the place where the Lord has led us. Here the Lord wishes us to take shelter."

The first months there were difficult. We had to find lodgings and work to support ourselves, and learn to live among aliens. Not that we had never been with foreigners, but here we were the foreigners. In this midsized city laid out on the grid pattern of Greek planning, the language was Greek, the coins were drachmas, the work schedule was without a day of rest. There was one small synagogue, but on every corner, so it seemed, were temples to their multitude of gods: Zeus and Apollo, and ones from farther away, like Isis and Serapis. The smell of roasting pig wafted from food stalls, and it had an unmistakable aroma, nothing like lamb or goat. Half-naked youths would swagger down the streets, munching on their shredded pork, their fingers greasy with it. They would be on their way to a gymnasium, where they would strip themselves of all clothes and parade around the wrestling field naked.

Although Symeon was our nominal leader, I was our true leader, for we were lost in this strange place, and only I was given instructions about how to live here. And so they looked to me, and I did my utmost to answer them, praying that I would not be led astray myself.

More out of courtesy than anything else, we visited the synagogue, but when we spoke of who we were, we were asked to leave—as I knew we would be. They had heard of us, had heard of this strange sect that believed the Messiah had already come, but did not want to hear more. A few followed us into our new quarters and asked more questions, but only a handful actually joined us.

As the months passed and the rains of autumn came, we were fairly well settled in our new home. Gradually the city and its surroundings began to grow on me; too much so. I found myself drawn to the temples and the beauty of the statues; dangerously, they began to seem no longer alien but beguiling. As I passed them, it became more and more of a test to make myself hurry away. After a little while, I had to forbid myself even to look inside, into the white interiors—so different from our dark and curtained Holy of Holies.

We clung together in this foreign place, meeting nightly in one little house or another. Were we to make this place a true home—or was it the briefest of sojourns?

"In our history," Symeon said, "short visits have a way of turning into very long stays. Jacob went down to Egypt to buy grain, and his descendants did not leave for four hundred years. Is this, then, our fate? To be with these Greeks and pork-eaters for generations?" He spoke after one of our services, when we had our community meeting.

It was up to God, and we all knew he could be surprising. "I say we will wait," I said. "Remember how in the desert the Israelites were to stay still until the cloud and pillar of fire moved from over the Tabernacle? Sometimes it was years. Now we are faced with the same test."

For it was a test, I had no doubt. Would we wait for God's instructions, or take things into our own hands, and either melt back into the synagogue or lapse into the pagan life of the Greeks around us? It was, in fact, a severe test. And only I knew about the personal test for me: temples and beautiful statues and idols all around me.

Some of us worked to compile sayings of Jesus, so that when people inquired about him we could pass them on. Others wanted to gather as complete a list of them as possible, so that new believers could relive our experience of hearing him speak. There were many such collections of sayings in circulation, being passed from church to church, but none was complete or very long.

We also began to fashion a course of teaching for seekers, whom we called "catechumens," which means "instructed." There were certain things they should know before they could be admitted to our fellowship—the life of Jesus, his teachings, his commission to us, his death, and his glorious life afterward. And we constructed a baptismal formula, to be recited over the person as he or she emerged from the waters: "For all of you who were baptized into Christ have clothed yourself with Christ. There is neither Jew nor Greek, there is neither slave nor free person, there is neither male nor female, for you are all one in Christ Jesus." And we would lead the wet new member back into our hall, where he or she would be admitted to the memorial supper and full fellowship with great rejoicing. Someone would offer to be the new Christian's sponsor and guide for the first few months, and that person became like a blood relative.

There were still some who maintained that this was too legalistic, and that the only requirement should be a conviction of the heart and a public acclamation that "Jesus is Lord!" But gradually our minimum requirements won out.

What was most astounding to us in those days was the way Jesus could draw people to him, even through the clumsy methods of his imperfect followers, even after the passage of time, and, most important, even without his own physical presence.

We received news about the Romans and Jerusalem. The rebels in the city had had great and unexpected success, enough so that they could claim God had protected them as he had in ages past. They managed to capture most of the city, and when Gallus, the governor of Syria, was ordered by Nero to march south and secure Jerusalem, they routed him, killing his entire four-hundred-man rearguard. This first round ended in a victory for the Zealots, which seemed divine. They set up their own government and administrative districts, free of their hated overlord at last.

But this was not the victory of Moses with Pharaoh, only the beginning of the war. The Romans were masters of the world, and a skirmish or two meant nothing in the overall picture.

Nero ordered one of his ablest generals, Vespasian, to crush this rebellion. Vespasian was a prudent commander, having learned in Britain how to parry ambushes. He commanded the Fifth and Tenth Legions. He ordered his commander-son, Titus, to bring up the Fifteenth Legion from Egypt, and called out the troops from client kings. Soon there were some sixty thousand soldiers, including auxiliaries and cavalry, bearing down on the rebels.

God had said, long ago with Gideon, that overwhelming odds only gave him the opportunity to show his strength, but he fell oddly silent with the advance of the Roman army, the mightiest force the world had ever known.

Coming down from Syria, Vespasian had to pass through the northern regions and Galilee to reach Jerusalem, and hard battles were fought in Jotapata—and Tiberias and Magdala, where a band of fierce rebels had fled.

∽ LXVII ∽

Magdala! They were headed for Magdala! And Tiberias, where my dearest earthly treasure resided!

That vision . . . that bloody vision I had once had of the battle with boats, and all the people killed, and the lake red with the blood of men—was it now to come true? I had to go there, I had to rescue, I had to find my daughter.

"No!" Symeon said. "You cannot go! You are—forgive me—old. But pillaging soldiers do not spare old women."

"I am not afraid." And I was not. God's miracle, I was not!

"Think of the others. Think of your responsibility. You led us here. And even if you had not, you are one of the last survivors to have met Jesus face to face. You cannot just toss that aside. They need you—all these young people who are joining us. They need to hear what only you can tell them."

"I must go."

"Is this from the Lord? Or from your own desires?" Symeon looked fierce.

"Both," I could answer honestly. I had had that vision many years ago, and I knew it was true. But the call of motherhood was so strong— I *had* to go.

"And what if I told you that Jesus had forbidden it?" he said.

I hoped with all my heart he had not. But perhaps he had. I thought a moment and finally said, "Then I must disobey him, and ask his forgiveness afterward. I am not . . . as strong as he was." I paused. "But he knew that when he chose me."

· · ·

Symeon assigned a young man to accompany me on the journey, a new believer from Pella named Jason, and we set out across the Jordan, wading through the cold knee-deep waters, emerging on the other side, the side of Israel, expecting to see hordes of Roman troops lined up on the banks. But no one was there. The land was empty and tranquil; the late-summer crops were ready to harvest, golden in the sunlight.

Subduing Jotapata had taken Vespasian forty-seven days, and left him in a bad temper. Now he was in no mood to brook interference. Resolutely he was marching eastward toward the other fortified cities, Tiberias and Magdala.

We managed to reach Magdala before Vespasian. We scurried through the gates—heavily fortified now, manned by guards. "Not one of you will survive the Romans." That revelation came to me as I passed through the gates, and I was burdened and saddened by it. I looked at their impressive shields and swords and saw them in a smoldering heap in a few days. We hurried to Eli's home. Frantically beating on the door knocker, not caring about our reception, only wanting to warn him, we panted and kept knocking.

At length the door opened, cautiously. It was Dinah. I recognized her even after decades.

"Dinah—it is I, Mary. I have come to warn you. The Roman general Vespasian is bearing down upon you even as I speak. You must protect yourself! Flee!"

She stared at me. "Mary . . . Joel's wife? Oh, so long ago." She looked carefully, trying to locate the young woman she had known in my aged eyes. Then she shook her head. "How do you know this?"

"It has been revealed to me." That was all I could say. It was the truth. She looked skeptical. "I see."

"Where is Eli? May I speak to him?" It was necessary to find him quickly.

"He has gone to his ancestors, and is gathered to God," she answered.

"I am grieved." I felt sadness, I wept inwardly for Eli. "But you must flee this place, or die."

"This is my home," she said, proudly. "And I will be protected."

We managed to reach Tiberias ahead of the fighting.

The city had high walls, recently fortified to withstand an attack. But they had not reckoned on the strength of the Romans. As soon as I saw them, I knew they would be paper before the Roman legions.

"Let me in! Let me in!" I cried, beating on the gates, which were shut fast even at midday.

"Who are you?" a guard called out.

"A mother!" I said. "A mother, who must pass inside!"

Slowly the gates creaked open, and the soldiers manning them looked at us suspiciously. We passed through quickly. I must find my child! I must!

My "child" would now be a middle-aged woman, but no matter. I could still see her eyes, could see their brightness in her childish face, their roundness, their astuteness. Those eyes would be the same. The eyes never changed.

At last we stood before the house, all out of breath. I stopped and breathed slowly. Then I knocked on the door.

Oh, let her answer! Let me behold her face to face! The door gave way, pulled open by a servant.

"The lady Elisheba," I said. "May I see her?"

"She is not here," he said.

"Is she truly not here, or does she not wish to receive visitors?" I asked.

"She is truly not here," he said. He waited a moment. "Who are you?"

"I am her mother," I said.

He looked startled. "I understood she had no mother."

"She has a mother, one who loves her fiercely, and who has come to warn her. Where is she?"

"She went out into the hills," the servant said. "There did not seem to be any danger."

"There is great danger," I said. "Vespasian is on his way to destroy this city. He will be here by tomorrow. She must flee. Everyone must flee!"

"I will give her your message," he said curtly, and closed the door.

I sank back against the wall. Should I wait here for her return? But who knew when that might be? And up in the hills, seeing the approaching soldiers, she might well decide not to return to the surrounded Tiberias but to go elsewhere, someplace I could not even guess. And I would be trapped in here, perhaps killed in the melee, leaving the church at Pella without a leader. No, I must go, and commit her to God's safekeeping.

Already the streets were filling with worried people, for the ordinary citizens of Tiberias had no wish to be involved in a war; a rebel faction fleeing Jerusalem had taken a stand in their city, and now the inhabitants might pay the price. Jason and I fought our way out, in the opposite direction from the crowd, and pushed through the gates and into the open air. We took to the hills ourselves, keeping high above the flat ground that would soon serve as a battlefield, and hoping, as we rounded each clump of shrub, each boulder, that I might, miraculously, come upon Elisheba, and we would recognize one another and embrace, erasing the years.

Months later, when it was all over, the battles done and the Romans victorious, we had full accounting of it in Pella. Shortly after my visit, the rebels had attacked a peaceful emissary from the Romans; the citizens of Tiberias, not ready for the reprisal, fled to the Roman camp and threw themselves on their overlords' mercy, professing that they had nothing to do with the rebels. The Romans accepted their submission and demanded that the gates be opened to them, and they were. The Romans then swept into the city to a fine welcome, while the rebels fled in the other direction, straight for Magdala.

Oh, thanks be to God that Elisheba was in Tiberias and not in Magdala! For in Magdala the most dreadful slaughter took place after Titus gave a long ringing speech in which he said, "For, as to us Romans, no part of the habitable earth has been able, hitherto, to escape our hands": a stark summary of our world. The sea battle I had seen long ago in my vision now took place on the waters of the Sea of Galilee. Thousands were killed, and the rebels who commandeered boats—it was as my vision had foretold: they were slaughtered mercilessly. The surface of the lake was bright red with human blood, reflecting off the surface like swelling rubies.

And inside the city, innocent people perished, for the soldiers could not distinguish between the rebels and the inhabitants, and many buildings were set afire, and the destruction was great. (My old home . . . my father's warehouse . . . Eli's home . . . Dinah and all my relatives . . . all gone?) In the end, Vespasian sat in a judgment tribunal, trying to decide what to do with the innocent victims of the fighting. Then, being told that, since their homes had been destroyed, they were bound to turn rebel themselves, he yielded to the perfidious plan of one of his advisers. He addressed the people, assuring them of their safety and ordering them to go to Tiberias for settlement of their claims. But once they were there, he held them captive in the stadium while the old and infirm were killed, six thousand of the strongest young men were sent to labor for Nero's canal in Greece, and thirty thousand were sold into slavery. And that was what became of my home, and why I can no longer be Mary of Magdala, for Magdala has been destroyed.

We mourned for our land and our cities for forty days, grieving beyond words to describe. I prayed and prayed that Elisheba was safe, and the only hope I could cling to was that she lived in Tiberias and not in Magdala.

The Romans continued their southward march. The almost year-long battle for Jerusalem, fought house to house, is well known and chronicled elsewhere, unlike the battle at Magdala. Before the end came, the inhabitants of Jerusalem were starving and reduced almost to animals; and when the final day of the Temple's existence dawned, its downfall was not the stratagem of one man or a plan, but the flung torch of an angry soldier that set all its glory ablaze. Everything within perished, and days later a Roman soldier stepped on the smoke-stained and broken sign proclaiming that any Gentile who passed beyond the balustrade and "is taken shall be killed, and he alone shall be answerable for his death." Thus perished the Temple and all its boundaries, rules, sacrifices, hopes, and history, becoming the supreme lost treasure in the memory of the Jewish people.

The entire city was razed, except for three defense towers that withstood all assault; the inhabitants who were not slaughtered were sent into slavery. Titus and his soldiers carried off the golden menorah and the other Temple goods and used them in his triumphal parade in Rome, the sacred objects being reduced to booty exposed to the stares of the cheering crowd.

Our home was gone, the spiritual center of our universe. What were we to do now? Without our anchor in Jerusalem and the mother church, we were adrift.

And what of the daughter churches that were spread abroad? The churches Paul had left behind had not done well immediately after his death. The Jerusalem doctrine of strict interpretation of the Law had gained strength in the ten years when he was under arrest, and the future of Paul's more farsighted and liberal vision was dim. Then, with the fall of Jerusalem, all that changed in the wink of an eye. The only type of Christianity left was Paul's, and from then on the breach between the mother religion and its daughter was so wide, well-wishers could not see their fellows on the other side.

We remained in Pella for ten years, five years past the fall of Jerusalem. Symeon and a small group elected to return to Jerusalem, which was being painfully rebuilt and resettled. John and I decided to go to Ephesus. Matthew and Simon and Thaddeus had died in Pella, and now there were only two of us left.

"Why Ephesus?" Symeon asked us. "Why not come back to Jerusalem?"

"The church at Ephesus was a strong one while Paul was alive," John said. "But now there is danger it may wither away. The overwhelming influence of the cult of Artemis there is hard to overcome. And Ephesus is well situated to help the other struggling churches of the area. Paul founded ones in Derbe, in Lystra, in Iconium, in Pisidian Antioch; we have had no word of how they are managing."

"I hope you don't plan to go there yourself," said Symeon. "You will be fortunate to get to Ephesus."

John looked down at his sandaled feet. "These can walk well enough," he said.

"Man, you are almost eighty!" cried Symeon.

"In doing God's work, that's young!" said John. "Moses was eighty when he confronted Pharaoh. And what about Caleb, Moses's old warrior? Remember, he told Joshua, 'So here I am today, eighty-five years old! I am still as strong today as the day Moses sent me out; I'm just as vigorous to go out to battle now as I was then.'"

"And what happened?" Symeon asked.

"What, you don't know?" John asked teasingly. "He prevailed. He took the land."

"My, my." Symeon shook his head. "Well, perhaps you should take the name Caleb."

"There are still battles to be fought," said John. "And, truth to tell, I'm eager to fight them."

"Mary, you are settled on this?" asked Symeon. "We would value your knowledge and dedication in rebuilding the community in Jerusalem."

"Thank you," I said. "But I feel called to go forward, into the future. Jerusalem is my past." Starting with my visit there as a child, through Joel's accident there, through all the things that befell Jesus. I needed

something new; in my old age, I could not bear the burden of memories. I must go someplace that held none.

Ephesus is a fair city. It took us a long time to reach it, trudging along
at our slow pace with our fellow believers. We traveled up to Tyre,
where we caught a ship making its way slowly up the coast, hugging it
for fear of storms. We passed Seleucia, and Antioch, and the mouth of
the river Cydnus, where Tarsus, Paul's city, lay. And, bumping along like
a bulky ox along the huge bulge of the province of "Asia," we came at
last to Ephesus. Our ship tied up in the harbor, and as we disembarked
with shaky legs, we were struck by the opulence and sophistication of
this large provincial Roman city. A broad avenue, paved with marble
and called Harbor Road, led into the heart of the city, directly to the
theater. On each side were arched colonnades, and the street was
lighted by fifty lantern posts.

"You are walking where Antony and Cleopatra walked!" one of the
hawkers yelled. "Does it not stir your blood?" He thrust out a handful
of perfume vials.

I could not help laughing. This was a good sign. The people of Ephesus were full of life, incorrigible, if they tried to sell a seventy-five-
year-old woman perfume and reminded her of Cleopatra's legacy!

"You'll have some?" he asked. He unstoppered one of his bottles
and waved it under my nose.

"My dear son," I said, "it would be wasted on me. You must look to
younger customers."

"What do you mean?" he said, feigning surprise. "You are beautiful,
the kind of beauty that knows no age! How old are you? Thirty-five?"

Now I truly laughed. "Yes, I was once that. But no longer. My time
for perfume is past."

"Never!" he gallantly insisted.

For some odd reason, I had an urge to adapt Peter's proclamation
and tell the vendor, "Gold and silver I have none, but what I have I give
you: Jesus has kept me young!" and see him frown in confusion.

John and I settled in a snug stone house not far from the harbor. In
spite of what the perfume merchant said, our age protected us from
any suspicion of ill-doing, and we lived together in peace. We found the
church to be in sore need of attention, for it had been languishing since
Paul's departure. They welcomed us—indeed, made too much of us.
But it was a pleasure to work with the young people and instruct them,

and a great privilege to be able to tell them directly about Jesus, to pass on what we knew.

By this time, the Jewish religion had separated itself completely from the followers of Jesus. We could no longer go into synagogues to pray or read, because a proviso had been added to their liturgy stating, "May the Nazarenes and the heretics be suddenly destroyed and removed from the Book of Life."

How this would have saddened Jesus! In my prayers I asked him what response we should have to this, but I received no answer. Perhaps he was too grieved to say anything.

In the meantime, John and I toil on in "the vineyard," as Jesus would call it. And what a vineyard it is: a busy city with prosperous citizens entirely absorbed in their lives, but also deeply interested in things of the spirit. Every religion flourishes here, from the mystery cults to the great temple of Artemis. Under the very shadow of the columns of that stunning temple, we Christians are growing and becoming stronger.

And here, as Paul in his letters, I leave you, my brothers and sisters in Christ. My work is done; I am old and will spend the rest of my days here in Ephesus, far from where I thought my life would be lived. But as Paul said, God leads us in Jesus's triumphal procession, and, unlike those of Rome, which parade past a known route, ours is in unknown territory and often where we did not wish, or expect, to go. Peter in Rome, John and I in Ephesus—is not life, and the life Jesus opens to us, full of strange worlds?

Here concludes the testament of Mary of Magdala
✠

✿ LXVIII ✿

Address of Bishop Sebastian of Ephesus, upon the occasion of the celebration of the Feast of Saint Mary of Magdala, the twenty-second day of July, in the Year of Jesus the Christ Five Hundred and Ten, Church of St. John the Apostle: to be circulated among the churches of the Province

Greetings to you who have come today to honor our blessed saint Mary who walked beside the Lord Jesus in the days of his life on earth and died here at Ephesus, a martyr in her old age. We have been blessed in having two apostles here with us, for St. John of great fame lived here with St. Mary in chastity at the end of their lives. Here they preached the gospel and taught many about Christ, and here their lives were ended— Mary's in violence and John's in peace.

It is an altogether fitting testimony that Mary, who had been delivered of demons by our Lord, died repudiating them. At the time she lived in Ephesus, we were famed for the Great Temple of Artemis, one of the seven wonders of the ancient world. The temple seemed impregnable, the worship of the goddess invincible, and the little silver statues of her ubiquitous. But our Mary, in a fit of despair over the goddess worship, threw one of the idols to the ground, crying out that there was no help in such things. She was immediately set upon by the crowd, despite her frailty and old age, and attacked so viciously that she later died of her injuries, but she regarded it as a triumph. Her last words were, "You tempt me no more."

She was buried on the hill outside the city; because I know many of you will go in solemn procession there after the service, I will speak to you further about the tomb itself.

When they prepared her for burial, they found that, among her few earthly possessions, there was a letter, marked, "her last letter," and kept in a little box, along with an old child's amulet of some sort on a leather thong necklace. Thinking it might be of some churchly value, they read it, only to find it was from her daughter in faraway Tiberias. It said that at long last she was ready to come, to make the journey. They did not know what it meant, but they preserved it. You can see it in the reliquary case beside the altar.

Her companion, John, although harassed by the Roman emperor and sent briefly into exile, returned to us when he was almost a hundred years old and continued his ministry, traveling about the province and overseeing his churches.

In his extreme old age, he used to come to our church here and say no more than "Little children, love one another." His disciples asked why he always repeated the same words, and he said, "This is Jesus's command, and if this alone be done it is enough."

They thought John could never die. Yes, there was a belief that he would live until Jesus returned. So, when John fell ill, the believers in Ephesus prepared themselves for Jesus to come and stand among them.

But this did not happen, and so the last of the disciples, the last one living who had actually walked beside Jesus, passed from our midst.

The Artemis Temple fell. Which of you here can even find it? Mary's dashing of the idol to the ground was the harbinger of its downfall. Now its site is a muddy swamp, and its stones have been taken away and used in other buildings. The goddess has departed from our midst.

If you make your way out from Ephesus and into the countryside, follow the well-trodden path toward the city and you will soon find the venerable tomb of Mary of Magdala. For more than four hundred years, people have come to linger by it, to pray, and to speak to her. But pay special attention to a marble funerary monument beside the tomb. It depicts the disciple bidding farewell to all her children in the Lord. She is standing, a tall draped figure on the left, and on her right are the many spiritual offspring she left behind—men, women, and children. Examine it closely. It was put in place by her daughter, who had traveled here to see her mother, but arrived too late. To honor her, she ordered this grave stele. Her words have come down to us: "Mother, I kneel at your tomb and long to embrace you in the flesh. Farewell. I am come too late, too late."

May we live in today and never in the future or the past, or come too late to those we love. As John said, "Little children, love one another."

Author's Afterword

The Bible tantalizes readers, often telling them at great length things they have no pressing need to know, while leaving out the things they are most curious about. One example of this is the famous verse Exodus 1:15, which names two Hebrew midwives but fails to identify the pharaoh enslaving the Hebrews. This is the problem confronting any novelist or dramatist who is drawn to a Biblical subject.

In the case of Mary Magdalene, she is mentioned in the four canonical gospels—Matthew, Mark, Luke, and John—in connection with five events: (1) being delivered from seven demons by Jesus; (2) following Jesus, along with other women he had cured, and supporting him materially in his ministry; (3) being present at the crucifixion; (4) coming early to the tomb on Easter morning to anoint him; and (5) encountering the risen Christ. (In the Gospel of John, he appears first to her, commanding her to go tell the others, which earned her the title "Apostle to the Apostles.") An apostle is "someone who is sent." Disciples and apostles are not necessarily the same. St. Paul was an apostle but not a disciple. Mary Magdalene was both, as were Peter, John, and James.

Mary Magdalene reappears in the so-called apocryphal gospels, documents composed later (some as late as the third century A.D.). This includes the Gospel of Mary, the Gospel of Philip, the Gospel of Thomas, the Gospel of Peter, and the Pistis Sophia. In these gnostic writings, which emphasize secret teachings and wisdom, Mary Magdalene appears as a figure of enlightenment who possesses special spiritual knowledge and is honored by Jesus for it. Scholars hold that this may reflect a historical memory of the important position she once held among the disciples. These writings, however, give no personal details about her.

Thereafter, Mary Magdalene disappears into legend with the other disciples to have fantastic adventures in exotic locations.

In constructing a novel about Mary Magdalene, then, I had very few biographical facts to go on. Scholars assume her title, "Mary of Magdala," means that she was from the town of that name by the Sea of Galilee, a center for drying and salting fish. That she was able to contribute substantially to support Jesus's ministry indicates that she was a woman of means. There is no scriptural or historical basis for the idea that she was ever a prostitute, the sinful woman who washed Jesus's feet with her hair, or the same person as Mary of Bethany.

Therefore, I tried to create a life likely to have occurred—to make her typical of her time and class, not unusual. So I gave her a living mother and father, and two brothers. I made the family religiously observant, and, to illustrate one of the tensions in Jewish life at the time, made one brother strict in his religion and the other more assimilated to the Greeks and Romans around him.

I made her a married woman and a mother, for that would have been the usual life. I also wanted to illustrate that she left a family to follow Jesus, that there were personal sacrifices in being a disciple.

Although there is no specific mention of her role in the early church, I felt it likely that she carried on her mission with the other disciples. An early tradition is that she ended her days in Ephesus, in Asia Minor, where she was martyred. Her tomb, near those of the Seven Sleepers of Ephesus, was a place of pilgrimage. The first record of her feast day on July 22 is at Ephesus in 510 A.D.

I made her age coincide with the century: born around 1 A.D. and died around 90 A.D. That would make her twenty-seven when she first joined Jesus, in her thirties when he was crucified, and middle-aged and older as she became a "pillar of the church." It is likely that the original followers of Jesus and eyewitnesses of his life became spiritual celebrities as they grew older, and that people would seek them out for their remembrances.

As to the demons, my research indicated that often they gain access to a person because of some object or possession brought into the house that is connected with demonic activity. Sometimes this is done unwittingly, other times naïvely. There were certainly exorcisms then, but they were not the elaborate rituals of medieval Catholicism. Prayer and fasting, followed by a command for the demon to depart, was the usual practice. As for the other manifestations—unclear thoughts, scratches and welts (sometimes forming letters or words on the victim's skin), abnormally cold surroundings—these are seen today in cases of possession.

It must be made clear that possession was recognized as distinct from illness; they did not confuse the two, as we are wont to do today.

I included an interlude with Jesus and his family in childhood to illustrate that he always had unusual discernment and powers of expression.

I sent Mary out into the desert as a final resort against her demons because that was one known remedy. There are later legends linking her to a stay in the desert.

The romantic feelings of Jesus and Mary, Mary and Judas: I assume that Jesus was an attractive person, and it would be unusual if none of his female followers developed heightened feelings for him. This happens often between a mentor and mentee, a teacher and pupil, a master and disciple. It would also be unusual if, among a mixed group of men and women disciples in the prime of life, such attachments did not also occur. (In fact, it would seem naïve to assume they did not.)

The scene where Mary and Joanna are able to spy on Judas at Antipas's palace is, of course, fiction. But, again, Joanna's husband was part of Antipas's household, and so it is certainly possible. It would be surprising if Jesus's disciples did not want to find out what the authorities were planning to do about him.

We know from the Epistles of St. Paul that some churches expected Jesus's second coming any moment and had withdrawn from life to await him. The church in Jezreel that I created to illustrate that is therefore based on fact.

The Christians from Jerusalem did withdraw to the safety of Pella, in modern-day Jordan, before the Temple fell.

Jesus's brother James was a belated convert to the cause, and his other relatives did play an important part in church leadership in the first century.

The battle in Magdala was described by the historian Josephus.

Although there is some claim that the Virgin Mary died in Ephesus, the tradition that she died in Jerusalem is stronger and older, so I have chosen that.

In general, it is Mary Magdalene's personal background—age, family, appearance, education—that I have had to construct, making educated guesses. Her actions after she joins Jesus, and the overall historical and geographical context, are based on research and what is on record.

For those interested in my sources and in further reading, I include some suggestions. For the extra-canonical books: James M. Robinson, *The Nag Hammadi Library in English* (San Francisco: Harper, 1990); Willis Barnstone, *The Other Bible* (San Francisco: Harper, 1984). For background: Henri Daniel-Rops, *Daily Life in the Time of Jesus* (London: Weidenfeld & Nicholson, 1962); Jerome Murphy-O'Connor, *The Holy Land* (New York: Oxford University Press, 1999); Mendel Nun, *The Sea of Galilee and Its Fishermen in the New Testament* (Kibbutz Ein Gev, Israel, 1989); Mendel Nun, "Galilee Harbors from the Time of Jesus," *Biblical Archaeology*

Review, July–August 1999. For demonic possession: Malachi Martin, *Hostage to the Devil* (San Francisco: Harper, 1976).

For studies of women and the early church: Elisabeth Schüssler Fiorenza, *In Memory of Her: A Feminist Theological Reconstruction of Christian Origins* (New York: Crossroads Publishing Company, 1983); Rose Shepard Kraemer and Mary Rose D'Angelo, *Women & Christian Origins* (New York: Oxford University Press, 1999); Elaine Pagels, *The Gnostic Gospels* (New York: Random House, 1979).

Among the enormous number of books on Jesus: Michael Grant, *Jesus: An Historian's Review of the Gospels* (New York: Scribner, 1977); Bart D. Ehrman, *Jesus: Apocalyptic Prophet of the New Millennium* (New York: Oxford University Press, 1999); and Charlotte Allen, *The Human Christ* (New York: Free Press, 1998), were especially helpful.

There are many books on Mary Magdalene. Susan Haskins, *Mary Magdalen: Myth and Metaphor* (New York: Riverhead Books, 1993), is a study of both the historical Mary and the various interpretations of her in legend, art, and literature through the ages. Recent scholarly attempts to interpret Mary's life include: Mary R. Thompson, *Mary of Magdala, Apostle and Leader* (Mahwah, N.J.: Paulist Press, 1995); Ingrid Maisch, *Mary Magdalene: The Image of a Woman Through the Centuries* (Collegeville, Minn.: Liturgical Press, 1998); Esther de Boer, *Mary Magdalene—Beyond the Myth* (London: SCM Press, 1997); Carla Ricci, *Mary Magdalene and Many Others: Women Who Followed Jesus* (Tunbridge Wells, Kent: Burns & Oates, 1994); Elisabeth Moltmann-Wendel, *The Women Around Jesus* (London: SCM Press, 1982). An older book, Marjorie M. Malvern, *Venus in Sackcloth: The Magdalen's Origins and Metamorphoses* (Carbondale and Edwardsville: Southern Illinois University Press, 1975), was one of the first to explore the historical basis of the life of Mary Magdalene and how it had become distorted.

A PENGUIN READERS GUIDE TO

MARY, CALLED MAGDALENE

Margaret George

AN INTRODUCTION TO
Mary, Called Magdalene

Weaving together hints from the New Testament, Gnostic Gospels, and other ancient texts, *Mary, Called Magdalene* portrays the life of the mysterious figure of Mary Magdalene, "Apostle to the Apostles," and companion to Jesus. Here Margaret George creates a new portrait of one of the most controversial figures in biblical scholarship: a strong, independent woman, given to visions and endowed with a unique faith in Jesus and his message.

The daughter of a successful fish processor, Mary is raised in a religiously observant family in the town of Magdala on the Sea of Galilee. As a girl, she finds an idol made of ivory, an image with half-closed eyes and sensual lips. Though it is against the strict Jewish teachings to keep graven images, she cannot resist the power of the idol and takes it with her, hiding it from her family. The idol turns out to be a demon who begins speaking to Mary and then ultimately possesses her.

Though she marries and has a baby girl, the demons that haunt her persist and multiply, until finally she is near death from madness. Seeking a cure, she leaves her family and small daughter. After a powerful rabbi is unable to heal her, she travels into the desert alone, determined either to be killed by the evil spirits that possess her or to mount a final struggle and be rid of them forever. Soon after their victory over her, Mary comes upon the river Jordan, where a crowd of people have gathered around a wild-looking man preaching repentance: John the Baptist. It is here that she meets Jesus. When he commands the evil spirits to leave her, they do, and through this healing she is initiated as his disciple.

The book's depiction of Jesus' travels throughout the region—with Mary and his disciples at his side—will be familiar to those acquainted with the gospels of the New Testament. Just as in the Gospels of Matthew, Mark, Luke, and John, the Jesus of *Mary, Called Magdalene* is able to cure blindness, lameness, and leprosy, and perform other miracles. George's interpretation of the message that Jesus has come to share with the world is simple and compelling: The kingdom of God is at hand, and to be prepared one must love God with all one's heart, worship sincerely rather than just for show, and love one's neighbors and enemies alike.

Assuming her family will rejoice at the good news of her cure, Mary is devastated to learn on her return to Magdala that her family has cast her out and has no interest in Jesus' message. Now fully in the realm of fiction—the New Testament offers no details of Mary's personal life—George's depiction of her family's reaction mirrors the Biblical reaction of Jesus' own family when he first returns home. Through these domestic conflicts George explores the themes of earthly versus heavenly family and the necessity of sacrifice in any hero's journey.

Early legends depicted Mary Magdalene as a reformed sinner or prostitute; recently some have speculated that she was Jesus' wife. Neither has any scholarly validity. George avoids both of these images, depicting Mary as a spiritual seeker and bereaved mother and widow, whose feelings for Jesus inevitably heighten over the course of their companionship, as she struggles with her desire for his love as a man, not just as a messenger of God. That Jesus is unable to offer her the earthly love she seeks compounds her suffering and sacrifice.

George portrays Mary and the other disciples not as evolved beings like Jesus, but as mere humans suddenly faced with the opportunity to live a most unordinary life. Though Mary has the gift of prophesy, she fears her visions and the way they set her apart. Her gift—and her closeness to Jesus—inspires some jealousy among the disciples, who, despite their faith, continue to struggle with their own pettiness and prejudices about the proper role of women. At times even Mary would trade it all—her visions and her special relationship to Jesus—to be the simple wife and mother she imagined she would be.

Jesus, of course, is betrayed, executed, resurrected, and ascends to heaven, leaving Mary and his disciples to face the challenge of spreading the message without the messenger. Mary spends her life tending to the persecuted believers, always expecting Jesus' return. For the rest of her days, she struggles with the loss of her family and daughter.

A gripping story of one woman's deepest despair and journey of faith, *Mary, Called Magdalene* explores themes of dedication and deliverance, the tension between romantic love and love of God, and the necessity of suffering and persecution to test the heart. Torn between her belief in

Jesus' message and her love for her family, her love of Jesus as a man and her love for him as God, Mary bravely and painfully remains faithful to her heart's calling to the truth. Through her example, George calls on us to consider life's biggest questions: what it means to be called by God, and how each of us might answer.

A Conversation with
Margaret George

1. The Bible hardly mentions Mary Magdalene. What other primary sources did you turn to for information on this historical figure? How much did you rely on the Gnostic Gospels, specifically the Gospel of Mary?

Scanty though they are, the four canonical gospels remain our main source of information about Mary Magdalene. They recount her early possession by demons, her cure by Jesus, the fact that she was financially able to support Jesus' ministry, that she remained with him during the crucifixion, and, in coming to the tomb on Easter morning, became the first to see the risen Christ.

The Gospel of Mary, discovered in 1896, does not add any biographical information about her; it does stress her spiritual and visionary wisdom, her primacy among the disciples, and her closeness to Jesus. I wanted to bring these elements into the novel. They explain why she became so "famous" among the early Christians, which she certainly was.

Further details about her life appear in apocryphal writings in the fourth, fifth, sixth, and seventh centuries, but some of those facts are unreliable. She is also mentioned by church fathers in the early church, such as Irenaeus of Lyons, Tertullian, Origen, Pseudo-Clement of Rome, Augustine of Hippo, and Pope Gregory the Great.

2. How did you research the historical times in which this novel is set? Did you travel to the Middle East? If so, what was your experience there? Do you draw any parallels from the current violence in the Middle East to the conflict between the Romans and Jews at the time of Jesus?

Many excellent studies on the first-century world are available, and, in addition, I also did seven years of Bible study that covered sixty of the sixty-six books of the Bible.

I have traveled in Egypt, Syria, Jordan, and Turkey. I lived in Israel as a child in the 1950s and have returned six times since then. The last visit in 1999 was specifically to retrace all of Mary's footsteps as best I could. I found it a challenge to identify all the sites, and Magdala, Mary's hometown, was particularly hard to find. It was a calm period then, when there was a brief hope of peace. I feel a great similarity between what is happening now in the Middle East and what happened in Jesus' time: desperate people without leaders who can help them, despair, and fanatics and extremists driving each side further apart, with mounting bloodshed and violence. You can understand how the people put such hope in Jesus, wanting him only to be an earthly deliverer.

3. What drew you to Mary Magdalene as a historical figure? How did the experience of writing about Mary Magdalene differ from the subjects of your other historical novels? Do you personally relate to Mary Magdalene?

As poorly documented as Mary Magdalene is, she is more "historical" than many other characters in the New Testament, in that more details are cited about her life, personality, and behavior. Many of the disciples are simply names, with no attending facts. Still, compared to my other subjects, she presented much more empty space that had to be filled in by intelligent detective- and guesswork.

Yes, I do personally relate to Mary Magdalene, both as a spiritual seeker who must often choose between two mutually exclusive goals and as a strong, courageous woman I admire.

4. Past Church fathers have portrayed Mary Magdalene as a reformed prostitute; more recent feminist scholars have portrayed her as a female divinity figure, church leader, and even the wife of Christ. How did you decide on the role you gave her here—neither whore nor bride but beloved friend to Jesus?

Modern scholarship has given us new access into the world of the first century, and we are much better at deciphering the meaning behind customs and words than earlier ages. The recent claims that Mary Magdalene was a church leader, based on what we now know about the early church, seemed persuasive to me. Also, there is the fact that, as one scholar says, "she was famous"—but famous for what? It seems that the Gospel of Mary, as well as some of the other apocryphal, Gnostic Gospels, have preserved a hint of what made her so special: spiritual gifts that Jesus respected and that made her close to him. It is not necessary to assert that she was actually his wife. Nowhere in any writings is there any indication that Jesus was married.

As for the prostitute label, that did not arise until the sixth century, and it was formally refuted by the Vatican in 1969. So any novel taking that route now would definitely be historically incorrect.

The female divinity figure is an interesting perspective, because in spite of thunderings by the Biblical prophets against the rites of Astarte and the Queen of Heaven, people longed for a goddess and missed the female half of creativity. The goddess is a powerful figure who refuses to go away—and one that we honor in many ways as she is being rediscovered today. I wanted to bring that out with Mary's relationship to the goddess idol she found, which was forbidden but no less compelling. Mary herself is sometimes seen as a Christian version of the goddess, the earthly side representing sexuality and joy, whereas the Virgin Mary represents the ethereal. Perhaps in a twisted way that is why Mary Magdalene was saddled with the prostitute label—the early church had a hard time dealing with sexuality, so any female figure associated with it had to be a prostitute: the origins of the Whore/Madonna split.

5. *What is your own spiritual background?*

A long pilgrimage that has led me from my family background as a Baptist, to the traditions of the Episcopal and Catholic churches, married to a Jewish man, and now discovering New Age spirituality.

6. *Where does Mary's longing for Jesus as a husband come from? Is it a residual effect of her demonic possession or rather the understandable cravings of a woman who has lost her husband?*

I think it is really neither; it is a response to the magnetism of Jesus himself. One commentator has said that Jesus' greatest temptation could have been the doors his own charm opened to him; everyone wanted him to come to dinner. In such an unusual (for those times) close relationship between a man and a woman, as equals, it would be surprising if someone as human and lonely as Mary did not feel an attraction to Jesus and a wish to have him always with her as a husband.

7. Why did you have Judas propose to Mary? Are you implying that Mary's rejection of him had anything to do with his later betrayal of Jesus?

I tried to portray Judas as an intellectual who was never able to overcome his cynicism, which in the end doomed his attempt to follow Jesus. I thought of Judas as the type of person who tries everything to find fulfillment: in his artwork, in his knowledge and learning, in his sophistication. One last remedy had not been tried: marriage and commitment. He reached out to the one other disciple he felt was similar to himself, to whom he also was attracted. Perhaps if she had accepted him, he might have posed for a while as a church worker alongside her, but it would not have lasted. No, I did not mean to imply that her rejection made him reject Jesus; she was just the last branch he tried to grasp before his final fall.

8. Until the very end, even after the crucifixion, Mary doubts. It is not until he is resurrected that she fully believes. Is her lack of complete faith until that moment meant to be understood as a weakness? Or is it an understandable human response to a profoundly complex individual?

None of the disciples understood what Jesus was about, nor anticipated Easter morning. This is not weakness but common sense, as the resurrection was beyond expectation. Jesus was also mysterious in what he predicted, speaking in parables and strange wordings. I think the last sentence above describes it perfectly: an understandable human response to a profoundly complex individual.

9. Are there other women in the Bible you are drawn to or have considered writing about?

I always sympathized with Leah, the unwanted wife who had to share her husband, Jacob, with her younger sister Rachel. (This is in the Book of Genesis.) In competition with Rachel, who was the beloved one, she nonetheless gave Jacob six sons and a daughter—half the Twelve Tribes of Israel. I think the psychological tension in her life must have been phenomenal.

I also like the story of Tamar, David's daughter. Her brother Amnon's passion for her ignited the civil war between David and his son Absalom, her other brother who avenged her honor (II Samuel 13–19:33). For sheer operatic drama, it is hard to top this story, ending in the famous cry "O my son Absalom, my son, my son Absalom! Would God I had died for thee, O Absalom, my son, my son!"

QUESTIONS FOR DISCUSSION

1. Jesus' family rejects him when they learn his intention to travel and preach rather than run the family business. Mary's family casts her out when she joins with Jesus. What does this say about the nature of family? Is it possible to find one's true family outside of blood ties?

2. The people of Jesus' hometown of Nazareth do not welcome him or wish to hear his message. Why would the people he grew up with reject him? Why would it be easier to preach to strangers than to longtime family and friends?

3. Compare Judas' conversion (finding Jesus' answers to be "rational" and "persuasive") to that of the other disciples. What is the difference between believing with your head and believing with your heart? Does it make a difference?

4. Mary is unhappy that she has the gift of visions and says she would rather be ordinary. What does it mean to live an ordinary life? Given the choice, would she have chosen an ordinary life?

5. Why does Jesus reject Mary's proclamation of love? Do you think Jesus loved her in the same way as she loved him but felt unable to act

on it, or do you think he was truly only interested in her as a spiritual companion? Could Jesus have done what he did had he had a wife?

6. Jesus is persecuted by the Romans and suffers in death on the cross. Mary is also persecuted, by opponents of Jesus and by her own family. She suffers her entire life over her separation from her daughter. Is it necessary to suffer? Is that the only way humans are able to deepen spiritually? Could Jesus have spread his message without suffering? Compare his life to the life of Mohammed, who lived to be an old man and died peacefully.

7. Does a person's commitment to the truth necessarily mean that he or she will be persecuted by society?

8. There is a desire among Jesus' followers to make him the King of Israel who will throw out the Romans. Why are the crowds more interested in Jesus as a secular king than a heavenly one? How does this compare to the current struggle for power in the Middle East?

9. The Bible mentions very little about Mary Magdalene. Why would the Bible not mention her more? Throughout *Mary, Called Magdalene* there is resistance to Mary's spiritual leadership because she is a woman. Why would men not want women in positions of spiritual leadership? What is it that women threaten?

10. Mary Magdalene, in the novel, is forced to choose between her commitment to Jesus and her commitment to her daughter. How do you think a mother could make that choice? How hard would it be?

11. People who have visions are discounted as crazy in our culture. If you began having visions, would you believe them? What would it take for you to believe them? Do you think you could give up your own life, your spouse, and your child if you felt you were being called by God to spread the truth?

For more information about or to order other Penguin Readers Guides, please email the Penguin Marketing Department at reading@us.penguingroup.com or write to us at:

Penguin Books Marketing Dept.
Readers Guides
375 Hudson Street
New York, NY 10014-3657

Please allow 4–6 weeks for delivery.
To access Penguin Readers Guides online, visit the Penguin Group (USA) Web site at www.penguin.com

FOR THE BEST IN PAPERBACKS, LOOK FOR THE

In every corner of the world, on every subject under the sun, Penguin represents quality and variety—the very best in publishing today.

For complete information about books available from Penguin—including Penguin Classics, Penguin Compass, and Puffins—and how to order them, write to us at the appropriate address below. Please note that for copyright reasons the selection of books varies from country to country.

In the United States: Please write to *Penguin Group (USA), P.O. Box 12289 Dept. B, Newark, New Jersey 07101-5289* or call 1-800-788-6262.

In the United Kingdom: Please write to *Dept. EP, Penguin Books Ltd, Bath Road, Harmondsworth, West Drayton, Middlesex UB7 0DA.*

In Canada: Please write to *Penguin Books Canada Ltd, 10 Alcorn Avenue, Suite 300, Toronto, Ontario M4V 3B2.*

In Australia: Please write to *Penguin Books Australia Ltd, P.O. Box 257, Ringwood, Victoria 3134.*

In New Zealand: Please write to *Penguin Books (NZ) Ltd, Private Bag 102902, North Shore Mail Centre, Auckland 10.*

In India: Please write to *Penguin Books India Pvt Ltd, 11 Panchsheel Shopping Centre, Panchsheel Park, New Delhi 110 017.*

In the Netherlands: Please write to *Penguin Books Netherlands bv, Postbus 3507, NL-1001 AH Amsterdam.*

In Germany: Please write to *Penguin Books Deutschland GmbH, Metzlerstrasse 26, 60594 Frankfurt am Main.*

In Spain: Please write to *Penguin Books S. A., Bravo Murillo 19, 1° B, 28015 Madrid.*

In Italy: Please write to *Penguin Italia s.r.l., Via Benedetto Croce 2, 20094 Corsico, Milano.*

In France: Please write to *Penguin France, Le Carré Wilson, 62 rue Benjamin Baillaud, 31500 Toulouse.*

In Japan: Please write to *Penguin Books Japan Ltd, Kaneko Building, 2-3-25 Koraku, Bunkyo-Ku, Tokyo 112.*

In South Africa: Please write to *Penguin Books South Africa (Pty) Ltd, Private Bag X14, Parkview, 2122 Johannesburg.*